CRITICAL ACCLAIM FOR THE SPLENDID ROMANCES OF . . . JUDITH McNAUGHT

WHITNEY, MY LOVE

"A love story that often heats up the page . . . totally gratifying."

—*West Coast Review of Books*

"A very special and rare romance . . . an exquisite love story that will bring tears of happiness to your eyes. Judith McNaught's characters are engaging, her story is fast-paced, her dialogue is realistic and her love story is genuine. . . . *Whitney, My Love* is exceptional . . . the ultimate love story—one you will dream about forever."

—*Romantic Times*

ONCE AND ALWAYS

"The legend of Judith McNaught continues. . . . The range of her talent is truly extraordinary. . . . *Once and Always* is absolute perfection . . . goes beyond the heart and into the realm of dreams, a triumph of joy to enchant readers everywhere. When you need a dream, *Once and Always* is quite simply the best there is."

—*Rave Reviews*

"This delightful adventure will have you laughing, crying, and enjoying it until the very end. A must read."

—*Rendezvous*

A KINGDOM OF DREAMS

"Wonderful! . . . Judith McNaught is a master story-teller, weaving a marvelous tale that will bring out your deepest emotions and nurture your dearest dreams. *A Kingdom of Dreams* has a beauty that is eternally touching. . . . Judith McNaught is truly the spellbinding storyteller of our times."

—*Affaire de Cœur*

"There is pageantry, chivalry and heraldry. . . . There is grace, passion and love. . . . It is all here in *A Kingdom of Dreams*. . . . One of the best ever!"

—*Rendezvous*

"Tender, tempestuous and adventurous . . . Ms. McNaught's characters deeply touched my emotions. . . . Judith McNaught is a magical dreamspinner, a sensitive writer who draws on our childhood hopes and fantasies (some of the sad moments, too) and reminds us of the beauty of love. . . . This is a love story that will stay in your heart forever."

—*Romantic Times*

Books by Judith McNaught

Almost Heaven
Double Standards
A Kingdom of Dreams
Once and Always
Something Wonderful
Tender Triumph
Whitney, My Love

Published by POCKET BOOKS

Judith McNaught

Almost Heaven

POCKET BOOKS

New York   London   Toronto   Sydney   Tokyo   Singapore

To quiet, reassuring strength, and a smile that lights up my
    life;
To tuxedos, champagne, and an impromptu wedding aboard
    a boat.
To a man who can laugh when his new wife confuses a birdie
    with a bogey . . . and cheers him for the wrong one.
To my husband, Don Smith.
Happy marriage, darling.

An *Original* Publication of POCKET BOOKS

POCKET BOOKS, a division of Simon & Schuster Inc.
1230 Avenue of the Americas, New York, NY 10020

ISBN: 0-671-67915-5

First Pocket Books printing April 1990

10 9 8 7 6 5 4

POCKET and colophon are registered trademarks of
Simon & Schuster Inc.

Printed in the U.S.A.

Acknowledgments

To my editor, Linda Marrow—
For the years of harmony, for the long nights we've worked together when deadlines drew near, and most of all, for the tremendous skill and enthusiasm you bring to everything you do.

To Perry Knowlton, who is everything an agent—and a trusted friend—ought to be. I'm not certain what has meant more to me over the years . . . your confidence in me, your excellent advice, or your endless graciousness.

To Diana Gabaldon, whose knowledge of Scotland is only surpassed by her kindness in sharing this information. Thank you for your help.

and

To Susan Prigozen who *does* know how to recognize all those constellations and where to look for them. Elizabeth Cameron and I are both very grateful to you.

Fifteen servants wearing the traditional blue and silver livery of the Earl of Cameron left Havenhurst at dawn on the same day. All of them carried identical, urgent messages that Lady Elizabeth's uncle, Mr. Julius Cameron, had directed them to deliver at fifteen homes throughout England.

The recipients of these messages all had only one thing in common: They had once offered for Lady Elizabeth's hand in marriage.

All fifteen of these gentlemen, upon reading the message, exhibited shock at its contents. Some of them were incredulous, others derisive, and still others cruelly satisfied. Twelve of them promptly wrote out replies declining Julius Cameron's outrageous suggestion, then they hurried off in search of friends with whom they could share this unsurpassed, delicious piece of incredible gossip.

Three of the recipients reacted differently.

Lord John Marchman had just returned from his favorite daily pastime of hunting when the Havenhurst servant arrived at his home, and a footman brought him the message. "I'll be damned," he breathed as he read. The message stated that Mr. Julius Cameron was desirous of seeing his niece, Lady Elizabeth Cameron, suitably and immediately wed. To that end, Mr. Cameron said he would now be willing to reconsider John's previously rejected offer for Lady Elizabeth's hand. Cognizant of the year and a half that had passed since they had been in each other's company, Julius Cameron volunteered to send his niece, properly chaperoned, to spend a sennight with John so that they might "renew their acquaintance."

Unable to believe what he was reading, Lord Marchman paced the floor and read the entire message twice more. "I'll be damned," he said again. Raking a hand through his sandy hair, he glanced distractedly at the wall beside him, which was completely covered with his most prized possessions—the heads of the animals he'd hunted in Europe and abroad. A moose stared back at him through glazed eyes; beside it a wild boar snarled. Reaching up, he scratched the moose behind its antlers in an affectionate, if ludicrous, gesture that expressed his gratitude for the splendid day of hunting that particular prize had afforded him.

A vision of Elizabeth Cameron danced enchantingly before his eyes—an incredibly lovely face with green eyes, cameo skin, and soft, smiling lips. A year and a half ago, when he'd met her, he'd thought her the most beautiful girl he'd ever seen. After meeting her only twice he'd been so taken with the charming, unaffected seventeen-year-old girl that he'd dashed off to her brother and offered for her, only to be coldly rejected.

Evidently Elizabeth's uncle, who was now her guardian, judged John by different standards.

Perhaps the lovely Lady Elizabeth herself had been behind this decision; perhaps their two meetings in the park had meant as much to her as they had to him.

Getting up, John wandered over to the third wall, which held a variety of fishing poles, and thoughtfully selected one. The trout would be biting this afternoon, he decided as he remembered Elizabeth's magnificent honey-colored hair. Her hair had glistened in the sunlight, reminding him of the shimmering scales of a beautiful trout as it breaks the water. The analogy seemed so perfect and so poetic that Lord

Marchman stopped, spellbound by his own phrasing, and put the fishing pole down. He would compliment Elizabeth's hair in exactly those words, he decided, when he accepted her uncle's offer and she came to his home next month.

Sir Francis Belhaven, the fourteenth recipient of Julius Cameron's message, read it while sitting in his bedchamber wrapped in a satin dressing gown, his mistress naked and waiting for him in his bed across the room.

"Francis, darling," she purred, raking her long fingernails down the satin sheets, "what's important enough about that message to keep you over there instead of here?"

He looked up and frowned at the sound her nails were making. "Don't scratch the sheets, love," he said. "They cost £30 apiece."

"If you cared about me," she countered, careful not to sound as if she was whining, "you wouldn't give a thought to the cost." Francis Belhaven was so tightfisted that there were times Eloise wondered if marrying him would gain her more than a gown or two a year.

"If you cared about me," he countered smoothly, "you'd be more careful with my coin."

At five and forty Francis Belhaven had never been married, but he'd never lacked for feminine companionship. He enjoyed women immensely—their bodies, their faces, their bodies . . .

Now, however, he needed a legitimate heir, and for that he needed a wife. During the last year he'd been giving a good deal of thought to his rather stringent requirements for the lucky young lady he would eventually choose. He wanted a young wife as well as a beautiful wife with money of her own so she wouldn't squander his.

Glancing up from Julius's message, he gazed hungrily at Eloise's breasts and mentally added a new requirement for his future wife: She must be understanding about his sensual appetite and his need for variety on his sexual menu. It would not do for her to pucker up like a prune merely because he was involved in one trivial little affair or another. At the age of forty-five, he had no intention of being ruled by some chit with pious notions of morality and fidelity.

A vision of Elizabeth Cameron was superimposed against his naked mistress. What a lush little beauty she'd been when he'd offered for her nearly two years ago. Her breasts had been ripe, her waist tiny, her face . . . unforgettable. Her fortune . . . adequate. Since then gossip had it that she was practically destitute after her brother's mysterious disappearance, but her uncle had indicated that she would bring a sizable dowry, which meant the gossip was as wrong as always.

"Francis!"

Arising, he walked over to the bed and sat down beside Eloise. Caressingly he laid a hand on her hip, but he reached for the bell pull with his other hand. "A moment, my darling," he said as a servant rushed into the bedchamber. He handed over the note and said, "Instruct my secretary to send an affirmative reply."

The last invitation was forwarded from Ian Thornton's London town house to Montmayne, his country estate, where it appeared on his desk among a mountain of business and social correspondence awaiting his attention. Ian opened Julius Cameron's missive while he was in the midst of rapid-fire dictation to his new secretary, and he did not take nearly so long to make a decision as Lord John Marchman or Sir Francis Belhaven.

He stared at it in utter disbelief while his secretary, Peters, who'd only been with him for a fortnight, muttered a silent prayer of gratitude for the break and continued scribbling as fast as he could, trying futilely to catch up with his employer's dictation.

"This," said Ian curtly, "was sent to me either by mistake or as a joke. In either case, it's in excruciatingly bad taste." A memory of Elizabeth Cameron flickered across Ian's mind—a mercenary, shallow little flirt with a face and body that had drugged his mind. She'd been betrothed to a viscount when he'd met her. Obviously she hadn't married her viscount—no doubt she'd jilted him in favor of someone with even better prospects. The English nobility, as he well knew, married only for prestige and money, then looked elsewhere for sexual fulfillment. Evidently Elizabeth Cameron's relatives were putting her back on the marriage block. If so, they must be damned eager to unload her if they were willing to forsake a title for Ian's money. . . . That line of conjecture seemed so unlikely that Ian dismissed it. This note was obviously a stupid prank, perpetrated, no doubt, by someone who remembered the gossip that had exploded over that weekend house party—someone who thought he'd find the note amusing.

Completely dismissing the prankster and Elizabeth Cameron from his mind, Ian glanced at his harassed secretary who was frantically scribbling away. "No reply is necessary," he said. As he spoke he flipped the message across his desk toward his secretary, but the white parchment slid across the polished oak and floated to the floor. Peters made an awkward dive to catch it, but as he lurched sideways all the other correspondence that went with his dictation slid off his lap onto the floor. "I—I'm sorry, sir," he stammered, leaping up and trying to collect the dozens of pieces of paper he'd scattered on the carpet. "Extremely sorry, Mr. Thornton," he added, frantically snatching up contracts, invitations and letters and shoving them into a disorderly pile.

His employer appeared not to hear him. He was already rapping out more instructions and passing the corresponding invitations and letters across the desk. "Decline the first three, accept the fourth, decline the fifth. Send my condolences on this one. On this one, explain that I'm going to be in Scotland, and send an invitation to join me there, along with directions to the cottage."

Clutching the papers to his chest, Peters poked his face up on the opposite side of the desk. "Yes, Mr. Thornton!" he said, trying to sound confident. But it was hard to be confident when one was on one's knees. Harder still when one wasn't entirely certain which instructions of the morning went with which invitation or piece of correspondence.

Ian Thornton spent the rest of the afternoon closeted with Peters, heaping more dictation on the inundated clerk.

He spent the evening with the Earl of Melbourne, his future father-in-law, discussing the betrothal contract being drawn up between the earl's daughter and himself.

Peters spent part of his evening trying to learn from the butler which invitations his employer was likely to accept or reject.

2

With the help of her footman, who did double duty as a groom when the occasion required (which it usually did), Lady Elizabeth Cameron, Countess of Havenhurst, hopped down from her aging mare. "Thank you, Charles," she said, grinning affectionately at the old retainer.

At the moment the young countess did not remotely resemble the conventional image of a noblewoman, nor even a lady of fashion: Her hair was covered with a blue kerchief that was tied at the nape; her gown was simple, unadorned, and somewhat outdated; and over her arm was the woven basket she used to do her marketing in the village. But not even her drab clothing, her ancient horse, or the market basket over her arm could make Elizabeth Cameron look "common." Beneath her kerchief her shining gold hair fell in a luxurious tumble over her shoulders and back; left unbound, as it normally was, it framed a face of striking, flawless beauty. Her finely molded cheekbones were slightly high, her skin creamy and glowing with health, her lips generous and soft. But her eyes were her most striking feature; beneath delicately winged eyebrows long, curly lashes fringed eyes that were a vivid, startling green. Not hazel or aqua, but green; wonderfully expressive eyes that sparkled like emeralds when she was happy or darkened when she was pensive.

The footman peered hopefully at the contents of the basket, which were wrapped in paper, but Elizabeth shook her head with a rueful grin. "There are no tarts in there, Charles. They were much too expensive, and Mr. Jenkins would not be reasonable. I told him I would buy a whole dozen, but he would not reduce the price by so much as a penny, so I refused to buy even one—on principle. Do you know," she confided with a chuckle, "last week when he saw me coming into his shop he hid behind the flour sacks?"

"He's a coward!" Charles said, grinning, for it was a known fact among tradesmen and shopkeepers that Elizabeth Cameron pinched a shilling until it squeaked, and that when it came to bargaining for price—which it always did with her—they rarely came out the winner. Her intellect, not her beauty, was her greatest asset in these transactions, for she could not only add and multiply in her head, but she was so sweetly reasonable, and so inventive when she listed her reasons for expecting a better price, that she either wore out her opponents or confused them into agreeing with her.

Her concern with money didn't stop with tradesmen; at Havenhurst there was scarcely an economy she didn't practice, but her methods were successful. At nineteen years old, with the burden of her small ancestral estate and eighteen of its original ninety servants on her youthful shoulders, she was managing with limited financial help from her grudging uncle to do the nearly impossible: She was keeping Havenhurst off the auctioneer's block, as well as feeding and clothing the servants who had remained there. The only "luxury" Elizabeth permitted herself was Miss Lucinda Throckmorton-Jones, who had been Elizabeth's duenna and was now her paid companion at severely reduced wages. Although Elizabeth felt perfectly capable of living alone at Havenhurst, she knew that, were she to do it, what little was left of her reputation would have been blackened beyond redemption.

Elizabeth handed her basket to her footman and said cheerfully, "Instead of tarts I bought strawberries. Mr.

Thergood is more reasonable than Mr. Jenkins. *He* agrees that when a person buys multiples of something, it is only reasonable that she should pay less per each."

Charles scratched his head at these complicated notions, but he tried to look as if he understood. "O' course," he agreed as he led her horse away. "Any fool could understand that."

"My feelings *exactly,*" she said, then she turned and ran lightly up the front steps, her mind set on going over the account books. Bentner swung open the front door, the stout, elderly butler's features tense with excitement. In the tone of one who is bursting with delight but is too dignified to show it, he announced, "You have a *visitor,* Miss Elizabeth!"

For a year and a half there had been no visitors at Havenhurst, and so it was little wonder that Elizabeth felt an absurd burst of pleasure followed by confusion. It couldn't be another creditor; Elizabeth had paid them off by stripping Havenhurst of all its valuables and most of its furniture. "Who is it?" she asked, stepping into the hall and reaching up to pull off her kerchief.

A beaming grin broke across Bentner's entire face. "It is Alexandra Lawrence! Er—Townsende," he corrected himself, recalling that their visitor was married now.

Joyous disbelief held Elizabeth immobilized for a split second, then she turned and burst into an unladylike run, pulling off her kerchief as she dashed toward the drawing room. In the doorway she came to an abrupt halt, the kerchief dangling from her fingertips, her eyes riveted to the lovely young brunette who was standing in the middle of the room, clad in an elegant red traveling suit. The brunette turned, and the two girls looked at each other while slow smiles dawned across their faces and glowed in their eyes. Elizabeth's voice was a whisper, filled with admiration, disbelief, and pure delight. *"Alex?* Is it really you?"

The brunette nodded, her smile widening.

They stood still, uncertain, each one noting the dramatic changes in the other in the past year and a half, each one wondering a little apprehensively if the changes went too deep. In the silent room the ties of childhood friendship and long-standing affection began to tighten around them, pulling them forward a hesitant step, then another, and suddenly they were running toward each other, flinging their arms around one another in fierce hugs, laughing and crying with joy.

"Oh, Alex, you look wonderful! I've missed you so!" Elizabeth laughed, hugging her again. To society "Alex" was Alexandra, Duchess of Hawthorne, but to Elizabeth she was "Alex," her oldest friend in the world—the friend who'd been on a prolonged honeymoon trip and so was unlikely to have heard yet of the awful mess Elizabeth was in.

Pulling her down onto the sofa, Elizabeth launched into a torrent of questions. "When did you return from your honeymoon trip? Are you happy? What brings you here? How long can you stay?"

"I've missed you, too," Alex replied, chuckling, and she began answering Elizabeth's questions in the order they'd been asked. "We returned three weeks ago. I'm *ecstatically* happy. I'm here to see you, of course, and I can stay for a few days, if you wish me to."

"Of course I wish it!" Elizabeth said gaily. "I have absolutely nothing planned, except for today. My uncle is coming to see me." Actually, Elizabeth's social schedule was perfectly blank for the next twelve months, and her uncle's occasional visits were *worse* than having nothing to do. But none of that mattered anymore. Elizabeth was so absurdly happy to see her friend that she couldn't stop smiling.

As they had done when they were youngsters, both girls kicked off their slippers, curled their legs beneath them, and talked for hours with the easy camaraderie of kindred spirits separated for years, yet eternally united by girlhood memories, happy, tender, and sad. "Will you ever forget," Elizabeth laughingly asked two hours later, "those wonderful mock tournaments we used to have whenever Mary Ellen's family had a birthday?"

"Never," Alex said feelingly, smiling with the memories.

"You unseated me every time we had a joust," Elizabeth said.

"Yes, but you won every single shooting contest. At least, you did until your parents found out and decided you were too old—and too refined—to join us." Alex sobered. "We missed you after that."

"Not as much as I missed you. I always knew exactly which days those jousts were taking place, and I would mope around here in complete gloom, imagining what fun you were having. Then Robert and I decided to start our own tournaments, and we made all the servants participate," she added, laughing as she thought of her half-brother and herself in those bygone days.

After a moment Alex's smile faded. "Where *is* Robert? You haven't mentioned him at all."

"He . . ." She hesitated, knowing that she couldn't talk of her half-brother's disappearance without revealing everything that had preceded it. On the other hand, there was something in Alexandra's sympathetic eyes that made Elizabeth wonder uneasily if her friend had already heard the whole awful story. In a matter-of-fact voice she said, "Robert disappeared a year and a half ago. I think it may have had something to do with—well, debts. Let's not talk of it," she said hastily.

"Very well," Alex agreed with an artificially bright smile. "What shall we ta . about?"

"You," Elizabeth said promptly.

Alex was older than Elizabeth, and time flew past as Alexandra talked of the husband she had wed, whom she obviously adored. Elizabeth listened attentively to the descriptions of the wondrous places all over the world that he had taken her to see on their honeymoon trip.

"Tell me about London," Elizabeth said when Alex ran out of conversation about foreign cities.

"What do you want to know?" she asked, sobering.

Elizabeth leaned forward in her chair and opened her mouth to ask the questions that mattered most to her, but pride prevented her from voicing them. "Oh—nothing in particular," she lied. I want to know if my friends ridicule me or condemn me—or worse, if they pity me, she thought. I want to know if it's common gossip that I'm penniless now. Most of all, I want to know why none of them has bothered to visit me or even to send me a message.

A year and a half ago, when she'd made her debut, she had

been an instant success, and offers for her hand were made in record numbers. Now, at nineteen, she was an outcast from the same society that had once imitated, praised, and petted her. Elizabeth had broken their rules, and in doing so she had become the focus of a scandal that raged through the *ton* like wildfire.

As Elizabeth looked uneasily at Alexandra she wondered if society knew the whole story or only the scandal; she wondered if they still talked about it or if it had finally been laid to rest. Alex had left on her prolonged trip just before it all happened, and she wondered if Alex had heard about it since her return.

The questions tumbled in her mind, desperate to be voiced, but she could not risk asking for two reasons: In the first place, the answers, when they came, might make her cry, and she would *not* give in to tears. In the second, in order to ask Alex the questions she longed to ask she would have to first inform her friend of all that had happened. And the simple truth was that Elizabeth was too lonely and bereft to risk the possibility that Alex might also abandon her if she knew.

"What sorts of things do you want to know?" Alex asked with a determinedly blank, cheerful smile pinned to her face—a smile designed to conceal her pity and sorrow from her proud friend.

"Anything!" Elizabeth immediately replied.

"Well, then," Alex said, eager to banish the pall of Elizabeth's painful, unspoken questions from the room, "Lord Dusenberry just became betrothed to Cecelia Lacroix!"

"How nice," Elizabeth replied with a soft, winsome smile, her voice filled with genuine happiness. "He's very wealthy and from one of the finest families."

"He's an inveterate philanderer, and he'll take a mistress within a month of their vows," Alex countered with the directness that had always shocked and rather delighted Elizabeth.

"I hope you're mistaken."

"I'm not. But if you think I am, would you care to place a wager on it?" Alex continued, so happy to see the laughter rekindle in her friend's eyes that she spoke without thinking. "Say £30?"

Suddenly Elizabeth couldn't bear the uncertainty any longer. She needed to know whether loyalty had brought Alex to her—or whether she was here because she mistakenly believed Elizabeth was still the most sought-after female in London. Lifting her eyes to Alex's blue ones, Elizabeth said with quiet dignity, "I do not have £30, Alex."

Alex returned her somber gaze, trying to blink back tears of sympathy. "I know."

Elizabeth had learned to deal with relentless adversity, to hide her fear and hold her head high. Now, faced with kindness and loyalty, she nearly gave in to the hated tears that tragedy had not wrung from her. Scarcely able to drag the words past the tears clogging her throat, Elizabeth said humbly, "Thank you."

"There's nothing for which to thank me. I've heard the whole sordid story, and I don't believe a word of it! Furthermore, I want you to come to London for the Season and stay with us." Leaning forward, Alex took her hand. "For the sake of your own pride, you have to face them all down. I'll help you. Better yet, I'll convince my husband's grandmother to lend *her* consequence to you. Believe me," Alex finished feelingly, but with a fond smile, "no one will *dare* to cut you if the Dowager Duchess of Hawthorne stands behind you."

"Please, Alex, stop. You don't know what you're saying. Even if I were willing, which I'm not, she would never agree. I don't know her, but she'll surely know *all* about me. About what people say about me, I mean."

Alex held her gaze steadily. "You're right on one account —she had heard the gossip while I was away. I've talked the matter over with her, however, and she is willing to meet you and then make her own decision. She'll love you, just as I do. And when that happens she'll move heaven and earth to make society accept you."

Elizabeth shook her head, swallowing back a constricting lump of emotion that was part gratitude, part humiliation. "I appreciate it, really I do, but I couldn't endure it."

"I've quite made up my mind," Alex warned gently. "My

husband respects my judgment, and he'll agree, I have no doubt. As to gowns for a Season, I have many I've not yet worn. I'll lend—"

"Absolutely not!" Elizabeth burst out. "Please, Alex," she implored, realizing how ungrateful she must sound. "At least leave me some pride. Besides," she added with a gentle smile, "I am not quite so unlucky as you seem to think. I have you. And I have Havenhurst."

"I know that," Alex said. "But I also know that you cannot stay here all your life. You don't have to go out in company when you're in London, if you don't wish to do so. But we'll spend time together. I've missed you."

"You'll be too busy to do it," Elizabeth said, recalling the frenetic whirlwind of social activities that marked the Season.

"I won't be that busy," Alexandra said with a mysterious smile glowing in her eyes. "I'm with child."

Elizabeth caught her in a fierce hug. "I'll come!" she agreed before she could think better of it. "But I can stay at my uncle's town house if he isn't there."

"Ours," Alexandra said stubbornly.

"We'll see," Elizabeth countered just as stubbornly. And then she said rapturously, "A baby!"

"Excuse me, Miss Alex," Bentner interrupted, then he turned to Elizabeth, looking uneasy. "Your uncle has just arrived," he said. "He wishes to see you *at once* in the study."

Alex looked quizzically from the butler to Elizabeth. "Havenhurst seemed rather deserted when I arrived. How many servants are here?"

"Eighteen," Elizabeth said. "Before Robert left we were down to forty-five of the original ninety, but my uncle turned them all away. He said we didn't need them, and after examining the estate books he showed me that we couldn't possibly afford to give them anything but a roof and food. Eighteen of them remained anyway, though," she added, smiling up at Bentner as she continued, "They've lived at Havenhurst all their lives. It's their home, too."

Standing up, Elizabeth stifled the spurt of dread that was

nothing more than an automatic reflex at the prospect of confronting her uncle. "This shouldn't take long. Uncle Julius never likes to remain here any longer than he absolutely must."

Bentner hung back, ostensibly gathering up the tea things, watching Elizabeth leave. When she was out of earshot he turned to the Duchess of Hawthorne, whom he'd known when she was a dab of a girl running wild in boys' breeches. "Begging your pardon, Your Grace," he said formally, his kindly old face filled with concern, "but may I say how glad I am that you're here, especially now with Mr. Cameron just arriving?"

"Why, thank you, Bentner. It's lovely to see you again, too. Is anything particularly amiss with Mr. Cameron?"

"It looks like there might be." He paused to walk over to the doorway and steal a furtive glance down the hall, then he returned to her and confided, "Aaron—our coachman, that is—and I both don't like the look of Mr. Cameron today. And there's one thing more," he stated, picking up the tea tray. "None of us who've stayed on here remained because of affection for Havenhurst." An embarrassed flush stole up his white cheeks, and his voice turned gruff with emotion. "We stayed for our young mistress. We are all she has left, you see."

His gruffly spoken avowal of loyalty made Alex's eyes sting with tears even before he added, "We must not let her uncle send her into the gloom, which is what he always does."

"Is there a means to stop him?" Alex asked, smiling.

Bentner straightened, nodded, and said with dignified force, "I, for one, am in favor of shoving him off London Bridge. Aaron favors poison."

There was anger and frustration in his words, but no real menace, and Alex responded with a conspiratorial smile. "I think I prefer your method, Bentner—it's tidier."

Alexandra's remark had been teasing, and Bentner's reply was a formal bow, but as they looked at each other for a moment they both acknowledged the unspoken communication they'd just exchanged. The butler had informed her that, should the staff's help be needed in any way in future, the duchess could depend upon their complete, unquestioning loyalty. The duchess's answer had assured him that, far from resenting his intrusion, she appreciated the information and would keep it in mind should such an occasion occur.

3

Julius Cameron looked up as his niece entered his study, and his eyes narrowed with annoyance; even now, when she was little more than an impoverished orphan, there was regal grace in her carriage and stubborn pride in the set of her small chin. She was up to her ears in debt and sinking deeper every month, but she still walked about with her head high, just like her arrogant, reckless father had done. At the age of thirty-five he had drowned in a yachting accident, along with Elizabeth's mother, and by then he'd already gambled away his substantial inheritance and secretly mortgaged his lands. Even so, he'd continued to walk with arrogance, and to live, until the very last day, like a privileged aristocrat.

As the younger son of the Earl of Havenhurst, Julius had inherited neither title nor fortune nor substantial lands, yet *he* had managed by dint of unstinting work and vigilant frugality to amass a considerable fortune. He had gone without all but the barest necessities in his ceaseless efforts to better his lot in life; he had eschewed the glamour and temptations of society, not only because of the incredible expense, but because he refused to hang about on the fringes of the nobility.

After all of his sacrifices, after the Spartan existence he

and his wife had led, fate had still contrived to cheat him, for his wife was barren. To his everlasting bitterness, he had no heir for his fortune or his lands—no heir except the son Elizabeth would bear after she was wed.

Now, as he watched her seating herself across the desk from him, the irony of it all struck him with renewed, painful force: In actuality, he'd spent a lifetime working and scrimping . . . and all he'd accomplished was to replenish the wealth of his reckless brother's future grandson. And if that wasn't infuriating enough, he'd also been left with the task of cleaning up the mess Elizabeth's half-brother, Robert, had left behind when he'd vanished almost two years ago. As a result, it now fell to Julius to honor her father's written instructions to see her wed to a man possessed of *both* title and wealth, if possible. A month ago, when Julius had launched his search for a suitable husband for her, he'd expected the task to be fairly easy. After all, when she'd made her debut the year before last, her beauty, her impeccable lineage, and her alleged wealth had won her a record fifteen marital offers in four short weeks. To Julius's surprise, only three of those men had answered his letters of inquiry in the affirmative, and several hadn't bothered to answer at all. Of course, it was no secret that she was poor now, but Julius had offered a respectable dowry to get her off his hands. To Julius, who thought of everything in terms of money, her dowry alone should have made her desirable enough. Of the dreadful scandal surrounding her Julius knew little and cared less. He shunned society along with all its gossip, frivolity, and excesses.

Elizabeth's question pulled him from his angry reverie: "What did you wish to discuss with me, Uncle Julius?"

Animosity, combined with resentment over what was sure to be an angry outburst from Elizabeth, made his voice more curt than normal. "I have come here today to discuss your impending marriage."

"My—my what?" Elizabeth gasped, so taken aback that her tight facade of dignity dropped, and for a split second she looked and felt like a child, forlorn and bewildered and trapped.

"I believe you heard me." Leaning back in his chair, Julius said brusquely, "I've narrowed it down to three men.

Two of them are titled, the third is not. Since titles were paramount to your father, I shall choose the man with the highest rank who offers for you, assuming I *have* such a choice to make."

"How—" Elizabeth had to pause to gather her wits before she could speak. "How did you happen to select these men?"

"I asked Lucinda for the names of any men who, during your debut, had discussed marrying you with Robert. She gave me their names, and I sent messengers to each of them, stating your willingness and mine—as your guardian—to reconsider them as possible husbands for you."

Elizabeth clutched the arms of her chair, trying to control her horror. "Do you mean," she said in a strangled whisper, "you made some sort of public offering of my hand in marriage to any of those men who'd take me?"

"Yes!" he bit out, bristling at her implied accusation that he'd not behaved in a manner befitting his station or hers. "Furthermore, it may do you good to hear that your legendary attraction for the opposite sex has apparently ended. Only three of those fifteen men expressed a willingness to renew their acquaintance with you."

Humiliated to the depths of her being, Elizabeth stared blankly at the wall behind him. "I cannot believe you've *done* this."

His open palm hit the desk like a thunderclap. "I've acted within my rights, niece, and in accordance with your wastrel father's specific instructions. May I remind you that when I die, it is *my* money that will be entrusted to your husband and ultimately to your son. *Mine.*"

For months now Elizabeth had tried to understand her uncle, and somewhere in her heart she comprehended the cause of his bitterness and even empathized with it. "I wish you had been blessed with a son of your own," she said in a suffocated voice. "But I am not to blame because you were not. I've done you no harm, given you no cause to hate me enough to do this to me. . . ." Her voice trailed off when she saw his expression harden at what he regarded as pleading. Elizabeth's chin rose, and she clung to what was left of her dignity. "Who are the men?"

"Sir Francis Belhaven," he said shortly.

Elizabeth stared at him in stupefaction and shook her head. "I met hundreds of new people during my debut, but I don't recall that name at all."

"The second man is Lord John Marchman, Earl of Canford."

Again Elizabeth shook her head. "The name is somewhat familiar, but I can't recall a face to go with it."

Obviously disappointed in her reaction, her uncle said irritably, "You apparently have a poor memory. If you can't recall a knight or an earl," he added sarcastically, "I doubt you'll remember a mere mister."

Stung by his unprovoked remark, she said stiffly, "Who is the third?"

"Mr. Ian Thornton. He's—"

That name sent Elizabeth jolting to her feet while a blaze of animosity and a shock of terror erupted through her entire body. *"Ian Thornton!"* she cried, leaning her palms on the desk to steady herself. "Ian Thornton!" she repeated, her voice rising with a mixture of anger and hysterical laughter. "Uncle, if Ian Thornton discussed marrying me, it was at the *point of Robert's gun!* His interest in me was never marriage, and Robert dueled with him over his behavior. In fact, Robert *shot* him!"

Instead of relenting or being upset, her uncle merely regarded her with blank indifference, and Elizabeth said fiercely, "Don't you understand?"

"What I understand," he said, glowering, "is that he replied to my message in the affirmative and was very cordial. Perhaps he regrets his earlier behavior and wishes to make amends."

"Amends!" she cried. "I've no idea whether he feels loathing for me or merely contempt, but I can assure you he does *not* and has *never* wished to wed me! He's the reason I can't show my face in society!"

"In my opinion, you're better off away from that decadent London influence; however, that's not to the point. He has accepted my terms."

"What *terms?*"

Inured to Elizabeth's quaking alarm, Julius stated matter-of-factly, "Each of the three candidates has agreed that you will come to visit him briefly in order to allow you to decide if you suit. Lucinda will accompany you as chaperon. You're to leave in five days. Belhaven is first, then Marchman, then Thornton."

The room swam before Elizabeth's eyes. "I can't *believe* this!" she burst out, and in her misery she seized on the least of her problems. "Lucinda has taken her first holiday in years! She's in Devon visiting her sister."

"Then take Berta instead and have Lucinda join you later when you go to visit Thornton in Scotland."

"Berta! Berta is a maid. My reputation will be in shreds if I spend a week in the home of a man with no one but a maid for a chaperon."

"Then don't say she's a maid," he snapped. "Since I already referred to Lucinda Throckmorton-Jones as your chaperon in my letters, you can say that Berta is your aunt. No more objections, miss," he finished, "the matter is settled. That will be all for now. You may go."

"It's *not* settled! There's been some sort of horrible mistake, I tell you. Ian Thornton would never want to see me, any more than I wish to see him!"

"There's no mistake," Julius said with complete finality. "Ian Thornton received my letter and accepted our offer. He even sent directions to his place in Scotland."

"*Your* offer," Elizabeth cried, "not mine!"

"I'll not debate technicalities any further with you, Elizabeth. This discussion is at an end."

4

Elizabeth walked slowly down the hall and turned a corner, intending to rejoin Alexandra, but her knees were shaking so violently that she had to stop and put her hand against the wall to steady herself. Ian Thornton . . . In a matter of days she would confront Ian Thornton.

His name whirled through her mind, making her head spin with a combination of loathing, humiliation, and dread, and she finally turned and walked into the small salon where she sank down onto the sofa, staring blankly at the bright patch of wallpaper where a painting by Rubens had once hung.

Not for one moment did Elizabeth believe Ian Thornton had ever wanted to marry her, and she could not imagine what possible motive he might now have for accepting her uncle's outrageous offer. She had been a naïve, gullible fool where he was concerned.

Now, as she leaned her head back and closed her eyes, she could hardly believe she'd ever been as reckless—or as carefree—as she'd been the weekend she met him. She'd been so certain that her future would be bright, but then, she'd had no reason to think otherwise.

Her parents' death when she was eleven years old had been a dark time for her, but Robert had been there to comfort her and cheer her and promise her that everything would soon look bright again. Robert was eight years older than she, and although he was actually her half-brother—her mother's son by her first marriage—Elizabeth had loved and relied on him for as long as she could remember. Her parents had been gone so often that they had seemed more like beautiful visitors who flitted in and out of her life three or four times a year, bringing her presents and then vanishing soon after in a wave of gay good-byes.

Except for the loss of her parents, Elizabeth's childhood had been very pleasant indeed. Her sunny disposition had made her a favorite with all the servants, who doted on her. Cook gave her sweets; the butler taught her to play chess; Aaron, the head coachman, taught her to play whist, and years later he taught her to use a pistol should the occasion ever occur when she needed to protect herself.

But of all her "friends" at Havenhurst, the one with whom Elizabeth spent the most time was Oliver, the head gardener who'd come to Havenhurst when she was eleven. A quiet man with gentle eyes, Oliver labored in Havenhurst's greenhouse and flowerbeds, talking softly to his cuttings and plants. "Plants need affection," he'd explained when she surprised him one day in the greenhouse, speaking encouragements to a wilting violet, "just like people. Go ahead," he'd invited her, nodding toward the drooping violet, "give that pretty violet an encouragin' word."

Elizabeth had felt a little foolish, but she had done as instructed, for Oliver's expertise as a gardener was unquestionable—Havenhurst's gardens had improved dramatically in the months since he'd come there. And so she had leaned toward the violet and earnestly told it, "I hope you are soon completely recovered and your old lovely self again!" Then she had stepped back and waited expectantly for the yellowing, drooping leaves to lift toward the sun.

"I've given her a dose of my special medicine," Oliver said as he carefully moved the potted plant to the benches where he kept all his ailing patients. "In a few days, you come back and see if she isn't anxious to show you how much better she feels." Oliver, Elizabeth later realized, regarded all flowering plants as "she," while all others were "he."

The very next day Elizabeth went to the greenhouse, but the violet looked as miserable as ever. Five days later she'd all but forgotten the plant and had merely gone to the greenhouse to share some tarts with Oliver.

"You've a friend over there waiting to see you, missy," he told her.

Elizabeth had wandered over to the table with the ailing plants and discovered the violet, its delicate flowers standing sturdily on fragile little stems, its leaves perked up. "Oliver!" she'd cried delightedly. "How did you *do* that?"

"'Twas *your* kind words and a bit o' my medicine what pulled her through," he said, and because he could see the glimmerings of genuine fascination—or perhaps because he wished to distract the newly orphaned girl from her woes—he'd taken her through the greenhouse, naming the plants and showing her grafts he was trying to make. Afterward he'd asked if she would like a small garden for her own, and when Elizabeth nodded they'd strolled through the seedlings in the greenhouse, beginning to plan what flowers she ought to plant.

That day marked the beginning of Elizabeth's enduring love affair with growing things. Working at Oliver's side, an apron tied around her waist to protect her dress, she learned all he could tell her of his "medicines" and mulches and attempts to graft one plant to another.

And when Oliver had taught her all *he* knew, Elizabeth began to teach him, for she had a distinct advantage— Elizabeth could read, and Havenhurst's library had been the pride of her grandfather. Side by side they sat upon the garden bench until twilight made reading impossible, while Elizabeth read to him about ancient and modern methods of helping plants grow stronger and more vibrant. Within five years Elizabeth's "little" garden encompassed most of the main beds. Wherever she knelt with her small spade, flowers seemed to burst into bloom about her. "They know you love 'em," Oliver told her with one of his rare grins as she knelt in a bed of gaily colored pansies one day, "and they're showin' you they love you back by givin' you their very best."

When Oliver's health required he go to a warmer clime, Elizabeth missed him greatly and spent even more time in her gardens. There she gave full rein to her own ideas, sketching out planting arrangements and bringing them to life, recruiting footmen and grooms to help her enlarge the beds until they covered a newly terraced section that stretched across the entire back of the house.

In addition to her gardening and the companionship of the servants, Elizabeth took great pleasure in her friendship with Alexandra Lawrence. Alex was the closest neighbor of Elizabeth's approximate age, and although Alex was older, they shared the same exuberant pleasure in lying in bed at night, telling blood-chilling stories of ghosts until they were giggling with nervous fear, or sitting in Elizabeth's large tree house, confiding girlish secrets and private dreams.

Even after Alex had married and gone away, Elizabeth never regarded herself as lonely, because she had something else she loved that occupied all her plans and most of her time: She had Havenhurst. Originally a castle, complete with moat and high stone enclosures, Havenhurst had been the dower house of a twelfth-century grandmother of Elizabeth's. The husband of that particular grandmother had taken advantage of his influence with the king to have several unusual codicils attached to Havenhurst's entailment—codicils to ensure that it would belong to his wife and their successors for as long as they wished to keep it, be those successors male or female.

As a result, at the age of eleven when her father died, Elizabeth had become the Countess of Havenhurst, and although the title itself meant little to her, Havenhurst, with its colorful history, meant everything. By the time she was seventeen she was as familiar with that history as she was with her own. She knew everything about the sieges it had withstood, complete with the names of the attackers and the strategies the earls and countesses of Havenhurst had employed to keep it safe. She knew all there was to know of its former owners, their accomplishments and their foibles—from the first earl, whose daring and skill in battle had made him a legend (but who was secretly terrified of his wife), to his son, who'd had his unfortunate horse shot when the young earl fell off while practicing at the quintain in Havenhurst's bailey.

The moat had been filled in centuries before, the castle

walls removed, and the house itself enlarged and altered until it now looked like a picturesque, rambling country house that bore little or no resemblance to its original self. But even so, Elizabeth knew from parchments and paintings in the library *exactly* where everything had been, including the moat, the wall, and probably the quintain.

As a result of all that, by the time she was seventeen Elizabeth Cameron was very unlike most well-born young ladies. Extraordinarily well-read, poised, and with a streak of practicality that was evidencing itself more each day, she was already learning from the bailiff about the running of her own estate. Surrounded by trusted adults for all her life, she was naïvely optimistic that all people must be as nice and as dependable as she and everyone else at Havenhurst.

It was little wonder that on that fateful day when Robert unexpectedly arrived from London, dragged her away from the roses she was pruning, and, grinning broadly, informed her that she was going to make her debut in London in six months, Elizabeth had reacted with pleasure and no concern at all about encountering any difficulties.

"It's all arranged," he'd told her excitedly. "Lady Jamison has agreed to sponsor you—out of fondness for our mother's memory. The thing's going to cost a bloody fortune, but it'll be worth it."

Elizabeth had stared at him in surprise. "You've never mentioned the cost of anything before. We aren't in any sort of financial difficulty, are we, Robert?"

"Not anymore," he'd lied. "We have a fortune right here, only I didn't realize it."

"Where?" Elizabeth asked, completely baffled by everything she was hearing as well as by the uneasy feeling she had.

Laughing, he tugged her over to the mirror, cupped her face in his hands, and made her look at herself.

After casting him a puzzled glance she looked at her face in the mirror, then she laughed. "Why didn't you just say I had a smudge?" she said, rubbing at the small streak on her cheek with her fingertips.

"Elizabeth," he chuckled, "is that all you see in that mirror—a smudge on your cheek?"

"No, I see my face," she answered.

"How does it look to you?"

"Like my face," she replied in amused exasperation.

"Elizabeth, that face of yours is our fortune now!" he cried. "I never thought of it until yesterday, when Bertie Krandell told me about the splendid offer his sister just got from Lord Cheverley."

Elizabeth was stupefied. "What are you talking about?"

"I'm talking about your marriage," he explained with his reckless grin. "You're twice as beautiful as Bertie's sister. With your face and Havenhurst as your dowry, you'll be able to make a marriage that will make all England buzz. That marriage will bring you jewels and gowns and beautiful homes, and it will bring *me* connections that will be worth more than money. Besides," he teased, "if I run short now and then, I know you'll throw a few thousand pounds my way—from your pin money."

"We *are* short of money, aren't we?" Elizabeth persisted, too concerned about that to care about a London debut. Robert's gaze dropped from hers, and with a weary sigh he gestured toward the sofa. "We're in a bit of a fix," he admitted when she sat down beside him. Elizabeth might have been barely seventeen, but she knew when he was gulling her, and her expression made it clear she suspected he was doing exactly that. "Actually," he admitted reluctantly, "we're in a bad fix. Very bad."

"How can that be?" she asked, and despite the fear beginning to quake through her, she managed to sound calm.

Embarrassment tinted his handsome face with a ruddy hue. "For one thing, Father left behind a staggering amount of debts, some of them from gaming. I've accumulated more than a few debts of that sort of my own. I've been holding his creditors and mine off for the last several years as best I can, but they're getting nasty now. And it's not just that. Havenhurst costs a bloody ransom to run, Elizabeth. Its income doesn't match its expenses by a long way, and it never has. The end result is that we're mortgaged up to our ears, you and I both. We're going to have to mortgage the contents of the house to pay off some of these debts or neither of us will be able to show a face in London, and that's not the worst of it. Havenhurst is yours, not mine, but if you can't make a good marriage, it's going to end up on the auction block, and soon."

Her voice shook only slightly, but inwardly Elizabeth was a roiling mass of bewilderment and alarm. "You just said a London Season would cost a fortune, and we obviously don't have it," she pointed out practically.

"The creditors will back away the minute they see you're betrothed to a man of means and consequence, and I promise you we won't have a problem finding one of those."

Elizabeth thought the whole scheme sounded mercenary and cold, but Robert shook his head. This time he was the practical one: "You're a female, love, and you have to wed, you know that—all women must wed. You're not going to meet anyone eligible cooped up at Havenhurst. And I'm *not* suggesting we accept an offer from just anyone. I'll choose someone you can develop a lasting affection for, and then," he promised sincerely, "I'll bargain for a long engagement on the basis of your youth. No respectable man would want to rush a seventeen-year-old girl into matrimony before she was ready for it. It's the only way," he warned her when she looked as if she was going to argue.

Sheltered though she'd been, Elizabeth knew he was not being unreasonable about expecting her to wed. Before her parent's death they'd made it very clear that it was her duty to marry in accordance with her family's wishes. In this case, her half-brother was in charge of making the selection, and Elizabeth trusted him implicitly.

"Fess up," Robert teased gently, "haven't you ever dreamed of wearing beautiful gowns and being courted by handsome beaux?"

"Perhaps a few times," Elizabeth admitted with an embarrassed sidewise smile, and it was something of an understatement. She was a normal, healthy girl, filled with affection, and she'd read her share of romantic novels. That last part of what Robert said had much appeal. "Very well," she said with a decisive chuckle. "We'll give it a try."

"We'll have to do more than *try*, Elizabeth, we'll have to pull it off, or you'll end up as a landless governess to someone else's children instead of a countess or better, with children of your own. I'll land in debtors' gaol." The idea of Robert in a dank cell and herself without Havenhurst was enough to make Elizabeth agree to almost anything. "Leave everything to me," he said, and Elizabeth did.

In the next six months Robert set about to overcome every obstacle that might prevent Elizabeth from making a spectacular impression on the London scene. A woman named Mrs. Porter was employed to teach Elizabeth those intricate social skills her mother and former governess had not. From Mrs. Porter Elizabeth learned that she must never betray that she was intelligent, well-read, or the slightest bit interested in horticulture.

An expensive couturier in London was employed to design and make all the gowns Mrs. Porter deemed necessary for the Season.

Miss Lucinda Throckmorton-Jones, former paid companion to several of the *ton's* most successful debutantes of prior seasons, came to Havenhurst to fill the position of Elizabeth's duenna. A woman of fifty with wiry gray hair she scraped back into a bun and the posture of a ramrod, she had a permanently pinched face, as if she smelled something disagreeable but was too well-bred to remark upon it. In addition to the duenna's daunting physical appearance, Elizabeth observed shortly after their first meeting that Miss Throckmorton-Jones possessed an astonishing ability to sit serenely for hours without twitching so much as a finger.

Elizabeth refused to be put off by her stony demeanor and set about finding a way to thaw her. Teasingly, she called her "Lucy," and when the casually affectionate nickname won a thunderous frown from the lady, Elizabeth tried to find a different means. She discovered it very soon: A few days after Lucinda came to live at Havenhurst the duenna discovered her curled up in a chair in Havenhurst's huge library, engrossed in a book. "You enjoy reading?" Lucinda had said gruffly—and with surprise—as she noted the gold embossed title on the volume.

"Yes," Elizabeth had assured her, smiling. "Do you?"

"Have you read Christopher Marlowe?"

"Yes, but I prefer Shakespeare."

Thereafter it became their policy each night after supper to debate the merits of the individual books they'd read. Before long Elizabeth realized that she'd won the duenna's reluctant respect. It was impossible to be certain she'd won

Lucinda's affection, for the only emotion the lady ever displayed was anger, and that only once, at a miscreant tradesman in the village. Even so, it was a display Elizabeth never forgot. Wielding her ever-present umbrella, Lucinda had advanced on the hapless man, backing him clear around his own shop, while from her lips in a icy voice poured the most amazing torrent of eloquent, biting fury Elizabeth had ever heard.

"My temper," Lucinda had primly informed her—by way of apology, Elizabeth supposed—"is my *only* shortcoming."

Privately, Elizabeth thought Lucy must bottle up all her emotions inside herself as she sat perfectly still on sofas and chairs, for years at a time, until it finally exploded like one of those mountains she'd read about that poured forth molten rock when the pressure finally reached a peak.

By the time the Camerons, along with Lucinda and the necessary servants, arrived in London for Elizabeth's debut, Elizabeth had learned all that Mrs. Porter could teach her, and she felt quite capable of meeting the challenges Mrs. Porter described. Actually, other than memorizing the rules of etiquette she was a little baffled over the huge fuss being made. After all, she'd learned to dance in the six months she was being prepared for her debut, and she'd been conversing since she was three years old, and as closely as she could tell, her only duties as a debutante were to converse politely on trivial subjects only, conceal her intelligence at all costs, and dance.

The day after they settled into their rented town house her sponsor into the ranks of the *ton,* Lady Jamison, called on Elizabeth and Robert. With her were two daughters, Valerie and Charise. Valerie was a year older than Elizabeth and had made her debut the year before; Charise was five years older—the young widow of old Lord Dumont who cocked up his toes a month after the nuptials, leaving his new wife wealthy, relieved, and entirely independent.

In the two weeks before the Season began Elizabeth spent considerable time with the wealthy young debutantes who gathered in the Jamison drawing room to gossip happily about everything and anyone. All of them had come to

London with the same noble duty and familial objective: to marry, in accordance with their family's wishes, the wealthiest possible suitor while at the same time increasing their family's wealth and social standing.

It was in that drawing room that Elizabeth's education was continued and completed. She discovered to her shock that Mrs. Porter had been right about name-dropping. She also discovered that it was apparently not considered bad manners among the *ton* to discuss another person's financial status—particularly the status and prospects of an unmarried gentleman. The very first day it was all she could do not to betray her ignorance with a horrified gasp at the conversation swirling around her: "Lord Peters is an excellent catch. Why, he has an income of £20,000 and every prospect of being named heir to his uncle's baronetcy if his uncle dies of his heart ailment, which there's every reason to expect he will," one of the girls had announced, and the others chimed in: "Shoreham has that splendid estate in Wiltshire, and Mama is living on tenterhooks waiting to see if he'll declare himself. . . . Think of it, the Shoreham emeralds! . . . Robelsly is driving a splendid blue baroche, but Papa said he's up to his ears in debt and that I may on no account consider him. . . . Elizabeth, wait until you meet Richard Shipley! Do not under any circumstances let his charm fool you; he's a complete scoundrel, and though he dresses to the nines, he hasn't a feather to fly with!" That last advice came from Valerie Jamison, whom Elizabeth regarded as her very closest friend among the girls.

Elizabeth had gladly accepted their collective friendship and, outwardly, their advice. However, she felt increasingly uneasy about some of their attitudes toward people they judged as their inferiors—which wasn't surprising from a young lady who regarded her butler and coachman as *her* equals.

On the other hand, she was in love with London, with its bustling streets, manicured parks, and air of excited expectation, and she adored having friends who, when they weren't gossiping about someone, were merry companions.

On the night of her first ball, however, much of Elizabeth's confidence and delight had suddenly vanished. As she walked up the Jamisons' staircase beside Robert, she felt suddenly more terrified than she'd ever felt in her life. Her head was whirling with all the dos and don'ts she'd not really bothered to memorize, and she was morbidly certain she was going to be the Season's most notorious wallflower. But when she walked into the ballroom, the sight that greeted her made her forget all her self-conscious terrors and made her eyes shine with wonder. Chandeliers sparkled with hundreds of thousands of candles; handsome men and gorgeously gowned women strolled about in silks and satins.

Oblivious to the young men turning to stare at her, she lifted her shining eyes to her smiling brother. "Robert," she whispered, her green eyes radiant, "have you ever *imagined* there were such beautiful people and such grand rooms in the entire world?"

Clad in a filmy, gold-spangled white gauze gown with white roses entwined in her golden hair and her green eyes sparkling, Elizabeth Cameron looked like a fairy-tale princess.

She was enchanted, and her enchantment lent her an almost ethereal glow as she finally recovered herself enough to smile and acknowledge Valerie and her friends.

By the end of the evening Elizabeth *felt* as if she were in a fairy tale. Young men had flocked around her, begging for introductions and dances and for the opportunity to bring her punch. She smiled and danced, but she never resorted to the flirtatious contrivances used by some of the other girls; instead she listened with genuine interest and a warm smile to the beaux who spoke to her; she made them comfortable and drew them out as they led her to the dance floor. In truth, she was thrilled by the contagious gaiety, beguiled by the wondrous music, dazzled by so much attention, and all those emotions were displayed in her shining eyes and winsome smile. She was a mythical princess at her first ball, bewitching, entrancing, twirling around and around on the dance floor beneath glittering chandeliers, surrounded by charming princes, with no thought that it would ever end. Elizabeth Cameron, with her angelic beauty, golden hair, and shining green eyes, had taken London by storm. She was not a rage. She was *the* rage.

The callers began arriving at her house the next morning in an endless stream, and it was there, not in the ballrooms, where Elizabeth made her greatest conquests, for she was not merely lovely to look at, she was even easier to be with than she had been at the ball. Within three weeks fourteen gentlemen had offered for her, and London was abuzz with such an unprecedented occurrence. Not even Miss Mary Gladstone, the reigning beauty for two consecutive seasons, had received so many offers as that.

Twelve of Elizabeth's suitors were young, besotted, and eligible; two were much older and equally besotted. Robert, with great pride and equal lack of tact, boasted of her suitors and ruthlessly rejected them as unsuitable and inadequate. He waited, faithfully keeping his promise to Elizabeth to choose for her an *ideal* husband with whom she could be happy.

The fifteenth applicant for her hand filled all his requirements. Extremely wealthy, handsome, and personable, Viscount Mondevale, at twenty-five, was unquestionably one of the season's best catches. Robert knew it, and as he told Elizabeth that evening, he'd been so excited that he had nearly forgotten himself and leapt across his desk to congratulate the young viscount on his impending nuptials.

Elizabeth had been very pleased and touched that the gentleman she had most particularly admired was the very one who had offered for her and been chosen. "Oh, Robert, he's excessively nice. I—I wasn't entirely certain he liked me enough to offer for me."

Robert had pressed an affectionate kiss on her forehead. "Princess," he'd teased, "any man who takes a look at you loses his head entirely. It's only a matter of time."

Elizabeth had given him a brief smile and shrugged. She was heartily sick of people talking about her face as if there were no mind behind it. Moreover, all the frantic activities and brittle gaiety of the season, which had originally enthralled her, were rapidly beginning to pall. In fact, the strongest emotion she felt at Robert's announcement was relief that her marriage was settled.

"Mondevale plans to call on you this afternoon," Robert had continued, "but I don't mean to give him my answer for a week or two. Waiting will only strengthen his resolve, and besides, you deserve another few days of freedom before you become an engaged woman."

An engaged woman. Elizabeth felt an oddly queasy and distinctly uneasy feeling at the sound of that, though she realized she was being very foolish.

"I'll confess I dreaded telling him that your dowry is only £5,000, but he didn't seem to care. Said as much. Said all he wanted was you. Told me he meant to shower you with rubies the size of your palm."

"That's . . . wonderful," Elizabeth said weakly, trying very hard to feel something more than relief and an inexplicable twinge of apprehension.

"You're wonderful," he said, rumpling her hair. "You've pulled Father, me, and Havenhurst out of the briars."

At three o'clock Viscount Mondevale arrived. Elizabeth met with him in the yellow salon. He walked in, glanced around the room, then took her hands in his and smiled warmly into her eyes. "The answer is yes, isn't it?" he said, but it was more a statement than a question.

"You've already spoken to my brother?" Elizabeth said in surprise.

"No, I haven't."

"Then how do you know the answer is yes?" she asked, smiling and mystified.

"Because," he said, "the ever-present, eagle-eyed Miss Lucinda Throckmorton-Jones is absent from your side for the first time in a month!" He pressed a brief kiss to her forehead, which caught her off-guard, and she blushed. "Do you have any idea how beautiful you are?" he asked.

Elizabeth had a vague idea, since everyone was always telling her, and she supressed a worried impulse to reply, "Do you have any idea how *intelligent* I am?" It wasn't that she was an intellectual by any stretch of the imagination, but she *did* like to read and think and even debate issues, and she wasn't at all certain he would like that in her. He never expressed an opinion on anything except the most trivial generalities and he never asked for hers.

"You're enchanting," he whispered, and Elizabeth wondered, very seriously, *why* he thought that. He didn't know how much she loved to fish, or to laugh, or that she could

34

shoot a pistol so well she was almost a marksman. He didn't know she'd once had chariot races across the yard at Havenhurst, or that flowers seemed to bloom especially well for her. She didn't even know if he'd like to hear all the wonderful tales of Havenhurst and its colorful former inhabitants. He knew so little of her; she knew even less about him.

She wished she could ask Lucinda's advice, but Lucinda was ill with a high fever, raw throat, and bad digestion that had kept her in her chamber since the day before.

Elizabeth was still a little worried about all those things late the next afternoon when she left to attend the weekend party that would put her in the way of Ian Thornton and change her life. The party took place at the lovely country house belonging to Valerie's older sister, Lady Charise Dumont. By the time Elizabeth arrived the grounds of the estate were already filled with guests who were flirting and laughing and drinking liberal quantities of the champagne that gurgled forth from crystal fountains in the garden. By London standards, the gathering at this party was small; no more than one hundred fifty guests were present, and only twenty-five of them, including Elizabeth and her three friends, were actually staying the full weekend. If she hadn't been so sheltered and so naïve, she'd have recognized "the fast set" when she saw it that evening; she'd have realized at a glance that the guests at this party were much older, more experienced, and far more freewheeling than any she'd ever been around. And she'd have left.

Now, as Elizabeth sat in the salon at Havenhurst, reflecting on her disastrous folly that weekend, she marveled at her gullibility and naïveté.

Leaning her head back against the sofa, she closed her eyes, swallowing against the painful lump of humiliation that swelled in her throat. Why, she wondered despairingly, did happy memories fade and blur until one could scarcely recall them at all, while horrible memories seemed to retain their blinding clarity and painful sharpness? Even now she could remember that night—see it, hear it, smell it.

Flowers had been blooming riotously in the formal gardens when she walked outside looking for her friends. Roses. Everywhere there had been the intoxicating fragrance of roses. In the ballroom the orchestra was tuning up, and suddenly the opening strains of a lovely waltz drifted into the garden, filling it with music. Twilight was descending, and servants moved about the terraced garden paths lighting gay torches. Not all the paths would be lit, of course—those below the terraced steps would be left in convenient darkness for couples who later wished for intimacy in the hedge maze or the greenhouse, but Elizabeth hadn't realized that until later.

It had taken her nearly a half hour to find her friends, because they had gathered for a gay gossip at the far end of the garden where they were partially concealed from view by a high, clipped hedge. As she neared the girls she realized they weren't standing by the hedge, they were peeking through it, chattering excitedly about someone they were watching—someone who seemed to be sending them into raptures of excitement and speculation. "Now that," Valerie giggled, peering through the hedge, "is what my sister calls 'manly allure'!" In brief, reverent silence all three of the girls studied this paragon of masculinity who had earned such high praise from Valerie's gorgeous and very discerning sister, Charise. Elizabeth had just noticed a grass stain on her lavender slipper and was unhappily contemplating the exorbitant cost of a new pair while wondering if it was possible to buy only *one* shoe. "I still can't believe it's him!" Valerie whispered. "Charise said he might be here, but I wouldn't credit it. Won't everyone simply die when we return to London and tell them we've seen him?" Valerie added, then she noticed Elizabeth and beckoned her to the hedge. "Look, Elizabeth, isn't he *divine* in a sort of mysterious, *wicked* way?"

Instead of peering through the hedge Elizabeth glanced around the end of it, scanning the garden, which was filled with gorgeously garbed men and women who were laughing and chatting as they moved languidly toward the ballroom where dancing would take place, followed by a late supper. Her gaze drifted idly over the men in pastel satin breeches and colorful waistcoats and jackets, which made them resemble bright peacocks and flashy macaws. "Who am I supposed to see?"

"Mr. Ian Thornton, silly! No, wait, you can't see him now. He moved away from the torches."

"Who is Ian Thornton?"

"That's just it; nobody knows—not really!" In the tone of one imparting delicious and startling news she added, "Some say he's the grandson of the Duke of Stanhope."

Like all young debutantes, Elizabeth had been required to study *Debrett's Peerage,* a book the *ton* revered with almost as much fervor as a devout Presbyterian felt for his Bible. "The Duke of Stanhope is an old man," she remarked after thoughtful consideration, "and he has no heir."

"Yes, everyone knows that. But it's said Ian Thornton is his"—Valerie's voice dropped to a whisper—*"illegitimate* grandson."

"You see," Penelope contributed authoritatively, "the Duke of Stanhope did have a son, but he disowned him years ago. My mama told me all about it—it was quite a scandal." At the word "scandal" they all turned inquisitively, and she continued, "The old duke's son married the daughter of a Scottish peasant who was part Irish to boot! She was a perfectly dreadful person of no consequence whatsoever. So this could be his grandson."

"People think that's who he is simply because of his surname," Georgina provided with typical practicality, "yet it's a common enough name."

"I heard he's so rich," Valerie put in, "that he wagered £25,000 on a single hand of cards one night at a polite gaming hall in Paris."

"Oh, for heaven's sake," said Georgina with derision, "he didn't do that because he's rich, he did it because he's a gambler! My brother knows him, and *he* said Ian Thornton is a common *gambler*—a person without background, breeding, connections, *or* wealth!"

"I've heard that, too," Valerie admitted, peering through the hedge again. *"Look"*—she broke off—"you can see him now. Lady Mary Watterly is practically throwing herself at him!"

The girls leaned so far forward they almost fell into the shrubbery.

"I know I'd melt if he looked at me."

"I'm sure you would not," Elizabeth said with a wry smile, because she felt she ought to contribute something to the conversation.

"You haven't seen him yet!"

Elizabeth didn't *need* to look at him; she knew exactly the sort of handsome young men who made all her friends swoon—blond, blue-eyed Corinthians between twenty-one and twenty-four.

"I suppose Elizabeth has too many wealthy beaux of her own to care about a mere mister, no matter how handsome or intriguing he might be," Valerie said when Elizabeth remained politely aloof, and it seemed to Elizabeth the compliment was coated with a layer of envy and malice. The suspicion was so unpleasant that she quickly rejected it. She'd done nothing to Valerie, or to anyone, to deserve animosity. Not once since she'd come to London had she uttered an unkind word against anyone; in fact, she never took part in gossip that turned malicious or repeated a word of it to anyone else. Even now she was extremely uneasy with some of the things they were saying about the man they were watching. It seemed to Elizabeth that a person had a right to dignity regardless of his rank or lack thereof. That, of course, was a minority opinion that verged on heresy in the *ton*'s eyes, and so she kept her odd notions to herself.

At the time Elizabeth had felt such thoughts were disloyal to her friends, and, moreover, that she was probably being churlish by not joining in their fun and trying to share their excitement with Mr. Ian Thornton. Trying to throw herself into the spirit of the moment, she smiled at Valerie and said, "I don't have as many beaux as *that,* and I'm sure if I could see him, I'd be as intrigued as everyone else."

For some reason Elizabeth's words caused Valerie and Penelope to exchange pleased, conspiratorial glances, then Valerie explained the reason for it: "Thank heavens you agree, Elizabeth, because the three of us are in a bit of a coil. We were counting on you to help us out of it."

"What sort of coil?"

"Well, you see," Valerie explained with a breathless exuberance that Elizabeth blamed on the glasses of heady wine the servants had been pressing on all the guests, including them, "I had to wheedle forever before Charise would agree to let us be here this weekend."

Since she already knew that, Elizabeth nodded and waited.

"The thing is, when Charise said earlier today that Ian Thornton was really going to be here, we were all up in the boughs about it. But she said he wouldn't pay any of us the slightest notice, because we're too young and not at all in his style—"

"She's probably correct," Elizabeth said with an unconcerned smile.

"Oh, but he must!" Glancing at the other girls as if for reinforcement, Valerie finished eagerly, "He absolutely must, because the three of us wagered our entire quarter's allowance with Charise that he would ask one of us to dance tonight. And he's not likely to do *that* unless his interest is piqued beforehand."

"Your entire allowance?" Elizabeth said, horrified at such an extravagant gamble. "But you were planning to use it to buy those amethysts you saw at the jeweler's on Westpool Street."

"And I intended to use mine," Penelope added as she turned to peer through the hedge again, "to buy that marvelous little mare Papa has refused me."

"I—I could probably withdraw from the wager," Georgina put in, looking acutely uneasy about more than the money. "I don't think—" she started, but Penelope burst out eagerly, "He's starting across the garden in this direction, and he's alone! There'll never be a better opportunity to try to attract his notice than right now, if he doesn't change direction."

Suddenly the outrageous wager did seem like forbidden fun, and Elizabeth chuckled. "In that case, I nominate Valerie for the task of piquing his interest, since it was her idea and she particularly admires him."

"We nominate *you*," Valerie said in a giddy, determined voice.

"Me? Why should it be me?"

"Because you're the one who's already received fourteen offers, so it's perfectly obvious you're the most likely to succeed. Besides," she added when Elizabeth balked, "Viscount Mondevale cannot help but be impressed when he hears that Ian Thornton—a mysterious older man at whom Mary Jane Morrison flung herself last year to no avail—asked *you* to dance and paid *you* particular attention. As soon as Mondevale hears about it he'll come up to scratch in a trice!"

In accordance with the dictates of Polite Society, Elizabeth had never allowed herself to show the slightest partiality for the viscount, and she was startled to learn that her friends had guessed her secret feelings. Of course, they couldn't know that the handsome young man had already made his offer and was about to be accepted.

"Make up your mind quickly, he's nearly here!" Penelope implored amid a chorus of nervous giggles from Georgina.

"Well, will you do it?" Valerie demanded urgently as the other two girls began backing away and turning toward the house.

Elizabeth took her first swallow of the wine she'd been given as soon as she stepped from the house into the garden. She hesitated. "Very well, I suppose so," she said, flashing a smile at her friend.

"Excellent. Don't forget—he has to dance with you tonight or we'll lose our allowances!" Laughing, she gave Elizabeth a light, encouraging shove, then turned on her satin-shod heels and fled after their laughing friends.

The clipped hedge the girls had been peering around and through blocked Elizabeth from view as she hastily walked down two wide brick steps onto the grass and glanced around, trying to decide whether to stand where she was or be seated upon the little white stone bench to her left. She darted to the bench and sat down just as booted heels struck the steps, once—twice, and there he was.

Oblivious to her presence for the moment, Ian Thornton walked forward another pace, then stopped near a lighted torch and withdrew a thin cheroot from his jacket pocket. Elizabeth watched him, suffused with trepidation and an unfamiliar, tingling excitement that was due as much to his appearance as to her secret assignment. He was *nothing* like she'd expected him to be. Besides being older than she'd imagined—she guessed him to be at *least* twenty-seven—he was startlingly tall, more than six feet, with powerful shoulders and long, muscular legs. His thick hair was not blond, but a rich brown-black that looked as if it had a tendency to curl. Instead of wearing the customary bright satin coat and white breeches that the other men wore he was clad in raven black from head to foot, with the exception of his snowy shirt and neckcloth, which were so white they seemed to gleam against the stark black of his jacket and waistcoat. Elizabeth had the uneasy thought that Ian Thornton was like a large, predatory hawk in the midst of a gathering of tame, colorful peacocks. As she studied him he lit the cheroot, bending his dark head and cupping his hands over the flame. White cuffs peeped from beneath his black jacket, and in the bright orange glow of the flame she saw that his hands and face were deeply tanned.

Elizabeth expelled the breath she hadn't realized she'd been holding, and the tiny sound made him glance up sharply. His eyes narrowed in surprise or displeasure—Elizabeth wasn't certain. Caught in the act of lurking in the shadows and staring at him, Elizabeth blurted the first idiotic thing that came to mind. "I've never seen a man smoke a cigar before. It—they always retire to another room."

His dark brows lifted a fraction in bland inquiry. "Do you mind?" he asked as he finished lighting the cigar.

Two things hit Elizabeth at once: His piercing eyes were the strange color of gleaming amber, while his voice was richly textured and deep; the combination sent a peculiar warmth up her spine. "Mind?" she repeated stupidly.

"The cigar," he said.

"Oh—no. No, I don't," she hastily assured him, but she had the oddest impression that he had come here seeking privacy and to enjoy a cigar, and that if she had said yes, she did mind, he would have turned around abruptly and left rather than extinguish his cigar so that he could remain in her presence. Fifty yards away, at the far end of the long, narrow grassy ledge on which they stood, girlish laughter sounded, and Elizabeth turned involuntarily, catching a glimpse in the torchlight of Valerie's pink gown and

Georgina's yellow one before they darted around the hedge and were blocked from sight.

A flush stained her cheeks at the embarrassing way her friends were acting, and when she turned back she found her companion studying her, his hands shoved into his pockets, the cigar clamped between teeth as white as his shirt. With an imperceptible inclination of his head he indicated the place the girls had been. "Friends of yours?" he asked, and Elizabeth had the horrible, guilty feeling that he somehow knew the whole thing had been plotted in advance.

She considered telling a small fib, but she didn't like to lie, and those disturbing eyes of his were leveled on hers. "Yes, they are." Pausing to arrange her lavender skirts to their best advantage, she raised her face to his and smiled tentatively. It occurred to her that they hadn't been introduced, and since there was no one about to do the thing properly, she hastily and uneasily remedied the matter herself. "I am Elizabeth Cameron," she announced.

Inclining his head in the merest mockery of a bow, he acknowledged her by saying simply, "Miss Cameron."

Left with no other choice, Elizabeth prodded, "And you are?"

"Ian Thornton."

"How do you do, Mr. Thornton," she replied, and she extended her hand to him as was proper. The gesture made him smile suddenly, a slow, startlingly glamorous white smile as he did the only thing he could do—which was to step forward and take her hand. "A pleasure," he said, but his voice was lightly tinged with mockery.

Already beginning to regret ever agreeing to this plan, Elizabeth racked her brain for an opening, which in the past she'd left to the besotted boys who desperately wanted to engage *her* in conversation. The subject of whom one knew was always appropriate among the *ton,* and Elizabeth seized on that with relief. Gesturing with her fan toward the place they'd last seen her friends, she said, "The young lady in the pink gown was Miss Valerie Jamison, and Miss Georgina Granger was in the yellow one." When he showed no sign of recognition, she provided helpfully, "Miss Jamison is the daughter of Lord and Lady Jamison." When he merely continued to watch her with mild interest, Elizabeth added a little desperately, "They are the Herfordshire Jamisons. You know—the earl and countess."

"Really?" he responded with amused indulgence.

"Yes indeed," Elizabeth rambled, feeling more ill at ease by the second, "and Miss Granger is the daughter of the Wiltshire Grangers—the Baron and Baroness of Grangerley."

"Really?" he mocked, watching her in speculative silence.

It hit her then, what the girls had said about his questionable parentage, and she felt faint with shame for thoughtlessly speaking of titles to someone who might have been cheated of his own. The palms of her hands grew damp; she rubbed them against her knees, realized what she was doing, and hastily stopped. Then she cleared her throat, fanning herself vigorously. "We—are all here for the Season," she finished lamely.

The cool amber eyes warmed suddenly with a mixture of amusement and sympathy, and there was a smile in his deep voice as he asked, "And are you enjoying yourselves?"

"Yes, very much," Elizabeth said with a sigh of relief that he was finally participating a little in the conversation. "Miss Granger, though you couldn't see her at all well from here, is excessively pretty, with the sweetest manners imaginable. She has dozens of beaux."

"All titled, I imagine?"

Still thinking he might be longing for a ducal title he'd missed having, Elizabeth bit her lip and nodded in sublime discomfort. "I'm afraid so," she admitted abjectly, and to her astonishment, *that* made him grin—a slow, dazzling smile swept across his bronzed features, and its effect on his face was almost as dramatic as its effect on Elizabeth's nervous system. Her heart gave a hard bump, and she suddenly stood up, feeling unaccountably jumpy. "Miss Jamison is lovely also," she said, reverting to the discussion of her friends and smiling uncertainly at him.

"How many contenders have there been for *her* hand?"

Elizabeth finally realized he was teasing, and his irreverent view of what everyone else regarded as a matter of the utmost gravity startled an irrepressible, relieved chuckle

43

from her. "I have it on the best authority," she replied, trying to match his grave, teasing tone, "that her beaux have paraded to her papa in record numbers."

His eyes warmed with laughter, and as she stood there, smiling back at him, her tension and nervousness evaporated. Suddenly and inexplicably she felt quite as if they were old friends sharing the same secret irreverence—only he was bold enough to admit his feelings, while she still tried to repress her own.

"And what about you?"

"What about me?"

"How many offers have you had?"

A bubble of startled laughter escaped her, and she shook her head. To have told him proudly about her friends' achievements was acceptable, but to boast about her own was beyond all bounds, and she had no doubt he knew it. "Now *that,*" she admonished with laughing severity, "was really too bad of you."

"I apologize," he said, inclining his head in a mocking little bow, the smile still lurking at his mouth.

Darkness had fallen over the garden, and Elizabeth realized she ought to go inside, yet she lingered, somehow reluctant to leave the enveloping intimacy of the garden. Clasping her hands lightly behind her back, she gazed up at the stars beginning to twinkle in the night sky. "This is my favorite time of day," she admitted softly. She glanced sideways at him to see if he was bored with the topic, but he'd turned slightly and was looking up at the sky as if he, too, found something of interest there.

She searched for the Big Dipper and located it. "Look," she said, nodding toward a particularly bright light in the sky. "There's Venus. Or is it Jupiter? I'm never completely certain."

"It's Jupiter. Over there is Ursa Major."

Elizabeth chuckled and shook her head, pulling her gaze from the sky and sending him a wry, sideways glance. "It may look like the Great Bear to you and everyone else, but to me all the constellations just look like a big bunch of scattered stars. In the spring I can find Cassiopeia, but not because it looks like a lion to me, and in the autumn I can pick out Arcturus, but how they ever saw an archer in all that clutter is quite beyond my comprehension. Do you suppose there are people up there anywhere?"

He turned his head, regarding her with fascinated amusement. "What do *you* think?"

"I think there are. In fact, I think it's rather arrogant to assume that out of all those thousands of stars and planets up there, *we* are the only ones who exist. It seems as arrogant as the old belief that the earth is the center of the entire universe and everything revolves around us. Although people didn't exactly *thank* Galileo for disproving it, did they? Imagine being hauled before the Inquisition and forced to renounce what you absolutely knew—and could prove was right!"

"When did debutantes start studying astronomy?" he asked as Elizabeth stepped over to the bench to retrieve her wineglass.

"I've had years and years to read," she admitted ingenuously. Unaware of the searching intensity of his gaze, she picked up her wineglass and turned back to him. "I really must go inside now and change for the evening."

He nodded in silence, and Elizabeth started to walk forward and step past him. Then she changed her mind and hesitated, remembering her friends' wagers and how much they were counting on her. "I have a rather odd request—a favor to ask of you," she said slowly, praying that he felt, as she did, that they'd enjoyed a very brief and very pleasant sort of friendship out there. Smiling uncertainly into his inscrutable eyes, she said, "Could you possibly—for reasons I can't explain . . ." she trailed off, suddenly and acutely embarrassed.

"What is the favor?"

Elizabeth expelled her breath in a rush. "Could you possibly ask me to dance this evening?" He looked neither shocked nor flattered by her bold request, and she watched his firmly molded lips form his answer:

"No."

Elizabeth was mortified and shocked by his refusal, but she was even more stunned by the unmistakable regret she'd heard in his voice and glimpsed on his face. For a long moment she searched his shuttered features, and then the sound of laughing voices from somewhere nearby broke the spell. Trying to retreat from a predicament into which she should never have put herself in the first place, Elizabeth picked up her skirts, intending to leave. Making a conscious effort to keep all emotion from her voice, she said with calm dignity, "Good evening, Mr. Thornton."

He flipped the cheroot away and nodded. "Good evening, Miss Cameron." And then he left.

The rest of her friends had gone upstairs to change their gowns for the evening's dancing, but the moment Elizabeth entered the rooms set aside for them the conversation and laughter stopped abruptly—leaving Elizabeth with a fleeting, uneasy feeling that they had been laughing and talking about *her*.

"Well?" Penelope asked with an expectant laugh. "Don't keep us in suspense. Did you make an impression?"

The uneasy sensation of being the brunt of some secret joke left Elizabeth as she looked about at their smiling, open faces. Only Valerie looked a little cool and aloof.

"I made an impression, to be sure," Elizabeth said with an embarrassed smile, "but 'twas not a particularly favorable one."

"He remained by your side for ever so long," another girl prodded her. "We were watching from the far end of the garden. What did you talk about?"

Elizabeth felt a warmth creep through her veins and steal up her cheeks as she remembered his handsome, tanned face and the way his smile had glinted and softened his features as he looked at her. "I don't actually remember what we spoke of." That much was true. All she could remember was the odd way her knees had shaken and her heart had beaten when he looked at her.

"Well, what was he like?"

"Handsome," Elizabeth said a little dreamily before she could catch herself. "Charming. He has a beautiful voice."

"And, no doubt," Valerie said with a thread of sarcasm, "he's even now trying to discover your brother's whereabouts so that he can dash over there and apply for your hand."

That notion was so absurd that Elizabeth would have

burst out laughing if she weren't so embarrassed and oddly let down by the way he'd left her in the garden. "My brother's evening is safe from any interruption in that quarter, I can promise you. In fact," she added with a rueful smile, "I fear you've all lost your quarterly allowances as well, for there isn't the slightest chance he'll ask me to dance." With an apologetic wave she left to change her gown for the ball that was already underway on the third floor.

Once Elizabeth had gained the privacy of her bedchamber, however, the breezy smile she'd worn in front of the other girls faded to an expression of thoughtful bewilderment. Wandering over to the bed, she sat down, idly tracing the golden threads of the rose brocade coverlet with the tip of her finger, trying to understand the feelings she'd experienced in the presence of Ian Thornton.

Standing with him in the garden, she'd felt frightened and exhilarated at the same time—drawn to him against her very will by a compelling magnetism that he seemed to radiate. Out there she'd felt almost driven to win his approval, alarmed when she'd failed, joyous when she'd succeeded. Even now, just the memory of the way he smiled, of the intimacy of his heavy-lidded gaze, made her feel hot and cold all over.

Music drifted from the ballroom on another floor, and Elizabeth finally shook herself from her reverie and rang for Berta to help her dress.

"What do you think?" she asked Berta a half hour later as she pirouetted before the mirror for the inspection of her nursemaid-turned–lady's maid.

Berta twisted her plump hands as she stood back, nervously surveying her glowing young mistress's more sophisticated appearance, unable to supress her affectionate smile. Elizabeth's hair had been caught up into an elegant chignon at the crown with soft tendrils framing her face, and her mother's sapphire and diamond eardrops sparkled at her ears.

Unlike Elizabeth's other gowns, which were nearly all pastel and high-waisted, this one was a sapphire blue, by far the most unusual and alluring of them all. Panels of blue silk drifted from a flattened bow upon her left shoulder and fell straight to the floor, leaving her other shoulder bare. Despite the fact that the gown was little more than a straight tube of silk, it flattered her figure, emphasizing her breasts and hinting at the narrow waist beneath. "I think," Berta said finally, "it's a wonder Mrs. Porter ordered such a gown for you. It's not a bit like your others."

Elizabeth tossed her a jaunty, conspiratorial smile as she pulled on the sapphire gloves that encased her arms to above the elbows. "It's the only one Mrs. Porter didn't choose," she admitted. "And Lucinda hasn't seen it either."

"I don't doubt it."

Elizabeth turned back to the mirror, frowning as she surveyed her appearance. "The other girls are barely seventeen, but I'll be eighteen in a few months. Besides," she explained, picking up her mother's sapphire and diamond bracelet and fastening it over the glove on her left wrist, "as I tried to tell Mrs. Porter, it's a great waste to spend so much for gowns that won't be at all suitable for me next year or the year after. I'll be able to wear this one even when I'm twenty."

Berta rolled her eyes and shook her head, setting the streamers on her cap bobbing. "I doubt your Viscount Mondevale will want you wearin' the same gown more'n twice, let alone until you wear it out," she said as she bent over to straighten the hem on the blue gown.

5

Berta's reminder that she was virtually betrothed had a distinctly sobering effect on Elizabeth, and the mood stayed with her as she walked toward the flight of steps leading down to the ballroom. The prospect of confronting Mr. Ian Thornton no longer made her pulse race, and she refused to regret his refusal to dance with her, or even to think of him. With natural grace she started down to the ballroom, where couples were dancing, but most seemed to be clustered about in groups, talking and laughing.

A few steps from the bottom she paused momentarily to scan the guests, wondering where her friends had gathered. She saw them only a few yards away, and when Penelope lifted her hand in a beckoning wave Elizabeth nodded and smiled.

The smile still on her lips, she started to look away, then froze as her gaze locked with a pair of startled amber eyes. Standing with a group of men near the foot of the staircase, Ian Thornton was staring at her, his wineglass arrested halfway to his lips. His bold gaze swept from the top of her shining blond hair, over her breasts and hips, right down to her blue satin slippers, then it lifted abruptly to her face, and there was a smile of frank admiration gleaming in his eyes. As if to confirm it, he cocked an eyebrow very slightly and lifted his glass in the merest subtle gesture of a toast before he drank his wine.

Somehow Elizabeth managed to keep her expression serene as she continued gracefully down the stairs, but her treacherous pulse was racing double-time, and her mind was in complete confusion. Had any other man looked at her or behaved to her the way Ian Thornton just had, she would have been indignant, amused, or both. Instead the smile in his eyes—the mocking little toast—had made her feel as if they were sharing some private, intimate conversation, and she had returned his smile.

Lord Howard, who was Viscount Mondevale's cousin, was waiting at the bottom of the stairs. An urbane man with pleasing manners, he had never been one of her beaux, but he had become something of a friend, and he'd always done his utmost to further Viscount Mondevale's suit with her. Beside him was Lord Everly, one of Elizabeth's most determined suitors, a rash, handsome young man who, like Elizabeth, had inherited his title and lands as a youth. Unlike Elizabeth, he'd inherited a fortune along with them.

"I say!" Lord Everly burst out, offering Elizabeth his arm. "We heard you were here. You're looking ravishing tonight."

"Ravishing," echoed Lord Howard. With a meaningful grin at Thomas Everly's outstretched arm he said, "Everly, one usually asks a lady for the honor of escorting her forward—he does not thrust his arm in her way." Turning to Elizabeth, he bowed, said, "May I?" and offered his arm.

Elizabeth chuckled, and now that she was betrothed she permitted herself to break a tiny rule of decorum: "Certainly, my lords," she replied, and she placed a gloved hand on *each* of their arms. "I hope you appreciate the lengths to which I'm going to prevent the two of you from coming to fisticuffs," she teased as they led her forward. "I look like an elderly lady, too weak to walk without someone on each side to hold her upright!"

The two gentlemen laughed, and so did Elizabeth—and that was the scene Ian Thornton witnessed as the trio strolled by the group he was with. Elizabeth managed to stop herself from so much as glancing his way until they were nearly past him, but then someone called out to Lord

Howard, and he stopped momentarily to reply. Yielding to temptation, Elizabeth stole a split-second glance at the tall, broad-shouldered man in the midst of the group. His dark head was bent, and he appeared to be absorbed in listening to a laughing commentary from the only woman among them. If he was aware Elizabeth was standing there, he gave not the slightest indication of it.

"I must say," Lord Howard told her a moment later as he escorted her forward again, "I was a bit surprised to hear you were here."

"Why is that?" Elizabeth asked, adamantly vowing not to think of Ian Thornton again. She was becoming quite obsessed with a man who was a complete stranger, and moreover, she was very nearly an engaged woman!

"Because Charise Dumont runs with a bit of a fast set," he explained.

Startled, Elizabeth turned her full attention on the attractive blond man. "But Miss Throckmorton-Jones—my companion—has never raised the slightest objection in London to my visiting any member of the family. Besides, Charise's mama was a friend of my own mama's."

Lord Howard's smile was both concerned and reassuring. "In London," he emphasized, "Charise is a model hostess. In the country, however, her soirees tend to be, shall we say, somewhat less structured and restricted." He paused to stop a servant who was carrying a silver tray with glasses of champagne, then he handed one of the glasses to Elizabeth before continuing: "I never meant to imply your reputation would be ruined for being here. After all," he teased, "Everly and I are here, which indicates that at least a few of us are among the first stare of society."

"Unlike some of her *other* guests," Lord Everly put in contemptuously, tipping his head toward Ian Thornton, "who wouldn't be admitted to a *respectable* drawing room in all of London!"

Consumed with a mixture of curiosity and alarm, Elizabeth couldn't stop herself from asking, "Are you referring to Mr. Thornton?"

"None other."

She took a sip of her champagne, using that as an excuse

to study the tall, tanned man who'd occupied too many of her thoughts since the moment she'd first spoken to him. To Elizabeth he looked every inch the elegant, understated gentleman: His dark claret jacket and trousers set off his broad shoulders and emphasized his long, muscular legs with a perfection that bespoke the finest London tailoring; his snowy white neckcloth was tied to perfection, and his dark hair was perfectly groomed. Even in his relaxed pose his tall body gave off the muscular power of a discus thrower, while his tanned features were stamped with the cool arrogance of nobility. "Is—is he as bad as that?" she asked, tearing her gaze from his chiseled profile.

She was caught up in her private impressions of his elegance, so it took a moment for Lord Everly's scathing answer to register on Elizabeth's brain: "He's *worse!* The man's a common gambler, a pirate, a blackguard, and worse!"

"I—I can't believe all that," Elizabeth said, too stunned and disappointed to keep silent.

Lord Howard shot a quelling glance at Everly, then smiled reassuringly at a stricken Elizabeth, misunderstanding the cause of her dismay. "Don't pay any heed to Lord Everly, my lady. He's merely put out because Thornton relieved him of £10,000 two weeks ago in a polite gaming hall. Cease, Thom!" he added when the irate earl started to protest. "You'll have Lady Elizabeth afraid to sleep in her bed tonight."

Her mind still on Ian Thornton, Elizabeth only half heard what her girlfriends were talking about when her two escorts led her to them. "I don't know what men see in her," Georgina was saying. "She's no prettier than any of us."

"Have you ever noticed," Penelope put in philosophically, "what sheep men are? Where one goes they all follow."

"I just wish she'd choose one to wed and leave the rest to us," said Georgina.

"I think she's attracted to him."

"She's wasting her time in that quarter," Valerie sneered, giving her rose gown an angry twitch. "As I told you earlier, Charise assured me he has no interest in 'innocent young things.' Still," she said with an exasperated sigh, "it would be delightful if she did develop a tendre for him. A dance or two together, a few longing looks, and we'd be rid of her completely as soon as the gossip reached her adoring beaux—good heavens, Elizabeth!" she exclaimed, finally noticing Elizabeth, who was standing beside and slightly behind her. "We thought you were dancing with Lord Howard."

"An excellent idea," Lord Howard seconded. "I'd claimed the next dance, Lady Cameron, but if you have no objection to this one instead?"

"Before you usurp her completely," Lord Everly cut in with a dark look at Lord Howard, whom he mistakenly deemed his rival for Elizabeth's hand. Turning to Elizabeth, he continued, "There's to be an all-day jaunt to the village tomorrow, leaving in the morning. Would you do me the honor of permitting me to be your escort?"

Uneasy around the sort of vicious gossip in which the girls had been indulging, Elizabeth gratefully accepted Lord Everly's offer and then agreed to Lord Howard's invitation to dance. On the dance floor he smiled down at her and said, "I understand we're to become cousins." Seeing her surprised reaction to his premature remark, he explained, "Mondevale confided in me that you're about to make him the happiest of men—assuming your brother doesn't decide there's a nonexistent skeleton in his closet."

Since Robert had specifically said he wished Viscount Mondevale to be kept waiting, Elizabeth said the only thing she could say: "The decision is in my brother's hands."

"Which is where it should be," he said approvingly.

An hour later Elizabeth realized that Lord Howard's almost continual presence at her side indicated that he'd evidently appointed himself her guardian at this gathering, which he deemed to be of questionable suitability for the young and innocent. She also realized, as he left to get her a glass of punch, that the male population of the ballroom, as well as some of the female, was dwindling by the moment as guests disappeared into the adjoining card room. Normally the card room was an exclusively male province at balls—a place provided by hostesses for those men (usually married or of advancing years) who were forced to attend a ball, but who adamantly refused to spend an entire evening engaged in frivolous social discourse. Ian Thornton, she knew, had gone in there early in the evening and remained, and now even her girlfriends were looking longingly in that direction. "Is something special happening in the card room?" she asked Lord Howard when he returned with her punch and began guiding her over to her friends.

He nodded with a sardonic smile. "Thornton is losing heavily and has been most of the night—very unusual for him."

Penelope and the others heard his comment with avidly curious, even eager expressions. "Lord Tilbury told us that he thinks everything Mr. Thornton owns is lying on the table, either in chips or promissory notes," she said.

Elizabeth's stomach gave a sickening lurch. "He—he's wagering everything?" she asked her self-appointed protector. "On a turn of the cards? Why would he *do* such a thing?"

"For the thrill, I imagine. Gamblers often do just that."

Elizabeth could not imagine why her father, her brother, or other men seemed to enjoy risking large sums of money on anything as meaningless as a game of chance, but she had no opportunity to comment because Penelope was gesturing to Georgina, Valerie, and even Elizabeth and saying with a pretty smile, "We would all very much like to go and watch, Lord Howard, and if you would accompany us, there's no reason why we shouldn't. It's so very exciting, and half the people here are already in there."

Lord Howard wasn't immune to the three pretty faces watching him with such hope, but he hesitated anyway, glancing uncertainly at Elizabeth as his guardianship came into conflict with his personal desire to see the proceedings firsthand.

"It's not the least inappropriate," Valerie urged, "since there are other ladies in there."

"Very well," he acceded with a helpless grin. With Elizabeth on his arm he escorted the bevy of girls forward through the open doorway and into the hallowed male confines of the card room.

Suppressing the urge to cry out that she did not want to

watch Ian Thornton be beggared, Elizabeth forced herself to keep her expression blank as she looked around at the groups of people clustered about the largest of the oaken tables, obscuring the view of the players seated around it. Dark paneling on the walls and burgundy carpet on the floor made the room seem very dim in comparison to the ballroom. A pair of beautifully carved billiard tables with large chandeliers hanging above them occupied the front of the large room, and eight other tables were scattered about. Although those tables were unoccupied for the moment, cards had been left on them, carefully turned face down, and piles of chips remained in the center of each.

Elizabeth assumed the players at those tables had left their own card games and were now part of the spectators clustered around the large table where all the excitement was being generated. Just as she thought it, one of the spectators at the big table announced it was time to return to their own game, and four men backed away. Lord Howard neatly guided his ladies into the spot the men had just vacated, and Elizabeth found herself in the last place she wanted to be—standing almost at Ian Thornton's elbow with a perfect, unobscured view of what was purportedly the scene of his financial massacre.

Four other men were seated at the round table along with him, including Lord Everly, whose young face was flushed with triumph. Besides being the youngest man there, Lord Everly was the only one whose expression and posture clearly betrayed his emotions. In complete contrast to Lord Everly, Ian Thornton was lounging indifferently in his chair, his expression bland, his long legs stretched out beneath the table, his claret jacket open at the front. The other three men appeared to be concentrating on the cards in their hands, their expressions unreadable.

The Duke of Hammund, who was seated across from where Elizabeth stood, broke the silence: "I think you're bluffing, Thorn," he said with a brief smile. "Moreover, you've been on a losing streak all night. I'll raise you £500," he added, sliding five chips forward.

Two things hit Elizabeth at once: Evidently Ian's nickname was Thorn, and His Grace, the Duke of Hammund, a premier duke of the realm, had addressed him as if they were on friendly terms. The other men, however, continued to regard Ian coolly as they in turn plucked five chips from their individual stacks and pushed them into the pile that had already accumulated in the center of the table.

When it was Ian's turn Elizabeth noticed with a surge of alarm that he had no stack of chips at all, but only five lonely white ones. Her heart sank as she watched him pluck all five chips up and flip them onto the pile in the center. Unknowingly, she held her breath, wondering a little wildly why any sane human being would wager everything he had on anything as stupid as a game of chance.

The last wager had been placed, and the Duke of Hammund showed his cards—a pair of aces. The other two men apparently had less than that, because they withdrew. "I've got you beaten!" Lord Everly said to the duke with a triumphant grin, and he turned over three kings. Reaching forward, he started to pull the pile of chips toward him, but Ian's lazy drawl stopped him short: "I believe that's mine," he said, and he turned over his own cards—three nines and a pair of fours.

Without realizing it, Elizabeth expelled a lusty sigh of relief, and Ian's gaze abruptly snapped to her face, registering not only her presence for the first time, but her worried green eyes and wan smile as well. A brief impersonal smile touched the corner of his mouth before he glanced at the other men and said lightly, "Perhaps the presence of such lovely ladies has changed my luck at last."

He had said "ladies," but Elizabeth felt . . . she *knew* . . . his words had been meant for her.

Unfortunately, his prediction about his luck changing was wrong. For the next half hour Elizabeth stood stock still, watching with a sinking heart and unbearable tension as he lost most of the money he'd won when she first came to stand at the table. And during all that time he continued to lounge in his chair, his expression never betraying a single emotion. Elizabeth, however, could no longer endure watching him lose, and she waited for the last hand to end so that she could leave without disturbing the players. As soon as it was over the Duke of Hammund announced, "I think some refreshment would stand us in good stead." He nodded to a nearby servant, who promptly came to collect the empty glasses from the gentlemen's elbows and replace them with filled ones, and Elizabeth turned quickly to Lord Howard. "Excuse me," she said in a tense, quiet voice, picking up her skirts to leave. Ian had not so much as glanced at her since he'd joked about his luck changing, and she'd assumed he'd forgotten her presence, but at her words he lifted his head and looked straight at her. "Afraid to stay to the bitter end?" he asked lightly, and three of the men at the table, who'd already won most of his money, laughed heartily but without warmth.

Elizabeth hesitated, thinking she must be going quite mad, because she honestly sensed that he wanted her to stay. Uncertain whether she was merely imagining his feelings, she smiled bravely at him. "I was merely going for some wine, sir," she prevaricated. "I have every faith you'll"— she groped for the right term—"you'll come about!" she declared, recalling Robert's occasional gambling cant. A servant heard her and rushed forward to hand her a glass of wine, and Elizabeth remained standing at Ian Thornton's elbow.

Their hostess swept into the card room at that moment, and bent a reproving look on all the occupants of the card table. Then she turned to Ian, smiling gorgeously at him despite the severity of her words. "Now really, Thorn, this has gone on too long. Do finish your play and rejoin us in the ballroom." As if it took an effort, she dragged her gaze from him and looked at the other men around the table. "Gentlemen," she warned laughingly, "I shall cut off your supply of cigars and brandy in twenty minutes." Several of the spectators followed her out, either from guilt at having neglected their roles as courteous guests or from boredom at watching Ian lose everything.

"I've had enough cards for one night," the Duke of Hammund announced.

"So have I," another echoed.

"One more game," Lord Everly insisted. "Thornton still has some of my money, and I aim to win it back on the next hand."

The men at the table exchanged resigned glances, then the duke nodded agreement. "All right, Everly, one more game and then we return to the ballroom."

"No limit on the stakes, since it's the last game?" asked Lord Everly eagerly. All the men nodded as if assent were natural, and Ian dealt the first round of cards to each player.

The opening bet was £1,000. During the next five minutes the amount represented by the pile of chips in the center escalated to £25,000. One by one the remaining players dropped out until only Lord Everly and Ian were left, and only one card remained to be dealt after the wagers were placed. Silence stretched taut in the room, and Elizabeth nervously clasped and unclasped her hands as Lord Everly picked up his fourth card.

He looked at it, then at Ian, and Elizabeth saw the triumph gleaming in the young man's eyes. Her heart sank to her stomach as he said, "Thornton, this card will cost you £10,000 if you want to stay in the game long enough to see it."

Elizabeth felt a strong urge to throttle the wealthy young lord and an equally strong urge to kick Ian Thornton in his shin, which was within reach of her toe beneath the table, when he took the bet and *raised* it by £5,000!

She could not believe Ian's lack of perception; even *she* could tell from Everly's face that he had an unbeatable hand! Unable to endure it another moment, she glanced at the spectators gathered around the table who were watching Everly to see if he took the bet, then she picked up her skirts to leave. Her slight movement seemed to pull Ian's attention from his opponent, and for the third time that night he looked up at her—and for the second time his gaze checked her. As Elizabeth looked at him in taut misery, he very slightly, almost imperceptibly turned his cards so she could see them.

He was holding four tens.

Relief soared through her, followed instantly by terror that her face would betray her emotions. Turning swiftly, she almost knocked poor Lord Howard over in her haste to leave the immediate area of the table. "I need a moment of air," she told him, and he was so engrossed in waiting to see if Everly would match Ian's bet that he nodded and let her move away without protest. Elizabeth realized that in showing her his hand to relieve her fear, Ian had taken the risk that she would do or say something foolish that would give him away, and she couldn't think why he would have done that for her. Except that, as she'd stood beside him, she'd known somehow that he was as aware of her presence as she was of his, and that he rather liked having her stand at his side.

Now that she'd made good her escape, however, Elizabeth couldn't decide how to cover her hasty retreat and still remain in the card room, so she wandered over to a painting depicting a hunting scene and studied it with feigned fascination.

"It's your bet, Everly," she heard Ian prod.

Lord Everly's answer made Elizabeth tremble: "Twenty-five thousand pounds," he drawled.

"Don't be a fool!" the duke told him. "That's too much to wager on one hand, even for you."

Certain now that she had her facial expression under control, Elizabeth wandered back to the table.

"I can afford it," Everly reminded them all smoothly. "What concerns me, Thornton, is whether or not *you* can cover your bet when you lose."

Elizabeth flinched as if the insult had been hurled at her, but Ian merely leaned back in his chair and regarded Everly in steady, glacial silence. After a long, tense moment he said in a dangerously soft voice, "I can afford to raise you another £10,000."

"You don't *have* another £10,000 to your cursed name," Everly spat, "and I'm not putting up my money against a worthless chit signed by you!"

"Enough!" snapped the Duke of Hammund. "You go too far, Everly. I'll vouch for his credit. Now take the bet or fold."

Everly glowered furiously at Hammund and then nodded at Ian with contempt. "Ten thousand more it is. Now let's see what you're holding!"

Wordlessly Ian turned his hand palm up, and the cards spilled gracefully onto the table in a perfect fan of four tens.

Everly exploded from his chair. "You miserable *cheat!* I saw you deal that last card from the bottom of the deck. I *knew* it, but I refused to believe my own eyes."

A babble of conversation rumbled through the room at this unforgivable insult, but with the exception of the muscle that leapt in Ian's taut jaw, his expression didn't change.

"Name your seconds, you bastard!" Everly hissed, leaning his balled fists on the table and glowering his rage at Ian.

"Under the circumstances," Ian replied in a bored, icy drawl, "I believe *I* am the one with the right to decide if *I* want satisfaction."

"Don't be an ass, Everly!" someone hissed. "He'll drop you like a fly." Elizabeth scarcely heard that; all she knew was that there was going to be a duel when there shouldn't be.

"This is all a terrible mistake!" she burst out, and a roomful of annoyed, incredulous male faces turned toward her. "Mr. Thornton did not cheat," she explained quickly. "He was holding all four of those tens before he drew the last card. I stole a look at them when I was about to leave a few minutes ago, and I saw them in his hand."

To her surprise, no one showed any sign of believing her or of even caring what she said, including Lord Everly, who slapped his hand on the table and bit out, "Damn you, I've called you a cheat. Now I call you a co—"

"For heaven's sake!" Elizabeth cried, cutting off the word "coward," which she knew would force any man of honor into a duel. "Didn't any of you understand what I said?" she implored, rounding on the men standing about, thinking that since they were uninvolved, they would see reason more quickly than Lord Everly. "I just said Mr. Thornton was already holding all four tens and—"

Not one haughty male face showed a change in expression, and in a moment of crystal clarity Elizabeth saw what was happening and realized why none of them would intercede: In a roomful of lords and knights who were supremely conscious of their mutual superiority, Ian Thornton was outranked and outnumbered. He was the outsider, Everly was one of them, and they would never side with an outsider against one of their own. Moreover, by blandly refusing to accept Everly's challenge Ian was subtly making it appear that the younger man wasn't worth his time or effort, and they were all taking that insult personally.

Lord Everly knew it, and it made him more angry and more reckless as he glared murderously at Ian. "If you won't agree to a duel tomorrow morning, I'll come looking for you, you low—"

"You can't, milord!" Elizabeth burst out. Everly tore his gaze from Ian to gape at her in angry surprise, and with a presence of mind she didn't know she possessed Elizabeth targeted the one male in the room likely to be vulnerable to her wiles—she smiled brightly at Thomas Everly, speaking to him in a light, flirtatious tone, counting on his infatuation with her to sway him. "What a silly you are, sir, to be contemplating a duel tomorrow when you're already promised to *me* for a jaunt into the village."

"Now, really, Lady Elizabeth, this is—"

"No, I'm very sorry, milord, but I insist," Elizabeth interrupted with a look of vapid innocence. "I shan't be pushed aside like a—like a—I shan't!" she finished desperately. "It is very provoking of you to consider treating me so shabbily. And I—I'm *shocked* you would consider breaking your *word* to me." He looked as if he were caught on the tines of a fork as Elizabeth focused the full force of her dazzling green gaze and entrancing smile on him.

In a strangled voice he said fiercely, "I'll escort you to the village *after* I have satisfaction at dawn from this cad."

"Dawn?" Elizabeth cried in feigned dismay. "You will be too weary to be cheerful company for me if you arise so early. And besides, there isn't going to be a duel unless Mr. Thornton chooses to call *you* out, which I'm certain he won't wish to do because"—she turned to Ian Thornton, as she finished triumphantly—"because he could not be so disagreeable as to shoot you when that would deprive me of your escort tomorrow!" Without giving Ian an opportunity to argue she turned to the other men in the room and exclaimed brightly, "There now, it's all settled. No one cheated at cards, and no one is going to shoot anyone."

For her efforts Elizabeth received angry, censorious looks from every male in the room but two—the Duke of Hammund, who looked as if he was trying to decide if she were an imbecile or a gifted diplomat, and Ian, who was watching her with one eyebrow cocked, as if waiting to see what absurd stunt she might try next.

When no one else seemed capable of moving, Elizabeth took the rest of the matter into her own hands. "Lord Everly, I believe this is a waltz, and you did promise me a waltz." Male guffaws at the back of the room, which Lord Everly mistook for being aimed at him, not Elizabeth, made him turn almost scarlet. With a glance of furious contempt at her he turned on his heel and strode from the room, leaving her standing there feeling both ridiculous and relieved. Lord Howard, however, finally recovered from his private shock and calmly extended his arm to Elizabeth. "Allow me to stand in for Lord Everly," he said.

Not until they entered the ballroom did Elizabeth permit herself to react, and then it was all she could do to stand upright on her quaking limbs. "You're new to town," Lord Howard said gently, "and I hope you won't take me in dislike for telling you that what you did in there—interfering in men's affairs—is not at all the thing."

"I know," Elizabeth admitted with a sigh. "At least, I know it now. At the time I didn't stop to think."

"My cousin," Lord Howard said gently, referring to Viscount Mondevale, "is of an understanding nature. I'll make certain he hears the truth from me before he hears what is bound to be exaggerated gossip from everyone else."

When the dance ended Elizabeth excused herself and went to the withdrawing room, hoping to have a minute alone. Unfortunately, it was already occupied by several women who were talking about the events in the card room. She would have liked to retire to the safety of her bedchamber, skipping the late supper that would be served at midnight, but wisdom warned her that cowering would be the worst thing she could do. Left with no other choice, Elizabeth pinned a serene smile on her face and walked out on the terrace for a breath of air.

Moonlight spilled down the terrace steps and into the lantern-lit garden, and after a moment's blissful peace Elizabeth sought more of it. She wandered forward, nodding politely to the few couples she passed. At the edge of the garden she stopped and then turned to the right and stepped into the arbor. The voices died away, leaving only distant strains of soothing music. She had been standing there for several minutes when a husky voice like rough velvet spoke behind her: "Dance with me, Elizabeth."

Startled by Ian's silent arrival, Elizabeth whirled around and stared at him, her hand automatically at her throat. She'd thought he'd been angry with her in the card room, but the expression on his face was both somber and tender. The lilting notes of the waltz floated around her, and he opened his arms. "Dance with me," he repeated in that same husky voice.

Feeling as if she were in a dream, Elizabeth walked into his arms and felt his right arm slide around her waist, bringing her close against the solid strength of his body. His left hand closed around her fingers, engulfing them, and suddenly she was being whirled gently around in the arms of a man who danced to the waltz with the relaxed grace of one who has danced it a thousand times.

Beneath her gloved hand his shoulder was thick and broad with hard muscle, not padding, and the arm encircling her waist like a band of steel was holding her much closer than was seemly. She should have felt threatened, overpowered—especially out in the starlit darkness—but she felt safe and protected instead. She was, however, beginning to feel a little awkward, and she decided some form of conversation was in order. "I thought you were angry with me for interfering," she said to his shoulder.

There was a smile in his voice as he answered, "Not angry. Stunned."

"Well, I couldn't let them call you a cheat when I knew perfectly well you weren't."

"I imagine I've been called worse," he said mildly. "Particularly by your hotheaded young friend Everly."

Elizabeth wondered what could be worse than being called a cheat, but good manners forbade her asking. Lifting her head, she gazed apprehensively into his eyes and asked, "You don't mean to demand satisfaction from Lord Everly at a later date, do you?"

"I hope," he teased, grinning, "that I'm not so ungrateful as to spoil all your handiwork in the card room by doing such a thing. Besides, it would be very impolite of me to kill him when you'd just made it very clear he'd already engaged himself to escort you tomorrow."

Elizabeth chuckled, her cheeks warm with embarrassment. "I know I sounded like the veriest peagoose, but it was the only thing I could think of to say. My brother is hot-tempered, too, you see. I discovered long ago that whenever he flies into the boughs, if I tease or cajole him, he recovers his spirits much more quickly than if I try to reason with him."

"I very much fear," Ian told her, "that you'll still be without Everly's escort tomorrow."

"Because he'll be angry at me for interfering, do you mean?"

"Because at this moment his beleaguered valet has probably been rudely awakened from his sleep and ordered to pack his lordship's bags. He won't want to stay here, Elizabeth, after what happened in the card room. I'm afraid you humiliated him in your effort to save his life, and I compounded it by refusing to duel with him."

Elizabeth's wide green eyes shadowed, and he added reassuringly, "Regardless of that, he's better off alive and humbled than dead and proud."

That, Elizabeth thought to herself, was probably the difference between a gentleman born, like Lord Everly, and a gentleman made, like Ian Thornton: A true gentleman preferred death to disgrace—according to Robert, at least, who was forever pointing out the distinguishing factors of his own class.

"You disagree?"

Too immersed in her own thoughts to think how her words would sound, she nodded and said, "Lord Everly is a gentleman and a noble—as such, he would probably prefer death to dishonor."

"Lord Everly," he contradicted mildly, "is a reckless young fool to risk his life over a game of cards. Life is too precious for that. He'll thank me some day for refusing him."

"It's a gentleman's code of honor," she repeated.

"Dying over an argument isn't honor, it's a waste of a man's life. A man volunteers to die for a cause he believes in, or to protect others he cares about. Any other reason is nothing more than stupidity."

"If I hadn't interfered, would you have accepted his challenge?"

"No."

"No? Do you mean," she uttered in surprise, "you'd have let him call you a cheat and not lifted a finger to defend your honor or your good name?"

"I don't think my 'honor' was at stake, and even if it was, I fail to see how murdering a boy would redeem it. As far as my 'good name' is concerned, it, too, has been questioned more than once."

"If so, why does the Duke of Hammund champion you in society, which he obviously has done tonight?"

His gaze lost its softness, and his smile faded. "Does it matter?"

Gazing up into those mesmerizing amber eyes, with his arms around her, Elizabeth couldn't think very clearly. She wasn't certain anything mattered at that moment except the sound of his deep, compelling voice. "I suppose not," she said shakily.

"If it will reassure you that I'm not a coward, I suppose I could rearrange his face." Quietly he added, "The music has ended," and for the first time Elizabeth realized they were no longer waltzing but were only swaying lightly together. With no other excuse to stand in his arms, Elizabeth tried to ignore her disappointment and step back, but just then the musicians began another melody, and their bodies began to move together in perfect time to the music.

"Since I've already deprived you of your escort for the outing to the village tomorrow," he said after a minute, "would you consider an alternative?"

Her heart soared, because she thought he was going to offer to escort her himself. Again he read her thoughts, but his words were dampening.

"I cannot escort you there," he said flatly.

Her smile faded. "Why not?"

"Don't be a henwit. Being seen in my company is hardly the sort of thing to enhance a debutante's reputation."

Her mind whirled, trying to tally some sort of balance sheet that would disprove his claim. After all, he was a favorite of the Duke of Hammund's . . . but while the duke was considered a great matrimonial prize, his reputation as a libertine and rake made mamas fear him as much as they coveted him as a son-in-law. On the other hand, Charise Dumont was considered perfectly respectable by the *ton,* and so this country gathering was above reproach. Except it wasn't, according to Lord Howard. "Is that why you refused to dance with me when I asked you to earlier?"

"That was part of the reason."

"What was the rest of it?" she asked curiously.

His chuckle was grim. "Call it a well-developed instinct for self-preservation."

"What?"

"Your eyes are more lethal than dueling pistols, my sweet," he said wryly. "They could make a saint forget his goal."

Elizabeth had heard many flowery praises sung to her beauty, and she endured them with polite disinterest, but Ian's blunt, almost reluctant flattery made her chuckle. Later she would realize that at this moment she had made her greatest mistake of all—she had been lulled into regarding him as an equal, a gently bred person whom she could trust, even relax with. "What sort of alternative were you going to suggest for tomorrow?"

"Luncheon," he said. "Somewhere private where we can talk, and where we won't be seen together."

A cozy picnic luncheon for two was definitely not on Lucinda's list of acceptable pastimes for London debutantes, but even so, Elizabeth was reluctant to refuse. "Outdoors . . . by the lake?" she speculated aloud, trying to justify the idea by making it public.

"I think it's going to rain tomorrow, and besides, we'd risk being seen together there."

"Then where?"

"In the woods. I'll meet you at the woodcutter's cottage at the south end of the property near the stream at eleven. There's a path that leads to it two miles from the gate—off the main road." Elizabeth was too alarmed by such a prospect to stop to wonder how and when Ian Thornton had become so familiar with Charise's property and all its secluded haunts.

"Absolutely not," she said in a shaky, breathless voice. Even she was not naïve enough to consider being alone with a man in a cottage, and she was terribly disappointed that he'd suggested it. Gentlemen didn't make such suggestions, and well-bred ladies never accepted them. Lucinda's warnings about such things had been eloquent and, Elizabeth felt, sensible. Elizabeth gave a sharp jerk, trying to pull out of his arms.

His arms tightened just enough to keep her close, and his lips nearly brushed her hair as he said with amusement, "Didn't anyone ever tell you that a lady never deserts her partner before the dance is over?"

"It's over!" Elizabeth said in a choked whisper, and they both knew she referred to more than just the dancing. "I'm not nearly the greenhead you must take me for," she warned, frowning darkly at his frilled shirtfront. A ruby winked back at her from the folds of his white neckcloth.

"I give you my word," he said quietly, "not to force myself upon you tomorrow."

Oddly, Elizabeth believed him, but even so she knew she could never keep such an assignation.

"I give you my word as a gentleman," he said again.

"If you were a gentleman, you'd never make me such a proposition," Elizabeth said, trying to ignore the dull ache of disappointment in her chest.

"Now there's an unarguable piece of logic," he replied grimly. "On the other hand, it's the only choice open to us."

"It's no choice at all. We shouldn't even be out here."

"I'll wait for you at the cottage until noon tomorrow."

"I won't be there."

"I'll wait until noon," he insisted.

"You will be wasting your time. Let go of me, please. This has all been a mistake!"

"Then we may as well make two of them," he said harshly, and his arm abruptly tightened, bringing her closer to his body. "Look at me, Elizabeth," he whispered, and his warm breath stirred the hair at her temple.

Warning bells screamed through her, belated but loud. If she lifted her head, he was going to kiss her. "I do not want you to kiss me," she warned him, but it wasn't completely true.

"Then say good-bye to me now."

Elizabeth lifted her head, dragging her eyes past his finely sculpted mouth to meet his gaze. "Good-bye," she told him, amazed that her voice didn't shake.

His eyes moved down her face as if he were memorizing it, then they fixed on her lips. His hands slid down her arms and abruptly released her as he stepped back. "Good-bye, Elizabeth."

Elizabeth turned and took a step, but the regret in his deep voice made her turn back . . . or perhaps it had been her own heart that had twisted as if she was leaving something behind—something she'd regret. Separated by less than two feet physically and a chasm socially, they looked at each other in silence. "They've probably noticed our absence," she said lamely, and she wasn't certain whether she was making excuses for leaving him there or hoping he'd convince her to remain.

"Possibly." His expression was impassive, his voice coolly polite, as if he was already beyond her reach again.

"I really must go back."

"Of course."

"You do understand, don't you . . ." Elizabeth's voice trailed off as she looked at the tall, handsome man whom society deemed unsuitable merely because he wasn't a blue blood, and suddenly she hated all the restrictions of the stupid social system that was trying to enslave her. Swallowing, she tried again, wishing that he'd either tell her to go or open his arms to her as he had when he'd asked her to dance. "You do understand that I can't possibly be with you tomorrow. . . ."

"Elizabeth," he interrupted in a husky whisper, and suddenly his eyes were smiling again as he held out his hand, sensing victory before Elizabeth ever realized she was defeated. "Come here."

Of its own accord Elizabeth's hand lifted, his fingers closed around it, and suddenly she was hauled forward;

arms like steel bands encircled her, and a warm, searching mouth descended on hers. Parted lips, tender and insistent, stroked hers, molding and shaping them to fit his, and then the kiss deepened abruptly while hands tightened on her back and shoulders, caressing and possessive. A soft moan interrupted the silence, but Elizabeth didn't know the sound came from her; she was reaching up, her hands grasping broad shoulders, clinging to them for support in a world that had suddenly become dark and exquisitely sensual, where nothing mattered except the body and mouth locked hungrily to hers.

When he finally dragged his mouth from hers Ian kept his arms around her, and Elizabeth laid her cheek against his crisp white shirt, feeling his lips brush the hair atop her head. "That was an even bigger mistake than I feared it would be," he said, and then he added almost absently, "God help us both."

Strangely, it was that last remark that frightened Elizabeth back to her senses. The fact that *he* thought they'd gone so far that they'd both need some sort of divine assistance hit her like a bucket of ice water. She pulled out of his arms and began smoothing creases from her skirt. When she felt able, she lifted her face to his and said with a poise born of sheer terror, "None of this should have happened. However, if we both return to the ballroom and contrive to spend time with others, perhaps no one will think we were together out here. Good-bye, Mr. Thornton."

"*Good night,* Miss Cameron."

Elizabeth was too desperate to escape to remark on his gentle emphasis on the words "good night," which he'd deliberately used instead of "good-bye," nor did she notice at the time that he didn't seem to realize she was correctly Lady Cameron, not Miss Cameron.

Choosing one of the side doors off the balcony rather than the ones entering directly into the ballroom, Elizabeth tried the handle and gave a sigh of relief when the door opened. She slipped into what looked to be a small salon with a door at the opposite end leading, she hoped, into an empty hallway. After the relative silence of the night the house seemed to be a crashing cacophony of laughter, voices, and music that rubbed on her raw nerves as she tiptoed across the little salon.

Luck seemed to be smiling on her, because the hall was deserted, and once there she changed her mind and decided to go to her chamber, where she could quickly freshen up. She hurried up the staircase and had just crossed the landing when she heard Penelope ask in a puzzled voice from the lower landing, "Has anyone seen Elizabeth? We're going down to supper shortly, and Lord Howard wishes to escort her."

Inspired, Elizabeth hastily smoothed her hair, shook out her skirt, and uttered a silent prayer that she didn't *look* like someone who had been engaging in a forbidden assignation in the arbor only minutes before.

"I believe," Valerie said in a cool voice, "that she was last seen going out into the garden. And it appears Mr. Thornton has also vanished—" She broke off in astonishment as Elizabeth made her poised descent down the staircase she'd hurtled up only moments before.

"Heavens," Elizabeth said sheepishly, smiling at Penelope and then Valerie, "I don't know why the heat seems so oppressive this evening. I thought to escape it in the garden, and when that failed I went upstairs to lie down for a short while."

Together the girls strolled through the ballroom, then past the card room, where several gentlemen were playing billiards. Elizabeth's pulse gave a nervous leap when she saw Ian Thornton leaning over the table closest to the door, a billiard cue poised in his hand. He glanced up and saw the three young ladies, two of whom were staring at him. With cool civility he nodded to all three of them, then he let fly with the cue stick. Elizabeth listened to the sound of balls flying against wood and dropping into pockets, followed by the Duke of Hammund's admiring laugh.

"He *is* wondrously handsome in a dark, frightening sort of way," admitted Georgina in a whisper. "There's something—well—dangerous about him, too," she added with a delicate shiver of delight.

"True," remarked Valerie with a shrug, "but you were

right earlier—he *is* without background, breeding, or connections."

Elizabeth heard the gist of their whispered conversation, but she paid it little heed. Her miraculous good fortune of the last few minutes had convinced her that there *was* a God who watched over her now and then, and she was uttering a silent prayer of thanks to Him, along with a promise that she would never, *ever* put herself in such a compromising situation again. She had just said a silent "Amen" when it occurred to her that she'd counted four billiard balls dropping into the pockets after Ian had taken his shot. *Four!* When she played with Robert, the most he'd ever been able to drop was three, and he claimed to excel at billiards.

Elizabeth's sense of buoyant relief remained with her as she went down to supper on Lord Howard's arm. Oddly, it began to disintegrate as she talked with the gentlemen and ladies seated around them at their table. Despite their lively conversation, it took all Elizabeth's control to keep herself from looking about the lavishly decorated, huge room to see at which of the blue-linen–covered tables Ian was seated. A footman who was serving lobster stopped at her elbow, offering to serve her, and Elizabeth looked up at him and nodded. Unable to endure the suspense any longer, she used the footman's presence as an excuse to idly glance about the room. She scanned the sea of jeweled coiffures that shifted and bobbed like brightly colored corks, the glasses being raised and lowered, and then she saw him—seated at the head table between the Duke of Hammund and Valerie's beautiful sister Charise. The duke was talking with a gorgeous blonde who was said to be his current mistress; Ian was listening attentively to Charise's animated discourse, a lazy grin on his tanned face, her hand resting possessively on the sleeve of his jacket. He laughed at something she said, and Elizabeth snapped her gaze from the pair, but her stomach felt as if she'd been punched. They seemed so right together—both of them sophisticated, dark-haired, and striking; no doubt they had much in common, she thought a little dismally as she picked up her knife and fork and went to work on her lobster.

Beside her, Lord Howard leaned close and teased, "It's dead, you know."

Elizabeth glanced blankly at him, and he nodded to the lobster she was still sawing needlessly upon. "It's dead," he repeated. "There's no need to try to kill it twice."

Mortified, Elizabeth smiled and sighed and thereafter made an all-out effort to ingratiate herself with the rest of the party at their table. As Lord Howard had forewarned, the gentlemen, who by now had all seen or heard about her escapade in the card room, were noticeably cooler, and so Elizabeth tried ever harder to be her most engaging self. It was only the second time in her life she'd actually used the feminine wiles she was born with—the first time being her first encounter with Ian Thornton in the garden —and she was a little amazed by her easy success. One by one the men at the table unbent enough to talk and laugh with her. During that long, trying hour Elizabeth repeatedly had the strange feeling that Ian was watching her, and toward the end, when she could endure it no longer, she did glance at the place where he was seated. His narrowed amber eyes were leveled on her face, and Elizabeth couldn't tell whether he disapproved of this flirtatious side of her or whether he was puzzled by it.

"Would you permit me to offer to stand in for my cousin tomorrow," Lord Howard offered as the endless meal came to an end and the guests began to arise, "and escort you to the village?"

It was the moment of reckoning, the moment when Elizabeth had to decide whether she was going to meet Ian at the cottage or not. Actually, there was no real decision to make, and she knew it. With a bright, artificial smile Elizabeth said, "Thank you."

"We're to leave at half past ten, and I understand there are to be the usual entertainments—shopping and a late luncheon at the local inn, followed by a ride to enjoy the various prospects of the local countryside."

It sounded horribly dull to Elizabeth at that moment. "It sounds lovely," she exclaimed with such fervor that Lord Howard shot her a startled look.

"Are you feeling well?" he asked, his worried gaze taking in her flushed cheeks and overbright eyes.

"I've never felt better," she said, her mind on getting away—upstairs to the sanity and quiet of her bedchamber. "And now, if you'll excuse me, I have the headache and should like to retire," she said, leaving behind her a baffled Lord Howard.

She was partway up the stairs before it dawned on her what she'd actually said. She stopped in midstep, then gave her head a shake and slowly continued on. She didn't particularly care what Lord Howard—her fiancé's own cousin—thought. And she was too miserable to stop and consider how very odd that was.

"Wake me at eight, please, Berta," she said as her maid helped her undress. Without answering Berta bustled about, dropping objects onto the dressing table and floor—a sure sign the nervous maid was in a taking over something. "What's wrong?" Elizabeth asked, pausing as she brushed her hair.

"The whole staff is gossipin' about what you did in the card room, and that hatchet-faced duenna of yours is going to blame me for it, you'll see," Berta replied miserably. "She'll say the first time she let you out of her sight and left you in my charge you got yourself in the briars!"

"I'll explain to her what happened," Elizabeth promised wearily.

"Well, what *did* happen?" Berta cried, almost wringing her hands in dismayed anticipation of the tongue-lashing she anticipated from the formidable Miss Throckmorton-Jones.

Elizabeth wearily related the tale, and Berta's expression softened as her young mistress spoke. She turned back the rose brocade coverlet and helped Elizabeth into bed. "So you see," Elizabeth finished with a yawn, "I couldn't just keep quiet and let everyone think he'd cheated, which was what they *would* do, because he isn't one of them."

Lightning streaked across the sky, illuminating the entire room, and thunder boomed until the windows shook. Elizabeth closed her eyes and prayed the jaunt to the village would take place, because the thought of spending the entire day in the same house with Ian Thornton—without being able to look at him or speak to him—was more than she wanted to contemplate. I'm almost obsessed, she thought to herself, and exhaustion overtook her.

She dreamed of wild storms, of strong arms reaching out to rescue her, drawing her forward, then pitching her into the storm-tossed sea. . . .

6

Watery sunlight filled the room, and Elizabeth rolled reluctantly onto her back. No matter how much or how little sleep she got, she was the sort of person who always woke up feeling dazed and disoriented. While Robert could bound out of bed feeling fit and alert, she had to drag herself up onto the pillows, where she usually spent a full half hour staring vacantly at the room, forcing herself to wakefulness. On the other hand, when Robert was stifling yawns at ten P.M., Elizabeth was wide awake and ready to play cards or billiards or read for hours more. For that reason she was ideally suited to the London season, during which one slept until noon at least and then stayed out until dawn. Last night had been the rare exception.

Her head felt like a leaden weight upon the pillow as she forced her eyes open. On the table beside her bed was a tray with her customary breakfast: a small pot of hot chocolate and a slice of buttered toast. Sighing, Elizabeth forced herself to go through the ritual of waking up. Bracing her hands on the bed, she shoved herself upright until she was sitting back against the pillows, then she stared blankly at her hands—willing them to reach for the pot of hot, restorative chocolate.

This morning it took more of an effort than ever; her head

ached dully, and she had the uneasy feeling that something disturbing had happened.

Still caught somewhere between sleep and awareness, she removed the quilted cover from the porcelain pot and poured chocolate into the delicate cup beside it. And then she remembered, and her stomach plummeted: Today a dark-haired man would be waiting for her in the woodcutter's cottage. He would wait for an hour, and then he would leave—because Elizabeth wasn't going to be there. She couldn't. She absolutely could not!

Her hands trembled a little as she lifted the cup and saucer and raised it to her lips. Over the cup's rim she watched Berta bustle into the room with a worried look on her face that faded to a relieved smile. "Oh, good. I was worried you'd taken ill."

"Why?" Elizabeth asked as she took a sip of the chocolate. It was cold as ice!

"Because I couldn't wake—"

"What *time* is it?" Elizabeth cried.

"Nearly eleven."

"Eleven! But I told you to wake me at eight! How could you let me oversleep this way?" she said, her sleep-drugged mind already groping wildly for a solution. She could dress quickly and catch up with everyone. Or . . .

"I *did* try," Berta exclaimed, hurt by the uncharacteristic sharpness in Elizabeth's tone, "but you didn't want to wake up."

"I *never* want to awaken, Berta, you know that!"

"But you were worse this morning than normal. You said your head ached."

"I *always* say things like that. I don't know what I'm saying when I'm asleep. I'll say anything to bargain for a few minutes' more sleep. You've known that for years, and you always shake me awake anyway."

"But you said," Berta persisted, tugging unhappily at her apron, "that since it rained so much last night you were sure the trip to the village wouldn't take place, so you didn't have to arise at all."

"Berta, for heaven's sake!" Elizabeth cried, throwing off the covers and jumping out of bed with more energy than she'd ever shown after such a short period of wakefulness.

"I've told you I'm dying of diphtheria to make you go away, and that didn't succeed!"

"Well," Berta shot back, marching over to the bell pull and ringing for a bath to be brought up, "when you told me *that,* your face wasn't pale and your head didn't feel hot to my touch. And you hadn't dragged yourself into bed as if you could hardly stand when it was but half past one in the morning!"

Contrite, Elizabeth slumped down on the bed. "It's not your fault that I sleep like a hibernating bear. And besides, if they didn't go to the village, it makes no difference at all that I overslept." She was trying to resign herself to the notion of spending the day in the house with a man who could look at her across a roomful of diners and make her heart leap when Berta said, "They did go to the village. Last night's storm was more noise and threat than rain."

Closing her eyes for a brief moment, Elizabeth emitted a long sigh. It was already eleven, which meant Ian had already begun his useless vigil at the cottage. "Very well, I'll ride to the village and catch up with them there. There's no need to hurry," she said firmly when Berta rushed to the door to admit the maids carrying buckets of hot water for Elizabeth's bath.

It was already half past noon when Elizabeth descended the stairs clad in a festive peach riding habit. A matching bonnet with a feather curling at her right ear hid her hair, and riding gloves covered her hands to the wrists. A few masculine voices could be heard in the game room, testifying to the fact that not all the guests had chosen to make the jaunt to the village. Elizabeth's steps faltered in the hallway as she deliberated whether or not to take a peek into the room to see if Ian Thornton had already returned from the cottage. Certain that he had, and unwilling to see him, she turned in the opposite direction and left the house by the front door.

Elizabeth waited at the stable while the grooms saddled a horse for her, but her heart seemed to be beating in heavy time to the passing minutes, and her mind kept tormenting her with a picture of a solitary man who'd waited alone in the cottage for a woman who hadn't come.

"Will you be wantin' a groom ter ride wit' ye, milady?"

the stablekeep asked. "We're shorthanded, what with so many o' them bein' needed by the party what went for the day's outin' to the village. Some of 'em ought to be comin' back here in an hour or less, if you'd want to wait. If not, the road is safe, and no harm will come t'you. Her ladyship rides alone to the village all the time."

The thing Elizabeth wanted most was to gallop hell-bent down a country lane and leave everything else behind her. "I'll go alone," she said, smiling at him with the same friendly candor to which she treated Havenhurst's grooms. "We passed the village the day we arrived—it's straight down the main road about five miles, isn't it?"

"Aye," he said. A flash of heat lightning lit up the pale sky, and Elizabeth cast an anxious glance overhead. She did *not* want to stay there, yet the prospect of being caught in a summer downpour wasn't pleasant, either.

"I doubt it'll rain 'til tonight," the stablekeep told her when she hesitated. "We gets this kinda lightnin' hereabout this time 'o year. Did it all night, it did, and nary a drop o' rain fell."

It was all the encouragement Elizabeth needed.

The first hard drops of rain fell when she'd ridden a mile down the main road. "Wonderful," she said aloud, reining her horse to a halt and scanning the sky. Then she dug her heel into the mare's side and sent her bolting onward toward the village. A few minutes later Elizabeth realized that the wind, which had been sighing through the trees, suddenly seemed to be whipping the branches about, and the temperature was dropping alarmingly. Rain began to fall in large, fat drops that soon became a steady downpour. By the time she saw the path leading off the main road into the woods, Elizabeth was half-drenched. Seeking some form of shelter among the trees, she reined her mare off the road and onto the path. Here at least the leaves acted like an umbrella, albeit a very leaky one.

Lightning streaked and forked above, followed by the ominous boom of thunder, and despite the stablekeep's prediction Elizabeth realized a full-fledged storm was brewing and about to break. The little mare sensed it, too, but though she flinched with the thunder, she remained docile and obedient. "What a little treasure you are," Elizabeth said softly, patting her satiny flank, but her mind was on the cottage she knew would be at the end of the path. She bit her lip with indecision, trying to judge the time. It was surely after one o'clock, so Ian Thornton would be long gone.

In the few additional moments Elizabeth sat there contemplating her alternatives she reached the obvious conclusion that she was vainly putting far too much emphasis on her importance to Ian. Last night she'd seen how easily he had been able to flirt with Charise only an hour after he'd kissed her in the arbor. No doubt she'd been nothing but a momentary diversion to him. How melodramatic and stupid she'd been to imagine him pacing the cottage floor, watching the door. He was a gambler, after all—a gambler and probably a skilled flirt. No doubt he'd left at noon and gone back to the house in search of more willing company, which he'd be able to find without the slightest problem. On the other hand, if by some outlandish chance he was still there, she would be able to see his horse, and then she would simply turn around and ride back to the manor house.

The cottage came into view several minutes later. Set deep in the steamy woods, it was a welcome sight, and Elizabeth strained her eyes to see through the dense trees and rising fog, looking for signs of Ian's horse. Her heart began to pound in expectation and alarm as she scanned the front of the little thatched cottage; but, as she soon realized, she had no reason for excitement or alarm. The place was deserted. So much for the depth of his sudden attachment to her, she thought, refusing to acknowledge the funny little ache she felt.

She dismounted and walked her horse around the back, where she found a lean-to under which she could tie the little mare. "Did you ever notice how very fickle males are?" she asked the horse. "And how very foolish females are about them?" she added, aware of how inexplicably deflated she felt. She realized as well that she was being completely irrational—she had not intended to come here, had not wanted him to be waiting, and now she felt almost like crying because he wasn't!

Giving the ribbons of her bonnet an impatient jerk, she untied them. Pulling the bonnet off, she pushed the back door of the cottage open, stepped inside—and froze in shock!

Standing at the opposite side of the small room, his back to her, was Ian Thornton. His dark head was slightly bent as he gazed at the cheery little fire crackling in the fireplace, his hands shoved into the back waistband of his gray riding breeches, his booted foot upon the grate. He'd taken off his jacket, and beneath his soft lawn shirt his muscles flexed as he withdrew his right hand and shoved it through the side of his hair. Elizabeth's gaze took in the sheer male beauty of his wide, masculine shoulders, his broad back and narrow waist.

Something in the somber way he was standing—added to the fact that he'd waited more than two hours for her— made her doubt her earlier conviction that he hadn't truly cared whether she came or not. And that was before she glanced sideways and saw the table. Her heart turned over when she saw the trouble he'd taken: A cream linen tablecloth covered the crude boards, and two places had been set with blue and gold china, obviously borrowed from Charise's house. In the center of the table a candle was lit, and a half-empty bottle of wine stood beside a platter of cold meat and cheese.

In all her life Elizabeth had never known that a man could actually arrange a luncheon and set a table. Women did that. Women and servants. Not men who were so handsome they made one's pulse race. It seemed she'd been standing there for several minutes, not mere seconds, when he stiffened suddenly, as if sensing her presence. He turned, and his harsh face softened with a wry smile: "You aren't very punctual."

"I didn't intend to come," Elizabeth admitted, fighting to recover her balance and ignore the tug of his eyes and voice. "I got caught in the rain on my way to the village."

"You're wet."

"I know."

"Come over by the fire."

When she continued to watch him warily, he took his foot off the grate and walked over to her. Elizabeth stood rooted to the floor, while all of Lucinda's dark warnings about being alone with a man rushed through her mind. "What do you want?" she asked him breathlessly, feeling dwarfed by his towering height.

"Your jacket."

"No—I think I'd like to keep it on."

"Off," he insisted quietly. "It's wet."

"Now see here!" she burst out backing toward the open door, clutching the edges of her jacket.

"Elizabeth," he said with reassuring calm, "I gave you my word you'd be safe if you came today."

Elizabeth briefly closed her eyes and nodded. "I know. I also know I shouldn't be here. I really ought to leave. I should, shouldn't I?" Opening her eyes again, she looked beseechingly into his—the seduced asking the seducer for advice.

"Under the circumstances, I don't think I'm the one you ought to ask."

"I'll stay," she said after a moment and saw the tension in his shoulders relax. Unbuttoning her jacket, she gave it to him, along with her bonnet, and he took them over to the fireplace, hanging them on the pegs in the wall. "Stand by the fire," he ordered, walking over to the table and filling two glasses with wine, watching as she obeyed.

The front of her hair that had not been covered by her bonnet was damp, and Elizabeth reached up automatically, pulling out the combs that held it off her face on the sides and giving the mass a hard shake. Unconscious of the seductiveness of her gesture, she raised her hands, combing her fingers through the sides of it and lifting it.

She glanced toward Ian and saw him standing perfectly still beside the table, watching her. Something in his expression made her hastily drop her hands, and the spell was broken, but the effect of that warmly intimate look in his eyes was vibrantly, alarmingly alive, and the full import of the risk she was taking by being here made Elizabeth begin to quake inside. She did not *know* this man at all; she'd only met him hours ago; and yet even now he was watching her with a look that was much too . . . personal. And possessive. He handed her the glass, then he nodded toward the threadbare sofa that nearly filled the tiny room. "If you're warm enough, the sofa is clean." Upholstered in what might have been green and white stripes at one time, it had faded to shades of gray and was obviously a castoff from the main house.

Elizabeth sat down as far from him as the sofa permitted and curled her legs beneath the skirt of her riding habit to warm them. He'd promised she would be "safe," which she now realized left a great deal of room for personal interpretation. "If I'm going to remain," she said uneasily, "I think we ought to agree to observe all the proprieties and conventions."

"Such as?"

"Well, for a beginning, you really shouldn't be calling me by my given name."

"Considering the kiss we exchanged in the arbor last night, it seems a little absurd to call you Miss Cameron."

It was the time to tell him she was Lady Cameron, but Elizabeth was too unstrung by his reference to those unforgettable—and wholly forbidden—moments in his arms to bother with that. "That isn't the point," she said firmly. "The point is that although last night did happen, it must not influence our behavior today. Today we ought—ought to be *twice* as correct in our behavior," she continued, a little desperately and illogically, "to atone for what happened last night!"

"Is *that* how it's done?" he asked, his eyes beginning to glint with amusement. "Somehow I didn't quite imagine you allowed convention to dictate your every move."

To a gambler without ties or responsibility, the rules of social etiquette and convention must be tiresome in the extreme, and Elizabeth realized it was imperative to convince him he *must* yield to her viewpoint. "Oh, but I am," she prevaricated. "The Camerons are the most conventional people in the world! As you know from last night, I believe in death before dishonor. We also believe in God and country, motherhood and the king, and . . . and all the proprieties. We're quite intolerably boring on the subject, actually."

"I see," he said, his lips twitching. "Tell me something," he asked mildly, "why would such a conventional person as yourself have crossed swords with a roomful of men last night in order to protect a stranger's reputation?"

"Oh, that," Elizabeth said. "That was just—well, my *conventional* notion of justice. Besides," she said, her ire coming to the fore as she recalled the scene in the card room last night, "it made me excessively angry when I realized that the only reason none of them would try to dissuade Lord Everly from shooting you was because *you* were not their social equal, while Everly is."

"Social equality?" he teased with a lazy, devastating smile. "What an unusual notion to spring from such a conventional person as yourself."

Elizabeth was trapped, and she knew it. "The truth is," she said shakily, "that I am scared to death of being here."

"I know you are," he said, sobering, "but I am the last person in the world you'll ever have to fear."

His words and his tone made the quaking in her limbs, the hammering of her heart, begin again, and Elizabeth hastily drank a liberal amount of her wine, praying it would calm her rioting nerves. As if he saw her distress, he smoothly changed the topic. "Have you given any more thought to the injustice done Galileo?"

She shook her head. "I must have sounded very silly last night, going on about how wrong it was to bring him up before the Inquisition. It was an absurd thing to discuss with anyone, especially a gentleman."

"I thought it was a refreshing alternative to the usual insipid trivialities."

"Did you *really?*" Elizabeth asked, her eyes searching his with a mixture of disbelief and hope, unaware that she was being neatly distracted from her woes and drawn into a discussion she'd find easier.

"I did."

"I *wish* society felt that way."

He grinned sympathetically. "How long have you been required to hide the fact that you have a mind?"

"Four weeks," she admitted, chuckling at his phrasing. "You cannot imagine how awful it is to mouth platitudes to people when you're *longing* to ask them about things they've seen and things they know. If they're male, they wouldn't tell you, of course, even if you did ask."

"What would they say?" he teased.

"They would say," she said wryly, "that the answer would be beyond a female's comprehension—or that they fear offending my tender sensibilities."

"What sorts of questions have you been asking?"

Her eyes lit up with a mixture of laughter and frustration. "I asked Sir Elston Greeley, who had just returned from extensive travels, if he had happened to journey to the colonies, and he said that he had. But when I asked him to describe to me how the natives looked and how they lived, he coughed and sputtered and told me it wasn't at all 'the thing' to discuss 'savages' with a female, and that I'd swoon if he did."

"Their appearance and living habits depend upon their tribe," Ian told her, beginning to answer her questions. "Some of the tribes are 'savage' by our standards, not theirs, and some of the tribes are peaceful by any standards. . . ."

Two hours flew by as Elizabeth asked him questions and listened in fascination to stories of places he had seen, and not once in all that time did he refuse to answer or treat her comments lightly. He spoke to her like an equal and seemed to enjoy it whenever she debated an opinion with him. They'd eaten lunch and returned to the sofa; she knew it was past time for her to leave, and yet she was loath to end their stolen afternoon.

"I can't help thinking," she confided when he finished answering a question about women in India who covered their faces and hair in public, "that it is grossly unfair that I was born a female and so must never know such adventures, or see but a few of those places. Even if I were to journey there, I'd only be allowed to go where everything was as civilized as—as London!"

"There does seem to be a case of extreme disparity between the privileges accorded the sexes," Ian agreed.

"Still, we each have our duty to perform," she informed him with sham solemnity. "And there's said to be great satisfaction in that."

"How do you view your—er—duty?" he countered, responding to her teasing tone with a lazy white smile.

"That's easy. It is a female's duty to be a wife who is an asset to her husband in every way. It is a male's duty to do whatever he wishes, whenever he wishes, so long as he is prepared to defend his country should the occasion demand it in his lifetime—which it very likely won't. Men," she informed him, "gain honor by sacrificing themselves on the field of battle while *we* sacrifice ourselves on the altar of matrimony."

He laughed aloud then, and Elizabeth smiled back at him, enjoying herself hugely. "Which, when one considers it, only proves that *our* sacrifice is by far the greater and more noble."

"How is that?" he asked, still chuckling.

"It's perfectly obvious—battles last mere days or weeks, months at the very most. While *matrimony* lasts a lifetime! Which brings to mind something else I've often wondered about," she continued gaily, giving full rein to her innermost thoughts.

"And that is?" he prompted, grinning, watching her as if he never wanted to stop.

"Why do you suppose, after all that, they call *us* the weaker sex?" Their laughing gazes held, and then Elizabeth realized how outrageous he must be finding some of her remarks. "I don't usually go off on such tangents," she said ruefully. "You must think I'm dreadfully ill-bred."

"I think," he softly said, "that you are magnificent."

The husky sincerity in his deep voice snatched her breath away. She opened her mouth, thinking frantically for some light reply that could restore the easy camaraderie of a minute before, but instead of speaking she could only draw a long, shaky breath.

"And," he continued quietly, "I think you know it."

This was not, *not* the sort of foolish, flirtatious repartee she was accustomed to from her London beaux, and it terrified her as much as the sensual look in those golden eyes. Pressing imperceptibly back against the arm of the sofa, she told herself she was only overreacting to what was nothing more than empty flattery. "I think," she managed with a light laugh that stuck in her throat, "that you must find whatever female you're with 'magnificent.'"

"Why would you say a thing like that?"

Elizabeth shrugged. "Last night at supper, for one thing." When he frowned at her as if she were speaking in a foreign language, she prodded, "You remember Lady Charise

Dumont, our hostess, the same lovely brunette on whose every word you were hanging at supper last night?"

His frown became a grin. "Jealous?"

Elizabeth lifted her elegant little chin and shook her head. "No more than you were of Lord Howard."

She felt a small bit of satisfaction as his amusement vanished. "The fellow who couldn't seem to talk to you without touching your arm?" he inquired in a silky-soft voice. "That Lord Howard? As a matter of fact, my love, I spent most of my meal trying to decide whether I wanted to shove his nose under his right ear or his left."

Startled, musical laughter erupted from her before she could stop it. "You did nothing of the sort," she chuckled. "Besides, if you wouldn't duel with Lord Everly when *he* called you a *cheat*, you certainly wouldn't harm poor Lord Howard merely for touching my arm."

"Wouldn't I?" he asked softly. "Those are two very different issues."

Not for the first time, Elizabeth found herself at a loss to understand him. Suddenly his presence was vaguely threatening again; whenever he stopped playing the amusing gallant he became a dark, mysterious stranger. Raking her hair off her forehead, she glanced out the window. "It must be after three already. I really must leave." She surged to her feet, smoothing her skirts. "Thank you for a lovely afternoon. I don't know why I remained. I shouldn't have, but I *am* glad I did. . . ."

She ran out of words and watched in wary alarm as he stood up. "Don't you?" he asked softly.

"Don't I what?"

"Know why you're still here with me?"

"I don't even know who *you* are!" she cried. "I know about places you've been, but not your family, your people. I know you gamble great sums of money at cards, and I disapprove of that—"

"I also gamble great sums of money on ships and cargo—will that improve my character in your eyes?"

"And I know," she continued desperately, watching his gaze turn warm and sensual, "I absolutely *know* you make me excessively uneasy when you look at me the way you're doing now!"

"Elizabeth," he said in a tone of tender finality, "you're here because we're already half in love with each other."

"Whaaat?" she gasped.

"And as to needing to know who I am, that's very simple to answer." His hand lifted, grazing her pale cheek, then smoothing backward, cupping her head. Gently he explained, "I am the man you're going to marry."

"Oh, my *God!*"

"I think it's too late to start praying," he teased huskily.

"You—you must be mad," she said, her voice quavering.

"My thoughts exactly," he whispered, and, bending his head, he pressed his lips to her forehead, drawing her against his chest, holding her as if he knew she would struggle if he tried to do more than that. "You were not in my plans, Miss Cameron."

"Oh, please," Elizabeth implored helplessly, "don't do this to me. I don't understand any of this. I don't know what you want."

"I want you." He took her chin between his thumb and forefinger and lifted it, forcing her to meet his steady gaze as he quietly added, "And you want *me."*

Elizabeth's entire body started to tremble as his lips began descending to hers, and she sought to forestall what her heart knew was inevitable by reasoning with him. "A gently bred Englishwoman," she shakily quoted Lucinda's lecture, "feels nothing stronger than affection. We do *not* fall in love."

His warm lips covered hers. "I'm a Scot," he murmured huskily. "We do."

"A *Scot!"* she uttered when he lifted his mouth from hers.

He laughed at her appalled expression. "I said 'Scot,' not 'ax murderer.'"

A Scot who was a gambler to boot! Havenhurst would land on the auction block, the servants turned off, and the world would fall apart. "I cannot, *cannot* marry you."

"Yes, Elizabeth," he whispered as his lips trailed a hot path over her cheek to her ear, "you *can."*

His lips brushed back and forth across her ear, then his tongue touched the lobe and began delicately tracing each curve, slowly probing each crevice, until Elizabeth shivered with the waves of tension shooting through her. The instant he felt her trembling response, his arm tightened, supporting her, while his tongue plunged boldly into her ear. His hand curved round her nape, sensually stroking it, and he began trailing scorching kisses down her neck to her shoulder. His warm breath stirred her hair and his whisper was achingly gentle as his mouth began retracing its stirring path to her ear again. "Don't be afraid, I'll stop whenever you tell me to."

Imprisoned by his protective embrace, reassured by his promise, and seduced by his mouth and caressing hands, Elizabeth clung to him, sliding slowly into a dark abyss of desire where he was deliberately sending them both.

He dragged his mouth roughly across her cheek, and when his lips touched the corner of hers, Elizabeth helplessly turned her head to fully receive his kiss. The sweet offering of her mouth wrung a half-groan, half-laugh from him, and his lips seized hers in a kiss of melting hunger that deepened to scorching demand.

Suddenly, Elizabeth was being lifted and lowered onto his lap, then shifted down onto the sofa, his mouth locked fiercely to hers as he leaned over her. His tongue traced a hot line between her lips, coaxing, urging them to part, and then insisting. The moment they yielded, his tongue plunged into her mouth, stroking and caressing. Her body jerked convulsively with the primitive sensations jarring through her entire nerve stream, and Elizabeth surrendered mindlessly to the stormy splendor of the pagan kiss. Her hands shifted restlessly over his heavily muscled shoulders and forearms, her lips moving against his with increasing abandon as she fed his hunger and unwittingly increased it.

When he finally pulled his mouth from hers an eternity later, their breaths were coming in mingled gasps. Feeling almost bereft, Elizabeth surfaced slightly from the sensual Eden where he had sent her, and forced her heavy eyelids to open so that she could look at him. Stretched out beside her on the sofa, he was leaning over her, his tanned face hard and flushed with passion, his amber eyes smoldering. Lifting his hand, he tenderly brushed a golden lock of hair off her cheek, and he tried to smile, but his breathing was as ragged as hers. Unaware of the effort he was making to keep their passion under control, Elizabeth let her gaze drop to his finely chiseled mouth, and she watched him draw an unsteady breath. "Don't," he warned her in a husky, tender voice, "look at my mouth unless you want it on yours again."

Too naïive to know how to hide her feelings, Elizabeth lifted her green eyes to his, and her longing for his kiss was in their soft depths. Ian drew a steadying breath, and yielded to temptation again, gently telling her how to show him what she wanted. "Put your hand around my neck," he whispered tenderly.

Her long fingers lifted to his nape, and he lowered his mouth to hers, so close their breaths mingled. Understanding finally dawned, and Elizabeth put firmer pressure on his nape. And even though she was braced for it, the shock of his parted lips on hers again was wild, indescribable sweetness. This time it was Elizabeth who touched her tongue to his lips, and when she felt him shudder, instinct told her she was doing something right.

It told him the same thing, and he jerked his mouth from hers. "Don't do this, Elizabeth," he warned.

In answer, she tightened her hand at his nape and at the same time turned into his arms. His mouth came down hard on hers, but instead of struggling, her body arched against him and she drew his tongue into her mouth. Against her breasts, she felt his heart slam into his ribs, and he began kissing her with unleashed passion, his tongue tangling with hers, then plunging and slowly retreating in some wildly exciting, forbidden rhythm that made the blood roar in Elizabeth's ears. His hand slid up her side to her breast, covering it possessively, and Elizabeth jumped in shocked protest.

"Don't," he whispered against her lips. "God, don't. Not yet . . ."

Stunned into stillness by the harsh need in his voice, Elizabeth gazed up into his face as he lifted his head, his eyes moving restlessly over the bodice of her dress. Despite his protest, his hand was still, and in her befuddled senses, she finally realized he was honoring his promise to stop whenever she asked him to stop. Helpless to stop or encourage him, she looked at the masculine fingers, still and tanned against her white shirt, then she dragged her eyes to his.

Heat was beating behind them, and with a silent moan, Elizabeth curled her hand behind his head and turned into his body.

It was all the encouragement Ian needed. His fingers moved and spread across her breast, but his gaze was locked with hers, watching the way her beautiful face reflected first fear then pleasure. Breasts, to Elizabeth, had heretofore been like legs—they both had a purpose; legs were to walk on and breasts were to hold up and fill out the bodice of a gown. She had no idea they could give such sensation, and kissed into insensibility, she lay quiescent while his fingers unfastened her shirt, pulling down her chemise, baring her breasts to his hot gaze. Reflexively she reached to cover herself, but he swiftly lowered his head, distracting her by the expedient means of kissing her fingers, then drawing a fingertip into his mouth and sucking hard against it. Elizabeth stiffened in shock and pulled her hand away, but his lips only found a breast and did the same thing to her nipple. Raw pleasure streaked through her, and she moaned, her fingers sliding into the soft dark hair at his nape, her heart hammering out a frantic warning to tell him to *stop*.

He nuzzled the other breast, his lips closing tightly around the taut nipple and her body arched, her hands tightening on his nape. Suddenly, he raised up, his eyes restlessly caressing her swollen breasts, then he swallowed and drew a long, tortured breath. "Elizabeth, we're going to have to stop."

Elizabeth's swirling senses began to return to reality, slowly at first, and then with a sickening plummet. Passion gave way to fear and then to anguished shame as she realized she was lying in a man's arms, her shirt unfastened, her flesh exposed to his gaze and touch. Closing her eyes, she fought back the sting of tears and shoved his hand away, lurching into an upright position. "Let me rise, please," she whispered, her voice strangled with self-revulsion. Her skin flinched as he began to fasten her shirt, but in order to do it he had to release his hold on her, and the moment he did, she scrambled to her feet.

Turning her back to him, she fastened her shirt with shaking hands and snatched her jacket from the peg beside the fire. He moved so silently that she had no idea he'd stood until his hands settled on her stiff shoulders. "Don't be frightened of what is between us. I'll be able to provide for you—"

All of Elizabeth's confusion and anguish exploded in a burst of tempestuous, sobbing fury that was directed at herself, but which she hurtled at him. Tearing free of his grasp, she whirled around. "Provide for me," she cried. "Provide what? A—a hovel in Scotland where I'll stay while you dress the part of an English gentleman so you can gamble away everything—"

"If things go on as I expect," he interrupted her in a voice of taut calm, "I'll be one of the richest men in England within a year—two at the most. If they don't, you'll still be well provided for."

Elizabeth snatched her bonnet and backed away from him in a fear that was partly of him and partly of her own weakness. "This is madness. Utter madness." Turning, she headed for the door.

"I know," he said gently. She reached for the door handle and jerked the door open. Behind her, his voice stopped her in midstep. "If you change your mind after we leave in the morning, you can reach me at Hammund's town house in Upper Brook Street until Wednesday. After that I'd intended to leave for India. I'll be gone until winter."

"I—I hope you have a safe voyage," she said, too overwrought to wonder about the sharp tug of loss she felt at the realization he was leaving.

"If you change your mind in time," he teased, "I'll take you with me."

Elizabeth fled in sheer terror from the gentle confidence she'd heard in his smiling voice. As she galloped through the thick fog and wet underbrush she was no longer the sensible, confident young lady she'd been before; instead she was a terrified, bewildered girl with a mountain of responsibilities and an upbringing that convinced her the wild attraction she felt for Ian Thornton was sordid and unforgivable.

As she left the horse in the stable and saw with sinking horror that the party had already returned from the village jaunt, she didn't think of anything except sending Robert a note begging him to fetch her that night, instead of in the morning.

Elizabeth had supper in her room while Berta packed, and

she scrupulously avoided the window of her bedchamber, which happened to look out over the gardens below. Twice she'd glanced outside, and both times she'd seen Ian. The first time he'd been standing alone on the terrace, a cheroot clamped between his teeth, staring out across the lawns, and his solitary stance made her heart ache because he seemed lonely somehow. The next time she saw him, he was surrounded by females who'd not been there last night— new arrivals at the house party, Elizabeth supposed—and all five of them seemed to find him irresistible. She told herself it didn't matter, could *not* matter to her. She had responsibilities to Robert and Havenhurst, and they had to come first. Despite what Ian obviously thought, she could not link her future with that of a reckless gambler, even if he was probably the handsomest Scotsman ever born—and the gentlest—

Elizabeth closed her eyes, trying to shut out these thoughts. It was incredibly silly to think of Ian in this way. Silly and dangerous, for Valerie and some of the others seemed to suspect where she'd been all afternoon, and with whom. Wrapping her arms around herself, Elizabeth shivered as she remembered how neatly she'd been trapped by her own guilt that afternoon as soon as she'd walked into the house.

"Good heavens, you're wet," Valerie had exclaimed in a cry of sympathy. "The stable said you've been gone all afternoon. Don't say you were lost and in the rain all that time!"

"No, I—I came upon a cottage in the woods and stayed there until the rain let up a little while ago." It had seemed the wisest thing to say, since Ian's horse had been nowhere in sight and hers had been perfectly visible, should anyone have cared to look.

"What time was that?"

"Close to one o'clock, I think."

"Did you happen to come upon Mr. Thornton while you were out?" Valerie inquired with a malicious smile, and everyone in the salon seemed to stop talking and turn toward them. "The gamekeeper said he saw a tall, dark man mounted on a big sorrel stallion go into the cottage. He assumed the man was a guest, and so he didn't challenge his presence."

"I—I didn't see him," Elizabeth said. "It was . . . very foggy. I hope nothing untoward happened to him."

"We aren't certain. He isn't back yet. Charise is concerned, although," Valerie continued, watching Elizabeth closely, "I told her she needn't be. The scullery maids gave him a luncheon à deux to take with him."

Stepping aside to let a couple pass, Elizabeth explained to Valerie that she'd decided to leave tonight instead of tomorrow, and without giving Valerie an opportunity to question her reason she quickly excused herself to change out of her wet clothing.

Berta had taken one look at Elizabeth's pale face and guessed at once that something was terribly wrong, particularly when Elizabeth insisted on sending word to Robert to fetch them home tonight. By the time Elizabeth had sent the note off Berta had managed to pry most of the story out of Elizabeth, and Elizabeth was forced to spend the rest of her afternoon and early evening trying to soothe her maid.

It won't do you a bit of good to wear a path through the carpet," Berta told her. "We'll both be spending time enough on the carpet when that Miss Throckmorton-Jones hears what you've been about."

"She won't hear anything," Elizabeth said with more determination than conviction, and she sank into a chair, nervously plucking at the skirt of her bright green traveling costume. Her bonnet and gloves were on the bed beside their packed valises, waiting to be brought downstairs when Robert arrived. Even though she'd been expecting it, the knock on her door made her nerves jump. Instead of telling her that her brother had arrived, the footman handed her a note when she opened the door.

With clammy hands she unfolded it, praying that it wasn't news from London that Robert couldn't be found to fetch them. For a moment she frowned in blank incomprehension at the hastily scrawled, almost illegible note that said *"Meet me in greenhowse—Must talk to you."*

The footman had already started down the hall, and Elizabeth called after him, "Who gave you this note?"

"Miss Valerie, my lady."

Elizabeth's relief that it wasn't from Ian was immediately replaced by guilty terror that Valerie had somehow discovered more about Elizabeth's disappearance this afternoon. "Valerie wants me to meet her in the greenhouse right away," she told Berta.

Berta's color drained. "She knows what happened, doesn't she? Is that why she wants to see you? It's not my place to say it, but I can't like that girl. She has mean eyes."

Elizabeth had never in her life been embroiled in intrigue or deceit, and everything that was happening seemed unbearably complicated and tinged with malice. Without replying to Berta's comment about her friend she looked at the clock and realized it was only six. "Robert can't possibly be here for at least an hour. In the meantime I'll go and find out why Valerie needs to see me."

Walking over to the windows, Elizabeth parted the draperies, studying the guests who were standing on the terrace or strolling about the gardens. The last thing she wanted was for Ian to see her go to the greenhouse and follow her there. Such a possibility seemed extremely remote, but even so, it seemed wise to take no further chances. She almost sagged with relief when she saw his tall form on the terrace below. Clearly illuminated by a pair of torches, he was occupied with three women who were flirting with him while a footman hovered on the edge of their group, patiently waiting for recognition. She saw Ian glance at the footman, who then handed him something she supposed to be a drink.

Ignoring the sharp tug of her senses as she looked down on his dark head, Elizabeth turned away from the windows. Rather than leaving the house by the back doors, which opened out onto the terrace where she knew Ian was, she left by the side doors and stayed away from the lit torches.

In the doorway to the greenhouse Elizabeth hesitated. "Valerie?" she called in a low voice, looking around.

Moonlight poured in through the glass panels of the roof, and when no one answered, Elizabeth walked inside and looked about her. Pots of flowers bloomed everywhere—in orderly rows upon the tables and on benches. More delicate species adorned the shelves beneath the tables, sheltered from the direct rays of the sun that would pour through the glass ceiling in the daytime. Trying to calm her nerves, Elizabeth strolled down the aisles, studying the blooms.

The greenhouse was larger than the one at Havenhurst, she noted, and part of it was apparently used as a sort of solarium, for there were trees growing in pots, and beside them were ornate stone benches with colorful cushions on them.

Elizabeth wandered down the aisle, oblivious to the dark shadow looming in the doorway, moving silently down the aisle. Her hands clasped behind her back, she bent down to sniff a gardenia.

"Elizabeth?" Ian said in a clipped voice.

She whirled around, her heart slamming against her ribs, her hand flying to her throat, her knees turning to jelly.

"What's wrong?" he asked.

"You—you startled me," she said as he strolled up to her, his expression oddly impassive. "I didn't expect you to come here," she added nervously.

"Really?" he mocked. "Whom did you expect after that note—the Prince of Wales?"

The note! Crazily, her first thought after realizing it was from him, not Valerie, was that for an articulate man his handwriting verged on the illiterate. Her second thought was that he seemed angry about something. He didn't keep her long in doubt as to the reason.

"Suppose you tell me how, during the entire afternoon we spent together, you neglected to mention that you are *Lady* Elizabeth?"

Elizabeth wondered a little frantically how he'd feel if he knew she was the Countess of Havenhurst, not merely the eldest daughter of some minor noble or knight.

"Start talking, love. I'm listening."

Elizabeth backed away a step.

"Since you don't want to talk," he bit out, reaching for her arms, "is *this* all you wanted from me?"

"No!" she said hastily, backing out of his reach. "I'd rather talk."

He stepped forward, and Elizabeth took another step backward, exclaiming, "I mean, there are so *many* interesting topics for conversation, are there not?"

"Are there?" he asked, moving forward again.

"Yes," she exclaimed, taking two steps back this time. Snatching at the first topic she could think of, she pointed to the table of hyacinths beside her and exclaimed, "A-Aren't these hyacinths lovely?"

"Lovely," he agreed without looking at them, and he reached for her shoulders, obviously intending to draw her forward.

Elizabeth jumped back so swiftly that his fingers merely grazed the gauze fabric of her gown. "Hyacinths," she babbled with frantic determination as he began stalking her step for step, past the table of potted pansies, past the table of potted lilies, "are part of genus Hyacinthus, although the cultivated variety, which we have here, is commonly called the Dutch hyacinth, which is part of H. orientalis—"

"Elizabeth," he interrupted silkily, "I'm not interested in flowers." He reached for her again, and Elizabeth, in a frantic attempt to evade his grasp, snatched up a pot of hyacinths and dumped it into his outstretched hands.

"There is a *mythological* background to hyacinths that you may find more interesting than the flower itself," she continued fiercely, and an indescribable expression of disbelief, amusement, and fascination suddenly seemed to flicker across his face. "You see, the hyacinth is actually named for a handsome Spartan youth—Hyacinthus—who was loved by Apollo and by Zephyrus, god of the west wind. One day Zephyrus was teaching Hyacinthus to throw the discus, and he accidentally killed him. It is said that Hyacinthus's blood caused a flower to spring up, and each petal was inscribed with the Greek exclamation of sorrow." Her voice trembled a little as he purposefully set the pot of hyacinths on the table. "A-Actually, the flower that sprang up would have been the iris or larkspur, not the modern hyacinth, but that is how it earned its name."

"Fascinating." His unfathomable eyes locked onto hers.

Elizabeth knew he was referring to her and not the history of the hyacinth, and though she commanded herself to move out of his reach, her legs refused to budge.

"Absolutely fascinating," he murmured again, and in slow motion she watched his hands reach out and gently grasp her shoulders, rubbing lightly. "Last night you were ready to do battle with a roomful of men because they dared believe I'd cheated, yet now *you're* afraid. Is it me you fear, sweetheart? Or something else?"

The endearment spoken in his rich baritone voice had the same stirring effect on her as the touch of his lips. "I'm afraid of the things you make me feel," she admitted desperately, trying to get control of herself and the situation. "I realize that this is merely a—a little weekend dalliance—"

"Liar," he teased, and he took her lips in a sweet, swift kiss. Her mind reeled from the brief touch, but the moment he lifted his mouth from hers she rushed into frightened speech. "Thank you," she blurted inanely. "H-Hyacinths are not the only flower with an interesting history. There are lilies, too, which are also part of the genus—"

A lazy, seductive grin swept across his handsome face, and, to Elizabeth's helpless horror, her gaze fastened on his mouth. She couldn't still the shiver of anticipation as he bent his head. Her brain warned her she was mad, but her heart knew this truly was good-bye, and the knowledge made her lean up on her toes and kiss him back with all the helpless, confused longing she felt. The sweetness of her yielding, combined with the way her hand slid up his chest and rested against his heart while her other hand curved around his nape, would have seemed to any man to be either the actions of a woman who was falling in love or else those of an experienced flirt. Elizabeth—naïve, inexperienced, and very young—was acting on pure instinct and was unaware that everything she did was convincing him she was the former.

She was, however, not so lost as to the ramifications of her actions that she forgot about Robert's impending arrival. Unfortunately, she had never imagined Robert might have been on his way there before her note ever arrived.

"Please listen to me," she whispered desperately. "My brother is coming to take me home."

"Then I'll talk to him. Your father may have some objections, even after he understands that I'll be able to provide for your future—"

"My future!" Elizabeth interrupted in genuine terror at the way he was taking charge—a gambler, just like her father. She thought of the rooms at Havenhurst, stripped almost bare of valuables, the servants counting on her, the *ancestors* counting on her. At that moment she would have said anything, *anything* to make him stop pursuing her before she lost control completely and gave in to the mindless, wicked weakness he seemed to inspire in her. She leaned back in his arms, trying to make her shaking voice sound cool and amused: "And what will you provide, sir? Will you promise me a ruby large enough to cover my palm, as Viscount Mondevale has? Sables to cover my shoulders and mink to carpet the floor, as Lord Seabury has?"

"Is that what you want?"

"Of course," she said with brittle gaiety, but she was choking back a sob. "Isn't that what all females want and all gentlemen promise?"

His face hardened into an expressionless mask, but his eyes were probing hers like daggers, looking for answers—as if he couldn't completely believe that jewels and furs mattered to her more than feelings.

"Oh, please let me go," she cried on a choked sob, shoving hard at his chest.

So intent were they that neither of them noticed the man striding swiftly down the aisle. "You *miserable bastard!*" Robert thundered, "you heard what she said! Take your filthy hands off my sister!"

Ian's arms started to tighten protectively, but Elizabeth tore free of his grasp and ran to Robert, tears streaking down her face. "Robert, listen to me. It's not what you think!" Robert put his arm around her shoulder, and Elizabeth started to launch into explanations. "This is Mr. Ian Thornton," she began, "and—"

"And despite the way this looks," Ian interrupted with amazing calm, "my intentions toward Miss Cameron are perfectly honorable."

"You arrogant *son of a bitch!*" Robert exploded, his voice vibrating with fury and contempt. "My sister is *Countess Cameron* to the likes of you! And I don't need an introduction. I know all about you. As to your intentions—or should I say *pretentions*—I wouldn't let her marry scum like you even if she weren't *already* bethrothed."

At those words Ian's gaze jerked to Elizabeth. He saw the truth on her guilt-stricken face, and Elizabeth almost cried out at the cynical contempt blazing in his eyes.

"You've compromised my sister, you misbegotten pig, and you'll answer for it!"

Pulling his gaze from Elizabeth, Ian looked at Robert, his hard face wiped clean of all expression now. Acceding to Robert's demand for a duel, he nodded curtly and said almost politely, "Of course." Then he moved as if to leave.

"No!" Elizabeth cried wildly, clutching at Robert's arm, and for the second time in twenty-four hours she found herself trying to stop someone from spilling Ian Thornton's blood. "I won't permit this, Robert, do you hear me? It wasn't all his—"

"This is none of your affair, Elizabeth!" Robert snapped, too enraged to listen to her. Removing her hand from his arm, he said, "Berta is already in my carriage in the drive. Go around the far side of the house and get in with her. This man," he said with scathing sarcasm, "and I have some things to discuss."

"You can't—" Elizabeth tried again, but Ian Thornton's murderous voice stopped her cold.

"Get *out* of here!" he said between his teeth, and while Elizabeth was willing to ignore Robert's order, Ian Thornton's made her quake. Her chest heaving with fright, she looked at his rigid face, at the muscle leaping in his jaw, and then at Robert. Not certain whether her presence was making things worse or forestalling a calamity, she tried once again to appeal to Robert: "Please—promise me you won't do anything until tomorrow, when you've had time to think and we've talked."

Elizabeth watched him make a herculean effort not to further terrify her and to agree with what she asked. "Fine," he bit out. "I'll be only a moment behind you," he promised. "Now go on to my carriage before that crowd out there who's been watching this whole scene decides to come in here where they can hear as well as see."

Elizabeth felt physically ill when she stepped out of the greenhouse and saw many of the people from the ballroom gathered outdoors. Penelope was there, and Georgina and the others, and the expressions on their faces ranged from amusement among the older people to icy condemnation among the younger.

A short while later her brother strode to the chaise and climbed inside. His manner was more rigidly controlled than it had been. "The matter is settled," he said, but regardless of how much she pleaded, he would not say more.

In helpless misery Elizabeth leaned back against the squabs, listening to Berta, who was sniffling in anticipation of the blame she felt she would ultimately receive from Lucinda Throckmorton-Jones. "My note couldn't have reached you more than two hours ago," Elizabeth whispered after a few minutes. "How could you have gotten here so quickly?"

"I never got your note," he replied stiffly. "This afternoon Lucinda felt well enough to come downstairs for a bit. When I told her where you'd gone this weekend, she gave me some startling news about the sorts of goings-on your friend Charise permits at her country parties. I left three hours ago to fetch you and Berta home early. Unfortunately, I was too late."

"It's not as bad as you think," Elizabeth lied lamely.

"We'll discuss it tomorrow!" he snapped, and she slumped with relief, thinking he meant to do nothing, at least until then. "Elizabeth, how could you be such a fool? Even you should have realized the man's a complete scoundrel! He's not fit to . . ." He broke off and drew a long breath, striving to get control of his temper. When he spoke again he seemed more composed. "The damage, whatever it may be, has already been done. I'm to blame for this— you're too young and inexperienced to go anywhere without Lucinda to keep you out of harm's way. I can only pray that your affianced husband will take an equally understanding view of the matter."

It dawned on Elizabeth that this was the second time tonight that Robert had openly spoken of her engagement as if it was finalized. "Since it hasn't been settled or made public, I can't see why my actions should reflect on Viscount Mondevale," she said with more hope than conviction. "If there is a little scandal, he may want to delay announcing it for a while, Robert, but I can't think he'll be so very embarrassed."

"We signed the contracts today," Robert gritted. "Mondevale and I had no difficulty agreeing on your settlement—he was extremely generous, by the way. The proud bridegroom was eager to send an announcement to the papers, and I saw no reason why he should not. It will be in the *Gazette* tomorrow."

That piece of alarming news made Berta let out a muted sob before she lapsed again to sniffling and blowing her nose. Elizabeth squeezed her eyes closed and held back her own tears while her mind tormented her with more pressing problems than her handsome young fiancé.

In bed Elizabeth lay awake for hours, tortured with memories of the weekend and with terror that she might not be able to dissuade Robert from dueling with Ian Thornton, which she was almost certain he still meant to do. Staring up at the ceiling, she feared alternately for Robert and then for Ian. Lord Howard had made it sound as if Ian was a deadly duelist, yet Ian had refused to defend his honor when Lord Everly called him a cheat—an act many might view as cowardice. Perhaps gossip about Ian's skill was totally wrong. Robert was a fair shot, and Elizabeth's body grew clammy thinking of Ian, proud and alone, being felled by a ball from Robert's pistol. *No.* She told herself she was thinking hysterically. The possibility of either of them actually shooting the other was outlandish.

Dueling was illegal, and in this instance the code of honor would dictate that Ian appear—which he'd already agreed to do in the greenhouse—and that Robert would delope— fire in the air. In so doing, Ian would be tentatively admitting his guilt by putting his life in Robert's hands, which would give Robert the satisfaction a duel provided without the bloodshed, and Robert could then delope. That was the way gentlemen usually dealt with such matters these days.

Usually, Elizabeth's terrified mind reminded her, but Robert's temper was explosive, and he was so infuriated tonight that instead of raging he'd been coldly, murderously silent—and that alarmed Elizabeth more than his outburst would have done.

Shortly before dawn she fell into an uneasy slumber, only to wake what seemed like minutes later to the sound of someone moving down the hall. A servant, she thought, glancing at the window where pale rays of gray were tinting the inky night sky. She was about to drift off to sleep again when she heard the front door downstairs open and then close.

Dawn—duels. Robert had *promised* to talk to her today before doing anything, she thought hysterically, and for once Elizabeth had no trouble waking up. Fear sent her bolting from beneath the covers. Still pulling on a dressing robe, she ran flying down the stairs and jerked open the front door in time to see Robert's carriage rounding the corner.

"Oh my *God!*" she said to the empty hall, and because she was too overwrought to wait and wonder alone, she went upstairs to awaken the one person whose good judgment could be depended upon no matter how chaotic the world became. Lucinda had been waiting up for them last night, and she knew most of what had happened this weekend, with the exception, of course, of the interlude in the gamekeeper's cottage.

"Lucinda," she whispered, and the gray-haired woman's eyes opened, their pale hazel orbs alert and unclouded. "Robert has just left the house. I'm certain he means to duel with Mr. Thornton."

Miss Lucinda Throckmorton-Jones, whose career as a duenna had heretofore included the unblemished chaperonage of the daughters of three dukes, eleven earls, and six viscounts, pushed herself upright against the pillows and gazed narrowly at the young lady who had just spoiled her brilliant record. "Inasmuch as Robert is not an early riser," she said, "that would seem to be an obvious conclusion."

"Whatever shall I *do?*"

"For a start, I suggest you cease wringing your hands in that unbecoming fashion and then go to the kitchen and make some tea."

"I don't want any tea."

"I shall require some tea if we are to wait downstairs for your brother's return, which I foresee is what you wish to do."

"Oh, Lucy," Elizabeth said, looking at the gruff spinster with love and gratitude, "whatever would I do without you?"

"You would get yourself into a deal of trouble, which you

have already done." Seeing the torment in Elizabeth's face, she relented slightly as she climbed out of bed. "Custom dictates that Thornton present himself and that your brother have the satisfaction of seeing him do so, and then Robert must delope. There's nothing else that *can* happen."

It was the first time in Elizabeth's acquaintance with Lucinda that the stalwart duenna was wrong.

The clock was just chiming the hour of eight A.M. when Robert returned with Lord Howard. He stalked past the drawing room, saw Elizabeth huddled on the sofa across from Lucinda, who was doing needlework, paused, and stepped back. "What are you doing up so early?" he asked her tersely.

"Waiting for you," Elizabeth told him, hurtling out of her chair. Lord Howard's presence confused her for a moment, and then it hit her—Robert would have needed a second to attend the duel. "You dueled with him, didn't you, Robert?"

"Yes!"

Elizabeth's voice was a strangled whisper. "Is he *hurt?*"

Robert stalked over to the side table and poured whiskey in a glass.

"Robert," she cried, grabbing him by the arms. "What *happened?*"

"I shot him in the arm," Robert snapped savagely. "I was aiming for his black heart, and I missed! That's what happened." Shaking off Elizabeth's hands, he downed the contents of his glass, then turned to refill it.

Sensing that there was more, Elizabeth searched his face. "Is that all?"

"No, that's not all!" Robert exploded. "After I wounded him, that bastard lifted his pistol and stood there, making me sweat. Then he blew the tassel off the top of my goddamned boot!"

"He—he what?" Elizabeth said, recognizing Robert's roiling fury and unable to understand it. "Surely you aren't angry because he missed!"

"Damn it, don't you understand anything? He *didn't* miss! It was an *insult*. He stood there with blood pouring down his arm, his pistol aimed at my heart, then he changed his aim at the last possible second and shot the tassel off my boot instead. He meant to show me he *could* have killed me if he'd chosen, and everyone who was there saw it! It was the final insult, damn his rotten soul!"

"*You* not only refused to delope," Lord Howard bit out, sounding as angry as Robert, "you fired before the call was given. You disgraced yourself *and* me. Moreover, if word of this duel becomes public, you'll have the lot of us arrested for participating. Thornton gave you satisfaction by appearing this morning and refusing to raise his pistol. He admitted guilt. What more did you expect?" As if unable to bear the sight of Robert any longer, Lord Howard turned on his heel. Elizabeth followed him helplessly into the hall, desperately trying to think of something eloquent to say in Robert's defense. "You must be cold and weary," she began, stalling for time. "Won't you at least stay for some tea?"

Lord Howard shook his head and kept walking. "I only returned to get my carriage."

"Then I'll see you out," Elizabeth persisted. She walked him to the door, and for a moment she thought he actually meant to leave without even saying good day. Standing in the open doorway, he hesitated and then turned back to her. "Good-bye, Lady Elizabeth," he said in an odd, regretful voice, and then he left.

Elizabeth scarcely noticed his tone or even his departure. She realized for the first time that this morning—perhaps at this very minute—a surgeon somewhere was digging a ball out of Ian's arm. Sagging against the door, she swallowed convulsively, fighting the urge to vomit at the thought of the pain she'd caused him. Last night she'd been too terrified by the prospect of a duel to consider how Ian must have felt when Robert told him she was engaged. Now it was finally beginning to hit her, and her stomach clenched. Ian had spoken of marrying her, had kissed and held her with tender, possessive passion and told her he was falling in love with her. In return for that, Robert had barged in on him and contemptuously told him she was beyond his touch socially and already engaged besides. And this morning he had shot him for daring to reach too high.

Leaning her head back against the door, Elizabeth stifled a moan of contrition. Ian might not have a title nor any claim to being a gentleman in the *ton*'s interpretation of the term, but Elizabeth sensed instinctively that he was a proud man. That pride had been stamped on his bronzed features, in the way he carried himself, in his every movement—and she and Robert had trampled it to pieces. They had made a fool of him in the greenhouse last night and forced him into a duel today.

At that moment, if Elizabeth had known where to find him, she really thought she would have braved his anger and gone to him to explain about Havenhurst and all her responsibilities, to try to make him understand that it was those things, not any lack in him, that had made it impossible for her to consider marrying him.

Shoving herself away from the door, Elizabeth walked slowly down the hall and into the drawing room where Robert was sitting with his head in his hands. "This isn't finished," Robert gritted, lifting his head to look at her. "I'll kill him one day for this!"

"No you will *not!*" Elizabeth said, her words shaking with alarm. "Bobbie, listen to me—you don't understand about Ian Thornton. He didn't do anything wrong, not really. You see," she said in a suffocated voice, "he thought he was—well, falling in love with me. He wanted to *marry* me—"

Robert's sharp bark of derisive laughter rang through the room. "Is *that* what he told you?" he sneered, his face purpling with fury at her lack of familial loyalty. "Well, then let me set you straight, you little idiot! To put it bluntly and in his own words, all he wanted from you was a tumble between the sheets!"

Elizabeth felt the blood drain from her face, then she slowly shook her head in denial. "No, you're wrong. When you first found us he said his intentions were honorable, remember?"

"He changed his mind damned quick when I told him you are penniless," Robert flung back, looking at her with a mixture of pity and scorn.

Too weak to continue standing, Elizabeth sank down on the sofa beside her brother, crushed by the full weight of responsibility for her stupidity, her gullibility, and all that those two traits had brought down on them. "I'm sorry," she whispered helplessly. "I'm so sorry. You risked your life for me this morning, and I haven't even thanked you for caring enough to do that." Because she couldn't think of anything else to say or do, she put her arm around his slumped shoulders. "Things will work out for us—they always have," she promised unconvincingly.

"Not this time," he said, his eyes harsh with despair. "I think we're ruined, Elizabeth."

"I can't believe it's as bad as that. There's a chance none of this will come out," she continued, not believing her own words. "And Lord Mondevale cares for me, I think. Surely he'll listen to reason."

"In the meantime," Lucinda said at last, with typical cool practicality, "Elizabeth must go out as usual—as if nothing untoward has happened. If she hides in the house, gossip will feed on itself. You, sir, will have to escort her."

"It won't matter, I tell you!" Robert said. "We're ruined."

He was right. That night, while Elizabeth bravely attended a ball with her fiancé, who seemed to be blessedly unaware of her weekend debacle, lurid versions of her activities were already spreading like wildfire throughout the *ton*. The story of the episode in the greenhouse was circulated, along with the added slander that she had purportedly sent him a note *inviting* him to join her there. More damning by far was the titillating gossip that she'd spent an afternoon with Ian Thornton alone in a secluded cottage.

"That bastard is the one who's spreading those stories," Robert had raged the next day when the tales reached his ears. "He's trying to whiten his own hands by saying you sent him a note inviting him to the greenhouse, and that you were pursuing him. You're not the first female to lose your head over him, you know. You're just the youngest and the most naïve. This year alone there've been Charise Dumont and several others whose names have been linked with his. None of them, however, was unsophisticated enough to behave with such wanton indiscretion."

Elizabeth was too humiliated to argue or protest. Now that she was no longer under the influence of Ian Thornton's sensual magnetism she realized that his actions were, in retrospect, exactly what one would expect of an unscrupulous rake who was bent on seduction. After only a few hours' acquaintance he'd claimed to be half in love with her and to want to marry her—just the sort of impossible lie a libertine would tell to his victim. She'd read enough novels to know that fortune hunters and dissolute libertines intent on seduction often claimed to be in love with their victims when all they wanted was another conquest. Like an utter fool, Elizabeth had thought of him as a victim of unfair social prejudice.

Now she realized too late that the social prejudices that would have excluded him from respectable *ton* activities had existed to protect her from men like him.

Elizabeth didn't have a great deal of time to devote to her private misery, however. Friends of Viscount Mondevale, upon learning of his betrothal in the papers, finally felt it incumbent upon them to disclose to the happy bridegroom the gossip about the female to whom he'd offered his hand.

The next morning he called at the town house on Ripple Street and withdrew his offer. Since Robert had not been at home, Elizabeth had met with him in the drawing room. One look at his rigid stance and unsmiling mouth and Elizabeth had felt as if the floor was falling away from beneath her.

"I trust there won't need to be an unpleasant scene over this," he'd said stiffly, without preamble.

Unable to speak past the tears of shame and sorrow choking her, Elizabeth had shaken her head. He turned and started for the door, but as he strode past her he swung around and grasped her by the shoulders. "Why, Elizabeth?" he demanded, his handsome face twisted with angry regret. "Tell me why. At least give me *that.*"

"Why?" she repeated, stupidly longing to throw herself into his arms and beg his forgiveness.

"I can understand that you might have accidentally encountered him at some cottage in the woods in the rain, which is what my cousin, Lord Howard, tells me *he* believes happened. But *why* would you have sent him a note to meet you alone in the greenhouse?"

"I didn't!" she cried, and only her stubborn pride kept her from collapsing in a sobbing heap at his feet.

"You're lying," he said flatly, his hands falling away. "Valerie saw the note after he tossed it away and went looking for you."

"She's mistaken!" Elizabeth choked, but he was already walking out of the room.

Elizabeth had thought she could not feel more humiliated than she did at that moment, but she soon discovered she was mistaken. Viscount Mondevale's desertion was taken as proof that she was guilty, and from that day onward no more invitations or callers arrived at the town house on Ripple Street. At Lucinda's insistence Elizabeth finally got up the courage to attend the one function she'd been invited to *before* the scandal became public—a ball at Lord and Lady Hinton's home. She stayed for fifteen minutes, and then she left—because no one except the host and hostess, who had no choice, would speak to her or acknowledge her in any way.

In the eyes of the *ton* she was a shameless wanton, soiled and used, unfit company for unsullied young ladies and gullible young heirs, unfit to mingle in Polite Society. She had broken the rules governing moral conduct, and not even with someone of her own class, but with a man whose reputation was black, his social standing nonexistent. She hadn't merely broken the rules, she'd flung them in their faces.

One week after the duel Robert disappeared without word or warning. Elizabeth was terrified for his safety, unwilling to believe he would desert her because of what she'd done, and unable to think of any other, less tormenting explanation. The actual explanation, however, was not long in coming. While Elizabeth sat alone in the drawing room, waiting and praying for his return, news of his disappearance was spreading all over the city. Creditors began arriving on her doorstep, demanding payment for huge debts that had accrued not only for her debut, but over many years for Robert's gambling and even that of her father.

Three weeks after Charise Dumont's party, on a brilliantly sunny afternoon, Elizabeth and Lucinda closed the door on the rented town house for the last time and climbed into their carriage. As her carriage drove past the park the same people who had flattered her and sought her out saw her and coldly turned their backs. Through the blur of her hot, humiliated tears Elizabeth saw a handsome young man with a pretty girl in his carriage. Viscount Mondevale was taking Valerie for a drive, and the look she gave Elizabeth was meant to be pitying. But Elizabeth, in her private torment, thought it was tinged with triumph. Her fear that Robert had met with foul play had already given way to the far more believable possibility that he had fled to avoid debtors' gaol.

Elizabeth returned to Havenhurst and sold off every valuable she owned to pay off Robert's gaming debts, her father's gaming debts, and those from her debut. And then she picked up the threads of her life. With courage and determination she devoted herself to preserving Havenhurst and to the well-being of the eighteen servants who elected to stay with her for only a home, food, and new livery once each year.

Slowly her smiles returned and the guilt and confusion receded. She learned to avoid looking back on her grievous mistakes during her season, because it hurt too much to remember them and the awful retribution that had followed. At seventeen years old she was her own mistress, and she had come home, where she had always belonged. She resumed her chess games with Bentner and her target practice with Aaron; she lavished her love on this peculiar family of hers and on Havenhurst—and they returned it. She was contented and busy, and she adamantly refused to think of Ian Thornton or of the events that had led up to her self-imposed exile. Now her uncle's actions were forcing her not only to think of him but to see him. Without her uncle's modest financial support for two more years there was no way Elizabeth could avoid giving up Havenhurst. Until she could accumulate the money to have Havenhurst properly irrigated, as it should have been long ago, it could never be productive enough to attract cottagers and support itself.

With a reluctant sigh Elizabeth opened her eyes and gazed blankly at the empty room, then she slowly stood up. She'd confronted more difficult problems than *this,* she told herself bracingly. Wherever there was a problem, there were solutions; one simply had to look carefully for the best one. And Alex was here now. Between the two of them they could surely think of a way to circumvent Uncle Julius.

She would take it as a challenge, she decided firmly as she

headed off in search of Alex. At nineteen she still enjoyed challenges, and life at Havenhurst had become a little bit routine. A few short trips—two of the three, at least— might be exciting.

By the time she finally located Alex in the garden, Elizabeth had almost convinced herself of all those things.

Alexandra took one look at Elizabeth's carefully composed features and fixed smile and was not fooled for a
moment, nor was Bentner, who'd been entertaining Alex
with stories about Elizabeth's efforts in the gardens. They
both turned to her with matched expressions of alarm.
"What's wrong?" Alex asked, anxiety already driving her to
her feet.

"I don't quite know how to tell you," Elizabeth admitted
frankly, sitting down beside Alex while Bentner hovered
worriedly about, pretending to pluck withered roses
from their stems so that he might hear and, if needed, lend
advice or assistance. The more Elizabeth considered what
she had to tell Alex, the more bizarre—almost comical—
it began to seem to her dazed mind. "My uncle," she explained, "has endeavored to find a willing husband for
me."

"Really?" Alex said, her gaze searching Elizabeth's bemused expression.

"Yes. In fact, I think it's safe to say he's gone to rather
extraordinary lengths to accomplish that feat."

"What do you mean?"

Elizabeth swallowed a completely unexpected bubble of
hysterical laughter. "He sent messages to all fifteen of my

112

former suitors, asking if they were still interested in marrying me—"

"Oh, my *God*," Alex breathed.

"—and, if they were, he volunteered to send me to them for a sennight, properly chaperoned by Lucinda," Elizabeth recited in that same strangled tone, "so that we could both discover if we still suit."

"Oh, my *God*," Alex said again, with more force.

"Twelve of them declined," she continued, and she watched Alex wince in embarrassed sympathy. "But three of them agreed, and now I am to be sent off to visit them. Since Lucinda can't return from Devon until I go to visit the third—*suitor,* who's in Scotland," she said, almost choking on the word as she applied it to Ian Thornton, "I shall have to pass Berta off as my aunt to the first two."

"Berta!" Bentner burst out in disgust. "Your aunt? The silly widgeon's afraid of her shadow."

Threatened by another uncontrollable surge of mirth, Elizabeth looked at both her friends. "Berta is the least of my problems. However, do continue invoking God's name, for it's going to take a miracle to survive this."

"Who are the suitors?" Alex asked, her alarm increased by Elizabeth's odd smile as she replied, "I don't *recall* two of them. It's quite remarkable, isn't it," she continued with dazed mirth, "that two grown men could have met a young girl at her debut and hared off to her brother to ask for her hand, and *she* can't remember anything about them, except one of their names."

"No," Alex said cautiously, "it isn't remarkable. You were, are, very beautiful, and that is the way it's done. A young girl makes her debut at seventeen, and gentlemen look her over, often in the most cursory fashion, and decide if they want her. Then they apply for her hand. I can't think it is reasonable or just to betroth a young girl to someone with whom she's scarcely acquainted and then expect her to develop a lasting affection for him *after* she is wed, but the *ton* does regard it as the *civilized* way to manage marriages."

"It's actually quite the opposite—it's rather barbaric, when you reflect on it," Elizabeth stated, willing to be diverted from her personal calamity by a discussion of almost anything else.

113

"Elizabeth, who are the suitors? Perhaps I know of them and can help you remember."

Elizabeth sighed. "The first is Sir Francis Belhaven—"

"You're joking!" Alex exploded, drawing an alarmed glance from Bentner. When Elizabeth merely lifted her delicate brows and waited for information, Alex continued angrily, "Why, he's—he's a dreadful old roue. There's no polite way to describe him. He's stout and balding, and his debauchery is a joke among the *ton* because he's so flagrant and foolish. He's an unparalleled pinchpenny to boot—a nipsqueeze!"

"At least we have that last in common," Elizabeth tried to tease, but her glance was on Bentner, who in his agitation was deflowering an entire healthy bush. "Bentner," she said gently, touched by how much he obviously cared for her plight, "you can tell the dead blooms from the live ones by their color."

"Who's the second suitor?" Alex persisted in growing alarm.

"Lord John Marchman." When Alex looked blank, Elizabeth added, "The Earl of Canford."

Comprehension dawned, and Alex nodded slowly. "I'm not acquainted with him, but I have heard of him."

"Well, don't keep me in suspense," Elizabeth said, choking back a laugh, because everything seemed more absurd, more unreal by the moment. "What do you know of him?"

"That's just it, I can't recall, but there was—wait, I have it! He's"—she shot a discouraged look at Elizabeth—"he's an inveterate sportsman who rarely comes near London. He's said to have entire walls of his home covered in the stuffed heads of animals he's hunted and fish he's caught. I remember some joking remarks being made that the reason he'd never married was that he couldn't tear himself away from his sport long enough to look for a wife. He doesn't sound at all suitable for you," Alex added miserably, glaring absently at the toe of her red kid slipper.

"Suitability hasn't anything to do with it, since I haven't any intention of wedding anyone if I can possibly avoid it. If I can just hold out for two more years, my grandmother's trust will come to me. With that money I should be able to manage here on my own for a long time. The problem is that

I can't hold ends together until then without my uncle's support, and he threatens to withdraw it almost weekly. If I don't at least appear to go along with this mad scheme of his, I've no doubt he'll do exactly that."

"Elizabeth," Alex ventured cautiously, "I could help if you'd let me. My husband—"

"Don't, please," Elizabeth interrupted. "You know I could never take money from you. Among other things, I wouldn't be able to pay it back. The trust should cover Havenhurst's expenses, but only barely. For now, my most pressing problem is to find some way out of this coil my uncle has created."

"What I cannot understand is how your uncle could consider these two men suitable when they aren't. Not one whit!"

"*We* know that," Elizabeth said wryly, bending down to pull a blade of grass from between the flagstones beneath the bench, "but evidently my 'suitors' do not, and that's the problem." As she said the words a thought began to form in her mind; her fingers touched the blade, and she went perfectly still. Beside her on the bench Alex drew a breath as if to speak, then stopped short, and in that pulsebeat of still silence the same idea was born in both their fertile minds.

"Alex," Elizabeth breathed, "all I have to—"

"Elizabeth," Alex whispered, "it's not as bad as it seems. All you have to—"

Elizabeth straightened slowly and turned.

In that prolonged moment of silence two longtime friends sat in a rose garden, looking raptly at each other while time rolled back and they were girls again—lying awake in the dark, confiding their dreams and troubles and inventing schemes to solve them that always began with *"If only . . ."*

"If only," Elizabeth said as a smile dawned across her face and was matched by the one on Alex's, "I could convince them that we *don't* suit—"

"Which shouldn't be hard to do," Alex cried enthusiastically, "because it's true!"

The joyous relief of having a plan, of being able to take control of a situation that minutes before had threatened her entire life, sent Elizabeth to her feet, her face aglow with laughter. "Poor Sir Francis," she chuckled, looking delightedly from Bentner to Alex as both grinned at her. "I greatly fear he's in for the most disagreeable surprise when he realizes what a—a"—she hesitated, thinking of everything an old roue would most dislike in his future wife—"a complete prude I am!"

"And," Alex added, "what a shocking *spendthrift* you are!"

"Exactly!" Elizabeth agreed, almost twirling around in her glee. Sunlight danced off her gilded hair and lit her green eyes as she looked delightedly at her friends. "I shall make perfectly certain to give him glaring evidence I am both. Now then, as to the Earl of Canford . . ."

"What a pity," Alex said in a voice of exaggerated gloom, "you won't be able to show him what a capital hand you are with a fishing pole."

"Fish?" Elizabeth returned with a mock shudder. "Why, the mere thought of those scaly creatures positively makes me *swoon!"*

"Except for that prime one you caught yesterday," Bentner put in wryly.

"You're right," she returned with an affectionate grin at the man who'd taught her to fish. "Will you find Berta and break the news to her about going with me? By the time we come back to the house she ought to be over her hysterics, and I'll reason with her." Bentner trotted off, his threadbare black coattails flapping behind him.

"That only leaves the third contender to discourage," Alex said happily. "Who is he, and what do we know of him? Do I know him?"

It was the moment Elizabeth had been dreading. "You never heard of him until a few weeks ago, when you returned."

"What?" she asked, nonplussed.

Elizabeth drew a steadying breath and nervously rubbed her hands against the sides of her blue skirts. "I think," she said slowly, "I ought to tell you exactly what happened a year and a half ago—with Ian Thornton."

"There's no need to ever tell me if it will cause you unhappiness to speak of it. And right now, we surely ought to be thinking of the third man—"

"The third man," Elizabeth interrupted tightly, "is Ian Thornton."

"Dear *God!*" Alex gasped in horror. "Why? I mean—"

"I don't know why," Elizabeth admitted with angry confusion. "He accepted my uncle's proposition. So it is either some sort of complete misunderstanding or it is his idea of a joke, and neither makes much sense—"

"A joke! He ruined you. He must be a complete monster to find it amusing now."

"The last time I saw him, he did not find the situation amusing, believe me," Elizabeth said, and, sitting down, she told the whole story, trying desperately to keep her emotions under control so that she would be able to think clearly when she and Alex finalized their plans.

9

Berta, we've arrived," Elizabeth said as their traveling chaise drew up before the expansive estate belonging to Sir Francis Belhaven. Berta's eyes had been squeezed closed for the last hour, but Elizabeth saw her bosom rising and falling with rapid, shallow breaths and knew she was not asleep. Berta had been terrified at the prospect of playing the role of Elizabeth's aunt, and none of Elizabeth's soothing or promises had eased her fear one bit in the last several days. She had not wanted to come, and now that she was there, she was still praying for deliverance.

"Aunt Berta!" she said forcefully as the front door of the great, rambling house was swung open. The butler stepped aside, and footmen hurried forward. "Aunt Berta!" she said urgently, and in desperation Elizabeth reached for the maid's tightly clenched eyelid. She pried it open and looked straight into a frightened brown orb. "Please do not do this to me, Berta. I'm counting on you to act like an aunt, not a timid mouse. They're almost upon us."

Berta nodded, swallowed, and straightened in her seat, then she smoothed her black bombazine skirts.

"How do I look?" Elizabeth whispered urgently.

"Dreadful," said Berta, eyeing the severe, high-necked black linen gown Elizabeth had carefully chosen to wear at this, her first meeting with the prospective husband whom Alexandra had described as a lecherous old roué. To add to her nunlike appearance, Elizabeth's hair was scraped back off her face, pinned into a bun à la Lucinda, and covered with a short veil. Around her neck she wore the only piece of "jewelry" she intended to wear for as long as she was here—a large, ugly iron crucifix she'd borrowed from the family chapel.

"Completely dreadful, milady," Berta added with more strength to her voice. Ever since Robert's disappearance, Berta had elected to address Elizabeth as her mistress instead of in the more familiar ways she'd used before.

"Excellent," Elizabeth said with an encouraging smile. "So do you."

The footman opened the door and let down the steps, and Elizabeth went first, followed by her "aunt." She let Berta step forward, then she turned and looked up at Aaron, who was atop the coach. Her uncle had permitted her to take six servants from Havenhurst, and Elizabeth had chosen them with care. "Don't forget," she warned Aaron needlessly. "Gossip freely about me with any servant who'll listen to you. You know what to say."

"Aye," he said with a devilish grin. "We'll tell them all what a skinny ogress you are—prim 'n proper enough to scare the devil himself into leading a holy life."

Elizabeth nodded and reluctantly turned toward the house. Fate had dealt her this hand, and she had no choice but to play it out as best she could. With head held high and knees shaking violently she walked forward until she drew even with Berta. The butler stood in the doorway, studying Elizabeth with bold interest, giving her the incredible impression that he was actually trying to locate her breasts beneath the shapeless black gown she wore. He stepped back from the door to permit them to enter. "My lord is with guests at the moment and will join you shortly," he explained. "In the meantime, Curbes will show you to your chambers." His eyes shifted to Berta and began to gleam appreciatively as they settled on her plump derriere, then he turned and nodded to the head footman.

With a white-faced, tight-lipped Berta beside her, Elizabeth climbed the long flight of stairs, glancing curiously about her at the gloomy hall and the crimson carpet on the steps. The carpet was thick and soft at the edges, attesting to its original cost, but it was threadbare beneath her feet and in immediate need of being replaced. There were gilt sconces on the wall with candles in them, but they had not been lit, and the staircase and landing above it were shrouded in darkness. So was the bedchamber she'd been assigned, Elizabeth realized as the footman opened the door and ushered them inside.

"Lady Berta's chamber is just through this door," the footman spoke up. Elizabeth squinted, peering in the darkness, and saw him walk over to what she assumed must be a wall. Hinges creaked slightly, hinting at the fact that a door had just been opened by the footman.

"It's dark as a tomb in here," she said, unable to see more than shadows. "Will you light the candles, please," she asked, "assuming there *are* candles in here?"

"Aye, milady, right there, next to the bed." His shadow crossed before her, and Elizabeth focused on a large, oddly shaped object that she supposed could be a bed, given its size.

"Will you light them, please?" she urged. "I—I can't see a thing in here."

"His lordship don't like more'n one candle lit in the bedchambers," the footman said. "He says it's a waste o' beeswax."

Elizabeth blinked in the darkness, torn somewhere between laughter and tears at her plight. "Oh," she said, nonplussed. The footman lit a small candle at the far end of the room and left, closing the door behind him. "Milady?" Berta whispered, peering through the dark, impenetrable gloom. "Where are you?"

"I'm over here," Elizabeth replied, walking cautiously forward, her arms outstretched, her hands groping about for possible obstructions in her path as she headed for what she hoped was the outside wall of the bedchamber, where there was bound to be a window with draperies hiding its light.

"Where?" Berta asked in a frightened whisper, and Elizabeth could hear the maid's teeth chattering halfway across the room.

"Here—on your left."

Berta followed the sound of her mistress's voice and let out a terrified gasp at the sight of the ghostlike figure moving eerily through the darkness, arms outstretched. "Raise your arm," she said urgently, "so I'll know 'tis you."

Elizabeth, knowing Berta's timid nature, complied immediately. She raised her arm, which, while calming poor Berta, unfortunately caused Elizabeth to walk straight into a slender, fluted pillar with a marble bust upon it, and they both began to topple. "Good God!" Elizabeth burst out, wrapping her arms protectively around the pillar and the marble object upon it. "Berta!" she said urgently. "This is no time to be afraid of the dark. Help me, please. I've bumped into something—a bust and its stand, I think—and I daren't let go of them until I can see how to set them upright. There are draperies over here, right in front of me. All you have to do is follow my voice and open them. Once we do, 'twill be bright as day in here."

"I'm coming, milady," Berta said bravely, and Elizabeth breathed a sigh of relief. "I've found them!" Berta cried softly a few minutes later. "They're heavy—velvet they are, with another panel behind them." Berta pulled one heavy panel back across the wall, and then, with renewed urgency and vigor, she yanked back the other and turned around to survey the room.

"Light at last!" Elizabeth said with relief. Dazzling late-afternoon sunlight poured into the windows directly in front of her, blinding her momentarily. "That's much better," she said, blinking. Satisfied that the pillar was quite sturdy enough to stand without her aid, Elizabeth was about to place the bust back upon it, but Berta's cry stopped her.

"Saints preserve us!"

With the fragile bust clutched protectively to her chest Elizabeth swung sharply around. There, spread out before her, furnished entirely in red and gold, was the most shocking room Elizabeth had ever beheld: Six enormous gold cupids seemed to hover in thin air above a gigantic bed clutching crimson velvet bed draperies in one pudgy fist and holding bows and arrows in the other; more cupids adorned the headboard. Elizabeth's eyes widened, first in disbelief, and a moment later in mirth. "Berta," she breathed on a smothered giggle, "will you *look* at this place!"

Mesmerized by the gilt ghastliness of it all, Elizabeth slowly turned in a full circle. Above the fireplace there was a gilt-framed painting of a lady attired in nothing whatsoever but a scrap of nearly-transparent red silk that had been draped across her hips. Elizabeth jerked her eyes away from that shocking display of nudity and found herself confronted by a veritable army of cavorting cupids. They reposed in chubby, gilt splendor atop the mantel and the bed tables; a cluster of them formed the tall candelabra beside the bed, which held twelve candles—one of which the footman had lit—and more cupids surrounded an enormous mirror.

"It's . . ." Berta uttered as she gazed through eyes the size of saucers, "it's . . . I can't find words," she breathed, but Elizabeth had passed through her own state of shock and was perilously close to hilarity.

"Unspeakable?" Elizabeth suggested helpfully, and a giggle bubbled up from her throat. "U-Unbelievable?" she volunteered, her shoulders beginning to shake with mirth.

Berta made a nervous, strangled sound, and suddenly it was too much for both of them. Days of relentless tension erupted into gales of hilarity, and they gave in to it with shared abandon. Great gusty shouts of laughter erupted from them, sending tears trickling down their cheeks. Berta snatched for her missing apron, then remembered her new, elevated station in life and instead withdrew a handkerchief from her sleeve, dabbing at the corners of her eyes; Elizabeth simply clutched the forgotten bust to her cheek, perched her chin upon its smooth head, and laughed until she ached. So complete was their absorption that neither of them realized their host was entering the bedchamber until Sir Francis boomed enthusiastically, "Lady Elizabeth and Lady Berta!"

Berta let out a muffled scream of surprised alarm and quickly shifted her handkerchief from the corners of her eyes to her mouth.

Elizabeth took one look at the satin-clad figure who rather resembled the cupids he obviously admired, and the dire reality of her predicament hit her like a bucket of icy water, banishing all thoughts of laughter. She dropped her gaze to the floor, trying wildly to remember her plan and to believe she could make it work. She *had* to make it work, for if she failed, this aging roue with the penchant for gilded cupids could very likely become her husband.

"My dear, dear ladies," Sir Francis effused as he hastened forward, "what a long-awaited delight this is!" Courtesy demanded that he acknowledge the older lady first, and so he turned to her. Picking up Berta's limp hand from her side, he pressed his lips to it and said, "Permit me to introduce myself. I am Sir Francis Belhaven."

Lady Berta curtsied, her fear-widened eyes fastened on his face, and continued to press her handkerchief to her lips. To his astonishment, she did not acknowledge him at all; she did not say she was charmed to meet him or inquire after his health. Instead, the woman curtsied again. And once again. "There's hardly a need for all that," he said, covering his puzzlement with forced joviality. "I'm only a knight, you know. Not a duke or even an earl."

Lady Berta curtsied again, and Elizabeth nudged her sharply with her elbow. "How do!" burst out the plump lady.

"My aunt is a trifle—er—shy with strangers," Elizabeth managed weakly.

The sound of Elizabeth Cameron's soft, musical voice made Sir Francis's blood sing. He turned with unhidden eagerness to his future bride and realized that it was a bust of himself that Elizabeth was clutching so protectively, so very *affectionately* to her bosom. He could scarcely contain his delight. "I *knew* it would be this way between us—no pretense, no maidenly shyness," he burst out, beaming at her blank, wary expression as he gently took the bust of himself from Elizabeth's arms. "But, my lovely, there's no need for you to caress a hunk of clay when *I* am here in the *flesh*."

Momentarily struck dumb, Elizabeth gaped at the bust she'd been holding as he first set it gently upon its stand, then turned expectantly to her, leaving her with the horrifying—and accurate—thought that he now expected her to reach out and draw his balding head to her bosom. She stared at him, her mind in paralyzed chaos. "I—I would ask a favor of you, Sir Francis," she burst out finally.

"Anything, my dear," he said huskily.

"I would like to—to rest before supper."

He stepped back, looking disappointed, but then he recalled his manners and reluctantly nodded. "We don't keep country hours. Supper is at eight-thirty." For the first time he took a moment to really look at her. His memories of her exquisite face and delicious body had been so strong, so clear, that until then he'd been seeing the Lady Elizabeth Cameron he'd met long ago. Now he belatedly registered the stark, unattractive gown she wore and the severe way her hair was dressed. His gaze dropped to the ugly iron cross that hung about her neck, and he recoiled in shock. "Oh, and my dear, I've invited a few guests," he added pointedly, his eyes on her unattractive gown. "I thought you would want to know, in order to attire yourself more appropriately."

Elizabeth suffered that insult with the same numb paralysis she'd felt since she set eyes on him. Not until the door closed behind him did she feel able to move. "Berta," she burst out, flopping disconsolately onto the chair beside her, "how *could* you curtsy like that—he'll know you for a lady's maid before the night is out! We'll never pull this off."

"Well!" Berta exclaimed, hurt and indignant. "Twasn't *I* who was clutching his head to *my* bosom when he came in."

"We'll do better after this," Elizabeth vowed with an apologetic glance over her shoulder, and the trepidation was gone from her voice, replaced by steely determination and urgency. "We have to do better. I want us both out of here tomorrow. The day after at the very latest."

"The butler stared at my bosom," Berta complained. "I *saw* him!"

Elizabeth sent her a wry, mirthless smile. "The footman stared at mine. No woman is safe in this place. We only had a bit of—of stage fright just now. We're new to playacting, but tonight I'll carry it off. You'll see. No matter what it takes, I'll do it."

* * *

124

When Elizabeth finally descended the stairs on her way to the dining room she was two hours late. Deliberately.

"Good heavens, you're tardy, my dear!" Sir Francis said, shoving back his chair and rushing to the doorway where Elizabeth had been standing, trying to gather her courage to do what needed to be done. "Come and meet my guests," he said, drawing her forward after a swift, disappointed look at her drab attire and severe coiffure. "We did as you suggested in your note and went ahead with supper. What kept you abovestairs so long?"

"I was at prayer," Elizabeth said, managing to look him straight in the eye.

Sir Francis recovered from his surprise in time to introduce her to the three other people at the table—two men who resembled him in age and features and two women of perhaps five and thirty who were both attired in the most shockingly revealing gowns Elizabeth had ever seen.

Elizabeth accepted a helping of cold meat to silence her protesting stomach while both women studied her with unhidden scorn. "That is a most unusual ensemble you're wearing, I must say," remarked the woman named Eloise. "Is it the custom where you come from to dress so . . . simply?"

Elizabeth took a dainty bite of meat. "Not really. I disapprove of too much personal adornment." She turned to Sir Francis with an innocent stare. "Gowns are expensive. I consider them a great waste of money."

Sir Francis was suddenly inclined to agree, particularly since he intended to keep her naked as much as possible. "Quite right!" he beamed, eyeing the other ladies with pointed disapproval. "No point in spending all that money on gowns. No point in spending money at all."

"My sentiments exactly," Elizabeth said, nodding. "I prefer to give every shilling I can find to charity instead."

"*Give* it away?" he said in a muted roar, half rising out of his chair. Then he forced himself to sit back down and reconsider the wisdom of wedding her. She was lovely—her face more mature than he remembered it, but not even the black veil and scraped-back hair could detract from the beauty of her emerald-green eyes with their long, sooty lashes. Her eyes had dark circles beneath them—shadows he didn't recall seeing there earlier in the day. He put the shadows down to her far-too-serious nature. Her dowry was creditable, and her body beneath that shapeless black gown . . . he wished he could see her shape. Perhaps it, too, had changed, and not for the better, in the past few years.

"I had hoped, my dear," Sir Francis said, covering her hand with his and squeezing it affectionately, "that you might wear something else down to supper, as I suggested you should."

Elizabeth gave him an innocent stare. "This is all I brought."

"All you brought?" he uttered. "B-But I distinctly saw my footmen carrying several trunks upstairs."

"They belong to my aunt—only one of them is mine," she fabricated hastily, already anticipating his next question and thinking madly for some satisfactory answer.

"Really?" He continued to eye her gown with great dissatisfaction, and then he asked exactly the question she'd expected: "What, may I ask, does your one trunk contain if not gowns?"

Inspiration struck, and Elizabeth smiled radiantly. "Something of great value. Priceless value," she confided.

All faces at the table watched her with alert fascination—particularly the greedy Sir Francis. "Well, don't keep us in suspense, love. What's in it?"

"The mortal remains of Saint Jacob."

Lady Eloise and Lady Mortand screamed in unison, Sir William choked on his wine, and Sir Francis gaped at her in horror, but Elizabeth wasn't quite finished. She saved the coup de grace until the meal was over. As soon as everyone arose she insisted that they sit back down so a proper prayer of gratitude could be said. Raising her hands heavenward, Elizabeth turned a simple grace into a stinging tirade against the sins of lust and promiscuity that rose to a crescendo as she called down the vengeance of doomsday on all transgressors and culminated in a terrifyingly lurid description of the terrors that awaited all who strayed down the path of lechery—terrors that combined dragon lore with mythology, a smattering of religion, and a liberal dash of her own vivid imagination. When it was done Elizabeth dropped her eyes, praying in earnest that tonight would loose her from her predicament. There was no more she could do; she'd played out her hand with all her might; she'd given it her all.

It was enough. After supper Sir Francis escorted her to her chamber and, with a poor attempt at regret, announced that he greatly feared they wouldn't suit. Not at all.

Elizabeth and Berta departed at dawn the following morning, an hour before Sir Francis's servants stirred themselves. Clad in a dressing robe, Sir Francis watched from his bedchamber window as Elizabeth's coachman helped her into her conveyance. He was about to turn away when a sudden gust of wind caught Elizabeth's black gown, exposing a long and exceptionally shapely leg to Sir Francis's riveted gaze. He was still staring at the coach as it circled the drive; through its open window he saw Elizabeth laugh and reach up, unpinning her hair. Clouds of golden tresses whipped about the open window, obscuring her face, and Sir Francis thoughtfully wet his lips.

10

The country seat of Lord John Marchman, Earl of Canford, was a place of such unhampered, unplanned, raw beauty that Elizabeth temporarily forgot the purpose of her visit as she stared out the window. The house was the largest she'd ever seen—a sprawling, half-timbered Tudor structure—but it was the grounds that held her enthralled. Weeping willows marched along a stream that ran through a park at the front of the property, and lilacs bloomed unhampered and untamed beside the willows, their soft colors blending in natural splendor with blue columbine and wild lilies.

Before their chaise drew to a complete halt in front of the house a door was already being flung open, and a tall, stocky man was bounding down the steps.

"It would appear that our greeting here is going to be far more enthusiastic than the one we received at our last stop," Elizabeth said in a resolute voice that still shook with nerves as she drew on her gloves, bravely preparing to meet and defy the next obstacle to her happiness and independence.

The door of their chaise was wrenched open with enough force to pull it from its hinges, and a masculine face poked inside. "Lady Elizabeth!" boomed Lord Marchman, his face flushed with eagerness—or drink; Elizabeth wasn't certain. "This is indeed a long-awaited surprise," and then, as if dumbstruck by his inane remark, he shook his large head and hastily said, "A long-awaited *pleasure,* that is! The *surprise* is that you've arrived early."

Elizabeth firmly repressed a surge of compassion for his obvious embarrassment, along with the thought that he might be rather likable. "I hope we haven't inconvenienced you overmuch," she said.

"Not overmuch. That is," he corrected, gazing into her wide eyes and feeling himself drowning, "not at *all.*"

Elizabeth smiled and introduced "Aunt Berta," then allowed their exuberant host to escort them up the steps. Beside her Berta whispered with some satisfaction, "I think he's as nervous as I am."

The interior of the house seemed drab and rather gloomy after the sunny splendor outside. As their host led her forward Elizabeth glimpsed the furnishings in the salon and drawing room—all of which were upholstered in dark leathers that appeared to have once been maroon and brown. Lord Marchman, who was watching her closely and hopefully, glanced about and suddenly saw his home as she must be seeing it. Trying to explain away the inadequacies of his furnishings, he said hastily, "This home is in need of a woman's touch. I'm an old bachelor, you see, as was my father."

Berta's eyes snapped to his face. "Well, I never!" she exclaimed in outraged reaction to his apparent admission of being a bastard.

"I didn't mean," Lord Marchman hastily assured, "that my father was *never* married. I meant"—he paused to nervously tug on his neckcloth, as if trying to loosen it—"that my mother died when I was very young, and my father never remarried. We lived here together."

At the juncture of two hallways and the stairs Lord Marchman turned and looked at Berta and Elizabeth. "Would you care for refreshment, or would you rather go straight to bed?"

Elizabeth wanted a rest, and she particularly wanted to spend as little time in his company as was possible. "The latter, if you please."

"In that case," he said with a sweeping gesture of his arm toward the staircase, "let's go."

Berta let out a gasp of indignant outrage at what she perceived to be a clear indication that he was no better than Sir Francis. "Now see here, milord! I've been putting her to bed for nigh onto two score, and I don't need help from the likes of you!" And then, as if she realized her true station, she ruined the whole magnificent effect by curtsying and adding in a servile whisper, "if you don't mind, sir."

"Mind? No, I—" It finally occurred to John Marchman what she thought, and he colored up clear to the roots of his hair. "I—I only meant to show you how," he began, and then he leaned his head back and briefly closed his eyes as if praying for deliverance from his own tongue. "How to find *the way*," he finished with a gusty sigh of relief.

Elizabeth was secretly touched by his sincerity and his awkwardness, and were the situation less threatening, she would have gone out of her way to put him at his ease.

Reluctantly opening her eyes, Elizabeth rolled over onto her back. Sunlight was streaming in through the windows, and a faint smile teased the corners of her lips as she stretched and thought back on the previous night's meal. Lord Marchman had turned out to be as endearing, awkward, and eager to please as he'd seemed upon their arrival.

Berta bustled in, still managing to look like a maid despite her stylish puce gown. "That man," she announced huffily, referring to their host, "can't put two words together without losing his meaning!" Obviously she'd expected better of the quality during the time she was allowed to mix with them.

"He's afraid of us, I think," Elizabeth replied, climbing out of bed. "Do you know the time? He desired me to accompany him fishing this morning at seven."

"Half past ten," Berta replied, opening drawers and turning toward Elizabeth for her decision as to which gown to wear. "He waited until a few minutes ago, then went off without you. He was carrying two poles. Said you could join him when you arose."

"In that case, I think I'll wear the pink muslin," she decided with a mischievous smile.

The Earl of Marchman could scarcely believe his eyes when he finally saw his intended making her way toward him. Decked out in a frothy pink gown with an equally frothy pink parasol and a delicate pink bonnet, she came tripping across the bank. Amazed at the vagaries of the female mind, he quickly turned his attention back to the grandfather trout he'd been trying to catch for five years. Ever so gently he jiggled his pole, trying to entice or else annoy the wily old fish into taking his fly. The giant fish swam around his hook as if he knew it might be a trick and then he suddenly charged it, nearly jerking the pole out of John's hands. The fish hurtled out of the water, breaking the surface in a tremendous, thrilling arch at the same moment John's intended bride deliberately chose to let out a piercing shriek: *"Snake!"*

Startled, John jerked his head in her direction and saw her charging at him as if Lucifer himself was on her heels, screaming, "Snake! *Snake! Snnnaaaaake!"* And in that instant his concentration was broken; he let his line go slack, and the fish dislodged the hook, exactly as Elizabeth had hoped.

"I saw a snake," she lied, panting and stopping just short of the arms he'd stretched out to catch her—or strangle her, Elizabeth thought, smothering a smile. She stole a quick searching glance at the water, hoping for a glimpse of the magnificent trout he'd nearly caught, her hands itching to hold the pole and try her own luck.

Lord Marchman's disgruntled question snapped her attention back to him. "Would you like to fish, or would you rather sit and watch for a bit, until you recover from your flight from the serpent?"

Elizabeth looked around in feigned shock. "Goodness, sir, I don't fish!"

"Do you sit?" he asked with what *might* have been sarcasm.

Elizabeth lowered her lashes to hide her smile at the mounting impatience in his voice. "Of course I sit," she proudly told him. "Sitting is an excessively ladylike occupation, but fishing, in my opinion, is not. I shall *adore* watching you do it, however."

For the next two hours she sat on the boulder beside him,

complaining about its hardness, the brightness of the sun and the dampness of the air, and when she ran out of matters to complain about she proceeded to completely spoil his morning by chattering his ears off about every inane topic she could think of while occasionally tossing rocks into the stream to scare off his fish.

When at last he finally hooked one, despite Elizabeth's best efforts to prevent it, she scrambled to her feet and backed up a step. "You—you're hurting it!" she cried as he pulled the hook from its mouth.

"Hurting what? The fish?" he asked in disbelief.

"Yes!"

"Nonsense," said he, looking at her as if she was daft, then he tossed the fish on the bank.

"It can't breathe, I tell you!" she wailed, her eyes fixed on the flapping fish.

"It doesn't need to *breathe,*" he retorted. "We're going to eat it for lunch."

"I certainly won't!" she cried, managing to look at him as if he were a cold-blooded murderer.

"Lady Cameron," he said sternly, "am I to believe you've never eaten fish?"

"Well, of course I have."

"And *where* do you think the fish you've eaten came from?" he continued with irate logic.

"It came from a nice tidy package wrapped in paper," Elizabeth announced with a vacuous look. "They come in nice, tidy paper wrapping."

"Well, they weren't born in that tidy paper," he replied, and Elizabeth had a dreadful time hiding her admiration for his patience as well as for the firm tone he was finally taking with her. He was not, as she had originally thought, a fool or a namby-pamby. "Before that," he persisted, "where was the fish? How did that fish *get* to the market in the first place?"

Elizabeth gave her head a haughty toss, glanced sympathetically at the flapping fish, then gazed at him with haughty condemnation in her eyes. "I assume they used nets or something, but I'm perfectly certain they didn't do it this way."

"What way?" he demanded.

"The way you have—sneaking up on it in its own little watery home, tricking it by covering up your hook with that poor fuzzy thing, and then jerking the poor fish away from its family and tossing it on the bank to die. It's quite inhumane!" she said, and she gave her skirts an irate twitch.

Lord Marchman stared at her in frowning disbelief, then he shook his head as if trying to clear it. A few minutes later he escorted her home.

Elizabeth made him carry the basket containing the fish on the opposite side from where she walked. And when that didn't seem to discomfit the poor man she insisted he hold his arm straight out—to keep the basket even further from her person.

She was not at all surprised when Lord Marchman excused himself until supper, nor when he remained moody and thoughtful throughout their uncomfortable meal. She covered the silence, however, by chattering earnestly about the difference between French and English fashions and the importance of using only the best kid for gloves, and then she regaled him with detailed descriptions of every gown she could remember seeing. By the end of the meal Lord Marchman looked dazed and angry; Elizabeth was a little hoarse and very encouraged.

"I think," Berta remarked with a proud little smile when she was seated alone in the drawing room beside Elizabeth, "he's having second thoughts about proposing, milady."

"I think he was silently contemplating the easiest way to murder me at dinner," Elizabeth said, chuckling. She was about to say more when the butler interrupted them to announce that Lord Marchman wished to have a private word with Lady Cameron in his study.

Elizabeth prepared for another battle of wits—or witlessness, she thought with an inner smile—and dutifully followed the butler down a dark hall furnished in brown and into a very large study where the earl was seated in a maroon chair at a desk on her right.

"You wished to see—" she began as she stepped into his study, but something on the wall beside her brushed against her hair. Elizabeth turned her head, expecting to see a portrait hanging there, and instead found herself eye-to-fang with an enormous bear's head. The little scream that tore from her was very real this time, although it owed to shock, not to fear.

"It's quite dead," the earl said in a voice of weary resignation, watching her back away from his most prized hunting trophy with her hand over her mouth.

Elizabeth recovered instantly, her gaze sweeping over the wall of hunting trophies, then she turned around.

"You may take your hand away from your mouth," he stated. Elizabeth fixed him with another accusing glare, biting her lip to hide her smile. She would have dearly loved to hear how he had stalked that bear or where he had found that monstrous-big boar, but she knew better than to ask. "Please, my lord," she said instead, "tell me these poor creatures didn't die at your hands."

"I'm afraid they did. Or more correctly, at the point of my gun. Please sit down." He nodded toward an overstuffed leather wingback chair in front of his desk, and Elizabeth settled into its enveloping comfort. "Tell me, if you will," he inquired, his eyes softening as he gazed upon her upturned face, "in the event we were wed, how would you envision our lives together?"

Elizabeth hadn't expected such a frontal attack, and she both respected him for it and was disconcerted by it. Taking a long breath, she tried systematically to describe the sort of life she knew he'd probably loathe: "Naturally, we'd live in London," she began, leaning forward in her chair in a pose of eager enthusiasm. "I do so adore the city and its amusements."

His brows drew together at the mention of living in London. "What sort of amusements do you enjoy?"

"Amusements?" Elizabeth said brightly, considering. "Balls and routs and the opera. I adore giving balls and attending them. In fact, I simply cannot bear to miss a ball. Why, during my season there were days I managed to make it to as many as fifteen different balls! And I adore gambling," she added, trying to give him the impression that she would cost him a great deal more than the dowry she would bring. "I have dreadful luck, however, and am forever having to borrow money."

"I see," he said. "Is there anything else?"

Elizabeth faltered, feeling she ought to think of more, but

his steady, speculative gaze was unnerving her. "What else matters in life," she said with forced gaiety, "other than balls and gaming and sophisticated companions?"

His face had grown so thoughtful that Elizabeth sensed he was working up the courage to cry off, and she waited in expectant silence so as not to distract him. The moment he began to speak, she knew he was going to do it because his speech became awkward, as it seemed to do whenever he addressed her on matters he perceived to be important. "Lady . . . er . . ." he began lamely, running his fingers around his neckcloth.

"Cameron," Elizabeth provided helpfully.

"Yes—Cameron," he agreed, and he fell silent for a moment, regathering his thoughts. "Lady Cameron," he began, "I am a simple country lord without any aspirations to spend the season in London and cut a dash among the *ton*. I go there as seldom as possible. I can see that disappoints you."

Elizabeth nodded sadly.

"I greatly fear," he said, flushing at the neck, "that we won't suit, Lady . . . er . . ." He trailed off uneasily at his rudeness.

"Cameron," Elizabeth provided, eager to have him complete his thought.

"Yes, of course. Cameron. I knew that. What I was trying to say was that . . . ah . . ."

"We won't suit?" Elizabeth prodded helpfully.

"Exactly!" Misinterpreting her last sentence as being her own thought instead of his, he sighed with relief and nodded emphatically. "I must say I'm happy to hear you agree with me."

"Naturally, I regret that this is so," Elizabeth added kindly, feeling that some sort of balm was due him for the emotional torment she'd put him through at the stream. "My uncle will be most disappointed also," she continued. It was all she could do not to leap to her feet and put the quill in his hand as she added, "Would you like to write to him now and explain your decision?"

"*Our* decision," he corrected gallantly.

"Yes, but . . ." She hesitated, framing her answer carefully. "My uncle will be so very disappointed, and I—I shouldn't like him to lay the blame at my door." Sir Francis might well have blamed her in his inevitable letter to her uncle, and she didn't dare risk having the earl do likewise. Uncle Julius was no fool, and she couldn't risk his retribution if he realized she'd been deliberately discouraging her beaux and intentionally thwarting him.

"I see," he said, observing her with disturbing concentration, then he picked up a quill and trimmed it. A sigh of relief escaped Elizabeth as she watched him write his note. "Now that that distasteful matter is out of the way, may I ask you something?" he said, shoving the note aside.

Elizabeth nodded happily.

"Why did you come here—that is, why did you agree to reconsider my proposal?"

The question alarmed and startled her. Now that she'd seen him she had only the dimmest, possibly even erroneous recollection of having spoken to him at a ball. Moreover, she couldn't tell him she was in danger of being cut off by her uncle, for that whole explanation was too humiliating to bear mentioning.

He waited for her to reply, and when she seemed unable to give one he prompted, "Did I do or say something during our brief meetings the year before last to mislead you, perhaps, into believing I might yearn for the city life?"

"It's hard to say," Elizabeth said with absolute honesty.

"Lady Cameron, do you even remember our meeting?"

"Oh, yes, of course. Certainly," Elizabeth replied, belatedly recalling a man who looked very like him being presented to her at Lady Markham's. That was it! "We met at Lady Markham's ball."

His gaze never left her face. "We met in the park."

"In the park?" Elizabeth repeated in sublime embarrassment.

"You had stopped to admire the flowers, and the young gentleman who was your escort that day introduced us."

"I see," Elizabeth replied, her gaze skating away from his.

"Would you care to know what we discussed that day and the next day when I escorted you back to the park?"

Curiosity and embarrassment warred, and curiosity won out. "Yes, I would."

"Fishing."

"F-Fishing?" Elizabeth gasped.

He nodded. "Within minutes after we were introduced I mentioned that I had not come to London for the Season, as you supposed, but that I was on my way to Scotland to do some fishing and was leaving London the very next day."

An awful feeling of foreboding crept over Elizabeth as something stirred in her memory. "We had a charming chat," he continued. "You spoke enthusiastically of a particularly challenging trout you were once able to land."

Elizabeth's face felt as hot as red coals as he continued, "We quite forgot the time and your poor escort as we shared fishing stories."

He was quiet, waiting, and when Elizabeth couldn't endure the damning silence anymore she said uneasily, "Was there . . . more?"

"Very little. I did not leave for Scotland the next day but stayed instead to call upon you. You abandoned the half-dozen young bucks who'd come to escort you to some sort of fancy soiree and chose instead to go for another impromptu walk in the park with me."

Elizabeth swallowed audibly, unable to meet his eyes.

"Would you like to know what we talked about that day?"

"No, I don't think so."

He chuckled but ignored her reply. "You professed to be somewhat weary of the social whirl and confessed to a longing to be in the country that day—which is why we went to the park. We had a charming time, I thought."

When he fell silent, Elizabeth forced herself to meet his gaze and say with resignation, "And we talked of fishing?"

"No," he said. "Of boar hunting."

Elizabeth closed her eyes in sublime shame.

"You related an exciting tale of a wild boar your father had shot long ago, and of how you watched the hunt—without permission—from the very tree below which the boar was ultimately felled. As I recall," he finished kindly, "you told me that it was your impulsive cheer that revealed your hiding place to the hunters—and that caused you to be seriously reprimanded by your father."

Elizabeth saw the twinkle lighting his eyes, and suddenly they both laughed.

"I remember your laugh, too," he said, still smiling, "I

thought it was the loveliest sound imaginable. So much so that between it and our delightful conversation I felt very much at ease in your company." Realizing he'd just flattered her, he flushed, tugged at his neckcloth, and self-consciously looked away.

Seeing his discomfort, Elizabeth waited until he'd recovered his composure and was looking at her. "I remember you, too," she said, tipping her head sideways when he started to turn his head and refusing to let him break their gaze. "I do," she said quietly and honestly. "I had forgotten until just a moment ago."

He looked gratified and puzzled as he leaned back in his chair and studied her. "Why did you choose to reconsider my proposal, when I scarcely made the merest impression on you?"

He was so nice, so kind, that Elizabeth felt she owed him a truthful answer. Moreover, she was rapidly revising her opinion of Lord Marchman's acuity. Now that the possibility of romantic involvement had vanished, his speech had become incisive and his perception alarmingly astute.

"You might as well confide the whole of it to me, you know," he urged, smiling as he read her thoughts. "I'm not quite the simpleton I'm sure I've seemed to be. It is only that I am not . . . er . . . comfortable around females in a courtship situation. Since I am not going to be your husband, however," he said with only a twinge of regret, "perhaps we could be friends?"

Elizabeth knew instinctively that he would not mock her situation if she explained it, and that he would continue probing until she did. "It was my uncle's decision," she said with an embarrassed smile, trying to gloss matters over and still explain to him why he'd been put through this inconvenience. "My uncle has no children, you see, and he is most determ—that is, concerned—to see me well wed. He knew of those gentlemen who'd offered for me—and so my uncle—that is to say . . ." Elizabeth trailed off helplessly. It was not so easy to explain as she'd hoped.

"Selected me?" the earl suggested.

Elizabeth nodded.

"Amazing. I distinctly recall hearing that you'd had several—no, *many* offers of marriage the Season we met.

Yet your uncle chose me. I must say I'm flattered. And very surprised. Considering the substantial difference in our ages, not to mention our interests, I should have expected him to choose a younger man. I apologize for prying," he said, studying her very closely.

Elizabeth almost bolted out of her chair in dismay when he asked bluntly, "Who *else* did he chose?"

Biting her lip, she looked away, unaware that Lord Marchman could see from her stricken expression that although the question embarrassed her, the answer distressed her terribly.

"Whoever he is, he must be even less suited to you than I, from the look on your face," he said, watching her. "Shall I guess? Or shall I tell you frankly that an hour ago, when I returned, I overheard your aunt and your coachman laughing about something that occurred at the home of Sir Francis Belhaven. Is Belhaven the other man?" he asked gently.

The color drained from Elizabeth's face, and it was answer enough.

"Damnation!" expostulated the earl, grimacing in revulsion. "The very thought of an innocent like yourself being offered to that old—"

"I've dissuaded him," Elizabeth hastily assured him, but she was profoundly touched that the earl, who knew her so slightly, was angered on her behalf.

"You're certain?"

"I think so."

After a moment's hesitation he nodded and leaned back in his chair, his disturbingly astute gaze on her face while a slow smile drifted across his own. "May I ask how you accomplished it?"

"I'd truly rather you wouldn't."

Again he nodded, but his smile widened and his blue eyes lit with amusement. "Would I be far off the mark if I were to assume you used the same tactics on Marchman that I think you've used here?"

"I'm—not certain I understand your question," Elizabeth replied warily, but his grin was contagious, and she found herself having to bite her lip to stop from smiling back at him.

"Well, either the interest you exhibited in fishing two years ago was real, or it was your courteous way of putting me at ease and letting me talk about the things that interested me. If the former is true, then I can only assume your terror of fish yesterday isn't quite . . . shall we say . . . as profound as you would have had me believe?"

They looked at each other, he with a knowing smile, Elizabeth with brimming laughter. "Perhaps it is not *quite* so profound, my lord."

His eyes positively twinkled. "Would you care to make a try for that trout you cost me this morning? He's still out there taunting me, you know."

Elizabeth burst out laughing, and the earl joined her. When their laughter had died away Elizabeth looked across the desk at him, feeling as if they were truly friends. It would have been so lovely to sit by the stream without her slippers, waiting to test her own considerable skill with pole and line. On the other hand, she wanted neither to put him to the inconvenience of keeping them as house guests nor to risk that he might change his mind about their betrothal. "All things considered," she said slowly, "I think it best if my aunt and I were on our way tomorrow to our last . . . to our destination."

The next day dawned clear and fine with birds singing outside in the trees and sun shining gaily in an azure sky. Unfortunately, it was one of those days when solutions to the problems of the night before did *not* automatically present themselves, and as Lord Marchman handed Berta and her into their coach Elizabeth had still not resolved her dilemma: She could not remain here now that her task was accomplished; on the other hand, the prospect of arriving at Ian Thornton's home in Scotland, nearly a fortnight before she was expected and with Berta instead of Lucinda, did not appeal to her at all. In order to confront *that* man, she wanted Lucinda with her—Lucinda, who cowered before no one and who would be able to advise Elizabeth when advice was needed. The obvious solution was therefore to proceed to the inn where Lucinda was to meet them and to remain there until she arrived. Uncle Julius, with typical reverence for a shilling and unswerving practicality, had worked out what he called a budget and had given her only enough extra money to cover emergencies. Elizabeth told herself this was an emergency and resolved to spend the money and worry about explanations later.

Aaron was still waiting for instruction as to where to go, and Elizabeth made up her mind. "To Carrington, Aaron," she said. "We'll wait for Lucinda at the inn there."

Turning, she smiled with genuine affection at Lord Marchman and offered him her hand through the open window of the coach. "Thank you," she said shyly but with great sincerity, "for being all the things you are, my lord."

His face scarlet with pleasure at her compliment, John Marchman stepped back and watched her coach pull out of his drive. He watched it until the horses turned onto the road, then he slowly walked back toward the house and went into his study. Sitting down at his desk, he looked at the note he'd written her uncle and idly drummed his fingers upon his desk, recalling her disturbing answer when he asked if she'd dissuaded old Belhaven from pressing his suit. *"I think I have,"* she'd said. And then John made his decision.

Feeling rather like an absurd knight in shining armor rushing to save an unwilling damsel in the event of future distress, he took out a fresh sheet of paper and wrote out a new message to her uncle. As it always happened the moment courtship was involved, Lord Marchman lost his ability to be articulate. His note read:

> If Belhaven asks for her, please advise me of it. I think I want her first.

11

Ian Thornton stood in the center of the large cottage in Scotland where he had been born. Now he used it as a hunting box, but it was much more than that to him: It was the place where he knew he could always find peace and reality; the one place where he could escape, for a while, the hectic pace of his life. With his hands thrust deep in his pockets he looked about him, seeing it again through the eyes of an adult. "Every time I come back it's smaller than I remembered," he told the ruddy-faced, middle-aged man who was trudging through the front doors with heavy sacks of provisions slung over his shoulder.

"Things always look bigger when yer little," Jake said, unceremoniously dumping the sacks onto the dusty sideboard. "That's the lot o' it, 'cept my gear," he said. He pulled his pistol out of his belt and put it on the table. "I'll put the horses away."

Ian nodded absently, but his attention was on the cottage. An aching nostalgia swelled inside him as he remembered the years he'd lived here as a child. In his heart he heard his father's deep voice and his mother's answering laughter. To his right was the hearth where his mother had once prepared their meals before the arrival of their stove. At right angles to the hearth were the two tan high-backed chairs in which his parents had spent long, cozy evenings before the fire, talking in low voices so that Ian and his younger sister wouldn't be disturbed in their bedrooms above. Across from that was a sofa upholstered in a sturdy tan and brown plaid.

It was all here, just as Ian remembered. Turning, he looked down at the dust-covered table beside him, and with a smile he reached out and touched the surface, his long fingers searching the surface for a specific set of scratches. It took several seconds of rubbing, but slowly they came into view—four clumsily formed letters: I.G.B.T.—his initials, scratched into the surface when he was a little over three years old. That piece of mischief had nearly gotten him a good shaking until his mother realized he'd been teaching himself his letters without her help.

His lessons had begun the next day, and when his mother's considerable learning had been exhausted his father took over, teaching him geometry and physics and everything he'd learned at Eton and Cambridge. When Ian was fourteen Jake Wiley had joined the household as a jack-of-all-trades, and from him Ian had learned firsthand of the sea, and ships, and mysterious lands on the other side of the world. Later he had gone with Jake to see them himself and to put his education to use.

He'd returned home three years afterward, eager to see his family, only to discover that a few days earlier they had died in a fire at an inn where they had gone to await his impending return. Even now Ian felt the wrenching loss of his mother and father, the proud man who had turned his back on his noble heritage and instead married the sister of a poor Scottish vicar. By his actions he had forfeited a dukedom . . . and had never given a blessed damn. Or so he said. The poignancy of being here after two long years was almost past bearing, and Ian tipped his head back, closing his eyes against the bittersweet ache of it. He saw his father grinning and shaking his hand as Ian prepared to depart on his first voyage with Jake. "Take care," he had said. "Remember, no matter how far you go, we'll always be with you."

Ian had left that day, the impecunious son of a disowned English lord whose entire fortune was a small bag of gold his father had given him on his sixteenth birthday. Now, fourteen years later, there were fleets of ships flying Ian's flag and carrying his cargo; mines filled with his silver and tin; warehouses loaded with precious goods that he owned. But it was land that had originally made him rich. A large parcel of barren-looking land that he'd won at cards from a colonial who swore the old mine there had gold in it. And it had. Gold that bought more mines, and ships, and palatial homes in Italy and India.

Gambling everything on a series of investments had paid off for Ian again and again. Once society had called him a gambler; now he was regarded as some sort of mythical king with a golden touch. Rumors flew and prices soared on the 'change every time he bought a stock. He could not set foot into a ball without the butler bellowing out his name. Where once he had been a social pariah, those same people who had shunned him now courted his favor—or, more precisely, his financial advice, or his money for their daughters. His wealth had brought Ian many luxuries, but no extraordinary joy. It was the gamble he loved best—the challenge of selecting exactly the right venture and the thrill of wagering a fortune on it. Moreover, success had come with a price— it had cost him his right to privacy, and he resented that.

Now his grandfather's actions were adding to his unwanted notoriety. The death of Ian's father had evidently caused the old duke to feel some belated regret for the estrangement, and for the last twelve years he'd been writing to Ian periodically. At first he had pleaded with Ian to come and visit him at Stanhope. When Ian ignored his letters, he'd tried bribing him with promises to name Ian his legitimate heir. Those letters had gone unanswered, and for the last two years the old man's silence had misled Ian into thinking he'd given up. Four months ago, however, another letter bearing Stanhope's ducal crest had been delivered to Ian, and this one infuriated him.

The old man had imperiously given Ian four months in which to appear at Stanhope and meet with him to discuss arrangements for the transfer of six estates—estates that would have been Ian's father's inheritance had the duke not disowned him. According to the letter, if Ian did not appear, the duke planned to proceed without him, publicly naming him his heir.

Ian had written to his grandfather for the first time in his life; the note had been short and final. It was also eloquent proof that Ian Thornton was as unforgiving as his grandfather, who'd rejected his own son for two decades:

Try it and you'll look a fool. I'll disclaim all knowledge of any relationship with you, and if you still persist, I'll let your title and your estates rot.

The four months had elapsed now, and there had been no more communications from the duke, but in London gossip was still rampant that Stanhope was about to name an heir. And that the heir would be his natural grandson, Ian Thornton. Now invitations to balls and soirees arrived in tidal waves from the same people who had long ago shunned him as an undesirable, and their hypocrisy alternately amused and disgusted him.

"That black horse we used for packin' up here is the most cantankerous beast alive," Jake grumbled, rubbing his arm.

Ian lifted his gaze from the initials on the tabletop and turned to Jake, making no attempt to hide his amusement. "Bit you, did he?"

"Damn right he bit me!" the older man said bitterly. "He's been after a chunk of me since we left the coach at Hayborn and loaded those sacks on his back to bring up here."

"I warned you he bites anything he can reach. Keep your arm out of his way when you're saddling him."

"It weren't my arm he was after, it was my arse! Opened his mouth and went for it, only I saw him outter the corner of my eye and swung around, so he missed." Jake's frown darkened when he saw the amusement in Ian's expression. "Can't see why you've bothered to feed him all these years. He doesn't deserve to share a stable with your other horses—beauties they are, every one but him."

"Try slinging packs over the backs of one of those and you'll *see* why I took him. He was suitable for using as a pack mule; none of my other cattle would have been," Ian said, frowning as he lifted his head and looked about at the months of accumulated dirt covering everything.

"He's *slower'n* a pack mule," Jake replied. "Mean and

stubborn and slow," he concluded, but he, too, was frowning a little as he looked around at the thick layers of dust coating every surface. "Thought you said you'd arranged for some village wenches to come up here and clean and cook fer us. This place is a mess."

"I did, I dictated a message to Peters for the caretaker, asking him to stock the place with food and to have two women come up here to clean and cook. The food is here, and there are chickens out in the barn. He must be having difficulty finding two women to stay up here."

"Comely women, I hope," Jake said. "Did you tell him to make the wenches comely?"

Ian paused in his study of the spiderwebs strewn across the ceiling and cast him an amused look. "You wanted me to tell a seventy-year-old caretaker who's half-blind to make certain the wenches were comely?"

"Couldn'ta hurt t' mention it," Jake grumbled, but he looked chastened.

"The village is only twelve miles away. You can always stroll down there if you've urgent need of a woman while we're here. Of course, the trip back up here may kill you," he joked referring to the winding path up the cliff that seemed to be almost vertical.

"Never mind women," Jake said in an abrupt change of heart, his tanned, weathered face breaking into a broad grin. "I'm here for a fortnight of fishin' and relaxin', and that's enough for any man. It'll be like the old days, Ian—peace and quiet and naught else. No hoity-toity servants hearin' every word what's spoke, no carriages and barouches and matchmaking mamas arrivin' at your house. I tell you, my boy, though I've not wanted to complain about the way you've been livin' this past year, I don't like these servants o' yours above half. That's why I didn't come t'visit you very often. Yer butler at Montmayne holds his nose so far in t'air, it's amazin' he gets any oxhegen, and that French chef o' yers practically threw me out of his kitchens. That what he called 'em—*his* kitchens, and—" The old seaman abruptly broke off, his expression going from irate to crestfallen, "Ian," he said anxiously, "did you ever learn t' cook while we was apart?"

"No, did you?"

"Hell and damnation, no!" Jake said, appalled at the prospect of having to eat anything he fixed himself.

"Lucinda," Elizabeth said for the third time in an hour, "I cannot tell you how sorry I am about this." Five days ago, Lucinda had arrived at the inn at the Scottish border where she joined Elizabeth for the journey to Ian Thornton's house. This morning, their hired coach broke an axle, and they were now ignominiously ensconced on the back of a hay wagon belonging to a farmer, their trunks and valises tipping precariously to and fro along the rutted path that evidently passed for a road in Scotland. The prospect of arriving in a hay wagon on Ian Thornton's doorstep was so horrible that Elizabeth *preferred* to concentrate on her guilt, rather than her forthcoming meeting with the monster who had ruined her life.

"As I said the last time you apologized, Elizabeth," Lucinda replied, "it is not your fault, and therefore not your responsibility to apologize, for the deplorable lack of roads and conveyances in this heathen country."

"Yes, but if it weren't for me you wouldn't be here."

Lucinda sighed impatiently, clutched the side of the hay wagon as it made a particularly sharp lurch, and righted herself. "And as I have already admitted, if *I* hadn't been deceived into mentioning Mr. Thornton's name to your uncle, *neither* of us would be here. You are merely experiencing some nervousness at the disagreeable prospect of confronting the man, and there is no reason in the world—" The wagon tipped horribly and they both clutched at the sides of it for leverage. "—no reason in the world to continue apologizing. Your time would be better spent preparing yourself for the unhappy occasion."

"You're right, of course."

"Of course," Lucinda agreed unhesitatingly. "I am always right, as you know. *Nearly* always," she amended, obviously thinking of how she had been misled by Julius Cameron into revealing the name of Ian Thornton as one of Elizabeth's former suitors. As she'd explained to Elizabeth as soon as she arrived at the inn, she'd only given his name as a suitor because Julius had begun asking questions about Elizabeth's reputation during her debut, and about whether she'd been popular or not. Thinking he'd heard some of the malicious gossip about Elizabeth's involvement with Ian Thornton, Lucinda had tried to put a better face on things by including his name among Elizabeth's many suitors.

"I would rather face the devil himself than that man," Elizabeth said with a repressed shudder.

"I daresay," Lucinda agreed, clutching her umbrella with one hand and the side of the cart with her other.

The nearer the time came, the more angry and confused Elizabeth became about this meeting. For the first four days of their journey, her tension had been greatly allayed by the scenic grandeur of Scotland with its rolling hills and deep valleys carpeted in bluebells and hawthorne. Now, however, as the hour of confronting him drew near, not even the sight of the mountains decked out in spring flowers or the bright blue lakes below could calm her mounting tension. "Furthermore, I cannot believe he has the slightest desire to see me."

"We shall soon find out."

In the hills above the high, winding track that passed for a road, a shepherd paused to gape at an old wooden wagon making its laborious way along the road below. "Lookee there, Will," he told his brother. "Do you see what I see?"

The brother looked down and gaped, his lips parting in a toothless grin of glee at the comical sight of two ladies—bonnets, gloves, and all—who were perched primly and precariously on the back of Sean MacLaesh's haywagon, their backs ramrod-stiff, their feet sticking straight out beyond the wagon.

"Don't that beat all," Will laughed, and high above the haywagon he swept off his cap in a mocking salute to the ladies. "I heerd in the village Ian Thornton was acomin' home. I'll wager 'e's arrived, and them two are his fancy pieces, come to warm 'is bed an' see to 'is needs."

Blessedly unaware of the conjecture taking place between the two spectators up in the hills, Miss Throckmorton-Jones brushed angrily and ineffectually at the coating of dust clinging to her black skirts. "I have *never* in all my life been *subjected* to such treatment!" she hissed furiously as the wagon they were riding in gave another violent, creaking lurch and her shoulder banged into Elizabeth's. "You may depend on this—I shall give Mr. Ian Thornton a piece of my mind for inviting two gentlewomen to this godforsaken wilderness, and never even *mentioning* that a traveling baroche is too wide for the roads!"

Elizabeth opened her mouth to say something soothing, but just then the wagon gave another teeth-jarring lurch, and she clutched at the wooden side. "From what little I know of him, Lucy," she managed finally when the wagon righted, "he wouldn't care in the least what we've been through. He's rude and inconsiderate—and *those* are his *good* points—"

"Whoa there, *whoa,"* the farmer called out, sawing back on the swayback nag's reins and bringing the wagon to a groaning stop. "That's the Thornton place up there atop yon hill," the farmer said, pointing.

Lucinda gazed in mounting anger at the large, but unimpressive cottage that was barely visible through the thick trees, then she turned the full force of her authority on the hapless farmer. "You're mistaken, my good man," she said stoutly. "No gentleman of consequence or sense would live in such a godforsaken place as this. Kindly turn this decrepit vehicle around and return us to the village whence we came so that we can ask directions again. There was obviously a misunderstanding."

At that, both the horse and the farmer swung their heads around and looked at her with identical expressions of weary resentment.

The horse remained silent, but the farmer had heard Lucinda's irate complaints for the last twelve miles, and he was heartily sick of them. "See here, my lady," he began, but Lucinda cut him off.

"Do not address me as 'my lady.' 'Miss Throckmorton-Jones' will do very well."

"Aye. Well, whoever ye be, this is as far as I'm takin' ye, and that thar is the Thornton cottage."

"You can't mean to abandon us here!" she said as the tired old man exhibited a surge of renewed energy—obviously brought on by the prospect of ridding himself of his unwanted guests—and leapt off the wagon, whereupon he began to drag their trunks and bandboxes off the wagon and onto the side of the narrow ledge that passed for a road.

"What if they aren't home?" she gasped as Elizabeth took

pity on the elderly farmer and began helping him drag one of the trunks down.

"Then we'll simply come down here and wait for another farmer to be kind enough to give us a ride," Elizabeth said with a courage she didn't quite feel.

"I wouldna plan on't," said the farmer as Elizabeth withdrew a coin and placed it in her hand. "Thankee, milady, thankee kindly," he said, touching his cap and smiling a little at the younger lady, with the breathtaking face and shimmering blond hair.

"Why shouldn't we count on it?" Lucinda demanded.

"Because," said the farmer as he climbed back onto his wagon, "there ain't likely to be nobody comin' along for a week or two, mebbe more. There's rain comin' on—tomorrow, I'd guess, or the day after. Can't get a wagon through here when it rains hard. Besides," he said, taking pity on the young miss, who'd gone a little pale, "I see smoke comin' out o' yon chimney, so there's someone up there."

With a snap of the worn reins he drove off, and for a minute Elizabeth and Lucinda just stood there while a fresh cloud of dust settled all around them. Finally Elizabeth gave herself a firm mental shake and tried to take things in hand. "Lucy, if you'll take one end of that trunk there, I can take the other, and we can carry it up to the house."

"You'll do no such thing!" Lucinda cried angrily. "We shall leave everything right here and let Thornton send his servants down here."

"We could do that," Elizabeth said, "but it's a treacherous, steep climb, and the trunk is light enough, so there's no point in someone having to make an extra trip. Please, Lucy, I'm too exhausted to argue."

Lucinda turned a swift look upon Elizabeth's pale, apprehensive face and swallowed her argument. "You're quite right," she said briskly.

Elizabeth was not entirely right. The climb was steep enough, but the trunk, which originally felt quite light, seemed to gain a pound of weight with every step they took. A few yards from the house both ladies paused to rest again, then Elizabeth resolutely grabbed the handle on her end. "You go to the door, Lucy," she said breathlessly, worried for the older woman's health if she had to lug the trunk any further. "I'll just drag this along."

Miss Throckmorton-Jones took one look at her poor, bedraggled charge, and rage exploded in her breast that they'd been brought so low as this. Like an angry general she gave her gloves an irate yank, turned on her heel, marched up to the front door, and lifted her umbrella. Using its handle like a club, she rapped hard upon the door.

Behind her Elizabeth doggedly dragged the trunk. "You don't suppose there's no one home?" She panted, hauling the trunk the last few feet.

"If they're in there, they must be deaf!" said Lucinda. She brought up her umbrella again and began swinging at the door in a way that sent rhythmic thunder through the house. "Open up, I say!" she shouted, and on the third downswing the door suddenly lurched open to reveal a startled middle-aged man who was struck on the head by the handle of the descending umbrella.

"God's teeth!" Jake swore, grabbing his head and glowering a little dizzily at the homely woman who was glowering right back at him, her black bonnet crazily askew atop her wiry gray hair.

"It's God's *ears*, you need, not his teeth!" the sour-faced woman informed him as she caught Elizabeth's sleeve and pulled her one step into the house. "We are expected," she informed Jake. In his understandably dazed state, Jake took another look at the bedraggled, dusty ladies and erroneously assumed they were the women from the village come to clean and cook for Ian and him. His entire countenance changed, and a broad grin swept across his ruddy face. The growing lump on his head forgiven and forgotten, he stepped back. "Welcome, welcome," he said expansively, and he made a broad, sweeping gesture with his hand that encompassed the entire dusty room. "Where do you want to begin?"

"With a hot bath," said Lucinda, "followed by some tea and refreshments."

From the corner of her eye Elizabeth glimpsed a tall man who was stalking in from a room behind the one where they stood, and an uncontrollable tremor of dread shot through her.

"Don't know as I want a bath just now," Jake said.

"Not for you, you dolt, for Lady Cameron."

Elizabeth could have sworn Ian Thornton stiffened with shock. His head jerked toward her as if trying to see past the rim of her bonnet, but Elizabeth was absolutely besieged with cowardice and kept her head averted.

"You want a bath?" Jake repeated dumbly, staring at Lucinda.

"Indeed, but Lady Cameron's must come first. Don't just stand there," she snapped, threatening his midsection with her umbrella. "Send servants down to the road to fetch our trunks at once." The point of the umbrella swung meaningfully toward the door, then returned to jab Jake's middle. "But before you do that, inform your master that we have arrived."

"His master," said a biting voice from a rear doorway, "is aware of that."

Elizabeth swung around at the scathing tone of Ian's voice, and her fantasy of seeing him fall to his knees in remorse the moment he set eyes on her collapsed the instant she saw his face; it was as hard and forbidding as a granite sculpture. He did not bother to come forward but instead remained where he was, his shoulder propped negligently against the door frame, his arms folded across his chest, watching her through narrowed eyes. Until then Elizabeth had thought she remembered *exactly* what he looked like, but she hadn't. Not really. His suede jacket clung to wide shoulders that were broader and more muscular than she'd remembered, and his thick hair was almost black. His face was one of leashed sensuality and arrogant handsomeness with its sculpted mouth and striking eyes, but now she noticed the cynicism in those golden eyes and the ruthless set of his jaw—things she'd obviously been too young and naïve to see before. Everything about him exuded brute strength, and that in turn made her feel even more helpless as she searched his features for some sign that this aloof, forbidding man had actually held and kissed her with seductive tenderness.

"Have you had an edifying look at me, Countess?" he snapped, and before she could recover from the shock of that rude greeting his next words rendered her nearly speechless. "You are a remarkable young woman, Lady Cameron—you must possess the instincts of a bloodhound to track me here. Now that you've succeeded, there is the door. Use it."

Elizabeth's momentary shock gave way to a sudden, almost uncontrollable burst of wrath. "I beg your pardon?" she said tightly.

"You heard me."

"I was *invited* here."

"Of course you were," Ian mocked, realizing in a flash of surprise that the letter he'd had from her uncle must not have been a prank, and that Julius Cameron had obviously decided to regard Ian's lack of reply as willingness, which was nothing less than absurd and obnoxious. In the last months, since news of his wealth and his possible connection to the Duke of Stanhope had been made public, he'd become accustomed to being pursued by the same socialites who had once cut him. Normally he found it annoying; from Elizabeth Cameron he found it revolting.

He stared at her in insolent silence, unable to believe the alluring, impulsive girl he remembered had become this coolly aloof, self-possessed young woman. Even with her dusty clothes and the smear of dirt on her cheek, Elizabeth Cameron was strikingly beautiful, but she'd changed so much that—except for the eyes—he scarcely recognized her. One thing hadn't changed: She was still a schemer and a liar.

Straightening abruptly from his stance in the doorway, Ian walked forward. "I've had enough of this charade, Miss Cameron. No one invited you here, and you damn well know it."

Blinded with wrath and humiliation, Elizabeth groped in her reticule and snatched out the handwritten letter her uncle had received inviting Elizabeth to join Ian there. Marching up to him, she slapped the invitation against his chest. Instinctively he caught it but didn't open it.

"Explain that," she commanded, backing away and then waiting.

"Another note, I'll wager," he drawled sarcastically, thinking of the night he'd gone to the greenhouse to meet her and recalling what a fool he'd been about her.

Elizabeth stood beside the table, determined to have the satisfaction of hearing his explanation before she left—not that anything he said could make her stay. When he showed no sign of opening it, she turned furiously to Jake, who was sorely disappointed that Ian was deliberately chasing off two females who could surely be persuaded to do the cooking if they stayed. "Make him read it aloud!" she ordered the startled Jake.

"Now, Ian," Jake said, thinking of his empty stomach and the bleak future that lay ahead for it if the ladies went away, "why don't you jes' read that there little note, like the lady asked?"

When Ian Thornton ignored the older man's suggestion, Elizabeth lost control of her temper. Without thinking what she was actually doing, she reached out and snatched the pistol off the table, primed it, cocked it, and leveled it at Ian Thornton's broad chest. "Read that note!"

Jake, whose concern was still on his stomach, held up his hands as if the gun were pointed at him. "Ian, it could be a misunderstanding, you know, and it's not nice to be rude to these ladies. Why don't you read it, and then we'll all sit down and have a nice"—he inclined his head meaningfully to the sack of provisions on the table—*"supper."*

"I don't need to read it," Ian snapped. "The last time I read a note from Lady Cameron I met her in a greenhouse and got shot in the arm for my trouble."

"Are you implying *I* invited *you* into that greenhouse?" Elizabeth scoffed furiously.

With an impatient sigh Ian said, "Since you're obviously determined to enact a Cheltenham tragedy, let's get it over with before you're on your way."

"Do you deny you sent me a note?" she snapped.

"Of course I deny it!"

"Then what were *you* doing in the greenhouse?" she shot back at him.

"I came in response to that nearly illegible note you sent me," he said in a bored, insulting drawl. "May I suggest that in future you devote less of your time to theatrics and some of it to improving your handwriting?" His gaze shifted to the pistol. "Put the gun down before you hurt yourself."

Elizabeth raised it higher in her shaking hand. "You have

insulted me and degraded me every time I've been in your presence. If my brother were here, he'd call you out! Since he is not here," she continued almost mindlessly, "I shall demand my own satisfaction. If I were a man, I'd have the right to satisfaction on the field of honor, and as a woman I refuse to be denied that right."

"You're ridiculous."

"Perhaps," Elizabeth said softly, "but I also happen to be an excellent shot. I'm a far worthier opponent for you on the dueling field than my brother. Now, will you meet me outside, or shall I—I finish you here?" she threatened, so beside herself with fury that she never stopped to think how reckless, how utterly empty her threat was. Her coachman had insisted she learn to fire a weapon for her own protection, but although her aim was excellent when she'd practiced with targets, she had never shot a living thing.

"I'll do no such silly damned thing."

Elizabeth raised the gun higher. "Then I'll have your apology right now."

"What am I to apologize for?" he asked, still infuriatingly calm.

"You may start by apologizing for luring me into the greenhouse with that note."

"I didn't write a note. I *received* a note from you."

"You have great difficulty sorting out the notes you send and don't send, do you not?" she said. Without waiting for a reply she continued, "Next, you can apologize for trying to seduce me in England, and for ruining my reputation—"

"Ian!" Jake said, thunderstruck. "It's one thing to insult a lady's handwriting, but spoilin' her reputation is another. A thing like *that* could ruin her whole life!"

Ian shot him an ironic glance. "Thank you, Jake, for that helpful bit of inflammatory information. Would you now like to help her pull the trigger?"

Elizabeth's emotions veered crazily from fury to mirth as the absurdity of the bizarre tableau suddenly struck her: Here she was, holding a gun on a man in his own home, while poor Lucinda held another man at umbrella-point—a man who was trying ineffectually to soothe matters by inadvertently heaping more fuel on the volatile situation. And then she recognized the stupid futility of it all, and that banished her flicker of mirth. Once again this unspeakable man had caused her to make a complete fool of herself, and the realization made her eyes blaze with renewed fury as she turned her head and looked at him.

Despite Ian's apparent nonchalance he had been watching her closely, and he stiffened, sensing instinctively that she was suddenly and inexplicably angrier than before. He nodded to the gun, and when he spoke there was no more mockery in his voice; instead it was carefully neutral. "I think there are a few things you ought to consider before you use that."

Though she had no intention of using it, Elizabeth listened attentively as he continued in that same helpful voice. "First of all, you'll have to be very fast and very calm if you intend to shoot me and reload before Jake there gets to you. Second, I think it's only fair to warn you that there's going to be a great deal of blood all over the place. I'm not complaining, you understand, but I think it's only right to warn you that you're never again going to be able to wear that charming gown you have on." Elizabeth felt her stomach lurch. "You'll hang, of course," he continued conversationally, "but that won't be nearly as distressing as the *scandal* you'll have to face first."

Too disgusted with herself and with him to react to that last mocking remark, Elizabeth put her chin up and managed to say with great dignity, "I've had enough of this, Mr. Thornton. I did not think anything could equal your swinish behavior at our prior meetings, but you've managed to do it. Unfortunately, I am not so ill-bred as you and therefore have scruples against assaulting someone who is weaker than I, which is what I would be doing if I were to shoot an unarmed man. Lucinda, we are leaving," she said, then she glanced back at her silent adversary, who'd taken a threatening step, and she shook her head, saying with extreme, mocking civility, "No, please—do not bother to see us out, sir, there's no need. Besides, I wish to remember you just as you are at this moment—helpless and thwarted." It was odd, but now, at the low point of her life, Elizabeth felt almost exhilarated because she was finally doing *something* to avenge her pride instead of meekly accepting her fate.

Lucinda had marched out onto the porch already, and

Elizabeth tried to think of something to dissuade him from retrieving his gun when she threw it away outside. She decided to repeat his own advice, which she began to do as she backed away toward the door. "I know you're loath to see us leave like this," she said, her voice and her hand betraying a slight, fearful tremor. "However, before you consider coming after us, I beg you will take your own excellent advice and pause to consider if killing me is worth hanging for."

Whirling on her heel, Elizabeth took one running step, then cried out in pained surprise as she was jerked off her feet and a hard blow to her forearm sent the gun flying to the floor at the same time her arm was yanked up and twisted behind her back. "Yes," he said in an awful voice near her ear, "I actually think it would be worth it."

Just when she thought her arm would surely snap, her captor gave her a hard shove that sent her stumbling headlong out into the yard, and the door slammed shut behind her.

"Well! I never," Lucinda said, her bosom heaving with rage as she glowered at the closed door.

"Neither have I," said Elizabeth, shaking dirt off her hem and deciding to retreat with as much dignity as possible. "We can talk about what a madman he is once we're down the path, out of sight of the house. So if you'll please take that end of the trunk?"

With a black look Lucinda complied, and they marched down the path, both of them concentrating on keeping their backs as straight as possible.

In the house Jake shoved his hands deep in his pockets as he stood at the window watching the women, his expression a mixture of stupefaction and ire. "Gawdamighty," he breathed, glancing at Ian, who was scowling at the unopened note in his hand. "The women are chasin' you clear into Scotland! That'll stop soon as the news is out that yer betrothed." Reaching up, he idly scratched his bushy red hair and turned back to the window, peering down the path. The women had vanished from view, and he left the window. Unable to hide a tinge of admiration, he added, "Tell you one thing, that blond gel had spunk, you have to give her that. Cool as can be, she stood there tauntin' you with your own words and callin' you a swine. I don't know a man what would dare to do that!"

"She'd dare anything," Ian said, remembering the young temptress he'd known. When most girls her age were blushing and simpering, Elizabeth Cameron had asked *him* to dance at their first meeting. That same night she'd defied a group of men in the card room; the next day she'd risked her reputation to meet him in a cottage in the woods—and all that merely to indulge in what she'd described in the greenhouse as a "little weekend dalliance." Since then she must have been indulging in more of those—and indiscriminately—or else her uncle wouldn't be sending out letters offering to marry her off to virtual strangers. That was the only possible explanation for her uncle's action, an action that struck Ian as unprecedented in its flagrant lack of tact and taste. The only other possible explanation would be a desperate need of a moneyed husband, and Ian discounted that. Elizabeth had been gorgeously and expensively dressed when they met; moreover, the gathering at the country house had been composed almost exclusively of the social elite. And what few snatches of gossip he'd heard of her shortly after that fateful weekend had indicated that she moved among the highest circles of the *ton*, as befitted her rank.

"I wonder where they'll go," Jake continued, frowning a little. "There's wolves out there, and all sorts of beasts."

"No self-respecting wolf would dare to confront that duenna of hers, not with that umbrella she wields," Ian snapped, but he felt a little uneasy.

"Oho!" said Jake with a hearty laugh "So that's what she was? I thought they'd come to court you together. Personally, I'd be afraid to close my eyes with that gray-haired hag in bed next to me."

Ian was not listening. Idly he unfolded the note, knowing that Elizabeth Cameron probably wasn't foolish enough to have written it in her own girlish, illegible scrawl. His first thought as he scanned the neat, scratchy script was that she'd gotten someone else to write it for her . . . but then he recognized the words, which were strangely familiar, because he'd spoken them himself:

Your suggestion has merit. I'm leaving for Scotland on the first of next month and cannot delay the trip again. Would prefer the meeting take place there, in any case. A map is enclosed for direction to the cottage. Cordially—Ian.

"God help that silly bastard if he ever crosses my path!" Ian said savagely.

"Who d'you mean?"

"Peters!"

"Peters?" Jake said, gaping. "Your secretary? The one you sacked for mixin' up all your letters?"

"I should have *strangled* him! This is the note I meant for Dickinson Verley. He sent it to Cameron instead."

In furious disgust Ian raked his hand through his hair. As much as he wanted Elizabeth Cameron out of his sight and out of his life, he could not cause two women to spend the night in their carriage or whatever vehicle they'd brought, when it was his fault they'd come here. He nodded curtly to Jake. "Go and get them."

"Me? Why me?"

"Because," Ian said bitterly, walking over to the cabinet and putting away the gun, "it's starting to rain, for one thing. For another, if you don't bring them back, you'll be doing the cooking."

"If I have to go after that woman, I want a stout glass of something fortifying first. They're carrying a trunk, so they won't get too far ahead of me."

"On foot?" Ian asked in surprise.

"How did you think they got up here?"

"I was too angry to think."

At the end of the lane Elizabeth put down her side of the trunk and sank down wearily beside Lucinda upon its hard top, emotionally exhausted. A wayward chuckle bubbled up inside her, brought on by exhaustion, fright, defeat, and the last remnants of triumph over having gotten just a little of her own back from the man who'd ruined her life. The only possible explanation for Ian Thornton's behavior today was that he was a complete madman.

With a shake of her head Elizabeth made herself stop thinking of him. At the moment she had so many new worries she hardly knew how to begin to cope. She glanced sideways at her stalwart duenna, and an amused smile touched her lips as she recalled Lucinda's actions at the cottage. On the one hand, Lucinda rejected all emotional displays as totally unseemly—yet at the same time she herself was possessed of the most formidable temper Elizabeth had ever witnessed. It was as if Lucinda did not regard her own outbursts of ire as emotional. Without the slightest hesitation or regret Lucinda could verbally flay a wrongdoer into small, bite-sized pieces and then mentally stamp him into the ground and grind him beneath the heel of her sturdy shoe.

On the other hand, were Elizabeth to exhibit the smallest bit of fear right now over their daunting predicament, Lucinda would instantly stiffen up with disapproval and deliver one of her sharp reprimands.

Cognizant of that, Elizabeth glanced worriedly at the sky, where black clouds were rolling in, heralding a storm; but when she spoke she sounded deliberately and absurdly bland. "I believe it's starting to rain, Lucinda," she remarked while cold drizzle began to slap the leaves of the tree over their heads.

"So it would seem," said Lucinda. She opened her umbrella with a smart snap, holding it over them both.

"It's fortunate you have your umbrella."

"I always have my umbrella."

"We aren't likely to drown from a little rain."

"I shouldn't think so."

Elizabeth drew a steadying breath, looking around at the harsh Scottish cliffs. In the tone of one asking someone's opinion on a rhetorical question, Elizabeth said, "Do you suppose there are wolves out here?"

"I believe," Lucinda replied, "they probably constitute a larger threat to our health at present than the rain."

The sun was setting, and the early spring air had a sharp bite in it; Elizabeth was almost positive they'd be freezing by nightfall. "It's a bit chilly."

"Rather."

"We have warmer clothes in the trunks, though."

"I daresay we won't be too uncomfortable, in that case."

Elizabeth's wayward sense of humor chose that unlikely moment to assert itself. "No, we shall be snug as can be while the wolves gather around us."

"Quite."

Hysteria, hunger, and exhaustion—combined with Lucinda's unswerving calm and her earlier unprecedented entry into the cottage with umbrella flailing—were making Elizabeth almost giddy. "Of course, if the wolves realize how hungry *we* are, there's every chance they'll give us a wide berth."

"A cheering possibility."

"We'll build a fire," Elizabeth said, her lips twitching. "That will keep them at bay, I believe." When Lucinda remained silent for several moments, occupied with her own thoughts, Elizabeth confided with an odd surge of happiness, "Do you know something, Lucinda? I don't think I would have missed today for *anything.*"

Lucinda's thin gray brows shot up, and she cast a dubious sideways glance at Elizabeth.

"I realize that must sound extremely peculiar, but can you imagine how absolutely exhilarating it was to have that man at the point of a gun for just a few minutes? Do you find that—odd?" Elizabeth asked when Lucinda stared straight ahead in angry, thoughtful silence.

"What I find odd," she said in a tone of frosty disapproval mingled with surprise, "is that you evoke such animosity in that man."

"I think he's quite demented."

"I would have said embittered."

"About what?"

"That is an interesting question."

Elizabeth sighed. When Lucinda decided to work out a problem that puzzled her she would not leave it alone. She could not countenance behavior of any sort that she didn't understand. Rather than wonder about Ian Thornton's motivations, Elizabeth decided to concentrate on what they ought to do in the next few hours. Her uncle had adamantly refused to waste a coach and coachman in idleness while she spent the requisite time here. At his instructions they'd sent Aaron back to England as soon as they reached the Scottish border, where they'd then hired a coach at the Wakeley Inn. In a sennight Aaron would come here to fetch them. They could, of course, return to the Wakeley Inn and wait for Aaron's return, but Elizabeth didn't have enough money to pay for a room for Lucinda and herself.

She might be able to hire a coach at the inn and pay for it when she reached Havenhurst, but the cost might be more than she could manage, even if she did her most brilliant bargaining.

And worse than all of that was the problem of her Uncle Julius. He was bound to be furious if she returned in two weeks' less time than she was to have been gone—providing she could manage to return. And once she arrived home, what would he say?

At the moment, however, she had an even larger problem: what to do now, when two defenseless women were completely lost in the wilds of Scotland, at night, in the rain and cold.

Shuffling footsteps sounded on the gravel path, and both women straightened, both suppressing the hope soaring in their breasts and keeping their faces carefully expressionless.

"Well, well, well," Jake boomed. "Glad I caught up with you and—" He lost his thought as he beheld the utterly comic sight of two stiff-backed women seated on a trunk together, prim and proper as you please, beneath a black umbrella in the middle of nowhere. "Uh—where are your horses?"

"We have no horses," Lucinda informed him in a disdainful voice that implied such beasts would have been an intrusion on their tête-à-tête.

"No? How did you get here?"

"A wheeled conveyance carried us to this godforsaken place."

"I see." He lapsed into daunted silence, and Elizabeth started to say something at least slightly pleasant when Lucinda lost patience.

"You have, I collect, come to urge us to return?"

"Ah—yes. Yes, I have."

"Then do so. We haven't all night." Lucinda's words struck Elizabeth as a bald lie.

When Jake seemed at a loss as to how to go about it, Lucinda stood up and assisted him. "I gather Mr. Thornton is extremely regretful for his unforgivable and inexcusable behavior?"

"Well, yes, I guess that's the way it is. In a way."

"No doubt he intends to tell us that when we return?"

Jake hesitated, weighing his certainty that Ian had no intention of saying anything of the kind against the certainty that if the women didn't return, he'd be eating his own cooking and sleeping with a bad conscience and a bad stomach. "Why don't we let him make his own apologies?" he prevaricated.

Lucinda turned up the path toward the house and nodded grandly. "Bring the trunks. Come, Elizabeth."

By the time they reached the house Elizabeth was torn between relishing an apology and turning to flee. A fire had been lit in the fireplace, and she was vastly relieved to see that their unwilling host was absent from the room.

He reappeared within moments, however, minus his jacket, carrying an armload of firewood, which he dumped beside the hearth.

Straightening, he turned to Elizabeth, who was watching him with a carefully blank expression on her face. "It appears a mistake has been made," he said shortly.

"Does that mean you've remembered sending the message?"

"It was sent to you in error. Another man was being invited up here to join us. Unfortunately, his message went to your uncle."

Until that moment Elizabeth wouldn't have believed she could feel more humiliated than she already did. Robbed of even the defense of righteous indignation, she faced the fact that she was the unwanted guest of someone who'd made a fool of her not once but twice.

"How did you get here? I didn't hear any horses, and a carriage sure as hell can't make the climb."

"A wheeled conveyance brought us most of the way," she prevaricated, seizing on Lucinda's earlier explanation, "and it's gone on now." She saw his eyes narrow with angry disgust as he realized he was stuck with them unless he wanted to spend several days escorting them back to the inn.

Terrified that the tears burning the backs of her eyes were going to fall, Elizabeth tipped her head back and turned it, pretending to be inspecting the ceiling, the staircase, the walls, anything. Through the haze of tears she noticed for the first time that the place looked as if it hadn't been cleaned in a year.

Beside her Lucinda glanced around through narrowed eyes and arrived at the same conclusion.

Jake, anticipating that the old woman was about to make some disparaging comment about Ian's house, leapt into the breach with forced joviality.

"Well, now," he burst out, rubbing his hands together and striding forward to the fire. "Now that's all settled, shall we all be properly introduced? Then we'll see about supper." He looked expectantly at Ian, waiting for him to handle the introductions, but instead of doing the thing properly he merely nodded curtly to the beautiful blond girl and said, "Elizabeth Cameron—Jake Wiley."

"How do you do, Mr. Wiley," Elizabeth said.

"Call me Jake," he said cheerfully, then he turned expectantly to the scowling duenna. "And you are?"

Fearing that Lucinda was about to rip up at Ian for his cavalier handling of the introductions, Elizabeth hastily said, "This is my companion, Miss Lucinda Throckmorton-Jones."

"Good heavens! Two names. Well, no need to stand on formality, since we're going to be cooped up together for at least a few days! Just call me Jake. What shall I call you?"

"You may call me Miss Throckmorton-Jones," she informed him, looking down the length of her beaklike nose.

"Er—very well," he replied, casting an anxious look of appeal to Ian, who seemed to be momentarily enjoying Jake's futile efforts to create an atmosphere of conviviality. Disconcerted, Jake ran his hands through his disheveled hair and arranged a forced smile on his face. Nervously, he gestured about the untidy room. "Well, now, if we'd known we were going to have such . . . ah . . . gra . . . that is, illustrious company, we'd have—"

"Swept off the chairs?" Lucinda suggested acidly. "Shoveled off the floor?"

"Lucinda!" Elizabeth whispered desperately. "They didn't know we were coming."

"No respectable person would dwell in such a place even for a night," she snapped, and Elizabeth watched in mingled distress and admiration as the redoubtable woman turned around and directed her attack on their unwilling host. "The responsibility for our being here is yours, whether it was a mistake or not! I shall expect you to rout your servants from their hiding places and have them bring clean linens up to us at once. I shall also expect them to have this squalor remedied by morning! It is obvious from your behavior that you are no gentleman; however, *we* are ladies, and we shall expect to be treated as such."

From the corner of her eye Elizabeth had been watching Ian Thornton, who was listening to all of this, his jaw rigid, a muscle beginning to twitch dangerously in the side of his neck.

Lucinda, however, was either unaware of or unconcerned with his reaction, for, as she picked up her skirts and turned toward the stairs, she turned on Jake. "You may show us to our chambers. We wish to retire."

"Retire!" cried Jake, thunderstruck. "But—but what about supper?" he sputtered.

"You may bring it up to us."

Elizabeth saw the blank look on Jake's face, and she endeavored to translate, politely, what the irate woman was saying to the startled red-haired man.

"What Miss Throckmorton-Jones means is that we're rather exhausted from our trip and not very good company, sir, and so we prefer to dine in our rooms."

"You will dine," Ian Thornton said in an awful voice that made Elizabeth freeze, "on what *you* cook for yourself, madam. If you want clean linens, you'll get them yourself from the cabinet. If you want clean rooms, clean them! Am I making myself clear?"

"Perfectly!" Elizabeth began furiously, but Lucinda interrupted in a voice shaking with ire: "Are you suggesting, sirrah, that we are to do the work of servants?"

Ian's experience with the *ton* and with Elizabeth had given him a lively contempt for ambitious, shallow, self-indulgent young women whose single goal in life was to acquire as many gowns and jewels as possible with the least amount of effort, and he aimed his attack at Elizabeth. "I am suggesting that you look after yourself for the first time in your silly, aimless life. In return for that, I am willing to give you a roof over your head and to share our food with you until I can get you to the village. If that is too overwhelming a task for you, then my original invitation still stands: There's the door. Use it!"

Elizabeth knew the man was irrational, and it wasn't worth riling herself to reply to him, so she turned instead to Lucinda. "Lucinda," she said with weary resignation, "do not upset yourself by trying to make Mr. Thornton understand that *his* mistake has inconvenienced *us*, not the other way around. You will only waste your time. A gentleman of breeding would be perfectly able to understand that he should be apologizing instead of ranting and raving. However, as I told you before we came here, Mr. Thornton is no gentleman. The simple fact is that he enjoys humiliating people, and he will continue trying to humiliate us for as long as we stand here."

Elizabeth cast a look of well-bred disdain over Ian and said, "Good night, Mr. Thornton." Turning, she softened her voice a little and said, "Good evening, Mr. Wiley."

When the ladies had both retired to their bedchambers Jake wandered over to the table and rummaged through the provisions. Taking out some cheese and bread, he listened to the sounds of their footsteps on the wooden floor as they went about opening cabinets and making up their beds. When he'd finished eating he had two glasses of Madeira, then he glanced at Ian. "You ought to eat something," he said.

"I'm not hungry," his friend replied shortly. Jake's eyes filled with puzzlement as he gazed at the enigmatic man who was staring out the window into the darkness, his profile taut.

Although there had been no sounds of movement from the bedchambers above for the last half hour, Jake felt guilty that the ladies hadn't eaten. Hesitantly, he said, "Shall I bring some of this up to them?"

"No," Ian said. "If they want to eat, they can damn well come down here and feed themselves."

"We're not being very hospitable to 'em, Ian."

"Not hospitable?" he repeated with a sarcastic glance over his shoulder. "In case you haven't realized it, they've taken two of the bedchambers, which means one of us will be sleeping on the sofa tonight."

"The sofa's too short. I'll sleep out in the barn, like I used to do. Don't mind it a bit. I like the way hay smells, and it's soft. Your caretaker's brought up a cow and some chickens, just like the note said, so we'll have fresh milk and eggs. Looks to me like the only thing he didn't do was have someone clean this place up."

When Ian made no reply to that but continued staring off into the dark, Jake said hesitantly, "Would you be willing to tell me how the ladies came to be here? I mean, who are they?"

Ian drew a long, impatient breath, tipped his head back, and absently massaged the muscles at the back of his neck. "I met Elizabeth a year and a half ago at a party. She'd just made her debut, was already betrothed to some unfortunate nobleman, and was eager to test her wiles on me."

"Test her wiles on you? I thought you said she was engaged to another."

Sighing irritably at his friend's naïveté, Ian said curtly, "Debutantes are a different breed from any women you've known. Twice a year their mamas bring them to London to make their debut. They're paraded about during the Season like horses at an auction, then their parents sell them as wives to whoever bids the highest. The winning bidder is selected by the expedient measure of choosing whoever has the most important title and the most money."

"Barbaric!" said Jake indignantly.

Ian shot him an ironic look. "Don't waste your pity. It suits them perfectly. All they want from marriage is jewels, gowns, and the freedom to have discreet liaisons with whomever they please, once they produce the requisite heir. They've no notion of fidelity or honest human feeling."

Jake's brows lifted at that. "Can't say as I ever noticed you took the petticoat set in aversion," he remarked, thinking of the women who'd warmed Ian's bed in the last two years—some with titles of their own.

"Speaking of debutantes," Jake continued cautiously when Ian remained silent, "what about the one upstairs? Do you dislike her especially, or just on general principle?"

Ian walked over to the table and poured some Scotch into a glass. He took a swallow, shrugged, and said, "Miss Cameron was more inventive than some of her vapid little friends. She accosted me in a garden at a party."

"I can see how bothersome that musta been," Jake joked, "having someone like her, with a face that men dream about, tryin' to seduce you, usin' feminine wiles on you. Did they work?"

Slamming the glass down on the table, Ian said curtly, "They worked." Coldly dismissing Elizabeth from his mind, he opened the deerskin case on the table, removed some papers he needed to review, and sat down in front of the fire.

Trying to suppress his avid curiosity, Jake waited a few minutes before asking, "Then what happened?"

Already engrossed in reading the documents in his hand, Ian said absently and without looking up, "I asked her to marry me; she sent me a note inviting me to meet her in the greenhouse; I went there; her brother barged in on us and informed me she was a countess, and that she was already betrothed."

The topic thrust from his mind, Ian reached for the quill lying on the small table beside his chair and made a note in the margin of the contract.

"And?" Jake demanded avidly.

"And what?"

"And *then* what happened—after the brother barged in?"

"He took exception to my having contemplated marrying so far above myself and challenged me to a duel," Ian replied in a preoccupied voice as he made another note on the contract.

"So what's the girl doin' here now?" Jake asked, scratching his head in bafflement over the doings of the Quality.

"Who the hell knows," Ian murmured irritably. "Based on her behavior with me, my guess is she finally got caught in some sleazy affair or another, and her reputation's beyond repair."

"What's that got to do with you?"

Ian expelled his breath in a long, irritated sigh and glanced at Jake with an expression that made it clear he was finished answering questions. "I assume," he bit out, "that her family, recalling my absurd obsession with her two years ago, hoped I'd come up to scratch again and take her off their hands."

"You think it's got somethin' to do with the old duke talking about you bein' his natural grandson and wantin' to make you his heir?" He waited expectantly, hoping for more information, but Ian ignored him, reading his documents. Left with no other choice and no prospect for further confidences, Jake picked up a candle, gathered up some blankets, and started for the barn. He paused at the door, struck by a sudden thought. "She said she didn't send you any note about meetin' her in the greenhouse."

"She's a liar and an excellent little actress," Ian said icily, without taking his gaze from the papers. "Tomorrow I'll think of some way to get her out of here and off my hands."

Something in Ian's face made Jake ask, "Why the hurry? You afraid of fallin' fer her wiles again?"

"Hardly."

"Then you must be made of stone," he teased. "That woman's so beautiful she'd tempt any man who was alone with her for an hour—includin' me, and you know I ain't in the petticoat line at all."

"Don't let her catch you alone," Ian replied mildly.

"I don't think I'd mind." Jake laughed as he left.

Upstairs in the bedchamber at the end of the hall over the kitchen, Elizabeth had wearily pulled off her clothes, climbed into bed, and fallen into an exhausted slumber.

In the bedchamber that opened off the landing above the parlor where the two men talked, Lucinda Throckmorton-Jones had seen no reason to break her normal retiring routine. Refusing to yield to weariness merely because she'd been jounced about on the back of a wagon, ignobly ejected from a dirty cottage into the rain, where she'd contemplated the feeding habits of predatory beasts, and then been rudely forced to retire without so much as a morsel of bread for sustenance, she nevertheless prepared for bed exactly as she would have done had she spent the day over her embroidery. After removing and folding her black bombazine gown she had unpinned her hair, given it the requisite one hundred slow strokes, and then carefully braided it and tucked it beneath her white nightcap.

Two things, however, put Lucinda so out of countenance that once she had climbed into bed and pulled the scratchy blankets up to her chin she actually could not sleep. First and foremost, there had not been a ewer and basin in her crude bedchamber that she could use to wash her face and body, which she always did before retiring. Second, the bed upon which her bony frame was expected to repose had lumps in it.

Those two things had resulted in her still being awake when the men below began to talk, and their voices had drifted up between the floorboards, muted but distinct. Because of that she had been forced to be an eavesdropper. In her entire fifty-six years Lucinda Throckmorton-Jones had never stooped to eavesdropping. She *deplored* eavesdroppers, a fact of which the servants in every house where she had ever dwelt were well aware. She ruthlessly reported any servant, no matter how high in the household hierarchy, if she caught him or her listening at doors or looking through keyholes.

Now, however, she had been relegated to their lowly level, for she had listened.

She had heard.

And now she was mentally going over every word Ian Thornton had spoken, examining it for truth, weighing each thing he'd said to that socially inept man who'd mistaken her for a menial. Despite her inner turmoil, as she lay upon her pallet Lucinda was perfectly composed, perfectly still. Her eyes were closed, her soft white hands folded across her flat bosom atop the coverlet. She did not fidget or pluck at the covers, she did not glower and frown at the ceiling. So still was she that had anyone peeked into the moonlit room and seen her lying there they might well have expected to find candles lit at her feet and a crucifix in her hands.

That impression, however, was no reflection on the activity in her mind. With scientific precision she was examining everything she'd heard and considering what, if anything, could or ought to be done. She knew it was possible that Ian Thornton had been lying to Jake Wiley—that he had been professing to have cared about Elizabeth, to have wanted to marry her—merely to cast himself in a better light. Robert Cameron had insisted that Thornton was nothing but a dissolute fortune hunter and an unprincipled rake; he'd specifically said that Thornton had admitted he'd been trying to seduce Elizabeth merely for sport. In this instance Lucinda was inclined to think Robert had been lying out of a desire to justify his shameful actions at the duel. Furthermore, although Lucinda had witnessed a certain fraternal devotion in Robert's attitude toward Elizabeth, his disappearance from England had proven him a coward.

For more than an hour Lucinda lay awake, weighing everything she'd heard for truth. The only thing she accepted unequivocally was the one thing that other people of inferior knowledge and intuition had wondered about and refused to believe for years: She did not doubt for an instant that Ian Thornton was directly related to the Duke of Stanhope. As was often said, an impostor might be able to pass himself off as Quality to another gentleman in an exclusive club, but he'd better not present himself at the gentleman's home—for an observant butler would know him as an impostor at a glance.

That same ability extended to skilled duennas whose job it was to protect their charges from social impostors. Of course, Lucinda had the advantage of having been, during her early career, companion to the niece of the Duke of Stanhope, which was why she'd taken one look at Ian Thornton tonight and placed him immediately as a close descendant of the old man, to whom he bore an absolutely startling resemblance. Based on Ian Thornton's age and her recollection of the scandal surrounding the Marquess of Kensington's break with his family over his unsuitable marriage to a Scottish girl, Lucinda had guessed Ian Thornton to be the old duke's grandson within thirty seconds of clapping eyes on him. In fact, the only thing she hadn't been able to deduce within a moment of meeting him downstairs was whether or not he was legitimate—but only because she had not been present at his conception, and so could not know whether he had been conceived before or after his parents' unsanctioned marriage thirty years before. But if Stanhope was trying to make Ian Thornton his heir, which was the rumor she'd heard time and again, then there was no question whatever of Thornton's parentage.

Given all that, Lucinda had only two more matters to contemplate. The first was whether Elizabeth would benefit from marriage to a future peer of the realm—not a mere earl or count, but a man who would someday bear the title of duke, the loftiest of all noble titles. Since Lucinda had made it her life's work to ensure that her charges made the best possible matches, it took her less than two seconds to decide that the answer to that was an emphatic affirmative.

The second matter gave her a trifle more difficulty: As things stood, *she* was the only one in favor of the match. And time was her enemy. Unless she was wrong—and Lucinda was *never* wrong in such matters—Ian Thornton was about to become the most sought-after bachelor in all Europe. Although she'd been locked away with poor Elizabeth at Havenhurst, Lucinda kept up correspondence with two other duennas. Their letters had often included casual mentions of him at various social functions. His desirability, which apparently had been increasing apace with news of his wealth, would increase a hundredfold when he was called by the title that had been his father's—the Marquess of Kensington. That title was rightfully his, and considering the trouble he'd caused Lucinda's charge, Lucinda felt he owed it to Elizabeth to bestow a coronet and marriage ring upon her without further delay.

Having decided that, she was faced with only one remaining problem, and it posed something of a moral dilemma. After a lifetime devoted to keeping unmarried persons of the opposite sex apart, she was now considering bringing them together. She contemplated Jake Wiley's last remark about Elizabeth: "That woman's so beautiful she'd tempt any man who was alone with her for an hour." As Lucinda knew, Ian Thornton had once been "tempted" by Elizabeth, and although Elizabeth was no longer a young girl, she was even more beautiful now than she'd been then. Elizabeth was also wiser; therefore she would not be so foolish as to let him carry things too far, if and when they were left alone for a very few hours. Of that Lucinda was certain. In fact, the only things of which Lucinda *wasn't* certain were whether or not Ian Thornton was now as immune to Elizabeth as he'd claimed to be . . . and how on earth she was going to contrive to see that they had those few hours alone. She entrusted those last two difficulties to the equally capable hands of her Creator and finally fell into her usual peaceful slumber.

12

Jake opened one eye and blinked confusedly at the sunlight pouring through the window high above. Disoriented, he rolled over on a lumpy, unfamiliar bed and found himself staring up at an enormous black animal who flattened his ears, bared his teeth, and tried to bite him through the slats of his stall. "You damned cannibal!" he swore at the evil-tempered horse. "Spawn of Lucifer!" Jake added, and for good measure he aimed a hard kick at the wooden slats by way of retaliation for the attempted bite. "Ouch, dammit!" he swore as his bootless foot hit the board.

Shoving himself to a sitting position, he raked his hands through his thick red hair and grimaced at the hay that stuck between his fingers. His foot hurt, and his head ached from the bottle of wine he'd drunk last night.

Heaving himself to his feet, he pulled on his boots and brushed off his woolen shirt, shivering in the damp chill. Fifteen years ago, when he'd come to work on the little farm, he'd slept in this barn every night. Now, with Ian successfully investing the money Jake made when they sailed together, he'd learned to appreciate the comforts of feather mattresses and satin covers, and he missed them sorely.

"From palaces to a damned cowshed," he grumbled, walking out of the empty stall he'd slept in. As he passed

Attila's stall, a hoof punched out with deadly aim, narrowly missing Jake's thigh. "That'll cost you an early breakfast, you miserable piece of living glue," he spat, and then he took considerable pleasure in feeding the other two horses while the black looked on. "You've put me in a sour mood," he said cheerfully as the jealous horse shifted angrily while the other two steeds were fed. "Maybe if it improves later on, I'll feed you—" He broke off in alarm as he noticed the way Ian's splendid chestnut gelding was standing with his right knee slightly bent, holding his right hoof off the ground. "Here now, Mayhem," he crooned softly, patting the horse's satiny neck, "let's see that hoof."

The well-trained animal, who'd won every race he'd ever run and who'd sired the winner of the last races at Heathton, put up no resistance when Jake lifted his hoof and bent over it. "You've picked up a stone," Jake told the animal, who was watching him with ears attentively forward, his brown eyes bright and intelligent. Jake paused, looking around for something to use as a pick, and found it on an old wooden ledge. "It's lodged in there good," he murmured to the horse as he lifted the hoof and crouched down, bracing the hoof on his knee. He picked away at the rock, leaning back against the slats of the next stall in an attempt to get leverage. "That's got it." The rock came loose, but Jake's satisfied grunt turned into a howl of outraged pain as a set of huge teeth in the next stall clamped into Jake's ample rear end. "You vicious bag of bones," he shouted, jumping to his feet and throwing himself half over the rail in an attempt to land a punch on Attila's body. As if the horse anticipated retribution, he sidled to the edge of his stall and regarded Jake from the corner of his eye with an expression that looked to Jake like complacent satisfaction. "I'll get you for that," Jake promised, and he started to shake his fist when he realized how absurd it was to threaten a dumb beast.

Rubbing his offended backside, he turned to Mayhem and carefully put his own rump against the outside wall of the barn. He checked the hoof to make certain it was clean, but the moment his fingers touched the place where the rock had been lodged the chestnut jerked in pain. "Bruised you, did it?" Jake said sympathetically. "It's not surprisin', considering the size and shape of the rock. But you never gave a sign yesterday that you were hurtin'," he continued. Raising his voice and infusing it with a wealth of exaggerated admiration, he patted the chestnut's flank and glanced disdainfully at Attila while he spoke to Mayhem. "That's because you're a true aristocrat and a fine, brave animal—not a miserable, sneaky mule who's not fit to be your stallmate!"

If Attila cared one way or another for Jake's opinion, he was disappointingly careful not to show it, which only made Jake's mood more stormy when he stomped into the cottage.

Ian was sitting at the table, a cup of steaming coffee cradled between his palms. "Good morning," he said to Jake, studying the older man's thunderous frown.

"Mebbe you think so, but I can't see it. Course, I've spent the night freezin' out there, bedded down next to a horse that wants to make a meal of me, and who broke his fast with a bit of my arse already this mornin'. And," he finished irately as he poured coffee from the tin pot into an earthenware mug and cast a quelling look at his amused friend, "your horse is lame!" Flinging himself into the chair beside Ian, he gulped down the scalding coffee without thinking what he was doing; his eyes bulged, and sweat popped out on his forehead.

Ian's grin faded. "He's what?"

"Picked up a rock, and he's favoring his left foreleg."

Ian's chair legs scraped against the wooden floor as he shoved his chair back and started to go out to the barn.

"There's no need. It's just a bruise."

As she finished washing, Elizabeth heard the indistinct murmur of masculine voices below. Wrapped in a thin towel, she went over to the trunks her unwilling host had carried upstairs and left outside her door this morning, along with two large pitchers of water. Even before she dragged them into her bedchamber she knew the gowns they contained were all a little fancy and fragile to wear in a place like this.

Elizabeth chose the least flamboyant—a high-waisted white lawn gown with a wide band of pink roses and green leaves embroidered at the hem and at the fitted cuffs of its full, billowy sleeves. A matching white ribbon with roses and leaves embroidered on it lay atop the gown, and she pulled it out, uncertain how to wear it, if at all.

Elizabeth struggled into the gown, smoothed it over her waist, and spent several minutes fighting to close the long row of tiny buttons down her back. She turned to survey her appearance in the small mirror above the washstand and nervously bit her lip. The rounded bodice, which had once been demure, now clung tightly to her ripened figure. "Wonderful," she said aloud with a grimace as she tugged on the bodice. No matter how she tried to pull it up, it persisted in falling lower as soon as she let it go, and she finally gave up the struggle. "They wore gowns cut lower than this during the season," she reminded the mirror in her own defense. Walking over to the bed, she retrieved the hair ribbon, debating what to do with her hair. In London, the last time she'd worn the gown, Berta had threaded the ribbon through Elizabeth's curls. At Havenhurst, however, her heavy hair was no longer twisted into elegant styles, but was left to hang partway down her back, where it ended in thick waves and curls.

With a shrug Elizabeth picked up her comb, parted her hair down the middle, and then caught it at the nape and gathered it together with the embroidered ribbon, which she tied in a simple bow; then she tugged two tendrils loose to soften the effect. She stood back to survey her appearance and sighed with resignation. Completely oblivious to the wide, bright green eyes looking back at her or the healthy glow of her skin, or any of the features that had made Jake say she had a face men dreamt of, Elizabeth looked for glaring flaws in her appearance, and when she didn't see anything out of the ordinary she lost interest. Turning away from the mirror, she sat down on the bed, going over last night's events as she'd been doing all morning. The thing that bothered her the most was relatively minor: Ian's claim that he'd received a note from her to meet her in the greenhouse. Of course, it was perfectly possible he was lying about that in an effort to acquit himself in front of Mr. Wiley. But Ian Thornton, as she well knew, was innately rude and blunt, so she couldn't quite see him bothering to shade the truth for his friend's sake. Closing her eyes, she tried to recall exactly what he'd said when he came to the greenhouse that night. Something like "Who were you expecting after that note—the prince regent?"

At the time she'd thought he was talking about the note he'd sent her. But he claimed *he'd* received one. And he had jabbed at her about her handwriting, which her tutors had described as both "scholarly and precise—a credit to an Oxford gentleman!" Why would Ian Thornton think he knew what her handwriting looked like unless he truly believed he'd received such a note from her? Perhaps he really *was* mad, but Elizabeth didn't think so. But then, she reminded herself impatiently, where he was concerned she had always been unable to see the truth. And no wonder! Even now, when she was older and hopefully wiser, it had not been easy to think clearly yesterday with those golden eyes raking over her. For the life of her she could *not* understand his attitude unless he was still angry because Robert had broken the rules and shot him. That must be it, she decided, turning her mind to the more difficult problem:

She and Lucinda were trapped there, only their host didn't realize it, and she couldn't bear the shame of explaining it. Therefore, she was going to have to find some way to remain here in relative harmony for the next week. In order to survive the ordeal she would simply have to ignore his inexplicable antagonism and take each moment as it came, never looking back or forward. And then it would all be over, and she and Lucinda could leave. But whatever happened during the next seven days, Elizabeth vowed, she would never again let him make her lose her composure as she had last night. The last time they'd been together he'd confused her so much that she scarcely knew right from wrong.

From this moment on, she vowed, things would be different. She would be poised and polite and completely imperturbable, no matter how rudely or outrageously he behaved. She was no longer an infatuated young girl whom he could seduce, hurt, or anger for his own amusement. She would prove it to him and also set an excellent example of how well-bred people behaved.

With that settled in her mind, Elizabeth stood up and headed for Lucinda's room.

Lucinda was already dressed, her black gown brushed free of every speck of yesterday's dust, her gray hair in its neat bun. She was seated in a wooden chair near the window, her spine too rigid to require any support from the back of the chair, her expression thoughtful and preoccupied. "Good morning," Elizabeth said as she carefully closed the door behind her.

"Hmmm? Oh, good morning, Elizabeth."

"I wanted to tell you," Elizabeth began in a rush, "how very sorry I am to have dragged you here and subjected you to such humiliation. Mr. Thornton's behavior was inexcusable, unforgivable."

"I daresay he was . . . surprised by our unexpected arrival."

"Surprised?" Elizabeth repeated, gaping at her. "He was *demented!* I know you must think—must be wondering what could have led me to have anything at all to do with him before," she began, "and I cannot honestly tell you what I could possibly have been thinking of."

"Oh, I don't find that much mystery," said Lucinda. "He's exceedingly handsome."

Elizabeth would not have been more shocked if Lucinda had called him the soul of amiability. "Handsome!" she began, then she shook her head, trying to clear it. "I must say you're being very tolerant and kind about all this."

Lucinda stood up and cast an appraising eye over Elizabeth. "I would not describe my attitude as 'kind,'" she thoughtfully replied. "Rather I would say it's one of practicality. The bodice on your gown is quite tight, but attractive for all that. Shall we go down to breakfast?"

13

"Good mornin'!" Jake boomed as Elizabeth and Lucinda walked downstairs.

"Good morning, Mr. Wiley," Elizabeth said with a gracious smile. Then, because she could think of nothing else to say, she added quickly, "Something smells wonderful. What is it?"

"Coffee," Ian replied bluntly, his gaze drifting over her. With her long, burnished honey hair tied back with a ribbon she looked extremely pretty and very young.

"Sit down, sit down!" Jake continued jovially. Someone had cleaned the chairs since last night, but he took out his handkerchief as Elizabeth approached and wiped off the chair seat again.

"Thank you," she said, bestowing a smile on him. "But the chair is just fine as it is." Deliberately she looked at the unsmiling man across from her and said, "Good morning."

In answer he lifted a brow, as if questioning her odd change in attitude. "You slept well, I take it?"

"Very well," Elizabeth said.

"How 'bout some coffee?" Jake said as he hurried over to the coffee pot on the stove and filled a mug with the remainder of the steaming brew. When he got to the table with it, however, he stopped and looked helplessly from Lucinda to Elizabeth, obviously not certain who ought properly to be served first.

"Coffee," Lucinda informed him dampeningly when he took a step toward her, "is a heathen brew, unfit for civilized people. I prefer tea."

"I'll have coffee," Elizabeth said hastily. Jake flashed her a grateful smile, put the mug before her, then returned to the stove. Rather than look at Ian, Elizabeth stared, as if fascinated, at Jake Wiley's back while she sipped her coffee.

For a moment he stood there, nervously rubbing the palms of his hands on the sides of his legs, looking uncertainly from the fresh eggs to the slab of bacon to the heavy iron skillet already starting to smoke near his elbow—as if he hadn't the faintest idea how to begin. "May as well get at it," he murmured, and he stretched his arms straight out in front of him, linked the fingers of both hands together, and made a horrible cracking sound with his knuckles. Then he snatched up the knife and began vigorously sawing at the bacon.

While Elizabeth watched in puzzled interest he tossed large chunks of bacon into the skillet until it was heaped with it. A minute later the delicious smell of bacon began to waft about the room, and Elizabeth felt her mouth water, thinking how good breakfast was going to be. Before the thought had fully formed she saw him pick up two eggs, crack them open on the edge of the stove, and dump them into the skillet full of raw bacon. Six more eggs followed in rapid succession, then he turned and looked over his shoulder. "D'you think I shoulda let the bacon cook a wee bit longer before I dumped in the eggs, Lady Elizabeth?"

"I—I'm not completely certain," Elizabeth admitted, scrupulously ignoring the smirking satisfaction on Ian's tanned face.

"D'you want to have a look at it and tell me what you think?" he asked, already sawing off chunks of bread.

With no choice but to offer her uneducated advice or submit to Ian's relentlessly mocking stare, Elizabeth chose the former, got up, and went to peer over Mr. Wiley's shoulder.

"How does it look to you?"

It looked to Elizabeth like large globs of eggs congealing in unappetizing bacon fat. "Delicious."

He grunted with satisfaction and turned to the skillet, this time with both hands loaded with bread chunks, which he was obviously considering adding to the mess. "What do you think?" he asked, his hands hovering over the pile of cooking food. "Should I dump this in there?"

"No!" Elizabeth said hastily and with force. "I definitely think the bread should be served . . . well . . . "

"Alone," Ian Thornton said in an amused drawl, and when Elizabeth automatically looked toward his voice she discovered that he'd turned halfway around in his chair to watch her.

"Not *entirely* alone," Elizabeth put in, feeling as if she ought to contribute additional advice on the meal preparation rather than show herself as ignorant of cooking as she actually was. "We could serve it with—with butter!"

"Of course! I shoulda thought of that," he said with a sheepish grin at Elizabeth. "If you don't mind standin' here and keepin' your eye on what's happenin' in this skillet, I'll go fetch it from the cold keg."

"I don't mind in the least," Elizabeth assured him, absolutely refusing to acknowledge the fact that Ian's relentless gaze was boring holes through her back. Since little of import was likely to happen to the contents of the skillet for several minutes, Elizabeth regretfully faced the fact that she couldn't continue avoiding Ian Thornton—not when she desperately needed to smooth things over enough to convince him to let her and Lucinda remain for the allotted week.

Straightening reluctantly, she strolled about the room with forced nonchalance, her hands clasped behind her back, looking blindly at the cobwebs in the corner of the ceiling, trying to think what to say. And then inspiration struck. The solution was demeaning but practical, and properly presented, it could appear she was graciously doing him a favor. She paused a moment to arrange her features into what she hoped was the right expression of enthusiasm and compassion, then she wheeled around abruptly. "Mr. Thornton!" Her voice seemed to explode in the room at the same time his startled amber gaze riveted on her face, then drifted down her bodice, roving boldly over her ripened curves. Unnerved but determined, Elizabeth forged shakily ahead: "It appears as if no one has occupied this house in quite some time."

"I commend you on that astute observation, Miss Cameron," Ian mocked lazily, watching the tension and emotion play across her expressive face. For the life of him he could not understand what she was doing here or why she seemed to be trying to ingratiate herself this morning. Last night the explanation he'd given Jake had made sense; now, looking at her, he couldn't quite believe any of it. Then he remembered that Elizabeth Cameron had always robbed him of the ability to think rationally.

"Houses do have a way of succumbing to dirt when no one looks after them," she stated with a bright look.

"Another creditable observation. You've certainly a quick mind."

"Must you make this so very difficult!" Elizabeth exclaimed.

"I apologize," he said with mocking gravity. "Do go on. You were saying?"

"Well, I was thinking, since we're quite stranded here—Lucinda and I, I mean—with absolutely *nothing* but time on our hands, that this house could certainly use a woman's touch."

"Capital idea!" burst out Jake, returning from his mission to locate the butter and casting a highly hopeful look at Lucinda.

He was rewarded with a glare from her that could have pulverized rock. "It could use an army of servants carrying shovels and wearing masks on their faces," the duenna countered ruthlessly.

"You needn't help, Lucinda," Elizabeth explained, aghast. "I never meant to imply you should. But I could! I—" She whirled around as Ian Thornton surged to his feet and took her elbow in a none-too-gentle grasp.

"Lady Cameron," he said, "I think you and I have something to discuss that may be better spoken in private. Shall we?"

He gestured to the open door and then practically dragged

her along in his wake. Outdoors in the sunlight he marched her forward several paces, then dropped her arm. "Let's hear it," he said.

"Hear what?" Elizabeth said nervously.

"An explanation—the truth, if you're capable of it. Last night you drew a gun on me, and this morning you're awash with excitement over the prospect of cleaning my house. I want to know why."

"Well," Elizabeth burst out in defense of her actions with the gun, "you were *extremely* disagreeable!"

"I am *still* disagreeable," he pointed out shortly, ignoring Elizabeth's raised brows. "*I* haven't changed. I am not the one who's suddenly oozing goodwill this morning."

Elizabeth turned her head to the lane, trying desperately to think of an explanation that wouldn't reveal to him her humiliating circumstances.

"The silence is deafening, Lady Cameron, and somewhat surprising. As I recall, the last time we met you could scarcely contain all the edifying information you were trying to impart to me." Elizabeth knew he was referring to her monologue on the history of hyacinths in the greenhouse. "I just don't know where to begin," she admitted.

"Let's stick to the salient points. What are you doing here?"

"That's a little awkward to explain," Elizabeth said. So off balance from his reference to the hyacinths was she that her mind went blank, and she said disjointedly, "My uncle is acting as my guardian now. He is childless, so everything he has will go to my child. I can't have any until I'm married, and he wants the matter settled with the least possible exp—*time,*" she amended hastily. "He's an impatient man, and he thinks I've taken too long to—well, settle down. He doesn't completely understand that you can't just pick out a few people and force someone—me—to make a choice from them."

"May I ask why the hell he would think I have any desire to marry you?"

Elizabeth wished she could sink into the ground and disappear. "I think," she said, choosing her words with great care in hope of preserving what little was left of her pride, "it was because of the duel. He heard about it and misunderstood what precipitated it. I tried to convince him it was merely a—a weekend flirtation, which of course it was— but he would not listen. He's rather stubborn and—well, *old,"* she finished lamely. "In any case, when your message arrived inviting Lucinda and me to join you, he made me come here."

"It's a shame you wasted a trip, but it's hardly a tragedy. You can turn around and go right back."

She bent down, feigning absorption in picking up a twig and inspecting it. "I was rather hoping that, if it wouldn't be too much trouble, Lucinda and I could stay here for the agreed-upon time."

"It's out of the question," he said curtly, and Elizabeth's heart sank. "Besides, I seem to recall you were already betrothed the night we met—to a peer of the realm, no less."

Angry, frightened, and mortified, Elizabeth nevertheless managed to lift her chin and meet his speculative gaze. "He—we decided we didn't suit."

"I'm sure you're better off without him," he mocked. "Husbands can be very disagreeable to wives who indulge in 'weekend flirtations' with clandestine visits to secluded cottages and dark greenhouses."

Elizabeth clenched her fists, her eyes shooting green fire. "I did *not* invite you to meet me in that greenhouse, and you know it!"

He stared at her in bored disgust. "All right, let's play this farce out to its revolting conclusion. If you didn't send me a note, suppose you tell me what you were doing there."

"I told you, I *received* a note, which I thought was from my friend, Valerie, and I went to the greenhouse to discover why she wanted to see me. I didn't send you a note to meet me there, I *received* a note. Good God!" she exploded, almost stamping her foot in frustration when he continued to regard her with visible disbelief. "I was terrified of you that night!"

A poignant memory, as fresh as the moment it happened, came back to Ian . . . a bewitchingly lovely girl thrusting flowerpots into his hands to keep him from kissing her . . . and then, moments later, melting in his arms.

"Now do you believe me?"

Try as he might, Ian could not completely blame or acquit

her. His instincts told him she was lying about something, keeping something back. Moreover, there was something very odd and entirely out of character in the way she seemed so eager to stay here. On the other hand, he knew desperation when he saw it, and for some incomprehensible reason Elizabeth Cameron seemed on the verge of desperation. "What I believe doesn't matter." He broke off as the smell of smoke drifted into the yard from an open window and reached them both at the same time. "What the—" he began, already heading toward the house, with Elizabeth walking quickly beside him.

Ian opened the front door just as Jake came hurrying in from the back of the cottage.

"I got some milk—" Jake began, then he stopped abruptly as the stench hit him. His gaze snapped from Ian and Elizabeth, who were just rushing inside, to Lucinda, who was sitting exactly where she had been, serenely indifferent to the smell of burning bacon and incinerated eggs as she fanned herself with a black silk fan. "I took the liberty of removing the utensil from the stove," she informed them. "However, I was not in time to save its contents, which I sincerely doubt were worth saving in any case."

"Couldn't you have moved 'em *before* they burned?" Jake burst out.

"I cannot cook, sir."

"Can you *smell?*" Ian demanded.

"Ian, there's nothing for it—I'll have to ride to the village and hire a pair o' wenches to come up here and get this place in order for us or we'll starve."

"My thoughts exactly!" Lucinda seconded promptly, already standing up. "I shall accompany you."

"Whaat?" Elizabeth burst out.

"What? Why?" Jake echoed, looking balky.

"Because selecting good female servants is best done by a woman. How far must we go?"

If Elizabeth weren't so appalled, she'd have laughed at Jake Wiley's expression. "We can be back late this afternoon, assumin' there's anyone in the village to do the work. But I—"

"Then we'd best be about it." Lucinda paused and turned

to Ian, passing a look of calculating consideration over him; then she glanced at Elizabeth. Giving her a look that clearly said "Trust me and do not argue," she said, "Elizabeth, if you would be so good as to excuse us, I'd like a word alone with Mr. Thornton." With no choice but to do as bidden, Elizabeth went out the front door and stared in utter confusion at the trees, wondering what bizarre scheme Lucinda might have hatched to solve their problems.

In the cottage Ian watched through narrowed eyes as the gray-haired harpy fixed him with her basilisk stare. "Mr. Thornton," she said finally, "*I* have decided you are a gentleman."

She made that pronouncement as if she were a queen bestowing knighthood on a lowly, possibly undeserving serf. Fascinated and irritated at the same time, Ian leaned his hip against the table, waiting to discover what game she was playing by leaving Elizabeth alone here, unchaperoned. "Don't keep me in suspense," he said coolly. "What have I done to earn your good opinion?"

"Absolutely nothing," she said without hesitation. "I'm basing my decision on my own excellent intuitive powers and on the fact that you were born a gentleman."

"What gave you that idea?" he inquired in a bored tone.

"I am not a fool. I'm acquainted with your grandsire, the Duke of Stanhope. I was a member of his niece's household when news of your parents' unsanctioned marriage caused a furor. Other, less informed persons may need to conjecture on your ancestry, but I do not. It's apparent in your face, your height, your voice, even your mannerisms. You are his grandson."

Ian was accustomed to having the English study his features circumspectly and, on rare occasions, to ask a probing question or two; he knew they wondered and debated and whispered among themselves, but it was the first time anyone had ever had the effrontery to *tell* him who he was. Reining in his mounting anger, he replied in a voice that implied she was deluding herself, "If you say so, it must be true."

"That is *exactly* the sort of patronizing tone your grandfather would use," she informed him on a note of pleased triumph. "However, that is not to the point."

"May I inquire what *is* the point?" he snapped impatiently.

"Indeed you may," Lucinda said, thinking madly for some way to prod him into remembering his long-ago desire for Elizabeth and to prick his conscience. "The point is that I am well apprised of all that transpired between Elizabeth and yourself when you were last together. I, however," she decreed grandly, "am inclined to place the blame for your behavior not on a lack of character, but rather a lack of judgment." He raised his brows but said nothing. Taking his silence as assent, she reiterated meaningfully, "A lack of judgment on *both* your parts."

"*Really?*" he drawled.

"Of course," she said, reaching out and brushing the dust from the back of a chair, then rubbing her fingers together and grimacing with disapproval. "What else except lack of judgment could have caused a seventeen-year-old girl to rush to the defense of a notorious gambler and bring down censure upon herself for doing it?"

"What indeed?" he asked with growing impatience.

Lucinda dusted off her hands, avoiding his gaze. "Who can possibly know except you and she? No doubt it was the same thing that prompted her to remain in the woodcutter's cottage rather than leaving it the instant she discovered your presence." Satisfied that she'd done the best she was able to on that score, she became brusque again—an attitude that was more normal and, therefore, far more convincing. "In any case, that is all water under the bridge. She has paid dearly for her lack of judgment, which is only right, and even though she is now in the most dire straits because of it, that, too, is justice."

She smiled to herself when his eyes narrowed with what she hoped was guilt, or at least concern. His next words disabused her of that hope: "Madam, I do not have all day to waste in aimless conversation. If you have something to say, say it and be done!"

"Very well," Lucinda said, gritting her teeth to stop herself from losing control of her temper. "My point is that it is my duty, my obligation to see to Lady Cameron's physical well-being as well as to chaperon her. In this case, given the condition of your dwelling, the former obligation seems more pressing than the latter, particularly since it is obvious to me that the two of you are not in the least need of a chaperon to keep you from behaving with impropriety. You may need a referee to keep you from murdering each other, but a chaperon is entirely superfluous. Therefore, I feel duty-bound to now ensure that adequate servants are brought here at once. In keeping with that, I would like your word as a gentleman not to abuse her verbally or physically while I am gone. She has already been ill-used by her uncle. I will not permit anyone else to make this terrible time in her life more difficult than it already is."

"Exactly what," Ian asked in spite of himself, "do you mean by a 'terrible time'?"

"I am not at liberty to discuss that, of course," she said, fighting to keep her triumph from her voice. "I am merely concerned that you behave as a gentleman. Will you give me your word?"

Since Ian had no intention of laying a finger on her, or even spending time with her, he didn't hesitate to nod. "She's perfectly safe from me."

"That is *exactly* what I hoped to hear," Lucinda lied ruthlessly.

A few minutes later Elizabeth watched Lucinda emerge from the cottage with Ian, but there was no way to guess from their closed expressions what they'd discussed.

In fact, the only person betraying any emotion at all was Jake Wiley as he led two horses into the yard. And *his* face, Elizabeth noted with confusion—which had been stormy when he went off to saddle the horses—was now wreathed in a smile of unrestrained glee. With a sweep of his arm and a bow he gestured toward a swaybacked black horse with an old sidesaddle upon its back. "Here's your mount, ma'am," he told Lucinda, grinning. "His name's Attila."

Lucinda cast a disdainful eye over the beast as she transferred her umbrella to her right hand and pulled on her black gloves. "Have you nothing better?"

"No, ma'am. Ian's horse has a hurt foot."

"Oh, very well," said Lucinda, walking briskly forward, but as she came within reach the black suddenly bared his teeth and lunged. Lucinda struck him between the ears with her umbrella without so much as a pause in her step.

"Cease!" she commanded, and, ignoring the animal's startled grunt of pain, she continued around to his other side to mount. "You brought it on yourself," she told the horse as Jake held Attila's head, and Ian Thornton helped her into the sidesaddle. The whites of Attila's eyes showed as he warily watched her land in his saddle and settle herself. The moment Jake handed Lucinda the reins Attila began to leap sideways and twist around in restless annoyance. "I do not countenance ill-tempered animals," she warned the horse in her severest tone, and when he refused to heed her and continued his threatening antics she hauled up sharply on his reins and simultaneously gave him a sharp jab in the flank with her umbrella. Attila let out a yelping complaint, broke into a quick, animated trot, and headed obediently down the drive.

"If that don't beat all!" Jake said furiously, glowering after the pair, and then at Ian. "That animal doesn't know the meaning of the word loyalty!" Without waiting for a reply Jake swung into his saddle and cantered down the lane after them.

Absolutely baffled over everyone's behavior this morning, Elizabeth cast a puzzled, sideways glance at the silent man beside her, then gaped at him in amazement. The unpredictable man was staring after Lucinda, his hands shoved into his pockets, a cigar clamped between his white teeth, his face transformed by a sweeping grin. Drawing the obvious conclusion that these odd reactions from the men were somehow related to Lucinda's skillful handling of an obstinate horse, Elizabeth commented, "Lucinda's uncle raised horses, I believe."

Almost reluctantly, Ian transferred his admiring gaze from Lucinda's rigid back to Elizabeth. His brows rose. "An amazing woman," he stated. "Is there any situation of which she can't take charge?"

"None that I've ever seen," Elizabeth said with a chuckle; then she felt self-conscious because his smile faded abruptly, and his manner became detached and cool.

Drawing a long breath, Elizabeth clasped her shaking hands behind her back and decided to try for a truce. "Mr. Thornton," she began quietly, "must there be enmity between us? I realize my coming here is an . . . an inconvenience, but it was your fault . . . your mistake," she corrected cautiously, "that brought us here. And you must surely see that we have been even more inconvenienced than you." Encouraged by his lack of argument, she continued. "Therefore, the obvious solution is that we should both try to make the best of things."

"The obvious solution," he countered, "is that I should apologize for 'inconveniencing' you, and then you should leave as soon as I can get you to a carriage or a wagon."

"I can't!" she cried, fighting to recover her calm.

"Why the hell not?"

"Because—well—my uncle is a harsh man who won't like having his instructions countermanded. I was supposed to stay a full sennight."

"I'll write him a letter and explain."

"No!" Elizabeth burst out, imagining her uncle's reaction if the third man also sent her packing straightaway. He was no fool. He'd suspect. "He'll blame me, you see."

Despite Ian's resolution not to give a damn what her problems were, he was a little unnerved by her visible fright and by her description of her uncle as "harsh." Based on her behavior two years ago, he had no doubt Elizabeth Cameron had done much to earn a well-deserved beating from her unfortunate guardian. Even so, Ian had no wish to be the cause of the old man laying a strap to that smooth white skin of hers. What had happened between them was folly on his part, but it had been over long ago. He was about to wed a beautiful, sensual woman who wanted him and who suited him perfectly. Why should he treat Elizabeth as if he harbored any feelings for her, including anger?

Elizabeth sensed that he was wavering a little, and she pressed home her advantage, using calm reason: "Surely nothing that happened between us should make us behave badly to each other now. I mean, when you think on it, it was nothing to us but a harmless weekend flirtation, wasn't it?"

"Obviously."

"Neither of us was hurt, were we?"

"No."

"Well then, there's no reason why we should not be cordial to each other now, is there?" she demanded with a bright, beguiling smile. "Good heavens, if every flirtation ended in enmity, no one in the *ton* would be speaking to anyone else!"

She had neatly managed to put him in the position of either agreeing with her or else, by disagreeing, admitting that she had been something more to him than a flirtation, and Ian realized it. He'd guessed where her calm arguments were leading, but even so, he was reluctantly impressed with how skillfully she was maneuvering him into having to agree with her. "Flirtations," he reminded her smoothly, "don't normally end in duels."

"I know, and I *am* sorry my brother shot you."

Ian was simply not proof against the appeal in those huge green eyes of hers. "Forget it," he said with an irritated sigh, capitulating to all she was asking. "Stay the seven days."

Suppressing the urge to twirl around with relief, she smiled into his eyes. "Then could we have a truce for the time I'm here?"

"That depends."

"On what?"

His brows lifted in mocking challenge. "On whether or not you can make a decent breakfast."

"Let's go in the house and see what we have."

With Ian standing beside her Elizabeth surveyed the eggs and cheese and bread, and then the stove. "I shall fix something right up," she promised with a smile that concealed her uncertainty.

"Are you sure you're up to the challenge?" Ian asked, but she seemed so eager, and her smile was so disarming, that he almost believed she knew how to cook.

"I shall prevail, you'll see," she told him brightly, reaching for a wide cloth and tying it around her narrow waist.

Her glance was so jaunty that Ian turned around to keep himself from grinning at her. She was obviously determined to attack the project with vigor and determination, and he was equally determined not to discourage her efforts. "You do that," he said, and he left her alone at the stove.

An hour later, her brow damp with perspiration, Elizabeth grabbed the skillet, burned her hand, and yelped as she snatched a cloth to use on the handle. She arranged the bacon on a platter and then debated what to do with the ten-inch biscuit that had actually been four small biscuits when she'd placed the pan in the oven. Deciding not to break it into irregular chunks, she placed the entire biscuit neatly in the center of the bacon and carried the platter over to the table, where Ian had just seated himself. Returning to the stove, she tried to dig the eggs out of the skillet, but they wouldn't come loose, so she brought the skillet and spatula to the table. "I—I thought you might like to serve," she offered formally, to hide her growing trepidation over the things she had prepared.

"Certainly," Ian replied, accepting the honor with the same grave formality with which she'd offered it; then he looked expectantly at the skillet. "What have we here?" he inquired sociably.

Scrupulously keeping her gaze lowered, Elizabeth sat down across from him. "Eggs," she answered, making an elaborate production of opening her napkin and placing it on her lap. "I'm afraid the yolks broke."

"It doesn't matter."

When he picked up the spatula Elizabeth pinned a bright, optimistic smile on her face and watched as he first tried to lift, and then began trying to *pry* the stuck eggs from the skillet. "They're stuck," she explained needlessly.

"No, they're *bonded*," he corrected, but at least he didn't sound angry. After another few moments he finally managed to pry a strip loose, and he placed it on her plate. A few moments more and he was able to gouge another piece loose, which he placed on his own plate.

In keeping with the agreed-upon truce they both began observing all the polite table rituals with scrupulous care. First Ian offered the platter of bacon with the biscuit centerpiece to Elizabeth. "Thank you," she said, choosing two black strips of bacon.

Ian took three strips of bacon and studied the flat brown object reposing on the center of the platter. "I recognize the bacon," he said with grave courtesy, "but what is that?" he asked, eyeing the brown object. "It looks quite exotic."

"It's a biscuit," Elizabeth informed him.

"Really?" he said, straight-faced. "Without any shape?"

"I call it a—a *pan* biscuit," Elizabeth fabricated hastily.

"Yes, I can see why you might," he agreed. "It rather resembles the shape of a pan."

Separately they surveyed their individual plates, trying to decide which item was most likely to be edible. They arrived at the same conclusion at the same moment; both of them picked up a strip of bacon and bit into it. Noisy crunching and cracking sounds ensued—like those of a large tree breaking in half and falling. Carefully avoiding each other's eyes, they continued crunching away until they'd both eaten all the bacon on their plates. That finished, Elizabeth summoned her courage and took a dainty bite of egg.

The egg tasted like tough, salted wrapping paper, but Elizabeth chewed manfully on it, her stomach churning with humiliation and a lump of tears starting to swell in her throat. She expected some scathing comment at any moment from her companion, and the more politely he continued eating, the more she wished he'd revert to his usual unpleasant self so that she'd at least have the defense of anger. Lately everything that happened to her was humiliating, and her pride and confidence were in tatters. Leaving the egg unfinished, she put down her fork and tried the biscuit. After several seconds of attempting to break a piece off with her fingers she picked up her knife and sawed away at it. A brown piece finally broke loose; she lifted it to her mouth and bit—but it was so tough her teeth only made grooves in the surface. Across the table she felt Ian's eyes on her, and the urge to weep doubled. "Would you like some coffee?" she asked in a suffocated little voice.

"Yes, thank you."

Relieved to have a moment to compose herself, Elizabeth arose and went to the stove, but her eyes blurred with tears as she blindly filled a mug with freshly brewed coffee. She brought it over to him, then sat down again.

Sliding a glance at the defeated girl sitting with her head bent and her hands folded in her lap, Ian felt a compulsive urge to either laugh or comfort her, but since chewing was requiring such an effort, he couldn't do either. Swallowing the last piece of egg, he finally managed to say, "That was . . . er . . . quite filling."

Thinking perhaps he hadn't found it so bad as she had,

Elizabeth hesitantly raised her eyes to his. "I haven't had a great deal of experience with cooking," she admitted in a small voice. She watched him take a mouthful of coffee, saw his eyes widen with shock—and he began to *chew* the coffee.

Elizabeth lurched to her feet, squared her shoulders, and said hoarsely, "I always take a stroll after breakfast. Excuse me."

Still chewing, Ian watched her flee from the house, then he gratefully got rid of the mouthful of coffee grounds.

14

Elizabeth's breakfast had cured Ian's hunger; in fact, the idea of ever eating again made his stomach churn as he started for the barn to check on Mayhem's injury.

He was partway there when he saw her off to the left, sitting on the hillside amid the bluebells, her arms wrapped around her knees, her forehead resting atop them. Even with her hair shining like newly minted gold in the sun, she looked like a picture of heartbreaking dejection. He started to turn away and leave her to moody privacy; then, with a sigh of irritation, he changed his mind and started down the hill toward her.

A few yards away he realized her shoulders were shaking with sobs, and he frowned in surprise. Obviously there was no point in pretending the meal had been good, so he injected a note of amusement into his voice and said, "I applaud your ingenuity—shooting me yesterday would have been too quick."

Elizabeth started violently at the sound of his voice. Snapping her head up, she stared off to the left, keeping her tear-streaked face averted from him. "Did you want something?"

"Dessert?" Ian suggested wryly, leaning slightly forward,

trying to see her face. He thought he saw a morose smile touch her lips, and he added, "I thought we could whip up a batch of cream and put it on the biscuit. Afterward we can take whatever is left, mix it with the leftover eggs, and use it to patch the roof."

A teary chuckle escaped her, and she drew a shaky breath but still refused to look at him as she said, "I'm surprised you're being so pleasant about it."

"There's no sense crying over burnt bacon."

"I wasn't crying over that," she said, feeling sheepish and bewildered. A snowy handkerchief appeared before her face, and Elizabeth accepted it, dabbing at her wet cheeks.

"Then why were you crying?"

She gazed straight ahead, her eyes focused on the surrounding hills splashed with bluebells and hawthorn, the handkerchief clenched in her hand. "I was crying for my own ineptitude, and for my inability to control my life," she admitted.

The word "ineptitude" startled Ian, and it occurred to him that for the shallow little flirt he supposed her to be she had an exceptionally fine vocabulary. She glanced up at him then, and Ian found himself gazing into a pair of green eyes the amazing color of wet leaves. With tears still sparkling on her long russet lashes, her long hair tied back in a girlish bow, and her full breasts thrusting against the bodice of her gown, she was a picture of alluring innocence and intoxicating sensuality. Ian jerked his gaze from her breasts and said abruptly, "I'm going to cut some wood so we'll have it for a fire tonight. Afterward I'm going to do some fishing for our supper. I trust you'll find a way to amuse yourself in the meantime."

Startled by his sudden brusqueness, Elizabeth nodded and stood up, dimly aware that he did not offer his hand to assist her. He'd already started to walk away when he turned and added, "Don't try to clean the house. Jake will be back before evening with women to do that."

After he left, Elizabeth went into the house, looking for something to do that would divert her mind from her predicament and help use her pent-up energy. Deciding the least she could do was to clean up the mess from the meal she'd made, she set to work doing that. As she scraped at the eggs in the blackened skillet she heard the rhythmic sound of an ax splitting wood. Reaching up to push a wisp of hair off her forehead, she glanced out the window and then stared, blushing. Without a semblance of modesty Ian Thornton was bare to the waist, his bronzed back tapering to narrow hips, his arms and shoulders rippling with thick, bunched muscle as he swung the ax in a graceful arc. Elizabeth had never seen a man's bare arms before, let alone an entire naked male torso, and she was shocked and fascinated and appalled that she was looking. Yanking her gaze from the window, she absolutely refused to yield to the heathen temptation of stealing another glance at him. She wondered instead where he had learned to cut wood with such ease and skill. He'd looked so right at Charise's party, so at ease in his beautifully tailored evening clothes, that she'd assumed he'd spent all his life on the fringes of society, supporting himself with his gambling. Yet he seemed equally at home here in the wilds of Scotland. More so here, she decided. Besides his powerful physique there was a harsh vitality, an invulnerability about him that was perfectly suited to this untamed land.

At that moment she suddenly recalled something she had long ago chosen to forget: She recalled the way he had waltzed with her in the arbor and the effortless grace of his movements. Evidently he had the ability to belong in whatever setting he happened to be in. For some reason that realization was unsettling—either because it made him seem almost admirable, or because it suddenly made her doubt her former ability to judge him correctly. For the first time since that disastrous week that had culminated in a duel, Elizabeth allowed herself to reexamine what had happened between Ian Thornton and herself—not the events, but the *causes*. Until now, the only way she'd been able to endure her subsequent disgrace was to categorically blame Ian for it, exactly as Robert had done.

Now, having come face to face with him again when she was older and wiser, she couldn't seem to do that anymore. Not even Ian's current unkindness could make her see him as completely at fault for past events anymore.

As she slowly washed a dish she saw herself as she had really been: foolish and dangerously infatuated and as guilty as he of breaking the rules.

Determined to be objective, Elizabeth reconsidered her actions and her own culpability two years before. And his. In the first place, she had been foolish beyond words to want so badly to protect him . . . and to be protected by him. At seventeen, when she should have been too frightened to *consider* meeting him at that cottage, she had only been frightened that she would yield to the irrational, nameless feelings he awakened in her with his voice, his eyes, his touch.

When she should rightfully have been terrified of *him,* she had only been terrified of herself, of throwing away Robert's future and Havenhurst. And she would have done it, Elizabeth realized bitterly. If she'd spent another day, a few more hours alone with Ian Thornton that weekend, she would have flung caution and reason to the winds and married him. She'd sensed it even then, and so she'd sent for Robert to come for her early.

No, Elizabeth corrected herself, she'd never really been in danger of marrying Ian. Despite what he'd said two years before about wanting to marry her, *marriage* was not what he'd intended; he'd admitted that to Robert.

And just when that memory started to make her genuinely angry, she remembered something else that had an oddly calming effect: For the first time in almost two years, Elizabeth recalled the warnings Lucinda had given her before she made her debut. Lucinda had been emphatic that a female must, by her every action, make a gentleman understand that he would be expected to *act* like a gentleman in her presence. Obviously, Lucinda had realized that although the men Elizabeth was going to meet were technically "gentlemen," their behavior could, on occasion, be ungentlemanly.

Allowing that Lucinda was right on both counts, Elizabeth began to wonder if she wasn't rather to blame for what had happened that weekend. After all, from their first meeting she'd certainly not given Ian the impression she was a proper and prim young lady who expected the highest standards of behavior from him. For one thing, *she* had asked *him* to request a dance from her.

Carrying that thought to its conclusion, she began to wonder if Ian hadn't perhaps done what many other socially acceptable "gentlemen" would have done. He had probably thought her more worldly than she was, and he had wanted a dalliance. If she had been wiser, more worldly, she undoubtedly would have known that and would have been able to act with the amused sophistication he must have expected of her. Now, with the belated understanding of a detached adult, Elizabeth realized that although Ian had not been as socially acceptable as many of the *ton's* flirts, he had actually behaved no worse than they. She had seen married women flirting at balls; she'd even inadvertently witnessed a stolen kiss or two, after which the gentleman received nothing worse than a slap on the arm from the lady's fan and a laughing warning that he must behave himself. She smiled at the realization that instead of a slap on the arm for his forwardness, Ian Thornton had gotten a ball from a pistol; she smiled—not with malicious satisfaction this time, but simply because it had a certain amusing irony to it. It also occurred to her that she might have survived the entire weekend with nothing worse than a mildly painful case of lingering infatuation for Ian Thornton—if only she hadn't been seen with him in the greenhouse.

In retrospect it seemed that her own naïveté was to blame for much of what had happened.

Somehow, all that made her feel better than she had in a very long time; it diffused the helpless anger that had been festering inside of her for nearly two years and left her feeling unburdened and almost weightless.

Elizabeth picked up a towel, then stood still, wondering if she was simply making excuses for the man. But why would she? she thought as she slowly dried the earthenware dishes. The answer was that she simply had more problems at the moment than she could deal with, and by ridding herself of her animosity for Ian Thornton she'd feel better able to cope. That seemed so sensible and so likely that Elizabeth decided it must be true.

When everything had been dried and put away she

emptied the pan of water outside, then wandered about the house, looking for something to do that would divert her mind. She went upstairs, unpacked her writing things, and brought them down to the kitchen table to write to Alexandra, but after a few minutes she was too restless to continue. It was so lovely outdoors, and from the silence she knew Ian had finished cutting wood. Putting down her quill, she wandered outside, visited with the horse in the barn, and finally decided to attack the large patch of weeds and struggling flowers at the rear of the cottage that had once been a garden. She went back into the cottage, found an old pair of men's gloves and a towel to kneel upon, and went back outside.

With ruthless determination Elizabeth yanked out the weeds that were choking some brave little heartsease struggling for air and light. By the time the sun started its lazy descent she had cleared the worst of the weeds and dug up some bluebells, transplanting them to the garden in neat rows, to give the best show of color in the future.

Occasionally she paused with her spade in hand and looked down into the valley below, where a thin ribbon of sparkling blue wound through the trees. Sometimes she saw a flash of movement—his arm, as he cast his line. Other times he simply stood there, his legs braced slightly apart, gazing up at the cliffs to the north.

It was late afternoon, and she was sitting back on her heels, studying the effect of the bluebells she'd transplanted. Beside her was a small pile of compost she'd mixed using decayed leaves and the coffee grounds of the morning. "There now," she said to the flowers in an encouraging tone, "you have food and air. You'll be very happy and pretty in no time."

"Are you talking to the *flowers?*" Ian asked from behind her.

Elizabeth started and turned around on an embarrassed laugh. "They like it when I talk to them." Knowing how peculiar that sounded, she reinforced it by adding, "Our gardener used to say all living things need affection, and that includes flowers." Turning back to the garden, she shoveled the last of the compost around the flowers, then she stood up and brushed off her hands. Her earlier ruminations about him had abolished so much of her antagonism that as she looked at him now she was able to regard him with perfect equanimity. It occurred to her, though, that it must seem odd to him that a guest was rooting about in his garden like a menial. "I hope you don't mind," she said, nodding toward the garden, "but the flowers couldn't breathe with so many weeds choking them. They were crying out for a little room and sustenance."

An indescribable expression flashed across his face. "You *heard* them?"

"Of course not," Elizabeth said with a chuckle. "But I did take the liberty of fixing a special meal—well, compost, actually—for them. It won't help them very much this year, but next year I think they'll be much happier. . . ."

She trailed off, belatedly noticing the worried look he gave the flowers when she mentioned fixing them "a meal." "You needn't look as if you expect them to collapse at my feet," she admonished, laughing. "They'll fare far better with their meal than we did with ours. I am a *much* better gardener than I am a cook."

Ian jerked his gaze from the flowers, then looked at her with an odd, contemplative expression. "I think I'll go inside and clean up." She walked away without looking back, and so she did not see Ian Thornton turn halfway around to watch her.

Stopping to fill a pitcher with the hot water she'd been heating on the stove, Elizabeth carried it upstairs, then made four more trips until she had enough water to use to bathe and wash her hair. Yesterday's travel and today's work in the garden had combined to make her feel positively grimy.

An hour later, her hair still damp, she put on a simple peach gown with short puffed sleeves and a narrow peach ribbon at the high waist. Sitting on the bed, she brushed her hair slowly, letting it dry, while she reflected with some amusement on how ill-suited her clothes were for this cottage in Scotland. When her hair was dry she stood at the mirror, gathering the mass at her nape, then shoving it high into a haphazard chignon she knew would come unbound in only the slightest breeze. With a light shrug she let go of it, and it fell over her shoulders; she decided to leave it that way. Her mood was still bright and cheerful, and she was inwardly convinced it might stay that way from now on.

Ian had started toward the back door with a blanket in his hand when Elizabeth came downstairs. "Since they aren't back yet," he said, "I thought we might as well eat something. We have cheese and bread outside."

He'd changed into a clean white shirt and fawn breeches, and as she followed him outside she saw that his dark hair was still damp at the nape.

Outside he spread a blanket on the grass, and she sat down on one side of it, gazing out across the hills. "What time do you suppose it is?" she asked several minutes after he'd sat down beside her.

"Around four, I imagine."

"Shouldn't they be back by now?"

"They probably had difficulty finding women who were willing to leave their own homes and come up here to work."

Elizabeth nodded and lost herself in the splendor of the view spread out before them. The cottage was situated on the back edge of a plateau, and where the backyard ended the plateau sloped sharply downward to a valley where a stream meandered among the trees. Surrounding the valley in the distance on all three sides were hills piled on top of one another, carpeted with wildflowers. The view was so beautiful, so wild and verdant, that Elizabeth sat for a long while, enthralled and strangely at peace. Finally a thought intruded, and she cast a worried look at him. "Did you catch any fish?"

"Several. I've already cleaned them."

"Yes, but can you *cook* them?" Elizabeth countered with a grin.

His lips twitched. "Yes."

"That's a relief, I must say."

Drawing up one leg, Ian rested his wrist on his knee and turned to regard her with frank curiosity. "Since when do debutantes include rooting around in the dirt among their preferred entertainments?"

"I am no longer a debutante," Elizabeth replied. When she realized he intended to continue waiting for some sort of explanation, she said quietly, "I'm told my grandfather on my mother's side was an amateur horticulturist, and perhaps I inherited my love of plants and flowers from him. The gardens at Havenhurst were his work. I've enlarged them and added some new species since."

Her face softened, and her magnificent eyes glowed like bright green jewels at the mention of Havenhurst. Against his better judgment Ian kept her talking about a subject that obviously meant something special to her. "What is Havenhurst?"

"My home," she said with a soft smile. "It's been in our family for seven centuries. The original earl built a castle on it, and it was so beautiful that fourteen different aggressors coveted it and laid siege to it, but no one could take it. The castle was razed centuries later by another ancestor who wished to build a mansion in the classic Greek style. Then the next six earls enhanced and enlarged and modernized it until it became the place it now is. Sometimes," she admitted, "it's a little overwhelming to know it's up to me to see that it is preserved."

"I'd think that responsibility falls to your uncle or your brother, not you."

"No, it's mine."

"How can it be yours?" he asked, curious that she would speak of the place as if it was everything in the world that mattered to her.

"Under the entailment Havenhurst must pass to the oldest son. If there is no son, it passes to the daughter, and through her, to her children. My uncle cannot inherit because he was younger than my father. I suppose that's why he never cared a snap for it and resents so bitterly the cost of its upkeep now."

"But you have a brother," Ian pointed out.

"Robert is my half-brother," Elizabeth said, so soothed by the view and by having come to grips with what had happened two years ago that she spoke to him quite freely. "My mother was widowed when she was but twenty-one, and Robert was a babe. She married my father after Robert was born. My father formally adopted him, but it doesn't change the entailment. Under the terms of the entailment the heir can sell the property outright, but ownership cannot be transferred to any relative. That was done to safeguard against one member or branch of the family coveting the property and exerting undue force on the heir to relinquish it. Something like that happened to one of my grandmothers in the fifteenth century, and that amendment was added to the entailment at her insistence many years later. Her daughter fell in love with a Welshman who was a black-guard," Elizabeth continued with a smile, "who coveted Havenhurst, *not* the daughter, and to keep him from getting it her parents had a final codicil added to the entailment."

"What was that?" Ian asked, drawn into the history she related with such entertaining skill.

"It states that if the heir is female, she cannot wed against her guardian's wishes. In theory it was to stop the females from falling prey to another obvious blackguard. It isn't always easy for a woman to hold her own property, you see."

Ian saw only that the beautiful girl who had daringly come to his defense in a roomful of men, who had kissed him with tender passion, now seemed to be passionately attached not to any man, but to a pile of stones instead. Two years ago he'd been furious when he discovered she was a countess, a shallow little debutante already betrothed—to some blood-less fop, no doubt—and merely looking about for someone more exciting to warm her bed. Now, however, he felt oddly uneasy that she hadn't married her fop. It was on the tip of his tongue to bluntly ask her why she had never married when she spoke again. "Scotland is different than I imagined it would be."

"In what way?"

"More wild, more primitive. I know gentlemen keep hunting boxes here, but I rather thought they'd have the usual conveniences and servants. What was your home like?"

"Wild and primitive," Ian replied. While Elizabeth looked on in surprised confusion, he gathered up the remains of their snack and rolled to his feet with lithe agility. "You're in it," he added in a mocking voice.

"In what?" Elizabeth automatically stood up, too.

"My home."

Hot, embarrassed color stained Elizabeth's smooth cheeks as they faced each other. He stood there with his dark hair blowing in the breeze, his sternly handsome face stamped with nobility and pride, his muscular body emanating raw power, and she thought he seemed as rugged and invulnerable as the cliffs of his homeland. She opened her mouth, intending to apologize; instead, she inadvertently spoke her private thoughts: "It suits you," she said softly.

Beneath his impassive gaze Elizabeth stood perfectly still, refusing to blush or look away, her delicately beautiful face framed by a halo of golden hair tossing in the restless breeze—a dainty image of fragility standing before a man who dwarfed her. Light and darkness, fragility and strength, stubborn pride and iron resolve—two opposites in almost every way. Once their differences had drawn them together; now they separated them. They were both older, wiser—and convinced they were strong enough to withstand and ignore the slow heat building between them on that grassy ledge. "It doesn't suit you, however," he remarked mildly.

His words pulled Elizabeth from the strange spell that had seemed to enclose them. "No," she agreed without rancor, knowing what a hothouse flower she must seem with her impractical gowns and fragile slippers.

Bending down, Elizabeth folded the blanket while Ian went into the house and began gathering the guns so that he could clean and and check them before hunting tomorrow. Elizabeth watched him removing the guns from the rack above the mantel, and she glanced at the letter she'd begun to Alexandra. There was no way to post it until she went home, so there was no reason to finish it quickly. On the other hand, there was little else to do, so she sat down and began writing.

In the midst of her letter a gun exploded outside, and she half rose in nervous surprise. Wondering what he'd shot so close to the house, she walked to the open door and looked outside, watching as he loaded the pistol that had been lying on the table yesterday. He raised it, aiming at some unknown target, and fired. Again he loaded and fired, until curiosity made her step outside, squinting to see what, if anything, he had hit.

From the corner of his eye Ian glimpsed a slight flash of peach gown and turned.

"Did you hit the target?" she asked, a little self-conscious at being caught watching him.

"Yes." Since she was stranded in the country and obviously knew how to load a gun, Ian realized good manners required that he at least offer her a little diversion. "Care to try your skill?"

"That depends on the size of the target," she answered, but Elizabeth was already walking forward, absurdly happy to have something to do besides write letters. She did not stop to consider—would never have let herself contemplate —that she enjoyed his company inordinately when he was pleasant.

"Who taught you to shoot?" he asked when she was standing beside him.

"Our coachman."

"Better the coachman than your brother," Ian mocked, handing her the loaded gun. "The target's that bare twig over there—the one with the leaf hanging off the middle of it."

Elizabeth flinched at his sarcastic reference to his duel with Robert. "I'm truly sorry about that duel," she said, then she concentrated all her attention for the moment on the small twig.

Propping his shoulder against the tree trunk, Ian watched with amusement as she grasped the heavy gun in both her hands and raised it, biting her lip in concentration. "Your brother was a very poor shot," he remarked.

She fired, nicking the leaf at its stem.

"I'm not," she said with a jaunty sidewise smile. And then, because the duel was finally out in the open and he seemed to want to joke about it, she tried to follow suit: "If I'd been there, I daresay I would have—"

His brows lifted. "Waited for the call to fire, I hope?"

"Well, that, too," she said, her smile fading as she waited for him to reject her words.

And at that moment Ian rather believed she would have

waited. Despite everything he knew her to be, when he looked at her he saw spirit and youthful courage. She handed the gun back to him, and he handed her another one he'd already loaded. "The last shot wasn't bad," he said, dropping the subject of the duel. "However, the target is the twig, not the leaves. The *end* of the twig," he added.

"You must have missed the twig yourself," she pointed out, lifting the gun and aiming it carefully, "since it's still there."

"True, but it's shorter than it was when I started."

Elizabeth momentarily forgot what she was doing as she stared at him in disbelief and amazement. "Do you mean you've been clipping the end off it?"

"A bit at a time," he said, concentrating on her next shot.

She hit another leaf on the twig and handed the gun back to him.

"You're not bad," he complimented.

She was an outstanding shot, and his smile said he knew it as he handed her a freshly loaded gun. Elizabeth shook her head. "I'd rather see *you* try it."

"You doubt my word?"

"Let's merely say I'm a little skeptical."

Taking the gun, Ian raised it in a swift arc, and without pausing to aim, he fired. Two inches of twig spun away and fell to the ground. Elizabeth was so impressed she laughed aloud. "Do you know," she exclaimed with an admiring smile, "I didn't entirely believe until this moment that you really *meant* to shoot the tassel off Robert's boot!"

He sent her an amused glance as he reloaded and handed her the gun. "At the time I was sorely tempted to aim for something more vulnerable."

"You wouldn't have, though," she reminded him, taking the gun and turning toward the twig.

"What makes you so certain?"

"You told me yourself you didn't believe in killing people over disagreements." She raised the gun, aimed, and fired, missing the target completely. "I have a very good memory."

Ian picked up the other gun. "I'm surprised to hear it," he drawled, turning to the target, "inasmuch as when we met you'd forgotten you were betrothed. Who was the fop, anyway?" he asked unemotionally, aiming, firing, and hitting true again.

Elizabeth had been reloading a gun, and she paused imperceptibly, then returned to the task. His casual question proved she'd been right in her earlier reflections. Flirtations were obviously not taken seriously by those mature enough to indulge in them. Afterward, like now, it was apparently accepted procedure to tease one another about them. While Ian loaded the other two guns Elizabeth considered how much nicer it was to joke openly about it than to lie awake in the dark, consumed with confusion and bitterness, as she had done. How foolish she'd been. How foolish she'd seem now if she didn't treat the matter openly and lightly. It did seem, however, a little strange—and rather funny—to discuss it while blasting away with guns. She was smiling about that very thing when he handed her a gun. "Viscount Mondevale was anything but a 'fop,'" she said, turning to aim.

He looked surprised, but his voice was bland. "Mondevale, was it?"

"Mmmm." Elizabeth blasted the end off the twig and laughed with delight. "I hit it! That's three for you and one for me."

"That's *six* for me," he pointed out drolly.

"In any case, I'm catching up, so beware!" He handed a gun to her, and Elizabeth squinted, taking careful aim.

"Why did you cry off?"

She stiffened in surprise; then, trying to match his light, mocking tone, she said, "Viscount Mondevale proved to be a trifle high in the instep about things like his fiancée cavorting about in cottages and greenhouses with you." She fired and missed.

"How many contenders are there this Season?" he asked conversationally as he turned to the target, pausing to wipe the gun.

She knew he meant contenders for her hand, and pride absolutely would not allow her to say there were none, nor had there been for a long time. "Well . . ." she said, suppressing a grimace as she thought of her stout suitor with a houseful of cherubs. Counting on the fact that he didn't move in the inner circles of the *ton,* she assumed he wouldn't know much about either suitor. He raised the gun as she said, "There's Sir Francis Belhaven, for one."

Instead of firing immediately as he had before, he seemed to require a long moment to adjust his aim. "Belhaven's an old man," he said. The gun exploded, and the twig snapped off.

When he looked at her his eyes had chilled, almost as if he thought less of her. Elizabeth told herself she was imagining that and determined to maintain their mood of light conviviality. Since it was her turn, she picked up a gun and lifted it.

"Who's the other one?"

Relieved that he couldn't possibly find fault with the age of her reclusive sportsman, she gave him a mildly haughty smile. "Lord John Marchman," she said, and she fired.

Ian's shout of laughter almost drowned out the report from the gun. "Marchman!" he said when she scowled at him and thrust the butt of the gun in his stomach. "You must be joking!"

"You spoiled my shot," she countered.

"Take it again," he said, looking at her with a mixture of derision, disbelief, and amusement.

"No, I can't shoot with you laughing. And I'll thank you to wipe that smirk off your face. Lord Marchman is a very nice man."

"He is indeed," said Ian with an irritating grin. "And it's a damned good thing you like to shoot, because he sleeps with his guns and fishing poles. You'll spend the rest of your life slogging through streams and trudging through the woods."

"I happen to like to fish," she informed him, striving unsuccessfully not to lose her composure. "And Sir Francis may be a trifle older than I, but an elderly husband might be more kind and tolerant than a younger one."

"He'll have to be tolerant," Ian said a little shortly, turning his attention back to the guns, "or else a damned good shot."

It angered Elizabeth that he was suddenly attacking her when she had just worked it out in her mind that they were supposed to be dealing with what had happened in a light, sophisticated fashion. "I must say, you aren't being very mature *or* very consistent!"

His dark brows snapped together as their truce began to disintegrate. "What the hell is that supposed to mean?"

Elizabeth bridled, looking at him like the haughty, disdainful young aristocrat she was born to be. "It means," she informed him, making a monumental effort to speak clearly and coolly, "that you have no right to act as if *I* did something evil, when in truth you yourself regarded it as nothing but a—a meaningless dalliance. You said as much, so there's no point in denying it!"

He finished loading the gun before he spoke. In contrast to his grim expression, his voice was perfectly bland. "My memory apparently isn't as good as yours. To whom did I say that?"

"My brother, for one," she said, impatient with his pretense.

"Ah, yes, the honorable Robert," he replied, putting sarcastic emphasis on the word "honorable." He turned to the target and fired, but the shot was wide of the mark.

"You didn't even hit the right *tree*," Elizabeth said in surprise. "I thought you said you were going to clean the guns," she added when he began methodically sliding them into leather cases, his expression preoccupied.

He looked up at her, but she had the feeling he'd almost forgotten she was there. "I've decided to do it tomorrow instead." Ian went into the house, automatically putting the guns back on the mantel; then he wandered over to the table, frowning thoughtfully as he reached for the bottle of Madeira and poured some into his glass. He told himself it made no difference how she might have felt when her brother told her that falsehood. For one thing, she was already engaged at the time, and, by her own admission, she'd regarded their relationship as a flirtation. Her pride might have suffered a richly deserved blow, but nothing worse than that. Furthermore, Ian reminded himself irritably, he was technically betrothed, and to a beautiful woman who deserved better from him than this stupid preoccupation with Elizabeth Cameron.

"Viscount Mondevale proved to be a trifle high in the instep about things like his fiancée cavorting about in cottages and greenhouses with you," she'd said.

Her fiancé had evidently cried off because of him, and Ian felt an uneasy pang of guilt he couldn't completely banish. Idly he reached for the bottle of Madeira, thinking of offering Elizabeth a glass. Lying beside the bottle was a note Elizabeth had been writing. It began, "Dearest Alex . . ." But it was not the words that made his jaw clench; it was the handwriting. Neat, scholarly, and precise. Suited to a monk. It was not a girlish, illegible scrawl like that note he'd had to decipher before he understood she wanted to see him in the greenhouse. He picked it up, staring at it in disbelief, his conscience beginning to smite him with a vengeance. He saw himself stalking her in that damned greenhouse, and guilt poured through him like acid.

Ian downed the Madeira as if it could wash away his self-disgust, then he turned and walked slowly outdoors. Elizabeth was standing at the edge of the grassy plateau, a few yards beyond where they'd held their shooting match. Wind ruffled through the trees, blowing her magnificent hair about her shoulders like a shimmering veil. He stopped a few steps away from her, looking at her, but seeing her as she had looked long ago—a young goddess in royal blue, descending a staircase, aloof, untouchable; an angry angel defying a roomful of men in a card room; a beguiling temptress in a woodcutter's cottage, lifting her wet hair in front of the fire—and at the end, a frightened girl thrusting flowerpots into his hands to keep him from kissing her. He drew in a deep breath and shoved his hands into his pockets to keep from reaching for her.

"It's a magnificent view," she commented, glancing at him.

Instead of replying to her remark, Ian drew a long, harsh breath and said curtly, "I'd like you to tell me again what happened that last night. Why were you in the greenhouse?"

Elizabeth suppressed her frustration. "You *know* why I was there. You sent me a note. I thought it was from Valerie—Charise's sister—and I went to the greenhouse."

"Elizabeth, I did *not* send you a note, but I did receive one."

Sighing with irritation, Elizabeth leaned her shoulders against the tree behind her. "I don't see why we have to go through this again. You won't believe me, and I can't believe you." She expected an angry outburst; instead he said, "I do believe you. I saw the letter you left on the table in the cottage. You have a lovely handwriting."

Caught completely off balance by his solemn tone and his quiet compliment, she stared at him. "Thank you," she said uncertainly.

"The note you received," he continued. "What was the handwriting like?"

"Awful," she replied, and she added with raised brows, "You misspelled 'greenhouse.'"

His lips quirked with a mirthless smile. "I assure you I can spell it, and while my handwriting may not be as attractive as yours, it's hardly an illegible scrawl. If you doubt me, I'll be happy to prove it inside."

Elizabeth realized at that moment he was not lying, and an awful feeling of betrayal began to seep through her as he finished, "We both received notes that neither of us wrote. Someone intended us to go there and, I think, to be discovered."

"No one could be so cruel!" Elizabeth burst out, shaking her head, her heart trying to deny what her mind was realizing must be true.

"Someone *was.*"

"Don't tell me that," she cried, unable to endure one more betrayal in her life. "I won't believe it! It must have been a mistake," she said fiercely, but scenes from that weekend were already parading through her memory: Valerie insisting that Elizabeth be the one to try to entice Ian Thornton into asking her for a dance . . . Valerie asking pointed questions after Elizabeth had gone to the woodcutter's cottage . . . the footman handing her a note he said was from Valerie. Valerie, whom she'd believed was her friend. Valerie with the pretty face and watchful eyes . . .

The pain of betrayal almost doubled Elizabeth over, and she wrapped her arms around herself, feeling as if she were crumbling into pieces. "It was Valerie," she managed chokingly. "I asked the footman who'd given him the note, and he said Valerie had." The unspeakable malice of the deed made her shudder. "Later I assumed you'd entrusted it to her, and she'd given it to the footman."

"I'd never have done anything of the sort," he said shortly. "You were terrified we'd be discovered as it was."

His anger at what had been done only made the whole thing seem worse, because even *he* couldn't shrug it off with casual urbanity. Swallowing, Elizabeth closed her eyes and saw Valerie riding in the park with Viscount Mondevale. Elizabeth's life had been shattered—and all because someone she believed was her friend had coveted her fiancé. Tears burned the backs of her eyes, and she said brokenly, "It was a trick. My life was ruined by a trick."

"Why?" he asked. "Why would she do a thing like that to you?"

"I think she wanted Mondevale, and—" Elizabeth knew she would cry if she tried to talk, and she shook her head and started to turn away, to find somewhere to weep out her anguish in privacy.

Helpless to let her go without at least trying to comfort her, Ian caught her shoulders and pulled her against his chest, tightening his arms when she tried to wrench free. "Don't, please," he whispered against her hair. "Don't go. She's not worth your tears."

The shock of being held in his arms again was almost as great as Elizabeth's misery, and the combination of emotions left her paralyzed. With her head bowed she stood silently in his arms, tears racing from her eyes, her body jerking with suppressed sobs.

Ian tightened his arms more, as if he could absorb her hurt by holding her closer, and when that didn't console her after several minutes, he began in sheer desperation to tease her. "If she'd known what a good shot you are," he whispered past the unfamiliar tightness in his throat, "she'd never have dared." His hand lifted to her wet cheek, holding it pressed against his chest. "You could always call her out, you know." The spasmodic shaking in Elizabeth's slender shoulders began to subside, and Ian added with forced tightness, "Better yet, Robert should stand in for you. He's not as fine a shot as you are, but he's a hell of a lot *faster. . . .*"

A teary giggle escaped the girl in his arms, and Ian continued, "On the other hand, if you're holding the pistol, you'll have some choices to make, and they're not easy. . . ."

When he didn't say more, Elizabeth drew a shaky breath. "What choices?" she finally whispered against his chest after a moment.

"What to shoot, for one thing," he joked, stroking her back. "Robert was wearing Hessians, so I had a tassel for a target. I suppose, though, you could always shoot the bow off Valerie's gown."

Elizabeth's shoulders gave a lurch, and a choked laugh escaped her.

Overwhelmed with relief, Ian kept his left arm around her and gently took her chin between his forefinger and thumb, tipping her face up to his. Her magnificent eyes were still wet with tears, but a smile was trembling on her rosy lips. Teasingly, he continued, "A bow isn't much of a challenge for an expert marksman like you. I suppose you could insist that she hold up an earring between her fingers so you could shoot that instead."

The image was so absurd that Elizabeth chuckled.

Without being conscious of what he was doing, Ian moved his thumb from her chin to her lower lip, rubbing lightly against its inviting fullness. He finally realized what he was doing and stopped.

Elizabeth saw his jaw tighten. She drew a shuddering breath, sensing he'd been on the verge of kissing her, and had just decided not to do it. After the last shattering minutes, Elizabeth no longer knew who was friend or foe, she only knew she'd felt safe and secure in his arms, and at that moment his arms were already beginning to loosen, and his expression was turning aloof. Not certain what she was going to say or even what she wanted, she whispered a single, shaky word, filled with confusion and a plea for understanding, her green eyes searching his: "Please—"

Ian realized what she was asking for, but he responded with a questioning lift of his brows.

"I—" she began, uncomfortably aware of the knowing look in his eyes.

"Yes?" he prompted.

"I don't know—exactly," she admitted. All she knew for certain was that, for just a few minutes more, she would have liked to be in his arms.

"Elizabeth, if you want to be kissed, all you have to do is put your lips on mine."

"What!"

"You heard me."

"Of all the arrogant—"

He shook his head in mild rebuke. "Spare me the maidenly protests. If you're suddenly as curious as I am to find out if it was as good between us as it now seems in retrospect, then say so." His own suggestion startled Ian, although having made it, he saw no great harm in exchanging a few kisses if that was what she wanted.

To Elizabeth, his statement that it had been "good between us" defused her ire and confused her at the same time. She stared at him in dazed wonder while his hands tightened imperceptibly on her arms. Self-conscious, she let her gaze drop to his finely molded lips, watching as a faint smile, a *challenging* smile lifted them at the corners, and inch by inch, the hands on her arms were drawing her closer.

"Afraid to find out?" he asked, and it was the trace of huskiness in his voice that she remembered, that worked its strange spell on her again, exactly as it had so long ago. His hands shifted to the curve of her waist. "Make up your mind," he whispered, and in her confused state of loneliness and longing, she made no protest when he bent his head. A shock jolted through her as his lips touched hers, warm, inviting—brushing slowly back and forth. Paralyzed, she waited for that shattering passion he'd shown her before, without realizing that her participation had done much to trigger it. Standing still and tense, she waited to experience that forbidden burst of exquisite delight . . . wanted to experience it, just once, just for a moment. Instead his kiss was feather-light, softly stroking . . . teasing!

She stiffened, pulling back an inch, and his gaze lifted lazily from her lips to her eyes. Dryly, he said, "That's not quite the way I remembered it."

"Nor I," Elizabeth admitted, unaware that he was referring to her lack of participation.

"Care to try it again?" Ian invited, still willing to indulge in a few pleasurable minutes of *shared* ardor, so long as there was no pretense that it was anything but that, and no loss of control on his part.

The bland amusement in his tone finally made her suspect he was treating this as some sort of diverting game or perhaps a challenge, and she looked at him in shock. "Is this a—a *contest?*"

"Do you want to make it into one?"

Elizabeth shook her head and abruptly surrendered her secret memories of tenderness and stormy passion. Like all her other former illusions about him, that too had evidently been false. With a mixture of exasperation and sadness, she looked at him and said, "I don't think so."

"Why not?"

"You're playing a game," she told him honestly, mentally throwing her hands up in weary despair, "and I don't understand the rules."

"They haven't changed," he informed her. "It's the same game we played before—I kiss you, *and,"* he emphasized meaningfully, *"you* kiss *me."*

His blunt criticism of her lack of participation left her caught between acute embarrassment and the urge to kick him in the shin, but his arm was tightening around her waist while his other hand was sliding slowly up her back, sensuously stroking her nape.

"How do you remember it?" he teased as his lips came closer. "Show me." He brushed his lips over hers, rubbing lightly, and despite his humorous tone, this time there was a demand as well as a challenge in the stroking touch; Elizabeth answered it slowly, leaning into his arms, her hand sliding softly up his silk shirt, feeling his muscles tauten, the reflexive tightening of his arm at her back. His mouth opened on hers, and Elizabeth felt her heart begin to beat in painful lurches. His tongue flicked against her lips, teasing, inviting, and Elizabeth lost control and retaliated in the only way she could. Sliding her hands around his shoulders, she kissed him back with fierce shyness, letting him part her lips and, when his tongue probed, she welcomed the invasion.

She felt his sharp intake of breath at the same time Ian felt desire begin to beat in his veins. He told himself to let her go, and he tried, but her hands were sliding into the hair at his nape, her mouth was yielding with tormenting sweetness to his intimate kiss. With an effort he jerked his head up, unable to move more than an inch from that romantic mouth of hers. *"Dammit!"* he whispered, but his arms were already dragging her fully against his hardening body.

Her heart hammering like a wild, captive bird, Elizabeth gazed into those smoldering eyes, while his hand plunged into her hair, holding her head captive as he abruptly bent his head. His mouth opened over hers with fiery demand, slanting fiercely, and Elizabeth's body responded helplessly to the intimate sensuality of it; her arms stole around his neck, and she leaned into him, kissing him back. With cruel pressure he parted her lips, his tongue probing, daring her to protest. But Elizabeth didn't protest; she drew his tongue into her mouth, her fingers sliding over his jaw and temple in an innocent, feather-light caress. Lust roared through Ian in tidal waves, and he splayed his hand across her spine, forcing her into vibrant contact with his rigid arousal, burying his mouth in hers, kissing her with a demanding savagery he couldn't control. His hands slid caressingly over her, then clenched convulsively when she fitted her body tighter to his, unaware of—or unconcerned with—the bold evidence of his desire thrusting insistently against her.

Automatically, his hands lifted toward her breasts, then he realized what he was doing, and he tore his mouth from hers, staring blindly over her head, as he debated whether to kiss her again or try to pass the entire matter off as some sort of joke. No woman he'd known had ever ignited this uncontrollable surge of pure lust with just a few kisses.

"It was the same as I remembered it," she whispered, sounding defeated and puzzled and shattered.

It was better than he remembered. Stronger, wilder . . . And the only reason she didn't know it was because he hadn't succumbed to temptation yet and kissed her once more. He had just rejected that idea as complete insanity when a male voice suddenly erupted behind them:

"Good God! What's going on here!"

Elizabeth jerked free in mindless panic, her gaze flying to a middle-aged elderly man wearing a clerical collar who was dashing across the yard. Ian put a steadying hand on her waist, and she stood there rigid with shock.

"I heard shooting—" The gray-haired man gasped, sagging against a nearby tree, his hand over his heart, his chest heaving. "I heard it all the way up the valley, and I thought—"

He broke off, his alert gaze moving from Elizabeth's flushed face and tousled hair to Ian's hand at her waist.

"You thought what?" Ian asked in a voice that struck Elizabeth as being amazingly calm, considering they'd just been caught in a lustful embrace by nothing less daunting than a Scottish vicar.

The thought had scarcely crossed her battered mind when the man's expression hardened with understanding. "I thought," he said ironically, straightening from the tree and coming forward, brushing pieces of bark from his black sleeve, "that you were trying to kill each other. Which," he continued more mildly as he stopped in front of Elizabeth, "Miss Throckmorton-Jones seemed to think was a distinct possibility when she dispatched me here."

"Lucinda?" Elizabeth gasped, feeling as if the world was turning upside down. "Lucinda sent you here?"

"Indeed," said the vicar, bending a reproachful glance on Ian's hand, which was resting on Elizabeth's waist. Mortified to the very depths of her being by the realization she'd remained standing in this near-embrace, Elizabeth hastily shoved Ian's hand away and stepped sideways. She braced herself for a richly deserved, thundering tirade on the sinfulness of their behavior, but the vicar continued to regard Ian with his bushy gray eyebrows lifted, waiting. Feeling as if she were going to break from the strain of the silence, Elizabeth cast a pleading look at Ian and found him regarding the vicar not with shame or apology, but with irritated amusement.

"Well?" demanded the vicar at last, looking at Ian. "What do you have to say to me?"

"Good afternoon?" Ian suggested drolly. And then he added, "I didn't expect to see you until tomorrow, Uncle."

"Obviously," retorted the vicar with unconcealed irony.

"Uncle!" blurted Elizabeth, gaping incredulously at Ian Thornton, who'd been flagrantly defying rules of morality with his passionate kisses and seeking hands from the first night she met him.

As if the vicar read her thoughts, he looked at her, his brown eyes amused. "Amazing, is it not, my dear? It quite convinces me that God has a sense of humor."

A hysterical giggle welled up in Elizabeth as she saw Ian's impervious expression begin to waver when the vicar promptly launched into a recitation of his tribulations as Ian's uncle: "You cannot imagine how trying it used to be when I was forced to console weeping young ladies who'd cast out lures in hopes Ian would come up to scratch," he told Elizabeth. "And that's nothing to how I felt when he raced his horse and one of my parishioners thought *I* would be the ideal person to keep track of the bets!" Elizabeth's burst of laughter rang like music through the hills, and the vicar, ignoring Ian's look of annoyance, continued blithely, "I have flat knees from the hours, the weeks, the months I've spent praying for his immortal soul—"

"When you're finished itemizing my transgressions, Duncan," Ian cut in, "I'll introduce you to my companion."

Instead of being irate at Ian's tone, the vicar looked satisfied. "By all means, Ian," he said smoothly. "We should always observe *all* the proprieties." At that moment Elizabeth realized with a jolt that the shaming tirade she'd expected the vicar to deliver when he first saw them had been delivered after all—skillfully and subtly. The only difference was that the kindly vicar had aimed it solely at Ian, absolving her from blame and sparing her any further humiliation.

Ian evidently realized it, too; reaching out to shake his uncle's hand, he said dryly, "You're looking well, Duncan— despite your flattened knees. And," he added, "I can assure you that your sermons are equally eloquent whether I'm standing up or sitting down."

"That is because you have a lamentable tendency to doze off in the middle of them either way," the vicar replied a little irritably, shaking Ian's hand.

Ian turned to introduce Elizabeth. "May I present Lady Elizabeth Cameron, my house guest."

Elizabeth thought *that* explanation sounded more damning than being seen kissing Ian, and she hastily shook her head. "Not exactly. I'm something of a—a—" Her mind went blank, and the vicar again came to her rescue.

"A stranded traveler," he provided. Smiling, he took her hand in his. "I understand perfectly—I've had the pleasure of meeting your Miss Throckmorton-Jones, and she is the one who dispatched me here posthaste, as I said. I promised to remain until tomorrow or the next day, when she can return."

"Tomorrow or the day after? But they were to return today."

"There's been an unfortunate accident—a *minor* one," he hastened to assure. "That evil-tempered horse she was riding has a tendency to kick, Jake tells me."

"Was Lucinda badly hurt?" Elizabeth asked, already trying to think of a way to go to her.

"The horse kicked Mr. Wiley," the vicar corrected, "and the only thing that was hurt was Mr. Wiley's pride and his . . . ah . . . nether region. However, Miss Throckmorton-Jones, rightly feeling that some form of discipline was due the horse, retaliated with the only means at her disposal, since she said her umbrella was unfortunately on the ground. She kicked the horse," he explained, "which unfortunately resulted in a severely sprained ankle for that worthy lady. She's been given laudanum, and my housekeeper is tending her injury. She should be well enough to put her foot in a stirrup in a day or two at the most."

Turning to Ian, he said, "I'm fully aware I've taken you by surprise, Ian. However, if you mean to retaliate by depriving me of a glass of your excellent Madeira, I may decide to remain here for months, rather than until Miss Throckmorton-Jones returns."

"I'll go ahead and . . . and get the glasses down," Elizabeth said, politely trying to leave them some privacy. As Elizabeth turned toward the house she heard Ian say, "If you're hoping for a good meal, you've come to the wrong place. Miss Cameron has already attempted to sacrifice herself on the altar of domesticity this morning, and we both narrowly escaped death from her efforts. I'm cooking supper," he finished, "and it may not be much better."

"I'll try my hand at breakfast," the vicar volunteered good-naturedly.

When Elizabeth was out of earshot, Ian said quietly, "How badly is the woman hurt?"

"It's hard to say, considering that she was almost too angry to be coherent. Or it might have been the laudanum that did it."

"Did what?"

The vicar paused a moment to watch a bird hop about in the rustling leaves overhead, then he said, "She was in a rare state. Quite confused. Angry, too. On the one hand, she was afraid you might decide to express your 'tender regard' for Lady Cameron, undoubtedly in much the way you were doing it when I arrived." When his gibe evoked nothing but a quirked eyebrow from his imperturbable nephew, Duncan sighed and continued, "At the same time, she was equally convinced that her young lady might try to shoot you with your own gun, which I distinctly understood her to say the young lady had *already* tried to do. It is that which I feared when I heard the gunshots that sent me galloping up here."

"We were shooting at targets."

The vicar nodded, but he was studying Ian with an intent frown.

"Is something else bothering you?" Ian asked, noting the look.

The vicar hesitated, then shook his head slightly, as if trying to dismiss something from his mind. "Miss Throckmorton-Jones had more to say, but I can scarcely credit it."

"No doubt it was the laudanum," Ian said, dismissing the matter with a shrug.

"Perhaps," he said, his frown returning. "Yet *I* have not taken laudanum, and *I* was under the impression you are about to betroth yourself to a young woman named Christina Taylor."

"I am."

His face turned censorious. "Then what excuse can you have for the scene I just witnessed a few minutes ago?"

Ian's voice was clipped. "Insanity."

They walked back to the house, the vicar silent and thoughtful, Ian grim. Duncan's untimely arrival had not bothered him, but now that his passion had finally cooled he was irritated as hell with his body's uncontrollable reaction to Elizabeth Cameron. The moment his mouth touched hers it was as if his brain went dead. Even though he knew exactly what she was, in his arms she became an alluring angel. Those tears she'd shed today were because she'd been tricked by a friend. Yet two years ago she'd virtually cuckolded poor Mondevale without a qualm. Today she had calmly talked about wedding old Belhaven or John Marchman and within the same hour had pressed her eager little body against Ian's, kissing him with desperate ardor. Disgust replaced his anger. She ought to marry Belhaven, he decided with grim humor. The old letch was perfect for her; they were a matched pair in everything but their ages. Marchman, on the other hand, deserved much better than Elizabeth's indiscriminate, well-used little body. She'd make his life a living hell.

Despite that angelic face of hers, Elizabeth Cameron was still what she had always been: a spoiled brat, a skillful flirt with more passion than sense.

With a glass of Scotch in his hand and the stars twinkling in the inky sky, Ian watched the fish cooking on the little fire he'd built. The quiet of the night, combined with his drink, had soothed him. Now, as he watched the cheery little fire, his only regret was that Elizabeth's arrival had deprived him of the badly needed peace and quiet he'd been seeking when he came here. He'd been working at a killing pace for almost a year, and he'd counted on finding the same peace he always found here whenever he returned.

Growing up, he'd known all along that he would leave this place, that he would make his own way in the world, and he'd succeeded. Yet he always came back here, looking for something he still hadn't found, some elusive thing to cure his restlessness. Now he led a life of power and wealth, a life that suited him in most ways. He'd gone too far, seen too much, changed too much to try to live here. He'd accepted that when he decided to marry Christina. She would never like this place, but she would preside over all his other homes with grace and poise.

She was beautiful, sophisticated, and passionate. She suited him perfectly, or he wouldn't have offered for her. Before doing so, he'd considered it with the same combination of dispassionate logic and unfailing instinct that marked all his business decisions—he'd calculated the odds for success, made his decision swiftly, and then acted. In fact, the only rash, ill-advised thing of any import he'd done in recent years was his behavior the weekend he'd met Elizabeth Cameron.

"It was poor-spirited of you in the extreme," Elizabeth smilingly informed him after dinner as she cleared away the dishes, "to make me cook this morning, when you are so very good at it."

"Not really," Ian said mildly as he poured brandy into two glasses and carried them over to the chairs by the fire. "The only thing I know how to cook is fish—exactly the way we just ate it." He handed one to Duncan, then he sat down and lifted the lid off a box on the table beside him, removing one of the thin cheroots that were made especially for him by a London tobacconist. He looked at Elizabeth and, with automatic courtesy, asked, "Do you mind?"

Elizabeth glanced at the cigar, smiled, and started to shake her head, then she stopped, assailed by a memory of him standing in a garden nearly two years ago. He'd been about to light one of those cheroots when he saw her standing there, watching him. She remembered it so clearly, she could still see the golden flame illuminating his chiseled features as he cupped his hands around it, lighting the cigar. Her smile wobbled a little with the piercing memory, and she lifted her eyes from the unlit cigar to Ian's face, wondering if he remembered it, too.

His eyes met hers in polite inquiry, flicked to the unlit cigar, and moved back to her face. He did not remember; she could see that he didn't. "No, I don't mind at all," she said, hiding her disappointment behind a smile.

The vicar, who had observed the exchange and noticed Elizabeth's overbright smile, found the incident as puzzling as Ian's treatment of Elizabeth during the meal. He lifted his brandy to his lips, surreptitiously watching Elizabeth, then he glanced at Ian, who was lighting his cigar.

It was Ian's attitude that struck Duncan as extremely odd. Women routinely found Ian almost irresistibly attractive, and as the vicar well knew, Ian had never felt morally compelled to decline what was freely and flagrantly offered to him. In the past, however, Ian had always treated the women who fell into his arms with a combination of amused tolerance and relaxed indulgence. To his credit, even after he lost interest in the female, he continued to treat her with unfailing charm and courtesy, regardless of whether she was a village maid or an earl's daughter.

Given all that, Duncan found it understandably surprising, even suspect, that two hours ago Ian had been holding Elizabeth Cameron in his arms as if he never intended to let her go, and now he was ignoring her. True, there'd been nothing to criticize about the *way* he was doing it, but ignoring her he was.

He continued to study Ian, half expecting to see him steal a glance at Elizabeth, but his nephew had picked up a book and was reading it as if he'd dismissed Elizabeth Cameron completely from his mind. After casting about for a conversational gambit, the vicar said to Ian, "Things have gone well for you this year, I gather?"

Glancing up, Ian said with a brief smile, "Not quite as well as I expected, but well enough."

"Your gambles didn't entirely pay off?"

"Not all of them."

Elizabeth stilled a moment, then picked up a towel and began to dry a plate, helpless to ignore what she'd heard. Two years ago Ian had told her that if things went well for him he'd be able to provide for her. Evidently they hadn't, which would explain why he lived here. Her heart filled with sympathy for what she imagined had been his grand dreams that had not come to fruition. On the other hand, he was not nearly so bad off as he might believe, she decided, thinking of the wild beauty of the hills all around and the coziness of the cottage, with its large windows overlooking the valley.

It was not Havenhurst by any stretch of the imagination, but it had an untamed splendor of its own. Furthermore, it did not cost a fortune in upkeep and servants, as

Havenhurst did, which was vastly to its credit. She did not own Havenhurst, not really; *it* owned *her*. This beautiful little cottage, with its quaint thatched roof and few spacious rooms, was rather wonderful in that regard. It gave shelter and warmth without requiring whoever lived here to lie awake at night, worrying about mortar coming loose from its stones and the cost of repairing its eleven chimneys.

Obviously Ian didn't realize how truly lucky he was, or he wouldn't waste his time in gentlemen's clubs or wherever he gambled in hopes of making his fortune. He'd stay here, in this rugged, beautiful place where he looked so completely at ease, where he belonged. . . . So intent was she on her thoughts that it did not occur to her that she was close to wishing *she* lived here.

When everything was dried and put away, Elizabeth decided to go upstairs. At supper she'd learned that Ian hadn't seen his uncle in a long while, and she felt the proper thing to do was leave them alone so they might talk privately.

Hanging the towel on a peg, she untied her makeshift apron and went to bid the men good night. The vicar smiled and wished her pleasant dreams. Ian glanced up and said a preoccupied "Good night."

After Elizabeth went upstairs, Duncan watched his nephew reading, remembering the lessons in the vicarage that he'd given Ian as a boy. Like Ian's father, Duncan was intelligent and university-educated, yet by the time Ian was thirteen he'd already read and absorbed all their university textbooks and was looking for more answers. His thirst for knowledge was unquenchable; his mind was so brilliant that Duncan and Ian's father had both been more than a little awed. Without requiring quill and parchment, Ian could calculate complicated mathematical probabilities and equations in his head, producing the answer before Duncan had decided how to go about finding it.

Among other things, that rare mathematical ability had enabled Ian to amass a fortune gaming; he could calculate the odds for or against a particular hand or a spin of the roulette wheel with frightening accuracy—something the vicar had long ago decried as a misuse of his God-given genius, to absolutely no avail. Ian had the calm arrogance of his noble British forebears, the hot temper and the proud intractability of his Scots ancestors; and the combination had produced a brilliant man who made his own decisions and who never permitted anyone to sway him when his mind was made up. And why would he, the vicar thought with an unhappy premonition of doom as he contemplated the topic he needed to discuss with his nephew. Ian's judgment in most things was as close to infallible as was human, and he relied on it, rather than on the opinions of anyone else.

Only in one area was his judgment clouded, in Duncan's opinion, and that was when it came to the matter of his English grandfather. The mere mention of the Duke of Stanhope made Ian furious, and while Duncan wanted to discuss the ancient topic once again, he was hesitant to broach the sore subject. Despite the deep affection and respect Ian had for Duncan, Duncan knew his nephew had an almost frightening ability to turn his back irrevocably on anyone who went too far or anything that hurt him too deeply.

A memory of the day Ian returned home at the age of nineteen from his first voyage made the vicar frown with remembered helplessness and pain. Ian's parents and sister, in an excess of eagerness to see him, had journeyed to Hernloch to meet his ship, thinking to surprise him.

Two nights before Ian's ship put into port, the little inn where the happy family had slept burned to the ground, and all three of them had died in the fire. Ian had ridden past the charred rubble on his way here, never knowing that the place he passed was his family's funeral pyre.

He'd arrived at the cottage, where Duncan was waiting to break the wrenching news to him. "Where is everyone?" he demanded, grinning and slinging his duffel to the floor, walking swiftly around the cottage, looking into its empty rooms. Ian's Labrador had been the only one to greet him, racing into the cottage, barking ecstatically, skidding to a stop at Ian's booted feet. Shadow—who'd been named not for her black color, but for her utter devotion to her master, whom she'd worshipped from puppyhood—had been delirious with joy at his return. "I missed you, too, girl," Ian had said, crouching down and ruffling her sleek black fur. "I brought you a present," he'd told her, and she'd instantly stopped rubbing against him and cocked her head to the side, listening and waiting, her intelligent eyes riveted on his face. It had always been that way between them, that odd, almost uncanny communication between the human and the intelligent dog that worshipped him.

"Ian," the vicar had said somberly, and as if he heard the anguish in the single word, Ian's hand had stilled. He'd straightened slowly and turned, his dog coming to heel beside him, looking at Duncan with the same sudden tension that was in her master's face.

As gently as he could, Duncan broke the news to Ian of his family's death, and despite the fact that Duncan was well-schooled in soothing the bereaved, he'd never before encountered the sort of pent-up, rigidly controlled grief that Ian displayed, and he was at a loss how to deal with it. Ian had not wept or raged; his whole face and body had gone stiff, bracing against unbearable anguish, rejecting it because he sensed it could destroy him. That night, when Duncan finally left, Ian had been standing at the window, staring out into the darkness, his dog beside him. "Take her with you to the village and give her to someone," he'd said to Duncan in a voice as final as death.

Confused, Duncan had halted with his hand on the door handle. "Take who with me?"

"The dog."

"But you said you intended to stay here for at least a half year to get things in order."

"Take her with you," Ian had clipped out. In that moment Duncan had understood what Ian was doing, and he'd feared it. "Ian, for the love of God, that dog worships you. Besides, she'll be company for you up here."

"Give her to the MacMurtys in Calgorin," Ian snapped, and Duncan had reluctantly taken the unwilling dog with him. It had, in fact, taken a rope about the Labrador's neck to make her leave him.

The following week the intrepid Shadow had found her way across the county and reappeared at the cottage.

Duncan had been there and had felt a lump of emotion in his throat when Ian resolutely refused to acknowledge the bewildered dog's presence. The next day Ian himself had taken her back to Calgorin with Duncan. After Ian dined with the family, Shadow waited while Ian mounted his horse in the front yard, but when she'd started to follow him Ian had turned and harshly commanded her to stay.

Shadow had stayed because Shadow had never disobeyed a command of Ian's.

Duncan had remained for several hours, and when he left, Shadow was still sitting in the yard, her eyes riveted on the bend in the road, her head tipped to the side, waiting, as if she refused to believe Ian actually meant to leave her there.

But Ian had never returned for her. It was the first time that Duncan had realized Ian's mind was so powerful that it could completely override all his emotions when he wished. With calm logic Ian had irrevocably decided to separate himself from anything whose loss could cause him further anguish. Pictures of his parents and his sister had been carefully packed away, along with their belongings, into trunks, until all that remained of them was the cottage. And his memories.

Shortly after their death a letter from Ian's grandfather, the Duke of Stanhope, had arrived. Two decades after disowning his son for marrying Ian's mother, the Duke had written to him asking to make amends; his letter arrived three days after the fire. Ian had read it and thrown it away, as he had done with the dozens of letters that followed it during the last eleven years, all addressed to him. When wronged Ian was as unyielding, as unforgiving as the jagged hills and harsh moors that had spawned him.

He was also the most stubborn human being Duncan had ever known. As a boy Ian's calm confidence, his brilliant mind, and his intractability had all combined to give his parents pause. As Ian's father had once jokingly remarked of their gifted son, "Ian *permits* us to raise him because he loves us, not because he thinks we're smarter than he is. He already knows we aren't, but he doesn't want to wound our sensibilities by saying so."

Given all that, and considering Ian's ability to coldly turn away from anyone who had wronged him, Duncan had little hope of softening Ian's attitude toward his grandfather now—not when he couldn't appeal to either Ian's intellect or his affection in the matter. Not when the Duke of Stanhope meant far less to Ian than his Labrador had.

Lost in his own reflections, Duncan stared moodily into the fire, while across from him Ian laid aside his papers and watched him in speculative silence. Finally he said, "Since my cooking was no worse than usual, I assume there's another reason for that ferocious scowl of yours."

Duncan nodded, and with a considerable amount of foreboding he stood up and walked over to the fire, mentally phrasing his opening arguments. "Ian, your grandfather has written to me," the vicar began, watching Ian's pleasant smile vanish and his face harden into chiseled stone. "He has asked me to intercede on his behalf and to urge you to reconsider meeting with him."

"You're wasting your time," Ian said, his voice steely.

"He's your family," Duncan tried again.

"My entire family is sitting in this room," Ian bit out. "I acknowledge no other."

"You're his only living heir," Duncan persisted doggedly.

"That's his problem, not mine."

"He's dying, Ian."

"I don't believe it."

"I do believe him. Furthermore, if your mother were alive, she would beg you to reconcile with him. It crushed her all her life that he disowned your father for marrying her. I shouldn't have to remind you that your mother was my only sister. I loved her, and if I can forgive the man for the hurt he dealt her by his actions, I don't see why you can't."

"You're in the business of forgiveness," Ian drawled with scathing sarcasm. "I'm not. I believe in an eye for an eye."

"He's dying, I tell you."

"And I tell *you*"—Ian enunciated each word with biting clarity—"I do not give a damn!"

"If you won't consider accepting the title for yourself, do it for your father. It was *his* by right, just as it is your future son's birthright. This is your last opportunity to relent, Ian.

Your grandfather allowed me a fortnight to sway you before he named another heir. Your arrival here was delayed for a full fortnight. It may be too late already—"

"It was too late eleven years ago," Ian replied with glacial calm, and then, while the vicar watched, Ian's expression underwent an abrupt and startling transformation. The rigidity left his jaw, and he began sliding papers back into their case. That finished, he glanced at Duncan and said with quiet amusement, "Your glass is empty, Vicar. Would you like another?"

Duncan sighed and shook his head. It was over, exactly as Duncan had anticipated and feared: Ian had mentally slammed the door on his grandfather, and nothing would ever change his mind. When he turned calm and pleasant like this, Duncan knew from experience, Ian was irrevocably beyond reach. Since he'd already ruined his first night with his nephew, Duncan decided there was nothing to be lost by broaching another sensitive subject that was bothering him. "Ian, about Elizabeth Cameron. Her duenna said some things—"

That alarmingly pleasant yet distant smile returned to Ian's face. "I'll spare you further conversation, Duncan. It's over."

"The discussion or—"

"*All* of it."

"It didn't look over to me!" Duncan snapped, nudged to the edge by Ian's infuriating calm. "That scene I witnessed—"

"You witnessed the end."

He said that, Duncan noted, with the same deadly finality, the same amused calm with which he'd spoken of his grandfather. It was as if he'd resolved matters to his complete satisfaction in his own mind, and nothing and no one could ever invade the place where he put them to rest. Based on Ian's last reaction to the matter of Elizabeth Cameron, she was now relegated to the same category as the Duke of Stanhope. Frustrated, Duncan jerked the bottle of brandy off the table at Ian's elbow and splashed some into his glass. "There's something I've never told you," he said angrily.

"And that is?" Ian inquired.

"I *hate* it when you turn all pleasant and amused. I'd rather see you furious! At least then I know I still have a chance of reaching you."

To Duncan's boundless annoyance, Ian merely picked up his book and started reading again.

15

"Ian, would you go out to the barn and see what's keeping Elizabeth?" the vicar asked as he expertly turned a piece of bacon frying in the skillet. "I sent her out there fifteen minutes ago to bring in some eggs."

Ian dumped an armload of wood beside the fireplace, dusted off his hands, and went searching for his house guest. The sight and sounds that greeted him when he reached the door of the barn halted him in his tracks. With her hands plunked upon her hips Elizabeth was glowering at the roosting hens, who were flapping and cackling furiously at her. "It's not my fault!" she was exclaiming. "I don't even *like* eggs. In fact, I don't even like the *smell* of chickens." As she spoke she started stealthily forward on tiptoe, her voice pleading and apologetic. "Now, if you'll just let me have four, I won't even eat any. Look," she added, reaching forward toward the flapping hen, "I won't disturb you for more than just one moment. I'll just slide my hand right in there—ouch!" she cried as the hen pecked furiously at her wrist.

Elizabeth jerked her hand free, then swung around in mortification at Ian's mocking voice: "You don't really need her permission, you know," he said, walking forward. "Just show her who's master by walking right up there like this. . . ."

. And without further ado he stole two eggs from beneath the hen, who did not so much as *try* to attack him; then he did the same thing beneath two more hens. "Haven't you ever been in a henhouse before?" Ian asked, noting with detached impartiality that Elizabeth Cameron looked adorable with her hair mussed and her face flushed with ire.

"No," she said shortly. "I haven't. Chickens stink."

He chuckled. "That's it, then. They sense how you feel about them—animals do, you know."

Elizabeth slid him a swift, searching glance while an uneasy, inexplicable feeling of change hit her. He was smiling at her, even joking, but his eyes were blank. In the times they'd been together she'd seen passion in those golden eyes, and anger, and even coldness. But she'd never seen *nothing*.

She wasn't at all certain anymore how she wanted him to feel, but she was quite certain she didn't like being looked at like an amusing stranger.

"Thank heaven!" said the vicar when they walked into the house. "Unless you like your bacon burned, you'd better sit down at the table while I fix these."

"Elizabeth and I *prefer* burned bacon," Ian said drolly.

Elizabeth returned his lazy smile, but her unease was growing.

"Do you perchance play cards?" the vicar asked her when breakfast was nearly over.

"I'm familiar with some card games," she replied.

"In that case, when Miss Throckmorton-Jones and Jake return, perhaps we could get up a game of whist one evening. Ian," he added, "would you join us?"

Ian glanced around from pouring coffee at the stove and said with a mocking smile, "Not a chance." Transferring his gaze to Elizabeth, he explained, "Duncan cheats."

The absurd notion of a vicar cheating at cards wrung a musical laugh from Elizabeth. "I'm sure he doesn't do anything of the sort."

"Ian is quite right, my dear," the vicar admitted, grinning sheepishly. "However, I never cheat when I'm playing against another person. I cheat when I play against the deck—you know, Napoleon at St. Helena."

"Oh, that," Elizabeth said, laughing up at Ian as he walked past her carrying his mug. "So do I!"

"But you do play whist?"

She nodded. "Aaron taught me to play when I was twelve, but he still trounces me regularly."

"Aaron?" the vicar asked, smiling at her.

"Our coachman," Elizabeth explained, always happy to speak of her "family" at Havenhurst. "I'm better at chess, however, which Bentner taught me to play."

"And he is?"

"Our butler."

"I see," said the vicar, and something made him persevere. "Dominoes, by any chance?"

"That was Mrs. Bodley's specialty," Elizabeth told him with a smile. "Our housekeeper. We've played many times, but she takes it very seriously and has strategy. I can't seem to get much enthusiasm over flat pieces of ivory with dots on them. Chess pieces, you know, are more interesting. They invite serious play."

Ian finally added to the conversation. Sending his uncle an amused look, he explained, "Lady Cameron is a very wealthy young woman, Duncan, in case you haven't guessed." His tone implied that she was actually an overindulged, spoiled brat whose every wish had been fulfilled by an army of servants.

Elizabeth stiffened, not certain whether the insult she'd sensed had been intentional or even real, and the vicar looked steadily at Ian as if he disapproved of the tone of the comment, if not its content.

Ian returned his gaze dispassionately, but inwardly he was startled by his verbal thrust and genuinely annoyed with himself for making it. Last night he'd decided to no longer feel anything whatsoever for Elizabeth, and that decision was final. Therefore, it followed that it could make no difference to him that she was a pampered, shallow little aristocrat. Yet he'd deliberately baited her just now, when she'd done nothing whatsoever to deserve it other than sitting across the table looking almost outrageously alluring, with her hair tied at the nape with a bright yellow bow that matched her gown. So irritated with himself was he that Ian realized he'd lost the thread of their conversation.

"What sorts of games did you play with your brothers and sisters?" Duncan was asking her.

"I had only one brother, and he was away at school or off in London most of the time."

"I imagine there were other children in the neighborhood, however," the vicar suggested kindly.

She shook her head, sipping her tea. "There were only a few cottagers, and none of them had children my age. Havenhurst was never properly irrigated, you see. My father didn't think it was worth the expense, so most of our cottagers moved to more fertile ground."

"Then who were your companions?"

"The servants mostly," Elizabeth said. "We had grand times, however."

"And now?" he prompted. "What do you do for amusement there?"

He'd drawn her out so completely and so expertly that Elizabeth answered without choosing her words or considering what conclusions he might later draw. "I'm very busy most of the time just looking after the place."

"You sound as if you enjoy it," he said with a smile.

"I do," she replied. "Very much. In fact," she confided, "do you know the part I enjoy most?"

"I can't imagine."

"The bargaining that goes with purchasing our foodstuffs and supplies. It's the most amazing thing, but Bentner—our butler—says I have a genius for it."

"The bargaining?" Duncan repeated, nonplussed.

"I think of it as being reasonable and helping someone else to see reason," she said ingenuously, warming to her subject. "For example, if the village baker were to make one single tart, it would take him, shall we say, an hour. Now, of that hour, half of his time would be used in getting out all his supplies and measuring everything out, and then putting everything away again."

The vicar nodded his tentative agreement, and Elizabeth continued. "However, if he were to make *twelve* tarts, it would not take him twelve times as long, would it—since he would put out all his supplies and measure everything only once?"

"No, it wouldn't take him nearly so long."

"Exactly my thinking!" Elizabeth said happily. "And so why should I be required to pay twelve times more for twelve tarts if it didn't take him twelve times longer to prepare them? And that's before one considers that by making things in great quantity, one buys one's supplies in quantity, and thus pays less for the single part. At least one *should* pay less," she finished, "if the other person is *reasonable.*"

"That's amazing," the vicar stated honestly. "I never thought of it that way."

"Neither, unfortunately, has the village baker," Elizabeth chuckled. "I do think he's coming around, though. He's stopped hiding behind his flour bags when I come in." Belatedly, Elizabeth realized how revealing her commentary might be to an astute man like the vicar, and she quickly added, "Actually, it's not the cost. Not really. It's the *principle,* you understand?"

"Of course," Duncan said smoothly. "Your home must be a lovely place. You smile whenever you mention it."

"It is," Elizabeth said, her fond smile widening to encompass both the vicar and Ian. "It's a wondrous place, and wherever you look there is something beautiful to see. There are hills and a lovely parkland and extravagant gardens," she explained as Ian picked up his plate and mug and stood up.

"How large a place is it?" inquired the vicar sociably.

"There are forty-one rooms," she began.

"And I'll wager that all of them," Ian put in smoothly as he put his plate and mug near the dishpan, "are carpeted with furs and filled with jewels the size of your palm." He stopped cold, glowering at his reflection in the window.

"Of course," Elizabeth replied with artificial gaiety, staring at Ian's rigid back, refusing to retreat from his unprovoked attack. "There are paintings by Rubens and Gainsborough, and chimneys by Adams. Carpets from Persia, too." That *had* been true, she told herself when her conscience pricked her for the lies, until she'd had to sell everything last year to pay her creditors.

To her complete bafflement, instead of continuing his attack, Ian Thornton turned around and met her stormy eyes, an odd expression on his handsome face. "I apologize, Elizabeth," he said grimly. "My remarks were uncalled for." And on that amazing note he strode off, saying that he intended to spend the day hunting.

Elizabeth tore her startled gaze from his departing back, but the vicar continued staring after him for several long moments. Then he turned and looked at Elizabeth. An odd, thoughtful smile slowly dawned across his face and lit his brown eyes as he continued gazing at her. "Is—is something amiss?" she asked.

His smile widened, and he leaned back in his chair, beaming thoughtfully at her. "Apparently there is," he answered, looking positively delighted. "And I, for one, am vastly pleased."

Elizabeth was beginning to wonder if a tiny streak of insanity ran in the family, and only good manners prevented her from remarking on it. Instead she stood up and began clearing the dishes.

When the dishes were washed and put away, she ignored the vicar's protest and went to work tidying the lower floor of the cottage and polishing the furniture. She stopped to have dinner with him and finished her house-keeping tasks in midafternoon. Her spirits buoyed up with a sense of grand accomplishment, she stood in the center of the cottage, admiring the results of her efforts.

"You've wrought wonders," he told her. "Now that you're finished, however, I *insist* you enjoy what's left of the fine day." Elizabeth would have loved a hot bath, but since that was impossible under the circumstances, she accepted his suggestion as her second choice and did just that. Outdoors the sky was bright blue, the air soft and balmy, and Elizabeth looked longingly at the stream below. As soon as Ian came home she'd go down there and bathe in the stream—her very first time to bathe anywhere but in the privacy of her own chamber. For the present, though, she'd have to wait, since she couldn't risk having him come upon her while she bathed.

She wandered about the yard, enjoying the view, but the

day seemed oddly flat with Ian gone. Whenever he was around the air seemed to vibrate with his presence, and her emotions fluctuated crazily. Cleaning his house this morning, which she'd decided to do out of a mixture of boredom and gratitude, had become an almost intimate act.

Standing at the edge of the ridge, she wrapped her arms around herself, gazing into the distance, seeing his ruggedly handsome face and amber eyes, remembering the tenderness in his deep voice and the way he had held her yesterday. She wondered what it would be like to be married, and to have a cozy home like this one that overlooked such breathtaking scenery. She wondered what sort of female Ian would bring here as his wife and imagined the two of them sitting side by side on the sofa near the fire, talking and dreaming together.

Mentally, Elizabeth gave herself a hard shake. She was thinking like—like a madwoman! It was herself she'd just imagined sitting on that sofa beside him. Shoving such outrageous ruminations aside, she looked about for something to occupy her time and her mind. She turned in a complete, aimless circle, glanced up at a rustling in the tree overhead . . . and then she saw it! A large tree house was almost completely concealed from view by the ancient branches of the huge tree. Her eyes alight with fascination, she gazed up at the tree house, then she called to the vicar, who'd stepped outside. "It's a tree house," she explained, in case he didn't know what was up there. "Do you think it would be all right if I have a look? I imagine the view from up there must be spectacular."

The vicar crossed the yard and studied the haphazard "steps," which were flat old boards nailed to the huge tree. "It might not be safe to step on those boards."

"Don't worry about that," Elizabeth said cheerfully. "Elbert always said I was half monkey."

"Who is Elbert?"

"One of our grooms," she explained. "He and two of our carpenters built a tree house for me at home."

The vicar looked at her shining face and could not deny her such a small pleasure. "I suppose it's all right, if you promise you'll take care."

"Oh, I will. I promise."

He watched her kick off her slippers. For several minutes she circled the tree, and then she vanished to the far side where there were no steps. To Duncan's shock, he saw a flash of jonquil skirts and realized she was climbing the tree without aid of the old boards. He started to call out a warning to her, then realized it wasn't necessary—with carefree abandon she'd already gained the middle branches and was edging her way along toward the tree house.

Elizabeth reached the floor of the tree house and bent over to get inside. Once through the door, however, the ceiling was high enough for her to stand without stooping—which made her think Ian Thornton must have been tall even in his youth. She glanced around with interest at the old table, chair, and large, flat wooden box that were the only items in the tree house. Dusting off her hands, she looked through the window in the side of the tree house and breathed in the splendor of the valley and hills, decked out in bright hawthorn, cherry, and bluebells, then she turned back to inspect the little room. Her gaze slid to the white-painted box, and she reached down to brush the grime and dust off the lid. Etched across the top were the words "Private property of Ian Thornton. Open at your own peril!" As if the young boy had felt that written warning was insufficient, he'd etched a gruesome skull and crossbones below the words.

Elizabeth stared at it, remembering her tree house at home, where she'd held lavish and lonely tea parties with her dolls. She'd had her own "treasure chest," too, although she hadn't needed to put a skull and crossbones across it. A smile touched her lips as she tried to remember exactly what treasures she'd kept in that large chest with the shiny brass hinges and latches . . . a necklace, she remembered, given to her by her father when she was six . . . and the miniature porcelain tea set her parents had given her for her dolls when she was seven . . . and ribbons for her dolls' hair.

Her gaze was drawn again to the battered box on the table while she accepted the evidence that the virile, indomitable male she knew had actually been a youth who had secret treasures and perhaps played make-believe as she had done. Against her will and the dictates of her conscience Elizabeth put her hand on the latch. The box would probably be empty, she told herself, so it wasn't really snooping. . . .

She raised the lid, then stared in smiling bafflement at the contents. On top was a bright green feather—from a parrot, she thought. There were three ordinary-looking gray stones, that, for some reason, must have been special to the boy Ian had been, because they'd been painstakingly polished and smoothed. Beside the stones was a large seashell with a smooth pink interior. Recalling the seashell her parents had once brought her, Elizabeth lifted the shell and held it to her ear, listening to the muted roaring of the sea; then she carefully laid it aside and picked up the drawing pencils strewn across the bottom of the box. Beneath them was something that looked like a small sketchbook. Elizabeth picked up the pad and lifted the cover. Her eyes widened with admiration as she beheld a skillfully executed pencil sketch of a beautiful young girl with long hair blowing in the wind, the sea in the background. She was seated on the sand, her legs curled beneath her, her head bent as she examined a large seashell that looked exactly like the shell in the box. The next sketch was of the same girl, looking sideways at the artist, smiling as if they shared some funny secret. Elizabeth was awed by the zest and sparkle Ian had captured with a pencil, as well as the detail. Even the locket the girl wore around her neck was finely drawn.

There were other sketches, not only of the same girl, but of a couple Elizabeth presumed to be his parents, and more sketches of ships and mountains and even a dog. A Labrador retriever, Elizabeth knew at a glance, and she found herself smiling again at the dog. Its ears were forward, its head cocked to one side, its eyes bright—as if it were just waiting for the chance to run at its master's feet.

So dumbfounded was she by the sensitivity and skill evidenced by the sketches that she stood stock still, trying to assimilate this unexpected facet of Ian. It was several minutes before she snapped out of her reverie and considered the only other object in the box—a small leather bag. Regardless of what the vicar had said when he gave her permission to explore to her heart's content, she already felt like a trespasser into Ian's private life, and she knew she shouldn't compound that transgression now by opening the bag. On the other hand, the compulsion to learn more about the enigmatic man who'd turned her life upside down from the moment she'd set eyes on him long ago was so strong it couldn't be denied. Loosening the string on the leather bag, she turned it over, and a heavy ring dropped into her hand. Elizabeth studied it, not quite able to believe what she was seeing: In the center of the massive gold ring an enormous square-cut emerald glowed and winked, and embedded in the emerald itself was an intricate gold crest depicting a rampant lion. She was no expert on jewels, but she had little doubt that a ring of such splendid craftsmanship was real—and worth a ransom in value. She studied the crest, trying to match it up with the pictures of crests she'd been required to memorize before making her debut, but though it seemed vaguely familiar, she could not positively identify it. Deciding the crest was probably more ornamental than real, Elizabeth slid the ring back into the leather bag, pulled the drawstring tight, and made up her mind: Apparently Ian had placed no more value on it than he did on three stones and a seashell when he was a youth, but she knew better, and she felt certain that if he saw it now he'd recognize its value and realize it had to be put somewhere for safekeeping. With an inward grimace she anticipated his anger when he realized she'd been snooping through his things, but even so she had to at least bring it to his attention. She'd bring the sketchbook, too, she decided. Those sketches were so beautifully executed they deserved to be framed, not left outdoors to eventually crumble.

Closing the box, Elizabeth put it back beside the wall where she'd found it, smiling at the skull and crossbones. Without her realizing what had happened, her heart had softened yet more toward a boy who'd carried his dreams up here and hidden them in a treasure chest. And the fact that the boy had become a man who was frequently cold and distant had little effect on her tender heart. Untying the scarf from her hair, Elizabeth put it around her waist; then she slid the sketchbook between the makeshift belt and her gown and slid the ring onto her thumb, for want of anywhere else to keep it while she climbed down.

Ian, who'd been coming toward the yard from the woods

to the west, had seen Elizabeth walk around the tree and vanish. Leaving the game he'd shot at the barn, he started for the house, then changed his direction and headed for the tree.

With his hands on his hips he stood beneath the tree, looking down the mossy slope that led to the stream, his forehead furrowed in a puzzled frown as he wondered how she'd scrambled down the incline fast enough to disappear. High overhead branches began to rustle and sway, and Ian glanced up. At first he saw nothing, and then what he did see made him doubt his vision. A long, shapely bare leg was poking out of the branches, toes feeling about for a sturdy branch on which to begin a descent. Another leg joined it, and the pair of them seemed to hang there, levitating.

Ian started to reach up for the hips to which the legs would surely be attached somewhere further up in the leaves, then he hesitated, since she seemed to be managing well enough on her own. "What in hell are you doing up there?" he demanded.

"Climbing down, of course," Elizabeth's voice said from among the leaves. Her right toes wiggled, reaching for the wooden step and finally touching it; then, as Ian looked on, still ready to catch her if she fell, she shimmied down the branch a bit more and got the toes of her left foot on the step.

Amazed by her daring, not to mention her agility, Ian was about to back away and let her finish decending unaided when the rotted step on which she stood gave way. "Help!" Elizabeth cried as she came plunging out of the tree into a pair of strong hands that caught her by the waist.

Her back to him, Elizabeth felt her body slide down Ian's hard chest, his flat stomach, and then his thighs. Embarrassed to the depths of her soul by her clumsy egress, by the boyhood treasures she'd discovered while snooping in the tree house, and by the odd feelings that shook through her at the intimate contact with him, Elizabeth drew a shaky breath and turned uneasily to face him. "I was snooping in your things," she confessed, lifting her green eyes to his. "I hope you won't be angry."

"Why should I be angry?"

"I saw your sketches," she admitted, and then, because her heart was still filled with the lingering tenderness of her discovery, she continued with smiling admiration, "They're wonderful, truly they are! You should never have taken up gambling. You should have been an artist!" She saw the confusion that narrowed his eyes, and in her eagerness to convince him of her sincerity she pulled the sketchbook from her "belt" and bent down, opening it carefully on the grass, smoothing the pages flat. "Just look at this!" she persisted, sitting down beside the sketches and smiling up at him.

After a moment's hesitation Ian crouched down beside her, his gaze on her entrancing smile, not the sketches.

"You aren't looking," she chided him gently, tapping the first sketch of the young girl with her tapered fingernail. "I can't believe how talented you are! You captured everything in the tiniest detail. Why, I can almost *feel* the wind blowing on her hair, and there's laughter in her eyes." His gaze shifted from her eyes to the open sketchbook, and Elizabeth watched in shock as he glanced at the sketch of the young girl and pain slashed across his tanned features.

Somehow Elizabeth knew from his expression that the girl was dead. "Who was she?" she asked softly. The pain she'd imagined vanished, and his features were already perfectly composed when he looked at her and quietly answered, "My sister." He hesitated, and for a moment Elizabeth thought he wasn't going to say more. When he did, his deep voice was strangely hesitant, almost as if he was testing his ability to talk about it: "She died in a fire when she was eleven."

"I'm sorry," Elizabeth whispered, and all the sympathy and warmth in her heart was mirrored in her eyes. "Truly sorry," she said, thinking of the beautiful girl with the laughing eyes. Reluctantly pulling her gaze from his, she tried lamely to lighten the mood by turning the page to a sketch that seemed to vibrate with life and exuberant joy. Seated on a large boulder by the sea was a man with his arm around a woman's shoulders; he was grinning at her up-turned face, and her hand was resting on his arm in a way that somehow bespoke a wealth of love. "Who are these people?" Elizabeth asked, smiling as she pointed to the sketch.

"My parents," Ian replied, but there was something in his voice again that made her look sharply at him. "The same fire," he added calmly.

Elizabeth turned her face away, feeling a lump of constricting sorrow in her chest.

"It happened a long time ago," he said after a moment, and reaching out slowly, he turned to the next sketch. A black Labrador looked back from the pages. This time when he spoke there was a slight smile in his voice. "If I could shoot it, she could find it."

Her own emotions under control again, Elizabeth looked at the sketch. "You have an amazing way of capturing the *essence* of things when you sketch, do you know that?"

His brows lifted in dubious amusement, then he reached out and turned the other pages, pausing when he came to a detailed sketch of a four-masted sailing ship. "I intended to build that one someday," he told her. "This is my own design."

"Really?" she said, looking as impressed as she felt.

"Really," he confirmed, grinning back at her. Their faces only inches apart, they smiled at each other; then Ian's gaze dropped to her mouth, and Elizabeth felt her heart begin to pound with helpless anticipation. His head bent imperceptibly, and Elizabeth knew, she *knew* he was going to kiss her; her hand lifted of its own accord, reaching toward his nape as if to draw him down to her; then the moment was abruptly shattered. Ian's head lifted sharply, and he stood up in one smooth motion, his jaw rigid. Stunned, Elizabeth hastily turned to the sketchbook and carefully closed it. Then she, too, stood up. "It's getting late," she said to cover her awkward confusion. "I'd like to bathe in the stream before the air turns chilly. Oh, wait," she said, and carefully she pulled the ring from her thumb, holding it out to him. "I found this in the same box where the sketches were," she added, putting it in his outstretched palm.

"My father gave it to me when I was a boy," he said in an

offhand voice. His long fingers closed around it, and he slipped it into his pocket.

"I think it may be very valuable," Elizabeth said, imagining the sorts of improvements he could make to his home and lands if he chose to sell the ring.

"As a matter of fact," Ian drawled blandly, "it's completely worthless."

16

To Elizabeth the meal they shared with the vicar that night was a period of mystified torment. Ian conversed with his uncle as if absolutely nothing of import had happened between them, while Elizabeth's mind tortured her with feelings she could neither understand nor vanquish. Every time Ian's amber gaze flickered to her, her heart began to pound. Whenever he wasn't looking she found her gaze straying to his mouth, remembering the way those lips had felt locked to hers yesterday. He raised a wineglass to his lips, and she looked at the long, strong fingers that had slid with such aching tenderness over her cheek and twined in her hair.

Two years ago she'd fallen under his spell; she was wiser now. She *knew* he was a libertine, and even so her heart rebelled against believing it. Yesterday, in his arms, she'd felt as if she was special to him—as if he not only wanted her close but needed her there.

Very vain, Elizabeth, she warned herself severely, and very foolish. Skilled libertines and accomplished flirts probably made every woman feel that she was special. No doubt they kissed a woman with demanding passion one moment and then, when the passion was over, forgot she was alive.

As she'd heard long ago, a libertine pretended violent interest in his quarry, then dropped her without compunction the instant that interest waned—exactly as Ian had done now. That was not a comforting thought, and Elizabeth was sorely in need of comfort as twilight deepened into night and supper dragged on, with Ian seemingly oblivious to her existence. Finally the meal was finished; she was about to volunteer to clear the table when she glanced at Ian and watched in paralyzed surprise as his gaze roved over her cheek and jaw, then shifted to her mouth, lingering there. Abruptly he looked away, and Elizabeth stood up to clear the table.

"I'll help," the vicar volunteered. "It's only fair, since you and Ian have done everything else."

"I won't hear of it," Elizabeth teased him, and for the fourth time in her entire life she tied a towel around her waist and washed dishes. Behind her the men remained at the table, talking about people Ian had evidently known for years. Although they'd both forgotten her presence, she felt strangely happy and content listening to them talk.

When she finished she draped the dishtowel on the handle of the door and wandered over to sit in a chair near the fireplace. From there she could see Ian clearly without being observed. With no one to write to but Alex, and little she could risk saying in a letter that might be seen by Ian, Elizabeth tried to concentrate on descriptions of Scotland and the cottage, but she wrote desultorily, her mind was on Ian, not the letter. In some ways it seemed wrong that he lived here now, in this solitary place. At least part of the time he ought to be walking into ballrooms and strolling into gardens in his superbly tailored black evening clothes, making feminine heartbeats triple. With a wan inner smile at her attempted impartiality, Elizabeth told herself men like Ian Thornton probably performed a great service to society—he gave them something to stare at and admire and even fear. Without men like him, ladies would have nothing to dream about. And much less to regret, she reminded herself.

Ian had not so much as turned to glance her way, and so it was little wonder that she jumped in surprise when he said without looking at her, "It's a lovely evening, Elizabeth. If you can spare the time from your letter, would you like to go for a walk?"

"Walk?" she repeated, stunned by the discovery that he was evidently as aware of what she was doing as she had been aware of him, sitting at the table. "It's dark out," she said mindlessly, searching his impassive features as he arose and walked over to her chair. He stood there, towering over her, and there was nothing about the expression on his handsome face to indicate he had any real desire to go anywhere with her. She cast a hesitant glance at the vicar, who seconded Ian's suggestion. "A walk is just the thing," Duncan said, standing up. "It aids the digestion, you know."

Elizabeth capitulated, smiling at the gray-haired man. "I'll just get a wrap from upstairs. Shall I bring something for you, sir?"

"Not for me," he said, wrinkling his nose. "I don't like tramping about at night." Belatedly realizing he was openly abdicating his duties as chaperon, Duncan added quickly, "Besides, my eyesight is not as good as it once was." Then he spoiled that excuse by picking up the book he'd been reading earlier, and—without any apparent need for spectacles—he sat down in a chair and began reading by the light of the candles.

The night air was chilly, and Elizabeth pulled her wool shawl tighter around her. Ian didn't speak as they walked slowly across the back of the house.

"It's a full moon," she said after several minutes, looking up at the huge yellow orb. When he didn't reply, she cast about for something else to say and inadvertently voiced her own thoughts: "I can't quite believe I'm really in Scotland."

"Neither can I." They were walking around the side of a hill, down a path he seemed to know by instinct, and behind them the lights from the cottage windows faded and then vanished completely.

Several silent minutes later they rounded the hill, and suddenly there was nothing in front of them but the darkness of a valley far below, the gentle slope of the hill behind them, a little clearing on their left, and a blanket of stars overhead. Ian stopped there and shoved his hands into his pockets, staring out across the valley. Uncertain of his mood, Elizabeth wandered a few paces to the end of the path on the left and stopped because there was nowhere else to go. It seemed colder here, and she absently pulled her shawl closer about her shoulders, stealing a surreptitious look at him. In the moonlight his profile was harsh, and he lifted his hand, rubbing the muscles in the back of his neck as if he was tense.

"I suppose we ought to go back," she said when several minutes had passed, and his silence became unsettling.

In answer Ian tipped his head back and closed his eyes, looking like a man in the throes of some deep, internal battle. "Why?" he said, still in that odd posture.

"Because there's nowhere else to walk," she answered, stating the obvious.

"We did not come out tonight to walk," he said flatly.

Elizabeth's sense of security began to disintegrate. "We didn't?"

"You know we didn't."

"Then—then why *are* we here?" she asked.

"Because we wanted to be alone together."

Horrified at the possibility that he'd somehow known what thoughts had been running through her mind at supper, she said uneasily, "Why should you think I want to be alone with you?"

He turned his head toward her, and his relentless gaze locked with hers. "Come here and I'll show you why."

Her entire body began to vibrate with a mixture of shock, desire, and fear, but somehow her mind remained in control. It was one thing to want to be kissed by him at the cottage where the vicar was nearby, but here, with absolute privacy and nothing to prevent him from taking all sorts of liberties, it was another matter entirely. Far more dangerous. More frightening. And based on her behavior in England, she couldn't even blame him for thinking she'd be willing now. Struggling desperately to ignore the sensual pull he was exerting on her, Elizabeth drew a long, shaky breath. "Mr. Thornton," she began quietly.

"My name is Ian," he interrupted. "Considering our long acquaintance—not to mention what has transpired between us—don't you think it's a little ridiculous to call me Mr. Thornton?"

Ignoring his tone, Elizabeth tried to keep hers nonjudgmental and continue her explanation. "I used to blame you entirely for what happened that weekend we were together," she began softly. "But I've come to see things more clearly." She paused in that valiant speech to swallow and then plunged in again. "The truth is that my actions that first night, when we met in the garden and I asked you to dance with me, were foolish—no, shameless." Elizabeth stopped, knowing that she could partly exonerate herself by explaining to him that she'd only done all that so her friends wouldn't lose their wagers, but he would undoubtedly find that degrading and insulting, and she wanted very much to soothe matters between them, not make them much, much worse. And so she said haltingly, "Every other time we were alone together after that I behaved like a shameless wanton. I can't completely blame you for thinking that's exactly what I was."

His voice was heavy with irony. "Is that what I thought, Elizabeth?"

His deep voice saying her name in the darkness made her senses jolt almost as much as the odd way he was looking at her across the distance that separated them. "Wh-what else *could* you have thought?"

Shoving his hands into his pockets, he turned fully toward her. "I thought," he gritted, "you were not only beautiful but intoxicatingly innocent. If I'd believed when we were standing in the garden that you realized what the hell you were asking for when you flirted with a man of my years and reputation, I'd have taken you up on your offer, and we'd both have missed the dancing."

Elizabeth gaped at him. "I don't believe you."

"What don't you believe—that I wanted to drag you behind the hedges then and there and make you melt in my arms? Or that I had scruples enough to ignore that ignoble impulse?"

A treacherous warmth was slowly beginning to seep up Elizabeth's arms and down her legs, and she fought the weakness with all her might. "Well, what happened to your scruples in the woodcutter's cottage? You *knew* I thought you'd already left when I went inside."

"Why did you stay," he countered smoothly, "when you realized I was still there?"

In confused distress Elizabeth raked her hair off her forehead. "I knew I shouldn't do it," she admitted. "I don't know why I remained."

"You stayed for the same reason I did," he informed her bluntly. "We wanted each other."

"It was wrong," she protested a little wildly. "Dangerous and—foolish!"

"Foolish or not," he said grimly, "I wanted you. I want you now." Elizabeth made the mistake of looking at him, and his amber eyes captured hers against her will, holding them imprisoned. The shawl she'd been clutching as if it was a lifeline to safety slid from her nerveless hand and dangled at her side, but Elizabeth didn't notice.

"Neither of us has anything to gain by continuing this pretense that the weekend in England is over and forgotten," he said bluntly. "Yesterday proved that it wasn't over, if it proved nothing else, and it's never been forgotten—I've remembered you all this time, and I know damn well you've remembered me."

Elizabeth wanted to deny it; she sensed that if she did, he'd be so disgusted with her deceit that he'd turn on his heel and leave her. She lifted her chin, unable to tear her gaze from his, but she was too affected by the things he'd just admitted to her to lie to him. "All right," she said shakily, "you win. I've never forgotten you or that weekend. How could I?" she added defensively.

He smiled at her angry retort, and his voice gentled to the timbre of rough velvet. "Come here, Elizabeth."

"Why?" she whispered shakily.

"So that we can finish what we began that weekend."

Elizabeth stared at him in paralyzed terror mixed with violent excitement and shook her head in a jerky refusal.

"I'll not force you," he said quietly, "nor will I force you to do anything you don't want to do once you're in my arms. Think carefully about that," he warned, "because if you come to me now, you won't be able to tell yourself in the morning that I made you do this against your will—or that

252

you didn't know what was going to happen. Yesterday neither of us knew what was going to happen. Now we do."

Some small, insidious voice in her mind urged her to obey, reminded her that after the public punishment she'd taken for the last time they were together she was entitled to some stolen passionate kisses, if she wanted them. Another voice warned her not to break the rules again. "I—I can't," she said in a soft cry.

"There are four steps separating us and a year and a half of wanting drawing us together," he said.

Elizabeth swallowed. "Couldn't you meet me halfway?"

The sweetness of the question was almost Ian's undoing, but he managed to shake his head. "Not this time. I want you, but I'll not have you looking at me like a monster in the morning. If you want me, all you have to do is walk into my arms."

"I don't know *what* I want," Elizabeth cried, looking a little wildly at the valley below, as if she were thinking of leaping off the path.

"Come here," he invited huskily, "and I'll show you."

It was his tone, not his words, that conquered her. As if drawn by a will stronger than her own, Elizabeth walked forward and straight into arms that closed around her with stunning force. "I didn't think you were going to do it," he whispered gruffly against her hair.

There was praise for her courage in his voice, and Elizabeth clung to that as she raised her head and looked up at him. His smoldering gaze dropped to her lips, riveting there, and Elizabeth felt her body ignite at the same instant his mouth swooped down, capturing hers in a kiss of demanding hunger. His hands bit into her back, molding her pliant body to the rigid contours of his, and Elizabeth fed his hunger. With a silent moan of desperation she slipped her hands up his chest, her fingers sliding into the soft hair at his nape, her body arching to his. A shudder shook his powerful frame as she fitted herself to him, and his lips crushed down on hers, parting them, his tongue driving into her mouth with hungry urgency, and their dormant passion exploded. Heedless of what he was doing, Ian forced her to give him back the sensual urgency he was offering her, driving his tongue into her mouth until Elizabeth began to match the pagan kiss. Lost in the heated magic, she touched her tongue to his lips and felt the gasp of his breath against her mouth, then she hesitated, not certain. . . . His mouth moved more urgently against hers. *"Yes,"* he whispered hoarsely, and when she did it again he groaned with pleasure.

Ian kissed her again and again until her nails were digging into his back and her breaths were coming in ragged gasps, mingling with his, and still he couldn't stop. The same uncontrollable compulsion to have her that had seized him two years ago had overtaken him again, and he kissed her until she was moaning and writhing in his arms and desire was pouring through him in hot tidal waves. Tearing his mouth from hers, he slid his lips across her cheek, his tongue seeking the inner crevice of her ear while his hand sought her breast. She jumped in dazed surprise at the intimate caress, and the innocent reaction wrung a choked laugh from him at the same time it sent a fresh surge of pure lust through him that almost sent him to his knees. Out of sheer self-preservation he forced his hands to stop the pleasurable torture of caressing her breasts, but his mouth sought hers again, sliding back and forth against her parted lips, but softer this time, gentling her. Gentling him . . . and then he started again.

An eternity later he lifted his head, his blood pounding in his ears, his heart thundering, his breathing labored. Elizabeth stayed in his arms, her hot cheek against his chest, her voluptuous body pressed to his, trembling in the aftermath of the most explosive, inexplicable passion Ian had ever experienced.

Until now he had managed to convince himself that his memory of the passion that erupted between them in England was faulty, exaggerated. But tonight had surpassed even his imaginings. It surpassed anything he'd ever felt. He stared into the darkness above her head, trying to ignore the way she felt in his arms.

Against her ear Elizabeth felt his heart slow to normal, his breathing even out, and the sounds of the night began penetrating her drugged senses. Wind rifled through the long grass, whispering in the trees; his hand stroked soothingly up and down her spine; tears of pure confusion stung her eyes, and she rubbed her cheek against his hard chest, brushing them away in what felt to Ian like a poignantly tender caress. Drawing a shattered breath, she tried to ask him why this was happening to her. "Why?" she whispered against his chest.

Ian heard the shattered sound in her voice, and he understood her question; it was the same one he'd been asking himself. Why did this explosion of passion happen every time he touched her; why could this one English girl make him lose his mind? "I don't know," he said, and his voice sounded curt and unnatural to his own ears. "Sometimes it just happens"—to the wrong people at the wrong time, he added silently. In England he'd been so blindly besotted that he'd brought up marriage twice in two days. He remembered her reply word for word. Moments after she'd melted in his arms and kissed him with desperate passion, exactly as she'd done tonight, he'd said,

"Your father will have some objections to our marriage, but once he understands that I'll be able to provide for you, the rest should suit him."

Elizabeth had leaned back in his arms and smiled with amusement. *"And what will you provide, sir? Will you promise me a ruby large enough to cover my palm, as Viscount Mondevale did? Sables to cover my shoulders as Lord Seabury did?"*

"Is that what you want?" he'd asked, unable to believe she was so mercenary that she'd decide whom to marry based on who gave her the most expensive jewels or the most lavish furs.

"Of course," she'd replied. *"Isn't that what all females want and all gentlemen promise?"*

You had to give her credit, Ian thought to himself, fighting down a surge of disgust—at least she was honest about what mattered to her. In retrospect, he rather admired her courage, if not her standards.

He glanced down at Elizabeth and saw her watching him, her apprehensive green eyes soft and deceptively innocent. "Don't worry," he said flippantly, taking her arm and starting to walk back toward the house. "I'm not going to make the ritualistic proposal that followed our last encounters. Marriage is out of the question. Among other things, I'm fresh out of large rubies and expensive furs this season."

Despite his joking tone, Elizabeth felt ill at how ugly those words sounded now, even though her reasons for saying them at the time had nothing to do with a desire for jewels or furs. You had to give him credit, she decided miserably, because he obviously took no offense at it. Evidently, in sophisticated flirtations, the rule was that no one took anything seriously.

"Who's the leading contender these days?" he asked in that same light tone as the cottage came into view. "There must be more than Belhaven and Marchman."

Elizabeth struggled valiantly to make the same transition from heated passion to flippancy that he seemed to find so easy. She wasn't quite so successful, however, and her light tone was threaded with confusion. "In my uncle's eyes, the leading contender is whoever has the most important title, followed by the most money."

"Of course," he said dryly. "In which case it sounds as if Marchman may be the lucky man."

His utter lack of caring made Elizabeth's heart squeeze in an awful, inexplicable way. Her chin lifted in self-defense. "Actually, I'm not in the market for a husband," she informed him, trying to sound as indifferent and as amused as he. "I may *have* to marry someone if I can't continue to outmaneuver my uncle, but I've come to the conclusion that I'd like to marry a much older man than I."

"Preferably a blind one," he said sardonically, "who'll not notice a little affair now and then?"

"I *meant,*" she informed him with a dark glance, "that I want my freedom. Independence. And that is something a young husband isn't likely to give me, while an elderly one might."

"Independence is *all* an old man will be able to give you," Ian said bluntly.

"That's quite enough," she said. "I'm excessively tired of being forever pushed about by the men in my life. I'd like to care for Havenhurst and do as I wish to do."

"Marry an old man," Ian interjected smoothly, "and you may be the *last* of the Camerons."

She looked at him blankly.

"He won't be able to give you children."

"Oh, that," Elizabeth said, feeling a little defeated and nonplussed. "I haven't been able to work that out yet."

"Let me know when you do," Ian replied with biting sarcasm, no longer able to find her either amusing or admirable. "There's a fortune to be made from a discovery like that one."

Elizabeth ignored him. She hadn't worked it out yet because she'd only made that outrageous decision after being held tenderly in Ian Thornton's arms one moment and then, for no comprehensible reason, treated at first like an amusing diversion and now as if she were contemptible. It was all too bewildering, too painful, too baffling. She'd had little enough experience with the opposite sex, and she was finding them a completely unpredictable, unreliable group. From her father to her brother to Viscount Mondevale, who'd wanted to marry her, to Ian Thornton, who didn't. The only one she could depend upon to act in the same reliable way was her uncle. He at least was unfailingly heartless and cold.

In her eagerness to escape to the privacy of her bedchamber, Elizabeth bade Ian a cool good night the instant she stepped over the threshold of the cottage, and then she walked past the high, wing-backed chair without ever noticing that the vicar was seated in it and watching her with an expression of bafflement and concern. "I trust you had a pleasant walk, Ian," he said when her door closed upstairs.

Ian stiffened slightly in the act of pouring some leftover coffee into a mug and glanced over his shoulder. One look at his uncle's expression told him that the older man was well aware that desire, not a need for fresh air, had caused Ian to take Elizabeth for a walk. "What do you think?" he asked irritably.

"I think you've upset her repeatedly and deliberately, which is not your ordinary behavior with women."

"There is nothing ordinary about Elizabeth Cameron."

"I completely agree," said the vicar with a smile in his voice. Closing his book, he put it aside. "I also think she is strongly attracted to you, and you are to her. That much is perfectly obvious."

257

"Then it should be equally obvious to a man of your discernment," Ian said in a low, implacable voice, "that we are completely ill-suited to each other. It's a moot issue in any case; I'm marrying someone else."

Duncan opened his mouth to comment on that, saw the expression on Ian's face, and gave up.

17

Ian left at first light the next morning to go hunting, and Duncan took advantage of his absence to try to glean from Elizabeth some answers to the problems that worried him. Repeatedly and without success he tried to question her about her original meeting with Ian in England, what sort of life she led there, and so on. By the time breakfast was over, however, he had received only the most offhand and superficial sort of replies—replies he sensed were designed to mislead him into believing her life was perfectly frivolous and very agreeable. Finally, she tried to divert him by asking about Ian's sketches.

In the hope that she would confide in him if she understood Ian better, Duncan went so far as to explain how Ian had dealt with his grief after his family's death and why he had banished the retriever. The ploy failed; although she exhibited sympathy and shock at the story, she was no more inclined to reveal anything about herself than she had been before.

For Elizabeth's part, she could scarcely wait for the meal to end so she could escape his steady gaze and probing questions. For all his kindness and Scots bluntness, he was also, she suspected, an extremely perceptive man who did not give up easily when he set his mind to get at the bottom of something. As soon as the dishes were put away she fled to her work in the garden, only to have him appear at her side a few minutes later, a worried expression on his face. "Your coachman is here," he said. "He's brought an urgent message from your uncle."

A feeling of dread swept through Elizabeth as she stood up, and she rushed into the house where Aaron was waiting.

"Aaron?" she said. "What's wrong? How on earth did you get the coach up here?"

In answer to the first question he handed her a folded message. In answer to the second he said gruffly, "Your uncle was so anxious to have you start home that he told us to rent whatever we needed, just so's we'd get you back posthaste. There's a pair o' horses out there for you and Miss Throckmorton-Jones, and a carriage down at the road we can use to get back to the inn where yer coach is waitin' to take ye home."

Elizabeth nodded absently, opened the message, and stared at it in dawning horror.

"Elizabeth," her uncle had written, "Come home at once. Belhaven has offered for you. There's no reason to waste time in Scotland. Belhaven would have been my choice over Thornton, as you know." Obviously anticipating that she would try some tactic to stall, he'd added, "If you return within a sennight, you may participate in the betrothal negotiations. Otherwise I shall proceed without you, which, as your guardian, I have every right to do."

Elizabeth crumpled the note in her hand, staring at her fist while her heart began to thud in helpless misery. A disturbance in the front yard beyond the open door of the cottage made her look up. Lucinda and Mr. Wiley were returning at last, and she ran to Lucinda, hastily stepping around the black horse, who laid his ears back evilly in warning. "Lucy!" she burst out while Lucinda waited calmly for Mr. Wiley to help her down. "Lucy! Disaster has struck."

"A moment, if you please, Elizabeth," said the unflappable woman. "Whatever it is, it will surely wait until we're inside and can be comfortable. I declare, I feel as if I were *born* atop this horse. You cannot imagine the time we had finding suitable servants. . . ."

Elizabeth scarcely heard the rest of what she was saying. In a torment of frantic helplessness she had to wait while Lucinda dismounted, limped into the house, and sat down upon the sofa. "Now then," said Lucinda, flicking a speck of dust off her skirts, "what has happened?"

Oblivious to the vicar, who was standing by the fireplace looking mystified and alarmed on her behalf, Elizabeth handed Lucinda the note. "Read this. It—it sounds as if he's already *accepted* him."

As she read the brief missive Lucinda's face turned an awful gray with two bright splotches of angry color standing out on her hollow cheeks. "He'd accept an offer from the devil," Lucinda gritted wrathfully, "so long as he had a noble title and money. This shouldn't come as a surprise."

"I was so certain I'd persuaded Belhaven that we couldn't possibly suit!" Elizabeth almost wailed, twisting her blue skirt in her hands in her agitation. "I did everything, Lucy, *everything* I told you about, and more." Agitation drove Elizabeth to her feet. "If we make haste, we can be home by the allotted time, and perhaps I can find a way to dissuade Uncle Julius."

Lucinda did not leap to her feet as Elizabeth did; she did not race for the stairs, dash into her room, and vent her helpless rage by slamming a door, as Elizabeth did. Her body rigid, Lucinda stood up very slowly and turned to the vicar. "Where is he?" she snapped.

"Ian?" the vicar said distractedly, alarmed by her pallid color. "He's gone hunting."

Deprived of her real prey, Lucinda unleashed her fury upon the hapless vicar instead. When she finished her tirade she hurled the crumpled note into the cold fireplace and said in a voice that shook with wrath, "When that spawn of Lucifer returns, you tell him that if he ever crosses my path, he'd better be wearing a suit of armor!" So saying, she marched upstairs.

It was dusk when Ian returned, and the house seemed unnaturally quiet. His uncle was sitting near the fire, watching him with an odd expression on his face that was half anger, half speculation. Against his will Ian glanced about the room, expecting to see Elizabeth's shiny golden hair and entrancing face. When he didn't, he put his gun back on the rack above the fireplace and casually asked, "Where is everyone?"

"If you mean Jake," the vicar said, angered yet more by the way Ian deliberately avoided asking about Elizabeth, "he took a bottle of ale with him to the stable and said he was planning to drink it until the last two days were washed from his memory."

"They're back, then?"

"Jake is back," the vicar corrected as Ian walked over to the table and poured some Madeira into a glass. "The servingwomen will arrive in the morn. Elizabeth and Miss Throckmorton-Jones are gone, however."

Thinking Duncan meant they'd gone for a walk, Ian flicked a glance toward the front door. "Where have they gone at this hour?"

"Back to England."

The glass in Ian's hand froze halfway to his lips. "Why?" he snapped.

"Because Miss Cameron's uncle has accepted an offer for her hand."

The vicar watched in angry satisfaction as Ian tossed down half the contents of his glass as if he wanted to wash away the bitterness of the news. When he spoke his voice was laced with cold sarcasm. "Who's the lucky bridegroom?"

"Sir Francis Belhaven, I believe."

Ian's lips twisted with excruciating distaste.

"You don't admire him, I gather?"

Ian shrugged. "Belhaven is an old lecher whose sexual tastes reportedly run to the bizarre. He's also three times her age."

"That's a pity," the vicar said, trying unsuccessfully to keep his voice blank as he leaned back in his chair and propped his long legs upon the footstool in front of him. "Because that beautiful, innocent child will have no choice but to wed the old . . . lecher. If she doesn't, her uncle will withdraw his financial support, and she'll lose that home she loves so much. He's perfectly satisfied with Belhaven, since he possesses the prerequisites of title and wealth, which I gather are his *only* prerequisites. That lovely girl will have to wed that old man; she has no way to avoid it."

"That's absurd," Ian snapped, draining his glass. "Elizabeth Cameron was considered the biggest success of her season two years ago. It was public knowledge she'd had more than a dozen offers. If that's all he cares about, he can choose from dozens of others."

Duncan's voice was laced with uncharacteristic sarcasm. "That was *before* she encountered you at some party or other. Since then it's been public knowledge that she's used goods."

"What the hell is that supposed to mean?"

"You tell me, Ian," the vicar bit out. "I only have the story in two parts from Miss Throckmorton-Jones. The first time she spoke she was under the influence of laudanum. Today she was under the influence of what I can only describe as the most formidable temper I've ever seen. However, while I may not have the complete story, I certainly have the gist of it, and if half what I've heard is true, then it's obvious that you are completely without either a heart or a conscience! My own heart breaks when I imagine Elizabeth enduring what she has for nearly two years. And when I think of how forgiving of you she has been—"

"What did the woman tell you?" Ian interrupted shortly, turning and walking over to the window.

His apparent lack of concern so enraged the vicar that he surged to his feet and stalked over to Ian's side, glowering at his profile. "She told me you ruined Elizabeth Cameron's reputation beyond recall," he snapped bitterly. "She told me that you convinced that innocent girl—who'd never been away from her country home until a few weeks before meeting you—that she should meet you in a secluded cottage, and later in a greenhouse. She told me that the scene was witnessed by individuals who made great haste to spread the gossip, and that it was all over the city in a matter of days. She told me Elizabeth's fiancé heard of it and withdrew his offer because of you. When he did that, society assumed Elizabeth's character must indeed be of the blackest nature, and she was summarily dropped by the *ton*. She told me that a few days later Elizabeth's brother fled

England to escape their creditors, who would have been paid off when Elizabeth made an advantageous marriage, and that he's never returned." With grim satisfaction the vicar observed the muscle that was beginning to twitch in Ian's rigid jaw. "She told me the reason for Elizabeth's going to London in the first place had been the necessity for making such a marriage—and that you destroyed any chance of that ever happening. Which is why that child will now have to marry a man you describe as a lecher three times her age!" Satisfied that his verbal shots were finding their mark, he fired his final, most killing round. "As a result of everything you have done, that brave, beautiful girl has been living in shamed seclusion for nearly two years. Her house, of which she spoke with such love, has been stripped of its valuables by creditors. I congratulate you, Ian. You have made an innocent girl into an impoverished leper! And all because she fell in love with you on sight. Knowing what I now know of you, I can only wonder what she saw in you!"

A muscle moved spasmodically in Ian's throat, but he made no effort to defend himself to his enraged uncle. Bracing his hands on either side of the window, he stared out into the darkness, his uncle's revelations pounding in his brain like a thousand hammers, combining with the torment of his own cruelty to Elizabeth the past few days.

He saw her as she'd been in England, courageous and lovely and filled with innocent passion in his arms, and he heard her words from yesterday: "You told my brother it was nothing but a meaningless dalliance"; he saw her shooting at the target with jaunty skill while he mocked at her suitors. He saw her kneeling in the grass, looking at his sketches of his dead family. "I'm so sorry," she'd whispered, her glorious eyes filled with soft compassion. He remembered her crying in his arms because her friends had betrayed her, too.

With a fresh surge of remorse he recalled her incredible sweetness and unselfish passion in his arms last night. She had driven him mad with desire, and afterward he had said, "I'll spare us both the ritualistic proposal. Marriage is out of the question—I'm fresh out of large rubies and expensive furs."

He remembered other things he'd said before that—"

Why the hell would your uncle think I have any desire to wed you?" "Miss Cameron is a very wealthy young lady, Duncan." "No doubt all the rooms at Havenhurst are covered with furs and filled with jewels."

And she'd been too proud to let him think anything else.

Scolding rage at his own blindness and stupidity poured through Ian. He should have *known*—the minute she started talking about bargaining for price with tradesmen, he damned well should have *known!* Ever since he'd set eyes on Elizabeth Cameron he'd been blind—no, he corrected himself with furious self-disgust, in England he'd recognized instinctively what she was—gentle and proud, brave and innocent and . . . rare. He'd known damned well she wasn't a promiscuous little flirt, yet he'd later convinced himself she was, and then he'd treated her like one here—and she had endured it the entire time she'd been here! She had let him say those things to her and then tried to excuse his behavior by blaming herself for behaving like "a shameless wanton" in England!

Bile rose up in his throat, suffocating him, and he closed his eyes. She was so damned sweet, and so forgiving, that she even did that for him.

Duncan hadn't moved; in taut silence he watched his nephew standing at the window, his eyes clenched shut, his stance like that of a man who was being stretched on the rack.

Finally Ian spoke, and his voice was rough with emotion, as if the words were being gouged out of him: "Did the woman say that, or was that your own opinion?"

"About what?"

Drawing a ragged breath, he asked, "Did she tell you that Elizabeth was in love with me two years ago, or was that your opinion?"

The answer to that obviously meant so much to Ian that Duncan almost smiled. At the moment, however, the vicar was more concerned with the two things he wanted above all else: He wanted Ian to wed Elizabeth and rectify the damage he'd done to her, and he wanted Ian to reconcile with his grandfather. In order to do the former, Ian would have to do the latter, for Elizabeth's uncle was evidently determined that her husband should have a title if possible. So badly did

Duncan want those two things to happen that he almost lied to help his cause, but the precepts of his conscience forbade it. "It was Miss Throckmorton-Jones's opinion when she was under the influence of laudanum. It is also *my* opinion, based on everything I saw in Elizabeth's character and behavior to you."

He waited through another long moment of awful suspense, knowing exactly where Ian's thoughts would have to turn next, and then he plunged in, ready to press home his advantage with hard, systematic logic. "You have no choice except to rescue her from that repugnant marriage."

Taking Ian's silence as assent, he continued with more force. "In order to do it, you'll have to dissuade her uncle from giving her to this man. I know from what Miss Throckmorton-Jones told me, and from what I saw with my own eyes in that note over there, that the uncle wants a title for her and will favor the man who has it. I also know that's not uncommon among the nobility, so you've no hope of persuading the man he's being unreasonable, if that's what you're thinking of trying to do." Duncan watched his words hit home with enough force to make Ian's skin whiten, and he made his final push: "That title is within your power, Ian. I realize how deep your hatred for your grandfather goes, but it no longer signifies. Either you let Elizabeth wed this despicable man Belhaven, or you reconcile with the Duke of Stanhope. It's one or the other, and you *know* it."

Ian tensed, his mind locked in furious combat against the idea of reconciling with his grandfather. Duncan watched him, knowing the battle raging inside him, and he waited in an agony of suspense for Ian to make his decision. He saw Ian bend his dark head, saw him clench his hands into fists. When at last he spoke, his infuriated curse was aimed at his grandfather: "That miserable son of a bitch!" he bit out between clenched teeth. "After eleven years he's going to have it his way. And all because I couldn't keep my hands off her."

The vicar could scarcely conceal his joyous relief. "There are worse things than having to marry a wonderful young woman who also had the excellent judgment to fall in love with *you,*" he pointed out.

Ian almost, but not quite, smiled at that. The impulse

passed in an instant, however, as reality crushed down on him, infuriating and complicated. "Whatever she felt for me, it was a long time ago. All she wants now is independence."

The vicar's brows shot up, and he chuckled with surprise. "Independence? Really? What an odd notion for a female. I'm sure you'll be able to disabuse her of such fanciful ideas."

"Don't count on it."

"Independence is vastly overrated. Give it to her and she'll hate it," he suggested.

Ian scarcely heard him; the fury at having to capitulate to his grandfather was building inside him again with terrible force. "*Damn* him!" he said in a murderous underbreath. "I'd have let him rot in hell, and his title with him."

Duncan's smile didn't fade as he said with asperity, "It's possible that it's fear of 'rotting in hell,' as you so picturesquely phrased it, that has made him so desperate to affirm you now as his heir. But consider that he has been trying to make amends for over a decade—long before his heart became weak."

"He was a decade too late!" Ian gritted. "My father was the rightful heir, and that old bastard never relented until after he died."

"I'm well aware of that. However, that's not the point, Ian. You've lost the battle to remain distant from him. You must lose it with the grace and dignity of your noble lineage, as your father would have done. You are rightfully the next Duke of Stanhope. Nothing can really change that. Furthermore, I fervently believe your father would have forgiven the duke if he'd had the chance that you now have."

In restless fury Ian shoved away from the wall. "I am not my father," he snapped.

The vicar, fearing that Ian was vacillating, said pointedly, "There's no time to lose. There's every chance you may arrive at your grandfather's only to be told he's already done what he said he meant to do last week—name a new heir."

"There's an equally good chance I'll be told to go to hell after my last letter to him."

"Then, too," said the vicar, "if you tary, you may arrive after Elizabeth's wedding to this Belhaven."

Ian hesitated an endless moment, and then he nodded curtly, shoved his hands into his pockets, and started reluctantly up the stairs.

"Ian?" he called after him.

Ian stopped and turned. "Now what?" he asked irritably.

"I'll need directions to Elizabeth's. You've changed brides, but I gather I'm still to have the honor of performing the ceremony in London?"

In answer his nephew nodded.

"You're doing the right thing," the vicar said quietly, unable to shake the fear that Ian's anger would cause him to deliberately alienate the old duke. "Regardless of how your marriage turns out, you have no choice. You wreaked havoc in her life."

"In more ways than you know," Ian said tersely.

"What in God's name does *that* mean?"

"I'm the reason her uncle is now her guardian," he said with a harsh sigh. "Her brother didn't leave to avoid debts or scandal, as Elizabeth evidently thinks."

"You're the cause? How could that be?"

"He called me out, and when he couldn't kill me in a legitimate duel he tried twice more—on the road—and damned near accomplished his goal both times. I had him hauled aboard the *Arianna* and shipped off to the Indies to cool his heels."

The vicar paled and sank down upon the sofa. "How could you do a thing like that?"

Ian stiffened under the unfair rebuke. "There were only two other alternatives—I could have let him blow a hole through my back, or I could have handed him over to the authorities. I didn't want him hanged for his overzealous determination to avenge his sister; I just wanted him out of my way."

"But two years!"

"He would have been back in less than one year, but the *Arianna* was damaged in a storm and put into San Delora for repairs. He jumped ship there and vanished. I assumed he'd made his way back here somehow. I had no idea," he finished as he turned and started back up the stairs, "that he had never returned until you told me a few minutes ago."

"Good God!" said the vicar. "Elizabeth couldn't be blamed if she took it in her mind to hate you for this."

"I don't intend to give her the opportunity," Ian replied in an implacable voice that warned his uncle not to interfere. "I'll hire an investigator to trace him, and *after* I find out what's happened to him, I'll tell her."

Duncan's common sense went to battle with his conscience, and this time his conscience lost. "It's probably the best way," he agreed reluctantly, knowing how hard Elizabeth would undoubtedly find it to forgive Ian for yet another, and worse, transgression against her. "This all could have been so much easier," he added with a sigh, "if you'd known sooner what was happening to Elizabeth. You have many acquaintances in English society; how is it they never mentioned it to you?"

"In the first place, I was away from England for almost a year after the episode. In the second place," Ian added with contempt, "among what is amusingly called Polite Society, matters that concern you are never discussed with *you.* They are discussed with everyone else, directly behind your back if possible."

Ian watched an inexplicable smile trace its way across his uncle's face. "Putting their gossip aside, you find them an uncommonly proud, autocratic, self-assured group, is that it?"

"For the most part, yes," Ian said shortly as he turned and strode up the stairs. When his door closed the vicar spoke to the empty room. "Ian," he said, his shoulders beginning to shake with laughter, "you may as well have the title—you were *born* with the traits."

After a moment, however, he sobered and lifted his eyes to the beamed ceiling, his expression one of sublime contentment. "Thank You," he said in the direction of heaven. "It took You a rather long time to answer the first prayer," he added, referring to the reconciliation with Ian's grandfather, "but You were wonderfully prompt with the one for Elizabeth."

18

It was nearly midnight four days later when Ian finally reached the White Stallion Inn. Leaving his horse with a hostler, he strode into the inn, past the common room filled with peasants drinking ale. The innkeeper, a fat man with a soiled apron around his belly, cast an appraising eye over Mr. Thornton's expensively tailored charcoal jacket and dove-gray riding breeches, his hard face and powerful physique, and wisely decided it wasn't necessary to charge his guest for the room in advance—something at which the gentry occasionally took offense.

A minute later, after Mr. Thornton had ordered a meal sent to his room, the innkeeper congratulated himself on the wisdom of that decision, because his new guest inquired about the magnificent estate belonging to an illustrious local noble.

"How far is it to Stanhope Park?"

"'Bout an hour's ride, gov'ner."

Ian hesitated, debating whether to arrive there in the morning unannounced and unexpected or to send a message. "I'll need a message brought there in the morning," he said after a hesitation.

"I'll have my boy take it there personal. What time will you be wantin' it taken over t' Stanhope Park?"

Ian hesitated again, knowing there was no way to avoid it. "Ten o'clock."

Standing alone in the inn's private parlor the next morning, Ian ignored the breakfast that had been put out for him long ago and glanced at his watch. The messenger had been gone for three hours—almost a full hour more than it should have taken him to return with a message from Stanhope, if there was going to *be* a message. He put his watch away and walked over to the fireplace, moodily slapping his riding gloves against his thigh. He had no idea if his grandfather was at Stanhope or if the old man had already named another heir and would now refuse to see Ian in retaliation for all the gestures of reconciliation Ian had rebuffed in the last decade. With each minute that passed Ian was more inclined to believe the latter.

Behind him the innkeeper appeared in the doorway and said, "My boy hasn't yet returned, though there's been time aplenty. I'll have to charge ye extra, Mr. Thornton, if he don't return within the hour."

Ian glanced at the innkeeper over his shoulder and made a sublime effort not to snap the man's head off. "Have my horse saddled and brought round," he replied curtly, not certain exactly what he meant to do now. He'd actually have preferred a public flogging to writing that curt message to his grandfather in the first place. Now he was being brushed off like a supplicant, and that infuriated him.

Behind him the innkeeper frowned at Ian's back with narrowed, suspicious eyes. Ordinarily male travelers who arrived without private coach or even a valet were required to pay for their rooms when they arrived. In this instance the innkeeper hadn't demanded advance payment because this particular guest had spoken with the clipped, authoritative accents of a wealthy gentleman and because his riding clothes bore the unmistakable stamp of elegant cloth and custom tailoring. Now, however, with Stanhope Park refusing even to answer the man's summons, the innkeeper had revised his earlier estimation of the worth of his guest, and he was bent on stopping the man from trying to mount his horse and galloping off without paying his blunt.

Belatedly noting the innkeeper's continued presence, Ian

pulled his scowling gaze from the empty grate. "Yes, what is it?"

"It's yer tick, gov'ner. I'll be wantin' payment now."

His greedy eyes widened in surprise as his guest extracted a fat roll of bills, yanked off enough to cover the cost of the night's lodgings, and thrust it at him.

Ian waited thirty minutes more and then faced the fact that his grandfather wasn't going to reply. Furious at having wasted valuable time, he strode out of the parlor, deciding to ride to London and try to *buy* Elizabeth's uncle's favor. His attention on pulling on his riding gloves, he strode through the common room without noticing the sudden tension sweeping across it as the rowdy peasants who'd been drinking ale at the scarred tables turned to gape in awed silence at the doorway. The innkeeper, who'd only moments before eyed Ian as if he might steal the pewter, was now standing a few feet away from the open front door, staring at Ian with slackened jaw. "My lord!" he burst out, and then, as if words had failed him completely, the stout man made a sweeping gesture toward the door.

Ian's gaze shifted from the last button on his glove to the innkeeper, who was now bowing reverently, then snapped to the doorway, where two footmen and a coachman stood at rigid attention, clad in formal livery of green and gold.

Unconcerned with the peasants' gaping stares, the coachman stepped forward, bowed deeply to Ian, and cleared his throat. In a grave, carrying voice he repeated a message from the duke that could leave no doubt in Ian's mind about his grandfather's feelings toward him or his unexpected visit: "His Grace the Duke of Stanhope bade me to extend his warmest greetings to the *Marquess of Kensington* . . . and to say that he is most eagerly awaiting your convenience at Stanhope Park."

By instructing the coachman to address Ian as the Marquess of Kensington the duke had just publicly informed Ian and everyone else in the inn that the title was now—and would continue to be—Ian's. The public gesture was beyond anything Ian had anticipated, and it proved two things to him simultaneously: first, that his grandfather bore him no ill will for repeatedly rejecting his peace offerings;

second, that the wily old man was still keen enough in his mind to have sensed that victory was now in his grasp.

That irritated Ian, and with a curt nod at the coachman he strode past the gaping villagers, who were respectfully tipping their caps to the man who'd just been publicly identified as the duke's heir. The vehicle waiting in the inn yard was another testament to his grandfather's eagerness to welcome him home in style: Instead of a carriage and horse he'd sent the closed coach with a team of four handsome horses decked out in silver trappings.

It occurred to Ian that this grand gesture might be his grandfather's way of treating Ian as a long-awaited and much-loved guest, but he refused to dwell on that possibility. He had not come to be reunited with his grandfather; he had come to accept the title that had been his father's. Beyond that, he wanted nothing whatever to do with the old man.

Despite his cold detachment, Ian felt an odd sensation of unreality as the coach pulled through the gates and swept along the drive of the estate that his father had called home until his marriage at the age of twenty-three. Being here made him feel uncharacteristically nostalgic, and at the same time it increased his loathing for the tyrannical aristocrat who'd deliberately disowned his own son and cast him out of this place. With a critical eye he looked over the neatly tended parkland and the sprawling stone mansion with chimneys dotting the roof. To most people Stanhope Park would look very grand and impressive; to Ian it was an old, sprawling estate, probably badly in need of modernization, and not nearly as lovely as the least of his own.

The coach drew up before the front steps, and before Ian alighted, the front door was already being opened by an ancient, thin butler clad in the usual black. Ian's father had rarely spoken of his own father, nor of the estate and possessions he'd left behind, but he had talked often and freely of those servants of whom he was particularly fond. As he ascended the steps Ian looked at the butler and knew he had to be Ormsley. According to Ian's father, it was Ormsley who'd found him secretly sampling Stanhope's best French brandy in a hayloft when he was ten years old. It was also Ormsley who took the blame for the missing bottle—and its priceless decanter—by confessing to drinking it himself and misplacing the decanter in his inebriated state.

At the moment Ormsley looked on the verge of tears as his damp, faded blue eyes roved almost lovingly over Ian's face. "Good afternoon, my lord," he intoned formally, but the ecstatic expression on his face gave Ian the impression the servant was restraining himself from wrapping his arms around him. "And—and may I say—" The elderly man stopped, his voice hoarse with emotion, and cleared his throat. "And may I say how very—how very very *good* it is to have you here at—" His voice choked, he flushed, and Ian's ire at his grandfather was momentarily forgotten.

"Good afternoon, Ormsley," Ian said, grinning at the look of sublime pleasure that crossed Ormsley's lined face when Ian knew his name. Sensing the butler was about to bow again, Ian put out his hand instead, forcing the loyal retainer to shake hands with him. "I trust," Ian joked gently, "that you've conquered your habit of overindulging in French brandy?"

The faded old eyes brightened like diamonds at this added proof that Ian's father had spoken of him to Ian.

"Welcome home. Welcome home at last, my lord," Ormsley said hoarsely, returning Ian's handshake.

"I'm only staying a few hours," Ian told him calmly, and the butler's hand went a little limp with disappointment. He recovered himself, however, and escorted Ian down a wide, oak-paneled hall. A small army of footmen and housemaids seemed to be lurking about, ostensibly dusting mirrors, paneling, and floors. As Ian passed, several of them stole long, lingering looks at him, then turned to exchange swift, gratified smiles. His mind on the looming meeting with his grandfather, Ian was oblivious to the searching scrutiny and startled glances he was receiving, but he was dimly aware that a few of the servants were hastily dabbing at their eyes and noses with handkerchiefs.

Ormsley headed toward a pair of double doors at the end of a long hall, and Ian kept his mind perfectly blank as he braced himself for his first meeting with his grandfather. Even as a boy he'd refused to permit himself the weakness of thinking about his relative, and on those rare occasions when he had contemplated the man he'd always imagined him as looking rather like his father, a man of average height with light brown hair and brown eyes. Ormsley threw open the doors to the study with a flourish, and Ian strode forward, walking toward the chair where a man was leaning upon a cane and arising with some difficulty. Now, as the man finally straightened and faced him, Ian felt an almost physical shock: Not only was he as tall as Ian's own 6'2"; to his inner disgust, Ian realized that his own face bore a startling resemblance to the duke's, whereas he'd scarcely resembled his own sire at all. It was, in fact, eerily like looking at a silver-haired, older version of his own face.

The duke was studying him, too, and apparently reached the same conclusion, although his reaction was diametrically opposite: He smiled slowly, sensing Ian's ire at the discovery of their resemblance to each other. "You didn't know?" he asked in a strong baritone voice very like Ian's.

"No," Ian said shortly, "I didn't."

"I have the advantage of you, then," the duke said, leaning on his cane, his eyes searching Ian's face much as the butler's had done. "You see, I *did* know."

Ian stolidly ignored the mistiness he saw in those amber eyes. "I'll be brief and to the point," he began, but his grandfather held up a long, aristocratic hand.

"Ian, please," he said gruffly, nodding to the chair across from him. "I've waited for this moment for more years than you can imagine. Do not deprive me, I implore you, of an old man's pleasure at welcoming home his prodigal grandson."

"I haven't come here to heal the family breach," Ian snapped. "Were it up to me, I'd never have set foot in this house!"

His grandfather stiffened at his tone, but the duke's voice was carefully mild. "I assume you've come to accept what is rightfully yours," he began, but an imperious female voice made Ian swing around toward the sofa, where two elderly ladies were sitting, their fragile bodies all but engulfed by the plump cushions. "Really, Stanhope," one of them said in a surprisingly sturdy voice, "how can you expect the boy to be civil when you've quite forgotten your own manners?

275

You haven't even bothered to offer him refreshment, or to acknowledge our presence to him." A thin smile touched her lips as she regarded a startled Ian. "I am your great-aunt Hortense," she advised him with a regal inclination of her head. "We met in London some years back, though you obviously do not recognize me."

Having met his two great-aunts only once, purely by accident, Ian had neither animosity nor affection for either of them. He bowed politely to Hortense, who tipped her head toward the elderly gray-haired lady beside her, who seemed to be dozing, her head drooping slightly forward. "And this person, you may recall, is my sister Charity, your other great-aunt, who has again dozed off as she so often does. It's her age, you understand."

The little gray head snapped up, and blue eyes popped open, leveling on Hortense in wounded affront. "I'm only *four* little years older than you, Hortense, and it's very mean-spirited of you to go about reminding everyone of it," she cried in a hurt voice; then she saw Ian standing in front of her, and a beatific smile lit her face. "Ian, dear boy, do you remember *me?*"

"Certainly, ma'am," Ian began courteously, but Charity interrupted him as she turned a triumphant glance on her sister. "There, you see, Hortense—he remembers *me,* and it is because, though I may be just a trifle older than you, *I* have not aged nearly so much as you in the last years! Have I?" she asked, turning hopefully to Ian.

"If you'll take my advice," his grandfather said dryly, "you won't answer that question. Ladies," he said, bending a stern look on his sisters, "Ian and I have much to discuss. I promised you could meet him as soon as he arrived. Now I must insist you leave us to our business and join us later for tea."

Rather than upset the elderly ladies by telling them he wouldn't be here long enough for tea, Ian waited while they both arose. Hortense extended her hand for his kiss, and Ian obliged. He was about to bestow the same courtesy on his other aunt, but Charity lifted her cheek, not her hand, and so he kissed that instead.

When the ladies left, so did the temporary diversion they'd provided, and the tension grew thick as the two men stood looking at each other—complete strangers with nothing in common except a startling physical resemblance and the blood that flowed in their veins. The duke stood perfectly still, rigidly erect and aristocratic, but his eyes were warm; Ian slapped his gloves impatiently against his thigh, his face cold and resolute—two men in an undeclared duel of silence and contest of wills. The duke yielded with a faint inclination of his head that acknowledged Ian as the winner as he finally broke the silence. "I think this occasion calls for champagne," he said, reaching out for the bell cord.

Ian's clipped, cynical reply stilled his hand. "I think it calls for something much stronger." The implication that Ian found the occasion repugnant, rather than cause for celebration, was not lost on the duke. Inclining his head with another faint, knowing smile, he pulled the bell cord. "Scotch, isn't it?" he asked.

Ian's surprise that the old man seemed to know what drink he preferred was eclipsed by his astonishment when Ormsley instantly whisked into the room bearing a silver tray with a decanter of Scotch, a bottle of champagne, and two appropriate glasses on it. The butler was clairvoyant or had wings, or else the tray had been ordered before Ian arrived.

With a quick, self-conscious smile directed at Ian, the butler withdrew, closing the doors behind him. "Do you think," the duke asked with mild amusement, "we could sit down, or are we now to have a contest to see who can *stand* the longest?"

"I intend to get this ordeal over with as quickly as possible," Ian countered icily.

Instead of being insulted, as Ian meant him to be, Edward Avery Thornton looked at his grandson, and his heart swelled with pride at the dynamic, forceful man who bore his name. For over a decade Ian had flung one of the most important titles in England back in Edward's face, and while that might have enraged another man, Edward recognized in the gesture the same proud arrogance and indomitable will that had marked all the Thornton men. At the moment, however, that indomitable will was on a collision course with his own, and so Edward was prepared to yield on almost anything in order to win what he wanted most in the world: his grandson. He wanted his respect, if he couldn't have his love; he wanted just one small, infinitesimal piece of his affection to carry in his heart. And he wanted absolution. Most of all he needed that. He needed to be forgiven for making what had been the biggest mistake of his life thirty-two years ago, and for waiting too long to admit to Ian's father that he was wrong. To that end, Edward was prepared to endure anything from Ian—except his immediate departure. If he couldn't have anything else—not Ian's affection or his respect or his forgiveness— he wanted his *time*. Just a little of it. Not much—a day or two, or even a few hours to cherish, a few memories to hoard in his heart during the dreary days before his life ended.

In hopes of gaining this time the duke said noncommittally, "I can probably have the papers drawn up within the week."

Ian lowered his glass of Scotch. In a cold, clear voice he said, *"Today."*

"There are legalities involved."

Ian, who dealt with thousands of legalities in his business ventures on a daily basis, lifted his brows in glacial challenge. "Today."

Edward hesitated, sighed, and nodded. "I suppose my clerk could begin drawing up the documents while we have a talk in here. It's a complicated and time-consuming business, however, and it will take a few days at least. There's the matter of the properties that are yours by right—"

"I don't want the properties," Ian said with contempt. "Nor the money, if there is any. I'll take the damned title and be done with it, but that's all."

"But—"

"Your clerk should be able to draw up a straightforward document naming me your heir in a quarter of an hour. I'm on my way to Brinshire and then to London. I'll leave as soon as the document is signed."

"Ian," Edward began, but he would not plead, particularly not when he could see it was useless. The pride and unbending will, the strength and determination that marked Ian as his grandson, also put him out of Edward's reach. It was too late. Surprised by Ian's willingness to take a title but not the wealth that accompanied it, he arose stiffly from his chair and went down the hall to tell his clerk to draw up the documents. He also told him to include all the properties and their substantial incomes. He was a Thornton, after all, with pride of his own. His luck had obviously run out, but not his pride. Ian would leave in an hour, but he would leave endowed with all the wealth and estates that were his birthright.

Ian was standing at the windows when his grandfather returned. "It's done," Edward said, sitting back down in his chair. Some of the rigidity went out of Ian's shoulders; the loathsome matter was finished. He nodded, then refilled his glass and sat down across from his grandfather.

After another long moment of pregnant silence he remarked conversationally, "I understand felicitations are in order."

Ian started. His betrothal to Christina, which was about to be broken, was not yet common knowledge.

"Christina Taylor is a lovely young woman. I knew her grandfather and her uncles, and, of course, her father, the Earl of Melbourne. She'll make you a fine wife, Ian."

"Inasmuch as bigamy is a crime in this country, I find that unlikely."

Startled by the discovery that his information was apparently incorrect, Edward took another swallow of champagne and asked, "May I ask who the fortunate young woman is, then?"

Ian opened his mouth to tell him to go to hell, but there was something alarming about the way his grandfather was slowly putting his glass down. He watched as the older man began to rise. "I'm not supposed to drink spirits," the duke said apologetically. "I believe I'll have a rest. Ring for Ormsley, if you please," he said in a harsh voice. "He'll know what to do."

There was an urgency about the scene that hit Ian as he did as bidden. An instant later Ormsley was helping his grandfather upstairs and a physician was being summoned. He arrived within a half hour, rushing up the stairs with his bag of instruments, and Ian waited in the drawing room, trying to ignore the uneasy feeling that he'd arrived just in time for his grandfather's death.

When the physician came downstairs, however, he

seemed relieved. "I've warned him repeatedly not to touch spirits," he said, looking harassed. "They affect his heart. He's resting now, however. You may go up after an hour or two."

Ian didn't want to care how ill he was. He told himself the old man who looked so much like him was nothing to him, and despite that he heard himself ask in a curt voice, "How long does he have?"

The physician lifted his hands, palms up. "Who's to say? A week, a month," he speculated, "a year, maybe more. His heart is weak, but his will is strong—more so now than ever," he continued, shrugging into the light cape Ormsley was putting over his shoulders.

"What do you mean, 'more now than ever'?"

The physician smiled in surprise. "Why, I meant that your coming here has meant a great deal to him, my lord. It's had an amazing effect on him—well, not amazing, really. I should say a *miraculous* effect. Normally he rails at me when he's ill. Today he almost hugged me in his eagerness to tell me you were here, and why. Actually, I was ordered to 'have a look at you,'" he continued in the confiding tone of an old family friend, "although I wasn't supposed to *tell* you I was doing so, of course." Grinning, he added, "He thinks you are a 'handsome devil.'"

Ian refused to react to that astonishing information with any emotion whatsoever.

"Good day, my lord," the doctor said. Turning to the duke's sisters, who'd been hovering worriedly in the hall, he tipped his hat. "Ladies," he said, and he departed.

"I'll just go up and look in on him," Hortense announced. Turning to Charity, she said sternly, "Do not bore Ian with too much chatter," she admonished, already climbing the stairs. In an odd, dire voice, she added, "And do *not* meddle."

For the next hour Ian paced the floor, with Charity watching him with great interest. The one thing he did not have was time, and time was what he was losing. At this rate Elizabeth would be giving birth to her first child before he got back to London. And before he could go to her uncle with his suit he had to deal with the unpleasant task of breaking off nuptial negotiations with Christina's father.

"You aren't really going to leave today, are you, dear boy?" Charity piped up suddenly.

Stifling a sigh of impatience, Ian bowed. "I'm afraid I must, ma'am."

"He'll be heartbroken."

Suppressing the urge to inform the elderly lady that Ian doubted the duke had a heart to break, he said curtly, "He'll survive."

She watched him so intently after that that Ian began to wonder if she was addled or trying to read his mind. Addled, he decided when she suddenly stood up and insisted he ought to see a drawing of some peacocks his father had made as a boy. "Another time, perhaps," he declined.

"I really think," she said, tipping her head to the side in her funny birdlike way, "it ought to be *now.*"

Silently wishing her to perdition, Ian started to decline and then changed his mind and relented. It might help the time to pass more quickly. She took him down a hall and into a room that appeared to be his grandfather's private study. Once inside she put her finger to her lips, thinking. "Now *where* was that drawing?" she wondered aloud, looking innocent and confused. "Oh, yes," she brightened, "I remember." Tripping over to the desk, she searched under the drawer for some sort of concealed lock. "You will adore it, I'm sure. Now where can that lock be?" she continued in the same vague, chatty manner of a confused elderly lady. "Here it is!" she cried, and the left-hand drawer slid open.

"You'll find it right in there," she said, pointing to the large open drawer. "Just rummage through those papers and you'll see it, I'm sure."

Ian refused to invade another man's desk, but Charity had no such compunction. Reaching her arms in to the elbows, she brought up a large stack of thick paper and dumped it on the desk. "Now which one am I looking for?" she mused aloud as she separated them. "My eyes are not what they once were. Do you see a bird among these, dear Ian?"

Ian dragged his impatient gaze from the clock to the littered desktop and then froze. Looking back at him in a hundred poses were sketches of himself. There were detailed sketches of Ian standing at the helm of the first ship of his fleet . . . Ian walking past the village church in Scotland with one of the village girls laughing up at him . . . Ian as a solemn six-year-old, riding his pony . . . Ian at seven and eight and nine and ten . . . In addition to the sketches, there were dozens of lengthy, written reports about Ian, some current, others dating all the way back to his youth.

"Is there a bird among them, dear boy?" Charity asked innocently, peering not at the things on the desk, but at his face, noting the muscle beginning to twitch at Ian's tense jaw.

"No."

"Then they must be in the schoolroom! Of course," she said cheerfully, "that's it. How like me, Hortense would say, to have made such a *silly* mistake."

Ian dragged his eyes from the proof that his grandfather had been keeping track of him almost from the day of his birth—certainly from the day when he was able to leave the cottage on his own two legs—to her face and said mockingly, "Hortense isn't very perceptive. I would say you are as wily as a fox."

She gave him a little knowing smile and pressed her finger to her lips. "Don't tell her, will you? She does so enjoy thinking *she* is the clever one."

"How did he manage to have these drawn?" Ian asked, stopping her as she turned away.

"A woman in the village near your home drew many of them. Later he hired an artist when he knew you were going to be somewhere at a specific time. I'll just leave you here where it's nice and quiet." She was leaving him, Ian knew, to look through the items on the desk. For a long moment he hesitated, and then he slowly sat down in the chair, looking over the confidential reports on himself. They were all written by one Mr. Edgard Norwich, and as Ian began scanning the thick stack of pages, his anger at his grandfather for this outrageous invasion of his privacy slowly became amusement. For one thing, nearly every letter from the investigator began with phrases that made it clear the duke had chastised him for not reporting in enough detail. The top letter began,

I apologize, Your Grace, for my unintentional laxness in failing to mention that indeed Mr. Thornton enjoys an occasional cheroot. . . .

The next one opened with,

I did not realize, Your Grace, that you would wish to know how fast his horse ran in the race—in addition to knowing that he won.

From the creases and folds in the hundreds of reports it was obvious to Ian that they'd been handled and read repeatedly, and it was equally obvious from some of the investigator's casual comments that his grandfather had apparently expressed his personal pride to him:

You will be pleased to know, Your Grace, that young Ian is a fine whip, just as you expected. . . .
I quite agree with you, as do many others, that Mr. Thornton is undoubtedly a genius. . . .
I assure you, Your Grace, that your concern over that duel is unfounded. It was a flesh wound in the arm, nothing more.

Ian flipped through them at random, unaware that the barricade he'd erected against his grandfather was beginning to crack very slightly.

"Your Grace," the investigator had written in a rare fit of exasperation when Ian was eleven,

"the suggestion that I should be able to find a physician who might secretly look at young Ian's sore throat is beyond all bounds of reason. Even if I could find one who was willing to pretend to be a lost traveler, I really cannot see how he could contrive to have a peek at the boy's throat without causing suspicion!"

The minutes became an hour, and Ian's disbelief increased as he scanned the entire history of his life, from his achievements to his peccadilloes. His gambling gains and losses appeared regularly; each ship he added to his fleet had been described, and sketches forwarded separately; his financial progress had been reported in minute and glowing detail.

Slowly Ian opened the drawer and shoved the papers into it, then he left the study, closing the door behind him. He was on his way to the drawing room when Ormsley found him to say the duke wished to visit with him now.

His grandfather was sitting in a chair near the fireplace, garbed in a dressing robe, when Ian walked in, and he looked surprisingly strong. "You look"—Ian hesitated, irritated with the relief he felt—"recovered," he finished curtly.

"I've rarely felt better in my life," the duke averred, and whether he meant it or was only exerting the will his doctor admired, Ian wasn't certain. "The papers are ready," he continued. "I've already signed them. I—er—took the liberty of ordering a meal sent up here, in hopes you'd share it with me before you leave. You'll have to eat somewhere, you know."

Ian hesitated, then nodded, and the tension seemed to leave the duke's body.

"Excellent!" He beamed and handed Ian the papers and a quill. He watched with inner satisfaction as Ian signed them without bothering to read them—and in so doing unwittingly accepted not only his father's title but all the wealth that went with it. "Now, where were we when our conversation had to be abandoned downstairs?" he said when Ian handed the papers back to him.

Ian's thoughts were still in the study, where a desk was filled with his likenesses and carefully maintained reports of every facet of his life, and for a moment he looked blankly at the older man.

"Ah, yes," the duke prodded as Ian sat down across from him, "we were discussing your future wife. Who is the fortunate young woman?"

Propping his ankle atop the opposite knee, Ian leaned back in his chair and regarded him in casual, speculative silence, one dark brow lifted in amused mockery. "Don't you know?" he asked dryly. *"I've* known for five days. Or is Mr. Norwich behind in his correspondence again?"

His grandfather stiffened and then seemed to age in his chair. "Charity," he said quietly. With a ragged sigh he lifted his eyes to Ian's, his gaze proud and beseeching at the same time. "Are you angry?"

"I don't know."

He nodded. "Do you have any idea how difficult it is to say 'I'm sorry'?"

"Don't say it," Ian said curtly.

His grandfather drew a long breath and nodded again, accepting Ian's answer. "Well, then, can we talk? For just a little while?"

"What do you want to talk about?"

"Your future wife, for one thing," he said warmly. "Who is she?"

"Elizabeth Cameron."

The duke gave a start. "Really? I thought you had done with that messy affair two years ago."

Ian suppressed a grim smile at his phrasing and his gall.

"I shall send her my congratulations at once," his grandfather announced.

"They'd be extremely premature," Ian said flatly. Yet over the next hour, soothed by brandy and lulled by exhaustion and his grandfather's perceptive, ceaseless questions, he reluctantly related the situation with Elizabeth's uncle. To his grim surprise, he did not need to explain about the ugly gossip that surrounded Elizabeth, or the fact that her reputation was in tatters. Even his grandfather was aware of it, as was, apparently, the entire *ton*, exactly as Lucinda Throckmorton-Jones had claimed.

"If you think," the duke warned him, "that society will forgive and forget and accept her merely because you're now prepared to marry her, Ian, you're quite wrong, I assure you. They'll ignore your part in the nasty affair, as they already have, because you are a man—and a rich one, not to mention that you're now the Marquess of Kensington. When you make Lady Cameron your marchioness, however, they'll tolerate her because they have no choice, but they'll cut her dead whenever the opportunity arises. It's going to take a show of force from some persons of great consequence to make society realize they must accept her. Otherwise they'll treat her like a pariah."

For himself Ian would have calmly and unhesitatingly told society to go to hell, but they'd already put Elizabeth through hell, and he wanted somehow to make it right for her again. He was idly considering how to go about it when his grandfather said firmly, "I shall go to London and be there when your betrothal is announced."

"No," Ian said, his jaw tightening in anger. It was one thing to relinquish his hatred for the man, but it was another entirely to allow him to insinuate himself into Ian's life as an ally or to accept help from him.

"I realize," his grandfather said calmly, "why you were so quick to reject my offer. However, I did not make it for my gratification alone. There are two other sound reasons: It will benefit Lady Elizabeth tremendously if society sees that *I* am fully willing to accept her as my granddaughter-in-law. I am the only one who has a prayer of swaying them. Second," the duke continued, pressing his advantage while he had one to press, "until society sees you and me together and in complete accord at least once, the gossip about your questionable parentage and our relationship will continue. In other words, you can call yourself my heir, but until they see that I regard you as such, they won't entirely believe what you say or what the newspapers print. Now then, if you want Lady Elizabeth treated with the respect due the Marchioness of Kensington, the *ton* will first have to accept you as Marquess of Kensington. The two things are tied together. It must be done *slowly,*" he emphasized, "one step at a time. Handled in that way, no one will dare to oppose me or to defy you, and they will then have to accept Lady Elizabeth and let the gossip be laid to rest."

Ian hesitated, a thousand emotions warring in his heart and mind. "I'll think about it," he agreed curtly.

"I understand," the duke said quietly. "In the event you decide to call upon my support, I will leave for London in the morn and stay at my town house."

Ian got up to leave, and his grandfather also arose. Awkwardly, the older man held out his hand, and hesitantly, Ian took it. His grandfather's grip was surprisingly strong, and it lasted a long time. "Ian," he said suddenly and desperately, "if I could undo what I did thirty-two years ago, I would do it. I swear to you."

"I'm sure you would," Ian said in a noncommittal tone.

"Do you think," he continued in a ragged voice, "that someday you might forgive me completely?"

Ian answered him honestly. "I don't know."

He nodded and took his hand away. "I shall be in London within the week. When do you plan to be there?"

"That depends on how long it takes to deal with Christina's father and Elizabeth's uncle and to explain things to Elizabeth. All things considered, I ought to be in London by the fifteenth."

19

Elizabeth stood up slowly, her hands clenched into nervous fists at her sides as she gaped at Alexandra Townsende across the young duchess's sumptuous green-and-cream London drawing room. "Alex, this is madness!" she burst out in frustrated disbelief. "My uncle gave me until the twenty-fourth, and it's already the fifteenth! How can you possibly expect me to consider attending a ball tonight, when my life is practically coming to an end, and we haven't thought of a single solution!"

"It might *be* a solution," Alex reasoned. "And it is the *only* one I've been able to think of since you arrived."

Elizabeth paused in her pacing to roll her eyes and shake her head in a gesture that clearly implied Alex had taken leave of her senses. Elizabeth had come racing back from Scotland to England, hoping to reason with her uncle, only to have him gleefully inform her that he'd just received a near-offer from Lord Marchman as well. "I prefer to wait in hope Marchman comes up to scratch. His title is greater, and so is his wealth; therefore he's less likely to squander my money. I've written to him and asked him to make his decision by the twenty-fourth."

Elizabeth had kept her senses and used his good mood to convince him to let her go to London in the meantime. Now that he knew he was about to get her off his hands, Uncle Julius was uncharacteristically agreeable. "Very well. Today is the tenth; you may remain there until the twenty-fourth. I shall send a message to you if Marchman offers."

"I—I think I'd like Alexandra Townsende's advice on the formalities of a wedding," Elizabeth had prevaricated on an impulse, hoping that Alex might somehow help her find a way to avoid marrying either man. "She is in London for the Season, and I can stay with her."

"You may use my town house if you bring your own servants," he offered magnanimously. "If Belhaven wants to press his suit with you in person in the meantime, he may call upon you in the city. In fact, while you are there you may order a wedding gown. Nothing too expensive," he added with a dark frown. "There's no reason for a big town wedding when a small one here at Havenhurst will do as well. And there's no reason for a wedding gown either, now that I reflect on it, since your mother's was only worn the one time."

Elizabeth didn't bother to remind him that her mother had been married in an elaborate ceremony at St. James's in a sumptuous, pearl-encrusted gown with a fifteen-foot train, and that such a gown for an intimate little wedding would look absurd. At the moment she was still hoping to avoid any ceremony at all, and she was much too anxious to flee to London to discuss finery. Now, after she'd spent five days with Alex, thinking of and discarding impossible solutions, Alex had suddenly decided it was imperative Elizabeth reenter society at a ball tonight. To make matters worse, in his excessive eagerness to continue his courtship, Sir Francis had arrived in London yesterday and was practically haunting Uncle Julius's town house on Promenade Street.

"Elizabeth." Alex's voice was filled with determination. "I'll admit I haven't had a great deal of time to work out all the details, since I only conceived of the plan three hours ago, but if you'll just sit down and have some of that tea, I'll try to explain the logic of it."

"Attending a ball tonight," Elizabeth said as she obediently sank down on a lovely little settee upholstered in green silk, "is *not* a solution, it's—it's a nightmare!"

"Will you just let me explain? There's no point arguing

289

about it, because I've already set wheels in motion, and I absolutely refuse to be gainsaid."

Elizabeth raked her hair off her forehead in a nervous gesture and nodded reluctantly. When Alexandra glanced pointedly at the tea her butler had just carried in Elizabeth sighed, picked up the dainty cup, and took a sip. "Explain."

"Not to put too fine a point on it, we have nine days left of your reprieve. Nine days to find you a more desirable suitor."

Elizabeth choked on her tea. "Another *suitor*? You are joking!" she sputtered, caught somewhere between hilarity and horror.

"Not at all," said Alex practically, daintily sipping her tea. "When you made your debut you received fifteen offers in four weeks. If you could accumulate an average of half a suitor per day before, then, even allowing for the scandal hanging over your head, there's no reason in the world why we oughtn't be able to find at least one suitor you like in nine full days. You're more beautiful now than you were as a girl."

Elizabeth paled at the mention of the scandal. "I can't do it," she said shakily. "I cannot face everyone. Not yet!"

"Not alone, perhaps, but you won't *be* alone tonight." In her desperation to convince Elizabeth of the feasibility and the necessity of the plan Alex leaned forward, propping her elbows on her knees. "I've been busy these past three hours since I conceived the plan. Since the Season is just beginning, not everyone has arrived yet, but I've already sent a note to my husband's grandmother asking her to call on me here today the moment she arrives in town. My husband is still at Hawthorne, but he'd planned to return tonight and spend the early evening at one of his clubs. I've already sent him a long note explaining the entire situation and asking him to join us at the Willingtons' ball at ten-thirty. I've also sent a note to my brother-in-law, Anthony, and he will escort you. So far that makes four of us to stand by you. That may not seem like many to you, but you cannot fully imagine the enormous influence my husband and his grandmother have." With a reassuring, affectionate grin she explained, "The Dowager Duchess of Hawthorne is a lady of *enormous* consequence, and she shamelessly adores forcing society to bend to her will. You haven't met my husband yet," Alex finished, her smile turning tender, "but Jordan has even more influence than the dowager, and he will not permit anyone to say an unkind word to you. They wouldn't even dare *try* if he is with us."

"Does he—does he know about me? Who I am, I mean, and what happened?"

"I explained in the note who you are—to me—and briefly what had happened to you two years ago. I would have told him before this, but I haven't seen him since I came to you at Havenhurst. He's been away, seeing to all the business and estate matters that were left to others for the year and a half we were traveling."

Elizabeth felt sick at the very real possibility that Alex's husband might return to London tonight and announce that Elizabeth was not a fit companion for his wife—or that he wanted nothing whatever to do with the scheme. The prospect was so repugnant that Elizabeth actually seized on an obstacle to the entire plan with enormous relief. "It won't work!" she said happily.

"Why not?" Alex asked.

"I have nothing to wear!"

"Yes, you do," Alex replied with a triumphant smile. "It's a gown I brought back from France."

She held up her hand to silence Elizabeth's cry of protest. "I cannot wear the gown," she said quietly. "My waist is enlarging already."

Elizabeth cast a dubious glance at Alex's slim waist as her friend finished reasonably, "By next year it will be quite out of style, so it's only right that one of us enjoy it. I've already sent word to Bentner to bring Berta here along with anything else you'll need," Alex admitted with a sheepish grin. "I've no intention of letting you go back to Promenade Street, because I fear you would send me a note later today announcing you have a violent headache and have taken to your bed with your salts."

Despite all the awful emotions warring in Elizabeth she had to bite back a guilty smile over that last astute remark. She'd already been thinking of doing exactly that. "I'll agree to the plan," she said slowly, her wide green eyes insistent, "but only if the dowager duchess has no reservations at all about sponsoring me tonight."

"Leave that to me," Alex said with a huge sigh of relief. She glanced up as the butler arrived in the doorway and grandly announced, "The dowager duchess has arrived, your grace. I've shown her into the yellow salon as you instructed." With a bright smile that displayed confidence she didn't completely feel, Alex stood up. "I just wanted to have a few words with her alone, to explain before she meets you," she said, already heading away. Partway across the room she stopped and turned back. "There's one small thing I ought to warn you about," she added hesitantly. "My husband's grandmother is occasionally a bit—brusque," she finished lamely.

The "few words" Alex needed with the dowager took considerably less than five minutes, but Elizabeth watched the clock in sublime misery, imagining the sort of indignant reluctance Alex must be confronting. When the drawing room door swung open Elizabeth was so tense that she shot to her feet and then had to stand there, feeling graceless and gauche, while the most formidable-looking woman she had ever beheld swept majestically into the room beside Alex.

Besides having the regal posture of a woman who was born with a ramrod down her back, the Dowager Duchess of Hawthorne was quite tall and possessed of a piercing pair of hazel eyes, an aristocratic nose, and an imperious expression that had been permanently stamped into her otherwise seamless white skin.

In aloof silence she waited while Alex performed the introductions, then she watched Elizabeth execute her curtsy and acknowledge the introduction. Still silent, the dowager then raised her lorgnette to her cold hazel eyes and inspected Elizabeth from the top of her hair to the tips of her toes, while Elizabeth mentally abandoned any notion that the old woman would lend her consequence tonight, willingly or otherwise.

When she finally deigned to speak, the dowager's voice had the cutting snap of a whip. "Young woman!" she said without preamble, "Alexandra has just explained to me that she is wishful of my assistance in reintroducing you to society this evening. However, as I told Alexandra, there was no need for her to describe to me the scandal that surrounded your association with a certain Mr. Ian Thornton the year before last. I am *well* aware of it—as is nearly everyone else in society." She let that unkind and unnecessary statement do its damage to Elizabeth's lacerated pride for a full moment before she demanded, "What I want to know is whether or not I can expect a repetition of it, if I were to agree with what Alexandra wants."

Drowning in angry mortification, Elizabeth nevertheless managed not to flinch or drop her gaze, and although her voice shook slightly, she managed to say calmly and clearly, "I have no control over wagging tongues, your grace. If I had, I would not have been the topic of scandal two years ago. However, *I* have no desire whatever to reenter your society. I still have scars enough from my last sortie among the Quality." Having deliberately injected a liberal amount of derision into the word "Quality," Elizabeth closed her mouth and braced herself to be verbally filleted by the old woman whose white brows had snapped together over the bridge of her thin nose. An instant later, however, the pale hazel eyes registered something that might have been approval, then they shifted to Alexandra. With a curt nod the dowager said, "I quite agree, Alexandra. She has spirit enough to endure what they will put her through. Amazing, is it not," continued the dowager to Elizabeth with a gruff smile, "that on the one hand we of the *ton* pride ourselves on our civilized manners, and yet many of us will dine on one another's reputations in preference to the most sumptuous meal." Leaving Elizabeth to sink slowly and dazedly into the chair she'd shot out of but moments before, the dowager then walked over to the sofa and seated herself, her eyes narrowed in thought. "The Willingtons' ball tonight will be a complete crush," she said after a moment. "That may be to our advantage—everyone of importance and otherwise will be there. Afterward there'll be less reason to gossip about Elizabeth's appearance, for everyone will have seen her for themselves."

"Your grace," Elizabeth said, flustered and feeling some

expression of gratitude was surely in order for the trouble the dowager was about to be put to, "it—it's beyond kind of you to do this—"

"Nonsense," the woman interrupted, looking appalled. "I am rarely kind. Pleasant, at times," she continued while Alexandra tried to hide her amusement. "Even gracious when the occasion demands, but I wouldn't say 'kind.' 'Kind' is so very bland. Like lukewarm tea. Now, if you will take my advice, my girl," she added, looking at Elizabeth's strained features and pale skin, "you will immediately take yourself upstairs and have a long and restorative nap. You're alarmingly peaked. While you rest"—she turned to Alexandra—"Alexandra and I will make our plans."

Elizabeth reacted to this peremptory order to go to bed exactly as everyone reacted to the dowager duchess's orders: After a moment of shocked affront she did exactly as she was bidden.

Alex hastily excused herself to accompany Elizabeth to a guest chamber, and once inside, Alex hugged her tightly. "I'm sorry for that awful moment—she said she wanted to reassure herself you had courage, but I never imagined she meant to do it *that* way. In any case," she finished happily, "I *knew* she would like you excessively, and she does!"

She departed in a flurry of rose skirts, leaving Elizabeth to lean weakly against the door of her bed chamber and wonder how the dowager treated people she liked only slightly.

The dowager was waiting in the drawing room when Alex returned, a bemused expression on her face. "Alexandra," she began at once, helping herself to tea, "it occurs to me there is something of which you may not be aware. . . ."

She broke off, glaring at the butler who appeared in the doorway and caused her to stop speaking. "Excuse me, your grace," he said to Alexandra, "but Mr. Bentner begs a word with you."

"Who is Mr. Bentner?" the dowager demanded irritably when Alexandra instantly agreed to see him in the drawing room.

"Elizabeth's butler," Alex explained with a smile. "He's the most delightful man—he's addicted to mystery novels."

A moment later, while the dowager looked on in sharp disapproval, a stout, white-haired man clad in slightly shabby black coat and trousers marched boldly into the drawing room and seated himself beside Alexandra without so much as a by-your-leave.

"Your note said you have a plan to help Miss Elizabeth out of her coil, Miss Alex," he said eagerly. "I brought Berta myself so I could hear it."

"It's a little vague yet, Bentner," Alex admitted. "Basically, we're going to re-present her to society tonight and see if we can't live down that old scandal over Mr. Thornton."

"That *blackguard!*" Bentner spat. "The sound of his name makes my knuckles ache for a poke at him!" For emphasis, he shook his fist.

"It has the same effect on me," Alex admitted wryly. "That's as far as we've planned."

He stood up to leave, patted Alexandra's shoulder, and blithely informed the elderly noblewoman who terrified half the ton with her stony hauteur, and who was already glowering at him for his familiarity with Alex, "You've got yourself a fine girl here, your grace. We've known Miss Alex since she was a girl chasin' frogs at our pond with Miss Elizabeth."

The dowager did not reply. She sat in frigid silence, and only her eyes moved, following his progress out the door.

"Alexandra," she said awfully, but Alex laughed and held up her hand. "Don't berate me for familiarity with the servants, I beg you, Grandmama. I cannot change, and it only upsets you. Besides, you were about to tell me something that seemed important when Bentner arrived."

Diverted from her ire at indecorous servants, the dowager said severely, "You were so concerned in the salon that we not keep Elizabeth in an agony of doubt in here that you gave me no time to discuss some pertinent facts that may cause you some grave concern—that is, if you aren't already aware of them."

"What facts?"

"Have you seen the newspaper today?"

"Not yet. Why?"

"According to the *Times* and the *Gazette*, Stanhope

himself is here in London and has just affirmed Ian Thornton as his grandson and legal heir. Of course, it's been whispered for years that Thornton is his grandson, but only a few knew it for a fact."

"I had no idea," Alex said absently, thinking how grossly unfair it was that the unprincipled libertine who'd brought so much unhappiness into Elizabeth's life should be enjoying such good fortune at the same moment Elizabeth's future looked so bleak. "I never heard of him until six weeks ago, when we returned from our trip and someone mentioned his name in connection with the scandal over Elizabeth."

"That's hardly surprising. Prior to this past year he was rarely mentioned in *polite* drawing rooms. You and Jordan left on your trip before the scandal over Elizabeth occurred, so there's no reason you would have heard of him in connection with that, either."

"How could such a wretched blackguard convince someone to legitimize him as his heir?" Alex said angrily.

"I daresay he didn't need to be 'legitimized,' if I take your meaning. He is Stanhope's natural and legitimate grandson. Your husband told me that in confidence years ago. I also know," she added meaningfully, "that *Jordan* is one of the very few people to whom Thornton has ever admitted it."

Alexandra's feeling of disaster increased, and she slowly put her teacup back in the saucer. "Jordan?" she repeated in an alarmed voice. "Why on earth would a scoundrel like that have confided in *Jordan,* of all people?"

"As you well know, Alexandra," the duchess said bluntly, "your husband did not always live a life that was above reproach. He and Thornton ran with much the same crowd in their wilder days—gaming and drinking and doing whatever debauched things men do. It was this friendship of theirs that I feared you might not know of."

Alex closed her eyes in misery. "I was counting on Jordan's support to help us launch Elizabeth tonight. I've written to him explaining how dreadfully Elizabeth was treated by the most unspeakable cad alive, but I didn't mention his name. I never imagined Jordan would know of

Ian Thornton, let alone be *acquainted* with such a person. I was so *certain,"* she added heavily, "that if he met Elizabeth, he would do everything in his power to help put the right face on things tonight."

Reaching across the settee, the dowager squeezed her hand and said with a gruff smile, "We both know that Jordan would give you his full support if you wished to stand against foe *or* friend, my dear. However, in this instance you may not have his unconditional *empathy* when he finds out who the 'unspeakable cad' is. It is that which I wished to warn you about."

"Elizabeth mustn't know of this," Alex said fiercely. "She'll be so uneasy around Jordan—and I couldn't blame her. There is simply no justice in life!" she added, glowering at the unopened issue of the *Times* lying on the side table. "If there were, that—that despoiler of innocents would never be a marquess now, while Elizabeth has to be afraid to show her face in society. I don't suppose there's the slightest chance," she added hopefully, "that he didn't get a shilling or a piece of property with the title? I could endure it better if he were still a penniless Scots cottager or a down-at-the-heel gambler."

The duchess snorted indelicately. "There's no chance of that, my dear, and if that's what Elizabeth believes he is, she's been duped."

"I don't think I want to hear this," Alex said with an angry sigh. "No, I have to know. Tell me, please."

"There's little to tell," the dowager said, reaching for her gloves and starting to draw them on. "Shortly after the scandal with Elizabeth, Thornton vanished. Then, less than a year ago, someone—whose name was not divulged for a long time—bought that splendid estate in Tilshire, named it Montmayne, and began renovations, with an army of carpenters employed to do the work. A few months later a magnificent town house in Brook Street was sold—again to an 'undivulged purchaser.' Massive renovations began the next week on it, too. Society was all agog, wondering who the owner was, and a few months ago Ian Thornton drew up in front of number eleven Upper Brook Street and walked into the house. Two years ago the rumor was that Thornton was a gambler and no more, and he was assuredly persona non grata in most respectable homes. Today, however, I have the sad task of telling you, he's said to be richer than Croesus, and he's welcome in almost any drawing room he cares to set foot in—not that he cares to very often, fortunately." Standing up to leave, she finished in a dire voice, "You may as well face the rest of it now, because you'll have to face it this evening."

"What do you mean?" Alex asked, wearily arising.

"I mean that Elizabeth's prospects for success tonight were drastically reduced by Stanhope's announcement this morning."

"Why?"

"The reason is simple: Now that Thornton has a title to go with his wealth, what happened between him and Elizabeth will be overlooked by the *ton* as a 'gentleman's sport,' but it will continue to stain her reputation. And there's one more thing," she added in her most dire tone yet.

"I'm not certain I can bear it. What is it?"

"I," her grace announced, "do *not* have a good feeling about this evening!"

Neither did Alex at that moment. "Tony has agreed to escort Elizabeth tonight, and Sally is in accord," she said idly, referring to her brother-in-law and his wife, who was still at home in the country. "I wish, though, her escort was someone else—an eligible bachelor above reproach— someone everyone looks up to, or better yet *fears*. Roddy Carstairs would have been the *perfect* one. I've sent him an urgent message to present himself to me here at his earliest convenience, but he is not expected back until tonight or tomorrow. He would be the perfect one, if I could convince him to do it. Why, most people in society positively tremble in fear of his cutting remarks."

"They tremble in fear of *me*," said the dowager with pride.

"Yes, I know," Alex said with a wan smile. "No one will dare to give Elizabeth the cut direct in front of you, but Roddy might be able to terrify everyone into actually accepting her."

"Perhaps. Perhaps not. When and where are we all to gather tonight for this ill-fated debacle?"

Alex rolled her eyes and smiled reassuringly. "We'll leave from here at ten-thirty. I asked Jordan to meet us at the Willingtons' receiving line so that we can all go down to the ballroom together."

20

At eight-thirty that night Ian stood on the steps outside Elizabeth's uncle's town house suppressing an almost overwhelming desire to murder Elizabeth's butler, who seemed to be inexplicably fighting down the impulse to do bodily injury to Ian. "I will ask you again, in case you misunderstood me the last time," Ian enunciated in a silky, ominous tone that made ordinary men blanch. *"Where is your mistress?"*

Bentner didn't change color by so much as a shade. *"Out!"* he informed the man who'd ruined his young mistress's life and had now appeared on her doorstep unexpected and uninvited, no doubt to try to ruin it again when she was at this very moment attending her first ball in years and trying bravely to live down the gossip *he* had caused.

"She is out, but you do not know where she is?"

"I did not say so, did I?"

"Then *where* is she?"

"That is for me to know and you to ponder."

In the last several days Ian had been forced to do a great many unpleasant things, including riding across half of England, dealing with Christina's irate father, and finally dealing with Elizabeth's repugnant uncle, who had driven a

300

bargain that still infuriated him. Ian had magnanimously declined her dowry as soon as the discussions began. Her uncle, however, had the finely honed bargaining instincts of a camel trader, and he immediately sensed Ian's determination to do whatever was necessary to get Julius's name on a betrothal contract. As a result, Ian was the first man to his knowledge who had ever been put in the position of *purchasing* his future wife for a ransom of £150,000.

Once he'd finished that repugnant ordeal he'd ridden off to Montmayne, where he'd stopped only long enough to switch his horse for a coach and get his valet out of bed. Then he'd charged off to London, stopped at his town house to bathe and change, and gone straight to the address Julius Cameron had given him. Now, after all that, Ian was not only confronted by Elizabeth's absence, he was confronted by the most insolent servant he'd ever had the misfortune to encounter. In angry silence he turned and walked down the steps. Behind him the door slammed shut with a thundering crash, and Ian paused a moment to turn back and contemplate the pleasure he was going to have when he sacked the butler tomorrow.

He climbed into his coach and instructed his driver to turn the horses back to his house in Upper Brook Street, and there he alighted. His own butler opened the door with proper respect, and Ian strode past him, scowling and restless. He was halfway up the staircase when he decided his evening would pass more quickly if he spent it somewhere other than here, contemplating the rebellion he'd probably face in Elizabeth tomorrow.

Twenty-five minutes later he emerged from the town house formally attired for an evening of faro, and instructed his coachman to take him to the Blackmore. He was still scowling when he strode into the dimly lit, exclusive gentlemen's club where he had gambled at high stakes for years. "Good evening, *my lord,*" the head footman intoned, and Ian nodded curtly, suppressing a grimace at the obsequious use of "my lord."

The card room was elegantly appointed and well populated by the crème de la crème of society who preferred straight gambling to the gossip that all too often made

White's a dead bore, and by less illustrious but equally wealthy gentlemen who preferred to play for only the very high stakes that were required at the Blackmore. Pausing at the entrance to the card room, Ian started to leave and head for the faro room when a laughing voice remarked from his immediate left, "For a man who's just inherited a small empire, Ian, you have a remarkably sour expression on your face. Would you care to join me for a drink and a few hands of cards, my lord?"

An ironic smile twisted Ian's lips as he turned to acknowledge one of the few aristocrats he respected and regarded as a friend. "Certainly," he mocked, *"Your Grace."*

Jordan Townsende laughed. "It gets a little tedious, does it not?"

Grinning, the two men shook hands and sat down. Since Jordan had also just arrived at the club, they had to wait for a table. When they were seated a few minutes later they enjoyed a drink together, caught up on events of the past year and a half, and then got down to the more serious and pleasurable occupation of gaming, combined with desultory conversation. Normally the gaming would have been a pleasurable occupation, but tonight Ian was preoccupied, and every man who walked by the table felt it incumbent to pause and talk to one or both of them.

"It's our long absence from the city that makes us so popular," Jordan joked, tossing chips into the center of the table.

Ian scarcely heard him. His mind was on Elizabeth, who had been at the mercy of her loathsome uncle for two years. The man had bartered his own flesh and blood—and Ian was the purchaser. It wasn't true, of course, but he had an uneasy feeling Elizabeth would see it that way as soon as she discovered what had been done without her knowledge or consent. In Scotland she'd drawn a gun on him. In London he wouldn't blame her if she fired it. He was toying with the idea of trying to court her for a few days before he told her they were already betrothed, and simultaneously wondering if she was going to hate the idea of marrying him. Belhaven might be a repulsive toad, but Ian had grievously and repeatedly wronged her. "I don't mean to criticize your strategy, my friend"—Jordan's drawl drew Ian's wandering attention—"but you have just wagered £1,000 on what appears to be a pair of absolutely nothing."

Ian glanced down at the hand he'd just turned over and actually felt a flush of embarrassment steal up his neck. "I have something on my mind," he explained.

"Whatever it is, it is assuredly not cards. Either that or you've lost your famous touch."

"I wouldn't be surprised," Ian said absently, stretching out his long legs and crossing them at the ankles.

"Do you want to play another hand?"

"I don't think I can afford it," Ian joked wearily.

Glancing over his shoulder, Jordan nodded to a footman to bring two more drinks to their table, then he shoved the cards aside. Leaning back in his chair, he stretched his own legs out, and the two men regarded each other, a portrait of indolent, masculine camaraderie. "I have time for only one drink," Jordan said, glancing at the ormolu clock on the opposite wall. "I've promised Alexandra to stand at her side at a ball tonight and beam approvingly at a friend of hers."

Whenever Jordan mentioned his wife's name, Ian noted with amusement, the other man's entire expression softened.

"Care to join us?"

Ian shook his head and accepted his drink from the footman. "It sounds boring as hell."

"I don't think it'll be boring, precisely. My wife has taken it upon herself to defy the entire *ton* and sponsor the girl back into the ranks. Based on some of the things Alexandra said in her note, that will be no mean feat."

"Why is that?" Ian inquired with more courtesy than interest.

Jordan sighed and leaned his head back, weary from the hours he'd been working for the last several weeks and unexcited at the prospect of dancing attendance on a damsel in distress—one he'd never set eyes on. "The girl fell into the clutches of some man two years ago, and an ugly scandal ensued."

Thinking of Elizabeth and himself, Ian said casually, "That's not an uncommon occurrence, evidently."

"From what Alex wrote me, it seems this case is rather extreme."

303

"In what way?"

"For one thing, there's every chance the young woman will get the cut direct tonight from half the *ton*—and that's the half that will be willing to acknowledge her. Alex has retaliated by calling in the heavy guns—my grandmother, to be exact, and Tony and myself, to a lesser degree. The object is to try to brave it out, but I don't envy the girl. Unless I miss my guess, she's going to be flayed alive by the wagging tongues tonight. Whatever the bastard did," Jordan finished, downing his drink and starting to straighten in his chair, "it was damaging as hell. The girl—who's purported to be incredibly beautiful, by the way—has been a social outcast for nearly two years."

Ian stiffened, his glass arrested partway to his mouth, his sharpened gaze on Jordan, who was already starting to rise. "Who's the girl?" he demanded tautly.

"Elizabeth Cameron."

"Oh, *Christ!*" Ian exploded, surging out of his chair and snatching up his evening jacket. "Where are they?"

"At the Willingtons'. Why?"

"Because," Ian bit out, impatiently shrugging into his jacket and tugging the frilled cuffs of his shirt into place, *"I'm* the bastard who did it."

An indescribable expression flashed across the Duke of Hawthorne's face as he, too, pulled on his evening jacket. *"You* are the man Alexandra described in her note as an 'unspeakable cad, vile libertine,' and 'despoiler of innocents'?"

"I'm all that and more," Ian replied grimly, stalking toward the door with Jordan Townsende beside him. "You go to the Willingtons' as quickly as you can," he instructed. "I'll be close behind you, but I've a stop to make first. And don't, for God's sake, tell Elizabeth I'm on my way."

Ian flung himself into his coach, snapped orders to his driver, and leaned back, counting minutes, telling himself it couldn't possibly be going as badly for her as he feared it would. And never once did he stop to think that Jordan Townsende had no idea what motives could possibly prompt Elizabeth Cameron's "despoiler" to be bent on meeting her at the Willingtons' ball.

His coach drew up before the Duke of Stanhope's town

house, and Ian walked swiftly up the front steps, almost knocking poor Ormsley, who opened the door, off his feet in his haste to get to his grandfather upstairs. A few minutes later he strode back down and into the library, where he flung himself into a chair, his eyes riveted on the clock. Upstairs the household was in an uproar as the duke called for his valet, his butler, and his footmen. Unlike Ian, however, the duke was ecstatic. "Ormsley, Ian *needs* me!" the duke said happily, stripping off his jacket and pulling off his neckcloth. "He walked right in here and *said* it."

Ormsley beamed. "He did indeed, your grace."

"I feel twenty years younger."

Ormsley nodded. "This is a very great day."

"What in hell is keeping Anderson? I need a shave. I want evening clothes—black, I think—a diamond stickpin and diamond studs. Stop thrusting that cane at me, man."

"You shouldn't overly exert yourself, your grace."

"Ormsley," said the duke as he walked over to an armoire and flung the doors open, "if you think I'm going to be leaning on that damned cane on the greatest night of my life, you're out of your mind. I'll walk in there beside my grandson unaided, thank you very much. Where the *devil* is *Anderson?*"

"We are late, Alexandra," said the dowager duchess as she stood in Alex's drawing room idly examining a magnificent fourteenth-century sculpture reposing on a satinwood table. "And I don't mind telling you, now that the time is upon us, I have a *worse* feeling about this now than I did earlier. And my instincts are never wrong."

Alexandra bit her lip, trying to fight down her own growing trepidation. "The Willingtons are just around the corner," she said, dealing with the matter of lateness before she faced more grim details. "We can be there in a matter of minutes. Besides, I want everyone there when Elizabeth makes her entrance. I was also hoping that Roddy might yet answer my note."

As if in response to that, the butler appeared in the drawing room. "Roderick Carstairs wishes to be announced, your grace," he informed Alex.

"Thank heavens!" she burst out.

305

"I showed him into the blue salon."

Alex mentally crossed her fingers.

"I have come, my lovely," Roddy said with his usual sardonic grin as he swept her a deep bow, "in answer to your urgent summons—and, I might add," he continued, *"before* I presented myself at the Willingtons', exactly as your message instructed." At 5'10", Roddy Carstairs was a slender man of athletic build with thinning brown hair and light blue eyes. In fact, his only distinguishing characteristics were his fastidiously tailored clothes, a much-envied ability to tie a neckcloth into magnificently intricate folds that never drooped, and an acid wit that accepted no boundaries when he chose a human target. "Did you hear about Kensington?"

"Who?" Alex said absently, trying to think of the best means to persuade him to do what she needed done.

"The new Marquess of Kensington, once known as Mr. Ian Thornton, persona non grata. Amazing, is it not, what wealth and title will do?" he continued, studying Alex's tense face as he continued, "Two years ago we wouldn't have let him past the front door. Six months ago word got out that he's worth a fortune, and we started inviting him to our parties. Tonight he's the heir to a dukedom, and we'll be coveting invitations to *his* parties. We are"—Roddy grinned—"when you consider matters from this point of view, a rather sickening and fickle lot."

In spite of herself, Alexandra laughed. "Oh, Roddy," she said, pressing a kiss on his cheek. "You *always* make me laugh, even when I'm in the most dreadful coil, which I am now. You could make things so very much better—if you would."

Roddy helped himself to a pinch of snuff, lifted his arrogant brows, and waited, his look both suspicious and intrigued. "I am, of course, your most obedient servant," he drawled with a little mocking bow.

Despite that claim, Alexandra knew better. While other men might be feared for their tempers or their skill with rapier and pistol, Roddy Carstairs was feared for his cutting barbs and razor tongue. And, while one could not carry a rapier or a pistol into a ball, Roddy could do his damage there unimpeded. Even sophisticated matrons lived in fear of being on the wrong side of him. Alex knew exactly how deadly he could be—and how helpful, for he had made her life a living hell when she came to London the first time. Later he had done a complete turnabout, and it had been Roddy who had forced the *ton* to accept her. He had done it not out of friendship or guilt; he had done it because he'd decided it would be amusing to test his power by building a reputation for a change, instead of shredding it.

"There is a young woman whose name I'll reveal in a moment," Alex began cautiously, "to whom you could be of great service. You could, in fact, rescue her as you did me long ago, Roddy, if only you would."

"Once was enough," he mocked. "I could hardly hold my head up for shame when I thought of my unprecedented gallantry."

"She's incredibly beautiful," Alex said.

A mild spark of interest showed in Roddy's eyes, but nothing stronger. While other men might be affected by feminine beauty, Roddy generally took pleasure in pointing out one's faults for the glee of it. He enjoyed flustering women and never hesitated to do it. But when he decided to be kind he was the most loyal of friends. "She was the victim of some very malicious gossip two years ago and left London in disgrace. She is also a very particular friend of mine from long ago."

She searched Roddy's bland features and couldn't tell whether she was getting his support or not. "All of us—the dowager duchess, Tony, and Jordan—intend to stand with her at the Willingtons' tonight. But if you could just pay her some small attention—or better yet, escort her yourself—it would be ever so helpful, and I would be grateful forever."

"Alex, if you were married to anyone but Jordan Townsende, I might consider asking you *how* you'd be willing to express your gratitude. However, since I haven't any real wish to see my life brought to a premature end, I shall refrain from doing so and say instead that your smile is gratitude enough."

"Don't joke, Roddy, I'm quite desperately in need of your help, and I would be eternally grateful for it."

"You are making me quake with trepidation, my sweet. Whoever she is, she must be in a deal of trouble if you need me."

"She's lovely and spirited, and you will admire her tremendously."

"In that case, I shall deem it an embarrassing honor to lend my support to her. Who—" His gaze flicked to a sudden movement in the doorway and riveted there, his eternally bland expression giving way to reverent admiration. "My God," he whispered.

Standing in the doorway like a vision from heaven was an unknown young woman clad in a shimmering silver-blue gown with a low, square neckline that offered a tantalizing view of smooth, voluptuous flesh, and a diagonally wrapped bodice that emphasized a tiny waist. Her glossy golden hair was swept back off her forehead and held in place with a sapphire clip, then left to fall artlessly about her shoulders and midway down her back, where it ended in luxurious waves and curls that gleamed brightly in the dancing candlelight. Beneath gracefully winged brows and long, curly lashes her glowing green eyes were neither jade nor emerald, but a startling color somewhere in between.

In that moment of stunned silence Roddy observed her with the impartiality of a true connoisseur, looking for flaws that others would miss and finding only perfection in the delicately sculpted cheekbones, slender white throat, and soft mouth.

The vision in the doorway moved imperceptibly. "Excuse me," she said to Alexandra with a melting smile, her voice like wind chimes, "I didn't realize you weren't alone."

In a graceful swirl of silvery blue skirts she turned and vanished, and still Roddy stared at the empty doorway while Alexandra's hopes soared. Never had she seen Roddy display the slightest genuine fascination for a feminine face and figure. His words sent her spirits even higher: "My God," he said again in a reverent whisper. "Was she *real?*"

"Very real," Alex eagerly assured him, "and very desperately in need of your help, though she mustn't know what I've asked of you. You will help, won't you?"

Dragging his gaze from the doorway, he shook his head as if to clear it. *"Help?"* he uttered dryly. "I'm tempted to offer her my very desirable hand in marriage! First I ought to know her name, though I'll tell you she suddenly seems damned familiar."

"You will help?"

"Didn't I just say so? Who is that delectable creature?"

"Elizabeth Cameron. She made her debut last—" Alex stopped as Roddy's smile turned harsh and sardonic.

"Little Elizabeth Cameron," he mused half to himself. "I should have guessed, of course. The chit set the city on its ear just after you left on your honeymoon trip, but she's changed. Who would have guessed," he continued in a more normal voice, "that fate would have seen fit to endow her with *more* looks than she had then."

"Roddy!" Alex said, sensing that his attitude toward helping was undergoing a change. "You already said you'd help."

"You don't need help, Alex," he snickered. "You need a *miracle.*"

"But—"

"Sorry. I've changed my mind."

"Is it the—the gossip about that old scandal that bothers you?"

"In a sense."

Alexandra's blue eyes began to spark with dangerous fire. "You're a fine one to believe gossip, Roddy! You above all know it's usually lies, because *you've* started your share of it!"

"I didn't say I believe it," he drawled coolly. "In fact, I'd find it hard to believe that any man's hands, *including* Thornton's, have ever touched that porcelain skin of hers. However," he said, abruptly closing the lid on his snuffbox and tucking it away, "society is *not* as discerning as I, or, in this instance, as kind. They will cut her dead tonight, never fear, and not even the influential Townsendes or my influential self could prevent it. Though I hate the thought of sinking any lower in your esteem than I can see I already have, I'm going to tell you an unlovely truth about myself, my sweet Alex," he added with a sardonic grin. "Tonight, any unattached bachelor who's foolish enough to show an interest in that girl is going to be the laughingstock of the Season, and *I* do *not* like being laughed at. I do not have the courage, which is why *I* am always the one to make jokes of others. Furthermore," he finished, reaching for his hat, "in society's eyes Elizabeth Cameron is used goods. Any bachelor who goes near her will be deemed a fool or a letch, and he'll suffer her fate."

At the door he stopped and turned, looking unperturbable and amused as usual. "For what it's worth, I shall make it a point to proclaim tonight that *I* for one don't believe she was with Thornton in a cottage or a greenhouse or anywhere else. That may slow down the tempest at first, but it won't stop it."

310

21

Less than an hour later, in the crowded, noisy, candlelit ballroom, Alexandra was painfully aware that all Roddy's predictions had been accurate. It was the first time in her recollection when she and Jordan were not completely surrounded by friends and acquaintances and even hangers-on eager to incur Jordan's favor and influence. Tonight, however, everyone was avoiding them. In the mistaken belief that Jordan and Alexandra would be deeply chagrined when they discovered the truth about Elizabeth Cameron, the Townsendes' friends were politely trying to lessen their inevitable embarrassment by simply pretending not to notice that the Townsendes were present and in the company of Elizabeth Cameron, whose reputation had sunk beneath reproach during their absence from England. Although they ignored Jordan and Alexandra out of courtesy, they, like everyone else at the ball, didn't hesitate to cast scathing glances at Elizabeth whenever they could do so without being seen by the few people she'd evidently duped into befriending her. Standing near the dance floor where dancers were whirling about—and stealing smirking glances at Elizabeth—Alexandra was caught between tears and fury. As she looked at Elizabeth, who was making a magnificent effort to smile at her, her throat constricted with guilt and sympathy. The laughter and music were so noisy that Alex had to lean forward in order to hear what Elizabeth was saying.

"If you don't mind," Elizabeth told her in a suffocated voice that belied her smile and made it obvious to Alex that she was drowning in humiliation, "I—I think I'll just find a retiring room and see to my gown."

There was nothing whatever wrong with Elizabeth's gown, and they both knew it. "I'll go with you."

Elizabeth shook her head. "Alex, if you don't mind . . . I'd like to be alone for just a few moments. It's the noise," she lied bravely.

Elizabeth moved away, keeping her head high, threading her way through six hundred people who either avoided meeting her gaze or turned away to laugh and whisper.

Tony, Jordan, the duchess, and Alexandra all watched her as she walked gracefully up the stairs. Jordan spoke first, careful to keep the emotion out of his voice for fear that if he showed how infuriated he was with all six hundred people in the ballroom, Alexandra would lose her slender thread of control, and the tears shining in her eyes would fall down her flushed cheeks. Putting his arm around her waist, he smiled into her tear-brightened eyes, but he spoke quickly because, as Elizabeth walked away, the acquaintances who'd been giving the Townsendes a wide berth were beginning to start their way.

"If it is any consolation, darling," Jordan told her, "*I* think Elizabeth Cameron is the most magnificently courageous young woman I've ever met. Except for you."

"Thank you." Alexandra tried to smile, but her gaze kept reaching for Elizabeth as she moved up the curving staircase.

"They will regret this!" the dowager said frigidly, and to prove it, she turned her back on two of her intimate friends who were now approaching her. The dowager's acquaintances had been the only ones to join the Townsendes tonight, because they were of her own age, and so several of them were unaware that Elizabeth Cameron was to be ridiculed, scorned, and snubbed.

Swallowing a lump of tears, Alex glanced at her husband. "At least," she said, trying to joke, "Elizabeth hasn't been completely without admirers. Belhaven's been hanging about her."

"Because," Jordan said without thinking, "he's on everybody's blacklist, and no one has condescended to share the gossip about Elizabeth with him—yet," he amended, watching with narrowed eyes as two elderly fops tugged Belhaven's sleeve, nodded toward Elizabeth's back, and began to speak rapidly.

Elizabeth spent the better part of a half hour standing alone in a small, dark salon, trying to compose herself. It was there that she heard the excited voices of guests discussing something that on any other night would at least have evoked a feeling of shock: Ian had just been named heir to the Duke of Stanhope. Elizabeth felt no emotion at all.

In her state of consuming misery she was incapable of feeling anything more. She remembered, though, Valerie's voice in the garden long ago as she looked through the hedge at Ian: "Some say he's the illegitimate grandson of the Duke of Stanhope." The memory drifted past Elizabeth's mind, aimless, meaningless. When she had no choice but to return to the ballroom she crossed the balcony and descended the stairs, wending her way through the crowd, avoiding the malicious eyes that made her skin burn and her heart contort. Despite her brief respite her head was pounding from the effort of maintaining her composure; the music she'd once loved blared discordantly in her ears, shouts of laughter and roars of conversation thundered around her, and above the din the butler, who was positioned at the top of the stairs leading down to the ballroom, called out the name of each new arrival like a sentry tolling the time. Many of the names he called out Elizabeth recalled from her debut, and each one identified another person who, she knew, was about to walk down the stairs and learn to their derision that Elizabeth Cameron was there. One more voice would repeat the old gossip; one more pair of ears would hear it; one more pair of cold eyes would look her way.

Her brother's arrogance in refusing her suitors two years ago would be recalled, and they would point out that only Sir Francis would have her now, and they would laugh. And in some ways, Elizabeth couldn't blame them. So utterly shamed was she that even the occasional faces that looked at her with sympathy and puzzlement, instead of contempt and condemnation, seemed vaguely threatening.

As she neared the Townsendes she noted that Sir Francis, clad in absurd pink britches and yellow satin jacket, was now carrying on an animated discussion with Alex and the Duke of Hawthorne. Elizabeth glanced about, looking for somewhere to hide until he went away, when she suddenly recognized a group of faces she had hoped never to see again. Less than twenty feet away Viscount Mondevale was watching her, and on both sides of him were several men and the girls Elizabeth had once called her friends. Elizabeth looked right through him and changed direction, then gave a start of surprise when he intercepted her just as she came to Alex and her husband. Short of walking over him, Elizabeth had no choice but to stop.

He looked very handsome, very sincere, and slightly ill at ease. "Elizabeth," he said quietly, "you are looking lovelier than ever."

He was the last person in the world she'd have expected to take pity on her plight, and Elizabeth wasn't certain whether she was grateful or angry, since the abrupt withdrawal of his offer had vastly contributed to it. "Thank you, my lord," she said in a noncommittal voice.

"I wanted to say," he began again, his eyes searching her composed features, "that I—I'm sorry."

That did it! Annoyance lifted Elizabeth's delicate chin an inch higher. "For what, sir?"

He swallowed, standing so close to her that his sleeve touched hers when he lifted his hand and then dropped it to his side. "For my part in what's happened to you."

"What am I to say to that?" she asked, and she honestly did not know.

"In your position," he said with a grim smile, "I think I'd slap my face for the belated apology."

A touch of Elizabeth's humor returned, and with a regal nod of her head she said, "I should like that very much."

Amazingly, the admiration in his eyes doubled. When he showed an inclination to linger at her side, Elizabeth had no choice but to turn and introduce him to the Townsendes— with whom, she discovered, he was already acquainted.

While he and Jordan exchanged pleasantries, however, Elizabeth watched with growing horror as Valerie, evidently resentful of Mondevale's brief desertion, began moving forward. Walking with her as if they were moving as one, were Penelope, Georgina, and all the others, closing in on a panicking Elizabeth. In a combined effort to sidle away from them and simultaneously rescue Alex from Sir Francis's boring monologue and roving eyes, Elizabeth turned to try to speak to her, but Sir Francis would not be silenced. By the time he finally finished his story Valerie had already arrived, and Elizabeth was trapped. Reeking with malice, Valerie cast a contemptuous look over Elizabeth's pale face and said, "Well, if it isn't Elizabeth Cameron. We certainly never expected to see you at a place like this."

"I'm sure you never did," Elizabeth managed to say in a controlled voice, but she was beginning to break under the strain.

"No, indeed," said Georgina with a twittering laugh.

Elizabeth felt as if she were suffocating, and the room began to undulate around her. The Townsende group had been like an isolated island all night; now people were turning to see who'd had the daring to go near them. The waltz was building to a roaring crescendo; the voices were getting louder; people were pouring down the staircase a few yards away; and the butler's endless monotone chant rose above the deafening din: *"The Count and Countess of Marsant!"* he boomed. *"The Earl of Norris! . . . Lord Wilson! . . . Lady Millicent Montgomery! . . ."*

Valerie and Georgina were looking at her pale face with amusement, saying words that were receding from Elizabeth's mind, drowned by the roaring in her ears and the butler's rhythmic calls: *"Sir William Fitzhugh! . . . Lord and Lady Enderly! . . ."*

Turning her back on Valerie's and Georgina's scorching hatred, Elizabeth said in a ragged whisper, "Alex, I'm not feeling well!" But Alex couldn't hear her because Sir Francis was droning on again.

"The Baron and Baronesss of Littlefield! . . . Sir Henry Hardin! . . ."

Elizabeth turned in desperation to the dowager, feeling as

if she was going to either scream or faint if she couldn't get out of there, not caring that Valerie and Georgina and everyone else in the room would know that she had fled from her own disgrace. "I have to leave," she told the dowager.

"The Earl of Titchley! . . . The Count and Countess of Rindell! . . ."

The dowager held up her hand to silence one of her friends and leaned toward Elizabeth. "What did you say, Elizabeth?"

"His Grace, the Duke of Stanhope! . . . The Marquess of Kensington!"

"I said," Elizabeth began, but the dowager's eyes had snapped to the landing where the butler was stationed, and her face was blanching. "I wish to leave!" Elizabeth cried, but an odd silence was sweeping over the room, and her voice was unnaturally loud.

Instead of replying to Elizabeth's statement, the dowager was doing what everyone else was doing: staring at the landing. "Tonight only wanted *this!*" the older woman said in a furious voice.

"I—I beg your pardon?" Elizabeth asked.

"Do you swoon?" the duchess demanded, dragging her eyes from the landing and pinning Elizabeth with the direst of looks.

"No, not in the past, but I really don't feel well." Behind her Valerie and Georgina erupted into laughter.

"Do not even *consider* leaving until I say you may," the dowager said tersely, sending a speaking look to Lord Anthony Townsende, a pleasant, unaffected man who'd been her escort tonight, and who suddenly clamped Elizabeth's elbow in a supporting grip. The entire crowd in the ballroom seemed to be pressing infinitesimally closer to the staircase, and the ones who weren't were turning to look at Elizabeth with raised brows. Elizabeth had been the cynosure of so many eyes tonight that she took no notice of the hundreds of pairs glancing her way now. But she felt the sudden tension growing in the room, the excitement building, and she glanced uncertainly in the direction of whatever seemed to be causing it. The vision she beheld made her knees tremble violently and a scream rise in her throat; for a split second she thought she was having a distorted double vision, and she blinked, but the vision didn't clear. Descending the staircase side by side were two men of identical height, clad in matching black evening clothes, wearing matching expressions of mild amusement on their very similar faces. And one of them was Ian Thornton.

"Elizabeth!" Tony whispered urgently. "Come with me. We're going to dance."

"Dance?" she uttered.

"Dance," he averred, half pulling her toward the dance floor. Once there, Elizabeth's shock was superseded by a blissful sense of unreality. Rather than deal with the horrible fact that the gossip about her former relationship with Ian was now going to erupt like a full-fledged volcano, and the equally appalling fact that Ian was there, her mind simply went blank, oblivious. No longer did the noise in the ballroom pound in her ears; she scarcely heard it at all. No longer did the watchful eyes wound her; she saw only Tony's shoulder, covered in dark blue superfine. Even when he reluctantly guided her back to the group around the Townsendes, which still included Valerie and Georgina and Viscount Mondevale, Elizabeth felt . . . nothing.

"Are you all right?" Tony asked worriedly.

"Perfectly," she replied with a sweet smile.

"Do you have any hartshorn with you?"

"I never faint."

"That's good. Your friends are still standing around to watch and listen, eager to see what happens now."

"Yes, they will not want to miss this."

"What do you think he will do?"

Elizabeth raised her eyes and looked at Ian without a tremor. He was still beside the gray-haired man who looked so like him, and they were both surrounded by people who were gathering around and seemed to be congratulating them on something. "Nothing."

"Nothing?"

"Why should he do anything?"

"Do you mean he'll cut you?"

"I never know what to expect from him. Does it matter?"

At that moment Ian lifted his gaze and saw her, and th only cut he thought of was a way to cut through the drive and good wishes so that he could get to her. But he couldn' yet. Even though she looked pale and stricken and hear breakingly beautiful, he had to meet her casually, if ther was any hope of putting the right face on it. With infuriatin persistence the well-wishers gathered around, the men toady ing, the women curtsying; and those who weren't, Ia noticed with fury, were whispering and looking at Elizabeth

Ian lasted five minutes before he signaled his grandfathe with a curt nod, and they both disengaged themselves from three dozen people who were waiting to be formally pre sented to the Marquess of Kensington. Together they starte through the crowd, Ian nodding absently to acquaintance and trying to avoid being waylaid, but pausing to bow an shake hands now and then so it wouldn't seem that he wa heading straight for Elizabeth. His grandfather, who ha been apprised of the plan in the coach, carried the whol thing off with aplomb. "Stanhope!" someone boomed "Introduce us to your grandson."

The stupid charade chafed against Ian's straining pa tience. He'd already been introduced to half these people a Ian Thornton, and the pretense that he *hadn't* was a infuriating farce. But he endured it for the sake of appear ances.

"How are you, Wilson?" Ian said at one of their innumer able pauses. "Suzanne," he said, smiling at Wilson's wif while he watched Elizabeth out of the corner of his eye. Sh hadn't moved, didn't seem to be capable of movement Someone had handed her a glass of champagne, and she wa holding it, smiling at Jordan Townsende, who seemed to b joking with her. Even from this distance Ian could see he smile lacked its entrancing sparkle, and his heart twisted "We'll have to do that," he heard himself say to someon who was inviting him to call at their house, and then he'c had all he was willing to endure. He turned in Elizabeth' direction, and his grandfather obligingly stopped conversa tion with a crony. The minute Ian started toward Elizabeth the whispers hit unprecedented volume.

Alexandra cast a worried look at her, then at Jordan. "As Elizabeth to dance, please!" she implored him urgently

318

For heaven's sake, get her out of here. That monster is coming straight in our direction."

Jordan hesitated and glanced at Ian, and whatever he saw in the other man's expression made him hesitate and shake his head. "It's going to be all right, love," he promised with only a twinge of doubt as he stepped forward to shake Ian's hand, exactly as if they hadn't been playing cards a short while ago. "Permit me to present you to my wife," Jordan said.

Jordan turned to the beautiful brunette who looked at him with blazing blue eyes. "A pleasure," he murmured, lifting her hand to his lips and feeling her exert pressure to yank it away. The dowager duchess acknowledged Ian's introduction with something that might, by a great stretch of the imagination, be considered an inclination of her regal white head and snapped, "I am *not* pleased to meet you."

Ian endured both ladies' rebuffs and then endured Jordan's deliberate ploy to "introduce" him to Elizabeth. A girl named Georgina curtsied to Ian, her eyes inviting. Another named Valerie curtsied, then stepped back in nervous fright from the blast from Ian's eyes as he nodded curtly to her. Mondevale was next, and Ian's first spurt of jealousy vanished when he saw Valerie clinging possessively to the young viscount's arm. *"I think Valerie did it because she wanted Mondevale,"* he recalled Elizabeth saying.

Elizabeth watched it all with interest and no emotion until Ian was finally standing in front of her, but the instant his golden eyes met hers she felt the shaking begin in her limbs. "Lady Elizabeth Cameron," Jordan intoned.

A slow, lazy smile swept across Ian's face, and Elizabeth braced her quaking self for him to say something mocking, but his deep voice was filled with admiration and teasing. "Lady Cameron," he said, raising his voice enough to be heard by the other girls. "I see you are still casting every other female into the shade. May I present my grandfather to you—"

Elizabeth *knew* she was dreaming. He had introduced his grandfather to no one but her, and the honor was both deliberate and noted by everyone within sight.

When he moved away Elizabeth felt herself sag with relief. "Well!" said the dowager with a reluctant nod of approval,

watching him. "I daresay he pulled that off well enough
Look there," she said several minutes later, "he's escortin
Evelyn Makepeace onto the dance floor. If Makepeac
didn't give him the cut direct, he's just been given the stam
of approval."

A hysterical giggle welled up inside Elizabeth. As if Ia
Thornton would care whether he was cut! As if he'd care
snap for a stamp of approval! Her disjointed thoughts wer
interrupted by the second man to ask her for a dance a
evening. With an elegant bow and a warm, searching smil
the Duke of Stanhope offered his arm to her. "Would yo
honor me with this dance, Lady Cameron?" he asked
blithely ignoring his duty to dance with the older wome
first.

Elizabeth considered refusing. She wasn't certain at th
moment she'd remember *how,* but there was somethin
imploring and almost urgent in the duke's look when sh
hesitated, and she reluctantly laid her gloved fingers on hi
arm.

As they walked through the crowd Elizabeth concentrate
on keeping her mind perfectly blank. So successful was sh
in that endeavor that they had nearly reached the danc
floor before she realized the older man's stride was slightl
slower than it needed to be. Rousing herself from he
lethargic misery, she cast a worried glance at his handsom
face, and he smiled. "An old riding injury," he explained
obviously guessing the cause of her concern. "I'm quit
adept at dealing with it, however, and I shan't disgrace us o
the dance floor." As he spoke he put his hand on her wais
and moved her into the midst of the dancers with easy grace
When they were safely blocked from view of the guests b
the other dancers, however, his face sobered. "Ian ha
charged me to give you a message," he told her gently.

It occurred to Elizabeth, not for the first time, that durin
every one of the five short days she'd spent in Ia
Thornton's company he had turned her emotions upsid
down and inside out, and she was not in a mood to let hin
do it again tonight. Lifting her eyes to the duke's, sh
regarded him politely but without any sign of interest i
hearing Ian's message.

"I am to tell you not to worry," the duke explained. "Al

you need do is remain here for another hour or so and trust him."

Elizabeth lost control of her expression completely; her eyes widened with shock, and her slender shoulders shook with laughter that was part hysteria and part exhaustion. "Trust him?" she repeated. Every time she was near Ian Thornton she felt as if she were a ball being slammed and bounced off his racket in whatever direction his whim chose to send her, and she was heartily and thoroughly weary of it. She smiled at the duke again and shook her head at the sheer absurdity of what his message suggested.

Among those dancers who were close enough to see what was happening, it was noted and immediately remarked upon that Lady Cameron seemed, amazingly, to be on the most amiable terms with the Duke of Stanhope. It was also being duly and uncomfortably noted by the entire assembly that not just one, but now two of the most influential families in England seemed to be championing her.

Ian, who had guessed before ever setting foot in the ballroom exactly how their collective minds would work, was standing amid the crowd, doing his skillful utmost to ensure their thoughts continued to move in the direction in which he pointed them. Since he couldn't stop the gossip about his relationship with Elizabeth, he set out to turn it in a new direction. With an indulgent cordiality he'd never before displayed to the *ton,* he allowed himself to be verbally feted while deliberately letting his admiring gaze rest periodically on her. His unhidden interest in the lady, combined with his lazy, sociable smile, positively invited questions from those who'd gathered around to speak to the new heir to the Stanhope prestige. They in turn were so emboldened by his attitude and so eager for a firsthand on-dit about his relationship with her that several of them ventured a hesitant but joking remark. Lord Newsom, a wealthy fop who'd attached himself to Ian's elbow, followed Ian's gaze on one of the occasions when it shifted to Elizabeth and went so far as to remark, in the amused tone of one exchanging manly confidences, "She's something, isn't she? It was the talk of the town when you got her off for an afternoon alone in that cottage two years ago."

Ian grinned and lifted his glass to his mouth, deliberately

looking at Elizabeth over its rim. "Was it?" he asked in a amused tone that was loud enough to reach the ears of th avidly interested gentlemen around him.

"Indeed it was."

"Did I enjoy it?"

"I beg your pardon?"

"I asked if I enjoyed being with her in that cottage."

"Why ask? You were there together."

Rather than deny it, which would never convince then Ian let the comment hang in the air until the other ma demanded, "Well, *weren't* you with her there?"

"No," he admitted with a rueful, conspiratorial grin, "bu it was not for want of trying on my part."

"Give over, Kensington," one of them chided with der sion. "There's no point in trying to protect the lady now You were seen with her in the greenhouse."

Instead of smashing his face, Ian quirked an amused brow at him. "As I said, it was not for want of trying to get her o alone."

Seven male faces gaped at him in disbelief that wa turning to disappointment; a moment later that gave way t shocked gratification when the new marquess asked the counsel: "I wonder," Ian remarked as if thinking aloud, "i she'd look with more favor on a marquess than she did on mere mister."

"Good God, man," one of them laughed sarcastically "The promise of a coronet will win you the hand of an woman you want."

"The promise of a coronet?" Ian repeated, frowning little. "I gather it's your opinion, then, that the lady woul settle for nothing less than marriage?"

The man, who'd thought nothing of the sort a momen ago, now nodded, though he wasn't exactly certain how he' come to agree.

When Ian departed he left behind six men who had th diverting impression that the Marquess of Kensington ha been rebuffed by Lady Cameron when he was a mere mister and *that* bit of gossip was far more delectable than th former gossip that he'd seduced her.

With democratic impartiality, all six of those men share their misinformation and erroneous conclusions with any one in the ballroom who wanted to listen. And everyone was more than eager to listen. Within thirty minutes the ballroom was alive with speculation on this new information, and several males were studying Elizabeth with new interest. Two of them hesitantly presented themselves to Ian's grandfather and requested introductions to her, and shortly afterward Ian saw her being drawn to the dance floor by one of them, with his grandfather beaming approval. Knowing that he had done all he could to stem the gossip about her for one night, Ian then performed the only other ritual he had to endure before he could ask her to dance without exposing her to further censure: He asked seven consecutive women of assorted ages and unimpeachable reputations to dance with him first.

When all seven duty-dances were over, Ian caught Jordan Townsende's eye and tipped his head very slightly toward the balcony, sending him the signal that Ian knew his grandfather had already forewarned Jordan to expect.

Elizabeth noticed none of that as she stood with the Townsendes, letting the conversations swirl around her. In a welcome state of calm unreality she listened to several gentlemen who seemed to have lost their aversion to her, but her only genuine feelings were of relief that the Townsendes were no longer ostracized, and a lingering frustration that when she had asked if she could leave, nearly an hour ago, Jordan Townsende had glanced at the Duke of Stanhope and then shaken his head and gently told her, "Not for a while." Thus she was forced to remain, surrounded by people whose faces and voices never quite penetrated her senses, even though she smiled politely at their remarks or nodded agreement at their comments or danced with a few of them.

She was not aware that while she danced, the Duke of Stanhope had relayed the rest of Ian's instructions to Jordan, and so she felt no warning tremor when Jordan tipped his head in acknowledgment of Ian's signal and abruptly said to Anthony Townsende, "I think the ladies would enjoy a stroll out on the balcony." Alex gave him a swift, questioning look but placed her hand on her husband's arm, while Elizabeth obediently turned and allowed Lord Anthony to offer her his. Along with the Duke of Stanhope, the party of five moved through the ballroom—

an honor guard to protect Elizabeth, arranged in advance by the same man who had caused the need to protect her.

The wide balcony was surrounded by a high stone balustrade, and several couples were standing near it, enjoying the refreshing night air and moonless night. Instead of walking out the French doors directly forward to the balustrade, as Elizabeth expected him to do, Jordan guided their party to the right, to the farthest end of the balcony, where it made a sharp right turn around the side of the house. He turned the corner, then stopped, as did the rest of the party. Grateful he'd sought some privacy for them, Elizabeth took her hand from Tony's arm and stepped up to the balustrade. Several feet to her left Jordan Townsende did a similar thing, except that he turned sideways and leaned his elbow atop the balustrade, his back blocking them from view of anyone who might decide to walk around the side of the house as they had done. From the corner of her eye she saw Jordan grin tenderly and speak to Alexandra, who was standing beside him at the railing. Turning her head away, Elizabeth gazed out at the night, letting the restless breeze cool her face.

Behind her, where Tony had been standing, shadows moved, then a hand gently grasped Elizabeth's elbow, and a deep, husky voice said near her ear, "Dance with me, Elizabeth."

Shock stiffened her body, slamming against the barricade of numbness that Elizabeth was trying to keep intact. Still gazing straight ahead, she said very calmly and politely, "Would you do me a great service?"

"Anything," he agreed.

"Go away. And stay away."

"Anything," he amended with a solemn smile in his voice, "but that."

She felt him move closer behind her, and the nervous quaking she'd conquered hours before jarred through her again, awakening her senses from their blissful anesthesia. His fingers lightly caressed her arm, and he bent his head closer to hers. "Dance with me."

In the arbor two years ago, when he had spoken those words, Elizabeth had let him take her in his arms. Tonight, despite the fact that she was no longer being totally ostracized, she was still teetering on the edge of scandal, and she shook her head. "I don't think that would be wise."

"Nothing we've ever done has been wise. Let's not spoil our score."

Elizabeth shook her head, refusing to turn, but the pressure on her elbow increased until she had no choice. "I insist."

Reluctantly she turned and looked at him. "Why?"

"Because," he said, smiling tenderly into her eyes, "I've already danced seven dances, all of them with ugly women of unimpeachable reputations, so that I'd be able to ask you, without causing more gossip to hurt you."

The words, as well as his softness, made her wary. "What do you mean by the last part of that?"

"I know what happened to you after the weekend we were together," he said gently. "Your Lucinda laid it all out for Duncan. Don't look so hurt—the only thing she did wrong was to tell Duncan rather than me."

The Ian Thornton who was talking to her tonight was almost achingly familiar; he was the man she'd met two years ago.

"Come inside with me," he urged, increasing the pressure on her elbow, "and I'll begin making it up to you."

Elizabeth let herself be drawn forward a few steps and hesitated. "This is a mistake. Everyone will see us and think we've started it all over again—"

"No, they won't," he promised. "There's a rumor spreading like fire in there that I *tried* to get you in my clutches two years ago, but without a title to tempt you I didn't have a chance. Since acquiring a title is a holy crusade for most of them, they'll admire your sense. Now that I have a title, I'm expected to use it to try to succeed where I failed before—as a way of bolstering my wounded male pride." Reaching up to brush a wisp of hair from her soft cheek, he said, "I'm sorry. It was the best I could do with what I had to work with—we were seen together in compromising circumstances. Since they'd never believe *nothing* happened, I could only make them think I was in pursuit and you were evading."

She flinched from his touch but didn't shove his hand away. "You don't understand. What's happening to me in there is no less than I deserve. I knew what the rules were, and I broke them when I stayed with you at the cottage. You didn't *force* me to stay. I broke the rules, and—"

"Elizabeth," he interrupted in a voice edged with harsh remorse, "if you won't do anything else for me, at least stop exonerating me for that weekend. I can't bear it. I exerted more force on you than you understand."

Longing to kiss her, Ian had to be satisfied instead with trying to convince her his plan would work, because he now needed her help to ensure its success. In a teasing voice he said, "I think you're underrating my gift for strategy and subtlety. Come and dance with me, and I'll prove to you how easily most of the male minds in there have been manipulated."

She nodded, but without any real interest or enthusiasm, and allowed him to guide her back through the French doors.

Despite his confidence, moments after they entered the ballroom Ian noticed the increasing coldness of the looks being directed at them, and he knew a moment of real alarm—until he glanced at Elizabeth as he took her in his arms for a waltz and realized the cause of it. "Elizabeth," he said in a low, urgent voice, gazing down at her bent head, "stop looking meek! Put your nose in the air and cut me dead or flirt with me, but do not on any account look humble, because these people will interpret it as guilt!"

Elizabeth, who had been staring at his shoulder, as she'd done with her other dancing partners, tipped her head back and looked at him in confusion. "What?"

Ian's heart turned over when the chandeliers overhead revealed the wounded look in her glorious green eyes. Realizing logic and lectures weren't going to help her give the performance he badly needed her to give, he tried the tack that had, in Scotland, made her stop crying and begin to laugh: He tried to tease her. Casting about for a subject, he said quickly, "Belhaven is certainly in fine looks tonight —*pink* satin pantaloons. I asked him for the name of his tailor so that I could order a pair for myself."

Elizabeth looked at him as if he'd taken leave of his senses; then his warning about looking meek hit home, and she began to understand what he wanted her to do. That added to the comic image of Ian's tall, masculine frame in those absurd pink pantaloons enabled her to manage a weak smile. "I have greatly admired those pantaloons myself," she said. "Will you also order a yellow satin coat to complement the look?"

He smiled. "I thought—puce."

"An unusual combination," she averred softly, "but one that I am sure will make you the envy of all who behold you."

Pride swelled in him at how valiantly she was rallying. To stop himself from saying things he wanted to say to her tomorrow, in private, Ian looked around for another topic to keep her talking. He mentioned the first one he saw. "Am I to assume the Valerie I was introduced to earlier was the Valerie of our greenhouse notes?" He realized his mistake the instant her eyes clouded over and she glanced in the direction he'd looked.

"Yes."

"Shall I ask Willington to clear his ballroom so you have the requisite twenty paces? Naturally, I'll stand as your second."

Elizabeth drew a shaky breath, and a smile curved her lips. "Is she wearing a bow?"

Ian looked and shook his head. "I'm afraid not."

"Does she have an earring?"

He glanced again and frowned. "I think that's a wart."

Her smile finally reached her eyes. "It's not a *large* target, but I suppose—"

"Allow *me*," he gravely replied, and she laughed.

The last strains of their waltz were dying away, and as they left the dance floor Ian watched Mondevale making his way toward the Townsendes, who'd returned to the ballroom.

"Now that you're a marquess," Elizabeth asked, "will you live in Scotland or in England?"

"I only accepted the title, not the money or the lands," he replied absently, watching Mondevale. "I'll explain everything to you tomorrow morning at your house. Mondevale is going to ask you to dance as soon as we reach the Townsendes, so listen closely—I'm going to ask you to dance again later. Turn me down."

She sent him a puzzled look, but she nodded. "Is there

anything else?" she asked when he was about to relinquish her to her friends.

"There's a great deal else, but it will have to wait until tomorrow."

Mystified, Elizabeth turned her attention to Viscount Mondevale.

Alex watched the byplay between Elizabeth and Ian but her mind was elsewhere. Earlier, Alex had told her husband exactly what she thought of Ian Thornton who'd first ruined Elizabeth's reputation and now deceived her into thinking he was still a man of very modest means. Instead of agreeing that Thornton was completely without principles, Jordan had calmly insisted that Ian intended to set matters aright this morning, and then he'd made her, and his grandmother, promise not to tell Elizabeth anything until Ian had been given the opportunity to do so himself. Alex had agreed, with great reluctance. Elizabeth was gentle and sweet, and Alex was fearful that gratitude might blind Elizabeth to his true nature. Dragging her thoughts back to the ballroom, Alex hoped more than anything that Ian Thornton would do nothing more to hurt her good friend.

By the end of the evening a majority of the guests at the Willington ball had drawn several conclusions: first, that Ian Thornton was definitely the natural grandson of the Duke of Stanhope (which everyone claimed to have always believed); second, that Elizabeth Cameron had very probably rebuffed his scandalous advances two years ago (which everyone claimed to have always believed); third, that since she had rejected his second request for a dance tonight, she might actually prefer her former suitor Viscount Mondevale (which hardly anyone could *really* believe).

22

Bentner carried a covered platter of scones into the morning room and placed it before Elizabeth and Alex, who were seated at the table discussing last night's ball. Lucinda, who rarely ate breakfast, was sitting upon a narrow window cushion, calmly applying herself to her needlework while she listened to their conversation.

The morning room, like all the other rooms in the spacious house on Promenade Street, was furnished in what Julius Cameron called "serviceable colors"—browns and grays. This morning, however, there was a bright rainbow of color in the center of it where the girls were seated at a table covered with a maize linen cloth, Alex in a dusty-pink day dress, Elizabeth in a mint-green morning gown.

Normally, Bentner would have beamed approvingly at the pretty portrait the girls made, but this morning, as he put out butter and jam, he had grim news to impart and a confession to make. As he swept the cover off the scones he gave his news and made his confession.

"We had a guest last night," he told Elizabeth. "I slammed the door on him."

"Who was it?"

"A Mr. Ian Thornton."

Elizabeth stifled a horrified chuckle at the image that called to mind, but before she could comment Bentner said fiercely, "I regretted my actions afterward! I *should* have invited him inside, offered him refreshment, and slipped some of that purgative powder into his drink. He'd have had a bellyache that lasted a month!"

"Bentner," Alex sputtered, "you are a treasure!"

"Do not encourage him in these fantasies," Elizabeth warned wryly. "Bentner is so addicted to mystery novels that he occasionally forgets that what one does in a novel cannot always be done in real life. He actually did a similar thing to my uncle last year."

"Yes, and he didn't return for six months," Bentner told Alex proudly.

"And when he does come," Elizabeth reminded him with a frown to sound severe, "he refuses to eat or drink anything."

"Which is why he never stays long," Bentner countered, undaunted. As was his habit whenever his mistress's future was being discussed, as it was now, Bentner hung about to make suggestions as they occurred to him. Since Elizabeth had always seemed to appreciate his advice and assistance, he found nothing odd about a butler sitting down at the table and contributing to the conversation when the only guest was someone he'd known since she was a girl.

"It's that odious Belhaven we have to rid you of first," Alexandra said, returning to their earlier conversation. "He hung about last night, glowering at anyone who might have approached you." She shuddered. "And the way he ogles you. It's revolting. It's worse than that; he's almost frightening."

Bentner heard that, and his elderly eyes grew thoughtful as he recalled something he'd read about in one of his novels. "As a solution it is a trifle extreme," he said, "but as a last resort it could work."

Two pairs of eyes turned to him with interest, and he continued, "I read it in *The Nefarious Gentleman*. We would have Aaron abduct this Belhaven in our carriage and bring him straightaway to the docks, where we'll sell him to the press gangs."

Shaking her head in amused affection, Elizabeth said, "I daresay he wouldn't just meekly go along with Aaron."

"And I don't think," Alex added, her smiling gaze meeting Elizabeth's, "a press gang would take him. They're not that desperate."

"There's always black magic," Bentner continued. "In *Deathly Endeavours* there was a perpetrator of ancient rites who cast an evil spell. We would require some rats' tails, as I recall, and tongues of—"

"No," Elizabeth said with finality.

"—lizards," Bentner finished determinedly.

"Absolutely not," his mistress returned.

"And fresh toad mold, but procuring that might be tricky. The novel didn't say how to tell fresh from—"

"Bentner!" Elizabeth exclaimed, laughing. "You'll cast us all into a swoon if you don't desist at once."

When Bentner had padded away to seek privacy for further contemplation of solutions, Elizabeth looked at Alex. "Rats' tails and lizards' tongues," she said, chuckling. "No wonder Bentner insists on having a lighted candle in his room all night."

"He must be afraid to close his eyes after reading such things," Alex agreed, but her thoughts had returned to last night. "One thing is certain—I was correct about having you go out in society. Last night was much harder than I imagined, but the rest will be easy. I have no doubt you'll be receiving offers within a sennight, so what we must do is decide whom you like and wish to encourage. I think," she continued gently, "that if you still want Mondevale—"

Elizabeth shook her head emphatically. "I don't want anyone, Alex. I mean that."

The dowager duchess, who had arrived to accompany Alex on a shopping expedition, swept in on the heels of an intimidated footman whom she'd waved off when he offered to announce her. "What are you saying, Elizabeth?" she demanded, looking extremely disgruntled that her efforts last night might be going for naught.

Elizabeth started at the sound of her imperious voice. Clad in silver-gray from head to foot, she exuded wealth, confidence, and superior breeding. Elizabeth still thought her the most intimidating woman she'd ever met, but, like Alex, she had seen past that to the reluctant warmth beneath the sound of disapproval in her stern voice.

"What Elizabeth meant," Alex explained while the dowager duchess seated herself at the table and arranged her silk skirts to her satisfaction, "is that she's only been back out in society for one day. After her unfortunate experiences with Mondevale and Mr. Thornton, she is naturally reluctant to misplace her affections."

"You're wrong, Alexandra," said the dowager stoutly, scrutinizing Elizabeth's face. "What she meant, I believe, is that she has no intention of wedding anyone now or in the future, if she can avoid it."

Elizabeth's smile faded, but she did not lie. "Exactly," she said quietly, buttering a scone.

"Foolish, my dear. You shall and you must wed."

"Grandmama is quite right," Alex said. "You can't hope to remain in society unwed without eventually encountering all manner of unpleasantness. Believe me, I know!"

"Exactly!" the dowager said, getting down to the reason for her early arrival. "And that is why I've decided that you ought to consider Kensington."

"Who?" Elizabeth said, and then she recognized Ian's new title. "Thank you, but no," she said firmly. "I feel much relieved that things came off as well as they did, and grateful to him for his help, but that is all." Elizabeth ignored the little tug on her heart when she recalled how handsome he'd looked last night, how gentle he'd been with her. He had caused her nothing but grief from the time she'd met him. He was unpredictable and dictatorial. Furthermore, having seen the special closeness Alex seemed to share with her handsome husband, Elizabeth was beginning to question the rightness of choosing husbands as if practicality were paramount. Elizabeth couldn't remember much about the gay, handsome couple who had been her own parents; they had breezed in and out of her life in a swirl of social activities that kept them away from home far more than they were there.

"Grateful?" repeated the duchess. "I would not have used that word. Besides, he did not handle it so well as he might have done. He should never have asked you to dance, for one thing."

"It might have looked more odd if he hadn't," Alex said reluctantly. "However, I, for one, am vastly relieved that Elizabeth has no interest in him."

The duchess frowned in surprise. "Why is that?"

"I cannot find it in my heart to forgive him for the misery he has caused her." Recalling again that he had let Elizabeth believe his home was a modest cottage in Scotland, she added, "And I cannot trust him." Turning to Lucinda for reinforcement, Alex asked for her opinion.

Lucinda, who'd been apprised of Ian's actions last night by Elizabeth, looked up from her needlework. "In the matter of Mr. Thornton," she replied noncommittally, "I now prefer to withhold judgment."

"I was not suggesting," the dowager said, irritated with such unprecedented opposition, "that you should fall into his arms if he made you an offer. His behavior, excepting last night, has been completely reprehensible." She broke off as Bentner appeared in the doorway, his expression one of distress and ire.

"Your uncle is here, Miss Elizabeth."

"There is no damned need to announce me," Julius informed him, striding down the hall to the morning room. "This is *my* house." Elizabeth stood up, intending to go somewhere private to hear whatever distressing thing he was bound to tell her, just as Uncle Julius stopped cold in the doorway, flushing a little at the realization she had female guests. "Have you seen Thornton?" he asked her.

"Yes, why?"

"I must say I'm proud of the way you've obviously taken it. I was afraid you'd fly into the boughs over not being told. There's a great deal of money involved here, and I'll not have you turning missish so that he wants it back."

"What are you talking about?"

"Perhaps we ought to leave," Alexandra suggested.

"There's no need for privacy," he said, tugging at his neckcloth, suddenly looking uncharacteristically apprehensive. "I'd as lief discuss this with Elizabeth in front of her friends. You are, I collect, her friends?"

Elizabeth had a horrible feeling that he was relying on her guests to keep her from making "a scene," which is how he described any sort of verbal opposition, no matter how quiet. "Shall we adjourn to the front drawing room?" he said in the tone of one issuing an instruction, not an invitation. "There's more room."

The duchess's face turned icy at his impertinence and lack of taste, but then she glanced at Elizabeth, noting her sudden stillness and her alarmed expression, and she nodded curtly.

"There's no point in rushing into the matter," Julius said as he started down the hall, accompanied by the group that had been in the morning room. It wasn't just the money that pleased Julius so much; it was the triumph he felt because, in dealing with a man as incredibly astute as Thornton was purported to be, Julius Cameron had emerged the absolute victor.

"I believe an introduction is in order, Elizabeth," Julius said when they entered the drawing room.

Elizabeth automatically presented him to the duchess, her mind ringing with alarm over an unknown threat, and when her uncle said, "I'd like some tea before we get into this," her alarm escalated to fear because he'd never partaken of anything since Bentner had put the purgative in his drink. He was stalling for time, she realized, to phrase his explanation; that alone meant it was news of the utmost import.

Oblivious to the park they were driving past on the way to Elizabeth's address, Ian idly tapped his gloves against his knee. Twice, women he'd met last night waved at him and smiled, but he didn't notice. His mind was occupied with the explanations he intended to make to Elizabeth. At all costs, she must not think he wanted to marry her out of pity or guilt, for Elizabeth was not only beautiful, she was proud; and her pride would make her oppose their betrothal. She was also courageous and stubborn, and if she discovered their betrothal was already an established fact, she sure as hell wasn't going to like that either, and Ian couldn't blame her. She had been the most sought-after beauty ever to hit the London scene two years ago; she was entitled to be courted properly.

No doubt she'd want to get a little of her own back by pretending she didn't want him, but that was one thing that didn't concern him. They had wanted each other from that first night in the garden. They had wanted each other every time they'd been together since then. She was innocence and courage; passion and shyness; fury and forgiveness. She was serene and regal in a ballroom; jaunty and skillful with a pistol in her hands; passionate and sweet in his arms. She was all of that, and much more.

And he loved her. If he was honest, he'd have to admit he had loved her from the moment she'd taken on a roomful of angry men in a card room—a young, golden princess, outnumbered by her subjects, dwarfed by their size, scornful of their attitude.

She had loved him, too; it was the only explanation for everything that had happened the weekend they met and the three days they were together in Scotland. The only difference was that Elizabeth didn't have the advantage of Ian's years and experience, or of his upbringing. She was a young, sheltered English girl who thought the strongest emotion two people could or should feel for one another was "a lasting attachment."

She didn't know, could not yet comprehend, that love was a gift that had been given to them in a torchlit garden the moment they met. A smile touched his lips as he thought of her in the garden the night they met; she could challenge a roomful of men, but in the garden, when she was flirting with him, she'd been so nervous that she'd rubbed her palms against her knees. That memory was one of the sweetest.

Ian smiled in amused self-mockery. In every other facet of his life he was coolly practical; where Elizabeth was concerned he was alternately blind and reactionary or, like now, positively besotted. On his way here this morning he'd stopped at London's most fashionable jeweler and made purchases that had left the proprietor, Mr. Phineas Weatherborne, caught somewhere between ecstasy and disbelief, bowing Ian out the front door. In fact, there was a betrothal ring in Ian's pocket, but he'd only taken it with him because he didn't think it needed to be sized. He would not put it on Elizabeth's finger until she was prepared to admit she loved him, or at least that she wanted to marry him. His own parents had loved one another unashamedly and without reservation. He wanted nothing less from Elizabeth, which, he thought wryly, was a little odd, given the fact that he hadn't expected or truly wanted the same thing from Christina.

The only problem that didn't concern him was Elizabeth's reaction to discovering that she was already betrothed to him, or worse, that he'd been made to pay to get her. There was no reason for her to know the former yet, and no reason for her *ever* to know the latter. He had specifically warned her uncle that he would deal with both those matters himself.

All the houses on Promenade Street were white with ornamental wrought-iron gates at the front. Although they were not nearly so imposing as the mansions on Upper Brook Street, it was a pretty street, with fashionable women in pastel bonnets and gowns strolling by on the arms of impeccably dressed men.

As Ian's driver pulled his grays to a stop before the Cameron house, Ian noticed the two carriages already waiting in the street in front of him, but he paid no heed to the rented hack behind him. Irritably contemplating the impending confrontation with Elizabeth's insolent butler, he was walking up the front steps when Duncan's voice called his name, and he turned in surprise.

"I arrived this morning," Duncan explained, turning to look askance at two dandies who were mincing down the street, garbed in wasp-waisted coats and chin-high shirt points dripping with fobs and seals. "Your butler informed me you were here. I thought—that is, I wondered how things were going."

"And since my butler didn't know," Ian concluded with amused irritation, "you decided to call on Elizabeth and see if you could discover for yourself?"

"Something like that," the vicar said calmly. "Elizabeth regards me as a friend, I think. And so I planned to call on her and, if you weren't here, to put in a good word for you."

"Only one?" Ian said mildly.

The vicar did not back down; he rarely did, particularly in matters of morality or justice. "Given your treatment of her,

I was hard pressed to think of *one*. How did matters turn out with your grandfather?"

"Well enough," Ian said, his mind on meeting with Elizabeth. "He's here in London."

"And?"

"And," Ian said sardonically, "you may now address me as 'my lord.' "

"I've come here," Duncan persisted implacably, "to address you as 'the bridegroom.' "

A flash of annoyance crossed Ian's tanned features. "You never stop pressing, do you? I've managed my own life for thirty years, Duncan. I think I can do it now."

Duncan had the grace to look slightly abashed. "You're right, of course. Shall I leave?"

Ian considered the benefits of Duncan's soothing presence and reluctantly shook his head. "No. In fact, since you're here," he continued as they neared the top step, "you may as well be the one to announce us to the butler. I can't get past him."

Duncan lifted the knocker while bestowing a mocking glance on Ian. "You can't get past the butler, and you think you're managing very well without me?"

Declining to rise to that bait, Ian remained silent. The door opened a moment later, and the butler looked politely from Duncan, who began to give his name, to Ian. To Duncan's startled disbelief, the door came crashing forward in his face. An instant before it banged into its frame Ian twisted, slamming his shoulder into it and sending the butler flying backward into the hall and ricocheting off the wall. In a low, savage voice he said, "Tell your mistress I'm here, or I'll find her myself and tell her."

With a glance of furious outrage the older man considered Ian's superior size and powerful frame, then turned and started reluctantly for a room ahead and to the left, where muted voices could be heard.

Duncan eyed Ian with one gray eyebrow lifted and said sardonically, "Very clever of you to ingratiate yourself so well with Elizabeth's servants."

The group in the drawing room reacted with diverse emotions to Bentner's announcement that "Thornton is here and forced his way into the house." The dowager duchess looked fascinated, Julius looked both relieved and dismayed, Alexandra looked wary, and Elizabeth, who was still preoccupied with her uncle's unstated purpose for his visit, looked nonplussed. Only Lucinda showed no expression at all, but she laid her needlework aside and lifted her face attentively toward the doorway.

"Show him in here, Bentner," her uncle said, his voice unnaturally loud in the emotionally charged silence.

Elizabeth felt a shock at seeing Duncan walk into the room beside Ian, and a greater one when Ian ignored everyone else and came directly to her, his gaze searching her face. "I trust you're suffering no ill effects from the ordeal last night?" he said in a gentle tone as he took her hand and lifted her fingertips to his lips.

Elizabeth thought he looked breathtakingly handsome in a coat and waistcoat of rust superfine that set off his wide shoulders, biscuit trousers that hugged his long legs, and a cream silk shirt that emphasized the tan of his face and throat. "Very well, thank you," she answered, trying to ignore the warmth tingling up her arm as he kept her hand for a long moment before he reluctantly released it and allowed her to handle the introductions.

Despite her grave concern over her uncle, Elizabeth chuckled inwardly as she introduced Duncan. Everyone exhibited the same stunned reaction she had when she'd discovered Ian Thornton's uncle was a cleric. Her uncle gaped, Alex stared, and the dowager duchess glowered at Ian in disbelief as Duncan politely bent over her hand. "Am I to understand, Kensington," she demanded of Ian, "that you are related to a man of the cloth?"

Ian's reply was a mocking bow and a sardonic lift of his brows, but Duncan, who was desperate to put a light face on things, tried ineffectually to joke about it. "The news always has a peculiar effect on people," he told her.

"One needn't think too hard to discover why," she replied gruffly.

Ian opened his mouth to give the outrageous harridan a richly deserved setdown, but Julius Cameron's presence was worrying him; a moment later it was infuriating him as the man strode to the center of the room and said in a bluff voice, "Now that we're all together, there's no reason to dissemble. Bentner, bring champagne. Elizabeth, congratulations. I trust you'll conduct yourself properly as a wife and not spend the man out of what money he has left."

In the deafening silence no one moved, except it seemed to Elizabeth that the entire room was beginning to move. "What?" she breathed finally.

"You're betrothed."

Anger rose up like flames licking inside her, spreading up her limbs. "Really?" she said in a voice of deadly calm, thinking of Sir Francis and John Marchman. "To whom?"

To her disbelief, Uncle Julius turned expectantly to Ian, who was looking at him with murder in his eyes. "To me," he clipped, his icy gaze still on her uncle.

"It's final," Julius warned her, and then, because he assumed she'd be as pleased as he to discover she had monetary value, he added, "He paid a fortune for the privilege. I didn't have to give him a shilling." Elizabeth, who had no idea the two men had ever met before, looked at Ian in wild confusion and mounting anger. "What does he mean?" she demanded in a strangled whisper.

"He means," Ian began tautly, unable to believe all his romantic plans were being demolished, "we are betrothed. The papers have been signed."

"Why, you—you arrogant, overbearing"—She choked back the tears that were cutting off her voice—"you couldn't even be bothered to *ask* me?"

Dragging his gaze from his prey with an effort, Ian turned to Elizabeth, and his heart wrenched at the way she was looking at him. "Why don't we go somewhere private where we can discuss this?" he said gently, walking forward and taking her elbow.

She twisted free, scorched by his touch. "Oh, no!" she exploded, her body shaking with wrath. "Why guard my sensibilities now? You've made a laughingstock of me since the day I set eyes on you. Why stop now?"

"Elizabeth," Duncan put in gently, "Ian is only trying to do the right thing by you, now that he realizes what a sad state you—"

339

"Shut up, Duncan!" Ian commanded furiously, but it was too late; Elizabeth's eyes had widened with horror at being pitied.

"And just what sort of 'sad state,'" she demanded, her magnificent eyes shining with tears of humiliation and wrath, "do you think I'm in?"

Ian caught her elbow. "Come with me, or I'll carry you out of here."

He meant it, and Elizabeth jerked her elbow free, but she nodded. "By all means," she said furiously.

Shoving open the door of the first room he came to, Ian drew Elizabeth inside and closed it behind them. She walked to the center of the little salon and whirled on him, her hands clenched into fists at her sides. "You monster!" she hissed. "How *dare* you pity me!"

It was exactly the conclusion Ian knew she'd draw, and exactly the reaction he would have expected from the proud beauty who'd let him believe in Scotland that her life was a frivolous social whirl, her home a virtual palace. Hoping to diffuse some of her anger, he tried to divert her with a logical debate over her choice of words. "There's a great difference between regretting one's actions and pitying the person who suffered for them."

"Don't you *dare* play word games with me!" she said, her voice trembling with fury.

Inwardly, Ian smiled with pride at her perspicacity; even in a state of shock, Elizabeth knew when she was being gulled. "I apologize," he conceded quietly. He walked forward, and Elizabeth retreated until her back touched a chair, then she held her ground, glaring at him. "Nothing but the truth will do in a situation like this," he agreed, putting his hands on her rigid shoulders. Knowing she'd laugh in his face if he tried to convince her now that he loved her, he told her something she should believe: "The truth is that I want you. I have *always* wanted you, and you know that."

"I *hate* that word," she burst out, trying unsuccessfully to break free of his grasp.

"I don't think you know what it means."

"I know you say it every time you force yourself on me."

"And every time I do, you melt in my arms."

"I will not marry you," Elizabeth said furiously, mentally circling for some way out. "I don't know you. I don't trust you."

"But you *do* want me," he told her with a knowing smile.

"Stop *saying* that, damn you! I *want* an old husband, I told you that," she cried, mindlessly saying anything she could think of to put him off. "I want my life to be mine. I told you that, too. And you came dashing to England and—and *bought* me." That brought her up short, and her eyes began to blaze.

"No," he stated firmly, though it was splitting hairs, "I made a settlement on your uncle."

The tears she'd been fighting valiantly to hide began to spill over her lashes. "I am not a pauper," she cried. "I am not a p-pauper," she repeated, her voice choking with tears. "I have—had—a dowry, damn you. And if you were so stu-stupid you let him swindle you out of it, it serves you right!"

Ian was torn between laughing, kissing her, and murdering her heartless uncle.

"How dare you make bargains I didn't agree to?" she blazed while tears spilled from her wondrous eyes. "I'm not a piece of chattel, no matter what my uncle thi-thinks. I'd have found some way out of marrying Belhaven. I *would* have," she cried fiercely. "I would have found a way to keep Havenhurst myself without my uncle. You had no right, no *right* to bargain with my uncle. You're no better than Belhaven!"

"You're right," Ian admitted grimly, longing to draw her into his arms and absorb some of her pain, and then it hit him—a possible way to neutralize some of her humiliation and opposition. Recalling how proud she'd been of her own bargaining ability with tradesmen when she'd spoken of it in Scotland, he tried to enlist her participation now. "As you said, you're perfectly capable of bargaining for yourself." Coaxingly, he said, "Will you bargain with *me,* Elizabeth?"

"Certainly," she flung back. "The agreement is off; I refuse the terms. The bargaining is over."

His lips twitched, but his voice was filled with finality.

"Your uncle means to unload you and the expense of that house you love, and nothing is going to stop him. Without him, you cannot keep Havenhurst. He explained the situation to me in detail."

Despite the fact that she shook her head, Elizabeth knew it was true, and the sense of impending doom she'd been struggling with for weeks began to overwhelm her. "A husband is the only possible solution to your problems."

"Don't you dare suggest a man as the solution for my troubles," she cried. "You're all the cause of them! My father gambled away the entire family fortune and left me in debt; my brother disappeared after getting me deeper in debt; you kissed me and destroyed my reputation; my fiancé left me at the first breath of a scandal *you* caused; and my uncle is trying to sell me! As far as I'm concerned," she finished, spitting fire, "men make excellent dancing partners, but beyond that I have no use for the lot of you. You're all quite detestable, actually, when one takes time to ponder it, which of course one rarely does, for it would only cause depression."

"Unfortunately, we're the only alternative," Ian pointed out. And because he would not give her up no matter what he had to do to keep her, he added, "In this case, I'm *your* only alternative. Your uncle and I have signed the betrothal contract, and the money has already changed hands. I am, however, willing to bargain with you on the terms."

"Why should you?" she said scornfully.

Ian recognized in her answer the same hostility he found whenever he negotiated with any proud man who was being forced by circumstances, not by Ian, to sell something he wanted to keep. Like those men, Elizabeth felt powerless; and, like them, her pride alone would force her to retaliate by making the whole ordeal as difficult as possible for Ian.

In a business matter, Ian certainly wouldn't have ruined his own negotiating position by helping his opponent to see the value of what he held and the advantageous terms he might wring from Ian because of it. In Elizabeth's case, however, Ian sought to do exactly that. "I'm willing to bargain with you," he said gently, "for the same reason anyone tries to bargain—you have something I want." Desperately trying to prove to her she wasn't powerless or empty-handed, he added, "I want it badly, Elizabeth."

"What is it?" she asked warily, but much of the resentment in her lovely face was already being replaced by surprise.

"This," he whispered huskily. His hands tightened on her shoulders, pulling her close as he bent his head and took her soft mouth in a slow, compelling kiss, sensually molding and shaping her lips to his. Although she stubbornly refused to respond, he felt the rigidity leaving her; and as soon as it did, Ian showed her just how badly he wanted it. His arms went around her, crushing her to him, his mouth moving against hers with hungry urgency, his hands shifting possessively over her spine and hips, fitting her to his hardened length. Dragging his mouth from hers, he drew an unsteady breath. "*Very* badly," he whispered.

Lifting his head, he gazed down at her, noting the telltale flush on her cheeks, the soft confusion in her searching green gaze, and the delicate hand she'd forgotten was resting against his chest. Keeping his own hand splayed against her lower back, he held her pressed to his rigid erection, torturing himself as he slid his knuckles against her cheek and quietly said, "For that privilege, and the others that follow it, I'm willing to agree to any reasonable terms you state. And I'll even forewarn you," he said with a tender smile at her upturned face, "I'm not a miserly man, nor a poor one."

Elizabeth swallowed, trying to keep her voice from shaking in reaction to his kiss. "What other privileges that follow kissing?" she asked suspiciously.

The question left him nonplussed. "Those that involve the creation of children," he said, studying her face curiously. "I want several of them—with your complete cooperation, of course," he added, suppressing a smile.

"Of course," she conceded without a second's hesitation. "I like children, too, very much."

Ian stopped while he was ahead, deciding it was wiser not to question his good fortune. Evidently Elizabeth had a very

343

frank attitude toward marital sex—rather an unusual thing for a sheltered, well-bred English girl.

"What are your terms?" he asked, and he made a final effort to tip the balance of power into her hands and out of his by adding, "I'm scarcely in a position to argue."

Elizabeth hesitated and then slowly began stating her terms: "I want to be allowed to look after Havenhurst without interference or criticism."

"Done," he agreed with alacrity while relief and delight built apace in him.

"And I'd like a stipulated amount set aside for that and given to me once each year. In return, the estate, once I've arranged for irrigation, will repay your loan with interest."

"Agreed," Ian said smoothly. Elizabeth hesitated, wondering if he could afford it, half-embarrassed that she'd mentioned it without knowing more about his circumstances. He'd said last night that he'd accepted the title but nothing else. "In return," she amended fairly, "I will endeavor to keep costs at an absolute minimum."

He grinned. "Never vacillate when you've already stipulated your terms and won a concession—it gives your opponent a subtle advantage in the next round."

Elizabeth's eyes narrowed suspiciously; he was agreeing to everything, and much too easily. "And I think," she announced decisively, "I want all this written down, witnessed, and made part of the original agreement."

Ian's eyes widened, a wry, admiring smile tugging at his lips as he nodded his consent. There was a roomful of witnesses in the next room, including her uncle, who'd signed the original agreement, and a vicar who could witness it. He decided it was wise to proceed now, when she was in the mood, rather than scruple over who knew about it. "With you as a partner a few years ago," he joked as he guided her from the room, "God knows how far I might have gone." Despite his tone and the fact that he'd been on *her* side during the negotiations, he was nevertheless impressed with the sheer daring of her requests.

Elizabeth saw the admiration in his smile and smiled a little in return. "At Havenhurst I purchase all our supplies and keep the books, since we have no bailiff. As I explained, I've learned to bargain."

Ian's grin faded as he imagined the creditors who'd descended on her after her brother left and how brave she'd had to be to keep them from dismantling her house stone by stone. Desperation had forced her to learn to bargain.

23

Duncan had been trying, with extreme difficulty, to keep a pleasant conversation going in the drawing room while Elizabeth and Ian were gone, but not even his lifelong experience in dealing with humans in the throes of emotion could aid him—because in this room everyone seemed to be in the throes of a *different* emotion. Lady Alexandra was obviously worried and tense; Elizabeth's loathsome uncle was cold and angry; the dowager and Miss Throckmorton-Jones were evidencing signs of enjoying the difficulty Ian was obviously having with this unusual betrothal.

With a sigh of relief, Duncan broke off his discourse on the likelihood of early snow and looked up as Elizabeth and Ian walked into the room. His relief doubled when he met Ian's eyes and saw softness there, and a touch of wry amusement.

"Elizabeth and I have come to an agreement," Ian told the occupants of the room without preamble. "She feels, and rightly so, that she and she alone has the right to give herself in marriage. Therefore, she has certain . . . ah . . . terms she wishes to be included in the betrothal agreement. Duncan, if you will be so kind as to write down what she stipulates?"

Duncan's brows rose, but he quickly got up and went over to the desk.

Ian turned to her uncle, his voice taking on a bite. "Do you have a copy of the betrothal contract with you?"

"Certainly," Julius said, his face reddening with anger. "I have it, but you're not changing one word, and I'm not giving back one shilling!" Rounding on Elizabeth, he continued, "He paid a fortune for you, you conceited little slut—"

Ian's savage voice cracked like a whiplash. *"Get out!"*

"Get out?" Julius repeated furiously. "I *own* this house. You didn't buy it when you bought her."

Without looking at Elizabeth, Ian snapped a question at her: "Do you *want* it?"

Although Julius didn't yet recognize the depth of Ian's fury, Elizabeth saw the taut rage emanating from every line of his powerful frame, and fear raced up her spine. "Do I—I want what?"

"The house!"

Elizabeth didn't know what he wanted her to say, and in the mood he was in, she was actually terrified of saying the wrong thing.

Lucinda's voice turned every head but Ian's as she eyed him with cool challenge. "Yes," she said. "She does."

Ian accepted that as if the woman spoke for Elizabeth, his gaze still boring through Julius. "See my banker in the morning," he clipped murderously. "Now *get out!"*

Belatedly, Julius seemed to realize that his life was in genuine jeopardy, and he picked up his hat and started for the door. "It won't come cheap!"

Slowly and with purposeful menace Ian turned around and looked at him, and whatever Julius saw in his metallic eyes made him leave without further discussion of price.

"I think," Elizabeth said shakily, when the front door banged closed behind him, "some refreshment is in order."

"An excellent idea, my dear," said the vicar.

Bentner appeared in answer to Elizabeth's summons, and after glowering at Ian he looked at her with outraged sympathy, then he left to fetch a tray of drinks and food.

"Well, now," said Duncan, rubbing his hands with satisfaction, "I believe I was to take down some—ah—new terms of betrothal."

For the next twenty minutes Elizabeth asked for concessions, Ian conceded, Duncan wrote, and the dowager duchess and Lucinda listened with ill-concealed glee. In the entire time Ian made but one stipulation, and only after he was finally driven to it out of sheer perversity over the way everyone was enjoying his discomfort: He stipulated that none of Elizabeth's freedoms could give rise to any gossip that she was cuckolding him.

The duchess and Miss Throckmorton-Jones scowled at such a word being mentioned in front of them, but Elizabeth acquiesced with a regal nod of her golden head and politely said to Duncan, "I agree. You may write that down." Ian grinned at her, and Elizabeth shyly returned his smile. Cuckolding, to the best of Elizabeth's knowledge, was some sort of disgraceful conduct that required a lady to be discovered in the bedroom with a man who was not her husband. She had obtained that incomplete piece of information from Lucinda Throckmorton-Jones, who, unfortunately, actually believed it.

"Is there anything more?" Duncan finally asked, and when Elizabeth shook her head, the dowager spoke up. "Indeed, though you may not need to write it down." Turning to Ian, she said severely, "If you've any thought of announcing this betrothal tomorrow, you may put it out of your head."

Ian was tempted to invite her to get out, in a slightly less wrathful tone than that in which he'd ordered Julius from the house, but he realized that what she was saying was lamentably true. "Last night you went to a deal of trouble to make it seem there had been little but flirtation between the two of you two years ago. Unless you go through the appropriate courtship rituals, which Elizabeth has every right to expect, no one will ever believe it."

"What do you have in mind?" Ian demanded shortly.

"One month," she said without hesitation. "One month of calling on her properly, escorting her to the normal functions, and so on."

"Two weeks," he countered with strained patience.

"Very well," she conceded, giving Ian the irritating certainty that two weeks was all she'd hoped for anyway. "Then you may announce your betrothal and be wed in—two months!"

"Two weeks," Ian said implacably, reaching for the drink the butler had just put in front of him.

"As you wish," said the dowager. Then two things happened simultaneously: Lucinda Throckmorton-Jones let out a snort that Ian realized was a laugh, and Elizabeth swept Ian's drink from beneath his fingertips. "There's—a speck of lint in it," she explained nervously, handing the drink to Bentner with a severe shake of her head.

Ian reached for the sandwich on his plate.

Elizabeth watched the satisfied look on Bentner's face and snatched that away, too. "A—a small insect seems to have gotten on it," she explained to Ian.

"I don't see anything," Ian remarked, his puzzled glance on his betrothed. Having been deprived of tea and sustenance, he reached for the glass of wine the butler had set before him, then he realized how much stress Elizabeth had been under and offered it to her instead.

"Thank you," she said with a sigh, looking a little harassed. Bentner's arm swooped down, scooping the wineglass out of her hand. *"Another* insect," he said.

"Bentner!" Elizabeth cried in exasperation, but her voice was drowned out by a peal of laughter from Alexandra Townsende, who slumped down on the settee, her shoulders shaking with unexplainable mirth.

Ian drew the only possible conclusion: They were all suffering from the strain of too much stress.

24

The dowager was of the opinion that the ritual of courtship should begin at once with a ball that very night, and Ian expected Elizabeth to look forward to such a prospect after almost two years of enforced rustication—particularly after she'd already conquered the highest hurdle last night. Instead, she evaded the issue by insisting that she wanted to show Havenhurst to Ian, and perhaps attend a ball or two later on.

The dowager remained adamant, Elizabeth remained resistant, and Ian watched the interchange with mild confusion. Since Havenhurst was only an hour and a half's drive from London, he couldn't see why doing one thing would preclude the other. He even said as much, watching as Elizabeth looked uneasily at Alexandra and then shook her head, as if refusing something being silently offered. In the end it was decided that Ian would go to Havenhurst tomorrow, and that Alexandra Townsende and her husband would play chaperon there, a notion that pleased Ian vastly more than having to endure the frosty, gloating face of Lucinda Throckmorton-Jones.

He was on his way home, contemplating with considerable amusement what Jordan's reaction would be when he learned his wife had volunteered him to spend a day and evening playing duenna to Ian, with whom he'd long ago gambled in most of London's polite, and impolite, gaming houses.

His smile faded, however, as his mind refused to stop wondering why Elizabeth wouldn't want to attend a ball after being banished to the country for so long. The logical answer finally hit him, and a fresh surge of pain stabbed at him. So convincingly had she played the frivolous socialite in Scotland that he still had difficulty remembering she'd been living in seclusion, pinching every shilling.

Leaning forward, Ian issued clipped instructions to his coachman, and a few minutes later he was striding swiftly into the establishment of London's most fashionable—and most discreet—modiste.

"It cannot be done, Monsieur Thornton," the proprietress gasped when he informed her he wanted a dozen ball gowns and an entire wardrobe designed and created for Lady Elizabeth Cameron at number fourteen Promenade Street within the week. "It would take two dozen experienced seamstresses a minimum of two weeks."

"Then hire four dozen," Monsieur Thornton replied in the politely impatient tone of one who was being forced to reason with an inferior intellect, "and you can do it in one." He took the sting out of that by flashing her a brief smile and writing her a bank draft in an amount that made her eyes widen. "Lady Cameron is leaving for the country early in the morning, which will give you all the rest of today and tonight to take whatever measurements you need," he continued. Tipping his quill toward the bolt of magnificent emerald silk embroidered with spidery golden threads lying on the counter beside his hand, he signed the draft and added, "And make the first of the ball gowns out of this. Have it ready on the twentieth."

Straightening, he thrust the bank draft at her. "That should cover it." It would have covered half again as much, and they both knew it. "If it doesn't, send the bills to me."

"Oui," the lady said in a slightly dazed voice, "but I *cannot* give you the emerald silk. That has already been selected by Lady Margaret Mitcham and promised to her."

Ian's expression took on a look of surprised displeasure. "I'm surprised you allowed her to choose it, madame. It will make her complexion look sallow. Tell her I said so."

He turned and left the shop without the slightest idea of who Lady Margaret Mitcham was. Behind him an assistant came to lift the shimmering emerald silk and take it back to the seamstresses. *"Non,"* the modiste said, her appreciative gaze on the tall, broad-shouldered man who was bounding into his carriage. "It is to be used for someone else."

"But Lady Mitcham chose it."

With a last wistful glance at the handsome man who obviously appreciated exquisite cloth, she dismissed her assistant's objection. "Lord Mitcham is an old man with bad eyes; he cannot appreciate the gown I can make from this cloth."

"But what shall I tell Lady Mitcham?" the harassed assistant implored.

"Tell her," her mistress said wryly, "that Monsieur Thornton—no, Lord Kensington—said it would make her complexion sallow."

25

Havenhurst was a pretty estate, Ian thought as his carriage
passed through the stone arch, but not nearly so imposing as
Elizabeth's proud description had led him to expect. Mortar
was missing from the portals, he noticed absently, and as the
carriage swayed down the drive he realized that the paving
was in need of repair, and the stately old trees dotting the
lawns were badly in need of pruning. A moment later the
house came into view, and Ian, who had a vast knowledge of
architecture, identified it in a single glance as a random
combination of Gothic and Tudor styles that somehow
managed to be pleasing to the eye, despite the inconsistencies of structure that would have sent a modern architect
straight to his drawing board.

The door was opened by a short footman, who looked Ian
over insolently from head to toe, his chin thrust out
pugnaciously. Ignoring the odd behavior of Elizabeth's
servants, Ian glanced with interest at the timbered ceiling
and then at the walls, where bright patches of wallpaper
marked the places where paintings had once hung. There
were no Persian carpets scattered on the polished floors, no
treasures reposing on tabletops; in fact, there was precious
little furniture anywhere in the hall or the salons off to his
right. Ian's heart squeezed with a combination of guilt and

admiration for how proudly she had pretended to him that she was still the carefree young heiress he'd thought her to be.

Realizing that the footman was still glowering at him, Ian looked down at the short man and said, "Your mistress is expecting me. Tell her I've arrived."

"I'm here, Aaron," Elizabeth's voice said softly, and Ian turned. One look at her and Ian forgot the footman, the state of the house, and any knowledge of architecture he'd ever possessed. Garbed in a simple gown of sky-blue gauze, with her hair twisted into thick curls bound with narrow blue ribbons, Elizabeth was standing in the hall with the poise of a Grecian goddess and the smile of an angel. "What do you think?" she asked expectantly.

"About what?" he asked huskily, walking forward, forcing his hands not to reach for her.

"About Havenhurst?" she asked with quiet pride. Ian thought it was rather small and in desperate need of repair, not to mention furnishings. In fact, he had an impulse to drag her into his arms and beg her forgiveness for all he'd cost her. Knowing such a thing would shame and hurt her, he smiled and said truthfully, "What I've seen is very picturesque."

"Would you like to see the rest?"

"Very much," he exaggerated, and it was worth it to see her face light up. "Where are the Townsendes?" he asked as they started up the staircase. "I didn't see a carriage in the drive."

"They haven't arrived yet."

Ian correctly supposed that was Jordan's doing and made a mental note to thank his friend.

Elizabeth gave him a grand tour of the old house that was saved from being boring by her charming stories about some of its former owners; then she took him outside to the front lawn. Nodding to the far edge of the lawn, she said, "Over there was the castle wall and the moat, which was filled, of course, centuries ago. This whole section was a bailey then—a courtyard," she clarified, "that was enclosed by the castle walls. In those days there were outbuildings here in the bailey that housed everything from livestock to the buttery, so that the entire castle was completely self-sufficient. Over there," she said a few minutes later as they rounded the side of the house, "was where the third Earl of Havenhurst fell off his horse and then had the horse shot for throwing him. He was most ill-tempered," she added with a jaunty grin.

"Obviously," Ian grinned back at her, longing to kiss the smile on her lips. He glanced at the spot on the lawn she'd mentioned and said instead, "How did he happen to fall off his horse in his own bailey?"

"Oh, that," she said with a laugh. "He was practicing at the quintain at the time. In the Middle Ages," she explained to Ian, whose knowledge of medieval history was as complete as his knowledge of architecture, and who knew exactly what a quintain was, "the knights used to practice for jousts and battles with a quintain. A quintain is a crossbar with a sandbag hanging off one arm and a shield in front of the sandbag. The knights would charge it, but if a knight didn't strike the shield squarely with his broadsword, then the crossbar whirled around and the sandbag hit the knight in his back and knocked him off his horse."

"Which, I gather, is what happened to the third earl?" Ian teased as they headed toward the largest tree on the far edge of the lawn.

"Exactly," she averred. When they came to the tree she linked her hands behind her back, looking like an enchanting little girl with a secret she was about to share. "Now," she said, "look up there."

Ian tipped his head back and laughed with amazed pleasure. Above him was an enormous and very unusual tree house. "Yours?" he asked.

"Of course."

He cast a swift, appraising look at the sturdy "steps" nailed into the tree and then quirked a brow at her. "Do you want to go first, or shall I?"

"You're joking!"

"If you could invade mine, I can't see why I shouldn't see yours."

The carpenters who'd built it for her had done their jobs well, Ian noted as he bent over in the middle of it, looking around. Elizabeth had been much smaller than he, and everything was scaled to her size, but it was large enough that she could nearly stand upright in it as an adult. "What's over there, in the little trunk?"

She sidled behind him, smiling. "I was trying to remember just that when I was in yours. I'll look. Just as I thought," she said a moment later as she opened the lid. "My doll and a tea service."

Ian grinned at it, and at her, but he saw the little girl she must have been, living alone in relative splendor, with a doll for her family and servants for friends. In comparison, his own youth had been much richer.

"There's just one more thing to show you," she said several minutes later when he'd extracted her from the tree limbs and they were heading toward the house.

Ian pulled himself from thoughts of her disadvantaged youth as she changed direction. They skirted the corner of the house, and when they came to the back of it Elizabeth stopped and raised her arm in a graceful, sweeping gesture. "Most of this is my contribution to Havenhurst," she told him proudly.

The sight that Ian beheld when he looked up made his grin fade as tenderness and awe shook through him. Spread out before him in colorful splendor were the most magnificent flower gardens Ian had ever beheld. The other heirs of Havenhurst might have added stone and mortar to the house, but Elizabeth had given it breathtaking beauty.

"When I was young," she confided softly, looking out at the sloping gardens and the hills beyond, "I used to think this was the most beautiful place on earth." Feeling a little foolish over her confidences, Elizabeth glanced up at him with an embarrassed smile. "What is the most beautiful place you've ever seen?"

Dragging his gaze from the beauty of the gardens, Ian looked down at the beauty beside him. "Any place," he said huskily, "where you are."

He saw the becoming flush of embarrassed pleasure that pinkened her cheeks, but when she spoke her voice was rueful. "You don't have to say such things to me, you know—I'll keep our bargain."

"I know you will," he said, trying not to overwhelm her with avowals of love she wouldn't yet believe. With a grin he added, "Besides, as it turned out after our bargaining session, *I'm* the one who's governed by all the conditions, not you."

Her sideways glance was filled with laughter. "You were much too lenient at times, you know. Toward the end I was asking for concessions just to see how far you'd go."

Ian, who had been multiplying his fortune for the last four years by buying shipping and import-export companies, as well as sundry others, was regarded as an extremely tough negotiator. He heard her announcement with a smile of genuine surprise. "You gave me the impression that every single concession was of paramount importance to you, and that if I didn't agree, you might call the whole thing off."

She nodded with satisfaction. "I rather *thought* that was how I ought to do it. Why are you laughing?"

"Because," he admitted, chuckling, "obviously I was not in my best form yesterday. In addition to completely misreading your feelings, I managed to buy a house on Promenade Street for which I will undoubtedly pay five times its worth."

"Oh, I don't think so," she said, and, as if she was embarrassed and needed a way to avoid meeting his gaze, she reached up and pulled a leaf off an overhanging branch. In a voice of careful nonchalance, she explained, "In matters of bargaining, *I* believe in being reasonable, but my uncle would assuredly have tried to cheat you. He's perfectly dreadful about money."

Ian nodded, remembering the fortune Julius Cameron had gouged out of him in order to sign the betrothal agreement.

"And so," she admitted, uneasily studying the azure-blue sky with feigned absorption, "I sent him a note after you left itemizing all the repairs that were needed at the house. I told him it was in poor condition and absolutely in need of complete redecoration."

"And?"

"And I told him you would consider paying a fair price for the house, but not one shilling more, because it needed all that."

"And?" Ian prodded.

"He has agreed to sell it for that figure."

Ian's mirth exploded in shouts of laughter. Snatching her

into his arms, he waited until he could finally catch his breath, then he tipped her face up to his. "Elizabeth," he said tenderly, "if you change your mind about marrying me, promise me you'll never represent the opposition at the bargaining table. I swear to God, I'd be lost." The temptation to kiss her was almost overwhelming, but the Townsende coach with its ducal crest was in the drive, and he had no idea where their chaperons might be. Elizabeth noticed the coach, too, and started toward the house.

"About the gowns," she said, stopping suddenly and looking up at him with an intensely earnest expression on her beautiful face. "I meant to thank you for your generosity as soon as you arrived, but I was so happy to—that is—" She realized she'd been about to blurt out that she was happy to see him, and she was so flustered by having admitted aloud what she hadn't admitted to herself that she completely lost her thought.

"Go on," Ian invited in a husky voice. "You were so happy to see me that you—"

"I forgot," she admitted lamely. "You shouldn't have done it, you know—ordered so very many things, and from her shop. Madame LaSalle is *horribly* expensive—I remember hearing about her when I made my debut."

"You are not to consider that sort of thing," he said firmly. Trying to lessen her lingering guilt over the gowns, he added jokingly, "At least we'll have the gowns to show for the expenditure. The night before I ordered them for you, *I* lost £1,000 on a hand of cards with Jordan Townsende."

"You're a gambler," she said curiously. "Don't you normally wager such sums on a hand?"

"Not," Ian said dryly, "when I'm not holding anything in that hand."

"You know," she told him gently as she led him across the lawn toward the front door, "if you persist in spending heedlessly, you'll end up just like my papa."

"How did he end up?"

"Up to his ears in debt. He liked to gamble, too."

When Ian was silent, Elizabeth ventured hesitantly, "We could always live here. There's no need for three establishments—it's very costly." She realized what she was saying and hastily said, "I didn't mean to imply I won't be perfectly comfortable wherever you live. I thought the cottage in Scotland was very beautiful, actually."

It delighted Ian that she evidently had no knowledge of the extent of his wealth and yet had still agreed to marry him, even if it meant living in a modest cottage or the town house on Promenade Street. If that was true, it gave him the proof that he desperately wanted—proof that she cared for him more than she was ready to admit.

"Let's decide the day after tomorrow when you see my house," he suggested mildly, already looking forward to what he hoped would be a shocked reaction.

"Do—do you think you could try to be more prudent with money?" she asked gently. "I could make out a budget, I'm quite good at that—"

Ian couldn't help it; he muffled a laugh and did what he'd been longing to do from the moment he saw her standing in the hall: He pulled her into his arms, covered her mouth with his, and kissed her with all the hungry ardor that being near her always evoked, and Elizabeth kissed him back with the same yielding sweetness that always drove him mad with desire.

When he reluctantly let her go, her face was flushed and her beautiful eyes were radiant. Lacing his fingers through hers, he walked slowly beside her toward the front door. Since he was in no hurry to join his chaperons, Ian diverted her by asking about a particularly interesting shrubbery, an unusual flower in the front bed, and even a perfectly ordinary rose.

Standing at the window overlooking the lawn, Jordan and Alexandra Townsende watched the couple heading toward them. "If you'd asked me to name the last man on earth I would have expected to fall head over heels for a slip of a girl, it would have been Ian Thornton," he told her.

His wife heard that with a sidewise look of extreme amusement. "If *I'd* been asked, I rather think I would have named *you.*"

"I'm sure you would have," he said, grinning. He saw her smile fade, and he put his arm around her waist, instantly concerned that her pregnancy was causing her discomfort. "Is it the babe, darling?"

She burst out laughing and shook her head, but she

sobered again almost instantly. "Do you think," she asked pensively, "he can be trusted not to hurt her? He's done so much damage that I—I just cannot like him, Jordan. He's handsome, I'll grant you that, extraordinarily handsome—"

"Not *that* handsome," Jordan said, stung. And this time Alexandra dissolved in mirth. Turning, she wrapped her arms around him and kissed him soundly. "Actually, he rather reminds me of you," she said, "in his coloring and height and build."

"I hope that hasn't anything to do with why you can't like him," her husband teased.

"Jordan, do stop. I'm worried, really I am. He's—well, he almost frightens me. Even though he seems very civilized on the surface, there's a forcefulness, maybe even a ruthlessness beneath his polished manners. And he stops at nothing when he wants something. I saw that yesterday when he came to the house and persuaded Elizabeth to agree to marry him."

Turning, Jordan looked at her with a mixture of intent interest, surprise, and amusement. "Go on," he said.

"Well, at this particular moment he wants Elizabeth, and I can't help fearing it's a whim."

"You wouldn't have thought that if you'd seen his face blanch the other night when he realized she was going to try to brave society without his help."

"Really? You're certain?"

"Positive."

"Are you certain you know him well enough to judge him?"

"Absolutely certain," he averred.

"How well do you know him?"

"Ian," Jordan said with a grin, "is my sixth cousin."

"Your what? You're joking! Why didn't you tell me before?"

"In the first place, the subject never came up until last night. Even if it had, I wouldn't have mentioned it, because until now Ian refused to acknowledge his relationship to Stanhope, which was within his rights. Knowing his feelings about that, I regarded it as a compliment that he was willing to admit *our* relationship. We're also partners in three shipping ventures."

He saw her staggered expression and chuckled. "If Ian isn't an actual genius, he's very close to it. He's a brilliant strategist. Intelligence," he teased, "runs in the family."

"Cousins!" Alex repeated blankly.

"That shouldn't surprise you. If you go back far enough, a vast number of the aristocracy have been connected at some point by what we called 'advantageous marriages.' I suspect, however, that the thing that confuses you about Ian is that he's half Scot. In many ways he's more Scot than English, which accounts for what you're calling a ruthless streak. He'll do what he pleases, when he pleases, and the devil fly with the consequences. He always has. He doesn't care what anyone thinks of him or of what he does."

Pausing, Jordan glanced meaningfully at the couple who'd paused to look at a shrubbery on the front lawn. Ian was listening to Elizabeth intently, an expression of tenderness on his rugged face. "The other night, however, he cared very much what people thought of your lovely friend. In fact, I don't like to think what he might have done had anyone actually dared to openly insult her in front of him. You're right when you aren't deceived by Ian's civilized veneer. Beneath that he's a Scot, and he has a temper to go with it, though he usually keeps it in check."

"I don't think you're reassuring me," Alex said shakily.

"I should be. He's committed himself completely to her. That commitment is so deep that he even reconciled with his grandfather and then appeared with him in public, which I know was because of Elizabeth."

"What on earth makes you think that?"

"For one thing, when I saw Ian at the Blackmore he had no plans for the evening until he discovered what Elizabeth was going to do at the Willingtons'. The next I knew, he was walking into that ball with his grandfather at his side. And that, my love, is what we call a show of strength."

She looked impressed by his powers of deduction, and Jordan grinned. "Don't admire me too much. I also asked him. So you see, you're worrying needlessly," he finished reassuringly. "Scots are a fiercely loyal lot, and Ian will protect her with his life."

"He certainly didn't protect her with his life two years ago, when she was ruined."

Sighing, Jordan looked out the window. "After the Willingtons' ball he told me a little of what happened that long-ago weekend. He didn't tell me much—Ian is a very private man—but reading between the lines, I'm guessing that he fell like a rock for her and then got the idea she was playing games with him."

"Would that have been so terrible?" Alex asked, her full sympathy still with Elizabeth.

Jordan smiled ruefully at her. "There's one thing Scots are besides loyal."

"What is that?"

"Unforgiving," he said flatly. "They expect the same loyalty as they give. Moreover, if you betray their loyalty, you're dead to them. Nothing you do or say will change their heart. That's why their feuds last from generation to generation."

"Barbaric," Alexandra said with a shiver of alarm.

"Perhaps it is. But then let's not forget Ian is also half English, and we are *very* civilized." Leaning down, Jordan nipped her ear. "Except in bed."

Ian had run out of diversions and resigned himself to going indoors, but as they reached the front steps Elizabeth turned and stopped. In the voice of one confessing to an action she isn't certain was entirely wrong, she said, "This morning I hired an investigator to try to locate my brother, or at least find out what has happened to him. I tried to do it before, but as soon as they realized I had no money they wouldn't accept my promise to pay them later. I thought I would use part of your loan for Havenhurst to pay him."

It took a conscious effort for Ian to keep his face expressionless. "And?" he asked.

"The dowager duchess assured me that Mr. Wordsworth is extremely good. He's frightfully expensive; however, we were finally able to come to terms."

"The good ones are always expensive," Ian said, thinking of the £3,000 retainer he'd paid to an investigator this morning for the same purpose. "How much did he charge you?" he asked, intending to add that amount to her allowance.

"Originally he wanted £1,000 whether he finds news of

Robert or not. But I offered to pay him twice his fee if he's successful."

"And if he isn't?"

"Oh, in *that* case I didn't think it was fair that he receive anything," she said. "I persuaded him I was right."

Ian's shout of laughter was still ringing in the hall when they entered the drawing room to greet the Townsendes.

Ian had never enjoyed a dinner of state, or dinner à deux, as much as he enjoyed the one that evening. Despite the scarcity of furnishings at Havenhurst, Elizabeth had turned the dining room and drawing room into an elegant bower of fresh-cut, artfully arranged flowers, and with the candles glowing in the candelabras, it was as beautiful a setting for dining as any he'd ever seen.

Only once did he have a bad moment, and that was when Elizabeth entered the dining room carrying a tray of food, and he thought she'd cooked the meal. A moment later a footman walked in bearing another tray, and Ian inwardly sighed with relief. "This is Winston, our footman and cook," she told Ian, guessing his thoughts. Straight-faced, she added, "Winston taught me everything I know about cooking." Ian's emotions veered from horror to hilarity, and the footman saw it.

"Miss Elizabeth," the footman pointedly informed Ian, "does not *know* how to cook. She has always been much too *busy* to learn."

Ian endured that reprimand without retort because he was thoroughly enjoying Elizabeth's relaxed mood, and because she had actually been teasing him. As the huffy footman departed, however, Ian glanced at Jordan and saw his narrowed gaze on the man's back, then he looked at Elizabeth, who was obviously embarrassed.

"They think they're acting out of loyalty to me," she explained. "They—well, they recognize your name from before. I'll speak to them."

"I'd appreciate that," Ian said with amused irritation. To Jordan he added, "Elizabeth's butler always tries to send me packing."

"Can he hear?" Jordan asked unsympathetically.

"Hear?" Ian repeated. "Of course he can."

"Then count yourself lucky," Jordan replied irritably, and the girls dissolved into gales of laughter.

"The Townsendes' butler, Penrose, is quite deaf, you see," Elizabeth explained.

Dinner progressed among bursts of merriment and revelations about both Alexandra and Elizabeth that amazed Ian, including the fact that Alexandra was evidently as handy with a rapier as Elizabeth was with a pistol. So entertaining was Elizabeth that Ian found himself ignoring his very satisfactory meal and simply lounging back in his chair, watching her with a mixture of amusement and pride. She sparkled like the wine in their crystal glasses, glowed like the candles in the centerpiece, and when she laughed, music floated through the room. With the instincts of a natural hostess she drew everyone into each topic of conversation, until even Jordan and Ian were participating in the raillery. But best of all, she was at ease in Ian's presence. Artless and elegant and sweet, she turned to him and teased him, or smiled at something he said, or listened attentively to an opinion. She wasn't ready to trust him yet, but she wasn't that far away from it, he sensed.

After dinner the ladies adhered to custom and adjourned to the drawing room, leaving the gentlemen to enjoy their port and cigars at the table.

"Ian was lighting a cigar the first moment I saw him," Elizabeth confided to Alex when they were comfortably seated in the drawing room. Glancing up, she saw the worried frown on Alexandra's face, and after a moment she quietly said, "You don't like him, do you?"

Alex's gaze flew to hers while the faint disappointment in Elizabeth's voice registered on her. "I—I don't like the things he's done to you," she admitted.

Tipping her head back, Elizabeth closed her eyes, trying to know what to say, what to think. A long time ago Ian had told her he was half in love with her, yet now that they were betrothed he'd never spoken a word of it, had not even pretended. She wasn't certain of his motives or his feelings; she wasn't certain of her own, either. All she really knew was that the sight of his hard, handsome face with its chiseled features, and bold amber eyes never failed to make her entire being feel tense and alive. She knew he liked to kiss her, and that she very much liked being kissed by him. Added to his other attractions was something else that drew her inexorably to him: From their very first meeting, Elizabeth had sensed that beneath his bland sophistication and rugged virility Ian Thornton had a depth that most people lacked. "It's so hard to know," she whispered, "how I ought to feel or what I ought to think. And I have the worst feeling it's not going to matter what I know or what I think," she added almost sadly, "because I *am* going to love him." She opened her eyes and looked at Alex. "It's happening, and I cannot stop it. It was happening two years ago, and I couldn't stop it then, either. So you see," she added with a sad little smile, "it would be so much nicer for me if you could love him just a little, too."

Alex reached across the table and took Elizabeth's hands in hers. "If you love him, then he must be the very *best* of men. I shall henceforth make it a point to see all his best qualities!" Alex hesitated, and then she hazarded the question: "Elizabeth, does he love you?"

Elizabeth shook her head. "He *wants* me, he says, and he wants children."

Alex swallowed embarrassed laughter. "He what?"

"He wants me, and he wants children."

A funny, knowing smile tugged at Alexandra's lips. "You didn't tell me he said the first part. I am much encouraged," she teased while a rosy blush stole over her cheeks.

"I think I am, too," Elizabeth admitted, drawing a swift, searching look from Alex.

"Elizabeth, this is scarcely the time to discuss this—in fact," Alex added, her flush deepening, "I don't think there *is* a really good time to discuss it—but has Lucinda explained to you how children are conceived?"

"Yes, of course," Elizabeth said without hesitation.

"Good, because I would have been the logical one otherwise, and I still remember *my* reaction when *I* found out. It was not a pretty sight," she laughed. "On the other hand, you were always much the wiser girl than I."

"I don't think so at all," Elizabeth said, but she couldn't imagine what there was, really, to blush about. Children, Lucinda had told her when she'd asked, were conceived when a husband kissed his wife in bed. And it hurt the first time. Ian's kisses were sometimes almost bruising, but they never actually hurt, and she enjoyed them terribly.

As if speaking her feelings aloud to Alexandra had somehow relieved her of the burden of trying to deal with them, Elizabeth was so joyously relaxed that she suspected Ian noticed it at once when the men joined them in the drawing room.

Ian did notice it; in fact, as they sat down to play a game of cards in accordance with Elizabeth's cheery suggestion, he noticed there was a subtle but distinct softening in the attitudes of *both* ladies toward him.

"Will you shuffle and deal?" Elizabeth asked. He nodded, and she handed the deck of cards to him, then watched in rapt fascination as the cards seemed to leap to life in Ian's hands, flying together with a whoosh and snap, then sliding out in neat little piles that flew together again beneath his fingers. "What would you like to play?" he asked her.

"I would like to see you cheat," Elizabeth said impulsively, smiling at him.

His hands stilled, his eyes intent on her face. "I beg your pardon?"

"What I meant," she hastily explained as he continued to idly shuffle the cards, watching her, "is that night in the card room at Charise's there was mention of someone being able to deal a card from the bottom of the deck, and I've always wondered if you could, if *it* could . . ." She trailed off, belatedly realizing she was insulting him and that his narrowed, speculative gaze proved that she'd made it sound as if she believed him to be dishonest at cards. "I beg your pardon," she said quietly. "That was truly awful of me."

Ian accepted her apology with a curt nod, and when Alex hastily interjected, "Why don't we use the chips for a shilling each," he wordlessly and immediately dealt the cards.

Too embarrassed even to look at him, Elizabeth bit her lip and picked up her hand.

In it there were four kings.

Her gaze flew to Ian, but he was lounging back in his chair, studying his own cards.

She won three shillings and was pleased as could be.

He passed the deck to her, but Elizabeth shook her head. "I don't like to deal. I always drop the cards, which Celton says is very irritating. Would you mind dealing for me?"

"Not at all," Ian said dispassionately, and Elizabeth realized with a sinking heart that he was still annoyed with her.

"Who is Celton?" Jordan inquired.

"Celton is a groom with whom I play cards," Elizabeth explained unhappily, picking up her hand.

In it there were four aces.

She knew it then, and laughter and relief trembled on her lips as she lifted her face and stared at her betrothed. There was not a sign, not so much as a hint anywhere on his perfectly composed features that anything unusual had been happening.

Lounging indolently in his chair, he quirked an indifferent brow and said, "Do you want to discard and draw more cards, Elizabeth?"

"Yes," she replied, swallowing her mirth, "I would like one more ace to go with the ones I have."

"There are only four," he explained mildly, and with such convincing blandness that Elizabeth whooped with laughter and dropped her cards. "You are a complete charlatan!" she gasped when she could finally speak, but her face was aglow with admiration.

"Thank you, darling," he replied tenderly. "I'm happy to know your opinion of me is already improving."

The laughter froze in Elizabeth's chest, replaced by warmth that quaked through her from head to foot. Gentlemen did not speak such tender endearments in front of other people, if at all. *"I'm a Scot,"* he'd whispered huskily to her long ago. *"We do."* The Townsendes had launched into swift, laughing conversation after a moment of stunned silence following his words, and it was just as well, because Elizabeth could not tear her gaze from Ian, could not seem to move. And in that endless moment when their gazes held, Elizabeth had an almost overwhelming desire to fling herself into his arms. He saw it, too, and the answering expression in his eyes made her feel she was melting.

"It occurs to me, Ian," Jordan joked a moment later, gently breaking their spell, "that we are wasting our time with honest pursuits."

Ian's gaze shifted reluctantly from Elizabeth's face, and then he smiled inquisitively at Jordan. "What did you have in mind?" he asked, shoving the deck toward Jordan while Elizabeth put back her unjustly won chips.

"With your skill at dealing whatever hand you want, we could gull half of London. If any of our victims had the temerity to object, Alex could run him through with her rapier, and Elizabeth could shoot him before he hit the ground."

Ian chuckled. "Not a bad idea. What would your role be?"

"Breaking us out of Newgate!" Elizabeth laughed.

"Exactly."

After Ian left for the Greenleaf Inn, where he planned to stop for the night before continuing the trip to his own home, Elizabeth stayed downstairs to put out the candles and tidy up the drawing room. In one of the guest chambers above, Jordan glanced at his wife's faint, preoccupied smile and suppressed a knowing grin. "Now what do you think of the Marquess of Kensington?" he asked.

Her eyes were shining as she lifted them to his. "I think," she softly said, "that unless he does something dreadful, I'm prepared to believe he could truly be your cousin."

"Thank you, darling," Jordan replied tenderly, paraphrasing Ian's words. "I'm happy to see your opinion of him is already improving."

26

Elizabeth was undeniably eager to see Ian again, and more than a little curious about the sort of house he lived in. He'd told her he had purchased Montmayne last year with his own money, and, after being with him in Scotland, she rather imagined a ruggedly built manor house would suit him. On the one hand it seemed a foolish waste not to live at Havenhurst, which would offer them every convenience, but she understood that Ian's pride would suffer if he had to live with her in her home.

She'd left Lucinda behind at the inn where they'd spent the night, and the coach had been traveling for more than two hours when Aaron finally turned off the road and pulled to a smart stop at a pair of massive iron gates that blocked their entry. Elizabeth glanced nervously out the window, saw the imposing entry, and reached the obvious conclusion that either they were in the wrong place or Aaron had pulled into the drive to ask directions. A gatekeeper emerged from the ornate little house beside the gates, and Elizabeth waited to hear what Aaron said.

"The Countess of Havenhurst," Aaron was informing the gatekeeper.

In shock, Elizabeth watched through the open window of the coach as the gatekeeper nodded and then walked over to the gates. The massive iron portals opened soundlessly on well-oiled hinges, and Aaron drove through as the gatekeeper was swinging them closed. Twisting her gloves in her hands, Elizabeth gazed out the window as the coach made its way along an endless, curving drive that wound through manicured parkland, offering a scenic view of an estate that surpassed anything Elizabeth had ever seen. Rolling hills dotted with lush trees bounded the estate on three sides, and a beautiful stream bubbled merrily beneath a stone bridge as the horses clattered across it.

Ahead of her the house came into view, and Elizabeth could not stop her exclamation at the exquisite beauty she beheld spread out before her. A majestic three-story house with two wings angled forward on the sides stretched out before her. Sunlight glinted on the large panes of glass that marched across its front; wide flights of shallow, terraced brick steps led from the drive to the massive front door, with stone urns containing clipped shrubs on both sides of every four steps. Swans drifted lazily on the mirror surface of a lake on the far end of the lawn, and beside the lake was a Grecian-style gazebo with white columns that was so immense a quarter of her own home could have fit inside it. The sheer magnitude of the grounds, combined with the precise positioning of every single scenic attribute, made it all seem both overwhelming and utterly breathtaking.

The coach finally drew up before the terraced steps, and four footmen descended, garbed in burgundy and gold. They helped a dazed Elizabeth to alight, and, positioning themselves on either side of her like an honor guard, they escorted her to the house.

A butler opened a massive front door and bowed to her, and Elizabeth stepped into a magnificent marble entryway with a glass ceiling three stories above. Entranced, she looked about her, trying to assimilate what was happening. "My lord is in his study with guests who arrived unexpectedly," the butler said, drawing Elizabeth's gaze from the graceful, curving Palladian staircases that swept upward on both sides of the great hall. "He asked that you be escorted to him the moment you arrived."

Elizabeth smiled uncertainly and followed him down a marble hallway, where he paused before a pair of polished double doors with ornate brass handles and knocked. Without waiting for an answer he opened the door. Elizabeth automatically started forward three steps, then halted, mesmerized. An acre of thick Aubusson carpet stretched across the book-lined room, and at the far end of it, seated behind a massive baronial desk with his shirtsleeves folded up on tanned forearms, was the man who had lived in the little cottage in Scotland and shot at a tree limb with her.

Oblivious to the other three men in the room who were politely coming to their feet, Elizabeth watched Ian arise with that same natural grace that seemed so much a part of him. With a growing sense of unreality she heard him excuse himself to his visitors, saw him move away from behind his desk, and watched him start toward her with long, purposeful strides. He grew larger as he neared, his broad shoulders blocking her view of the room, his amber eyes searching her face, his smile one of amusement and uncertainty. "Elizabeth?" he said.

Her eyes wide with embarrassed admiration, Elizabeth allowed him to lift her hand to his lips before she said softly, "I could kill you."

He grinned at the contrast between her words and her voice. "I know."

"You might have told me."

"I hoped to surprise you."

More correctly, he had hoped she didn't know, and now he had his proof: Just as he had thought, Elizabeth had agreed to marry him without knowing anything of his personal wealth. That expression of dazed disbelief on her face had been real. He'd needed to see it for himself, which was why he'd instructed his butler to bring her to him as soon as she arrived. Ian had his proof, and with it came the knowledge that no matter how much she refused to admit it to him or to herself, she loved him.

She could insist for now and all time that all she wanted from marriage was independence, and now Ian could endure it with equanimity. Because she loved him.

Elizabeth watched the expressions play across his face. Thinking he was waiting for her to say more about his splendid house, she gave him a jaunty smile and teasingly said, "'Twill be a sacrifice, to be sure, but I shall contrive to endure the hardship of living in such a place as this. How many rooms are there?" she asked.

His brows rose in mockery. "One hundred and eighty-two."

"A small place of modest proportions," she countered lightly. "I suppose we'll just have to make do."

Ian thought they were going to do very well.

He finished his meeting a few minutes later and almost rudely ejected his business acquaintances from his library, then he went in search of Elizabeth.

"She is out in the gardens, my lord," his butler informed him. A short while later Ian strolled out the French doors and started down the balcony steps to join her. She was bending down and snapping a withered rosebud from its stem. "It only hurts for a moment," she told the bush, "and it's for your own good. You'll see." With an embarrassed little smile she looked up at him. "It's a habit," she explained.

"It obviously works," he said with a tender smile, looking at the way the flowers bloomed about her skirts.

"How can you tell?"

"Because," he said quietly as she stood up, "until you walked into it, this was an ordinary garden."

Puzzled, Elizabeth tipped her head. "What is it now?"

"Heaven."

Elizabeth's breath caught in her chest at the husky timbre of his voice and the desire in his eyes. He held out his hand to her, and, without realizing what she was doing, she lifted her hand and gave it to him, then she walked straight into his arms. For one breathless moment his smoldering eyes studied her face feature by feature while the pressure of his arms slowly increased, and then he bent his head. His sensual mouth claimed hers in a kiss of violent tenderness and tormenting desire while his hands slid over the sides of her breasts, and Elizabeth felt all her resistance, all her will, begin to crumble and disintegrate, and she kissed him back with her whole heart.

All the love that had been accumulating through the lonely years of her childhood was in that kiss—Ian felt it in the soft lips parting willingly for his searching tongue, the delicate hands sliding through the hair at his nape. With unselfish ardor she offered it all to him, and Ian took it hungrily, feeling it moving from her to him, then flowing through his veins and mingling with his until the joy of it was shattering. She was everything he'd ever dreamed she could be and more.

With an effort that was almost painful he dragged his mouth from hers, his hand still cupping the rumpled satin of her hair, his other hand holding her pressed to his rigid body, and Elizabeth stayed in his arms, seeming neither frightened nor offended by his rigid erection. "I love you," he whispered, rubbing his jaw against her temple. "And you love me. I can feel it when you're in my arms." He felt her stiffen slightly and draw a shaky breath, but she either couldn't or wouldn't speak. She hadn't thrown the words back in his face, however, so Ian continued talking to her, his hand roving over her back. "I can feel it, Elizabeth, but if you don't admit it pretty soon, you're going to drive me out of my mind. I can't work. I can't think. I make decisions and then I change my mind. And," he teased, trying to lighten the mood by using the one topic sure to distract her, "that's nothing to the money I squander whenever I'm under this sort of violent stress. It wasn't just the gowns I bought, or the house on Promenade . . ."

Still talking to her, he tipped her chin up, glorying in the gentle passion in her eyes, overlooking the doubt in their green depths. "If you don't admit it pretty soon," he teased, "I'll spend us out of house and home." Her delicate brows drew together in blank confusion, and Ian grinned, taking her hand from his chest, the emerald betrothal ring he had bought her unnoticed in his fingers. "When I'm under stress," he emphasized, sliding the magnificent emerald onto her finger, "I buy everything in sight. It took my last ounce of control not to buy one of these in *every* color."

Her eyes lifted from his smiling lips, dropped to the enormous jewel on her finger, and then widened in shock. "Oh, but—" she exclaimed, staring at it and straightening in his arms. "It's *glorious,* I do mean that, but I couldn't let you—really, I couldn't. Ian," she burst out anxiously, sending a tremor through him when she called him by name, "I can't let you do this. You've been extravagantly generous already." She touched the huge stone almost reverently, then gave her head a practical shake. "I don't need jewels, really I don't. You're doing this because of that stupid remark I made about someone offering me jewels as large as my palm, and now you've bought one nearly that large!"

"Not quite," he chuckled.

"Why, a stone like this would pay for irrigating Havenhurst and all the servants' wages for years and years and years, and food to—"

She reached to slide it off her finger. "Don't!" he warned on a choked laugh, linking his hands behind her back. "I"—he thought madly for some way to stop her objections—"I cannot possibly return it," he said. "It's part of a matched set."

"You don't mean there's more!"

"I'm afraid so, though I meant to surprise you with them tonight. There's a necklace and bracelet and earrings."

"Oh, I see," she said, making a visible effort not to stare at her ring. "Well, I suppose . . . if it was a purchase of *several* pieces, the ring alone probably didn't cost as much as it would have . . . Do not tell me," she said severely, when his shoulders began to shake with suppressed mirth, "you actually paid full price for *all* of the pieces!"

Laughing, Ian put his forehead against hers, and he nodded.

"It's very fortunate," she said, protectively putting her fingers against the magnificent ring, "that I've agreed to marry you."

"If you hadn't," he laughed, "God knows what I would have bought."

"Or how much you would have *paid* for it," she chuckled, cuddling in his arms—for the first time of her own volition. "Do you really do that?" she asked a moment later.

"Do what?" he gasped, tears of mirth blurring his vision.

"Spend money heedlessly when you're disturbed about something?"

"Yes," he lied in a suffocated, laughing voice.

"You'll have to stop doing it."

"I'm going to try."

"I could help you."

"Please do."

"You may place yourself entirely in my hands."

"I'm very much looking forward to that."

It was the first time Ian had ever kissed a woman while he was laughing.

The afternoon passed as if it were minutes, not hours, and he kept glancing at the clock, willing it to stop. When there was no way to avoid it, he escorted her out to her carriage. "I'll see you in London tomorrow night at the ball. And don't worry. It will be fine."

"I know it will," she answered with complete confidence.

27

Five nights before, when she'd arrived at the Willingtons' ball, she'd been terrified and ashamed. Tonight, as the butler called out her name, Elizabeth felt neither dread nor even concern as she walked gracefully across the balcony and began slowly descending the steps to the ballroom beside the dowager duchess. With Jordan and Alexandra behind them she saw people turning to watch her, only tonight Elizabeth cared nothing for what expression was on all six hundred faces. Wrapped in an incredibly sumptuous gown of gold-embroidered emerald silk, with Ian's emerald and diamond necklace at her throat and her hair caught up in intricate curls at her crown, she felt carefree and calm.

Partway down the steps she let her gaze pass across the crowd, looking for the only face that mattered. He was exactly where he had been two years ago when she'd walked into Charise's ballroom—standing not far from the foot of the steps, listening to some people who were talking to him.

And just as she had known would happen, he looked up the moment she saw him, as if he'd been watching for her, too. His bold, admiring gaze swept over her, then it returned slowly to her face—and then, in shared memory, he lifted his glass and made that same subtle toast to her.

It was all sweetly, poignantly familiar; they'd played this

same scene two years ago, only then it had ended wrong. Tonight Elizabeth intended that it would end as it should have, and she didn't care a whit about any other reason for being here. The things he had said to her yesterday, the husky sound of his voice, the way he held her—they were like sweet music playing through her heart. He was daring and bold and passionate—he had *always* been those things —and Elizabeth was mightily tired of being fearful and prim and logical.

Ian's thoughts were also on the last time he'd watched her enter a ballroom—that is, they *had* been until he got a clear look at her and logical thinking fled his mind. The Elizabeth Cameron coming down the steps and passing within a few yards of him was *not* the beautiful girl in blue of two years ago.

A breathtaking vision in emerald silk, she was too exquisite to be flesh and blood; too regal and aloof to have ever let him touch her. He drew a long, strangled breath and realized he hadn't been breathing as he watched her. Neither had the four men beside him. "Good Lord," Count Dillard breathed, turning clear around and staring at her, "she cannot possibly be *real*."

"Exactly my thoughts when I first saw her," Roddy Carstairs averred, walking up behind them.

"I don't care what gossip says," Dillard continued, so besotted with her face that he forgot that one of the men in their circle was a part of that gossip. "I want an introduction."

He handed his glass to Roddy instead of the servant beside him and went off to seek an introduction from Jordan Townsende.

Watching him, it took a physical effort for Ian to maintain his carefully bland expression, tear his gaze from Dillard's back, and pay attention to Roddy Carstairs, who'd just greeted him. In fact, it took several moments before Ian could even remember his name. "How are you, Carstairs?" Ian said, finally recollecting it.

"Besotted, like half the males in here, it would seem," Roddy replied, tipping his head toward Elizabeth but scrutinizing Ian's bland face and annoyed eyes. "In fact, I'm so besotted that for the second time in my jaded career I've done the gallant for a damsel in distress. *Your* damsel, unless my intuition deceives me, and it never does, actually."

Ian lifted his glass to his lips, watching Dillard bow to Elizabeth. "You'll have to be more specific," he said impatiently.

"Specifically, I've been saying that in my august opinion no one, but no one, has ever besmirched that exquisite creature. Including you." Hearing him talk about Elizabeth as if she were a morsel for public delectation sent a blaze of fury through Ian.

He was spared having to form a reply to Carstairs's remark by the arrival of yet another group of people eager to be introduced to him, and he endured, as he had been enduring all night, a flurry of curtsies, flirtatious smiles, inviting glances, and overeager handshakes and bows.

"How does it feel," Roddy inquired as that group departed and another bore down on Ian, "to have become, overnight, England's most eligible bachelor?"

Ian answered him and abruptly walked off, and in so doing dashed the hopes of the new group that had been heading toward him. The gentleman beside Roddy, who'd been admiring Ian's magnificently tailored claret jacket and trousers, leaned closer to Roddy and raised his voice to be heard above the din. "I say, Roddy, how did Kensington say it feels to be our most eligible?"

Roddy lowered his glass, a sardonic smile twisting his lips. "He said it is a pain in the ass." He slid a sideways glance at his staggered companion and added wryly, "With Hawthorne wed and Kensington soon to be—in my opinion— the only remaining bachelor with a dukedom to offer is Clayton Westmoreland. Given the uproar Hawthorne and Kensington have both created with their courtships, one can only look forward with glee to observing Westmoreland's."

It took Ian twenty minutes to walk ten yards to his grandfather because he was interrupted at every step by someone else curtsying to him or insisting on a friendly word.

He spent the next hour on the same dance floor where Elizabeth danced with her own partners, and Ian realized she was now nearly as sought-after as he was. As the evening wore on, and he watched her laughing with her partners or listening to the compliments they lavished on her, he noted that while he found balls occasionally amusing but usually boring, Elizabeth thrived in their setting. She belonged here, he realized; this was the world, the setting where Elizabeth glowed and sparkled and reigned like a young queen. It was the world she obviously loved. Not once since she'd arrived had he seen her so much as glance his way, even though his gaze had constantly strayed to her. Which, he realized grimly as the time finally came to claim her for his waltz, put him among the majority of the men in the room. Like him, they were watching her, their eyes acquisitive, thoughtful.

In keeping with the farce he was forced to play, Ian approached the group around the Townsendes and went to Jordan first, who was standing between his wife and Elizabeth. After giving Ian a look of amused understanding Jordan dutifully turned aside to draw Elizabeth from her crowd of admirers into their own circle. "Lady Cameron," he said, playing his role with élan as he nodded toward Ian. "You recall our friend Lord Thornton, Marquess of Kensington, I hope?"

The radiant smile Elizabeth bestowed on Ian was not at all what the dowager had insisted ought to be "polite but impartial." It wasn't quite like any smile she'd ever given him. "Of course I remember you, my lord," Elizabeth said to Ian, graciously offering him her hand.

"I believe this waltz is mine," he said for the benefit of Elizabeth's avidly interested admirers. He waited until they were near the dancers, then he tried to sound more pleasant. "You seem to be enjoying yourself tonight."

"I am," she said idly, but when she looked up at his face she saw the coolness in his eyes; with her new understanding of her own feelings, she understood his more easily. A soft, knowing smile touched her lips as the musicians struck up a waltz; it stayed in her heart as Ian's arm slid around her waist, and his left hand closed around her fingers, engulfing them.

Overhead a hundred thousand candles burned in crystal chandeliers, but Elizabeth was back in a moonlit arbor long ago. Then as now, Ian moved to the music with effortless ease. That lovely waltz had begun something that had ended wrong, terribly wrong. Now, as she danced in his arms, she could make this waltz end much differently, and she knew it; the knowledge filled her with pride and a twinge of nervousness. She waited, expecting him to say something tender, as he had the last time.

"Belhaven's been devouring you with his eyes all night," Ian said instead. "So have half the men in this ballroom. For a country that prides itself on its delicate manners, they sure as hell don't extend to admiring beautiful women."

That, Elizabeth thought with a startled inner smile, was not the opening she'd been waiting for. With his current mood, Elizabeth realized, she was going to have to make her own opening. Lifting her eyes to his enigmatic golden ones, she said quietly, "Ian, have you ever wanted something very badly—something that was within your grasp—and yet you were afraid to reach out for it?"

Surprised by her grave question and her use of his name, Ian tried to ignore the jealousy that had been eating at him all night. "No," he said, scrupulously keeping the curtness from his voice as he gazed down at her alluring face. "Why do you ask? Is there something you want?"

Her gaze fell from his, and she nodded at his frilled white shirtfront.

"What is it you want?"

"You."

Ian's breath froze in his chest, and he stared down at her lustrous hair. "What did you just say?"

She raised her eyes to his. "I said I want you, only I'm afraid that I—"

Ian's heart slammed into his chest, and his fingers dug reflexively into her back, starting to pull her to him. "Elizabeth," he said in a strained voice, glancing a little wildly at their avidly curious audience and resisting the impossible impulse to take her out onto the balcony, "why in God's name would you say a thing like that to me when we're in the middle of a damned dance floor in a crowded ballroom?"

Her radiant smile widened. "I thought it seemed like *exactly* the right place," she told him, watching his eyes darken with desire.

"Because it's safer?" Ian asked in disbelief, meaning safer from his ardent reaction.

"No, because this is how it all began two years ago. We were in the arbor, and a waltz was playing," she reminded him needlessly. "And you came up behind me and said, 'Dance with me, Elizabeth.' And—and I did," she said, her voice trailing off at the odd expression darkening his eyes. "Remember?" she added shakily when he said absolutely nothing.

His gaze captured hers. "Love me, Elizabeth," he said with husky insistence.

Elizabeth felt a tremor run through her entire body, but she looked at him without flinching. "I do."

The waltz was dwindling away, and with a supreme effort he let her go. They walked through the crowd together, smiling politely at people who intercepted them without the slightest idea of anything that was said. When they neared the Townsendes' group Ian delayed her with a touch of his hand. "There's something I've wanted to tell you," he said. Scrupulously keeping up appearances, he reached out to take a drink from a tray being passed by a servant, using that to cover their having stopped. "I would have told you before, but until now you would have questioned my motives and not believed me."

Elizabeth nodded graciously to a woman who greeted her, then she slowly reached for the glass, listening to him as he quietly said, "I never told your brother I didn't want to wed you."

Her hand stayed, then she took the glass from him and walked beside him as they made their slowest possible way back to their friends. "Thank you," she said softly, pausing to sip from her glass in another delaying tactic.

"There's one more thing," he added irritably.

"What's that?" she asked.

"I hate this damn ball. I'd give half what I own to be anywhere else with you."

To his surprise, his thrifty fiancée nodded complete agreement. "So would I."

"Half?" he chided, grinning at her in complete defiance of the rules of propriety. "Really?"

"Well—at least a fourth," she amended helplessly, giving him her hand for the obligatory kiss as she reached for her skirts, preparing to curtsy.

"Don't you *dare* curtsy to me," he warned in a laughing underbreath, kissing her gloved fingers. "Everywhere I go women are falling to the floor like collapsing rigging on a ship."

Elizabeth's shoulders shook with mirth as she disobediently sank into a deep throne-room curtsy that was a miracle of grace and exaggeration. Above her she heard his throaty chuckle.

In an utter turnabout of his earlier feelings, Ian suddenly decided this ball was immensely enjoyable. With perfect equanimity he danced with enough old and respected pillars of the *ton* to ensure that he was guaranteed to be regarded as a perfectly acceptable escort for Elizabeth later on. In the entire endless evening his serenity received a jolt only a few times. The first was when someone who didn't know who he was confided that only two months ago Lady Elizabeth's uncle had sent out invitations to all her former suitors offering her hand in marriage.

Suppressing his shock and loathing for her uncle, Ian had pinned an amused smile on his face and confided, "I'm acquainted with the lady's uncle, and I regret to say he's a little mad. As you know, that sort of thing runs," Ian had finished smoothly, "in our *finest* families." The reference to England's hopeless King George was unmistakable, and the man had laughed uproariously at the joke. "True," he agreed. "Lamentably true." Then he went off to spread the word that Elizabeth's uncle was a confirmed loose screw.

Ian's method of dealing with Sir Francis Belhaven—who, his grandfather had discovered, was boasting that Elizabeth had spent several days with him—was less subtle and even more effective. "Belhaven," Ian said after spending a half hour searching for the repulsive knight.

The stout man had whirled around in surprise, leaving his acquaintances straining to hear Ian's low conversation with him. "I find your presence repugnant," Ian had said in a dangerously quiet voice. "I dislike your coat, I dislike your shirt, and I dislike the knot in your neckcloth. In fact, I dislike you. Have I offended you enough yet, or shall I continue?"

Belhaven's mouth dropped open, his pasty face turning a deathly gray. "Are—are you trying to force a—duel?"

"Normally one doesn't bother shooting a repulsive toad, but in this instance I'm prepared to make an exception, since this toad doesn't know how to keep his mouth shut!"

"A duel, with you?" he gasped. "Why, it would be no contest—none at all. Everyone knows what sort of marksman you are. It would be murder."

Ian leaned close, speaking between his clenched teeth. "It's going to be *murder*, you miserable little opium-eater, unless you suddenly remember very vocally that you've been joking about Elizabeth Cameron's visit."

At the mention of opium the glass slid from his fingers and crashed to the floor. "I have just realized I was joking."

"Good," Ian said, restraining the urge to strangle him. "Now start remembering it all over this ballroom!"

"Now that, Thornton," said an amused voice from Ian's shoulder as Belhaven scurried off to begin doing as bidden, "makes me hesitate to say that he is not lying." Still angry with Belhaven, Ian turned in surprise to see John Marchman standing there. "She was with me as well," Marchman said. "All aboveboard, for God's sake, so don't look at me like I'm Belhaven. Her aunt Berta was there every moment."

"Her what?" Ian said, caught between fury and amusement.

"Her Aunt Berta. Stout little woman who doesn't say much."

"See that you follow her example," Ian warned darkly.

John Marchman, who had been privileged to fish at Ian's marvelous stream in Scotland, gave his friend an offended look. "I daresay you've no business challenging *my* honor. I was considering marrying Elizabeth to keep her out of Belhaven's clutches; you were only going to *shoot* him. It seems to me that my sacrifice was—"

"You were what?" Ian said, feeling as if he'd walked in on a play in the middle of the second act and couldn't seem to hold onto the thread of the plot or the identity of the players.

"Her uncle turned me down. Got a better offer."

"Your life will be more peaceful, believe me," Ian said dryly, and he left to find a footman with a tray of drinks.

The last encounter was one Ian enjoyed, because Elizabeth was with him after they'd had their second—and last permissible—dance. Viscount Mondevale had approached them with Valerie hanging on his arm, and the rest of their group fanned around them. The sight of the young woman who'd caused them both so much pain evoked almost as much ire in Ian as the sight of Mondevale watching Elizabeth like a lovelorn swain.

"Mondevale," Ian had said curtly, feeling the tension in Elizabeth's fingers when she looked at Valerie, "I applaud your taste. I'm certain Miss Jamison will make you a fine wife, if you ever get up the spine to ask her. If you do, however, take my advice, and hire her a tutor, because she can't write and she can't spell." Transferring his blistering gaze to the gaping young woman, Ian clipped, "'Greenhouse' has a 'u' in it. Shall I spell 'malice' for you as well?"

"Ian," Elizabeth chided gently as they walked away. "It doesn't matter anymore." She looked up at him and smiled, and Ian grinned back at her. Suddenly he felt completely in harmony with the world.

The feeling was so lasting that he managed to endure the remaining three weeks—with all the requisite social and courtship rituals and betrothal formalities—with equanimity while he mentally marked off each day before he could make her his and join his starving body with hers.

With a polite smile on his face Ian appeared at teas and mentally composed letters to his secretary; he sat through the opera and slowly undressed her in his mind; he endured eleven Venetian breakfasts where he mentally designed an entirely new kind of mast for his fleet of ships; he escorted her to eighteen balls and politely refrained from acting out his recurring fantasy of dismembering the fops who clustered around her, eyeing her lush curves and mouthing platitudes to her.

It was the longest three weeks of his life.

It was the shortest three weeks of hers.

28

Nervous and happy, Elizabeth stood before the full-length mirror in her bedchamber on Promenade Street while Alexandra sat upon the bed, smiling at her and at four of the maids Ian had sent over to help her dress and do her packing. "Excuse me, milady," another maid said from the doorway, "Bentner said to tell you that Mr. Wordsworth is here and insists he must see you at once, even though we explained it is your wedding day."

"I'll be right down," Elizabeth said, already looking around for a dressing robe that would be acceptable apparel for greeting a male caller.

"Who is Wordsworth?" Alex asked, frowning a little at the idea of Elizabeth being interrupted in her bridal preparations.

"The investigator I hired to try to discover what has happened to Robert."

Wordsworth was prowling anxiously across the carpet, his hat in his hand, when Elizabeth stepped into the little salon. "I'm sorry to disturb you on your wedding day," he began, "but in truth, that is the very reason for my urgency. I think you ought to close the door," he added.

Elizabeth reached out a hand that was suddenly shaking and closed the door.

"Lady Cameron," he said in a worried voice, "I have reason to think your future husband could be involved in your brother's disappearance."

Elizabeth sank down on the sofa. "That is—is preposterous," she stated shakily. "Why would you say such a thing?"

He turned from the window and faced her. "Are you aware that Ian Thornton dueled with your brother only a week before Robert disappeared?"

"Oh, that!" Elizabeth said with relief. "Yes, I am. But no real harm was done."

"On the contrary, Thornton—er, Kensington—took a ball in the arm."

"Yes, I know."

"Did you also know your brother fired before the call to fire was given?"

"Yes."

"For now, it is important that you consider the mood that must have put Kensington in. He was caused pain by a dishonest act on your brother's part, and that in itself could be reason for him to seek retribution."

"Mr. Wordsworth," Elizabeth said with a faint smile, "if Ian—Lord Kensington—had wanted some sort of violent retribution, which I think is what you're implying, he'd have gotten it on that dueling field. He is an extraordinary marksman. He didn't, however," she continued, carried away with her loyal defense of Ian, "because he does not believe in dueling to the death over personal disagreements!"

"Really," said Wordsworth with unhidden sarcasm.

"Really," Elizabeth averred implacably. "Lord Thornton told me that himself, and I have reason to know it's true," she added, thinking of the way he'd declined Lord Everly's challenge when Everly called Ian a card cheat.

"And *I* have reason to know," Wordsworth said with equal implacability, "that the *Scotsman* you're marrying" —he loaded the word with all the scathing scorn many English felt for their "inferior" counterparts—"hasn't a qualm about taking a man's life in a duel."

"I don't—"

"He's killed at least five that I know of for certain."

Elizabeth swallowed. "I'm certain he had—had just cause, and that—that the duel was fair."

"If that is what you wish to believe . . . however, there is more."

Elizabeth felt her palms grow moist. Half of her wanted to get up and leave, and the other half was paralyzed. "What do you mean?"

"Let us remember, if you please, what we already know: Thornton was wounded and undoubtedly—even justifiably —furious at your brother's jumping the call to fire."

"I *know* that . . . at least, I'm willing to accept it. It makes sense."

"And did you also know, my lady, that three days after your brother's unsuccessful attempt to kill Thornton in a duel your brother tried again—this time on Marblemarle Road?"

Elizabeth slowly stood up. "You're wrong! How could you know such a thing? Why would Robert suddenly decide to . . ." Her voice trailed off. Three days after their duel Viscount Mondevale had withdrawn his offer, and with it all hope of financial reprieve for Robert and herself, and her brother had vanished.

"I know it because with the information you gave me I have been systematically re-creating every move your brother made during the week of his disappearance. It is standard procedure to go backward in time in order to pick up the threads that lead us forward through the mystery. Three days after his duel your brother spent the afternoon in the Knightbridge Club, where he became foxed and began talking about wanting to kill Thornton. He borrowed a carriage from an acquaintance and said he was going looking for his prey. I was able to ascertain that his 'prey' was in London that day, and that he left in the late afternoon for Derleshire, which would have meant he took Marblemarle Road. Since he would have had to change horses somewhere on the road, we began checking with the posting houses to discover if anyone meeting Thornton's or your brother's description could be recalled. We had luck at the Black Boar; the posting boy there remembered Thornton well because he gave him half a crown. What he *also* remembered, very fully, was a hole near the window of Thornton's coach and his conversation with Thornton's coachman, who was shaken up enough to talk about how the hole came to be there. It seems there had been an altercation a few miles back in which a man bearing Robert's description—a man Thornton told him was Robert Cameron—had ridden out on the road and tried to shoot Thornton through the window.

"Two days later your brother spoke of what he had done to cronies of his at the Knightbridge. He claimed that Thornton had ruined you and him, and that he would die before Thornton got away with it. According to one of Thornton's grooms, that very night your brother again rode out of the darkness and accosted Thornton on the road to London. This time, your brother shot him in the shoulder. Thornton managed to subdue him with his fists, but your brother fled on horseback. Since Thornton couldn't pursue him through the woods in his coach, your brother made good his escape. The next day, however, after leaving his club, your brother abruptly disappeared. He left everything behind in his rooms, you said. His clothes, his personal effects, everything. What does all this say to you, Lady Cameron?" he asked abruptly.

Elizabeth swallowed again, refusing to let herself think beyond what she knew. "It says that Robert was obsessed with avenging me, and that his methods were—were not exactly—well, aboveboard."

"Has Thornton never mentioned this to you?"

Shaking her head, Elizabeth added defensively, "Robert is something of a sore subject between us. We don't discuss him."

"You are not heeding me, my lady," he burst out in frustrated anger. "You are avoiding drawing obvious conclusions. I believe Thornton had your brother abducted, or worse, in order to prevent him from making additional attempts on his life."

"I'll *ask* him," Elizabeth cried as a tiny hammer of panic and pain began to pound in her head.

"Do *not* do any such thing," Wordsworth said, looking ready to shake her. "Our chances of discovering the truth lie in not alerting Thornton that we're seeking it. If all else fails, I may ask you to tell him what you know so that we can watch him, see where he goes, what he does next—not that he's likely to be overt about it. That is our last choice." Sympathetically, he finished, "I regret being the cause of your having to endure further gossip, but I felt you must be apprised before you actually married that murderous Scot!"

He sneered the word "Scot" again, and in the midst of all her turmoil and terror *that* foolish thing raised Elizabeth's hackles. "Stop saying 'Scot' in that insulting fashion," she cried. "And Ian—Lord Thornton—is half-English," she added a little wildly.

"That leaves him only *half*-barbarian," Wordsworth countered with scathing contempt. He softened his voice a little as he looked at the pale, beautiful girl who was glowering defiantly at him. "You cannot know the sort of people they can be, and usually are. My sister married one, and I cannot describe to you the hell he's made of her life."

"Ian Thornton is *not* your brother-in-law!"

"No, he is not," Wordsworth snapped. "He is a man who made his early fortune gambling, and who was more than once accused of being a cheat! Twelve years ago—it's common knowledge—he won the title deed to a small gold mine in a game of cards with a colonial while he was in port there on his first voyage. The gold mine panned out, and the miner who'd worked half his life in that mine tried to bring charges against Thornton in the colonies. He swore your fiancé cheated, and do you know what happened?"

Elizabeth shook her head.

"Your half-Scot killed him in cold blood. Do you hear me? He *killed* him. It is common knowledge, I tell you."

Elizabeth began to tremble so violently that her whole body shook.

"They dueled, and that barbarian *killed* him."

The word "duel" fell on Elizabeth's shattered senses like a numbing anesthetic. A duel was not quite murder . . . not really. "Was—was it a fair duel?"

Wordsworth shrugged. "Gossip has it that it was, but that is only gossip."

Elizabeth shot to her feet, but the angry accusation in her

eyes didn't hide her own misgivings. "You dismiss something as gossip when it vindicates him, yet when it incriminates him you rely on it completely, and you expect me to do so as well!"

"Please, my lady," he said, looking truly desperate. "I'm only trying to show you the folly of proceeding with this wedding. Don't do it, I implore you. You must wait."

"I'll be the one to decide that," she said, hiding her fright behind proud anger.

His jaw tight with frustration, he said finally, "If you are foolish enough to marry this man today, then I implore you not to tell him what I have learned, but to continue in whatever way you've been doing to avoid discussion of Robert Cameron. If you do *not*," he said in a terrible voice, "you are putting your brother's life in jeopardy, if he is still alive."

Elizabeth was trying so hard to concentrate and not to collapse that she dug her nails into her palms. "What are you talking about?" she demanded in a choked cry. "You're not making sense. I have to ask Ian. He has to have a chance to deny this slander, to explain, to—"

That drove Wordsworth to actually grab her shoulders in alarm. "Listen to me!" he barked. "If you do that, you may well get your own brother killed!" Embarrassed by his own vehemence, he dropped his hands, but his voice was still insistent to the point of pleading. "Consider the facts, if you won't consider conjecture: Your husband has just been named heir to one of the most important titles in Europe. He is going to marry you—a beautiful woman, a *countess*, who would have been above his touch until a few weeks ago. Do you think for a moment he'll risk all that by letting your brother be found and brought here to give evidence against him? If your brother wasn't killed, if Thornton only had him put to work in one of his mines, or impressed on one of his ships, and you start questioning him, Thornton will have little choice but to decide to dispose of the evidence. Are you listening to me, Lady Cameron? Do you understand?"

Elizabeth nodded.

"Then I'll bid you good day and resume the search for

your brother." He paused at the door and looked back at the girl in the middle of the room who was standing with her head bent, her face ghostly pale. "For your own sake, don't wed the man, at least until we know for sure."

"When will that be?" she asked in a shattered voice.

"Who knows? In a month, perhaps, or in a year. Or never." He paused and drew a long, frustrated breath. "If you do act in defiance of all sense and wed him, then for your brother's sake, if not for your own, keep your silence. You, too, would be in danger if he's guilty and he thinks you're going to discover it and perhaps expose him."

When he left, Elizabeth sank back down on the sofa and closed her eyes, trying to keep her tears at bay. In her mind she heard Wordsworth's voice. In her heart she saw Ian smiling down at her, his voice husky and filled with need: "Love me, Elizabeth." And then she saw him as he'd confronted her uncle, a muscle jerking in his cheek, his body emanating rage. She remembered him in the greenhouse, too, when Robert barged in on them and said Elizabeth was already betrothed; Ian had looked at *her* with murder in his eyes.

But he hadn't harmed Robert in that duel. Despite his justifiable wrath, he'd acted with cold control. Swallowing convulsively, Elizabeth brushed a tear from the corner of her eye, feeling as if she was being torn to pieces.

She saw his face, that hard face that could be transformed to almost boyishness by one of his lazy smiles. She saw his eyes—icy in Scotland, blazing at her uncle . . . and smiling down at her the day he came to Havenhurst.

But it was his voice that revolved in her mind, overcoming the doubt, that rich, compelling, husky voice—"Love me, Elizabeth."

Slowly Elizabeth stood up, and though she was still deathly pale, she had made her decision. If he was innocent and she stopped this wedding, Ian would be made to look a fool; she couldn't even give him a reason for doing it, and he would never forgive her. She would lose him forever. If she married him, if she followed her instincts, she might never know what became of Robert. Or Ian would be vindicated.

Or else she would find out that she was married to a monster, a murderer.

Alexandra took one look at Elizabeth's white face and hurtled off the bed, wrapping her arms around her friend. "What is it, Elizabeth? Is it bad news? Tell me—please, you look ready to drop."

Elizabeth wanted to tell her, would have told her, but she very much feared Alex would try to talk her out of proceeding with the wedding. The decision had been hard enough to make; now that she had decided, she didn't think she could bear to listen to arguments or she'd start to waver. She was determined to believe in Ian; and since she was, she wanted Alex's liking for him to continue to grow.

"It's nothing," she said lamely. "At least not yet. Mr. Wordsworth simply needed more information about Robert, and it's a difficult thing to talk about with him."

While Alexandra and a maid fussed with Elizabeth's train the bride waited at the back of the church, cold with nerves, torn with misgivings, telling herself this was nothing but wedding jitters.

She looked past the doors, knowing that in the entire packed cathedral there was not one relative of her own—not even a single male relative to give her away. At the front of the church she saw Jordan Townsende step out and take his place, followed by Ian, tall and dark and overwhelming in stature and will. There was no one who could make him abide by their bargain if he chose to ignore it. Not even the courts would force him to do that.

"Elizabeth?" the Duke of Stanhope said gently, and he held out his arm to her. "Don't be afraid, child," he said softly, smiling at her huge, stricken eyes. "It'll be over before you know it."

The organ gave forth with a blast of melody, then paused expectantly, and suddenly Elizabeth was walking down the aisle. Of the thousands of people watching her, she wondered how many were still recalling her publicized "liaison" with Ian and speculating on how much too soon a babe was likely to arrive.

Many of the faces were kind, though, she noticed distractedly. The duke's sister smiled as she passed; the other sister dabbed at her eyes. Roddy Carstairs gave her an audacious wink, and a hysterical chuckle bubbled inside her, then collided with a lump of terror and confusion. Ian was watching her, too, his expression unreadable. Only the vicar looked comforting as he waited, the marriage book open in his hands.

The Duke of Stanhope had insisted that a grand wedding banquet and reception, with everyone of social prominence in attendance, was just the thing to put a final end to the gossip about Ian and Elizabeth's past. As a result, the festivities were being held here, at Montmayne, rather than Havenhurst which lacked not only the size needed to accommodate one thousand guests but furnishings as well. Standing on the sidelines of the ballroom, which Ian's army of florists had transformed into a gigantic bower of flowers, complete with a miniature arbor at the far end, Elizabeth tried with every fiber of her being to ignore the haunting memory of Wordsworth's visit this morning. No matter how hard she tried, his words still hung over her like a wispy pall, not thick enough to prevent her from carrying on as if all were normal, but there, nonetheless.

Now she was dealing with it the only way she could: Whenever the gloom and dread closed around her, she looked for Ian. The sight of him, she had discovered in the long hours since their wedding, could banish her doubts and make Wordsworth's accusations seem as absurd as they undoubtedly were. If Ian weren't nearby, she did the only other thing she could—she pinned a bright smile on her face and pretended to herself, and to everyone else, that she was the radiantly happy, carefree bride she was supposed to be. The more she practiced, the more she *felt* like one.

Since Ian had gone to get her a glass of champagne and been waylaid by friends, Elizabeth devoted herself to smiling at the wedding guests who passed by her in an endless stream to wish her happiness, or compliment the lavish decorations or the sumptuous supper they'd been served. The coldness Elizabeth had thought she felt in church this morning now seemed to be a figment of her nervous imagination, and she realized she had misjudged many of these people. True, they had not approved of her conduct two years ago—and how could they?—yet now, most of them seemed genuinely anxious to let the past be laid to rest.

The fact that they were eager to pretend the past hadn't happened made Elizabeth smile inwardly as she looked again at the glorious decorations: No one but she had realized that the ballroom bore a rather startling resemblance to the gardens at Charise Dumont's country house, and that the arbor at the side, with its trellised entrance, was a virtual replica of the place where she and Ian had first waltzed that long-ago night.

Across the room, the vicar was standing with Jake Wiley, Lucinda, and the Duke of Stanhope, and he raised his glass to her. Elizabeth smiled and nodded back. Jake Wiley watched the silent communication and beamed upon his little group of companions. "Exquisite bride, isn't she?" he pronounced, not for the first time. For the past half-hour, the three men had been merrily congratulating themselves on their individual roles in bringing this marriage about, and the consumption of spirits was beginning to show in Duncan and Jake's increasingly gregarious behavior.

"Absolutely exquisite," Duncan agreed.

"She'll make Ian an excellent wife," said the duke. "We've done well, gentlemen," he added, lifting his glass in yet another congratulatory toast to his companions. "To you, Duncan," he said with a bow, "for making Ian see the light."

"To you, Edward," said the vicar to the duke, "for forcing society to accept them." Turning to Jake, he added, "And to you, old friend, for insisting on going to the village for the servingwomen and bringing old Attila and Miss Throckmorton-Jones with you."

That toast belatedly called to mind the silent duenna who was standing stiffly beside them, her face completely devoid of expression. "And to *you,* Miss Throckmorton-Jones," said Duncan with a deep, gallant bow, "for taking that laudanum and spilling the truth to me about what Ian did two years ago. 'Twas that, and that alone, which caused everything else to be put into motion, so to speak. But here," said Duncan, nonplussed as he waved to a servant bearing a tray of champagne, "you do not have a glass, my dear woman, to share in our toasts."

"I do not take strong spirits," Lucinda informed Duncan. "Furthermore, my good man," she added with a superior expression that might have been a smile or a smirk, "I do *not* take laudanum, either." And on that staggering announcement, she swept up her unbecoming gray skirts and walked off to dampen the spirits of another group. She left behind her three dumbstruck, staring men who gaped at each other and then suddenly erupted into shouts of laughter.

Elizabeth glanced up as Ian handed her a glass of champagne. "Thank you," she said, smiling up at him and gesturing to Duncan, the duke, and Jake, who were now convulsed with loud hilarity. "They certainly seem to be enjoying themselves," she remarked. Ian absently glanced at the group of laughing men, then back at her. "You're breathtaking when you smile."

Elizabeth heard the huskiness in his voice and saw the almost slumberous look in his eyes, and she was wondering about its cause when he said softly, "Shall we retire?"

That suggestion caused Elizabeth to assume his expression must be due to weariness. She, herself, was more than ready to seek the peace of her own chamber, but since she'd never been to a wedding reception before, she assumed that the protocol must be the same as at any other gala affair—which meant the host and hostess could not withdraw until the last of the guests had either left or retired. Tonight, every one of the guest chambers would be in use, and tomorrow a large wedding breakfast was planned, followed by a hunt. "I'm not sleepy—just a little fatigued from so much smiling," she told him, pausing to bestow another smile on a guest who caught her eye and waved. Turning her face up to

Ian, she offered graciously, "It's been a long day. If you wish to retire, I'm sure everyone will understand."

"I'm sure they will," he said dryly, and Elizabeth noted with puzzlement that his eyes were suddenly gleaming.

"I'll stay down here and stand in for you," she volunteered.

The gleam in his eyes brightened yet more. "You don't think that my retiring alone will look a little odd?"

Elizabeth knew it might seem impolite, if not precisely odd, but then inspiration struck, and she said reassuringly, "Leave everything to me. I'll make your excuses if anyone asks."

His lips twitched. "Just out of curiosity—what excuse will you make for me?"

"I'll say you're not feeling well. It can't be anything too dire though, or we'll be caught out in the fib when you appear looking fit for breakfast and the hunt in the morning." She hesitated, thinking, and then said decisively, "I'll say you have the headache."

His eyes widened with laughter. "It's kind of you to volunteer to dissemble for me, my lady, but that particular untruth would have me on the dueling field for the next month, trying to defend against the aspersions it would cause to be cast upon my . . . ah . . . manly character."

"Why? Don't gentlemen get headaches?"

"Not," he said with a roguish grin, "on their wedding night."

"I can't see why."

"Can you not?"

"No. And," she added with an irate whisper, "I don't see why everyone is staying down here this late. I've never been to a wedding reception, but it does seem as if they ought to be beginning to seek their beds."

"Elizabeth," he said, trying not to laugh. "At a wedding reception, the guests cannot leave until the bride and groom retire. If you look over there, you'll notice my great-aunts are already nodding in their chairs."

"Oh!" she exclaimed, instantly contrite. "I didn't know. Why didn't you tell me earlier?"

"Because," he said, taking her elbow and beginning to

guide her from the ballroom, "I wanted you to enjoy every minute of our ball, even if we had to prop the guests up on the shrubbery."

"Speaking of shrubbery," she teased, pausing on the balcony to cast a last fond look at the "arbor" of potted trees with silk blossoms that occupied one-fourth the length of the entire ballroom, "everyone is talking about having gardens and arbors as themes for future balls. I think you've started a new 'rage.'"

"You should have seen your face," he teased, drawing her away, "when you recognized what I had done."

"We are probably the only couple," she returned, her face turned up to his in laughing conspiracy, "ever to lead off a ball by dancing a waltz on the sidelines." When the orchestra had struck up the opening waltz, Ian had led her into the mock "arbor," and they had started the ball from there.

"Did you mind?"

"You know I didn't," she returned, walking beside him up the curving staircase.

He stopped outside her bed chamber, opened the door for her, and started to pull her into his arms, then checked himself as a pair of servants came marching down the hall bearing armloads of linens. "There's time for this later," he whispered. "All the time we want."

30

Oblivious to Berta's pinched face as the maid brushed her heavy hair, Elizabeth sat at her dressing table clad in a lacy cream silk nightdress that Madame LaSalle had insisted would be extremely pleasing to the marquess on his wedding night.

At the moment, however, Elizabeth wasn't worried about the way her breasts were revealed by the deep V of the bodice or the way her left leg was exposed to the knee by the seductive slash in the gown. For one thing, she knew the bedclothes would hide her; for another, now that she had solitude for the first time since this morning, she was finding it much harder to ignore the tormenting things Mr. Wordsworth had said.

Trying desperately to think of other things, Elizabeth shifted impatiently in her chair and concentrated on her wedding night instead. Staring at her hands folded in her lap, she bent her head to give Berta better access to her long tresses, her mind going over Lucinda's explanation about how babies were conceived. Since Ian had been very emphatic about wanting children, there was every chance he might wish to start tonight; if so, according to Lucinda, they would evidently share a bed.

She frowned as she reconsidered Lucinda's explanation; it

did not, in Elizabeth's opinion, make a great deal of sense. She was not ignorant of the way other species on earth created their young; on the other hand, she realized that people could not possibly behave in such an appalling fashion. But still, a kiss in bed from a spouse? If that were so, why had she heard occasional scandalous gossip about a certain married lady in the *ton* whose baby was purportedly *not* her husband's? Obviously there was more than one way to make a baby, or else Lucinda's information was incorrect.

That brought her to the matter of sleeping accommodations. Her suite adjoined his, and she had no idea whether, if he did wish to share a bed with her, it would be this one or his. As if in answer to her unspoken questions, the door that connected this chamber with Ian's opened, and Berta jumped in fright; then she glowered at Ian, whom she, like several of Elizabeth's servants, continued to fear and blame, and went scurrying out, closing the door behind her.

Elizabeth, however, felt only a swift surge of admiration, and she smiled a little as he walked toward her with those long, easy strides that always looked both certain and relaxed. Still clad in the formal black trousers he'd worn, he'd removed his coat, waistcoat, and neckcloth, and his white frilled shirt was open at the neck, revealing the strong, tanned column of his throat. He looked, she thought, as ruggedly virile and elegant in shirtsleeves as in formal attire. In the midst of that, Wordsworth's accusations slid insidiously through her mind, and Elizabeth thrust them away.

She stood up, self-conscious in her revealing gown, and took a step forward, then stopped, arrested by the spark flaring in those golden eyes as they moved over her body in the revealing gown. Unaccountably wary and shaky, she hastily turned back to the mirror and absently ran a hand over her hair. Ian came up behind her, and his hands settled on her shoulders. In the mirror she watched him bend his dark head, felt his warm lips against the curve of her neck, sending tingling sensations down her neck and arm. "You're trembling," he said in the gentlest voice she'd ever heard.

"I know," she admitted with a nervous tremor in her voice. "I don't know why."

His lips curved in a smile. "Don't you?" he asked softly.

Elizabeth shook her head, longing to turn to him and plead with him to tell her what had happened to Robert; afraid to hear his answer; afraid to ruin this night with her suspicions—suspicions she *knew* had to be unfounded. Afraid of what was in store for her in that bed . . .

Unable to tear her gaze from his, Elizabeth watched his hand slide around her waist from behind, pulling her against him until she felt his hard chest against her back, the imprint of his legs against her own. He bent his head again, his arm tightening as he lazily kissed her ear, and his other hand swept up her arm, sliding beneath the satin ribbon at her shoulder, his hand seeking the side of her breast, fingers splaying wide in a bold, possessive caress.

Slowly he turned her in his arms, and then he kissed her again, this time with slow ardor, his hands molding her close, and Elizabeth kissed him back, helplessly caught up in the stirring sensations his kiss always evoked, her arms sliding around his neck to hold him clasped to her . . . and the moment they did, he swung her into his arms, his mouth still claiming hers as he carried her through the doorway and into his spacious suite, where a huge bed stood upon a dais.

Lost in the stormy kiss, Elizabeth felt her legs gliding down his as he gently lowered her against him until her feet touched the floor. But when his fingers pulled at the ribbon that held her gown in place at her shoulder, she jerked free of his kiss, automatically clamping her hand over his. "What are you doing?" she asked in a quaking whisper. His fingers stilled, and Ian lifted his heavy-lidded gaze to hers.

The question took him by surprise, but as he stared into her green eyes Ian saw her apprehension, and he had a good idea what was causing it. "What do you think I'm doing?" he countered cautiously.

She hesitated, as if unwilling even to accuse him of such an unspeakable act, and then she admitted in a small, reluctant voice, "Disrobing me."

"And that surprises you?"

"Surprises me? Of course it does. Why wouldn't it?" Elizabeth asked, more suspicious than ever of what Lucinda had told her.

Quietly he said, "What exactly do you know about what takes place between a husband and wife in bed?"

"You—you mean 'as it pertains to the creation of children'?" she said, quoting his words to her the day she agreed to become betrothed to him.

He smiled with tender amusement at her phrasing. "I suppose you can call it that—for now."

"Only what Lucinda told me." He waited to hear an explanation, and Elizabeth reluctantly added, "She said a husband kisses his wife in bed and that it hurts the first time, and that is how it is done."

Ian hesitated, angry with himself for not having followed his own instincts and questioned her further when she seemed fully informed and without maidenly qualms about lovemaking. As gently as he could, he said, "You're a very intelligent young woman, love, not an overly fastidious spinster like your former duenna. Now, do you honestly believe the rules of nature would be completely set aside for people?"

His fingers slipped beneath the satin ribbons that held her shimmering gown on her shoulders, and he eased them off.

Ian felt her tremble beneath his hands, and he put his arms around her, only to have her stiffen more. "I promise you," he whispered, mentally cursing Lucinda Throckmorton-Jones to perdition, "that you'll find nothing disgusting about what happens between us in this bed." Realizing that the suspense was going to be worse than the actuality for her, he leaned down and blew out the candles beside the bed, then eased her satin nightdress off her shoulders. She flinched at his touch, and he sensed the jumbled emotions running through her. Tightening his hands on her shoulders to stop her from pulling away, he said quietly, "If I'd thought for a moment all this was going to come as a surprise, I'd have explained it to you weeks ago."

Oddly, it meant a great deal to Elizabeth to know that while Lucinda—and everyone else, evidently—had guarded the facts from her, Ian would have trusted her with them. She nodded jerkily and waited in stiff tension while he unfastened her gown and sent it sliding down around her ankles, then she hastily climbed beneath the sheets, trying not to panic.

This was not the way Ian intended his wedding night should be, and as he removed his clothes by the light of the single candle burning across the room, he was determined that it would at least end as he intended. Elizabeth felt the bed sink beneath his weight and drew her whole body into the smallest possible space. He moved onto his side, leaning up on an elbow, and his hand touched her cheek.

When he said nothing Elizabeth opened her eyes, staring straight ahead, and in her agitated state, lying naked next to a man who she knew was undoubtedly naked as well, she was a mass of disjointed emotions: Wordsworth's warnings tolled in one part of her mind while another part warned her that her own ignorance of the marital act didn't relieve her of keeping their bargain; she felt tricked somehow, as well.

Lying beside her, Ian put his hand on her arm, his thumb stroking soothingly across her arm, listening to her rapid breathing. She swallowed audibly and said, "I realize now what you expected from your part of the betrothal bargain and what rights I granted you this morning. You must think I am the most ignorant, uninformed female alive not to have known what—"

"Don't do this, darling!" he said, and Elizabeth heard the urgency in his voice; she felt it as he bent his head and seized her lips in a hard, insistent kiss and did not stop until he drew a response from her. Only then did he speak again, and his voice was low and forceful. "This has nothing to do with rights—not the ones you granted me at our betrothal nor the ones this morning in church. Had we been wed in Scotland, we could have spoken the old vows. Do you know what words, what promises we would have spoken had we been there, not here, this morning?" His hand slid up to her cheek, cupping it as if to soften the effect of his tone, and as Elizabeth gazed at his hard, beloved face in the candlelight her shyness and fears slid away. "No," she whispered.

"I would have said to you," he told her quietly and without shame, " 'With my body, I thee worship.' "

He spoke the words now, as a vow, and when Elizabeth realized it, the poignancy of it made her eyes sting with tears. Turning her face into his hand, she kissed his palm, covering his hand with hers, and a groan tore from his chest, his mouth descending on hers in a kiss that was both rough and tender as he parted her lips for the demanding invasion of his tongue. Her arms went around his broad shoulders, and he pulled her against his full length, clasping her against his rigid thighs while his tongue began to plunge into her mouth and then retreat, only to plunge again in an unmistakably suggestive rhythm that made desire streak through Elizabeth as she pressed herself closer.

He rolled her onto her back, his hand sliding caressingly over her breast, possessively cupping its fullness, then teasing her nipple, grazing it lightly, until it stood up proudly against his palm. He lifted his mouth from hers, and Elizabeth felt an aching sense of loss that was replaced by sweet torment as he slid his mouth down her neck to her breasts, nuzzling them slowly for endless moments before his lips closed tightly over her taut nipple. She moaned as he increased the pressure, her hands tangling in his hair, her back arching in helpless surrender, and all the while his hands were sliding and stroking with skillful reverence over her, heating her skin and making her ache with incomprehensible yearnings.

He kissed her flat stomach, trailing his lips ever lower, his tongue plunging into her navel, a low laugh coming from his chest when she gasped and gave a leap of surprise; then his hands slid lower, curving around her hips, his lips nuzzling closer to the curly triangle between her legs, deliberately taking his time. Elizabeth belatedly realized what he was going to do and panicked, her hands tightening. He hesitated, and she sensed his reluctance to stop an instant before he ignored her and kissed her there, too, but swiftly. Then he leaned up and over her again, his mouth at last claiming hers in another endless, drugging kiss as he drew her tongue into his mouth and his arms encircled her. She thought he would take her then, but the kiss continued, filled with exquisite promise and wild hunger. Rolling onto his side, he took her with him, his hand gliding down her spine, holding her hips pressed to his, forcing her into vibrant awareness of his raging desire. And then he gentled the pressure against her mouth until he was lightly brushing his parted lips against hers. By the time he lifted his head, Elizabeth's breathing was shattered, her hands were clutching his shoulders, and her heart was pounding like a maddened thing; again she waited with a mixture of excitement and fear for him to take her. Ian felt her escalating tension, and although he was already desperate for release, he brushed a kiss against her forehead. "Not yet," he whispered.

With a physical effort Elizabeth forced her eyes open and looked at him; what she saw made her heart beat almost painfully harder: In the candle glow his face was hard and dark with passion, and the eyes gazing at her upturned face were blazing with it—and yet there was as much tenderness in them as there was desire. The combination made her ache with sudden yearning to make him feel all the exquisite things he was making her feel, but she didn't know how. Instead, she did the one thing she *knew* he liked: Spreading her fingers across his smoothly shaven jaw, she gazed unashamedly into his eyes and achingly whispered, "I love you."

His eyes darkened, but instead of speaking he caught her wrist and drew her hand to his chest. Elizabeth knew a moment of disappointment at his silence—and then she realized what he had done: He had pressed her hand against his heart so that she could feel its violent pounding and know that he was as wildly aroused as she. Her eyes filled with wonder, she gazed at him, and then, because she was suddenly filled with an urge to really look at him, she lowered her eyes to his broad, muscled chest with its light furring of dark hair. In the dim light his skin glowed like oiled bronze; his shoulders and arms were hard with bunched muscles. He was, Elizabeth thought, incredibly beautiful. She started to move her fingers, then hesitated, not certain if it was proper to touch him, and raised her questioning eyes to his.

Ian saw her uncertainty. "Yes," he whispered hoarsely. Elizabeth realized that he was dying to be touched, and the knowledge filled her with a mixture of delight and pride as she slid her hands over the rigid muscles of his chest, watching as they flinched reflexively in passionate reaction to her feathery touch. He felt, she thought, like bunched satin, and she brushed a kiss near his arm, and then with more daring she kissed his nipple, touching her tongue to it, feeling his sharp intake of breath, the reflexive clenching of his hands on her back as she continued sliding her hands lower. In fact, she was so engrossed with the pleasure she was deriving from pleasing him as she pressed languid kisses down his chest that it was several seconds before she realized that his hand was no longer sliding up and down over her hip, but that it was forcing insistently between her legs.

Helpless to stop the instinctive reaction, Elizabeth clamped her legs together, her stricken gaze flying to his as nameless panic shot through her. "Don't, darling," he whispered thickly, his hot gaze on her while his fingers toyed amid the springy hair, stroking. "Don't close against me." Hiding her face against his chest, Elizabeth drew a shaky breath and forced herself to obey, then moaned with pleasure, not humiliation or pain, while the stroking continued and became increasingly intimate, and she wrapped her arms tightly around him when at last his finger slid deeply into her wet warmth. "I love you," she whispered fiercely against his neck, and the sweetness of her yielding was almost Ian's undoing.

Shifting her onto her back, he covered her mouth with his and began to increase the deep thrusts of his finger. When her hips started to move instinctively against his hand he eased himself between her legs, his rigid shaft poised at her entrance. Desperate to sheathe himself in her and simultaneously dreading the pain he was going to cause her, he lifted her slim hips to receive him. "I'm going to hurt you, sweetheart, because there's no other way. If I could take the pain for you, I would."

She did not turn her face away from him or try to twist free of his imprisoning grasp, and what she said made Ian's throat ache with emotion. "Do you know," she whispered with a teary smile, "how long I've waited to hear you call me 'sweetheart' again?"

"How long?" he asked hoarsely.

Putting her arms around his shoulders, Elizabeth braced herself for whatever pain was coming, knowing as he tensed that it was going to happen, talking as if she could calm herself. "Two years. I've waited and w—"

Her body jerked and a sharp gasp tore from her, but the pain was gone almost as quickly as the sound, and her husband was already easing deeper into her tight passage until she was filled with his heat and strength, holding him tightly to her, lost in the sheer beauty of the slow, deep strokes he was beginning to take. Guided by pure instinct and a wealth of love, Elizabeth willingly molded her hips to his and began to match his movements, and in doing so she unwittingly drove Ian to unparalleled agonies of desire as he held himself back, determined to ensure her climax before he had his own. He began to quicken his deep thrusts, circling his hips, and the young temptress in his arms matched his movements, clasping his pulsing shaft in her tight warmth.

Elizabeth felt something wild and primitive building inside her, racing through her veins, jarring through her body. Her head moved fitfully on the pillow as she waited for it, sought whatever it was that Ian was trying to give her as he drove into her again and again . . . and then it exploded, making her gasp against his mouth and cry out.

His shoulders and arms taut with the strain of holding back, Ian thrust into her in short sharp movements, matching the spasms shaking her and pulling at him. The instant they subsided he tightened his arms around her and drove into her full length, pouring himself into her, startled when the groan he heard was his own. His body jerked convulsively again and again, and he clasped her to him, breathing in deep pants against her cheek, his heart raging in frantic tempo with hers, his life merging into hers.

When a little of his strength returned he moved onto his side, taking her with him, still a part of her. Her hair spilled over his naked chest like a rumpled satin waterfall, and he lifted a shaking hand to smooth it off her face, feeling humbled and blessed by her sweetness and unselfish ardor.

Several minutes later Elizabeth stirred in his arms, and he tipped her chin up so that he could gaze into her eyes. "Have I ever told you that you are magnificent?"

She started to shake her head, then suddenly remembered that he had told her she was magnificent once before, and the recollection brought poignant tears to her eyes. "You did say that to me," she amended, brushing her fingers over his smooth shoulder because she couldn't seem to stop touching him. "You told me that when we were together—"

"In the woodcutter's cottage," he finished for her, recalling the occasion as well. In reply she had chided him for acting as if he also thought Charise Dumont was magnificent, Ian remembered, regretting all the time they had lost since then . . . the days and nights she could have been in his arms as she was now. "Do you know how I spent the rest of the afternoon after you left the cottage?" he asked softly. When she shook her head, he said with a wry smile, "I spent it pleasurably contemplating tonight. At the time, of course, I didn't realize tonight was years away." He paused to draw the sheet up over her back so she wouldn't be chilled, then he continued in the same quiet voice, "I wanted you so badly that day that I actually ached while I watched you fasten that shirt you were wearing. Although," he added dryly, "that *particular* condition, brought on by that particular cause, has become my normal state for the last four weeks, so I'm quite used to it now. I wonder if I'll miss it," he teased.

"What do you mean?" Elizabeth asked, realizing that he was perfectly serious despite his light tone.

"The agony of unfulfilled desire," he explained, brushing a kiss on her forehead, "brought on by wanting you."

"Wanting me?" she burst out, rearing up so abruptly that she nearly overturned him as she leaned up on an elbow, absently clutching the sheet to her breasts. "Is this—what we've just done, I mean—"

"The Scots think of it as making love," he interrupted gently. "Unlike most English," he added with flat scorn, "who prefer to regard it as 'performing one's marital duty.'"

"Yes," Elizabeth said absently, her mind on his earlier remark about wanting her until it caused him physical pain, "but is this what you meant all those times you've said you wanted me?"

His sensual lips quirked in a half smile. "Yes."

A rosy blush stained her smooth cheeks, and despite her effort to sound severe, her eyes were lit with laughter. "And the day we bargained about the betrothal, and you told me I had something you wanted very badly, what you wanted to do with me . . . was *this?*"

"Among other things," he agreed, tenderly brushing his knuckles over her flushed cheek.

"If I had known all this," she said with a rueful smile, "I'm certain I would have asked for additional concessions."

That startled him—the thought that she would have tried to drive a harder bargain if she'd realized exactly how much and what sort of power she really held. "What kind of additional concessions?" he asked, his face carefully expressionless.

She put her cheek against his shoulder, her arms curving around him. "A shorter betrothal," she whispered. "A shorter courtship, and a shorter ceremony."

A fresh surge of tenderness and profound pride swept through him at her sweetness and her candor, and he wrapped his arms tightly, protectively around her, smiling with joyous contentment. He had realized within minutes of meeting her that she was rare; he had known within hours that she was everything he wanted. Passionate and gentle, intelligent, sensitive, and witty. He loved all of her qualities, but he hadn't discovered the one he particularly admired until much later, and that was her courage. He was so proud of the courage that had enabled her to repeatedly confront adversity and adversaries—even when the adversary was him. Without it she'd have been lost to him long ago; she'd have done what most of her sex did, which was to find the first available male they could stomach and let him deal with life's unpleasantness. His Elizabeth hadn't done that; instead she'd tried to cope, not only with him, but with the terrible financial burdens she'd carried. That reminded him of how thrifty she was, and he promptly decided—at least for the moment—that her thriftiness was one of her most endearingly amusing qualities.

"What are you thinking about?" she asked.

He tipped his chin down so that he could better see her and brushed a stray lock of golden hair off her cheek. "I was thinking how wise I must be to have known within minutes of meeting you that you were wonderful."

She chuckled, thinking his words were teasing flattery. "How soon did my qualities become apparent?"

"I'd say," he thoughtfully replied, "I knew it when you took sympathy on Galileo."

She'd expected him to say something about her looks, not her conversation or her mind. "Truly?" she asked with unhidden pleasure.

He nodded, but he was studying her reaction with curiosity. "What did you think I was going to say?"

Her slim shoulders lifted in an embarrassed shrug. "I thought you would say it was my face you noticed first. People have the most *extraordinary* reaction to my face," she explained with a disgusted sigh.

"I can't imagine why," he said, grinning down at what was, in his opinion—in anyone's opinion—a heartbreakingly beautiful face belonging to a young woman who was sprawled across his chest looking like an innocent golden goddess.

"I think it's my eyes. They're an odd color."

"I see that now," he teased, then he said more solemnly, "but as it happens it was not your face which I found so beguiling when we met in the garden, because," he added when she looked unconvinced, "I couldn't *see* it."

"Of course you could. I could see yours well enough, even though night had fallen."

"Yes, but *I* was standing near a torch lamp, while you perversely remained in the shadows. I could tell that yours was a very *nice* face, with the requisite features in the right places, and I could also tell that your other—feminine assets—were definitely in all the right places, but that was all I could see. And then later that night I looked up and saw you walking down the staircase. I was so surprised, it took a considerable amount of will to keep from dropping the glass I was holding."

Her happy laughter drifted around the room and reminded him of music. "Elizabeth," he said dryly, "I am not such a fool that I would have let a beautiful face alone drive me to madness, or to asking you to marry me, or even to extremes of sexual desire."

She saw that he was perfectly serious, and she sobered. "Thank you," she said quietly. "That is the nicest compliment you could have paid me, my lord."

"Don't call me 'my lord,'" he told her with a mixture of gentleness and gravity, "unless you mean it. I dislike having you address me that way if it's merely a reference to my title."

Elizabeth snuggled her cheek against his hard chest and quietly replied, "As you wish. My lord."

Ian couldn't help it. He rolled her onto her back and devoured her with his mouth, claimed her with his hands and then his body.

"Haven't I tired you out yet, darling?" Ian whispered several hours later.

"Yes," she said with an exhausted laugh, her cheek nestled against his shoulder, her hand drifting over his chest in a sleepy caress. "But I'm too happy to sleep for a while yet."

So was Ian, but he felt compelled to at least suggest that she try. "You'll regret it in the morning when we have to appear for breakfast," he said with a grin, cuddling her closer to his side.

To his surprise, the remark made her smooth forehead furrow in a frown. She tipped her face up to his, opened her mouth as if to ask him a question, then she changed her mind and hastily looked away.

"What is it?" he asked, taking her chin between his thumb and forefinger and lifting her face up to his.

"Tomorrow morning," she said with a funny, bemused expression on her face. "When we go downstairs . . . will everyone know what we have done tonight?"

She expected him to try to evade the question.

"Yes," he said.

She nodded, accepting that, and turned into his arms. "Thank you for telling me the truth," she said with a sigh of contentment and gratitude.

"I'll always tell you the truth," he promised quietly, and she believed him.

It occurred to Elizabeth that she could ask him now, when he'd given that promise, if he'd had anything to do with Robert's disappearance. And as quickly as the thought crossed her mind, she pushed it angrily away. She would not defame their marriage bed by voicing ugly, unfounded suspicions carried to her by a man who obviously had a grudge against all Scots.

This morning, she had made a conscious decision to trust him and marry him; now, she was bound by her vows to honor him, and she had absolutely no intention of going back on her own decision or on the vow she made to him in church.

"Elizabeth?"

"Mmmm?"

"While we're on the subject of truth, I have a confession to make."

Her heart slammed into her ribs, and she went rigid. "What is it?" she asked tautly.

"The chamber next door is meant to be used as your dressing room and withdrawing room. I do not approve of the English custom of husband and wife sleeping in separate beds." She looked so pleased that Ian grinned. "I'm happy to see," he chuckled, kissing her forehead, "we agree on that."

31

In the weeks that followed, Elizabeth discovered to her pleasure that she could ask Ian any question about any subject and that he would answer her as fully as she wished. Not once did he ever patronize her when he replied, or fend her off by pointing out that, as a woman, the matter was truly none of her concern—or worse—that the answer would be beyond any female's ability to understand. Elizabeth found his respect for her intelligence enormously flattering—particularly after two astounding discoveries she made about him:

The first occurred three days after their wedding, when they both decided to spend the evening at home, reading.

That night after supper, Ian brought a book he wanted to read from their library—a heavy tome with an incomprehensible title—to the drawing room. Elizabeth brought *Pride and Prejudice,* which she'd been longing to read since first hearing of the uproar it was causing among the conservative members of the *ton.* After pressing a kiss on her forehead, Ian sat down in the high-backed chair beside hers. Reaching across the small table between them for her hand, he linked their fingers together, and opened his book. Elizabeth thought it was incredibly cozy to sit, curled up in a chair beside him, her hand held in his, with a book in her lap, and she didn't mind the small inconvenience of turning the pages with one hand.

Soon, she was so engrossed in her book that it was a full half-hour before she noticed how swiftly Ian turned the pages of his. From the corner of her eye, Elizabeth watched in puzzled fascination as his gaze seemed to slide swiftly down one page, then the facing page, and he turned to the next. Teasingly, she asked, "Are you reading that book, my lord, or only pretending for my benefit?"

He glanced up sharply, and Elizabeth saw a strange hesitant expression flicker across his tanned face. As if carefully phrasing his reply, he said slowly, "I have an—odd ability—to read very quickly."

"Oh," Elizabeth replied, "how lucky you are. I never heard of a talent like that."

A lazy glamorous smile swept across his face, and he squeezed her hand. "It's not nearly as uncommon as your eyes," he said.

Elizabeth thought it must be a great deal more uncommon, but she wasn't completely certain and she let it pass. The following day, that discovery was completely eclipsed by another one. At Ian's insistence, she'd spread the books from Havenhurst across his desk in order to go over the quarter's accounts, and as the morning wore on, the long columns of figures she'd been adding and multiplying began to blur together and transpose themselves in her mind—due in part, she thought with a weary smile, to the fact that her husband had kept her awake half the night making love to her. For the third time, she added the same long columns of expenditures, and for the third time, she came up with a different sum. So frustrated was she that she didn't realize Ian had come into the room, until he leaned over her from behind and put his hands on the desk on either side of her own. "Problems?" he asked, kissing the top of her head.

"Yes," she said, glancing at the clock and realizing that the business acquaintances he was expecting would be there momentarily. As she explained her problem to him, she started shoving loose papers into the books, hurriedly trying to reassemble everything and clear his desk. "For the last forty-five minutes, I've been adding the same four columns so that I could divide them by eighteen servants, multiply hat by forty servants, which we now have there, times four quarters. Once I know that, I can forecast the real cost of food and supplies with the increased staff. I've gotten three different answers to those miserable columns, and I haven't even tried the rest of the calculations. Tomorrow I'll have to start all over again," she finished irritably, "and it takes forever just to get all this laid out and organized." She reached out to close the book and shove her calculations into it, but Ian stopped her.

"Which columns are they?" he asked calmly, his surprised gaze studying the genuine ire on her face.

"Those long ones down the left-hand side. It doesn't matter, I'll fight it out tomorrow," she said. She shoved the chair back, dropped two sheets of paper, and bent over to pick them up. They'd slid beneath the kneehole of the desk, and in growing disgust Elizabeth crawled underneath to get them. Above her, Ian said, "£364."

"Pardon?" she asked when she reemerged, clutching the errant sheets of paper.

He was writing it down on a scrap of paper. "£364."

"Do not make light of my wanting to know the figures," she warned him with an exasperated smile. "Besides," she continued, leaning up and pressing an apologetic kiss on his cheek, loving the tangy scent of his cologne, "I usually enjoy the bookwork. I'm simply a little short of sleep today, because," she whispered, "my husband kept me awake half the night."

"Elizabeth," he began hesitantly, "there's something I—" Then he shook his head and changed his mind, and since Shipley was already standing in the doorway to announce the arrival of his business acquaintances, Elizabeth thought no more of it.

Until the next morning.

Rather than use his study again and disrupt his working schedule, she spread out her books and papers at a desk in the library. With her mind fresh and alert, she made quick progress and, within an hour, she'd gotten the answer she'd been seeking yesterday and double-checked it. Positive that £364 was correct, she smiled as she tried to recall what Ian's wild guess had been yesterday. When she couldn't recall it, she looked among her papers for the one he'd written his guess upon and found it tucked in between the sheets of the book.

With her own answer in one hand, she looked at what he had written . . . Shock sent her slowly to her feet, the paper with Ian's answer clutched in her other hand: £364. Trembling with an uneasy emotion she couldn't identify, she gazed at the answer he had calculated in his head, not on paper, in a matter of seconds, not three-quarters of an hour.

She was still standing there several moments later when Ian walked in to invite her to ride with him. "Still trying to find your answer, sweetheart?" he asked with a sympathetic grin, mistaking the cause of her wary stare.

"No, I found mine," she said, her voice unintentionally accusing as she thrust both pieces of paper toward him. "What I would like to know," she continued, unable to tear her gaze from him, "is how it happens to be the same answer you arrived at in a matter of moments."

His grin faded, and he shoved his hands into his pockets, ignoring the papers in her outthrust hand. His expression carefully impassive, he said, "That answer is a little more difficult than the one I wrote down for you—"

"You can do this—calculate all those figures in your *mind? In moments?"*

He nodded curtly, and when Elizabeth continued to stare at him warily, as if he was a being of unknown origin, his face hardened. In a clipped, cool voice he said, "I would appreciate it if you would stop staring at me as if I'm a freak."

Elizabeth's mouth dropped open at his tone and his words. "I'm not."

"Yes," he said implacably. "You are. Which is why I haven't told you before this."

Embarrassed regret surged through her at the understandable conclusion he'd drawn from her reaction. Recovering her composure, she started around the desk toward him. "What you saw on my face was wonder and awe, no matter how it must have seemed."

"The last thing I want from you is 'awe,'" he said tightly, and Elizabeth belatedly realized that, while he didn't care what anyone else thought of him, *her* reaction to all this was obviously terribly important to him. Rapidly concluding that he'd evidently had some experience with other people's reaction to what must surely be a form of genius—and which struck them as "freakish"—she bit her lip, trying to decide what to say. When nothing came to mind, she simply let love guide her and reacted without artifice. Leaning back against the desk, she sent him an amused, sidelong smile and said, "I gather you can calculate almost as rapidly as you can read?"

His response was short and chilly. "Not quite."

"I see," she continued lightly. "I would guess there are close to ten thousand books in your library here. Have you read them all?"

"No."

She nodded thoughtfully, but her eyes danced with admiring laughter as she continued, "Well, you've been quite busy the past few weeks—dancing attendance on me. No doubt that's kept you from finishing the last thousand or two." His face softened as she asked merrily, "Are you *planning* to read them all?"

With relief, she saw the answering smile tugging at his lips. "I thought I'd attend to that next week," he replied with sham gravity.

"A worthy endeavor," she agreed. "I hope you won't start without me. I'd like to watch."

Ian's shout of laughter was cut short as he snatched her into his arms and buried his face in her fragrant hair, his hands clenching her to him as if he could absorb her sweetness into himself.

"Do you have any other extraordinary skills I ought to know about, my lord?" she whispered, holding him as tightly as he was holding her.

The laughter in his voice was replaced by tender solemnity. "I'm rather good," he whispered, "at loving you."

In the weeks that followed, he proved it to her in a hundred ways. Among other things, he never objected to the times she was away from him at Havenhurst. To Elizabeth, whose entire life had once been wrapped up in Havenhurst's past and future, it came as something of a surprise to realize very quickly that she rather begrudged much of the time she had to spend there, overseeing the improvements that were getting under way.

To avoid spending more time there than was absolutely necessary, she began bringing home the drawings the architect had made, along with any other problems she'd encountered, so that she could consult with Ian. No matter how busy he was or who he was with, he made time for her. He would sit with her for hours, explaining alternatives to her in a step-by-step fashion which she soon realized was evidence of his inexhaustible patience with her, because Ian's mind did not reason in step-step fashion. With awesome speed, his mind went straight from point A to point Z, from problem to solution, without needing to plod through the normal steps between.

With the exception of the few times she had to stay at Havenhurst, they spent their nights together in his bed, and Elizabeth quickly discovered that their wedding night had been but a small preview of the wild beauty and primitive splendor of his lovemaking. There were times that he lingered over her endlessly, lavishing her senses with every exquisite sensation, prolonging their release, until Elizabeth was pleading with him to end the sweet torment; other nights, he turned to her in hunger and need and took her with tender roughness and few preliminaries. And Elizabeth could never quite decide which way she liked best. She admitted that to him one night, only to have him take her swiftly and then keep her awake for hours with his tender attentions, so that she might be better able to decide. He taught her to ask, without embarrassment, for what she wanted, and when shyness made her hesitate, he taught her by example that same night. It was a lesson Elizabeth found incredibly stirring as she listened to his husky voice grow thick with desire while he asked to be touched and caressed in particular ways, and when she did, his powerful muscles jumped beneath her touch, and a groan tore from his chest.

Toward the end of the summer, they went to London, although the city was still somewhat deserted, the Little Season having not yet begun. Elizabeth agreed because she thought it would be convenient for him to be nearer the men with whom he invested large sums of money in complex ventures, and because Alex would be there. Ian went because he wanted Elizabeth to enjoy the position of prestige in society she was entitled to—and because he enjoyed showing her off in the setting where she sparkled like the jewels he lavished on her. He knew she regarded him as a combination of loving benefactor and wise teacher, but in that last regard, Ian knew she was wrong, for Elizabeth was teaching him, too. By her own example, she taught him to be patient with servants; she taught him to relax; and she taught him that next to lovemaking, laughter was undoubtedly life's most pleasant diversion. At her insistence, he even learned to look tolerantly upon the foolish foibles of many of the *ton*'s members.

So successful was Elizabeth in this last endeavor that they were, within a matter of weeks, rather a favorite couple, much sought after for every sort of charitable and social event. Invitations arrived at the house in Upper Brook Street in large numbers, and together they laughingly invented excuses to avoid many of them so that Ian could work during the day and Elizabeth could occupy her time with something more interesting than social calls.

For Ian that was no problem at all; he was always busy. Elizabeth solved her problem by agreeing, at the urging of some of the *ton*'s most influential old guard, including the Dowager Duchess of Hawthorne, to join in a charitable endeavor to build a badly needed hospital on the outskirts of London. Unfortunately, the Hospital Fund Raising Committee, to which Elizabeth was assigned, spent most of its time mired down in petty trivialities and rarely made a decision on anything. In a fit of bored frustration, Elizabeth finally asked Ian to step into their drawing room one day, while the committee was meeting there, and to give them the benefit of his expertise. "And," she laughingly warned him in the privacy of his study when he agreed to join them, "no matter how they prose on about every tiny, meaningless expenditure—which they will—promise me you *won't* point out to them that you could build six hospitals with less effort and time."

"Could I do that?" he asked, grinning.

"Absolutely!" She sighed. "Between them, they must have half the money in Europe, yet they debate about every shilling to be spent as if it were coming out of their own reticules and likely to send them to debtors' gaol."

"If they offend *your* thrifty sensibilities, they must be a rare group," Ian teased. Elizabeth gave him a distracted smile, but when they neared the drawing room, where the committee was drinking tea in Ian's priceless Sèvres china cups, she turned to him and added hastily, "Oh, and *don't* comment on Lady Wiltshire's blue hat."

"Why not?"

"Because it's her hair."

"I wouldn't do such a thing," he protested, grinning at her.

"Yes, you would!" she whispered, trying to frown and chuckling instead. "The dowager duchess told me that, last night, you complimented the furry dog Lady Shirley had draped over her arm."

"Madam, I was following your specific instructions to be nice to the eccentric old harridan. Why shouldn't I have complimented her dog?"

"Because it was a new fur *muff* of a rare sort, of which she was extravagantly proud."

"There is no fur on earth that mangy, Elizabeth," he replied with an impenitent grin. "She's hoaxing the lot of you," he added seriously.

Elizabeth swallowed a startled laugh and said with an imploring look, "Promise me you'll be very nice, and very patient with the committee."

"I promise," he said gravely, but when she reached for the door handle and opened the door—when it was too late to step back and yank it closed—he leaned close to her ear and whispered, "Did you know a camel is the only animal invented by a committee, which is why it turned out the way it has?"

If the committee was surprised to see the formerly curt and irascible Marquess of Kensington stroll into their midst wearing a beatific smile worthy of a choir boy, they were doubtlessly shocked to see his wife's hands clamped over her face and her eyes tearing with mirth.

Elizabeth's concern that Ian might insult them, either intentionally or otherwise, soon gave way to admiration and then to helpless amusement as he sat for the next half-hour, charming them all with an occasional lazy smile or interjecting a gallant compliment, while they spent the entire time debating whether to sell the chocolates being donated by Gunther's for £5 or £6 per box. Despite Ian's outwardly bland demeanor, Elizabeth waited uneasily for him to say he'd buy the damned cartload of chocolates for £10 apiece, if it would get them on to the next problem, which she knew was what he was dying to say.

But she needn't have worried, for he continued to positively exude pleasant interest. Four times, the committee paused to solicit his advice; four times, he smilingly made excellent suggestions; four times, they ignored what he suggested. And four times, he seemed not to mind in the least or even to notice.

Making a mental note to thank him profusely for his incredible forbearance, Elizabeth kept her attention on her guests and the discussion, until she inadvertently glanced in his direction, and her breath caught. Seated on the opposite side of the gathering from her, he was now leaning back in his chair, his left ankle propped atop his right knee, and despite his apparent absorption in the topic being discussed, his heavy-lidded gaze was roving meaningfully over her breasts. One look at the smile tugging at his lips and Elizabeth realized that he wanted her to know it.

Obviously he'd decided that both she and he were wasting their time with the committee, and he was playing an amusing game designed to either divert her or discomfit her entirely, she wasn't certain which. Elizabeth drew a deep breath, ready to blast a warning look at him, and his gaze lifted slowly from her gently heaving bosom, traveled lazily up her throat, paused at her lips, and then lifted to her narrowed eyes.

Her quelling glance earned her nothing but a slight, challenging lift of his brows and a decidedly sensual smile, before his gaze reversed and began a lazy trip downward again.

Lady Wiltshire's voice rose, and she said for the second time, *"Lady Thornton,* what do you think?"

Elizabeth snapped her gaze from her provoking husband to Lady Wiltshire. "I—I agree," she said without the slightest idea of what she was agreeing with. For the next five minutes, she resisted the tug of Ian's caressing gaze, firmly refusing to even glance his way, but when the committee reembarked on the chocolate issue again, she stole a look at him. The moment she did, he captured her gaze, holding it, while he, with an outward appearance of a man in thoughtful contemplation of some weighty problem, absently rubbed his forefinger against his mouth, his elbow propped on the arm of his chair. Elizabeth's body responded to the caress he was offering her as if his lips were actually on hers, and she drew a long, steadying breath as he deliberately let his eyes slide to her breasts again. He knew *exactly* what his gaze was doing to her, and Elizabeth was thoroughly irate at her inability to ignore its effect.

The committee departed on schedule a half-hour later amid reminders that the next meeting would be held at Lady Wiltshire's house. Before the door closed behind them, Elizabeth rounded on her grinning, impenitent husband in the drawing room. "You wretch!" she exclaimed. "How *could* you?" she demanded, but in the midst of her indignant protest, Ian shoved his hands into her hair, turned her face up, and smothered her words with a ravenous kiss.

"I haven't forgiven you," she warned him in bed an hour later, her cheek against his chest. Laughter, rich and deep, rumbled beneath her ear.

"No?"

"Absolutely not. I'll repay you if it's the last thing I do."

"I think you already have," he said huskily, deliberately misunderstanding her meaning.

Shortly afterward, they returned to Montmayne to spend September in the country, where it was cooler. For Ian, life with Elizabeth was everything he ever hoped it could be, and more. It was so perfect that he had to fight down the nagging fear that things could not go on like this—a fear which he tried to convince himself was mere superstition brought on by the fact that two years ago fate had snatched her from him. But in his heart, he knew it was more than that. His investigators had not yet been able to find a trace of Elizabeth's brother, and he lived in daily dread that hers would succeed where his had not. And so he waited to discover the extent of his offense against her and her brother, knowing he was going to have to beg her forgiveness for it, and that—in marrying her without telling her what he *did* know—he was as guilty of duplicity as he was of her brother's abduction.

In the rational part of his mind, he knew that by having Robert tossed aboard the *Arianna,* he had spared the hotheaded young fool a far worse fate at the hands of the authorities. But now, without knowing what fate had actually befallen him, he couldn't be certain that Elizabeth would see his actions in that light. He couldn't see them in that light himself anymore, because now he knew something he hadn't known at the time: He knew that her parents had been long dead by then and that Robert had been her only buffer against her uncle.

Fear, the one emotion he despised above all others, grew apace with his love for Elizabeth until he actually began to wish someone would find out something, so that he could confess to her whatever sins he was guilty of, and either be forgiven or cast out of her life. In that, he knew his thinking was irrational, but he couldn't help himself. He had found something he treasured beyond all bounds; he had found Elizabeth, and loving her made him more vulnerable than he'd been since his family's death. The threat of losing her haunted him until he began to wonder how long he could bear the torment of uncertainty.

Blissfully unaware of all that, Elizabeth continued to love him without reservation or guile, and as she grew more certain of his love, she became more confident and more enchanting to Ian. On those occasions when she saw his expression become inexplicably grim, she teased him or kissed him, and, if those ploys failed, she presented him with little gifts—a flower arrangement from Havenhurst's gardens, a single rose that she stuck behind his ear, or left upon his pillow. "Shall I have to resort to buying you a jewel to make you smile, my lord?" she joked one day three months after they were married. "I understand that is how it is done when a lover begins to act distracted."

To Elizabeth's surprise, her remark made him snatch her into his arms in a suffocating embrace. "I am *not* losing interest in you, if that's what you're suggesting," he told her.

Elizabeth leaned back in his arms, surprised by the unwarranted force of his declaration, and continued to tease. "You're quite certain?"

"Positive."

"You wouldn't lie to me, would you?" she asked in a tone of mock severity.

"I would never lie to you," Ian said gravely, but then he realized that by withholding the truth from her, he was, in effect, deceiving her, which in turn, amounted to little less than lying outright.

Elizabeth knew something was bothering him, and that as time passed, it was bothering him with increasing frequency, but she never dreamed she was even remotely the cause of his silences or preoccupation. She thought of Robert often, but not since the day of her marriage had she permitted herself to think of Mr. Wordsworth's accusations, not even for an instant. In the first place, she couldn't bear it; in the second, she no longer believed there was the slightest possibility he was right.

"I have to go to Havenhurst tomorrow," she said reluctantly when Ian finally let her go. "The masons have started on the house and bridge, and the irrigation work has begun. If I spend the night, though, I shouldn't have to go back for at least a fortnight."

"I'll miss you," he said quietly, but there was no trace of resentment in his voice, nor did he attempt to dissuade her to postpone the trip. He was keeping to his bargain with the integrity that Elizabeth particularly admired in him.

"Not," she whispered, kissing the side of his mouth, "as much as I'll miss you."

32

Her mind on the list of provisions she was reading, Elizabeth walked slowly along the path from Havenhurst's storage buildings toward the main house. A tall hedge on her right shielded the utilitarian buildings from view of the main house where the masons were working. A footstep sounded behind her, and before she could turn or react, she was grabbed round the waist and dragged backward, a male hand clamped over her mouth, stifling her scream of frightened protest.

"Hush, Elizabeth, it's me," an achingly familiar voice said urgently. "Don't scream, all right?"

Elizabeth nodded, the hand loosened, and she whirled around into Robert's waiting arms. "Where have you *been?*" she demanded, laughing and crying and hugging him fiercely. "Why did you leave without telling me where you were going? I could kill you for worrying me so—"

His hands gripped her shoulders, moving her away, and there was urgency on his gaunt face. "There isn't time for explanations. Meet me in the arbor at dusk, and for God's sake don't tell anyone you've seen me."

"Not even Bentner—"

"No one! I have to get out of here before one of the

servants sees me. I'll be in the arbor near your favorite cherry tree at dusk."

He left her there, moving stealthily down the path, then vanishing into the arbor beside it after quickly glancing in both directions to ensure he hadn't been seen.

Elizabeth felt as if she'd imagined the whole brief encounter. The sense of unreality stayed with her as she paced across the drawing room, watching the sun set with nerve-wracking slowness, while she tried to imagine why Robert would fear being seen by their loyal old butler. Obviously he was in some sort of trouble, perhaps with the authorities. If so, she would ask Ian for advice and help. Robert was her brother, and she loved him despite his faults; Ian would understand that. In time, perhaps both men would come to treat one another as relatives, for her sake. She stole out of her own house, feeling like a thief.

Robert was sitting with his back against the old cherry tree, moodily contemplating his scuffed boots when Elizabeth first saw him, and he stood up quickly. "You didn't happen to bring food, did you?"

She'd been right, she realized; he *was* half-starved. "Yes, but only some bread and cheese," she explained, taking it out from behind her skirts. "I couldn't think of a way to carry more out here without causing someone to wonder whom I was feeding in the arbor. Robert," she burst out, no longer diverted by such commonplace needs as food, "where have you been, why did you leave me like that, and what—"

"I didn't leave you," he bit out furiously. "Your husband had me kidnapped the week after our duel and tossed onto one of his ships. I was supposed to die—"

Pain and disbelief streaked through Elizabeth.

"Don't say that to me," she cried, wildly shaking her head. "Don't—he wouldn't—"

Robert's jaw clamped down, and he yanked his shirt out of his waistband, jerked it up, and turned around. *"This* is a souvenir of one of his attempts."

A scream rose up in Elizabeth's throat, and she pressed her knuckles against her mouth, trying to stop it. Even then she felt as if she was going to vomit. "Oh, my God," she panted, looking at the vicious scars that crisscrossed almost every inch of Robert's thin back. "Oh, my God. Oh, my God."

"Don't faint," Robert said, clutching her arm to steady her. "You have to be strong, or he'll finish the deed."

Elizabeth sank to the ground and put her head against her knees, her arms clutched around her stomach, rocking helplessly to and fro. "Oh, my God," she kept saying over and over at the thought of his torn, battered flesh. "Oh, my God."

Forcing herself to take long, steadying breaths, she finally brought herself under control. All the doubts, the warnings, the hints, crystallized in her mind, focusing on the proof of Robert's battered back, and an icy cold stole through her, numbing her to everything, even the pain. Ian had been her love and her lover; she had lain in the arms of a man who knew what he had done to her brother.

Leaning a hand against the tree, she stood up unsteadily. "Tell me," she said hoarsely.

"Tell you why he did this? Or tell you about the months I've spent rotting in a mine, dragging coal out of it? Or tell you about the beatings I got the last time I tried to escape and come back to you?"

Elizabeth rubbed her arms; they felt cold and numb. "Tell me why," she said.

"How in hell do you expect me to explain the motives of a madman?" Robert hissed, and then with a sublime effort he got himself under control. "I've had two years to think about it, to try to understand, and when I heard he'd married you, it all came clear as glass. He tried to kill me on Marblemarle Road the week of our duel, did you know that?"

"I've hired investigators to try to find you," she said, nodding that she knew part of it, unaware that Robert had gone more pale than before. "But they thought *you* tried to kill *him.*"

"That's garbage!"

"It was—conjecture," she admitted. "But why would Ian want to kill you?"

"Why?" he sneered, tearing into the bread and cheese like a starving man while Elizabeth watched him, her heart wrenching. "For one thing, because I shot him in our duel.

427

But that's not really it. I foiled his plans when I barged in on him in the greenhouse. He knew he was reaching above himself when he reached for you, but I put the onus on him. Do you know," he continued with a harsh laugh, "there were people who turned their backs on him over that episode? Plenty, I heard before I was thrown in the hold of one of his ships."

Elizabeth drew a shaky breath. "What do you mean to do?"

Robert leaned his head back and closed his eyes, looking tormented. "He'll have me killed if he learns I'm still alive," he said with absolute conviction. "I couldn't take another whipping like the last one, Elizabeth. I was on the brink of death for a week."

A sob of pity and horror rose in her throat. "Legal charges, then?" she asked, and her voice dropped to an agonized whisper. "Do you mean to go to the authorities?"

"I've thought of it. I want it so badly I can hardly sleep at night, but they'd never take my word now. Your husband has become a rich and powerful man." When he said "your husband" he looked at her so accusingly that Elizabeth could scarcely meet his haunted eyes.

"I—" She lifted his haunted hand in helpless apology, but she didn't know what to apologize for, and tears were starting to blur her eyes and impede her speech. "Please," she cried helplessly. "I don't know what to do or say. Not yet. I can't think."

He dropped the bread and wrapped his arms around her. "Poor beautiful baby," he said. "I've lain awake nights scared out of my mind for you, trying not to think of his filthy hands on you. He owns mines—deep, endless pits in the ground where men live like animals and are beaten like oxen. That's where he gets the money for everything he buys."

Including all the jewels and furs he'd given her, Elizabeth realized, and the need to vomit was almost overwhelming. She shuddered repeatedly in Robert's embrace. "If you don't bring him up before the magistrates, what will you do?"

"What will *I* do?" he asked. "This isn't a question for me alone, Elizabeth. If he learns you know what he's done, your beautiful back won't take the punishment mine has. You won't survive what he has his people do to you."

At the moment, survival was unimportant to Elizabeth. Inside she was already battered, and she was already dying.

"We have to get away. Use new names. Find a new life."

It was the first time Elizabeth hadn't paused to consider Havenhurst before making a decision. "Where?" she asked in a shattered whisper.

"Leave that to me. How much money can you get your hands on in a few days' time?"

Tears dripped from her clenched eyes because she had no choice. No options. No Ian. "A great deal, I suppose," she said dully, "if I can find a way to sell some jewels."

His arms tightened, and he pressed a brotherly kiss on her temple. "You must follow my instructions exactly. Promise me you will?"

She nodded against his shoulder and swallowed painfully.

"No one must know you're leaving. He'll stop you if he knows what you mean to do."

Elizabeth nodded again; Ian would not let her go easily, and never without weeks of probing questions. After their torrid lovemaking, he certainly wouldn't believe she wished for a separation because she didn't want to live with him.

"Sell everything you possibly can without raising suspicion. Go to London; it's a big city, and if you use another name and try to make yourself look as different as you can, you aren't likely to be recognized. On Friday take a hack from London to Thurston Crossing on the Bernam Road. There's a posting house there, and I'll be waiting for you. Your husband will launch a search for you once your disappearance is noted. They'll be watching for a blond woman, and if they find me, I'm as good as dead. If you're with me, so are you, if he finds you first. We'll travel as man and wife; I think that will be the best way."

Elizabeth heard it all, she understood it all, but she could not seem to move or feel. "Where are we going?" she asked numbly.

"I haven't decided yet. To Brussels, maybe, but that's too close. Maybe to America. We'll travel north and stay in Helmshead. It's a little village on the seacoast, very secluded and provincial. They only get the newspapers irregularly, so they won't know of your disappearance. We'll wait for a ship going to the colonies up there."

His hands tightened, moving her away. "I have to leave. Do you understand what you need to do?"

She nodded.

"There's one thing more. I want you to quarrel with him—in front of someone, if possible. It doesn't need to be anything serious—just enough to make him think you're angry, so that when you leave he won't set investigators on your path so quickly. If you disappear for no apparent reason, he'll start searching for you at once. The other way will buy us time. Can you do that?"

"Yes," she said hoarsely. "I imagine so. But I wanted to be able to leave him a note, to tell him"—tears clogged her throat at the idea of writing Ian a note; he might be a monster, but her heart was refusing to let go of her love at the same speed her mind was accepting Ian's treachery—"to tell him *why* I'm leaving." Her voice broke, and her shoulders began to shake with wrenching sobs.

Robert gathered her into his arms again. Despite the comforting gesture, his voice was icy and implacable. *"No note!* Do you understand me? *No note.* Later," he promised, his voice softened and silky, "later, when we've made good our escape, you can write to him and tell him everything. You can write volumes to that bastard. Do you understand why it's imperative that you make it look like you're leaving over an ordinary quarrel?"

"Yes," she said hoarsely.

"I'll see you Friday," he promised, moving away from her and kissing her cheek. "Don't fail us."

"I won't."

Mechanically going through the motions of living and survival, Elizabeth sent a note to Ian that night announcing her intention to stay overnight at Havenhurst so that she could go over the books. The next day, Wednesday, she left for London, her jewels in a velvet sack concealed beneath her cloak. Everything was there, including her betrothal ring. Scrupulously adhering to the need for stealth, she had Aaron drop her in Bond Street, then she took a rented hack to the first jeweler she saw in a neighborhood where she wasn't likely to be recognized.

The jeweler was impressed with what she had to offer. Speechless, in fact. "They're all exceptionally fine stones, Mrs. . . ."

"Mrs. Roberts," Elizabeth provided with a kind of dumb inspiration. Now that nothing mattered anymore, it was easy to lie and dissemble.

The amount he offered her for the emeralds sent the first stab of feeling through her, but it was only a sense of mild dismay. "They must be worth twenty times that much."

"Thirty, more like, but I don't have the clientele that can pay those lofty prices. I have to sell them for what my clients are willing to pay." Elizabeth nodded numbly, her soul too dead to bargain, to point out to him that he could sell them to a Bond Street jeweler for ten times more than he was paying her. "I don't keep this kind of money around. You'll have to go to my bank."

Two hours later Elizabeth emerged from the designated bank with a fortune in notes filling the large sack and her reticule.

Before leaving for London she'd sent word to Ian that she intended to spend the night at the house on Promenade Street, using as an excuse a desire to do some shopping and look in on the servants. It was a lame excuse, but Elizabeth had passed the point of rational thought. She followed Robert's instructions automatically; she did not deviate or improvise; she did not feel. She felt like a person who had already died but whose body was still ghoulishly propelling itself around.

Sitting alone in her bed chamber on Promenade Street, she stared blankly out the window into the impenetrable night, her fingers idly twisting in her lap. She ought to send Alex a note to tell her good-bye, she thought. It was her first thought of the future in almost two days. Once the thinking began, however, she wished it hadn't. No sooner had she decided she couldn't risk writing to Alexandra than her mind began tormenting her with the single remaining ordeal before her: She still had to see Ian; she could not avoid him for two more days without awakening his suspicion. Or could she? she wondered helplessly. He had agreed to let her live her own life, and she'd stayed at Havenhurst occasionally since they'd been married. Of course, the reason had owed to foul weather, not whim.

Dawn was already lightening the sky when she fell asleep in her chair.

When Elizabeth's carriage drew up at Havenhurst the next day she half expected to see Ian's in the drive, but everything looked normal and peaceful. With Ian's money available, Havenhurst was filled with new servants; the grooms were walking a horse by the stable; the gardeners were laying mulch on the dormant flower beds. Normal and peaceful, she thought a little hysterically as Bentner opened the door. "Where have you been, missy?" he asked, anxiously searching her pale face. "The marquess sent word he wants you to come home."

Elizabeth should have expected that, but she actually hadn't. "I can't see why I must, Bentner," she said in a strained voice that was supposed to pass for annoyance. "My husband seems to forget we had a bargain when we wed."

Bentner, who still resented Ian for his past treatment of his mistress—not to mention for the assault on Bentner's person the day he forced his way into the house on Promenade Street—could not find any reason to defend the marquess now. Instead he trotted down the hall on Elizabeth's heels, stealing anxious glances at her face. "You don't look well, Miss Elizabeth," he said. "Shall I have Winston make you a nice hot pot of tea with some of his delicious scones?"

Elizabeth shook her head and went into the library, where she sat down at her writing desk and composed what she hoped was a politely evasive note to her husband stating her intention to remain at Havenhurst tonight to finish working on the account books. A footman left with the note shortly afterward, with instructions to make the carriage trip in no more than seven hours. Under no circumstances did Elizabeth want Ian leaving their house—*his* house—and barging in here in the morning—or worse, tonight.

After the footman left, the nerves that had seemed numb in Elizabeth came to vibrant life with a vengeance. The pendulum on the old grandfather clock in the hall began to swing ominously faster, and she began to imagine all sorts of vague, disastrous things happening. Sleep, she told herself; she needed sleep. Her imagination was running rampant because she'd had so little sleep.

Tomorrow she would have to face him, but only for a few hours. . . .

Elizabeth snapped awake in a terrified instant as the door to her bed chamber was flung open near dawn, and Ian stalked into the darkened room. "Do you want to go first, or shall I?" he said tightly, coming to stand at the side of her bed.

"What do you mean?" she asked in a trembling voice.

"I mean," he said, "that either you go first and tell me why in hell you suddenly find my company repugnant, or I'll go first and tell you how I feel when I don't know where you are or why you want to be there!"

"I've sent word to you both nights."

"You sent a damned note that arrived long after nightfall both times, informing me that you intended to sleep somewhere else. I want to know *why!*"

He has men beaten like animals, she reminded herself.

"Stop shouting at me," Elizabeth said shakily, getting out of bed and dragging the covers with her to hide herself from him.

His brows snapped together in an ominous frown. "Elizabeth?" he asked, reaching for her.

"Don't touch me!" she cried.

Bentner's voice came from the doorway. "Is aught amiss, my lady?" he asked, glaring bravely at Ian.

"Get out of here and close that damned door behind you!" Ian snapped furiously.

"Leave it open," Elizabeth said nervously, and the brave butler did exactly as she said.

In six long strides Ian was at the door, shoving it closed with a force that sent it crashing into its frame, and Elizabeth began to vibrate with terror. When he turned around and started toward her Elizabeth tried to back away, but she tripped on the coverlet and had to stay where she was.

Ian saw the fear in her eyes and stopped short only inches in front of her. His hand lifted, and she winced, but it came to rest on her cheek. "Darling, what is it?" he asked. It was his voice that made her want to weep at his feet, that beautiful baritone voice; and his face—that harsh, handsome face she'd adored. She wanted to beg him to tell her what Robert and Wordsworth had said were lies—all lies. *"My life depends on this, Elizabeth. So does yours. Don't fail me,"* Robert had pleaded. Yet, in that moment of weakness she actually considered telling Ian everything she knew and letting him kill her if he wanted to; she would have preferred death to the torment of living with the memory of the lie that had been their lives—to the torment of living without him.

"Are you ill?" he asked, frowning and minutely studying her face.

Snatching at the excuse he'd offered, she nodded hastily. "Yes. I haven't been feeling well."

"Is that why you went to London? To see a physician?"

She nodded a little wildly, and to her bewildered horror he started to smile—that lazy, tender smile that always made her senses leap. "Are you with child, darling? Is that why you're acting so strangely?" Elizabeth was silent, trying to debate the wisdom of saying yes or no—she should say no, she realized. He'd hunt her to the ends of the earth if he believed she was carrying his babe.

"No! He—the doctor said it is just—just—nerves."

"You've been working and playing too hard," Ian said, looking like the picture of a worried, devoted husband. "You need more rest."

Elizabeth couldn't bear any more of this—not his feigned tenderness or his concern or the memory of Robert's battered back. "I'm going to sleep now," she said in a strangled voice. *"Alone,"* she added, and his face whitened as if she had slapped him.

During his entire adult life Ian had relied almost as much on his intuition as on his intellect, and at that moment he didn't want to believe in the explanation they were both offering. His wife did not want him in her bed; she recoiled from his touch; she had been away for two consecutive nights; and—more alarming than any of that—guilt and fear were written all over her pale face.

"Do you know what a man thinks," he said in a calm voice that belied the pain streaking through him, "when his wife stays away at night and doesn't want him in her bed when she does return?"

Elizabeth shook her head.

"He thinks," Ian said dispassionately, "that perhaps someone else has been taking his place in it."

Fury sent bright flags of color to her pale cheeks.

"You're blushing, my dear," he said in an awful voice.

"I am furious!" she countered, momentarily forgetting that she was confronting a madman.

His stunned look was replaced almost instantly by an expression of relief and then bafflement. "I apologize, Elizabeth."

"Would you p-please get out of here!" Elizabeth burst out in a final explosion of strength. "Just go away and let me rest. I told you I was tired. And I don't see what right you have to be so upset! We had a bargain before we married—I was to be allowed to live my life without interference, and quizzing me like this is interference!" Her voice broke, and after another narrowed look he strode out of the room.

Numb with relief and pain, Elizabeth crawled back into bed and pulled the covers up under her chin, but not even their luxurious warmth could still the alternating chills and fever that quaked through her. Several minutes later a shadow crossed her bed, and she almost screamed with terror before she realized it was Ian, who had entered silently through the connecting door of their suite.

Since she'd gasped aloud when she saw him, it was useless to pretend she was sleeping. In silent dread she watched him walking toward her bed. Wordlessly he sat down beside her, and she realized there was a glass in his hand. He put it on the bedside table, then he reached behind her to prop up her pillows, leaving Elizabeth no choice but to sit up and lean back against them. "Drink this," he instructed in a calm tone.

"What is it?" she asked suspiciously.

"It's brandy. It will help you sleep."

He watched while she sipped it, and when he spoke again there was a tender smile in his voice. "Since we've ruled out another man as the explanation for all this, I can only assume something has gone wrong at Havenhurst. Is that it?"

Elizabeth seized on that excuse as if it were manna from heaven. "Yes," she whispered, nodding vigorously.

Leaning down, he pressed a kiss on her forehead and said teasingly, "Let me guess—you discovered the mill overcharged you?" Elizabeth thought she would die of the sweet torment when he continued tenderly teasing her about being thrifty. "Not the mill? Then it was the baker, and he refused to give you a better price for buying two loaves instead of one."

Tears swelled behind her eyes, treacherously close to the surface, and Ian saw them. *"That* bad?" he joked, looking at the suspicious sheen in her eyes. "Then it must be that you've overspent your allowance." When she didn't respond to his light probing, Ian smiled reassuringly and said, "Whatever it is, we'll work it out together tomorrow."

It sounded as though he planned to stay, and that shook Elizabeth out of her mute misery enough to say chokingly, "No—it's the—the masons. They're costing much more than I—I expected. I've spent part of my personal allowance on them besides the loan you made me for Havenhurst."

"Oh, so it's the *masons,*" he grinned, chuckling. "You have to keep your eye on them, to be sure. They'll put you in the poorhouse if you don't keep an eye on the mortar they charge you for. I'll have a talk with them in the morning."

"No!" she burst out, fabricating wildly. "That's just what has me so upset. I didn't want you to have to intercede. I wanted to do it all myself. I have it all settled now, but it's been exhausting. And so I went to the doctor to see why I felt tired. He—he said there's nothing in the world wrong with me. I'll come home to Montmayne the day after tomorrow. Don't wait here for me. I know how busy you are right now. Please," she implored desperately, "let me do this, I beg you!"

Ian straightened and shook his head in baffled disbelief. "I'd give you my life for the price of your smile, Elizabeth.

You don't have to beg me for anything. I do not want you spending your personal allowance on this place, however. If you do," he lied teasingly, "I may be forced to cut it off." Then, more seriously, he said, "If you need more money for Havenhurst, just tell me, but your allowance is to be spent exclusively on yourself. Finish your brandy," he ordered gently, and when she had, he pressed another kiss on her forehead. "Stay here as long as you must. I have business in Devon that I've been putting off because I didn't want to leave you. I'll go there and return to London on Tuesday. Would you like to join me there instead of at Montmayne?"

Elizabeth nodded.

"There's just one thing more," he finished, studying her pale face and strained features. "Will you give me your word the doctor didn't find anything at all to be alarmed about?"

"Yes," Elizabeth said. "I give you my word."

She watched him walk back into his own bed chamber. The moment his door clicked into its latch Elizabeth turned over and buried her face in the pillows. She wept until she thought there couldn't possibly be any more tears left in her, and then she wept harder.

Across the room the door leading out into the hall was opened a crack, and Berta peeked in, then quickly closed it. Turning to Bentner—who'd sought her counsel when Ian slammed the door in his face and ripped into Elizabeth— Berta said miserably, "She's crying like her heart will break, but he's not in there anymore."

"He ought to be shot!" Bentner said with blazing contempt.

Berta nodded timidly and clutched her dressing robe closer about her. "He's a frightening man, to be sure, Mr. Bentner."

33

When Elizabeth hadn't arrived at the town house in Upper Brook Street by Tuesday night, all the misgivings Ian had been trying to stifle came back with a vengeance. At eleven o'clock that night he sent two footmen to Havenhurst to ask if they knew where she was, and two others to Montmayne to see if she was there.

At ten-thirty the next morning he was apprised of the fact that the Havenhurst servants thought she'd gone to Montmayne five days ago, while his servants believed her to have been at Havenhurst the entire time. Elizabeth had vanished five days ago, and no one had thought to sound an alarm.

At one o'clock that afternoon Ian met with the head of Bow Street, and by four o'clock he'd hired a private team of one hundred investigators to search for her. There was little he could tell them. All anyone knew for certain was that Elizabeth had vanished from Havenhurst, where she had last been seen that night with him; that she had apparently taken nothing with her except whatever clothes she was wearing; and no one yet knew what clothes they were.

There was one other thing Ian knew, but he wasn't yet ready to reveal it unless he absolutely had to, and it was the sole reason he was desperately trying to keep her disappearance a secret: He knew his wife had been terrified of something, or someone, the last night she was with him. Blackmail was the only thing Ian could think of, but blackmailers didn't kidnap their victims, and for the life of him he couldn't imagine what in Elizabeth's innocent young life she might have done to attract a blackmailer. Without blackmail as a motive, no criminal would be demented enough to abduct a marchioness and set the entire English justice system on his heels.

Beyond all that, he could not bear to consider the one remaining possibility. He wouldn't let himself even imagine that she might have run away with some unknown lover. But as hour merged into day and day followed night, it became harder to banish the ugly, tormenting thought. He prowled around the house, he stood in her room to be closer to her, and then he drank. He drank to still the ache of her loss and the unnamed terror inside him.

On the sixth day the newspapers learned of the investigations into the disappearance of Lady Elizabeth Thornton, and the news was splashed across the front pages of the *Times* and the *Gazette*, along with a great deal of lurid speculation that included kidnapping, blackmail, and even broad hints that the Marchioness of Kensington might have decided to leave "for unknown reasons of her own."

After that, not even the combined power of the Thornton and Townsende families could keep the press from printing every word of truth, conjecture, or blatant falsehood they could discover or invent. They seemed to know, and to print, every morsel of information that Bow Street and Ian's investigators were discovering. Servants were questioned at all of Ian's houses and at Havenhurst, and their statements were "quoted" by the avid press. Details of Ian and Elizabeth's private life were fed to the insatiable public like shovelfuls of fodder.

In fact, it was from an article in the *Times* that Ian first learned that *he* was now a suspect. According to the *Times*, the butler at Havenhurst had supposedly witnessed a quarrel between Lord and Lady Thornton on the very night Lady Thornton was last seen. The cause of the quarrel, the butler said, had been Lord Thornton's vicious attack on Lady Thornton's moral character as it pertained to "certain things best left unsaid."

Lady Thornton's maid, according to the paper, had broken down and wept as she related having peeked in on her mistress and heard her "weeping like her heart would break." The maid had also said it was dark in the room, and so she could not see whether or not any physical abuse had been done to her mistress, "but she could not and would not say it wasn't likely."

Only one of the Havenhurst servants gave testimony that didn't incriminate Ian, and when he read it, it caused him more agony than anything they could have hinted about him: Four days before Lady Thornton's disappearance, a newly hired gardener named William Stokey had seen her ladyship go into the arbor from the back door of the house at dusk, and Stokey had started after her, intending to ask her a question about the mulch being laid on the flower beds. He had not approached her, however, because he had seen her embracing "a man who weren't her husband."

The papers promptly remarked that infidelity might cause a husband to do more than berate his wife, that it might provoke him into making her disappear . . . forever.

The authorities were still hesitant to believe Ian had done away with his wife merely because she'd purportedly met an unknown man in the arbor, which was the only motive he appeared to have.

At the end of the second week, however, a witness who had been away from England read the paper and reacted with instantaneous rage to the discovery that Lady Thornton had mysteriously disappeared. So damning, so shocking was the testimony of Mr. Wordsworth, a private investigator in the lady's employ, against the Marquess of Kensington that it was given under the utmost secrecy, and not even the press could discover it.

The following day the *Times* reported its most shocking and titillating piece of news yet: Ian Thornton, Marquess of Kensington, had been taken from his London town house and brought in for official questioning to ascertain his part in the disappearance of his wife.

Although Ian was not formally charged with responsibility for her disappearance, or imprisoned while the investigation continued, he was ordered not to leave London until a tribunal had met behind closed doors to decide whether or not there was enough reason to try him either for his wife's disappearance or on the new evidence provided by Wordsworth concerning his possible part in the disappearance of her brother two years before.

"They won't do it, Ian," Jordan Townsende said the night after Ian was released on his own recognizance. Pacing back and forth across Ian's drawing room, he said again, "They will not do it."

"They'll do it," Ian said dispassionately. The words were devoid of concern; not even his eyes showed interest. Days ago Ian had passed the point of caring about the investigation. Elizabeth was gone; there had been no ransom note, nothing whatever—no reason in the world to continue believing that she'd been taken against her will. Since Ian knew damned well he hadn't killed her or had her abducted, the only remaining conclusion was that Elizabeth had left him for someone else.

The authorities were still vacillating about the other man she'd allegedly met in the arbor because the gardener's eyesight had been proven to be extremely poor, and even he admitted that it "might have been tree limbs moving around her in the dim light, instead of a man's arms." Ian, however, did not doubt it. The existence of a lover was the only thing that made sense; he had even suspected it the night before she disappeared. She hadn't wanted him in her bed; if anything but a lover had been worrying her that night, she'd have sought the protection of his arms, even if she didn't confide in him. But *he* had been the last thing she'd wanted.

No, he hadn't actually *suspected* it—that would have been more pain than he could have endured then. Now, however, he not only suspected it, he knew it, and the pain was beyond anything he'd ever imagined existed.

"I tell you they won't bring you to trial," Jordan repeated. "Do you honestly think they will?" he demanded, looking first to Duncan and then to the Duke of Stanhope, who were seated in the drawing room. In answer, both men raised dazed, pain-filled eyes to Jordan's, shook their heads in an effort to seem decisive, then looked back down at their hands.

Under English law Ian was entitled to a trial before his peers; since he was a British lord, that meant he could only be tried in the House of Lords, and Jordan was clinging to that as if it were Ian's lifeline.

"You aren't the first man among us to have a spoiled wife turn missish on him and vanish for a while in hopes of bringing him to heel," Jordan continued, desperately trying to make it seem as if Elizabeth were merely sulking somewhere—no doubt unaware that her husband's reputation had been demolished and that his very life was going to be in jeopardy. "They aren't going to convene the whole damn House of Lords just to try a beleaguered husband whose wife has taken a start," he continued fiercely. "Hell, half the lords in the House can't control their wives. Why should you be any different?"

Alexandra looked up at him, her eyes filled with misery and disbelief. Like Ian, she knew Elizabeth wasn't indulging in a fit of the sullens. Unlike Ian, however, she could not and would not believe her friend had taken a lover and run away.

Ian's butler appeared in the doorway, a sealed message in his hand, which he handed to Jordan. "Who knows?" Jordan tried to joke as he opened it. "Maybe this is from Elizabeth—a note asking me to intercede with you before she dares present herself to you."

His smile faded abruptly.

"What is it?" Alex cried, seeing his haggard expression.

Jordan crumpled the summons in his hand and turned to Ian with angry regret. "They're convening the House of Lords."

"It's good to know," Ian said with cold indifference as he pushed out of his chair and started for his study, "that I'll have one friend and one relative there."

When he left, Jordan continued pacing. "This is a bunch of trumped-up conjecture and insult. That's all it is. The duel with Elizabeth's brother—all of it. Her brother's disappearance is easily explained."

"One disappearance is relatively easy to explain," the Duke of Stanhope said. "Two disappearances—in the same family—is another story, I'm afraid. They'll tear him to shreds if he doesn't do something to help himself."

"Everything that can be done is being done," Jordan assured him. "We have our own investigators turning the countryside upside down looking for a trace of Elizabeth. Bow Street thinks they've found their guilty party in Ian, and they've abandoned the theory of Elizabeth going away of her own volition."

Alexandra stood up to leave and loyally said, "If she did, you may be certain she will have an *excellent* explanation for it—rather than a fit of missish sulks, as all you men seem to want to believe."

When the Townsendes had left, the duke leaned his head wearily against the back of the chair and said to Duncan, "What sort of 'excellent' explanation could she possibly have?"

"It won't matter," Duncan said in a harsh voice. "Not to Ian. Unless she can make him believe that she was forcibly abducted, she's as good as dead to him."

"Don't say things like that!" Edward protested. "Ian loves her—he'll listen."

"I know him better than you, Edward," Duncan replied, remembering Ian's actions after his parents' death. "He'll never give her another chance to hurt him. If she's shamed him voluntarily, if she's betrayed his trust, she is dead to him. And he already believes that she has done both. Watch his face—he doesn't so much as flinch when her name is mentioned. He is already killing all the love he had for her."

"You can't just put someone out of your heart. Believe me, I know."

"Ian can," Duncan argued. "He'll do it so that she can never get close to him again." When the duke frowned in disbelief he said, "Let me tell you a story I told to Elizabeth not long ago when she asked me about some sketches of Ian's in Scotland. It's a story about his parents' death and the Labrador retriever that belonged to him. . . ."

When Duncan finished the tale, the two men sat in bleak silence while the clock chimed the hour of eleven. Both of them stared at the clock, listening . . . waiting for the inevitable sound of the door knocker . . . dreading it. They did not have long to wait. At a quarter past eleven, two men arrived, and Ian Thornton, Marquess of Kensington was formally charged with the murders of his wife and her half-brother, Mr. Robert Cameron. He was placed under arrest and told to prepare himself to stand trial before the House of Lords, four weeks hence. As a concession to his rank, he was not imprisoned prior to the trial, but guards were placed outside his home and he was warned that he would be under constant surveillance whenever he went about the city. His bail was set at £100,000.

34

Helmshead was a sleepy little village that overlooked a bright blue bay where sailing ships occasionally threaded their way into port, navigating between dozens of smaller fishing vessels dotting the harbor. Sometimes seamen came ashore hoping for a night of wenching and drinking; they sailed out again with the morning tide—reminding themselves not to bother leaving their ship next time they put in here. There were no brothels in Helmshead, nor taverns that catered to seamen, nor wenches who sold their wares.

It was a community of families, of hard-bitten fishermen with hands as tough as the ropes and nets they hauled each day; of women who carried their wash to the community well and gossiped with one another while their reddened hands worked lye soap into sun-bleached cloth; of small children playing at tag, and mongrel dogs barking in ecstatic delight at the chase. Faces there were suntanned and weathered and strong, with character lines and squint lines weathered and etched upon them. There were no elegant, bejeweled ladies in Helmshead, nor finely dressed gallants offering their arms so that gloved hands could be placed upon them; there were only women carrying heavy baskets of wet clothing back home and rough fishermen who overtook them and, grinning, hoisted the heavy burdens onto their own muscular shoulders.

Standing on a grassy ledge near the center of the village, Elizabeth leaned back against the tree behind her, watching them. She swallowed past the permanent lump of anguish that had been lodged in her throat and chest for four weeks and turned her face in a different direction, looking across at the steep cliff that rose upward from the sparkling bay below. Gnarled trees clung to the rock, their bodies disfigured by their lifelong battle with the elements—twisted and ugly and strangely beautiful in their showy autumn garb of red and gold.

She closed her eyes to shut out the view; beauty reminded her of Ian. Ruggedness reminded her of Ian. Splendor reminded her of Ian. Twisted things reminded her of Ian. . . .

Drawing in a long, shattered breath, she opened her eyes again. The roughened bark of the tree trunk bit into her back and shoulders, but she didn't move away; the pain proved to her that she was still living. Except for the pain, there was nothing. Emptiness. Emptiness and grief. And the sound of Ian's husky voice in her mind, whispering endearments when they made love . . . teasing her.

The sound of his voice . . . the sight of Robert's battered back.

"Where is he?" Jordan demanded of Ian's London butler, and when the servant replied he brushed past him, striding swiftly to the study. "I have news, Ian."

He waited while Ian finished dictating a brief memorandum, dismissed his secretary, and then finally gave him his attention. "God, I wish you'd stop this!" Jordan burst out.

"Stop what?" Ian asked, leaning back in his chair.

Jordan stared at him in helpless anger, not certain why Ian's attitude so upset him. Ian's shirtsleeves were rolled up, he was freshly shaven, and, except for a dramatic loss of weight, he looked like a man who was in control of a reasonably satisfactory life. "I wish you'd stop acting as if—as if everything is normal!"

"What would you have me do?" he replied, getting up and walking over to the tray of liquor. He poured some Scotch nto two glasses and handed one to Jordan. "If you're waiting for me to rant and weep, you're wasting your time."

"No, at the moment I'm glad you're not given to the masculine version of hysterics. I have news, as I said, and though you aren't going to find it pleasant from a personal viewpoint, it's the best possible news from the standpoint of our trial next week. Ian," he said uneasily, "our investigators—yours, I mean—have finally picked up Elizabeth's trail."

Ian's voice was cool, his expression unmoved. "Where is she?"

"We don't know yet, but we do know she was seen traveling in company of a man on the Bernam Road two nights after she disappeared. They put up at an inn about fifteen miles north of Lister. They"—he hesitated and expelled his breath in a rush—"they were traveling as man and wife, Ian."

Other than the merest tightening of Ian's hand upon the glass of Scotch, there was no visible reaction to this staggering news, or to all its heartbreaking and unsavory implications. "There's more news, and it's as good—I mean as valuable—to us."

Ian tossed down the contents of his glass and said with icy finality, "I can't see how any news could be better. She has now proven that I didn't kill her, and at the same time she's given me irrefutable grounds for divorce."

Biting off an expression of sympathy he knew Ian would only reject, Jordan watched him return to his desk, then he continued determinedly, "A prosecutor might try to contend that her traveling companion was a kidnapper in your pay. The next piece of news could help persuade everyone at our trial that she had planned and prepared in advance to leave you."

Ian regarded him in dispassionate silence as Jordan explained, "She sold her jewels to a jeweler in Fletcher Street four days before she disappeared. The jeweler said he hadn't come forward sooner because Lady Kensington, whom he knew as Mrs. Roberts, had seemed very frightened. He said he was reluctant to give her away if she'd run from you for some good reason."

"He was reluctant to give away the profit on the stones in

case they hadn't actually been hers to sell," Ian contradicted with calm cynicism. "Since the papers haven't reported them stolen or missing, he assumed he could safely come forward."

"Probably. But the point is that at least you won't be tried for that trumped-up charge of doing away with her. Of equal importance, since it's now obvious she 'disappeared' of her own will, things won't look so bad for you when they try you on the charges of having her brother . . ." He trailed off, unwilling to say the words.

Ian picked up his quill and a contract from the stack next to his elbow as Jordan finished, "The investigators failed to learn the jewels were missing because the staff at Havenhurst believed they were safely at your house, and your servants believed they were in London."

"I can see how it would have happened," Ian said without interest. "However, the odds are it won't carry any weight with the prosecution. They will insist I hired impostors to sell the jewels and travel together, and that argument will be believed. Now, do you want to proceed with that combined shipping venture we've been discussing, or would you rather forgo it?"

"Forgo it?" Jordan asked, completely unable to deal with Ian's ruthless lack of emotion.

"At the moment, my reputation for honesty and integrity has been destroyed. If your friends would rather withdraw from the venture, I'll understand."

"They've already withdrawn," Jordan admitted reluctantly. "I'm staying with you."

"It's just as well they have," Ian replied, reaching for the contracts and beginning to scratch out the names of the other parties. "In the end, there'll be greater profit for us both."

"Ian," Jordan said in a low, deliberate voice, "you are tempting me to take a swing at you, just to see if you'll wince when I hit you. I've taken about all I can of your indifference to everything that's happening." Ian glanced up from his documents, and Jordan saw it then—the muscle clamping in Ian's jaw, the merest automatic reaction to fury or torment, and he felt a mixture of relief and embarrassment. "I regret that remark more than I can say," he apologized quietly. "And if it's any consolation, I know firsthand how it feels to believe your wife has betrayed you."

"I don't need consolation," Ian clipped. "I need time."

"To get over it," Jordan agreed.

"Time," Ian drawled coolly, "to go over these documents."

As Jordan walked down the hall toward the front door he wasn't certain if he'd only imagined that minuscule sign of emotion.

Elizabeth stood near the same tree where she came to stand and look out at the sea every day. A ship was expected to arrive any time now—one that was bound for Jamaica, Robert said. He was eager to be away from Britain, nervously eager, and who could blame him, she thought, walking slowly over to the edge of the ledge. It fell off sharply, dropping several hundred feet to the rocks and sand below.

Robert had rented a room for them in a cottage belonging to a Mr. and Mrs. Hogan, and he was eating well now, gaining weight from Mrs. Hogan's excellent cooking. Like nearly everyone else in Helmshead, the Hogans were kind, hardworking people, and their four-year-old twin boys were a miracle of activity and lopsided grins. Elizabeth liked all four Hogans immensely, and if it were left to her, she rather thought she would like to stay there, hidden away forever.

Unlike Robert, she was not eager to leave Britain nor afraid of being found. In a strange sort of way she was finding a numb kind of peace there—she was close enough to Ian to almost feel his presence, far enough away from him to know that nothing he said or did could hurt her.

"That's a long way to fall, missus," Mr. Hogan said, coming up beside her and catching Elizabeth's arm in his calloused hand. "Come away from that ledge, y'hear?"

"I didn't realize I was this close to the edge," Elizabeth said, genuinely surprised to realize the toes of her slippers had been beyond solid ground.

"You come in and rest now. Yer husband explained ter us about the bad time ye've had and how ye need to be free o' worry for the time."

The revelation that Robert had confided something of their plight to anyone—especially the Hogans, who knew they were waiting for a ship bound for America or Jamaica or some other place he deemed suitable—pierced her pained daze enough to make her ask, "What did Rob—my husband—tell you about 'the bad time' I've had?"

"He explained yer not to hear nor see nothin' to worry you."

"What I'd like to see," Elizabeth said as she stepped over the threshold of their cottage and inhaled the smell of baking bread, "is a newspaper!"

"Especially no newspapers," Mr. Hogan said.

"There's not much chance of seeing one," Elizabeth said wearily, with an absent smile at one of the twins, who ran up to put his arms around her legs. "Although I can't conceive of anywhere in England that the newspapers don't eventually reach."

"Yer wouldn't want ter read none o' that stuff. It's allays the same—murder and mayhem and polytics and dances."

During the two years Elizabeth had remained in self-imposed isolation at Havenhurst she had rarely read the papers, because it only made her feel more isolated from London and life. Now, however, she wanted to see if there was any mention of her disappearance, and how much was being made of it. She supposed the Hogans couldn't read, which wasn't unusual, but she still thought it so very odd that Mr. Hogan couldn't locate even an old newspaper *anywhere* among the villagers.

"I really do need to see a newspaper," she said with more force than she intended, and the twin dropped his arms from her. "Would you like me to help you do something, Mrs. Hogan?" Elizabeth asked to take the sting out of her exclamation over the paper. Mrs. Hogan was in the seventh month of her pregnancy; she was constantly working and constantly cheerful.

"Not a thing, Miz Roberts. You just rest yerself right there at the table, and I'll get you a nice cup of tea."

"I need a newspaper," Elizabeth said under her breath, "more than I need tea."

"Timmy!" Mrs. Hogan hissed. "Put that away this minute, ye hear? *Timmy,"* she warned, but as usual the cheerful twin ignored her. Instead he tugged at Elizabeth's skirt just as his father swooped down and snatched something large out of his hand.

"For lady!" he shouted, climbing onto Elizabeth's lap. "I bring for lady!"

Elizabeth almost dumped the child on the floor in her surprise. "It's a newspaper!" she cried, her accusing gaze shifting from Mr. Hogan to Mrs. Hogan, who both had the grace to flush beneath their tanned skin. "Mr. Hogan, please—let me see that."

"Yer becomin' overwrought, jes' like yer husband said would happen if ye saw one."

"I'm becoming overwrought," Elizabeth said as patiently and politely as she could, "because you *won't* let me see it."

"It's old," he countered. "Mor'n three weeks."

Oddly, it was a quarrel over a stupid newspaper that made Elizabeth feel the first real emotion she'd felt in weeks. His refusal to hand it to her made her angry; his previous remarks about her needing to rest and becoming overwrought made her vaguely uneasy.

"I'm not the least overwrought," she said with a deliberate smile at Mrs. Hogan, who made most of the decisions in the household. "I merely wanted to see frivolous things— like what the fashions are this season."

"They're wearin' blue," Mrs. Hogan said, smiling back at her and shaking her head at her husband, indicating he wasn't to give Elizabeth the newspaper, "so now ye know. Ain't that nice—blue?"

"You can read, then?" Elizabeth said, forcing her fingers not to snatch the paper out of Mr. Hogan's hand, though she was fully prepared to do even that if necessary.

"Mama reads," one of the twins provided, grinning at her.

"Mr. and Mrs. Hogan," Elizabeth said in a calm, no-nonsense voice, "I am going to become extremely 'over-wrought' if you don't let me see that paper. In fact, I will go from cottage to cottage if I have to in order to find someone else who has one or who has read one."

It was the firm tone of a mother speaking to rowdy children who were close to getting on her nerves, and it seemed to register on Mrs. Hogan. "There's naught to be gained if you go about the village searching for other papers," Mrs. Hogan admitted. "There's but one paper among us, far as I know, and it was my turn to read it. Mr. Willys got it from a sea captain last week."

"Then may I see it, please?" Elizabeth persisted, her hand positively itching to snatch it out of Mr. Hogan's big fist while she had a hysterical vision of herself hopping about, reaching for it while he held it over her head.

"Feelin' as strong as you do about fashions and suchlike, I for one can't see that it will hurt, though yer husband was very firm you shouldn't—"

"My husband," Elizabeth said meaningfully, "does not dictate everything to me."

"Sounds ter me," said Mr. Hogan with a grin, "like she wears the trousers when she's feelin' up to snuff, jes' like you, Rose."

"Give her the paper, John," Rose said with an exasperated smile.

"I believe I'll take it into my room to read it," Elizabeth said as her fingers at last closed around it. From the way they watched her walk into her room, she realized Robert must have inadvertently made them think she was almost a refugee from Bedlam. Sitting down on the narrow bed, Elizabeth opened up the paper.

MARQUESS OF KENSINGTON CHARGED WITH
MURDERS OF WIFE AND BROTHER-IN-LAW
HOUSE OF LORDS CONVENED TO HEAR
TESTIMONY
CONVICTIONS EXPECTED
FOR BOTH MURDERS

A scream of hysteria and denial rose in her throat; she leapt to her feet, her gaze glued to the paper clutched in her fists. "No," she said, shaking her head in wild disbelief. "No," she said to the room. *"No!"* She read words, thousands of words, macabre words, grotesque lies, vicious innuendos—they swung past her gaze and made her senses reel. Then she read them again, because she couldn't comprehend them. It took three readings before Elizabeth could actually start to think, and even then she was panting like a cornered animal. In the next five minutes Elizabeth's emotions veered from hysterical panic to shaking rationality. With nervous swiftness she was weighing alternatives and trying to begin making choices. No matter what Ian had done to Robert, he had *not* murdered him, and he had not murdered her. According to the newspaper, evidence had been presented that Robert had twice tried to kill Ian, but at that moment none of that was truly registering on Elizabeth. All she knew was that the paper said the trial was to begin on the eighteenth—three days ago, and that there was every chance Ian would hang, and that the fastest way to London was by boat for the first leg of the journey, not by land.

Elizabeth dropped the paper, ran from her room, and dashed into the little parlor. "Mr. and Mrs. Hogan," she burst out, trying to remember they already thought she was a little unbalanced, "there is news in the paper—dire news that concerns me. I have to get back to London the quickest possible way."

"Now calm down, missus," Mr. Hogan said with gentle firmness. "You know you shouldn't have read that paper. Just like yer husband said, it got ye all upset."

"My *husband* is on trial for murder," Elizabeth argued desperately.

"Yer husband is down at the port, seein' 'bout a ship to take ye off explorin' the world."

"No, that is my *brother.*"

"He were yer husband this afternoon," Mr. Hogan reminded her.

"He was *never* my husband, he was *always* my brother," Elizabeth insisted. "My husband—my real husband is on trial for murdering me."

"Missus," he said gently, "you ain't dead."

"Oh, my *God!*" Elizabeth said in a low, explosive voice as she raked her hair off her forehead, trying to think what to do, how to convince them to have Mr. Hogan take her down the coast. She turned to Mrs. Hogan, who was watching her intently while mending her little boy's shirt. "Mrs. Hogan?" Crouching down, she took the woman's busy hands in her own, making her look at her, and in a voice that was almost calm and very imploring, Elizabeth began to plead her own case. "Mrs. Hogan, I am not a madwoman, I am not demented, but I am in trouble, and I need to explain it to you. Have you not noticed that I haven't been happy here?"

"Yes, we have noticed, my dear."

"Have you read the papers about Lady Thornton?"

"Every word, though I'm a slow reader and I don't understand any of that legal gobbledygook."

"Mrs. Hogan, I am Lady Thornton. No—don't look at your husband, look at me. Look at my face. I am worried and frightened, but do I really look demented to you?"

"I—I don't know."

"In all the time I've been here, have I ever done or said anything that would have made you think I was crazed? Or would you say I've merely seemed very unhappy and a little frightened?"

"I would not say you"—she hesitated, and in those moments there was an understanding, a communication that sometimes occurs when women reach out to one another for help—"I do *not* think you are crazed."

"Thank you," Elizabeth said feelingly, giving her hands a tight squeeze of gratitude as she continued speaking, half to herself. "Now that we've gotten this far, I need to find a way to prove to you who I am—who Robert and I are. In the paper," Elizabeth began, groping her way through the mire of explanations, mentally searching for the quickest, the easiest proof, and then *any* proof. "In the paper," she began hesitantly, "it said the Marquess of Kensington is believed to have killed his wife, Lady *Elizabeth* Thornton, and her brother, *Robert* Cameron, do you remember?"

Mrs. Hogan nodded. "But the names are commonplace," she protested.

"No, don't start thinking yet," Elizabeth said a little wildly. "I'll think of more proof in a minute. Wait, I have it. Come with me!" She nearly dragged the poor woman out of her chair and into the tiny bed chamber with the two narrow cots that she and Robert slept in. With Mr. Hogan standing in the doorway to watch, Elizabeth reached beneath her pillow and pulled out her reticule, jerking it open. "Look how much money I have with me. It's a great deal more than ordinary people such as Robert and I—such as you *think* Robert and I are—would have, isn't it?"

"I don't rightly know."

"No, of course you don't," Elizabeth said, realizing she was losing Mrs. Hogan's confidence. "Wait, I *have* it!" Elizabeth ran to the bed and pointed to the paper. "Read what it says they believe I was wearing when I left."

"I don't need to read it. They said it was green—green trimmed in black. Or they thought maybe it could be a brown skirt with a cream jacket—"

"Or," Elizabeth finished triumphantly as she opened the two valises that held what few articles of clothing she'd taken, "they thought it could be a gray traveling costume, didn't they?"

Mrs. Hogan nodded, and Elizabeth dragged all the clothes out of the valises and dumped them on the bed in triumph. She knew from the woman's face that she believed Elizabeth, and that she would be able to make her husband believe her as well.

Swinging around, Elizabeth began campaigning against a harassed Mr. Hogan. "I need to get back to London at once, and it would be much faster by boat."

"There's a ship due in next week what goes ter—"

"Mr. Hogan, I cannot wait. The trial began three days ago. For all I know, they've convicted my husband of murdering me, and they're planning to hang him."

"But," he cried irritably, "you ain't dead!"

"Exactly. Which is why I have to go there and prove it to them. And I can't wait for ships to come into port. I will give you anything you ask if you'll take me to Tilbery in your boat. From there the roads are good, and I can hire a coach for the rest of the journey."

"I don't know, missus. I'd like ter help, but the fishin' has been good jes' now, an' . . ." He saw her look of fierce alarm and glanced helplessly at his wife, lifting his hands in a shrug. Mrs. Hogan hesitated, then she nodded. "You will take her, John."

Wrapping the woman in a tight hug, Elizabeth said, "Thank you—both of you. Mr. Hogan, how much would you earn for a week's excellent catch?"

He told her, and Elizabeth reached into her reticule, extracted some bills, counted them, and thrust them into his hands, squeezing his fingers closed over them. "That is five times the amount you named," she told him. It was the first time in all her life Elizabeth Cameron Thornton had ever paid more than she absolutely had to for anything. "Can we leave tonight?"

"I—I s'pose, but it ain't wise to be out there at night."

"It has to be tonight. I can't spare a moment." Elizabeth shook off the unspeakable notion that she might already be too late.

"What's going on in here?" Robert's voice rose in surprise as he noticed Elizabeth's clothing tumbled onto the bed. Then his gaze riveted on the newspaper, and his eyes narrowed in anger. "I told you—" he began, turning furiously on the Hogans.

"Robert, you and I need to talk," Elizabeth interrupted. "Alone."

"John," said Mrs. Hogan, "I think we ought to go for a nice walk."

It was at that moment that Elizabeth realized for the first time that Robert must have had the newspaper hidden from her because he already knew what was in it. The idea that he knew and hadn't told her was almost as unspeakable as discovering that Ian was being accused of their murder. "Why?" she began on a sudden burst of anger.

"Why what?" he snapped.

"Why haven't you told me about the things in the paper?"

"I didn't want to upset you."

"You *what?*" she cried, then she realized she didn't have time to debate the technicalities with him. "We have to go back."

"Go back?" he jeered. "I'm not going back. He can hang for my murder. I hope he does, the bastard!"

"Well, he's not going to hang for mine," she said, shoving her clothes into her valise.

"I'm afraid he is, Elizabeth."

It was the sudden softness of his tone, his complete indifference, that made her heart freeze and an awful, unformed suspicion begin to tear through her. "If I had left a note, as I wanted to do," she began, "none of this would have been necessary. Ian could have showed the note to . . ." She broke off as a realization hit her: According to the testimony of witnesses published in the paper, Robert had twice tried to kill Ian, not the other way around. If he'd lied about that, then he could have—*would* have lied about the rest. The old, familiar pain of betrayal began to hammer in her mind, only this time it was Robert's betrayal, not Ian's. It had never been Ian's.

"It's all a dirty lie, isn't it?" she said with a calm that belied her rioting feelings.

"He destroyed my life," Robert hissed, wrathfully looking at her as if *she* were the traitor. "And it's *not* all a lie. He had me hauled aboard one of his ships, but I escaped in San Delora."

Elizabeth drew a shaky breath. "And your back? How did that happen?"

"I had no money, damn you—nothing but the clothes on my back when I escaped. I sold myself as a bond servant to pay for passage to America," he flung at her, "and *that* is how my master dealt with bond servants who sto—who didn't work fast enough."

"You said 'stole'!" Elizabeth flung back at him in shaking fury. "Don't lie to me—not again. What about the mines— the mines you talked about—black pits in the ground?"

"I worked in a mine for a few months," he gritted, walking toward her with menacing steps.

Elizabeth snatched up her reticule and stepped back as he grabbed her shoulders in a vicious grip. "I've seen unspeakable things, done unspeakable things—and all because I tried to defend your honor while you were playing the slut for that son of a bitch."

Elizabeth tried to twist free and couldn't, and fear began spiraling through her.

"When I finally made it back here, I picked up a paper and read all about how my little sister's been doing the elegant at all the *ton* parties while I was rotting in a jungle picking sugar cane—"

"Your little sister," Elizabeth cried in a shaking voice, "was selling everything we had to pay off *your* debts, damn you! You'd have landed in debtors' gaol if you showed your face here before I stripped Havenhurst of everything!" Her voice broke, and she panicked. "Robert, please," she choked, her tear-brightened eyes searching his hard face. "Please. You're my brother. And part of what you say is true—I *am* the reason for much of what's happened to you. Not Ian, *me*. He could have done much worse to you if he were truly cruel," she argued. "He could have turned you over to the authorities. That's what most men would have done, and you would have spent the rest of your life in a dungeon."

His grip tightened, and his jaw was rigid; Elizabeth lost the battle against her tears, and even her battle to hate Robert for what he had planned to do to Ian. Drawing a suffocated breath, she laid her hand against his lean cheek while tears danced in her eyes. "Robert," she said achingly, "I love you, and I think you love me. If you're going to stop me from going to London, I'm afraid you're going to have to kill me to do it."

He shoved her backward, as if the touch of her skin suddenly burned his hands, and Elizabeth landed on the bed, still clutching her open reticule. Filled with sorrow for all he had been through, she watched him pace the room like a caged animal. Carefully she pulled all her money out and put it on the bed, then she separated some bills to hire the coach she would need. "Bobby," she said quietly. She saw his shoulders stiffen at the use of his boyhood nickname. "Please come here."

She could see the battle going on in his mind as he continued to pace, then abruptly turned and stalked over to the bed as she stood up. "There's a small fortune here," she continued in the same gentle, sad voice. "It's yours. Use it to go anywhere you want." She touched his sleeve with her left hand. "Bobby?" she whispered, searching his face. "It's over. There'll be no more vengeance. Take the money and leave on the first boat going anywhere."

He opened his mouth, and she hastily shook her head. "Don't tell me where, if that's what you were going to do. There'll be questions about you, and if I don't know the answers, you'll know you're safe from me and Ian and even English law." She saw him swallow repeatedly, his forlorn gaze on the money lying on the bed. "In six months," she continued, as desperation lent an odd clarity to her thoughts, "I'll deposit more money into any bank you tell me to use. Put an ad in the *Times* for Elizabeth—Duncan," he fabricated hastily, "and I'll deposit it in the name of whoever signs the ad."

When he seemed unable to move, she clutched her reticule tighter. "Bobby, you have to decide now. There's no time to lose."

His throat worked as he struggled to ignore what she was saying, and after an endless minute he sighed harshly, and some of the tension drained from his face. "You always had," he said in a resigned voice as his eyes roved over her features, "the softest heart." Without another word he walked over to his valise, threw what few articles of clothing he possessed into it, then snatched the money from the bed.

Elizabeth blinked back a flood of tears. "Don't forget," he whispered hoarsely, "Elizabeth Duncan."

He paused with his hand on the door latch and looked back at her. "This is enough." For a long moment brother and sister looked at each other, knowing it would be the last time; then his lips quirked in an odd little smile of pain. "Good-bye," he said. "Beth," he added.

Not until she saw him striding swiftly past the window of their room, heading for the road that twisted down to the sea, did Elizabeth relax, and then she sagged onto the bed, boneless. She bowed her head, and tears slid down her cheeks, dropping onto the reticule that covered her hand; tears of sorrow mingled with tears of relief and fell from her lashes—but all the tears were for her brother, not for her.

Because inside the reticule was her pistol.

And from the moment she realized he might not agree to let her leave, she'd been pointing it at Robert.

35

Elizabeth made the four-day journey from Helmshead to London in two and a half days—a feat she managed to accomplish by the expedient, if dangerous and costly, method of paying exorbitant sums to coachmen who reluctantly agreed to drive at night, and by sleeping in the coach. The only pauses in her headlong journey were to change horses, change clothing, and gulp down an occasional meal. Wherever they stopped, everyone from post boys to barmaids talked about the trial of Ian Thornton, Marquess of Kensington.

As the miles rolled past, day receded into black night and gray dawn, then began the cycle again, and Elizabeth listened to the pounding hooves of the horses and the terrified pounding of her heart.

At ten o'clock in the morning, six days after Ian's trial had begun, the dusty coach she'd been traveling in drew up before the Dowager Duchess of Hawthorne's London town house, and Elizabeth hurtled out of it before the steps were down, tripping on her skirts when she hit the street, then stumbling up the steps and hammering on the door.

"What in heaven's name—" the dowager began as she paused in the hall, distracted from her worried pacing by the thundering of the brass knocker.

The butler opened the door, and Elizabeth rushed past him. "Your Grace!" she panted. "I—"

"*You!*" the dowager said, staring woodenly at the disheveled, dusty woman who'd deserted her husband, caused a furor of pain and scandal, and now presented herself looking like a beautiful dust mop in the dowager's front hall when it was all but too late. "Someone should take a strap to you," she snapped.

"Ian will undoubtedly want to attend to that himself, but later. Now I need"—Elizabeth paused, trying to still her panic, to carry out her plan step by step—"I need to get into Westminster. I need your help, because they'll not want to let a woman into the House of Lords."

"The trial is in its sixth day, and I don't mind telling you it is *not* going well."

"Tell me *later!*" Elizabeth said in a commanding tone that would have done credit to the dowager herself. "Just think of someone with influence who will get me in there— someone you know. I'll do the rest once I'm inside."

Belatedly, the dowager comprehended that regardless of her unforgivable behavior, Elizabeth was now Ian Thornton's best hope for acquittal, and she finally galvanized into action. "Faulkner!" she barked, turning to address what seemed to be the staircase.

"Your grace?" asked the dowager's personal maid, who materialized on the balcony above.

"Take this young woman upstairs. Get her clothing brushed and her hair into order. Ramsey!" she snapped, motioning to the butler to follow her into the blue salon, where she sat down at her writing desk. "Take this note directly to Westminster. Tell them that it is from me and that it is to be given *immediately* to Lord Kyleton. He'll be in his seat at the House of Lords." She wrote quickly, then thrust the missive at the butler. "I've told him to stop the trial *at once*. I've also told him that we will be waiting for him in front of Westminster in my coach in one hour. He is to meet us there so that he can get us into the House."

"At once, your grace," said Ramsey, already bowing himself out of the room.

She followed him out, still issuing orders. "On the off chance Kyleton has decided to be derelict in his duties and not attend the trial today, send a footman to his house, another to White's, and another to the home of that actress he thinks no one knows he keeps in Blorind Street. You," she said, bending an icy eye on Elizabeth, "come with me. You have much to explain, madam, and you can do it while Faulkner attends to your appearance."

"I am *not*," Elizabeth said in a burst of frustrated anger, "going to think of my appearance at a time like this."

The duchess's brows shot into her hairline. "Have you come to persuade them that your husband is innocent?"

"Well, of course I have. I—"

"Then don't shame him more than you already have! You look like a refugee from a dustbin in Bedlam. You'll be lucky if they don't hang *you* for putting them to all this trouble!" She started up the staircase with Elizabeth following slowly behind, listening to her tirade with only half her mind. "Now, if your misbegotten brother would do us the honor of showing himself, your husband might not have to spend the night in a dungeon, which is *exactly* where Jordan thinks he's going to land if the prosecutors have their way."

Elizabeth stopped on the third step. "Will you *please* listen to me for a moment—" she began angrily.

"I'll listen to you all the way to Westminster," the dowager snapped back sarcastically. "I daresay all London will be eager to hear what you have to say for yourself in tomorrow's paper!"

"For the love of God!" Elizabeth cried at her back, wondering madly to whom she could turn for speedier help. An hour was an eternity! "I have *not* come merely to show that I'm alive. I can prove that Robert is alive and that he came to no harm at Ian's hands, and—"

The duchess lurched around and started down the staircase, her gaze searching Elizabeth's face with a mixture of desperation and hope. "Faulkner!" she barked without turning, "bring whatever you need. You can attend Lady Thornton in the coach!"

Fifteen minutes after the duchess's coachman pulled the horses to a teeth-jarring stop in front of Westminster, Lord Kyleton came bounding up to their coach with Ramsey trotting doggedly at his heels. "What on earth—" he began.

462

"Help us down," the dowager said. "I'll tell you what I can on the way inside. But first tell me how it's going in there."

"Not well. Badly—very badly for Kensington. The head prosecutor is in rare form. So far he's managed to present a convincing argument that even though Lady Thornton is rumored to be alive, there's no real *proof* that she is."

He turned to help Elizabeth, whom he'd never met, down from the coach while continuing to summarize the prosecutors' tactics to the duchess: "As an explanation for the rumors that Lady Thornton was seen at an inn and a posting house with an unknown man, the prosecutors are implying that Kensington hired a young couple to impersonate her and an alleged lover—an implication that sounds very plausible, since it was a long time before she was supposedly traced, and an equally long time before the jeweler came forward to give his statement. Lastly," he finished as they rushed past the vaulted entryway, "the prosecutors have also managed to make it sound very logical that if she is still alive, she is obviously in fear for her life, or she would have shown herself by now. It follows, according to them, that Lady Thornton must know firsthand what a ruthless monster her husband is. And if he *is* a ruthless monster, then it follows that he'd be fully capable of having her brother killed. The brother's disappearance is the crime they believe they have enough evidence on to send him to the gallows."

"Well, the first part of that is no longer a worry. Have you stopped the trial?" the duchess said.

"Stopped the trial!" he expostulated. "My dear duchess, it would take the prince or God to stop this trial."

"They will have to settle for Lady Thornton," the dowager snapped.

Lord Kyleton swung around, his gaze riveting on Elizabeth, and his expression went from shock to relief to biting contempt. He withdrew his gaze and quickly turned, his hand reaching for a heavy door beside which sentries stood at attention. "Stay here. I'll get a note to Kensington's barrister that he is to meet us out here. Don't speak to a soul or reveal this woman's identity until Peterson Delham comes out here. I suspect he'll want to spring this as a surprise at the right moment."

Elizabeth stood stock still, braced against the pain of his blistering look, aware of its cause: In the eyes of everyone who'd followed the stories in the newspapers, Elizabeth was either dead or an adulteress who'd deserted her husband for an unidentified lover. Since she was here in the flesh and not dead, Lord Kyleton obviously believed the latter. And Elizabeth knew that every man in the cavernous chamber on the other side of that door—including her husband—was going to think exactly the same thing of her until she proved them wrong.

The duchess had hardly spoken at all in the coach during their ride here; she'd listened closely to Elizabeth's explanation, but she obviously wanted it proven in that chamber before she accepted it herself. That withholding of faith by the dowager, who'd believed in Elizabeth when scarcely anyone else had, hurt Elizabeth far more than Lord Kyleton's condemning glance.

A few minutes later Lord Kyleton returned to the hallway. "Peterson Delham was handed my note a moment ago. We'll see what happens next."

"Did you tell him Lady Thornton is here?"

"No, your grace," he said with strained patience. "In a trial, timing can mean everything. Delham must decide what he wants to do and when he wants to do it."

Elizabeth felt like screaming with frustration at this new delay. Ian was on the other side of those doors, and she wanted to burst past them and let him see her so badly that it took a physical effort to stand rigidly still. She told herself that in a few minutes he would see her and hear what she had to say. Just a few more minutes before she could explain to him that it was Robert she'd been traveling with, not a lover. Once he understood that, he would surely forgive her—eventually—for the rest of the pain she'd caused him. Elizabeth didn't care what the hundreds of lords in that chamber thought of her; she could endure their censure for as long as she lived, so long as Ian forgave her.

After what seemed like a lifetime, not a quarter-hour, the doors opened, and Peterson Delham, Ian's barrister, strode into the hall. "What in God's name do you want, Kyleton? I've got all I can do to keep this trial from becoming a massacre, and you drag me out here in the middle of the most damning testimony yet!"

Lord Kyleton looked uneasily at the few men strolling about the hall, then he cupped his hand near Peterson Delham's ear and spoke rapidly. Delham's gaze froze on Elizabeth's face at the same instant his hand locked on Elizabeth's arm, and he marched her forcibly across the hall toward a closed door. "We'll talk in there," he said tersely.

The room into which he hauled her contained a desk and six straight-back chairs; Delham went straight to the desk and flung himself into the chair behind it. Steepling his fingers, he gazed at Elizabeth over the tops of them, scrutinizing her every feature with eyes like blue daggers, and when he spoke his voice was like a blast of ice: "Lady Thornton, how very *good* of you to find the time to pay us a social call! Would it be too pushing of me to inquire as to your whereabouts during the last six weeks?"

At that moment Elizabeth's only thought was that if Ian's barrister felt this way about her, how much more hatred she would face when she confronted Ian himself. "I—I can imagine what you must be thinking," she began in a conciliatory manner.

He interrupted sarcastically, "Oh, I don't think you can, madam. If you could, you'd be quite horrified at this moment."

"I can explain everything," Elizabeth burst out.

"Really?" he drawled blightingly. "A pity you didn't try to do that six weeks ago!"

"I'm here to do it now," Elizabeth cried, clinging to a slender thread of control.

"Begin at your leisure," he drawled sarcastically. "There are only three hundred people across the hall awaiting your convenience."

Panic and frustration made Elizabeth's voice shake and her temper explode. "Now see here, sir, I have not traveled day and night so that I can stand here while you waste time insulting me! I came here the instant I read a paper and realized my husband is in trouble. I've come to prove I'm alive and unharmed, and that my brother is also alive!"

Instead of looking pleased or relieved he looked more

snide than before. "Do tell, madam. I am on tenterhooks to hear the whole of it."

"Why are you doing this?" Elizabeth cried. "For the love of heaven, I'm on your side!"

"Thank God we don't have more like you."

Elizabeth steadfastly ignored that and launched into a swift but complete version of everything that had happened from the moment Robert came up behind her at Havenhurst. Finished, she stood up, ready to go in and tell everyone across the hall the same thing, but Delham continued to pillory her with his gaze, watching her in silence above his steepled fingertips. "Are we supposed to believe that Banbury tale?" he snapped at last. "Your brother is alive, but he isn't here. Are we supposed to accept the word of a married woman who brazenly traveled as man and wife with another man—"

"With my *brother,*" Elizabeth retorted, bracing her palms on the desk, as if by sheer proximity she could make him understand.

"So *you* want us to believe. Why, Lady Thornton? Why this sudden interest in your husband's well-being?"

"Delham!" the duchess barked. "Are you mad? Anyone can see she's telling the truth—even I—and I wasn't inclined to believe a word she said when she arrived at my house! You are tearing into her for no reason—"

Without moving his eyes from Elizabeth, Mr. Delham said shortly, "Your grace, what I've been doing is nothing to what the prosecution will try to do to her story. If she can't hold up in here, she hasn't a chance out there!"

"I don't understand this at all!" Elizabeth cried with panic and fury. "By being here I can disprove that my husband has done away with me. And I have a letter from Mrs. Hogan describing my brother in detail and stating that we were together. She will come here herself if you need her, only she is with child and couldn't travel as quickly as I had to do. This is a trial to prove whether or not my husband is guilty of those crimes. I know the truth, and I can prove he isn't."

"You're mistaken, Lady Thornton," Delham said in a bitter voice. "Because of its sensational nature and the wild conjecture in the press, this is no longer a quest for truth and justice in the House of Lords. This is now an amphitheater, and the prosecution is in the center of the stage, playing a starring role before an audience of thousands all over England who will read about it in the papers. They're bent on giving a stellar performance, and they've been doing just that. Very well," he said after a moment. "Let's see how well you can deal with them."

Elizabeth was so relieved to see him stand up at last that not even his last remarks about the prosecution's motives had any weight with her. "I've told you everything exactly as it happened, and I've brought Mrs. Hogan's letter here to verify the part about Robert. She will come here herself, as I said, if it's necessary. She can describe him for everyone and even identify him from portraits I have of him—"

"Perhaps. Perhaps not. Perhaps you've described him well for her and paid her to do this," he remarked, again assuming the prosecutor's role. *"Have* you promised her money for coming here, by the way?"

"Yes, but—"

"Never mind," he clipped angrily. "It doesn't matter."

"It doesn't matter?" she repeated dumbly. "But Lord Kyleton said the prosecution's best case, and most damning case, has always been about my brother."

"As I've just told you," he said coldly, "it is not my primary concern at this moment. I'm going to put you where you can hear what I'm saying for the next few moments without being seen by anyone. My assistant will come to escort you to the witness box."

"Will—will you tell Ian I'm here?" she asked in a suffocated little voice.

"Absolutely not. I want him to have his first glimpse of you along with everyone else. I want them to see his initial reaction and judge its validity." With the duchess following behind he led them to another door, then stepped aside, and Elizabeth realized they were in a secluded alcove where they could see everything and everyone without being seen. Her pulse began to race as her senses tried to take in the entire kaleidoscope of color and movement and sound. The long, chamber with its high, vaulted ceilings was buzzing loudly with hundreds of muted conversations taking place in the galleries above and on the benches below, where lords of the realm sat, waiting impatiently for the trial to continue.

Not far from their alcove the scarlet-robed and bewigged Lord Chancellor was seated on the traditional red Woolsack, from where he would preside over the trial.

Below and about him were more grim-faced men in scarlet robes and powdered wigs, including eight judges and the Crown's prosecutors. Seated at another table were men whom Elizabeth presumed to be Ian's solicitors and their clerks, more grim-faced men in scarlet robes and powdered wigs. Elizabeth watched Peterson Delham striding forward down the aisle, and she tried desperately to see around him. Surely Ian would be seated at whatever table . . . her frantic gaze skidded to a stop, riveting on his beloved face. His name rose to her lips, and she bit down to stop herself from crying out to him that she was there. At the same time a teary smile touched her lips, because everything about him—even the nonchalant way he was sitting—was so achingly, beautifully familiar. Other accused men must surely have sat at rigid and respectful attention, but not Ian, she realized with a pang of pride and a twinge of alarm. As if he intended to display his utter contempt for the legality, the validity, of the proceedings against him, Ian was sitting in the accused box, his right elbow resting on the polished wooden ledge that surrounded him, his booted foot propped atop his knee. He looked dispassionate, cold, and in complete control.

"I trust that you're ready to begin again, Mr. Delham," the Lord Chancellor said irritably, and the instant his voice rose the great hall grew instantly quiet. In the galleries above and on the benches below, lords stiffened with attention and turned alertly toward the Chancellor—everyone did. Everyone, Elizabeth noted, except for Ian, who continued to lounge in his chair, looking impatient now, as if the trial was a farce taking his time away from weightier matters.

"I apologize again for this delay, my lords," Delham said after pausing to whisper something to the youngest of Ian's solicitors, who was seated at a table near Delham. The young man arose abruptly and started around the perimeter of the room—heading, Elizabeth realized, straight toward her. Turning back to the Lord Chancellor, Delham said with extreme courtesy, "My Lord, if you will permit me a little leeway in procedure at this time, I believe we can resolve the entire issue at hand without further debate or calling of witnesses."

"Explain your meaning, Mr. Delham," he commanded curtly.

"I wish to call a surprise witness to the witness box and to be permitted to ask her only one question. Afterward my lord prosecutor may question her at any length, and to any degree he desires."

The Lord Chancellor turned to consult with a man Elizabeth surmised must be the head prosecutor the Attorney-General. "Have you any objection, Lord Sutherland?"

Lord Sutherland arose, a tall man with a hawk nose and thin lips, garbed in the requisite scarlet robes and powdered wig. "Certainly not, my lord," he said in a tone that was almost snide. "We've waited for Mr. Delham twice already today. What is one more delay in the execution of English justice?"

"Bring your witness forward, Mr. Delham. And after this I'll countenance no more delays in these proceedings. Is that understood?"

Elizabeth actually jumped when the young solicitor stepped into the alcove and touched her arm. Her eyes riveted on Ian, she started forward on wooden legs, her heart thundering against her ribs, and that was *before* Peterson Delham said in a voice that carried to the highest tiers of seats, "My lords, we call to the witness box the Marchioness of Kensington!"

Waves of shock and tension seemed to scream through the huge chamber. Everyone leaned forward in their seats, but Elizabeth didn't notice that. Her eyes were on Ian; she saw his entire body stiffen, saw his gaze snap to her face . . . and then his face hardened into a mask of freezing rage, his amber eyes turning an icy, metallic gold.

Shaking beneath the blast of his gaze, Elizabeth walked into the witness box and repeated the oath that was being read to her. Then Peterson Delham was strolling forward. "Will you state your name, please, for the benefit and hearing of all within these chambers?"

Elizabeth swallowed and, tearing her gaze from Ian's, said as loudly as she could, "Elizabeth Marie Cameron."

Pandemonium erupted all around her, and white-wigged heads tipped toward one another while the Lord Chancellor called sharply for silence.

"Will the court permit me to verify this by asking the accused if this is indeed his wife?" Delham asked when order was restored.

The Lord Chancellor's narrowed gaze swung from Elizabeth's face to Ian. "Indeed."

"Lord Thornton," Delham asked calmly, watching Ian's reaction, "is this woman before us the wife whose disappearance—whose murder—you have been accused of causing?"

Ian's jaw clenched, and he nodded curtly.

"For the information of those present, Lord Thornton has identified this witness as his wife. I have no further questions."

Elizabeth clutched the wooden edge of the witness box, her widened eyes on Peterson Delham, unable to believe he wasn't going to question her about Robert.

"*I* have *several* questions, my lords," said the Attorney-General, Lord Sutherland.

With trepidation Elizabeth watched Lord Sutherland stroll forward, but when he spoke she was staggered by the kindness in his voice. Even in her state of fright and desperation Elizabeth could actually feel the contempt, the male fury, being blasted at her from all around the chamber —everywhere but from him.

"Lady Thornton," Lord Sutherland began, looking confused and almost relieved that she was here to clear up matters. "Please, there is no need to look frightened. I have only a few questions. Would you kindly tell us what brings you here at this late date, in what is obviously a state of great anxiety, to reveal your presence?"

"I—I came because I discovered that my husband is accused of murdering my brother and me," Elizabeth said, trying to speak loudly enough to be heard across the echoing chamber.

"Where have you been until now?"

"I've been in Helmshead with my brother, Rob—"

"Did she say *brother?*" demanded one of the Crown's solicitors. Lord Sutherland suffered the same shock that rocketed through the chambers causing another outbreak of conversation, which in turn caused the Lord Chancellor to call for order. The prosecutor's shock, however, did not last very long. Recovering almost at once, he said, "You have come here to tell us that not only are you alive and unharmed," he summarized thoughtfully, "but that you have been with the brother who has been missing for two years—the brother of whom no one has been able to find a trace—not your investigator, Mr. Wordsworth, nor the Crown's investigators, nor even those hired by your husband?"

Elizabeth's startled gaze flew to Ian and ricocheted in alarm from the glacial hatred on his face. "Yes, that's correct."

"And where is this brother?" For emphasis he made a sweeping gesture and looked around as if searching for Robert. "Have you brought him so that we can see him as we're seeing you—alive and unharmed?"

"No," Elizabeth said. "I haven't, but—"

"Please just answer my questions," Lord Sutherland admonished. For a long moment he looked nonplussed, then he said, "Lady Thornton, I believe we would all like to hear why you left the safety and comfort of your home six weeks ago, fled in secrecy from your husband, and have now returned at this last desperate hour to plead that we have all somehow made a mistake in thinking your life or your brother's life could be in danger. Begin at the beginning, if you please."

Elizabeth was so relieved that she was being given a chance to tell her story that she related it verbatim, just as she'd rehearsed it in the coach over and over again—carefully leaving out parts that would make Robert seem like a liar or a madman bent on having Ian hang for murders he didn't commit. With careful, rehearsed words she swiftly painted Robert as she truly saw him—a young man who had been driven by pain and deprivation to wrongly seek vengeance against her husband; a young man whom her husband had saved from the gallows or lifelong imprisonment by charitably having him put on a ship and taken abroad; a young man who had then suffered, through his own unintentional actions, great trials and even vicious beatings for which he had wrongly blamed Ian Thornton.

Because she was desperate and frightened and had practiced the speech so many times, Elizabeth delivered her testimony with the flat unemotionalism of a rehearsed speech, and in a surprisingly short time she was done. The only time she faltered was when she had to confess that she had actually believed her husband guilty of her brother's beatings. During that awful moment her gaze slid penitently to Ian, and the altered expression on his face was more terrifying because it was bored—as if she were a very poor actress playing a role in an exceedingly boring play he was being forced to watch.

Lord Sutherland broke the deafening silence that followed her testimony with a short, pitying laugh, and suddenly his eyes were piercing hers and his raised voice was hammering at her. "My dear woman, I have one question for you, and it is much like my earlier one: I want to know *why.*"

For an inexplicable reason, Elizabeth felt icy fear starting to quake through her, as if her heart understood that something awful was happening—that she had not been believed, and he was now going to make absolutely certain that she would never be. "Why—why what?" she stammered.

"*Why* have you come here to tell us such an amazing tale in hopes of saving the life of this man from whom you admit you fled weeks ago?"

Elizabeth looked beseechingly to Peterson Delham, who shrugged as if in resigned disgust. In her petrified state she remembered his words in the anteroom, and now she understood them: "*What I've been doing to her is nothing to what the prosecution will do to her story. . . . This is no longer a quest for truth and justice . . . this is an amphitheater, and the prosecution is bent on giving a stellar performance. . . .*"

"Lady Thornton!" the prosecutor rapped out, and he began firing questions at her so rapidly that she could scarcely keep track of them. "Tell us the truth, Lady Thornton. Did that man"—his finger pointed accusingly to where Ian was sitting, out of Elizabeth's vision—"find you and bribe you to come back here and tell us this absurd tale? Or did he find you and threaten your life if you didn't come here today? Isn't it true that you have no idea where your brother is? Isn't it true that by your own admission a few moments ago you fled in terror for your life from this cruel man? Isn't it true that you are afraid of further cruelty from him—"

"No!" Elizabeth cried. Her gaze raced over the male faces around and above her, and she could see not one that looked anything but either dubious or contemptuous of the truths she had told.

"No further questions!"

"Wait!" In that infinitesimal moment of time Elizabeth realized that if she couldn't convince them she was telling the truth, she might be able to convince them she was too stupid to make up such a lie. "Yes, my lord," her voice rang out. "I cannot deny it—about his cruelty, I mean."

Sutherland swung around, his eyes lighting up, and renewed excitement throbbed in the great chamber. "You admit this is a cruel man?"

"Yes, I do," Elizabeth emphatically declared.

"My dear, poor woman, could you tell us—all of us—some examples of his cruelty?"

"Yes, and when I do, I know you will all understand how truly cruel my husband can be and why I ran off with Robert—my brother, that is." Madly, she tried to think of half-truths that would not constitute perjury, and she remembered Ian's words the night he came looking for her at Havenhurst.

"Yes, go on." Everyone in the galleries leaned forward in unison, and Elizabeth had the feeling the whole building was tipping toward her. "When was the last time your husband was cruel?"

"Well, just before I left he threatened to cut off my allowance—I had overspent it, and I hated to admit it."

"You were afraid he would beat you for it?"

473

"No, I was afraid he wouldn't give me *more* until next quarter!"

Someone in the gallery laughed, then the sound was instantly choked. Sutherland started to frown darkly, but Elizabeth plunged ahead. "My husband and I were discussing that very thing—my allowance, I mean—two nights before I ran away with Bobbie."

"And did he become abusive during that discussion? Is that the night your maid testified that you were weeping?"

"Yes, I believe it was!"

"Why were you weeping, Lady Thornton?"

The galleries tipped further toward her.

"I was in a terrible taking," Elizabeth said, stating a fact. "I wanted to go away with Bobbie. In order to do it, I had to sell my lovely emeralds, which Lord Thornton gave me." Seized with inspiration, she leaned confiding inches toward the Lord Chancellor upon the woolsack. "I *knew* he would buy me more, you know." Startled laughter rang out from the galleries, and it was the encouragement Elizabeth desperately needed.

Lord Sutherland, however, wasn't laughing. He sensed that she was trying to dupe him, but with all the arrogance typical of most of his sex, he could not believe she was smart enough to actually attempt, let alone accomplish it. "I'm supposed to believe you sold your emeralds out of some freakish start—out of a frivolous desire to go off with a man you claim was your brother?"

"Goodness, I don't know what you are *supposed* to believe. I only know I did it."

"Madam!" he snapped. "You were on the verge of *tears*, according to the jeweler to whom you sold them. If you were in a frivolous mood, why were you on the verge of tears?"

Elizabeth gave him a vacuous look. "I *liked* my emeralds."

Guffaws erupted from the floor to the rafters. Elizabeth waited until they were finished before she leaned forward and said in a proud, confiding tone, "My husband often says that emeralds match my eyes. Isn't that sweet?"

Sutherland was beginning to grind his teeth, Elizabeth noted. Afraid to look at Ian, she cast a quick glance at

Peterson Delham and saw him watching her alertly with something that might well have been admiration.

"So!" Sutherland boomed in a voice that was nearly a rant. "We are *now* supposed to believe that you weren't really afraid of your husband?"

"Of course I was. Didn't I just explain how very cruel he can be?" she asked with another vacuous look. "Naturally, when Bobbie showed me his back I couldn't help thinking that a man who would threaten to cut off his wife's allowance would be capable of *anything*—"

Loud guffaws lasted much longer this time, and even after they died down, Elizabeth noticed derisive grins where before there had been condemnation and disbelief. "And," Sutherland boomed, when he could be heard again, "we are also supposed to believe that you ran off with a man you claim is your brother and have been cozily in England somewhere—"

Elizabeth nodded emphatically and helpfully provided, "In Helmshead—it is the *sweetest* village by the sea. I was having a very pleas—very *peaceful* time until I read the paper and realized my husband was on trial. Bobbie didn't think I should come back at all, because he was still provoked about being put on one of my husband's ships. But I thought I ought."

"And what," Sutherland gritted, "do you claim is the reason you decided you ought?"

"I didn't think Lord Thornton would like being hanged—" More mirth exploded through the House, and Elizabeth had to wait for a full minute before she could continue. "And so I gave Bobbie my money, and he went on to have his own agreeable life, as I said earlier."

"Lady Thornton," Sutherland said in an awful, silky voice that made Elizabeth shake inside, "does the word 'perjury' have any meaning to you?"

"I believe," Elizabeth said, "it means to tell a lie in a place like this."

"Do you know how the Crown punishes perjurers? They are sentenced to gaol, and they live their lives in a dark, dank cell. Would you want that to happen to you?"

"It certainly doesn't sound very agreeable," Elizabeth said. "Would I be able to take my jewels and gowns?"

Shouts of laughter shook the chandeliers that hung from the vaulted ceilings.

"No, you would not!"

"Then I'm certainly happy I haven't lied."

Sutherland was no longer certain whether he'd been duped, but he sensed that he'd lost his effort to make Elizabeth sound like a clever, scheming adulteress or a terrified, intimidated wife. The bizarre story of her flight with her brother had now taken on a certain absurd credibility, and he realized it with a sinking heart and a furious glower. "Madam, would you perjure yourself to protect that man?" His arm swung toward Ian, and Elizabeth's gaze followed helplessly. Her heart froze with terror when she saw that, if anything, Ian looked more bored, more coldly remote and unmoved than he had before.

"I asked you," Sutherland boomed, "if you would perjure yourself to save that man from going to the gallows next month."

Elizabeth would have died to save him. Tearing her gaze from Ian's terrifying face, she pinned a blank smile on her face. "Next month? What a disagreeable thing to suggest! Why, next month is—is Lady Northam's ball, and Kensington very specifically promised that we would go"— thunderous guffaws exploded, rocking the rafters, drowning out Elizabeth's last words—"and that I could have a new fur!"

Elizabeth waited, sensing that she had succeeded, not because her performance had been so convincing, but because many of the lords had wives who never thought beyond the next gown or ball or fur, and so she seemed entirely believable to them.

"No further questions!" Sutherland rapped out, casting a contemptuous glance over her.

Peterson Delham slowly arose, and though his expression was carefully blank, even bemused, Elizabeth sensed rather than saw that he was silently applauding her. "Lady Thornton," he said in formal tones, "is there anything else you have to say to this court?"

She realized that he *wanted* her to say something else, and in her state of relieved exhaustion Elizabeth couldn't think what it was. She said the only thing she could think of, and she knew soon after she began speaking that he was pleased. "Yes, my lord. I wish to say how very sorry I am for the bother Bobby and I have caused everyone. I was wrong to believe him and to dash off without a word to anyone. And it was wrong of him to remain so angry with my husband all this time over what was, after all, rather an act of kindness on his part." She sensed that she was going too far, sounding too sensible, and she hastily added, "If Kensington had had Bobby tossed into gaol for trying to shoot him, I daresay Bobby would have found it nearly as disagreeable a place as I. He is," she confided, "a very fastidious person!"

"Lady Thornton!" the Lord Chancellor said when the fresh waves of laughter had diminished to ripples. "You may step down." At the scathing tone in his voice Elizabeth dared a look in his direction, and then she almost missed her step when she saw the furious scorn on his face. The other lords might think her an incorrigible henwit, but the Lord Chancellor looked as if he would personally have enjoyed throttling her.

On shaking limbs Elizabeth permitted Peterson Delham's assistant to escort her from the hall, but when they came to the far wall and he reached for the door leading to the corridor, Elizabeth shook her head and looked imploringly into his eyes. "Please," she whispered, already watching over his shoulder, trying to see what would happen next, "let me stay over there in the alcove. Don't make me wait out there, wondering," she begged, watching a man striding swiftly down the long aisle from the main doors at the back of the chambers, heading straight for Peterson Delham.

"Very well," he agreed uneasily after a moment, "but don't make a sound. This will all be over soon," he added consolingly.

"Do you mean," she whispered, her gaze glued to the man walking up to Peterson Delham, "that I did well enough up here for them to release my husband now?"

"No, my lady. Hush, now. And don't worry."

Elizabeth was more puzzled than worried at that moment, because for the first time since she'd seen him, Ian seemed to take an interest in something that was happening. He glanced briefly toward the man talking to Peterson Delham, and for a split second she actually thought she saw a look of grim amusement flicker on Ian's impassive face. Following the assistant into the alcove, she stood beside the dowager, unaware of the gruff, approving look that lady was giving her. "What's happening?" she asked the assistant when he evidenced no sign of needing to return to his seat.

"He's going to pull it off!" the young man said, grinning.

"My Lord Chancellor." Peterson Delham raised his voice as he nodded quickly at the man who'd been talking to him. "With the court's permission—indulgence, I might say—I would like to present one more witness who, we believe, will provide indisputable proof that no harm came to Robert Cameron as a direct or indirect result of the time he spent on board the ship *Arianna*. If this proof is acceptable to the court, then I feel confident this entire matter can be put to rest in short order."

"I feel no such confidence!" snapped Lord Sutherland.

Even from there Elizabeth could see the Lord Chancellor's profile harden as he turned to glance at the prosecutor.

"Let us hope for the best," the Lord Chancellor told Lord Sutherland. "This trial has already exceeded the limits of decorum and taste, and that is due in no small part, my lord, to you." Glancing at Peterson Delham, he said irritably, "Proceed!"

"Thank you, my Lord Chancellor. We call to the witness box Captain George Granthome."

Elizabeth's breath stopped as a suspicion of what was going to happen was born in her mind. From the side of the room the doors opened, and a tall, muscular man came striding down the aisle. Behind him a cluster of burly, tanned, and weathered men gathered as if waiting to be called. Seamen. She'd seen enough fishermen in Helmshead to recognize those unmistakable features. The man named Captain Granthome took the witness box, and from the moment he began to answer Peterson Delham's questions, Elizabeth realized Ian's acquittal of Robert's "death" had been a foregone conclusion before she ever walked in. Captain Granthome testified to Robert's treatment on board the *Arianna* and to the fact that he had escaped when the ship made an unscheduled stop for repairs. And he smoothly managed to indicate that his entire crew was also prepared to testify.

It hit Elizabeth then that all her terror during the trip down, all her fears while she testified, were actually groundless. With Ian able to prove that Robert had come to no harm at his hands, Elizabeth's disappearance would have lost all sinister implications.

She rounded in angry stupefaction on the grinning assistant, who was listening attentively to the captain's testimony. "Why on earth didn't you say in the papers what had happened to my brother? Obviously my husband and Mr. Delham knew it. And you must have known you could provide the captain and crew to prove it."

Reluctantly, the assistant tore his gaze from the bench and said softly, "It was your husband's idea to wait until the trial was under way before springing his defense on them."

"But why?"

"Because our illustrious prosecutor and his staff showed no sign of dropping the case no matter what we claimed. They believed their evidence was enough for a conviction, and if we'd told them about the *Arianna,* they'd have kept stalling for time to look for more evidence to disprove Captain Granthome's potential testimony. Moreover, the *Arianna* and her crew were on a voyage, and we weren't completely certain we could locate them and get them back here in time to testify. Now our frustrated Lord Prosecutor has nothing readily at hand to use as rebuttal, because he didn't anticipate this. And if your brother is never seen again, there's still no point in his digging about for more circumstantial, incriminating evidence, because even if he found it—which he won't—your husband cannot be tried twice for the same crime."

Now Elizabeth understood why Ian had looked bored and disinterested, even though she still couldn't comprehend why he'd never softened when she'd explained it was Robert he was with, not a lover, and offered the proof of Mrs. Hogan's letter and even the promise of her testimony.

"Your husband orchestrated the entire maneuver," the assistant said, looking admiringly at Ian, who was being addressed by the Lord Chancellor. "Planned his own defense. Brilliant man, your husband. Oh, and by the by, Mr. Delham said to tell you that you were splendid up there."

From that point on, the rest of the proceedings seemed to

move with the swiftness of a necessary, but meaningless ritual. Obviously realizing that he hadn't a chance of discrediting the testimony of the *Arianna's* entire crew Lord Sutherland put only a few perfunctory questions to Captain Granthome, and then allowed him to be dismissed. After that, there remained only the closing statements of both barristers, and then the Lord Chancellor called for a vote.

In renewed tension, Elizabeth listened and watched as the Lord High Steward called out the name of each lord. One after another, each peer arose, placed his right hand upon his breast, and declared either "Not guilty upon my honor," or "Guilty upon my honor." The final vote was 324 to 14, in favor of acquittal. The dissenters, Peterson Delham's assistant whispered to Elizabeth were men who were either biased against Ian for personal reasons, or else they doubted the reliability of her testimony and Captain Granthome's.

Elizabeth scarcely heard that. All she cared about was that the majority were for acquittal, and that the Lord Chancellor had finally turned to pronounce judgment and was speaking:

"Lord Thornton," the Lord Chancellor was saying to Ian as Ian slowly rose, "it is the finding of this commission that you are innocent of all charges against you. You are free to leave." He paused as if debating something, then said, in what struck Elizabeth as a discordant note of humor, "I would like to suggest informally that if it is your intention to abide under the same roof as your wife tonight, you seriously reconsider that notion. In your place I would be sorely tempted to commit the act that you have already been accused of committing. Although," he added as laughter began to rumble through the galleries, "I feel certain you could count on an acquittal here on grounds of justifiable cause."

Elizabeth closed her eyes against the shame that she hadn't let herself feel over her testimony. She told herself that it was better to be mistaken for an absurd henwit than a scheming adulteress, but when she opened them again and saw Ian striding up the aisle, away from her, she no longer cared one way or another.

"Come, Elizabeth," the dowager said, gently putting her hand on Elizabeth's arm. "I've no doubt the press will be out there. The sooner we leave, the better our chance to evade them."

That proved to be pure whimsy, Elizabeth saw as soon as they emerged into the sunlight. The press, and a mob of spectators who'd come to hear firsthand news of the day's trial, had gathered in front of Ian's path. Instead of trying to dash around them Ian shouldered his way through them, his jaw clenched. Drowning in agony, Elizabeth watched as they called epithets and accusations at him. "Oh, my God," she said, "look what I've done to him."

The moment Ian's coach thundered away, the crowd turned, looking for new prey as the lords began emerging from the building.

"It's her!" a man from the *Gazette* who wrote about the doings of the *ton* shouted, pointing toward Elizabeth, and suddenly the press and the mob of spectators were descending on her in terrifying numbers. "Quick, Lady Thornton," an unfamiliar young man said urgently, dragging her back into the building, "follow me. There's another way out around the corner."

Elizabeth obeyed automatically, clutching the duchess's arm as they plowed back through the lords who were heading for the doors. "Which coach is yours?" he asked, looking from one to the other.

The duchess described her vehicle, and he nodded. "Stay here. Don't go out there. I'll have your coachman drive around this side to fetch you."

Ten minutes later the duchess's coach had made its way to the side, and they were inside its safety. Elizabeth leaned out the door. "Thank you," she told the young man, waiting for him to give his name.

He tipped his hat. "Thomas Tyson, Lady Thornton, from the *Times*. No, don't look panicked," he said reassuringly. "I haven't any notion of trying to barge in there with you now. Accosting ladies in coaches is not at all my style." For emphasis he closed the door of the coach.

"In that case," Elizabeth told him through the open window with her best attempt at a grateful smile, "I'm afraid you're not going to do very well as a journalist."

"Perhaps you'd consent to talk to me another time—in private?"

"Perhaps," Elizabeth said vaguely as their coachman sent the horses off at a slow trot, wending their way around the vehicles already crowding into the busy street.

Closing her eyes, Elizabeth leaned her head wearily against the squabs. The image of Ian being chased by a mob and called "Murderer!" and "Wife killer!" dug viciously into Elizabeth's battered senses. In an aching whisper she asked the duchess, "How long have they been doing that to him? Mobbing him and cursing him?"

"Over a month."

Elizabeth drew a shattered breath, her voice filled with tears. "Do you have any idea how proud Ian is?" she whispered brokenly. "He is so proud . . . and I made an accused murderer out of him. Tomorrow he'll be a public joke."

The dowager hesitated and then said brusquely, "He is a strong man who has never cared for anyone's opinion— except perhaps yours and Jordan's and a very few other's. In any case, I daresay you, not Kensington, will look the fool in tomorrow's papers."

"Will you take me to the house?"

"The one on Promenade?"

Elizabeth was momentarily shocked out of her misery. "No, of course not. Our house on Upper Brook Street."

"I do not think," the duchess said sternly, "that is a wise idea. You heard what the Lord Chancellor said."

Elizabeth disagreed, with only a tremor of doubt. "I would much rather face Ian now than dread doing it for an entire night."

The dowager, obviously determined to give Ian time to get his temper under control, remembered a pressing need to stop at the home of an ailing friend, and then at another. By the time they finally arrived in Upper Brook Street it was nearly dark, and Elizabeth was quaking with nerves—and that was before their own butler looked at her as if she were beneath contempt. Obviously Ian had returned, and the servants' grapevine already had the news of Elizabeth's testimony in the House of Lords. "Where is my husband, Dolton?" she asked him.

"In his study," Dolton said, stepping back from the door.

Elizabeth's gaze riveted on the trunks already standing in the hall and the servants carrying more of them downstairs. Her heart hammering wildly, she walked swiftly down the hall and into Ian's study, coming to a halt a few feet inside, pausing to gather her wits before he turned and saw her. He was holding a drink in his hand, staring down into the fireplace. He'd removed his jacket and rolled up his shirtsleeves, and Elizabeth saw with a fresh pang of remorse that he was even thinner than he'd seemed in the House. She tried to think how to begin, and because she was so overwhelmed with emotions and explanations she tackled the least important—but most immediate—problem first: the trunks in the hall. "Are—are you leaving?"

She saw his shoulders stiffen at the sound of her voice, and when he turned and looked at her, she could almost feel the effort he was exerting to keep his rage under control. *"You're* leaving," he bit out.

In silent, helpless protest Elizabeth shook her head and started slowly across the carpet, dimly aware that this was worse, much worse than merely standing up in front of several hundred lords in the House.

"I wouldn't do that, if I were you," he warned softly.

"Do—do what?" Elizabeth said shakily.

"Get any nearer to me."

She stopped cold, her mind registering the physical threat in his voice, refusing to believe it, her gaze searching his granite features.

"Ian," she began, stretching her hand out in a gesture of mute appeal, then letting it fall to her side when her beseeching move got nothing from him but a blast of contempt from his eyes. "I realize," she began again, her voice trembling with emotion while she tried to think how to begin to diffuse his wrath, "that you must despise me for what I've done."

"You're right."

"But," Elizabeth continued bravely, "I am prepared to do anything, *anything* to try to atone for it. No matter how it must seem to you now, I never stopped loving—"

His voice cracked like a whiplash. "Shut up!"

"No, you have to listen to me," she said, speaking more

quickly now, driven by panic and an awful sense of foreboding that nothing she could do or say would ever make him soften. "I never stopped loving you, even when I—"

"I'm *warning* you, Elizabeth," he said in a murderous voice, *"shut up* and get out! Get out of my house and out of my life!"

"Is—is it Robert? I mean, do you not believe Robert was the man I was with?"

"I don't give a damn *who* the son of a bitch was."

Elizabeth began to quake in genuine terror, because he meant that—she could see that he did. "It was Robert, exactly as I said," she continued haltingly. "I can prove it to you beyond any doubt, if you'll let me."

He laughed at that, a short, strangled laugh that was more deadly and final than his anger had been. "Elizabeth, I wouldn't believe you if I'd *seen* you with him. Am I making myself clear? You are a consummate liar and a magnificent actress."

"If you're saying that be-because of the foolish things I said in the witness box, you s-surely must know why I did it."

His contemptuous gaze raked her. "Of course I know why you did it! It was a means to an end—the same reason you've had for everything you do. You'd sleep with a snake if it gave you a means to an end."

"Why are you saying this?" she cried.

"Because on the same day your investigator told you I was responsible for your brother's disappearance, you stood beside me in a goddamned *church* and vowed to love me unto death! You were willing to marry a man you believed could be a murderer, to *sleep* with a murderer."

"You don't believe that! I can prove it somehow—I know I can, if you'll just give me a chance—"

"No."

"Ian—"

"I don't want proof."

"I love you," she said brokenly.

"I don't want your 'love,' and I don't want you. Now—" He glanced up when Dolton knocked on the door.

"Mr. Larimore is here, my lord."

"Tell him I'll be with him directly," Ian announced, and

Elizabeth gaped at him. "You—you're going to have a business meeting *now?*"

"Not exactly, my love. I've sent for Larimore for a different reason this time."

Nameless fright quaked down Elizabeth's spine at his tone. "What—what other reason would you have for summoning a solicitor at a time like this?"

"I'm starting divorce proceedings, Elizabeth."

"You're *what?*" she breathed, and she felt the room whirl. "On what grounds—my stupidity?"

"Desertion," he bit out.

At that moment Elizabeth would have said or done anything to reach him. She could not believe, actually could not comprehend that the tender, passionate man who had loved and teased her could be doing this to her—without listening to reason, without even giving her a chance to explain. Her eyes filled with tears of love and terror as she tried brokenly to tease him. "You're going to look extremely silly, darling, if you claim desertion in court, because I'll be standing right behind you claiming I'm more than willing to keep my vows."

Ian tore his gaze from the love in her eyes. "If you aren't out of this house in three minutes," he warned icily, "I'll change the grounds to adultery."

"I have *not* committed adultery."

"Maybe not, but you'll have a hell of a time proving you *haven't* done something. I've had some experience in that area. Now, for the last time, get out of my life. It's over." To prove it, he walked over and sat down at his desk, reaching behind him to pull the bell cord. "Bring Larimore in," he instructed Dolton, who appeared almost instantly.

Elizabeth stiffened, thinking wildly for some way to reach him before he took irrevocable steps to banish her. Every fiber of her being believed he loved her. Surely, if one loved another deeply enough to be hurt like this . . . It hit her then, what he was doing and why, and she turned on him while the vicar's story about Ian's actions after his parents' death seared her mind. She, however, was *not* a Labrador retriever who could be shoved away and out of his life.

Turning, she walked over to his desk, leaning her damp palms on it, waiting until he was forced to meet her gaze.

Looking like a courageous, heartbroken angel, Elizabeth faced her adversary across his desk, her voice shaking with love. "Listen carefully to me, darling, because I'm giving you fair warning that I won't let you do this to us. You gave me your love, and I will not let you take it away. The harder you try, the harder I'll fight you. I'll haunt your dreams at night, exactly the way you've haunted mine every night I was away from you. You'll lie awake in bed at night, wanting me, and you'll know I'm lying awake, wanting you. And when you cannot stand it anymore," she promised achingly, "you'll come back to me, and I'll be there, waiting for you. I'll cry in your arms, and I'll tell you I'm sorry for everything I've done, and you'll help me find a way to forgive myself—"

"Damn you!" he bit out, his face white with fury. "What does it take to make you stop?"

Elizabeth flinched from the hatred in the voice she loved and drew a shaking breath, praying she could finish without starting to cry. "I've hurt you terribly, my love, and I'll hurt you again during the next fifty years. And you are going to hurt me, Ian—never, I hope, as much as you are hurting me now. But if that's the way it has to be, then I'll endure it, because the only alternative is to live without you, and that is no life at all. The difference is that I know it, and you don't—not yet."

"Are you finished now?"

"Not quite," she said, straightening at the sound of footsteps in the hall. "There's one more thing," she informed him, lifting her quivering chin. *"I* am not a Labrador retriever! You cannot put me out of your life, because I won't stay."

When she left, Ian stared at the empty room that had been alive with her presence but moments before, wondering what in hell she meant by her last comment. He glanced toward the door as Larimore walked in, then he nodded curtly toward the chairs in front of his desk, silently ordering the solicitor to sit down.

"I gathered from your message," Larimore said quietly, opening his legal case, "that you now wish to proceed with the divorce?"

Ian hesitated a moment while Elizabeth's heartbroken

words whirled through his mind, juxtaposed with the lies and omissions that had begun on the night they met and continued right up to their last night together. He recalled the torment of the first weeks after she'd left him and compared it to the cold, blessed numbness that had now taken its place. He looked at the solicitor, who was waiting for his answer.

And he nodded.

36

The next day Elizabeth was anxiously waiting in the hall on Promenade Street for deliveries of both the newspapers. The *Times* exonerated Ian by splashing across the front page:

MURDEROUS MARQUESS ACTUALLY HARASSED HUSBAND

The *Gazette* humorously remarked that "the Marquess of Kensington is deserving, not only of an acquittal, but of a medal for Restraint in the Face of Extreme Provocation!"

Beneath both those stories were lengthy and—for Elizabeth—deeply embarrassing accounts of her ridiculous explanations of her behavior.

The day before the trial, Ian had been shunned and suspect; the day after it, he was the recipient of most of an entire city's amused sympathy and goodwill. The balance of the populace believed that where there was accusation, there was bound to be some guilt, and that rich people bought their way out of things that poor people hanged for. Those people would continue to associate Ian's name with evil, Elizabeth knew.

Elizabeth's status had altered dramatically as well. No

longer was she an abused or adulterous wife; she was more of a celebrity admired by women with drab lives, ignored by women with no lives, and sternly frowned upon—but forgiven—by society's husbands, whose wives were very like the woman she'd seemed to be in the House of Lords. Still, in the month that followed Ian's acquittal, if it hadn't been for Roddy Carstairs, who insisted she appear in society the same week the papers announced the verdict, she might well have retired to the house on Promenade Street and hidden behind its wrought-iron gate, waiting for Ian.

That would have been the worst possible thing she could do, for she soon realized that despite her belief to the contrary, Ian evidently found it easy to thrust her out of his mind. Through Alexandra and Jordan, Elizabeth learned that Ian had resumed his work schedule as if nothing had happened, and within a week after his acquittal he was seen gambling at the Blackmore with friends, attending the opera with other friends, and generally leading the life of a busy socialite who enjoyed playing as hard as he worked.

It was not exactly the image Elizabeth had of her husband —this endless round of social activity—and she tried to ease the ache in her heart by telling herself sternly that his hectic social schedule merely proved that he was fighting a losing battle to forget that she was waiting for him. She wrote him letters; they were refused by the servants at his instruction.

Finally she decided to follow his example and keep busy, because it was the only way she could endure the waiting; but with each day that passed it became harder not to go to him and try again. They saw each other occasionally at a ball or the opera, and each time it happened Elizabeth's heart went wild and Ian's expression grew more distant. Ian's uncle had warned her it would be no use to ask Ian's forgiveness again, while his grandfather patted Elizabeth's hand and naïvely said, "He'll come around, my dear."

Alex ultimately convinced Elizabeth that perhaps a bit of competition would be the thing to bring him around. That night at Lord and Lady Franklin's ball, Elizabeth saw Ian talking with friends of his. Gathering up her courage, she flirted openly with Viscount Sheffield, watching Ian from the corner of her eye as she danced and laughed with the handsome viscount. Ian saw her—he looked straight at her, and straight through her. That evening he left the ball with Lady Jane Addison on his arm. It was the first time in their separation that he'd singled out any woman for particular attention or behaved in any way except like a married man who might not want his wife, but who was not interested in amorous affairs either.

His action made Alex angry and confused. "He's fighting the battle with *your* weapons!" she cried when Elizabeth and she were alone that night. "It is not at all the way the game is supposed to be played. He was supposed to feel jealous and come to heel! Perhaps," she said soothingly, "he *was* jealous, and he wanted to make *you* jealous."

Elizabeth smiled sadly and shook her head. "Ian once told me he's always been able to think like his opponent. He was showing me that he knew exactly what I was doing with Sheffield, and telling me not to bother trying it again. He really does want to drive me away, you see. He's not merely trying to punish me or to make me suffer a little before he takes me back."

"Do you truly think he wants to drive you away forever?" Alexandra asked miserably, sitting down on the sofa beside Elizabeth and putting her arm around her shoulders.

"I know he does," Elizabeth said.

"Then what will you do next?"

"Whatever I have to do—anything I can think of. So long as he knows there's a possibility he'll see me wherever he goes, he can't put me entirely out of his mind. I still have a chance to win."

In that Elizabeth was proved mistaken. One month after Ian's acquittal Bentner tapped on the door to the salon where Elizabeth was sitting with Alexandra. "There is a man—a Mr. Larimore," he said, recognizing the name of Ian's solicitor. "He says he has papers he must hand to you personally."

Elizabeth went pale. "Did he say what sort of papers they were?"

"He refused until I told him I wouldn't interrupt you without being able to tell you why I must."

"What sort of papers are they?" Elizabeth asked, but, God help her, she already knew.

Bentner's eyes slid away, his face harsh with sorrow. "He said they are documents pertaining to a petition for divorce."

The world reeled as Elizabeth tried to stand.

"I really think I could hate that man," Alexandra cried, wrapping her friend in a supportive hug, her voice choked with sorrow. "Even Jordan is becoming angry at him for letting this breach between you continue."

Elizabeth scarcely knew she was being consoled; the pain was so great it was actually numbing. Turning out of Alexandra's embrace, she looked at Bentner, knowing that if she accepted the papers there'd be no more delaying tactics she could use, no more hope, but the anguished uncertainty would end. That at least would give her a blessed respite from a terrible, draining torment. Gathering all her courage for one last herculean battle, Elizabeth spoke, slowly at first. "Tell Mr. Larimore that while you were having your dinner, I left the house. Tell him you checked with my maid, and that she said I planned to go to a play with"—she glanced at Alexandra for permission, and her friend nodded emphatically—"with the Duchess of Hawthorne tonight. Invent any schedule you want for me this afternoon and tomorrow—but give him details, Bentner—details that explain *why* I'm not here."

Another butler, who was not addicted to mysteries, might not have caught on so easily, but Bentner began to nod and grin. "You want to keep him looking elsewhere so you'll have time to pack and get away without his guessing you're leaving."

"Exactly," Elizabeth said with a grateful smile. "And after that," she added as he turned to do as bidden, "send a message to Mr. Thomas Tyson—the man from the *Times* who's been pleading for an interview. Tell him I will give him five minutes if he can be here this evening."

"Where will you go?" Alex asked.

"If I tell you, Alex, you must swear not to tell Ian."

"Of course I won't."

"Nor your husband. He's Ian's friend. It would be wrong to put him in the middle."

Alex nodded. "Jordan will understand that I've given my word and cannot reveal what I know, even to him."

"I'm going," Elizabeth confided quietly, "to the last place on earth Ian will think to look for me now—and the first place he'll go when he really believes he needs to find me, or find peace because he can't. I'm going to the cottage in Scotland."

"You should *not* have to do that!" Alex exclaimed loyally. "If he weren't so heartless, so unjust—"

"Before you say all that," Elizabeth said gently, "ask yourself how you would feel if Jordan made it look to all the world that you were a murderess, and then he breezed into the House of Lords in the nick of time, after putting you through humiliation and heartbreak, and made it all seem like one big joke." Alex didn't reply, but some of the anger drained from her face; more as Elizabeth continued wisely, "Ask yourself how you would feel when you found out that from the day he married you he believed there was a chance you really *were* a murderess—and how you would feel when you remembered the nights you spent together during that time. And when you've done all that, remember that in all the time I've known Ian, all he's ever done is to try in every way to make me happy."

"I—" Alex began, and then her shoulders drooped. "When you put it that way, it does give it a different perspective. I don't see how you can be so fair and objective when I cannot."

"Ian," Elizabeth teased sadly, "taught me that the quickest and best way to defeat an opponent is to first see things from his viewpoint." She sobered then. "Do you know what a post boy asked me yesterday when he realized who I was?"

When Alex shook her head, Elizabeth said guiltily, "He asked me if I was still afraid of my husband. They haven't all forgotten about it, you know. Many will never believe he's completely innocent. I made a terrible and lasting mess of things, you see."

Biting her lip to hold back her tears, Alex said, "If he hasn't gone to Scotland to get you by the time our baby comes in January, will you come to us at Hawthorne? I can't bear the thought of you spending all winter alone up there."

"Yes."

* * *

Leaning back in his chair, Ian listened to Larimore's irate summation of the wild and fruitless chase he'd been sent on for two days by Lady Thornton and her butler: "And after all that," Larimore flung out in high dudgeon, "I returned to the house on Promenade Street to demand the butler allow me past the stoop, only to have the man—"

"Slam the door in your face?" Ian suggested dispassionately.

"No, my lord, he *invited* me in," Larimore bit out. "He invited me to search the house to my complete satisfaction. She's left London," Larimore finished, avoiding his employer's narrowed gaze.

"She'll go to Havenhurst," Ian said decisively, and he gave Larimore directions to find the small estate.

When Larimore left, Ian picked up a contract he needed to read and approve; but before he'd read two lines Jordan stalked into his study unannounced, carrying a newspaper and wearing an expression Ian hadn't seen before. "Have you seen the paper today?"

Ian ignored the paper and studied his friend's angry face instead. "No, why?"

"Read it," Jordan said, slapping it down on the desk. "Elizabeth allowed herself to be questioned by a reporter from the *Times*. Read *that*." He jabbed his finger at a few lines near the bottom of the article about Elizabeth by one Mr. Thomas Tyson. "*That* was your wife's response when Tyson asked her how she felt when she saw you on trial before your peers."

Frowning at Jordan's tone, Ian read Elizabeth's reply:

> My husband was not tried before his peers.
> He was merely tried before the Lords of the
> British Realm. Ian Thornton has *no* peers.

Ian tore his gaze from the article, refusing to react to the incredible sweetness of her response, but Jordan would not let it go. "My compliments to you, Ian," he said angrily. "You serve your wife with a divorce petition, and *she* responds by giving *you* what constitutes a public apology!" He turned and stalked out of the room, leaving Ian behind to stare with clenched jaw at the article.

One month later Elizabeth had still not been found. Ian continued trying to purge her from his mind and tear her from his heart, but with decreasing success. He knew he was losing ground in the battle, just as he had been slowly losing it from the moment he'd looked up and seen her walking into the House of Lords.

Sitting alone before the fire in the drawing room, two months after her disappearance, he gazed into the flames, trying to concentrate on the meeting he was going to have with Jordan and some other business acquaintances the next day, but it was Elizabeth he saw in his mind, not profit and cost figures. . . . Elizabeth kneeling in a garden of flowers; Elizabeth firing pistols beside him; Elizabeth sinking into a mocking throne-room curtsy before him, her green eyes glowing with laughter; Elizabeth looking at him as she waltzed in his arms: *"Have you ever wanted something very badly—something that was within your grasp—and yet you were afraid to reach out for it?"*

That night he had answered no. Tonight he would have said yes. Among other things, he wanted to know where she was; a month ago he'd told himself it was because he wanted the divorce petition served. Tonight he was too exhausted from his long internal battle to bother lying to himself anymore. He wanted to know where she was because he *needed* to know. His grandfather claimed not to know; his uncle and Alexandra both knew, but they'd both refused to tell him, and he hadn't pressed them.

Wearily, Ian leaned his head against the back of his chair and closed his eyes, but he wouldn't sleep, and he knew it, even though it was three o'clock in the morning. He never slept anymore unless he'd either had a day of grueling physical activity or drunk enough brandy to knock himself out. And even when he did, he laid awake, wanting her, and knowing—because she'd told him—that she was somewhere out there, lying awake, wanting *him*.

A faint smile touched his lips as he remembered her standing in the witness box, looking heartbreakingly young and beautiful, first trying logically to explain to everyone what had happened—and when that failed, playing the part of an incorrigible henwit. Ian chuckled, as he'd been doing whenever he thought of her that day. Only Elizabeth would have dared to take on the entire House of Lords—and when she couldn't sway them with intelligent logic, she had changed tack and used their own stupidity and arrogance to defeat them. If he hadn't felt so furious and betrayed that day, he'd have stood up and given her the applause she deserved! It was exactly the same tactic she'd used the night he'd been accused of cheating at cards. When she couldn't convince Everly to withdraw from the duel because Ian was innocent, she'd turned on the hapless youth and outrageously taken him to task because he'd already engaged himself to *her* the next day.

Despite his accusation that her performance in the House of Lords had been motivated by self-interest, he knew it hadn't. She'd come to save him, she thought, from hanging.

When his rage and pain had finally diminished enough, he'd reconsidered Wordsworth's visit to her on her wedding day and put himself in her place. He had loved her that day and wanted her. If his own investigator had presented him with conjecture—even damning conjecture—about Elizabeth, his love for her would have made him reject it and proceed with the wedding.

The only reason she could have had for marrying him, other than love, was to save Havenhurst. In order to believe that, Ian had first to believe that he'd been fooled by her every kiss, every touch, every word, and *that* he could not accept. He no longer trusted his heart, but he trusted his intellect.

His intellect warned him that of all the women in the world, no one suited him better in every way than Elizabeth.

Only Elizabeth would have dared to confront him after the acquittal and, after he'd hurt and humiliated her, to tell him that they were going to have a battle of wills that he could not win: *"And when you cannot stand it anymore,"* she'd promised in that sweet, aching voice of hers, *"you'll come back to me, and I'll cry in your arms and tell you I'm sorry for everything I've done. And then you'll help me find a way to forgive myself."*

It was, Ian thought with a defeated sigh, damned hard to concede the battle of wills when he couldn't find the victor so that he could surrender.

Five hours later Ian awoke in the chair where he'd fallen

asleep, blinking in the pale sunlight filtering in through the draperies. Rubbing his stiff arms and shoulders, he went upstairs, bathed, and shaved, then came back downstairs to bury himself in his work again, which was what he had been doing ever since Elizabeth disappeared.

By midmorning he was already halfway through a stack of correspondence when his butler handed him an envelope from Alexandra Townsende. When Ian opened it a bank draft fell out onto his desk, but he ignored that to read her brief note first. "This is from Elizabeth," it said. "She has sold Havenhurst." A pang of guilt and shock sent Ian to his feet as he read the rest of the note: "I am to tell you that this is payment in full, plus appropriate interest, for the emeralds she sold, which, she feels, rightfully belonged to you."

Swallowing audibly, Ian picked up the bank draft and the small scrap of paper with it. On it Elizabeth herself had shown her calculation of the interest due him for the exact number of days since she'd sold the gems, until the date of her bank draft a week ago.

His eyes ached with unshed tears while his shoulders began to rock with silent laughter—Elizabeth had paid him half a percent less than the usual interest rate.

Thirty minutes later Ian presented himself to Jordan's butler and asked to see Alexandra. She walked into the room with accusation and ire shooting from her blue eyes as she said scornfully, "I wondered if that note would bring you here. Do you have any notion how much Havenhurst means—meant—to her?"

"I'll get it back for her," he promised with a somber smile. "Where is she?"

Alexandra's mouth fell open at the tenderness in his eyes and voice.

"Where is she?" he repeated with calm determination.

"I cannot tell you," Alex said with a twinge of regret. "You know I cannot. I gave my word."

"Would it have the slightest effect," Ian countered smoothly, "if I were to ask Jordan to exert his husbandly influence to persuade you to tell me anyway?"

"I'm afraid not," Alexandra assured him. She expected him to challenge that; instead a reluctant smile drifted across his handsome face. When he spoke, his voice was gentle. "You're very like Elizabeth. You remind me of her."

Still slightly mistrustful of his apparent change of heart, Alex said primly, "I deem that a great compliment, my lord."

To her utter disbelief, Ian Thornton reached out and chucked her under the chin. "I meant it as one," he informed her with a grin.

Turning, Ian started for the door, then stopped at the sight of Jordan, who was lounging in the doorway, an amused, knowing smile on his face. "If you'd keep track of your own wife, Ian, you would not have to search for similarities in mine." When their unexpected guest had left, Jordan asked Alex, "Are you going to send Elizabeth a message to let her know he's coming for her?"

Alex started to nod, then she hesitated. "I—I don't think so. I'll tell her that he *asked* where she is, which is all he really did."

"He'll go to her as soon as he figures it out."

"Perhaps."

"You still don't trust him, do you?" Jordan said with a surprised smile.

"I do after this last visit—to a certain extent—but *not* with Elizabeth's heart. He's hurt her terribly, and I won't give her false hopes and, in doing so, help him hurt her again."

Reaching out, Jordan chucked her under the chin as his cousin had done, then he pulled her into his arms. "She's hurt him, too, you know."

"Perhaps," Alex admitted reluctantly.

Jordan smiled against her hair. "You were more forgiving when I trampled your heart, my love," he teased.

"That's because I loved *you,*" she replied as she laid her cheek against his chest, her arms stealing around his waist.

"And will you love my cousin just a little if he makes amends to Elizabeth?"

"I might find it in my heart," she admitted, "if he gets Havenhurst back for her."

"It'll cost him a fortune if he tries," Jordan chuckled. "Do you know who bought it?"

"No, do you?"

He nodded. "Philip Demarcus."

She giggled against his chest. "Isn't he that dreadful man who told the prince he'd have to pay to ride in his new yacht up the Thames?"

"The very same."

"Do you suppose Mr. Demarcus cheated Elizabeth?"

"Not our Elizabeth," Jordan laughed. "But I wouldn't like to be in Ian's place if Demarcus realizes the place has sentimental value to Ian. The price will soar."

In the ensuing two weeks Ian managed to buy back Elizabeth's emeralds and Havenhurst, but he was unable to find a trace of his wife. The town house in London felt like a prison, not a home, and still he waited, sensing somehow that Elizabeth was putting him through this torment to teach him some kind of well-deserved lesson.

He returned to Montmayne, where, for several more weeks, he prowled about its rooms, paced a track in the drawing room carpet, and stared into its marble-fronted fireplaces as if the answer would be there in the flames. Finally he could stand it no more. He couldn't concentrate on his work, and when he tried, he made mistakes. Worse, he was beginning to be haunted with walking nightmares that she'd come to harm—or that she was falling in love with someone kinder than he—and the tormenting illusions followed him from room to room.

On a clear, cold day in early December, after leaving instructions with his footmen, butler, and even his cook that he was to be notified immediately if any word at all was received from Elizabeth, he left for the cottage in Scotland. It was the one place where he might find peace from the throbbing emptiness that was gnawing away at him with a pain that increased unbearably from day to day, because he no longer really believed she would ever contact him. Too much time had passed. If the beautiful, courageous girl he had married had wanted a reconciliation, she'd have done something else to bring it about by now. It was not in Elizabeth's nature to simply let things happen as they may. And so Ian went home to try to find peace, as he had always done before, except now it was not the pressures of his life that brought him up the lane to the cottage on that unusually frigid December night; it was the gaping emptiness of his life.

Inside the cottage Elizabeth stood at the window, watching the snow-covered lane, as she'd been doing ever since Ian's message to the caretaker had been delivered to her by the vicar three days before. Ian was coming home, she knew, but he obviously hadn't the slightest notion she was there. His message had simply said to have the cottage stocked with wood and food, and cleaned, because he intended to stay for two months. Standing at the window, Elizabeth watched the moonlit path, telling herself she was ridiculous to think he would arrive at night, more ridiculous yet to be dressed for his arrival in her favorite sapphire wool gown with her hair loose about her shoulders, as Ian liked best.

A tall, dark form appeared around the bend of the lane, and Elizabeth pulled shut the new, heavy curtains she'd made, her heart beginning to hammer with a mixture of hope and dread as she recalled that the last time she'd seen him, he'd been leaving a ball with Jane Addison on his arm. Suddenly the idea of being here, where he didn't expect her to be—and probably didn't want her to be—didn't seem good at all.

After putting his horse in the barn Ian rubbed him down, then made certain he had food. Dim light shone through the windows of the cottage as he walked through the snow, and the smell of woodsmoke rose from the chimney. The caretaker was evidently there, awaiting his arrival. Kicking the snow off his boots, he reached for the door handle.

In the center of the room Elizabeth stood stock still, clasping and unclasping her hands, watching the handle turn, unable to breathe with the tension. The door swung open, admitting a blast of frigid air and a tall, broad-shouldered man who glanced at Elizabeth in the firelight and said, "Henry, it wasn't necess—"

Ian broke off, the door still open, staring at what he momentarily thought was a hallucination, a trick of the flames dancing in the fireplace, and then he realized the vision was real: Elizabeth was standing perfectly still, looking at him. And lying at her feet was a young Labrador retriever.

Trying to buy time, Ian turned around and carefully closed the door as if latching it with precision were the most paramount thing in his life, while he tried to decide whether she'd looked happy or not to see him. In the long lonely nights without her, he'd rehearsed dozens of speeches to her—from stinging lectures to gentle discussions. Now, when the time was finally here, he could not remember one damn word of any of them.

Left with no other choice, he took the only neutral course available. Turning back to the room, Ian looked at the Labrador. "Who's this?" he asked, walking forward and crouching down to pet the dog, because he didn't know what the hell to say to his wife.

Elizabeth swallowed her disappointment as he ignored her and stroked the Labrador's glossy black head. "I—I call her Shadow."

The sound of her voice was so sweet, Ian almost pulled her down into his arms. Instead, he glanced at her, thinking it encouraging she'd named her dog after his. "Nice name."

Elizabeth bit her lip, trying to hide her sudden wayward smile. "Original, too."

The smile hit Ian like a blow to the head, snapping him out of his untimely and unsuitable preoccupation with the dog. Straightening, he backed up a step and leaned his hip against the table, his weight braced on his opposite leg.

Elizabeth instantly noticed the altering of his expression and watched nervously as he crossed his arms over his chest, watching her, his face inscrutable. "You—you look well," she said, thinking he looked unbearably handsome.

"I'm perfectly fine," he assured her, his gaze level. "Remarkably well, actually, for a man who hasn't seen the sun shine in more than three months, or been able to sleep without drinking a bottle of brandy."

His tone was so frank and unemotional that Elizabeth didn't immediately grasp what he was saying. When she did, tears of joy and relief sprang to her eyes as he continued: "I've been working very hard. Unfortunately, I rarely get anything accomplished, and when I do, it's generally wrong. All things considered, I would say that I'm doing very well—for a man who's been more than half dead for three months."

Ian saw the tears shimmering in her magnificent eyes, and one of them traced unheeded down her smooth cheek.

With a raw ache in his voice he said, "If you would take one step forward, darling, you could cry in my arms. And while you do, I'll tell you how sorry I am for everything I've done—" Unable to wait, Ian caught her, pulling her tightly against him. "And when I'm finished," he whispered hoarsely as she wrapped her arms around him and wept brokenly, "you can help me find a way to forgive myself."

Tortured by her tears, he clasped her tighter and rubbed his jaw against her temple, his voice a ravaged whisper: "I'm sorry," he told her. He cupped her face between his palms, tipping it up and gazing into her eyes, his thumbs moving over her wet cheeks. "I'm sorry." Slowly, he bent his head, covering her mouth with his. "I'm so damned sorry."

She kissed him back, holding him fiercely to her while shattered sobs racked her slender body and tears poured from her eyes. Tormented by her anguish, Ian dragged his mouth from hers, kissing her wet cheeks, running his hands over her shaking back and shoulders, trying to comfort her. "Please darling, don't cry anymore," he pleaded hoarsely. "Please don't." She held him tighter, weeping, her cheek pressed to his chest, her tears soaking his heavy woolen shirt and tearing at his heart.

"Don't," Ian whispered, his voice raw with his own unshed tears. "You're tearing me apart." An instant after he said those words, he realized that she'd stop crying to keep from hurting him, and he felt her shudder, trying valiantly to get control. He cupped the back of her head, crumpling the silk of her hair, holding her face pressed to his chest, imagining the nights he'd made her weep like this, despising himself with a virulence that was almost past bearing.

He'd driven her here, to hide from the vengeance of his divorce petition, and still she had been waiting for him. In all the endless weeks since she'd confronted him in his study and warned him she wouldn't let him put her out of his life, Ian had never imagined that she would be hurting like this.

She was twenty years old and she had loved him. In return, he had tried to divorce her, publicly scorned her, privately humiliated her, and then he had driven her here to weep in solitude and wait for him. Self-loathing and shame poured through him like hot acid, almost doubling him over. Humbly, he whispered, "Will you come upstairs with me?"

She nodded, her cheek rubbing his chest, and he swung her into his arms, cradling her tenderly against him, brushing his lips against her forehead. He carried her upstairs, intending to take her to bed and give her so much pleasure that—at least for tonight—she'd be able to forget the misery he'd caused her.

Elizabeth knew, the moment he put her down in the bed chamber and began gently undressing her, that something was different. Confusion fluttered through her as he took her in his arms in bed, his body rigid with desire, his mouth and hands skillful as he kissed and caressed her, but the moment she tried to caress him in return, he forced her back onto the pillows, evading her touch, gently imprisoning her wrists. Kissed and caressed into near insensibility, desperate to please him as he had taught her to do, Elizabeth reached for him the moment his grip loosened on her hands. His body jerked away from her touch. "Don't," he whispered, but she heard the passion thickening his voice, and so she obeyed.

Refusing to let her do anything to increase his pleasure, he brought her to the very brink of fulfillment with his hands and mouth before he shifted on top of her and entered her with one sure, powerful thrust. Elizabeth strained toward him in trembling need, her nails biting into his back as his rhythmic thrusts began, and then slowly, he started increasing their tempo. The sweetness of being filled by him again, combined with the fierce power of his body driving deeply into hers again and again, sent pleasure streaking through her and she instinctively arched herself upward in a fevered need to share it with him. His hands gripped her hips, while he quickened the pace of his deep plunging strokes, circling his hips, forcing the trembling ecstasy to overtake her until she cried out, shuddering with the sweet violence of it, her arms locked fiercely around his broad shoulders.

Slowly, Elizabeth began to surface from the stormy splendor of his lovemaking, aware in some passion-drugged part of her mind that she had been the only one to find that quaking fulfillment. She opened her eyes, and in the firelight, she could see the harsh effort Ian was exerting to stop himself from moving within her and finding his own release: His hands were braced on either side of her shoulders, and he was holding his upper body away from hers; his eyes were clenched shut, and a muscle jerked spasmodically in his cheek. They had been so attuned to each other during the months of their marriage, that Elizabeth instinctively realized what he was doing, and the knowledge filled her with poignant tenderness: He was trying to atone to her in the only way he could right now—by unselfishly prolonging their lovemaking. And in order to do that, he was deliberately denying himself the release that Elizabeth knew he desperately wanted. It was, she thought tenderly, a loving gesture—and a futile one. Because this was not at all what she wanted, and Ian had taught her to show him what she wanted. He had also taught her the power she had over his body—and he had shown her how to use it. Always an excellent student, Elizabeth put her knowledge into immediate—and very effective use.

Since his weight prevented any sort of seductive movement, Elizabeth used her hands and her voice to seduce him. Her voice shaking with love and desire, she shifted her hands down his back, caressing the bunched muscles of his shoulders and the hollow of his spine. "I love you," she whispered. He opened his eyes and Elizabeth met his smoldering gaze as she continued achingly, "I've dreamed of this for so long . . . dreamed of the way you always hold me in your arms after we make love—and of how beautiful it is to lie beside you, knowing a part of you is still inside of me and that you might have given me your child." Lifting her hands, Elizabeth took his face between her palms, her fingers moving over his hard cheekbones in a trembling caress as she slowly drew his mouth toward hers. "But most of all," she whispered, "I dreamed of how exquisite it feels to have you moving deep inside of me—"

Ian's restraint broke under her sweet assault. A tortured groan tore from his chest, and he seized her mouth in a devouring kiss, wrapped his arms tightly around her, and drove into her, thrusting fiercely again and again, seeking absolution within her . . . finding it when she molded herself to him while his body jerked convulsively, shuddering violently, and he poured himself into her. His heart thundering against his ribs, his breath coming in deep, painful pants, Ian kept thrusting into her, willing her body to again respond to the fierce hunger of his driving strokes, determined to pleasure her again. She cried out his name, her hips arching, her body racked with tremors.

When some of his strength returned, he slid one arm beneath her hips, the other around her shoulders, and moved onto his side, taking her with him, still intimately joined to her . . . his seed deep inside her. It was, he thought, the most profound moment of his life. Stroking her hair, he swallowed and spoke, but his voice was shattered. "I love you," he said, telling her what she had told him that terrible day in his study. "I never stopped loving you."

She raised her face to his, and her answer made his chest ache. "I know."

"How did you know, sweetheart?" he asked, trying to smile.

"Because," she said, "I wanted it so badly to be true, and you've always given me everything I wanted. I couldn't believe you wouldn't do it, just one more time. Just once more."

She moved slightly and Ian checked her, tightening his arms. "Stay still, darling," he whispered tenderly, and seeing her confusion, he told her, "because our child is being conceived."

Her eyes searched his. "Why do you think so?"

"Because," he said, slowly smoothing her hair off her cheek, "I want it so badly to be true, and *you've* always given me everything I wanted." A lump of emotion swelled in Ian's chest as she pressed closer against him, cradled in his arms, not moving. She was willing it to be true; he knew it as surely as he knew that, somehow, it was.

Bright morning sunlight was glancing off the windowpanes when Ian finally began to surface from his deep slumber. A sense of well-being, absent from his life for more than three months, filled him, and oddly, it was the very unfamiliarity of the sensation that awakened him. Thinking some dream had caused it, he rolled onto his stomach, keeping his eyes closed, reaching for the dream, for unconsciousness, rather than awakening to the emptiness that normally inhabited his waking hours.

But awareness was already returning. The bed felt smaller and harder than it should; and, thinking he was at Montmayne, he decided dully that he'd fallen asleep on the sofa in his bedchamber. He'd drunk himself into oblivion on that sofa dozens of times, and slept there, rather than in the cavernous emptiness of the huge bed he'd shared with Elizabeth. Ian felt it start again—the dull ache of regret and worry, and, knowing sleep would evade him now, he flung himself onto his back and opened his eyes. His pupils recoiled from the glaring sunlight, his dazed eyes taking in the familiarity of his unexpected surroundings. And then it hit him: where he was, who had spent the night with him in naked splendor and uninhibited sharing. Joy and relief swept over him and he closed his eyes, letting it wash over him.

Slowly, however, his nose became aware of something else—the aroma of bacon cooking. A smile tugged at his lips, evolving into a lazy grin as he remembered the last time she had cooked bacon for him. It had been here, and she had burned it. This morning, he happily decided, he would eat charred paper—so long as he could feast his eyes on her while he did.

Clad in a soft gown of green wool with a bright yellow apron tied around her waist, Elizabeth stood at the stove, pouring tea into her mug. Unaware that Ian had just sat down on the sofa, she glanced at Shadow who was concentrating hopefully on the bacon cooling in the skillet. "What do you think of your master?" Elizabeth asked the Labrador as she added milk to her tea. "Didn't I tell you he was handsome? Although," she confided with a smile, bending down to pat the satiny head, "I'll admit I'd forgotten just *how* handsome he is."

"Thank you," Ian said with a tender smile.

Surprise brought her head around so quickly that Elizabeth's hair spilled over her shoulder in a gilt waterfall. She stood up, smothering a laugh at the picture of absolute, masculine contentment she beheld before her: Clad in a chamois peasant shirt with coffee-colored breeches, Ian was sitting on the sofa, his hands linked behind his head, his feet crossed at the ankles and propped on the low table in front of him. "You look like a Scottish sultan," she said with a chuckle.

"I *feel* like one." His grin faded to a somber smile when she handed him a mug of coffee. "Can breakfast wait a little while?" he asked.

Elizabeth nodded. "I thought I heard you moving about almost an hour ago, and I put the bacon on then. I intended to make more when you finally came down. Why?" she finished, wondering if he was afraid to eat her cooking.

"Because we have some things to talk about."

Elizabeth felt an unexpected lurch of dread. Last night, she'd lain beside him and explained everything that had happened from the time Robert appeared at Havenhurst until she arrived at the House of Lords. By the time she was finished, she'd been so exhausted from her tale and from Ian's lovemaking that she'd fallen asleep before he could explain his own actions. Now he obviously wanted to discuss the subject, and she wasn't entirely certain she wanted to spoil the beauty of their reconciliation by reopening it.

"We've wronged each other," Ian said quietly, seeing her reluctant expression. "If we try to hide from it, to pretend it didn't happen, it will always be there, lurking. It will come back to haunt both of us at odd times, for odd reasons, and when it does, it will come between us. Some little thing I say or do will rip open your scar from this, and I won't know why you're angry or hurt or mistrustful. Neither will you. Last night, you made your explanations to me, and there's no need to go into it again. I think you have a right to some explanations from me."

"How did you become so wise?" she asked with a soft smile.

"If I were wise," he said dryly, "this separation would have ended months ago. However, I've had several agonizing weeks to try to think how we could best go on after his—assuming you ever let me find you, and it seemed to me that talking about it, openly and thoroughly, was the only way."

Elizabeth still hesitated, remembering the murderous fury he'd turned on her in his study the day of his acquittal. If talking about it would make him angry again, she wasn't certain it was worthwhile.

Reaching for her hand, Ian drew her down onto the sofa, watching as she tucked her skirts around her, fidgeted with each fold, and then looked apprehensively at the snow-covered windowpane. She was nervous, he realized with a pang. "Give me your hand, sweetheart. You can ask me anything you want to know without fear of any anger from me."

The sound of his deep, reassuring voice, combined with the feeling of his strong warm fingers closing around hers, did much to dissolve her misgivings. Her gaze searching his face, Elizabeth asked, "Why didn't you tell me Robert had tried to kill you and you'd had him taken aboard your ship? Why did you let me go on believing he'd simply vanished?"

For a moment he leaned his head against the back of the sofa, closing his eyes, and Elizabeth saw his regret, heard it in his voice when he looked at her and said, "Until the day you left here last spring, and Duncan greeted me with a list of my crimes against you, I had assumed your brother returned to England after he got off the *Arianna*. I had no idea you'd been living alone at Haven-hurst since he'd left, or that you'd become a social outcast because of what I did, or that you had no parents to protect you, or that you had no money. You have to believe that."

"I do," she said honestly. "Lucinda ripped up at Duncan and told him all that, and you came to London to find me. We talked about it before we were married, except the part about Robert. Why didn't you tell me about him as well?"

"When?" he asked, his voice harsh with self-recrimination and futility. "When could I have told you? Consider the way you felt about me when I came racing to London to ask you to marry me. You were already half-convinced my proposal was made out of pity and regret. If I'd have told you my part in Robert's disappearance, you'd

have been sure of it. Besides, you didn't like me very well a
it was, and you didn't particularly trust me, either," he
reminded her. "You'd have flung my 'bargain' in my face i
I'd confessed to kidnapping your brother, no matter how
valid my excuse was.

"There's one more reason I didn't tell you," Ian added
with blunt honesty. "I wanted you to marry me, and I wa:
prepared to do almost anything to bring it about."

She gave him one of the disarming, sideways smiles tha
always melted him and then she sobered. "Later, when yo
knew I loved you, why didn't you tell me then?"

"Ah yes, later," he said wryly. "When I'd finally made you
love me? For one thing, I wasn't anxious to give you a reason
to change your mind. For another, we were so damned
happy together, I didn't want to spoil it until I absolutely
had to. Lastly, I didn't know exactly what I was *guilty* of yet
My investigators couldn't find a trace—Yes," he said, seeing
her startled look, "I hired investigators the same time you
did. For all I knew, your brother had stayed away to hide
from his creditors, exactly as you suspected. On the other
hand, it was possible he died, somehow, trying to make hi:
way back here, in which case, I'd have had that crime to
confess to you."

"If no information, no word of him ever came, would you
have ever told me why he originally left England?"

He'd been looking down at her hand, his thumb idly
tracing her palm, but when he answered, he lifted his eyes to
hers. "Yes." After a silence, he added, "Shortly before you
vanished, I'd already decided to allow the investigators si>
more months. If no trace of him was discovered by then, I
intended to tell you what I *did* know."

"I'm glad," she said softly. "I wouldn't like to think you'e
have gone on deceiving me forever."

"It was not an entirely noble decision," Ian admitted
"Fear had something to do with it. I lived in daily dread of
Wordsworth appearing at the house one day and handing
you proof that I'd caused your brother some irreparable
harm, or worse. There were times," he added, "near the end
when I honestly wished one of the investigators woulc
produce evidence to either damn me or acquit me, so that I

could put an end to my uncertainty. I had no idea, you see, of what you'd do."

Ian watched her, waiting for her to comment, and when she didn't, he said, "It would mean a great deal to me, and to our future together, if you could believe the things I've told you. I swear to you it's the truth."

Her eyes lifted to his. "I *do* believe you."

"Thank you," he said humbly.

"There's nothing to thank me for," she said trying to tease. "The fact is that I married a brilliant man, who taught me to always put myself in the opponent's place and try to see things from his point of view. I did that, and I was able to guess long ago your reasons for keeping Robert's disappearance a secret from me." Her smile faded as she continued, "By putting myself in your place, I was even able to guess how you might react when I first came back. I knew, before I ever saw the expression on your face when you looked at me in the House of Lords, that you would find it extremely difficult to forgive me for hurting you, and for shaming you. I never imagined, though, the extent you would actually go to retaliate against me."

Ian saw the pain in her eyes, and despite his belief that all this had to be said, it took an almost physical effort not to try to ease her hurt with his hands and silence her with his mouth.

"You see," she explained slowly, "I anticipated that you might send me away until you got over your anger, or that you'd live with me and retaliate in private—things that an ordinary man might do. But I never imagined you would try to put a permanent end to our marriage. And to me. I should have anticipated that, knowing what Duncan had told me about you, but I was counting too much on the fact that, before I ran away, you'd said you loved me—"

"You know damned well I did. And I do. For God's sake, if you don't believe anything else I've ever said to you, at least believe that."

He expected her to argue, but she didn't, and Ian realized that she might be young, and inexperienced, but she was also very wise. "I know you did," she told him, softly. "If you hadn't loved me so deeply, I could never have hurt you as much as I did—and you wouldn't have needed to put an end to the possibility I could ever do it again. I realized that was what you were doing, when I stood in your study and you told me you were divorcing me. If I hadn't understood it, and you, I could never have kept fighting for you all this time."

"I won't argue with your conclusion, but I will swear to you not to ever do anything like that again to you."

"Thank you. I don't think I could bear it another time."

"Could you enlighten me as to what Duncan told you to make you arrive at all that?"

Her smile was filled with tenderness and understanding. "He told me what you did when you returned home and discovered your family had died."

"What did I do?"

"You severed yourself from the only other thing you loved—a black Labrador named Shadow. You did it so that you couldn't be hurt anymore—at least not by anything over which you had control. You did essentially the same thing, although far more drastically, when you tried to divorce me."

"In your place," Ian said, his voice rough with emotion as he laid his hand against her cheek, "I think I'd hate me."

His wife turned her face into his hand and kissed his palm. "Do you know," she said with a teary smile, "how it feels to know I am loved so *much* . . ." She shook her head as if trying to find a better way to explain, and began again, her voice shaking with love. "Do you know what I notice whenever we are out in company?"

Unable to restrain himself, Ian pulled her into his arms, holding her against his heart. "No," he whispered, "what do you notice?"

"I notice the way other men treat their wives, the way they look at them, or speak to them. And do you know what?"

"What?"

"I am the only wife," she whispered achingly, "with the exception of Alex, whose husband adores her and doesn't care if the whole world knows it. And I absolutely know," he added with a soft smile, "that I am the *only* wife whose usband has ever tried to seduce her in front of the Hospital Fund Raising Committee."

His arms tightened around her, and with a groaning augh, Ian tried, very successfully, to seduce his wife on the ofa.

Snowflakes were falling outside the windows, and a log umbled off the grate sending bright sparks up the chimney. Sated and happy, wrapped in Ian's arms beneath the blanket e'd drawn over them, Elizabeth's thoughts drifted lazily rom the breakfast they hadn't eaten yet to the sumptuous breakfast he would have undoubtedly been served, had they been at Montmayne. With a sigh, she moved away from him nd got dressed.

When she was turning the bacon, he came up behind her, is hands settling on her waist as he peered over her houlder. "That looks awfully edible," he teased. "I was ather counting on our 'traditional' breakfast."

She smiled and let him turn her around. "When do we ave to return?" she asked, thinking whimsically of how ozy it was up here with him.

"How does two months sound?"

"It sounds wonderful, but are you certain you won't be bored—or worried about neglecting your business ffairs?"

"If they were going to suffer overmuch from my neglect, ny love, we'd have pockets to let after the last three months. Evidently," he continued with a grin, "I'm much better organized than I thought. Besides, Jordan will let me now if there's a particular problem that needs my attention."

"Duncan has provided me with nearly a hundred books," he said, trying to think of ways he could occupy his time if hey stayed, "but you've probably read them already, and, ven if you haven't," she said with laughing exaggeration, "you'd be done with the lot of them by Wednesday. I'm fraid you'll be bored."

"It will be difficult for me," he agreed dryly. "Snowbound up here with you. Without books or business to occupy my ime, I wonder what I'll do," he added with a leer.

She blushed gorgeously, but her voice was serious as she studied his face. "If things hadn't gone so well for you—if you hadn't accumulated so much wealth—you could have been happy up here, couldn't you?"

"With you?"

"Of course."

His smile was as somber as hers. "Absolutely."

"Although," he added, linking her hands behind her back and drawing her a little closer, "you may not want to remain up here when you learn your emeralds are back in their cases at Montmayne."

Her head snapped up, and her eyes shone with love and relief. "I'm so glad. When I realized Robert's story had been fabrication, it hurt beyond belief to realize I'd sold them."

"It's going to hurt more," he teased outrageously, "when you realize your bank draft to cover their cost was a little bit short. It cost me £45,000 to buy back the pieces that had already been sold, and £5,000 to buy the rest back from the jeweler you sold them to."

"That—that unconscionable thief!" she burst out. "He only gave me £5,000 for all of them!" She shook her head in despair at Ian's lack of bargaining prowess. "He took dreadful advantage of you."

"I wasn't concerned, however," Ian continued teasing, enjoying himself hugely, "because I knew I'd get it all back out of *your* allowance. With interest, of course. According to my figures," he said, pausing to calculate in his mind what it would have taken Elizabeth several minutes to figure out on paper, "as of today, you now owe me roughly £151,126."

"One hundred and—what?" she cried, half laughing and half irate.

"There's the little matter of the cost of Havenhurst. added that in to the figure."

Tears of joy clouded her magnificent eyes. "You bought it back from that horrid Mr. Demarcus?"

"Yes. And he *is* 'horrid.' He and your uncle ought to be partners. They both possess the instincts of camel traders. paid £100,000 for it."

Her mouth fell open, and admiration lit her face. "£100,000! Oh, Ian—"

"I love it when you say my name."

She smiled at that, but her mind was still on the splendid bargain he'd gotten. "I could not have done a bit better!" she generously admitted. "That's exactly what he paid for it, and he told me after the papers were signed that he was certain he could get £150,000 if he waited a year or so."

"He probably could have."

"But not from you!" she announced proudly.

"Not from me," he agreed, grinning.

"Did he try?"

"He tried for £200,000 as soon as he realized how important it was to me to buy it back for you."

"You must have been very clever and skillful to make him agree to accept so much less."

Trying desperately not to laugh, Ian put his forehead against hers and nodded. "Very skillful," he agreed in a suffocated voice.

"Still, I wonder why he was so agreeable?"

Swallowing a surge of laughter, Ian said, "I imagine it was because I showed him that I had something he needed more than he needed an exorbitant profit."

"Really?" she said, fascinated and impressed. "What did you have?"

"His throat."

Epilogue

Standing on the terrace near the balustrade, Ian gazed out at the magnificent gardens of Montmayne, where Elizabeth and their three-year-old daughter, Caroline, were kneeling among the geraniums, examining the vivid blooms. Their heads were so close together that it was impossible to distinguish where Elizabeth's bright golden hair stopped and Caroline's began. Something Elizabeth said caused Caroline to give forth a peal of happy laughter, and Ian's eyes crinkled with a smile at the joyous sound.

Seated at a wrought-iron table behind him, his grandfather and Duncan were indulging in a game of chess. Tonight seven hundred guests would arrive to attend the ball Ian was giving to celebrate Elizabeth's birthday. The silent concentration of the chess players, was abruptly interrupted by the arrival of a six-year-old boy, who already bore a remarkable resemblance to Ian, and the boy's tutor, who looked like a man driven to the brink of despair at having to cope with a six-year-old intellect that also bore a remarkable resemblance to Ian's.

"I beg your pardon," Mr. Twindell said, bowing apologetically to the chess players, "but Master Jonathon and I have been engaged in a debate which I have just realized that you, Vicar, can settle, if you will be so kind?"

Dragging his gaze from the chessboard, and his mind from the victory that was almost in his grasp, Duncan smiled sympathetically at the harassed tutor. "How may I be of assistance?" he asked, looking from the tutor to the handsome six-year-old whose attention had momentarily shifted to the chessboard.

"It concerns," Mr. Twindell explained, "the issue of heaven, Vicar. Specifically, a description of said place which I have, all morning, been attempting to convince Master Jonathon is not loaded with impossible inconsistencies."

At that point Master Jonathon pulled his bemused gaze from the chessboard, clasped his hands behind his back, and regarded his great-uncle and his great-grandfather as if sharing a story too absurd to be believed. "Mr. Twindell," he explained, trying to hide his chuckle, "thinks heaven has streets made of gold. But of course, it can't."

"*Why* can't it?" said the duke in surprise.

"Because the streets would be too hot in summer for the horses' hooves," Jon said, looking a little stricken by his great-grandfather's shortsightedness. Turning expectantly to his great-uncle, Jon said, "Sir, do you not find the idea of metal streets in heaven a highly unlikely possibility?"

Duncan, who was recalling similar debates with Ian at a similar age, leaned back in his chair while an expression of gleeful anticipation dawned across his face. "Jon," said he with eager delight, "ask your *father*. He is right over there at the balustrade."

The little boy nodded agreeably, paused to cup his hand over the duke's ear and whisper something, then he turned to do as bidden.

"Why didn't you answer Jon's question, Duncan?" the duke asked curiously. "A description of heaven ought to be right in your line."

Duncan's brows lifted in mocking denial. "When Ian was six years old," he said dryly, *"he* used to engage me in theological and rhetorical debates just like this one. I used to lose. It was most disconcerting." Shifting his gaze to the little boy who was waiting for his father to notice him, Duncan said gleefully, "I have waited for this day for decades. By the by," he added, "what did Jon whisper to you just now?"

515

The duke flushed. "He . . . ah . . . said you'll have my queen in check in four moves if I don't move my knight."

It was the burst of laughter from the two men at the chess table that made Ian glance over his shoulder and see Jonathon waiting beside, and slightly behind, him. Smiling, he turned to give his full attention to the son who was conceived that snowy night he'd returned to the cottage in Scotland. "You look," he teased, "like a man with something on his mind." He glanced at the harassed expression on the tutor's face, then back at his son, and added sympathetically, "I gather you and Mr. Twindell have had another polite disagreement? What is it about this time?"

A relieved grin lit up Jon's face and he nodded. While everyone else might be shocked by his thoughts or baffled by his questions, his father, he knew, would not only understand but provide acceptable answers. "It's about heaven," Jon confided, almost rolling his eyes in amusement as he explained in a low, conspiratorial voice, "Mr. Twindell wants me to believe heaven is a place with gold streets. Can you imagine," he added with a chuckle, "the temperature pure gold would reach if the sun were to hit it for ten consecutive hours in July? No one would want to walk on the streets!"

"What did Mr. Twindell say when you mentioned that?" Ian asked with amused gravity.

"He said we probably wouldn't have feet."

"Now that's an alarming thought," Ian agreed. "What do *you* think heaven will be like?"

"I haven't the foggiest idea. Do you?"

"Yes, but it's only my opinion," Ian explained to his puzzled son. Crouching down, he put his arm around the little boy's shoulders and gestured toward the garden. As if Elizabeth and Caroline sensed that they were being observed, they both looked up at the terrace, and then they smiled and waved—two green-eyed girls with gilded hair and love shining in their eyes. "In my opinion," Ian solemnly confided to his son, "that is heaven, right there."

"There are no angels," Jon noted.

"I see two of them," his father quietly replied, then he glanced at his son and amended with a grin, *"three* of them."

The little boy nodded slowly, a smile of comprehension

drifting across his face. Turning to look up at the tall man beside him, he said, "You think heaven will have whatever a person most wants it to have, is that it?"

"I think it's very possible."

"So do I," Jon agreed after another moment's thought. He started to turn, saw his tutor and his relatives looking expectantly in his direction, then he turned back to his father and said with a helpless smile, "They're going to ask what you said. And if I tell Mr. Twindell you said heaven will be like this, he'll be very disappointed. He's counting, you know, on gold streets and angels and horses with wings."

"I see where that could be a problem," Ian agreed, and he tenderly laid his hand against his son's cheek. "In that case, you can tell him I said this is *almost* heaven."

Dear Reader,

It may come as a surprise to you to know that you are very much on my mind while I'm writing a book, particularly this one. Late at night, as I write, I often imagine you laughing at something a character says and, hopefully, experiencing all his or her other emotions as well. That has always been my goal—and my commitment to you.

You, in turn, have rewarded my efforts a thousandfold. You've taken the time to write to me, and you've made me feel that each of my novels is special and meaningful to you.

Considering all that, I'd say we have a rather unique relationship, you and I.

The appearance of Jordan and Alexandra Townsende in this novel is a direct result of that relationship. Thousands of you who read SOMETHING WONDERFUL and came to know them as the hero and heroine of that novel, later wrote to urge me to write another book about them. Rather than do that, I thought you would enjoy meeting them again as secondary characters, here in ALMOST HEAVEN. It is a great compliment, and a great pleasure, to know that the characters in my books have become so meaningful to you that you want to read more about them.

My next novel is well underway, and I'm already looking forward, with great anticipation, to your reaction to it. It is the romance I've been longing to write for years!

Judith McKnaught

P. S. If you would like to receive my free semi-annual newsletter, which will keep you informed about my books-in-progress as well as answer some of the questions I'm frequently asked about publishing, please send a self-addressed, stamped envelope to me at:

P. O. Box 795491
Dallas, TX 75379